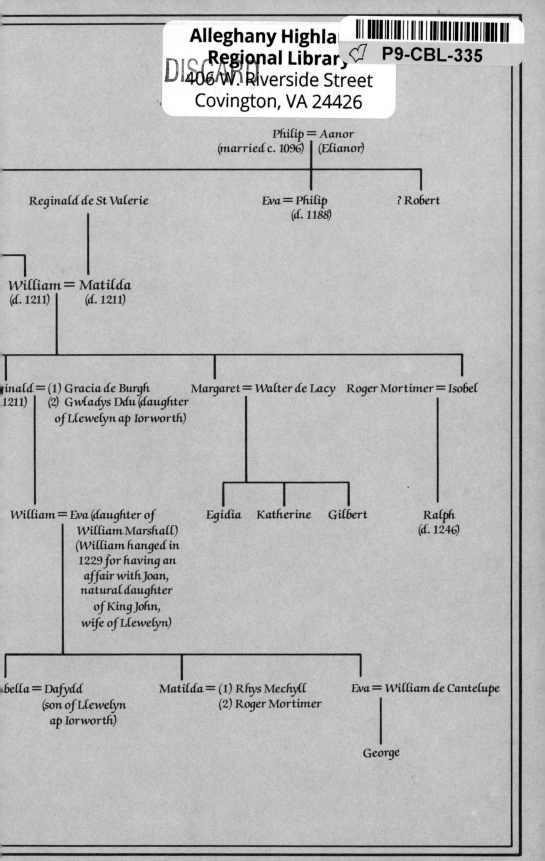

Philip = Aanor
(married c. 1096) (Elianor)

Reginald de St Valerie   Eva = Philip   ? Robert
                                      (d. 1188)

William = Matilda
(d. 1211)   (d. 1211)

inald = (1) Gracia de Burgh   Margaret = Walter de Lacy   Roger Mortimer = Isobel
1211)   (2) Gwladys Ddu (daughter
            of Llewelyn ap Iorworth)

William = Eva (daughter of   Egidia   Katherine   Gilbert   Ralph
            William Marshall)   (d. 1246)
            (William hanged in
            1229 for having an
            affair with Joan,
            natural daughter
            of King John,
            wife of Llewelyn)

bella = Dafydd   Matilda = (1) Rhys Mechyll   Eva = William de Cantelupe
         (son of Llewelyn   (2) Roger Mortimer
         ap Iorworth)

                                                                George

LADY of HAY

LADY of HAY

Barbara Erskine

DELACORTE PRESS/NEW YORK

For Michael

Published by
Delacorte Press
1 Dag Hammarskjold Plaza
New York, New York 10017

This work was first published in Great Britain by
Michael Joseph Ltd.

Manufactured in the United States of America

First U.S.A. printing

Library of Congress Cataloging in Publication Data

Erskine, Barbara.
Lady of Hay.

I. Title.
PR6055.R7L3   1986   823'.914   87–564
ISBN 0-385-29539-1

ACKNOWLEDGMENTS

I should like to thank all the people who have gone to such endless trouble to help me with the research for this book, particularly Professor Ann Matonis for her translations into Middle and Modern Welsh (for any mistakes in the transcriptions of which I must take the blame). I should also like to thank Dr. Brian Taylor, Dr. Michael Siddons, and Dr. Brian Blandford for their advice on matters medical, heraldic, and musical; my father, who has driven so many miles to double check on locations in the Welsh hills; and Carole Blake, for all her help and encouragement. And finally I must make special mention of Jean Walter, without whose meticulous typing this book might never have been finished!

Barbara Erskine
Llanigon and Great Tey, 1985

PROLOGUE

EDINBURGH 1970

It was snowing. Idly Sam Franklyn stared out of the dirty window up at the sky wondering if the leaden cloud would provide enough depth to ski by the weekend.

"Tape on now, Dr. Franklyn, if you please." Professor Cohen's quiet voice interrupted his thoughts. Sam turned, glancing at the young woman lying so calmly on the couch, and switched on the recorder. She was an attractive girl, slender and dark, with vivacious gray-green eyes, closed now beneath long curved lashes. He grinned to himself. When the session was over he intended to offer her a lift back into town.

The psychology labs were cold. As he picked up his notebook and began a new page, he leaned across and touched the grotesquely large cream radiator and grimaced. It was barely warm.

Cohen's office was small and cluttered, furnished with a huge desk buried beneath books and papers, some half-dozen chairs crowded together to accommodate tutorial students, when there were any, and the couch, covered by a bright tartan blanket, where most of his volunteers chose to lie while they were under hypnosis, "as if they are afraid they will fall down" he had commented once to Sam as yet another woman had lain nervously down as if on a sacrificial altar. The walls of the room were painted a light cold blue that did nothing to improve the temperature. Anyone who could relax comfortably in Michael Cohen's office, Sam used to think wryly, was halfway to being mesmerized already. Next to him the radiator let out a subterranean gurgle, but it grew no hotter.

Professor Cohen seated himself next to the couch and took the girl's hand in his. He had not bothered to do that for his last two victims, Sam noticed, and once more he grinned.

He picked up his pen and began to write:

Hypnotic Regression: Clinical Therapy Trials
Subject 224: Joanna Clifford 2nd year arts (English)
Age: 19
Attitude:

1

He chewed the end of the pen and glanced at her again. Then he put "enthusiastic but open minded" in the column.

Historical aptitude:

Again he paused. She had shrugged when they asked her the routine questions to determine roughly her predisposition to accurate invention.

"Average, I suppose," she had replied with a smile. "O-level history. Boring old Disraeli and people like that. Not much else. It's the present I'm interested in, not the past."

He eyed her sweater and figure-hugging jeans and wrote as he had written on so many other record sheets: *Probably average.*

Professor Cohen had finished his preliminary tests. He turned to Sam. "The girl's a good subject. There's a deep trance established already. I shall begin regressing her now."

Sam turned back to the window. At the beginning of the series of tests he had waited expectantly at this stage, wondering what would be revealed. Some subjects produced nothing, no memories, no inventions; some emerged as colorful characters who enthralled and amazed him. But for days now they had been working with routine ill-defined personalities who replied in dull monosyllables to all the questions put to them and who did little to further their research. The only different thing about this girl —as far as he knew—were her looks: those put her in a class by herself.

The snow was thickening, whirling sideways, blotting out the buildings on the far side of the street, muffling the sound of the car tires moving north toward the city. He did not bother to listen to the girl's words. Her soft English voice sounded tired and blurred under hypnosis, and he would have to listen again and again to the tape anyway as Cohen transcribed it and tried to fathom where her comments, if there were any, came from.

"And now, Joanna"—the professor's voice rose slightly as he shifted on the high stool to make himself more comfortable. "We'll go back again, if you please, back before the darkness, back before the dreams, back to when you were on this earth before." He is getting bored too, Sam thought dryly, catching sight of his boss glancing at his watch.

The girl suddenly flung out her arm, catching a pile of books on the table beside the couch and sending them crashing to the floor. Sam jumped, but she seemed not to have noticed. She was pushing herself up onto her elbow, her eyes open, staring in front of her.

Cohen was all attention. Quickly he slid from the stool, and as she stood up he moved it out of her way.

Sam recovered from his surprise and wrote hastily: *subject somnambulant; moved from couch. Eyes open; pupils dilated. Face pale and drawn.*

2

"Joanna." Cohen spoke softly. "Would you not like to sit down again, lassie, and tell us your name and where you are."

She swung around, but not to face him. Her eyes were fixed on some point in the middle of the room. She opened her mouth as if trying to speak and they saw her run her tongue across her lips. Then she drew herself up with a shudder, clutching at the neck of her sweater.

"William?" she whispered at last. Her voice was husky, barely audible. She took a step forward, her eyes still fixed on the same point. Sam felt the skin on the back of his neck prickle as he found himself looking at it too, half expecting someone or something to appear.

His notebook forgotten, he waited, holding his breath, for her to speak again, but she stayed silent, swaying slightly, her face drained of color as she began to stare around the room. Disconcerted, he saw that huge tears had begun to run slowly down her cheeks.

"Tell us where you are and why you are crying." The quiet insistent voice of Professor Cohen seemed to Sam a terrible intrusion on her grief, but to his surprise she turned and looked straight at him. Her face had become haggard and old. "William," she said again, and then gave a long desperate cry that tore through Sam, turning his guts to water. *"William!"* Slowly she raised her hands and stared at them. Sam dragged his eyes from her face and looked too. As he did so he heard a gasp and realized with a shock that the sound had come from his own throat.

Her hands had begun to bleed.

Electrified, he pushed himself away from the window and reached out toward her, but a sharp word from Cohen stopped him.

"Don't touch her. Don't do anything. It's incredible. *Incredible,"* the older man breathed. "It's autosuggestion, the stigmata of religious fanatics. I've never seen it before. Incredible!"

Sam stood only feet from her as she swayed once again, cradling her hands against her chest as if to ease their pain. Then, shivering uncontrollably, she fell to her knees. "William, don't leave me. Oh, God, save my child," she whispered brokenly. "Let someone come. Please . . . bring us . . . bring him . . . food. Please . . . I'm so cold . . . so cold . . ." Her voice trailed away to a sob and slowly she subsided onto the floor. "Oh, God . . . have mercy on . . . me." Her fingers grasped convulsively at the rush matting that carpeted the room, and Sam stared in horror as the blood seeped from her hands onto the sisal, soaking into the fibers, congealing as she lay there emitting dry, convulsive sobs.

"Joanna? Joanna!" Cohen knelt awkwardly beside her, and, defying his own instructions, he laid his hand on her shoulder. "Joanna, lass, I want you to listen to me." His face was compassionate as he touched her, lifting a strand of her heavy dark hair, gently stroking her cheek. "I want you to stop crying, do you hear me? Stop crying now and sit up, there's a good girl." His voice was calm, professionally confident as the two men watched

3

her, but there was growing anxiety in his eyes. Slowly her sobs grew quieter and she lay still, the harsh rasping in her throat dying away. Cohen bent closer, his hand still on her shoulder. "Joanna." Gently he shook her. "Joanna, are you hearing me? I want you to wake up. When I count three. Are you ready? One . . . two . . . three . . ."

Under his hand her head rolled sideways on the matting. Her eyes were open and unblinking, the pupils dilated. *"Joanna, do you hear me? One, two, three."* As he counted Cohen took her by the shoulders and half lifted her from the floor. "Joanna, for the love of God, hear me . . ."

The panic in the man's voice galvanized Sam into action. He dropped on his knees beside them, his fingers feeling rapidly for a pulse in the girl's throat.

"Christ! There's nothing there!"

"Joanna!" Cohen was shaking her now, his own face ashen. "Joanna! You must wake up, girl!" He calmed himself with a visible effort. "Listen to me. You are going to start to breathe now, slowly and calmly. Do you hear me? You are breathing now, slowly, and you are with William and you have both eaten. You are happy. You are warm. You are alive, Joanna! *You are alive!"*

Sam felt his throat constrict with panic. The girl's wrist, limp between his fingers, had begun to grow cold. Her face had taken on a deathly pallor, her lips were turning gray.

"I'll call for an ambulance." Cohen's voice had lost all its command. He sounded like an old man as he scrambled to his feet.

"No time." Sam pushed the professor aside. "Kneel here, by her head, and give her mouth to mouth. Now! When I say so!" Crouched over the girl, he laid his ear to her chest. Then, the heel of one hand over the other, he began to massage her heart, counting methodically as he did so. For a moment Cohen did not move. Then he bent toward her mouth. Just as his lips touched hers Joanna drew an agonizing, gasping breath. Sam sat back, his fingers once more to her pulse, his eyes fixed on her face as her eyelids flickered. "Go on talking to her," he said urgently under his breath, not taking his eyes from her face. Her color was beginning to return. His hands were once more on her ribs, gently feeling the slight flutter of returning life. One breath, then another; labored painful gulps of air. Gently Sam chafed her ice-cold hand, feeling the stickiness of her blood where it had dried on her fingers and over her palms. He stared down at the wounds. The cuts and grazes were real: lesions all around the finger-nails and on the pads of the fingers, blisters and cuts on her palms, and a raw graze across one knuckle.

Cohen, making a supreme effort to sound calm, began to talk her slowly out of her trance. "That's great, Joanna, good girl. You're relaxed now and warm and happy. As soon as you feel strong enough I want you to open your eyes and look at me. . . . That's lovely. . . . Good girl."

4

Sam watched as she slowly opened her eyes. She seemed not to see the room nor the anxious men kneeling beside her on the floor. Her gaze was focused on the middle distance, her expression wiped smooth and blank. Cohen smiled with relief. "That's it. Now, do you feel well enough to sit up?"

Gently he took her shoulders and raised her. "I am going to help you stand up so you can sit on the couch again." He glanced at Sam, who nodded. Carefully the two men helped her to her feet and guided her across the room; as she lay down obediently Cohen covered her with the blanket. Her face was still drawn and pale as she laid her head on the pillow. She curled up defensively, but her breathing had become normal.

Cohen hooked his stool toward him with his toe, and, perching himself on it, he leaned forward and took one of her hands in his. "Now, Joanna, I want you to listen carefully. I am going to wake you up in a moment and when I do you will remember nothing of what has happened to you here today, do you understand? Nothing, until we come and ask you if you would like to be regressed another time. Then you will allow us to hypnotize you once more. Once you are in a trance again, you will begin to relive all the events leading up to this terrible time when you died. Do you understand me, Joanna?"

"You can't do that." Sam stared at him in horror. "Christ! You're planting a time bomb in that girl's mind!"

Cohen glared back. "We have to know who she is and what happened to her. We have to try to document it. We don't even have a datefix—"

"Does that matter?" Sam tried to keep his voice calm. "For God's sake! She nearly died!"

Cohen smiled gently. "She did die. For a moment. What a subject! I can build a whole new program around her. Those hands! I wonder what the poor woman can have been doing to injure her hands like that. No, Dr. Franklyn, I can't leave it at that. I have to know what was happening to her, don't you see? Hers could be the case that proves everything!" He stared down at her again, putting his hands lightly on her face, ignoring Sam's protests. "Now, Joanna, my dear, you will wake up when I have counted to three and you will feel refreshed and happy and you will not think about what happened here today at all." He glanced up at Sam. "Is her pulse normal now, Dr. Franklyn?" he asked coldly.

Sam stared at him. Then he took her hand, his fingers on her wrist. "Absolutely normal, Professor," he said formally. "And her color is returning."

"We'll send her home now, then," Cohen said. "I don't want to risk any further trauma. You go with her and make sure she is all right. Her roommate is a technician at the labs here, that's how we got her name for the tests. I'll ask her to keep an eye on things too, to make sure there are no after-effects, though I'm sure there won't be any."

5

Sam walked over to the window, staring out at the snow as he tried to control his anger.

"There could well be after-effects. Death is a fairly debilitating experience physically," he said with quiet sarcasm.

It was lost on Cohen, who shook his head. "The lass won't remember a thing about it. We'll give her a couple of days to rest, then I'll have her back here." His eyes gleamed with excitement behind the thick lenses. "Under more controlled conditions we'll take her back to the same personality in the period prior to her death." He pursed his lips, took a handkerchief out of his pocket, and wiped his forehead with it. "All right. Here we go. Joanna, do you hear me? One . . . two . . . three."

Joanna lay still, looking from one to the other, dazed. Then she smiled shakily. "Sorry. Didn't hypnosis work on me? In my heart of hearts I thought it probably wouldn't." She sat up and pushed back the blanket, swinging her feet to the floor. Abruptly she stopped and put her hands to her head.

Sam swallowed. "You did fine. Every result is an interesting result to us, remember." He forced himself to smile, shuffling the papers on the table so that her notes were lost out of sight beneath the pile. The tape recorder caught his eye, the spools still turning, and he switched it off, unplugging it and coiling up the wire, not taking his eyes off her.

She stood up with an effort, her face still very pale, looking suddenly rather lost. "Don't I get a cup of tea or anything, like a blood donor?" She laughed. She sounded strained; her voice was hoarse.

Cohen smiled. "You do indeed. I think Dr. Franklyn has it in mind to take you out to tea in style, my dear. It's all part of the service here. To encourage you to return." He stood up and went over to the door, lifting her anorak down from the hook. "We ask our volunteers to come to a second session, if they can, to establish the consistency of the results," he said firmly.

"I see." She looked doubtful as she slipped into the warm jacket and pulled the scarf around her neck. As she groped in the pocket for her gloves, she gave a sudden cry of pain. "My hands! What's happened to them? There's blood on my scarf—there's blood everywhere!" Her voice rose in terror.

Cohen did not blink. "It must be the cold. You've been a naughty girl and not worn your gloves, that's nasty chapping."

"But—" She looked confused. "My hands weren't cold. I wore gloves. I don't even get chilblains. I don't understand . . ."

Sam reached for his raincoat. He suddenly felt very sick. "It's the heavy snow coming so soon on top of a warm spell," he said as reassuringly as he could. "I'll prescribe something for you if you like. But I suggest scones

6

and cream and hot tea might be the best medicines to start with, don't you think?" He took her arm. "Come on. My car is out back."

As he closed the door of the room behind them he knew that he would personally see to it that she did not return.

1

LONDON   THE PRESENT DAY

"**B**asically I like the idea," Bet Gun-
ning leaned across the table, her eyes, as they focused on Jo's face, intense
behind the large square lenses of her glasses.

Jo was watching her intently, admiring Bet's professionalism after the
relaxed lunch at Wheeler's.

Their eyes met and both women smiled appreciatively. They had been
friends for five years, ever since Bet had taken over as editor of *Women in
Action*. Jo had been on the staff then, learning the trade of journalism. She
learned fast. When she left to go freelance it was because she could name
her figure for the articles she was producing.

" 'Anything Ethnic,' 'Medieval Medicine,' 'Cosmic Consciousness'—my
God, what's that?—'Meditation and Religion'—you'll have to keep that
light—" Bet was going through the list in her head. " 'Regression: Is
history still alive?' That's the reincarnation one, yes? I read an article about
it somewhere quite recently. It was by an American woman, if I remember, and totally credulous. I must try to look it up. You will, of course, be
approaching it from quite the opposite standpoint."

Jo smiled. "They tried it on me once, at the university. That's what gave
me the idea. The world authority on the subject, Michael Cohen, tried to
put me under—and failed. He gave me the creeps! The whole thing is
rubbish."

Bet gave a mock sigh. "Okay, Jo, show me the outlines. I'm thinking in
terms of a New Year or spring slot so you've got plenty of time. Now,
what about illustrations? Are you fixed up or do you want them done in
house?"

"I want Tim Heacham."

"You'll be lucky! He's booked solid these days. And he'd cost."

"He'll do it for me."

Bet raised an eyebrow. "Does he know that?"

"He will soon."

"And what will Nick say?"

9

Jo's face tightened for a moment. "Nick Franklyn can go take a running jump, Bet."

"I see. That bad?"

"That bad."

"He's moved out?"

"He's moved out. With cream, please." Jo smiled up at the waiter who had approached with the coffeepot.

Bet waited until he had withdrawn. "Permanently?"

"That's right. I threw his camera across the room when I found out he'd been sleeping with Judy Curzon."

Bet laughed. "You cow." She sounded admiring.

"It was insured. But my nerves aren't. I'm not possessive, Bet, but he's not going to mess me about like that. If it's off it's off. I don't run a boardinghouse. What do you think about the title of the series?"

"Nostalgia Dissected?" Bet looked up, her head a little to one side. "Not bad. I'm not totally convinced, but it certainly puts the finger on your approach." She beckoned to the waiter for the bill. "Aren't you going to tell me any more about Nick?"

Jo put down her coffee cup and pushed it away. She stared down at her hand, extending it over the tablecloth, flexing her fingers as if amazed they still worked. "It is three years, four months, and eight days since I met Sam again and he introduced me to his brother. Doesn't that surprise you?"

"It surprises me that you counted, lovie," Bet said slightly acidly, tossing her American Express card down on the waiter's tray.

"I worked it out last night in the bath. It's too long, Bet. Too long to live in someone's pocket, however well one gets on. And, as you know, we don't all that often!"

"Bullshit. You're made for each other."

Jo picked up her coffee spoon and idly drew a cross in the surface of the sugar in the earthenware bowl in the center of the table, watching the crystals impact and crumble with a concentrated frown.

"Perhaps that's it. We're so awfully alike in a lot of ways. And we are competitive. That's bad in a relationship." She stood up, the drab olive of her dress emphasizing her tanned arms with their thin gold bangles as she unslung the canvas satchel from the back of the chair and swung it onto her shoulder.

"Tim said he'd be at his studio this afternoon so I'm going up to see him now. Are you going straight back across the river?"

" 'Fraid so. I've got a meeting at three." Bet was tucking the credit card back in her wallet. "I won't give you any good advice, Jo, because I know you won't listen, but don't hop straight into bed with Tim out of revenge, will you. He's a nice guy. Too nice to be used."

10

Jo smiled. "I didn't hear that, Miss Gunning. Besides, I'm a nice guy too, sometimes. Remember?"

She walked slowly, threading her way through the crowded streets, the June sun shining relentlessly on the exposed pavements. Here and there a restaurant had spilled umbrella-shaded tables out onto the pavement, where people dawdled over their coffee. In England, she thought affectionately, the sun makes people smile; that was good. In a hot climate it drove them to commit murder.

She ran up the dark uncarpeted staircase to Tim's studio in an old warehouse off Long Acre and let herself in without knocking. The studio was deserted, the lines of spots cold and dark as she walked in. She glanced around, wondering if Tim had forgotten, but he was there, alone, in shirt sleeves, reclining on the velvet chaise longue that was one of his favorite photographic props. There was a can of Long Life in his hand. Above him the sun, freed from the usual heavy blinds, streamed through huge open skylights. "Jo! How's life?" He managed to lever himself upright, a painfully thin man, six foot four in his bare feet, with wispy fair hair. His unbuttoned shirt swung open, revealing a heavy silver chain on which hung an engraved amulet.

"Beer or coffee, sweetheart? I'm right out of champagne."

Jo threw her bag on the floor and headed for the kitchenette next to one of the dark rooms. "Coffee, thanks. I'll make it. Are you sober, Tim?"

He raised his eyebrows, hurt. "When am I not?"

"Frequently. I've got a job for you. Six to be precise, and I want to talk about them. Then we'll go and see Bet Gunning in a week or two if you agree."

Jo reappeared with two mugs of black Nescafé, handing one to Tim. Then she pulled a sheaf of notes from her bag and peeled a copy off for him. "Take a look at the subjects, just to give you an idea."

He read down the page slowly, nodding critically, as she sipped her coffee. "Presumably it's the approach that's going to be new, sweetie? When's the deadline?"

"I've got months. There's quite a lot of research involved. Will you do them for me?"

He glanced up at her, his clear light-green eyes intense. "Of course. Some nice posed ones, some studio stuff—whole foods and weaving—the vox pops in *chiaroscuro*. Great. I like this one especially. Reincarnation. I can photograph a suburban mum under hypnosis who thinks she's Cleopatra as she has an orgasm with Antony, only Antony will be missing." He threw the notes to the floor and sipped his coffee thoughtfully. "I saw someone being hypnotized a few months back, you know. It was weird. He was talking baby talk and crying all over his suit. Then they took him

11

back to this so-called previous life and he spouted German, fluent as a native."

Jo's eyes narrowed. "Faked, of course."

"Uh-uh. I don't think so. The guy swore he'd never learned German at all, and there's no doubt he was speaking fluently. Really fluently. I just wish there had been someone there who knew anything about Germany in the 1880s, which is when he said it was, who could have cross-questioned him. It was someone in the audience who spoke German to him. The hypnotist couldn't manage more than a few words of schoolboy stuff himself."

Jo said, "Do you think it'll make a good article?"

"More like a book, love. Don't be too ready to belittle it, will you. I personally think there's a lot in it. Do you want me to introduce you to Bill Walton? That's the hypnotist."

Jo nodded. "Please, Tim. I have a lot of information on the subject from books and articles, but I certainly must sit in on a session or two. It's incredible that people really believe that it's regression into the past. It's not, you know." She was frowning at the wall in front of her where Tim had pinned a spread of huge black-and-white shots of a beautiful blonde nude in silhouette. "Is that who I think it is?"

He grinned. "Who else? Like them?"

"Does her husband?"

"I'm sure he will. It's the back lighting. Shows her hair and hides the tits. They really are a bit much in real life. I'd say she was the proverbial milch cow in a previous existence."

Jo looked back at him and laughed. "Okay, Tim. You tell your Mr. Walton he's got to convince me. Right?" She got up to examine the photos. "It's something called cryptomnesia. Memories that are completely buried and hidden. You'll probably find your man had a German au pair when he was three months old. He's genuinely forgotten he ever heard her talk, but he learned all the same and his subconscious can be persuaded to spit it all out. These are awfully good. You've made her look really beautiful."

"That's what they pay me for, Jo." He was watching her closely. "I was talking to Judy Curzon last week. She has an exhibition at the Beaufort Gallery, did you know?"

"I know." She turned. "So you know about it."

"About you and Nick? I thought he was fooling about. I'm surprised you took it seriously."

She picked up her cup again and began to walk up and down. "It's happened too often, Tim. And it's getting to hurt too much." She looked at him with a small grimace. "I'm not going to let myself get that involved. I just can't afford to. When a man starts causing me to lose sleep I begin to

12

resent him and that's not a good way to nurture a relationship. So better to cut him off quickly." She drew a finger across her throat expressively.

Tim hauled himself to his feet. "Ruthless lady. I'm glad I'm not one of your lovers." He took her cup from her and carried it through to the kitchen. "And you really can be grown up about it and not mind if I ask him and Judy to the party?"

"Not if I can bring someone too."

He turned from the sink where he had dumped the cups and spoons. "Someone?"

"I'll think of someone."

"Oh, that kind of someone. A spit-in-Nick's-eye someone." He laughed. "Course you can." He put his hands on her shoulders and stared at her for a moment. "It could always be me, you know, Jo."

She reached up and kissed him on the cheek. "It couldn't, Tim. I like you too much."

He groaned. "The most damning thing a woman can say to a man, a real castrating remark. 'I like you too much,'" he mimicked her, his voice sliding up into an uncomfortable falsetto. He burst out laughing. "At least you didn't say I was too old though. Now scram. I've got work to do. Consider yourself on for the photos, but let me know when as soon as you can."

Nick Franklyn walked into Bet Gunning's office. She was standing at the window of her office, staring down at the river eleven stories below as she lit a cigarette. A pleasure steamer was plodding up the center of the tideway, its bows creaming against the full force of water as it plied from Westminster Pier toward the Tower.

"What can I do for you, Nick?" She turned, drawing on the cigarette, and looked him up and down. He was dressed in jeans with a denim jacket, immaculately cut, which showed off his tall spare figure and tanned face.

He grinned. "You're looking great, Bet. So much hard work suits you."

"Meaning why the hell couldn't I see you three days ago when you called?"

"Meaning editor ladies are obviously busy if they can't see the guy who handles one of their largest advertising accounts." He sat down unasked opposite her desk and drew up one foot to rest across his knee.

She smiled. "Don't give me that, Nick. You're not here about the Wonda account."

"You're right. I've come to ask you a favor. As a friend."

She narrowed her eyes against the glare off the water and said, without turning around, "About?"

"Jo."

She waited in silence, conscious of his gaze on her back. Then slowly she

13

turned. He was watching her closely and he saw the guarded look in her eyes.

"Does Jo need any favors from me?" she asked.

"She's going to bring some ideas to you, Bet. I want you to kill one of them."

He saw the flash of anger in her face, swiftly hidden, as she sat down at her desk. Leaning forward, she glared at him. "I think you'd better explain, Nick."

"She's planning a series of articles that she's going to offer *Women in Action.* One of them is about hypnosis. I don't want her to write it."

"And who the hell are you to say what she writes or doesn't write?" Bet's voice was dangerously quiet. She kept her eyes fixed on Nick's face.

A muscle flickered slightly in his cheek. "I care about her, Bet."

Bet stood up. "Not from what I've been hearing. Your interests have veered to the artistic suddenly, the grapevine tells me, and that no longer qualifies you to interfere in Jo's life. If you ever had that right." She stubbed out her cigarette half smoked. "Sorry, Nick. No deal. Why the hell should you want to stop the article anyway?"

Nick rose to his feet. "I have good reasons, Bet. I don't know who the hell has been talking to you about me, but just because I'm seeing someone else doesn't mean I no longer care about Jo." He was pacing up and down the carpet. "She's a bloody good journalist, Bet. She'll research the article thoroughly . . ." He paused, running his fingers through his thatch of fair hair.

"And why shouldn't she?" Bet sat on the corner of her desk, watching him intently.

He reached the end of his trajectory across her carpet, and, turning to face her, he leaned against the wall, arms folded, his face worried. "If I tell you, I'm betraying a confidence."

"If you don't tell me, there's no way I'd ever consider stopping the article."

He shrugged. "You're a hard bitch, Bet. Okay. But keep this under your hat or you'll make it far worse for Jo. I happen to know that she is what is called a deep trance subject—that means if she gets hypnotized herself she's likely to get into trouble. She volunteered in the psychology lab at the university when she was a student. My brother Sam was doing a Ph.D. there and witnessed it. They were researching regression techniques as part of a medical program. She completely flipped. Jo doesn't know anything about it—they did that business of 'you won't remember when you wake up' on her, but Sam told me the professor in charge of the project had never seen such a dramatic reaction. Only very few people are quite that susceptible. She nearly died, Bet."

Bet picked up a pencil and began to chew the end of it, her eyes fixed on his face. "Are you serious?"

"Never more so."

"But that's fantastic, Nick! Think of the article she'll produce!"

"*Christ,* Bet!" Nick flung himself away from the wall and slammed his fist on the desk in front of her. "Can't you see, she *mustn't* do it?"

"No, I don't see. Jo's no fool, Nick. She won't take any risks. If she knows——"

"But she doesn't know." His voice had risen angrily. "I've asked her about it and she remembers nothing. *Nothing.* I've told her I think it's dangerous to meddle with hypnosis—which it is—but she laughs at me. Being her, if she thinks I'm against it she's keener to do it than ever. She thinks everything I say is hokum. Please, Bet. Just this once, take my word for it. When she brings the idea to you, squash it."

"I'll think about it." Bet reached for another cigarette. "Now if you'll forgive me I should be at a meeting downstairs." She smiled at him sweetly. "Did you know we were running a review of Judy Curzon's exhibition, by the way? She'll be pleased with it, I think. Pete Leveson wrote it, so the publicity should be good."

He glared at her. "It's a damn good exhibition." He reached out for the doorknob. "Bet——"

"I said I'd think about it, Nick."

She sat gazing at the desk in front of her for several minutes after he had left. Then she reached down to the bag that lay on the carpet at her feet and brought out Jo's sheaf of notes. The paragraph on hypnotic regression was right on top. Glancing through it, she smiled. Then she put the notes into the top drawer of her desk and locked it.

2

As Jo let herself into her flat she automatically stopped and listened. Then, throwing down her bag, she turned and closed the door behind her, slipping the deadlock into place; she had not really thought Nick might be there.

She went into the kitchen and plugged in the kettle. It was only for those few minutes when she first came in that she missed him: the clutter that surrounded him of cast-off jackets, papers, half-smoked cigarettes, and the endlessly playing radio. She shook her head, reaching into the refrigerator for the coffee beans. "No way, Nicholas," she said out loud. "You just get out from under my skin!"

On the table in the living room was a heap of books and papers. She pushed them aside to make room for her coffee cup and went to throw open the tall French windows that led onto the balcony which overlooked Cornwall Gardens. The scent of honeysuckle flooded the room from the plant, which trailed over the stone balustrade.

When the phone rang she actually jumped.

It was Tim Heacham. "Jo? I've fixed up for us to go and see my friend Bill Walton."

"Tim, you're an angel. When and where?" She groped for the pad and pencil.

"Six-fifteen Thursday, at Church Road, Richmond. I'm coming with you and I'll bring my Brownie."

She laughed. "Thanks. I'll see you at your party first."

"You and someone. Okay, Jo. Must go."

Tim always hurried on the phone. No time for preliminaries or goodbyes.

A broad strip of sunlight lay across the fawn carpet in front of the window, bringing with it the sounds of the London afternoon—the hum of traffic, the shouts of children playing in the gardens, the grinding monotony of a cement mixer somewhere. Reaching for her cup, Jo sank onto the carpet, stretching out her long legs in front of her as she flipped through the address book she had taken from the table and brought the phone down to rest on her knee as she dialed Pete Leveson's number.

"Pete? It's Jo."

"Well, well." The laconic voice at the other end of the wire feigned astonishment. "And how is the beautiful Joanna?"

"Partnerless for a party. Do you want to come?"

"Whose?"

"Tim Heacham."

There was a pause at the other end of the line. "I would be honored, of course. Do I gather that Nick is once more out of favor?"

"That's right."

Pete laughed. "Okay, Jo. But let me take you out to dinner first. How is work going?"

"Interesting. Have you heard of a guy called Bill Walton, Pete?" Her glance had fallen to the notepad in front of her.

"I don't think so. Should I?"

"He hypnotizes people and regresses them into their past lives." She kept her voice carefully neutral. To her surprise he didn't laugh.

"Therapeutically or for fun?"

"Therapeutically?" she echoed incredulously. "Don't tell me it's considered good for you!" She glanced across at the heap of books and articles that formed the basis of her researches. Half of them were still unread.

"As a matter of fact it is. Fascinating topic." Pete's voice faded a moment as if he had looked away from the phone, then it came back strongly. "This is work, I take it? I was just looking for a phone number. You remember David Simmons? His sister works for a hypnotherapist who uses regression techniques to cure people's phobias. I'll tell you about it if you're interested."

It was one-thirty in the morning when the phone rang, the bell echoing through the empty studio. Judy Curzon sat up in bed with a start, her red hair tousled. "Dear God, who is it at this hour?"

Nick groaned and rolled over, reaching for her. "Ignore it. It's a wrong number."

But she was already pulling herself out of bed. Standing up with a yawn, she snatched the sheet off him and, wrapping it around her, fumbled her way to the lamp. "It never is a wrong number at this hour of the morning. I expect someone is dead." She pushed through the bedroom door and into the studio.

Nick lay back, running his fingers through his hair, listening. He could hear the distant murmur of her voice. Then there was silence. She appeared in the doorway. "It's your bloody brother from Edinburgh. He says you left a message for him to call, however late."

17

Nick groaned again. "I spent most of yesterday trying to reach him. Sorry, Judy. I'll go into the sitting room. I've got to speak to him now."

He shut the door and picked up the receiver. "Sam? Can you hear me? It's about Jo. I need your advice."

There was a chuckle from the other end. "In bed with one and in love with the other. I'd say you need my advice badly."

"Sam, this is serious. Jo's set on writing an article on hypnotic regression. Can I tell her what happened to her last time?"

"No. No, Nick, it's too risky. I could do it perhaps, but not you. Hell! I can't postpone this trip. Can you get her to wait until I get back? It's only a week, then I'll fly direct to London and have a chat with her about it. Stall her till then, okay? Don't let her do it."

"I'll try to stop her." Nick grimaced to himself. "But you know Jo. Once she gets the bit between her teeth . . ."

"Nick, it's important." Sam's voice was very serious. "I may be wrong, but I suspect that there is a whole volcano simmering away in her unconscious. I discussed it with Michael Cohen dozens of times—he always wanted to get her back, you know, but I persuaded him in the end that it was too dangerous. The fact remains that her heart and breathing stopped —stopped, Nick. If that happened again and someone didn't know how to handle it—well, I don't have to spell it out, do I? It must not happen again. And just warning her is no good. If you were to tell her about it, cold, after posthypnotic suggestion that she forget the episode, she either won't believe you—that's the most likely—or, and this is the risk, she may suffer some kind of trauma or relapse or find she can't cope with the memory. You must make her wait, Nick, till I get there."

"Okay, Sam. Thanks for the advice. I'll do my best. The trouble is, she's not talking to me."

Sam laughed. "I'm not surprised when you're in another woman's bed." Nick put down the receiver.

"So. Why do you have to discuss Jo Clifford with your brother for half an hour in the middle of the night?"

He turned guiltily to see Judy, wearing a tightly belted bathrobe, standing in the doorway.

"Judy—"

"Yes. Judy! Judy's bed. Judy's apartment. Judy's fucking phone!"

"Honey." Nick went to her and put his hands on her shoulders. "It's nothing to do with you—with us. It's just . . . well." He groped for words. "Sam's a doctor."

"Sam's a psychiatrist." She drew in her breath sharply. "You mean there is something wrong with Jo?"

Nick grinned as casually as he could. "Not like that. Not so's you'd notice, anyway. Look, Judy. Sam is going to come and have a chat with her, that's all. Hell, he's known her for about fifteen years—Sam introduced her to me in the first place. She likes Sam and she trusts him. I had to talk to him tonight because he's going to Switzerland tomorrow. There is no more to it than that. He's going to help her with an article she's working on."

She looked doubtful. "What has this got to do with you, then?"

"Nothing. Except he's my brother and I'd like to think she is still a friend."

Something in his expression made her bite back the sarcastic retort that hovered in the air. She gave a small, lost smile.

Nick resisted the impulse to take her in his arms.

The next morning he drove over to Jo's apartment. Swinging her keys, he made for the pillared porch that supported her balcony. He glanced up to see the window open wide beneath its curtain of honeysuckle as he let himself in.

"Jo?" As the apartment door swung open he stuck his head around it and looked in. "Jo, are you there?"

She was sitting cross-legged on the floor, the typewriter on the low coffee table in front of her, dressed in jeans and a floppy turquoise sweater, her long dark hair caught back with a silk scarf. She did not appear to hear him.

He studied her face for a moment, the slim arched brows, the dark lashes that hid her eyes as she looked down at the page before her, the high planes of the cheekbones, and the delicately shaped mouth set off by the severe lines of the scarf—the face of a beautiful woman who would grow more beautiful as she grew older—and he found he was comparing it with Judy's girlish prettiness. He pushed the door shut behind him with a click.

"I'll have that key back before you go," she said without looking up.

He slipped it into his breast pocket with a grin. "You'll have to take it off me. Did you know your phone was out of order?"

"It's switched off. I'm working."

He picked up the top book on the pile by her typewriter and glanced at the title: *The Facts Behind Reincarnation.* He frowned.

"Jo, I want to talk to you about your article."

"Good. Discussing topics is always helpful."

"You know my views about this hypnotism business."

"And you know mine."

"Jo, will you promise me not to let yourself be hypnotized?"

She leaned forward. "I'll promise you nothing, Nick. Nothing at all."

"Christ, Jo! Don't you know how dangerous hypnosis can be? You hear awful stories of people permanently damaged by playing with something they don't understand."

"I'm not playing, Nick," she replied icily. "I'm working. Working, not

19

playing, on a series of articles. If I were a war correspondent I'd go to war. If I find my field of research is hypnotism I get hypnotized. If necessary." Furious, she got up and walked up and down the room a couple of times. "But if it worries you so much, perhaps you'd be consoled if I tell you that I can't be hypnotized. Some people can't. They tried it on me once at the university."

Nick sat up abruptly, his eyes on her face. "Sam told me about that time," he said with caution.

"So why the hell do you keep on then?" She turned on him. "Call up your brother and ask him all about it. Samuel Franklyn, M.D., D.P.M., et cetera! He will spell it out for you."

"Jo, Sam will be in London next week. Just hold on till then. Promise me. Once he's seen you—"

"Seen me?" she echoed. "For God's sake, Nick. What's the matter with you? I need to see your brother about as much as I need you at the moment, and that is not a lot!"

"Jo, it's important," he said desperately. "There is something you don't know. Something you don't remember—"

"What do you mean, I don't remember? I remember every bit of that session in Edinburgh. Better than Sam does obviously. Oh, I'm sure he doesn't want me to investigate the subject of regression. It's one of his pet theories, isn't it, and he doesn't want me to debunk it in the press. That wouldn't suit him at all! If your brother wants to see me, let him come and see me. I'll deal with him myself. You and I have nothing else to say to each other. Nothing!"

"Then I'd best leave," said Nick.

Jo closed the door behind him.

That same evening Pete Leveson called with the name of the hypnotherapist: Carl Bennet. Devonshire Place. Jo scribbled it down on the notepad on her desk. She stared at it thoughtfully for a while after she had hung up the phone, then she tore off the page and put it on top of her typewriter.

The night of the party the huge photography studio was already full of people when Jo and Pete arrived. They paused for a moment on the threshold to survey the crowd, the women colorfully glittering, the men in shirt sleeves, the noise already crescendoing wildly to drown the plaintive whine of a lone violin somewhere in the street below.

Someone pressed glasses of champagne into their hands.

Jo saw Nick almost at once, standing in front of Tim's photos, studying them. She recognized the set of his shoulders, the angle of his head. So he was angry. She wondered briefly who with, this time.

"You look wistful, Jo." Tim Heacham's voice came from immediately behind her. "And it does not suit you."

She turned to face him. "Wistful? Never. Happy birthday, Tim. I'm afraid I haven't brought you a present."

"Who has?" He laughed. "But I've got one for you. Judy's not here."

"Should I care?" She noticed suddenly that Pete was at the other end of the room.

"I don't think you should." He took the glass from her hand, sipped from it, and gave it back. "You and Nick are bad news for each other at the moment, Jo. You told me so yourself."

"And I haven't changed my mind."

"Nor about tomorrow, I hope?"

"Tomorrow?"

"Our visit to Bill Walton. He's going to arrange something special for us. We're going to see Cleopatra and her Antony! I find it all just the smallest bit weird."

She laughed. "I hope you won't be disappointed this time, Tim. It'll only be as good as the imagination of the people there, you know."

He held up his hand in mock horror. "No. No, you're not to spoil it for me. I believe."

"Jo?" The quiet voice behind her made her jump, slopping her champagne onto the floor. "Jo, I want to talk to you."

She spun around and found that Nick was standing behind them. Quickly she slipped her arm through Tim's. "Nick. I didn't expect to see you. Did you bring Judy? Or Sam? Perhaps Sam is here ready to psych me out. Is he?" Rudely she turned her back on him.

"Tim, will you dance with me?" She dragged her surprised host away, leaving Nick standing by himself looking after her.

"Jo, love, you're shaking." Tim put his arm around her and pulled her against him. "Come on. It's not like you to show your claws like that. Let's get another drink—most of yours went on the floor, and the rest is down my neck." He took her hand firmly. Then he made a rueful face. "You're in love with Nick, you know, Jo. The real thing."

She laughed. "No. No, Tim, you dear old-fashioned thing. I'm not in love with anyone. I'm fancy free and fully available. But you are right about one thing, I need another drink."

There was no way she would ever admit to herself or to anyone else that she loved Nick.

Behind her Tim glanced toward the door. He frowned. Judy Curzon stood there, dressed in a floor-length white dress embroidered with tiny flame and amber colored beads, her red hair brushed close to her head like a shining cap. Her huge eyes were fixed on Nick's face.

Tim shook his head slowly, then firmly he guided Jo into the most crowded part of the room.

It was the following evening.

"Why did you do it, Judy?" Nick pushed open the door of the studio and slammed it against the wall.

She was standing in front of the easel, once more dressed in her shirt and jeans, a brush in her hand. She did not turn around.

"You know why. How come it's taken you nineteen hours to come and ask?"

"Because, Judy, I have been at work today, and because I wasn't sure if I was going to come here ever again. I didn't realize you were such a bitch."

"Born and bred." She gave him a cold smile. "So now you know. I suppose you hate me."

Her face crumpled suddenly and she flung down the brush. "Oh, Nick, I'm so miserable."

"And so you should be. Telling Jo in front of all those people what Sam and I had talked about in confidence. Telling her at all was spiteful, but to do it like that, at a party—that was really vicious."

"She didn't turn a hair, Nick. She's so confident, so conceited. And she didn't believe it anyway. No one did. They all thought it was just me being bitchy."

She put her arms around his neck and nuzzled him. "Don't be angry. Please."

He disengaged himself. "I am angry. Very angry indeed."

"And I suppose you followed her last night?" Her voice was trembling slightly.

"No. She told me to go to hell, as you well know." He turned away from her, taking off his jacket and throwing it down on a chair. "Is there anything to drink?"

"You know damn well there is." She retrieved her paintbrush angrily and went back to her painting. "And get me one."

He glared at her. "The perfect hostess as ever."

"Better than Jo anyway!" she flashed back. She jabbed at the painting with a palette knife, laying on a thick *impasto* of vermilion.

"Leave Jo alone, Judy," Nick said quietly. "I'm not going to tell you again. You are beginning to bore me."

There was a long silence. Defiantly she laid on some more paint.

Nick sighed. He turned and went into the kitchen. There was wine in the refrigerator. He took it out and found two glasses. He had not told Judy the truth. Last night, at midnight, he had gone to Cornwall Gardens and, finding Jo's apartment in darkness, had cautiously let himself in. He had listened, then, realizing that there was still a light on in the kitchen, he had quietly pushed open the door. The room had been empty, the draining board piled high with clean, rinsed dishes, the sink spotless, the lids on all the jars, and the bread in the bin, when he had looked, new and crusty.

"What are you doing here?" Jo had appeared behind him silently, wearing a white bathrobe.

He had slammed down the lid of the bread bin. "Jo, I had to talk to you—"

"No, Nick, there is nothing to talk about." She had not smiled.

Staring at her, he had realized suddenly that he wanted to take her in his arms. "Oh, Jo, love. I'm sorry—"

"So am I, Nick. Very. Is it true what Judy said? Am I likely to go crazy?"

"That's not what she said, Jo."

"Is that what Sam said?"

"No, and you know it isn't. All he said was that you should be very careful." He had kept his voice deliberately light.

"How come Judy knows so much about it? Did you discuss it with her?"

"Of course I didn't. She listened to a private phone call. She had no business to. And she didn't hear very much, I promise. She made a lot of it up."

"But you had no business to make that call, Nick." Suddenly she had been blazingly angry with him. "*Christ!* I wish you would keep out of my affairs. I don't want you to meddle. I don't want your brother to meddle! I don't want anything to do with either of the Franklyns ever again. Now, get out!"

"No, Jo. Not till I know you're all right."

"I'm all right. Now, get out." Her voice had been shaking. "Get out, get out, *get out!*"

"Jo, for God's sake be quiet." Nick had backed away from her as her voice rose. "I'm going. But please promise me something—"

"Get out!"

He had gone.

Nick took a couple of gulps from his glass and topped it up again before going back into the studio.

Pete Leveson was standing next to Judy, staring at the canvas.

Nick groaned as Pete raised a hand. "I thought I'd find you here. Has anyone told you yet that you are five kinds of shit?"

Nick handed him one of the glasses. "You can't call me anything I haven't called myself already," he said dryly.

Judy whirled around. "All right, you guys. Stop being so bloody patronizing. I'm the one who said it all, I'm the one who told her, not Nick. If you've come here to reproach anyone, it should be me, not him." She put her hands on her hips defiantly.

Pete gave a small grin. "Right. It was you."

"Was Jo very upset later?" she was unable to resist asking after a moment.

"A little. Of course she was. She didn't believe anything you said, but you chose a pretty public place to make some very provocative statements."

"No one heard them—"

"Judy." Pete gave her a withering look. "You were heard by virtually every person in that party, including Nigel Dempster. I've been on the phone to him, but unfortunately he feels it was too juicy a tidbit to miss his column. After all, he's got a job to do, much like mine when you think about it. 'Well-known columnist accused of being a nut case by redheaded painter at Heacham party . . .' How could he resist a story like that? And he was there in person! It'll be in Friday's *Mail*."

"Hell!" Nick hit his forehead with the flat of his hand. "They'll crucify Jo. She's trodden on too many toes in her time."

"She'll be okay," Judy broke in. "She's tough."

"She's not half as tough as she makes out," Nick replied slowly. "Underneath she's very vulnerable."

Judy looked away. "And I'm not, I suppose?"

"We are not talking about you, Judy. It is not your sanity that is going to be questioned in the press."

"She can always sue them."

"If she sues anyone, it would be you. For defamation or slander. And it would serve you right."

Judy blanched. Without a word she took the glass out of Nick's hand and walked with it to the far end of the studio where she stood looking out of the window to the bare earth and washing lines of the garden below.

Pete frowned. "Just how much truth is there in any of this story?" he asked in a low voice.

"None at all. Judy misunderstood completely." Nick compressed his lips angrily. "Squash the story if you can, Pete. It's all rubbish anyway, but if it wasn't"—he paused fractionally—"if it wasn't, think how much damage it could do."

Pete nodded. "I had a reason for asking. You are sure that hypnosis can't hurt her in any way?"

"Of course not." Nick gave an uncomfortable little laugh. Then he looked at him sharply. "Why do you ask?"

"No reason. No reason at all. . . ."

24

3

While Tim locked the car, Jo stared up at the front of the house. It was a tall, shabby building in the center of a long terrace of once-elegant Edwardian town houses.

"Jo, about last night—" Tim was pocketing his car keys.

"I don't want to talk about it." Jo hunched her shoulders. "It was a great party for some. Now please forget about it."

"But the way Judy behaved was appalling—"

"She's a jealous lady, Tim, fighting for a man. Women are like that. Primeval!"

"And aren't you going to fight too?"

"For Nick? No." She gave him a bleak smile. "Come on, Tim. Let's go and see some regression!"

Tim glanced at her warningly. "Jo, love. Can you bear in mind that this chap is a friend of a friend? Go easy on the put-downs."

"I'm not going to put anyone down, Tim." She hitched her thumb through the strap of the bag on her shoulder. "I'm going strictly as an observer, I shan't say a word. Promise."

The front door was opened by a woman in a long Laura Ashley dress, her fair hair caught back in an untidy ponytail. She had a clipboard in her hand.

"Mr. Heacham and Miss Clifford?" she confirmed. "The others are all here. Follow me, please."

The dark hallway was carpeted wall to wall with a thick brown carpet that muffled their footsteps as they followed her past several closed doors and up a flight of stairs to the second floor. There, in a large room, facing onto the long narrow gardens that backed the houses, they found Bill Walton and some dozen other people, already seated on a semicircle of upright chairs.

Walton held out his hand to them. "How are you? As you requested, Tim, I've told everyone that a lady and gentleman of the press will be here. No one objects." He was a small, wizened man of about fifty, his

25

sandy hair standing out in wisps around his head. Jo looked apprehensively into his prominent green eyes as she shook hands.

Somewhere outside children were playing in the evening sunlight. She could hear their excited shouting and the dull thud as a foot connected with a ball. In the room there was a muted expectant silence. She could see two girls seated side by side at the end of the row. Both now looked distinctly frightened. Next to them a man in a turtleneck sweater whispered to his companion and laughed quietly.

The room was a study—a large, comfortable, untidy room, one end of the wall lined with books, the opposite one hung with a group of Japanese prints mounted on broad strips of fawn linen. Jo took her place on one of the remaining chairs while Tim slipped unobtrusively behind her, perching on the arm of a chair by the fire. He removed the lens cap from his camera and put it quietly down on the seat beside him.

Walton moved to the windows and half drew the curtains, shutting out the soft golden glow of the evening. Then he switched on a desk lamp. He grinned at the small audience before him.

"Ladies and gentlemen, first let me welcome you all. I hope you are going to find this evening instructive and entertaining. Let me say at the outset that there is nothing whatsoever to be afraid of. No one can be hypnotized who does not wish it." He glanced at Jo as, quietly, she slipped a notebook out of her bag. She rested it, still shut, on her knee. "My usual procedure is to make a few simple tests initially to find out how many of you are good hypnotic subjects, then from among those who seem to be suitable I shall ask for volunteers to be put into deep hypnosis and regressed if possible. I should emphasize that it does not always happen, and there have been occasions when I have found no one at all suitable among my audience." He laughed happily. "That is why I prefer to have a dozen or so people present. It gives us a better choice."

Jo shifted uncomfortably on the wooden chair and crossed her legs. Beside her the others were all staring at him, half hypnotized already, she suspected, by the quiet smoothness of his voice.

"Now," he continued, hitching himself up onto the desk so that he was sitting facing them, his legs swinging loosely, crossed at the ankle. "Perhaps you would all look at my finger." He raised it slowly until it was level with his eyes. "Now, as I raise my hand you will find that your own right hand rises into the air of its own accord."

Jo felt her fingers close convulsively around her pencil. Her hands remained firmly in her lap. Out of the corner of her eye she saw the hand of the man next to her as it twitched slightly and moved, then it too fell back onto his knee. She noticed his Adam's apple jump sharply as he swallowed. She looked back at Walton, who was watching them all with apparent lack of interest. "Fine. Now I want you all to sit back and relax against the back of your chairs. Perhaps you would fix your eyes on the light behind me

26

here on the desk. The light is bright and hard on the eyes. Perhaps if you were to close your eyes for a few moments and rest them." His voice had taken on a monotonous gentle tone that soothed the ears. "Fine. Now it may be that when you try to open them you will find that you can't. Your lids are sealed. The light is too bright to look at. The darkness is preferable." Jo could feel the nails of her hands biting into her palms. She leaned forward and stared down the line of seated people. Two were blinking at the light almost defiantly. The others all sat quietly, their eyes closed. Walton was smiling. Quietly he stood up and padded forward over the thick carpet. "Now I am going to touch your hands, one by one, and when I pick them up you will find that you cannot put them down." His voice had taken on a peremptory tone of command. He approached the man next to Jo, ignoring her completely. The man's eyes were open and he watched almost frightened as Walton caught his wrist and lifted the limp hand. He let go and to Jo's surprise the arm stayed where it was, uncomfortably suspended in midair. Walton made no comment. He passed on to the next person in the line. Behind her Jo heard the faint *click* of the camera shutter.

A moment later it was all over. Gently, almost casually, Walton spoke over his shoulder as he returned to his desk. "Fine, ladies and gentlemen. Thank you. You may lower your hands and open your eyes. And may I suggest that we all have some coffee at this stage while we consider what is going to happen next."

Jo licked her lips nervously. Her mouth had gone dry as she sat watching the man next to her. His hand had returned slowly to his lap, completely naturally, without any effort of will on his part, as far as she could see. She glanced over her shoulder at Tim. He winked and gave a thumbs-up sign. Then he sank back into his chair. As if at a signal the door had opened behind them and the young woman reappeared wheeling a cart on which sat two large earthenware coffeepots. Unobtrusively she moved up the line of chairs, never speaking, not raising her eyes to meet those of anyone in the room. Jo watched her and found herself wondering suddenly whether it was to stop herself from laughing at their solemn faces.

When they had all had their coffee, Walton sat down once more. He was looking preoccupied as he stirred the cup before him on the desk. Only when the woman had left the room did he speak.

"Now, I'm glad to say that several of you tonight have demonstrated that you are susceptible to hypnosis. What I intend to do is to ask if any one of those people would like to volunteer to come and sit over here." He indicated a deep leather armchair near the desk. "Bring your coffee with you, of course, and we'll discuss what is going to happen."

It was several minutes before anyone could be prevailed upon to move, but at last one stout, middle-aged woman rose to her feet. She looked flustered and clutched her cup tightly as she approached the chair and perched on the edge of it.

Walton rose from his desk. "It's Mrs. Potter, isn't it? Sarah Potter. Now, my dear, please make yourself comfortable." His voice had dropped once more and Jo again found herself sitting upright, consciously resisting the beguilement of the man's tone as she watched the woman lean back and close her eyes. Walton gently took the cup from her and without any preliminary comments began to talk her back into her childhood. After only a slight hesitancy she began to answer him, describing scenes from her early schooldays; they could all plainly hear the change in the quality of her voice as it rose and thinned girlishly. Tim stood up and, creeping forward, dropped on one knee before the woman with his camera raised. Walton ignored him. "Now, my dear, we are going back to the time before you were born. Tell me what you see."

There was a long silence. "Back, farther back into the time before you were little Sarah Fairly. Before, long before. You were on this earth before. Sarah. Tell me who you were."

"Betsy." The word came out slowly, puzzled, half hesitating, and Jo heard a sharp intake of breath from the people around her. She gripped the notepad on her knee and watched the woman's face intently.

"Betsy who?" Walton did not take his eyes from her face.

"Dunno. Just Betsy . . ."

"You were lucky this evening." Walton looked from Jo to Tim and back with a grin. "Here, let me offer you a drink."

The others had gone, leaving Tim packing his cameras and Jo still sitting on her wooden chair, lost in thought. "Three subjects who all produced more or less convincing past lives. That's not bad."

Jo looked up sharply. "More or less convincing? Are you saying you don't believe in this yourself?"

She saw Tim frown but Walton merely shrugged. He had poured three glasses of Scotch and he handed her one. "I am saying, as would any colleague, Miss Clifford, that the hypnosis is genuine. The response of the subject is genuine, in that it is not prompted by me, but where the personalities come from I have no idea. It is the people who come to these sessions who like to think they are reincarnated souls." His eyes twinkled roguishly.

Tim set his camera case on a chair and picked up his own glass. "It really is most intriguing. That Betsy woman. A respectable middle-aged housewife of unqualified boringness and she produces all those glorious words out of the gutter! I can't help wondering if that was merely her repressed self trying to get out." He chortled.

Walton nodded. "I find myself wondering that frequently. But there are occasions—and these are the ones of course that you as reporters should witness—when the character comes out with stuff which they could in no way have prepared, consciously or unconsciously. I have had people speaking languages they have never learned or revealing historical detail that is unimpeachable." He shook his head. "Very, very interesting."

Jo had stood up at last. She went to stand by the bookcase, still frowning slightly.

Walton watched her.

"Did you know, Miss Clifford, that you are potentially a good hypnotic subject yourself?"

She swung round. "Me? Oh, no. After all, none of your tests worked on me."

"No. Because you fought them. Did it not cross your mind that the fact that you had to resist so strenuously might mean something? I was watching you carefully and I suspect you were probably one of the most susceptible people here tonight."

Jo stared at him. She felt suddenly cold in spite of the warmth of the room. "I don't think so. Someone tried to hypnotize me once, at the university. It didn't work."

She looked into her glass, suddenly silent, aware that Walton was still watching her closely.

He shook his head. "You surprise me. Perhaps the person wasn't an experienced hypnotist. Although, of course, if you resisted as you did today, no one could—"

"Oh, but I didn't resist them. I wanted it to happen." She remembered suddenly the excitement and awe she had felt on her way to Professor Cohen's rooms, the abandon with which she had thrown herself into answering all his questions before the session started, the calm relaxation as she lay back on his couch watching Sam standing in the corner fighting with his notepad while outside the snow had started to fall . . .

She frowned. How strange that the details of that afternoon had slipped her mind until this moment. She could picture Sam now—he had been wearing a brown turtleneck sweater under a deplorably baggy sports jacket. When they had been introduced she had liked him at once. His calm relaxed manner had counteracted Cohen's stiff academic formality, putting her at ease. She had trusted Sam.

So why now did she have this sudden image of his tense face, his eyes wide with horror, peering at her out of the darkness, and with it the memory of pain . . .

She shrugged off a little shiver, sipping from her glass as she glanced back at Walton. "It was about fifteen years ago now—I've probably forgotten most of what happened."

He nodded slowly without taking his eyes from her face. Then he turned away. "Well, it might be interesting to try again," he said thoughtfully. "Would you like to?"

"No!" She answered more sharply than she intended. "At least, not yet. Perhaps when my research is a bit further advanced . . ." Warning bells were ringing in her mind; Sam's face was there again before her eyes, and with it she heard Nick's voice: "There is something you don't know, something you don't remember . . ."

Shakily she put down her glass, aware of Tim's puzzled eyes upon her. Furiously she tried to get a grip on herself as she realized suddenly that Bill Walton was addressing her while he straightened some papers on his desk.

"And were you pleased overall with what you saw this evening, Miss Clifford?"

She swallowed hard. "It was fascinating. Very interesting."

"But I suspect that you are going to debunk the reincarnation theory in your articles? My wife is a great fan of yours and she tells me your style of journalism can be quite sharp."

Jo grimaced. "She's right. If she told you that it's very brave of you to be so open with me."

"Why not? I've nothing to hide. As I told you, the hypnotism is real. The responses are real. I do not seek to explain them. Perhaps you will be able to do that."

He grinned.

Jo found herself smiling back. "I doubt it," she said as she picked up her bag, "but I daresay I'll give it a try."

"Come on, Jo. There's something wrong, isn't there?"

Tim put a double Scotch on the table in front of her and sat himself down in the chair facing her.

Jo summoned up a tired smile. "I'm exhausted, Tim, that's all. This'll put me right." She picked up her glass. "Thanks for arranging everything this evening."

"But Walton worried you, didn't he, and not just because you thought he was a fake."

She shook her head slowly. "He wasn't a fake. At least, I don't think so. A telepath perhaps—I don't know—" She was silent for a minute. "Yes, he did worry me, Tim. The stupid thing is, I don't know why. But it's something deep inside me. Something I can't put my finger on, floating at the edge of my mind. Every minute I think I'm going to remember what it is, but I can't quite catch it." She took a sip from her glass and grinned suddenly, her face animated. "Makes me sound pretty neurotic, doesn't it? No, Tim, I'm okay. I think I've been letting Nick get to me more than I realize, with his fearsome warnings. He's a bit paranoid about hypnosis. He told me once that he has this fear of losing consciousness—even on the edge of ordinary sleep. I think he thinks hypnosis is the same—like an anesthetic."

"And it is true he's been on to his brother about you?" Tim asked gently after a pause.

She drew a ring on the table with her finger in some spilled beer. "I could kill Judy." She looked up at him again and gave a rueful grimace. "I wouldn't be surprised if what she said was true. Nick told me he'd been in touch with Sam."

"You knew Sam well, of course."

She nodded. "He became a friend after—" She hesitated. "After they tried to hypnotize me, he and his boss, in Edinburgh, that first time. But we were never lovers or anything. The *coup de foudre* came with his kid brother."

Tim raised an eyebrow. "And the *foudre* has not yet run to earth, has it?"

"Oh, yes. After last night it has. Finished. Caput. Finis. Bye-bye Nicholas." She bit her lip hard.

Reaching over, Tim touched her hand lightly. "Poor Jo. Have another drink." He stood up and picked up her glass without waiting for her reply.

She watched him work his way to the bar, his tall, lanky frame moving easily between the crowded drinkers. She frowned. Tim reminded her of someone she had known when she was a child, but she could not quite remember who. Someone she had liked. She gave a rueful grin. Was that why she could never love him?

She held out her hand for her glass as he returned. "I've just thought of who it is you remind me." She gave a quick gurgle of laughter. "It's not someone from one of my previous lives. It's my Uncle James's Afghan hound. His name was Zarathustra!"

Tim poured himself another whisky as soon as he got in. He had dropped Jo off at her apartment, declining her offer of coffee. Throwing himself down in one of his low-sprung easy chairs, he reached for the phone.

"Hi, Nick. Can you talk?"

He shifted the receiver to his other hand and picked up his drink. "Listen, have you seen Pete Leveson?"

"He was here earlier." Nick sounded cautious.

"Did he manage to call off the press?"

"Apparently not. Have you warned Jo?"

Tim took a long drink from his glass. "I was hoping I wouldn't have to. Shit, if he can't do it, no one can. And I don't think Jo has a clue what is in store for her. She doesn't seem to realize anyone else heard at all. As far as she was concerned there were only two people in that room at that moment—Judy and herself. I hope that dolly of yours is really proud of herself. Listen, Nick, what is this about Jo and hypnotism? Is it serious?"

"Yes. It's serious. So if you've any influence with her, keep her away from it."

"We went to see a hypnotist tonight."

31

"Christ!"

"No, no. Not for Jo. Or at least only for her to watch other people being regressed. It was fascinating, but the fact is that Jo did behave a bit oddly. She didn't seem to be the least bit susceptible herself when he did his tests on everyone at the beginning, but afterward Walton said she was really, but she had been fighting it, and it upset her."

"It would." Nick's voice was grim. "Look, Tim, is she going to see him again? Or anyone else, do you know?"

"I don't think so. She did say that maybe she'd got enough material to be going on with."

"Thank God. Just pray she doesn't feel she needs to pursue any of this further. Sorry, Tim. Judy's just coming in. I've got to go." His voice had dropped suddenly to a whisper.

Tim grinned as he hung up. The henpecked Lothario role did not suit Nick Franklyn one bit.

4

Jo wanted to call Sam.

For hours she had lain tossing and turning thinking about Bill Walton and Sarah Potter, who had once been a street girl called Betsy; and about Tim and Judy Curzon; but her mind refused to focus. Instead again and again she saw images of Cohen's little Edinburgh study, with the huge antiquated radiator against which Sam had leaned, then the snow, whirling past the window, blotting out the sky, then her hands. Somehow her hands had been hurt; she remembered her fingers, blistered and bleeding, and Michael Cohen, his face pale and embarrassed talking about chilblains, and suddenly with startling clarity she remembered the bloodstains on the floor. How had the blood, her blood, come to be smeared all over the floor of his study?

She sat up abruptly, her body pouring with sweat, staring at the half-drawn curtains of her bedroom. The sheets were tangled and her pillow had fallen to the floor. Outside she could just see the faint light of dawn beginning to lighten the sky. Somewhere a bird had begun to sing, its whistle echoing mournfully between the tall houses. With her head aching she got up and staggered to the kitchen, turning on the light and staring around; automatically she reached for the kettle.

She found Sam's number in her old address book. After carrying a cup of black coffee through to the sitting room, she sat on the floor and picked up the phone. It was four thirty-two A.M. as she began to dial Edinburgh.

There was no reply.

She let the phone ring for five minutes before she gave up. Only then did she remember that Sam had gone abroad. She drank the coffee slowly, then she called Nick's apartment. There was no answer from his phone either and she slammed down the receiver.

"Goddamn you, Nick Franklyn!" she swore under her breath. She stood up and went to throw back the curtains, staring out over the sleeping square. On the coffee table behind her lay a scrap of paper. On it was written in Pete Leveson's neat italic script:

33

Dr. Carl Bennet, hypnotherapist. (Secretary Sarah Simmons: sister of David who you rather liked if I remember when he came to W I A as a features writer in '76.) Have made an appointment for you Friday, three p.m. to sit in on a session. Don't miss it; I had to grovel to fix it for you.

Jo turned and picked up the piece of paper yet again. She did not want to go.

It was two forty-five as she walked slowly up Devonshire Place, peering at the numbers and stopping at last outside one with a cream front door. Four brass plates were displayed on the elegantly washed paneling.

The door was opened by a white-coated receptionist. "Dr. Bennet?" she said in response to Jo's inquiry. "Just one minute and I'll call upstairs." The place smelled of antiseptic and jasmine. Jo waited in the hall, staring at herself in a huge gilt-framed mirror. Her eyes were shadowed from lack of sleep and she could see the strain in her face as she watched the woman on the telephone in the reflection behind her.

"You can go up, Miss Clifford," the woman said after a moment. "The second floor. His secretary will meet you."

Jo walked up slowly, aware of a figure waiting for her on the half landing at the head of the flight of stairs. Sarah Simmons was a tall fair-haired woman in a sweater and shirt, and Jo found herself sighing with relief. She had been afraid of another white coat.

"Jo Clifford?" Sarah extended her hand with a pleasant smile. "Pete Leveson spoke to us about you. It's a pleasure to meet you."

Jo grinned "Did he warn you I'm the world's most violent skeptic?"

She laughed. "He did, but Carl is very tolerant. Come and meet him."

Carl Bennet was sitting at a desk in a room that looked out over the street. It was a pleasant book-lined study, furnished with several deep armchairs and a sofa, all with discreet but expensive upholstery; the carpet was scattered with Afghan rugs—sufficiently worn to emphasize their antiquity. It was a comfortable room; a man's room, Jo thought with sudden amusement, the sort of room that should smell of cigars. It didn't. There was only the faintest suspicion of cologne.

Carl Bennet rose to greet her with a half-hesitant smile. "Miss Clifford. Please, come and sit down. Sarah will bring us some coffee—unless you would prefer tea?" He spoke with a barely perceptible mid-European accent. He nodded at Sarah, who disappeared through a door in the far wall, then he looked back at Jo. "I find my kitchen is the most important part of my office here," he said gently. "Now tell me, exactly how can I help you?"

Jo took out her notebook and, balancing it on her knee, sat down on one of the chairs. It was half turned with its back to the window. Her mouth had gone suddenly dry.

"As I believe Pete Leveson told you, I am writing an article on hypnotic regression. I'd like to ask you about it and if possible see how you work." She was watching his face intently. "Yesterday I attended a session with Bill Walton in Richmond. I wonder whether you know him?"

Bennet frowned. "I've heard of him, of course—"

"And you don't approve?"

"On the contrary. He has published some interesting papers. But we practice in very different ways."

"Can you tell me how your approach differs?" Jo kept her eyes fixed on his face as Sarah came in with a tray.

"Of course. Mr. Walton is an amateur, Miss Clifford. He does not, I believe, ever claim medical benefits from his work. I am a psychologist and I use this form of hypnosis in the treatment of specific conditions. I use it primarily in a medical context, and as such it is not something to be debunked by cheap journalism. If that is what you have in mind, then I would ask you to leave now."

Jo flushed angrily. "I feel sure, Dr. Bennet, that you will convince me so thoroughly that I will have no cause to debunk—as you put it—anything," she said a little sharply. She took a cup from Sarah.

"Good." He smiled disarmingly. He took off his glasses and polished them with the cloth from the eyeglass case that lay on his desk.

"Are you really going to allow me to sit in on a session with a patient?" Jo asked cautiously.

Bennet nodded. "She has agreed, with one proviso. That you do not mention her name."

"I'll give you a written guarantee if you wish," Jo said grimly. "Would you explain a little of what is going to happen before she gets here?"

"Of course." He stood up and, walking over to the sofa, sat down again. "It has been found that unexplained and hitherto incurable phobias frequently have their explanation in events that have occurred to a subject either in very early infancy or childhood, or in a previous existence. It is my job to regress the patient to that time, take them once more through the trauma involved—which is often, I may say, a deeply disturbing experience—to discover what it is that has led to the terror which has persisted into later life or even into another incarnation."

Jo strove to keep the disbelief out of her voice as she said, "Of course, this presupposes your absolute belief in reincarnation?"

"Of course."

She could feel his eyes steady on her face. She glanced away. "I am afraid you will have to convince me, Dr. Bennet. I must admit to being very dubious. If you were to affirm to me your belief in reincarnation as part of a religious philosophy, I should not presume to question it. It is this quasi-medical context—" She indicated the consulting room couch. "Are you saying therefore that everyone has lived before?"

He gave a tolerant smile. "In my experience, no. Some have lived on this earth many times, others are new souls."

She stared at him, swallowing with difficulty the bubble of laughter that threatened to overwhelm her as he stood up again, a solid graying man in his sixties, and walked over to her chair. "I can see you are derisive, Miss Clifford," he said severely, his eyes on hers, magnified a little by the thick lenses of his glasses. "One grows used to it as an initial, perhaps defensive response. All I ask is that you keep an open mind while you are here. Are you objective enough to be able to do that?"

Jo looked away. "I am sorry, I really am. I pride myself on my objectivity and I will try. In fact"—she set her cup down at her feet—"you have aroused my curiosity intensely. Can you tell before you start whether people have lived before?"

He smiled. "In some cases, yes. Sometimes it is harder."

Jo took a deep breath. "Can you tell by looking at me?"

He stared at her, holding her gaze for a while, until she dropped her eyes and looked away.

"I think you have been on this earth before, yes."

She felt her skin creep. "How can you tell?"

He shrugged. "I might be wrong. It is an instinct I have developed after years of studying the subject." He frowned. "I have a suspicion that the patient you are about to meet may not in fact have done so," he said with a grimace. "I can't promise anything from her that will necessarily help you with your article. I have had one preliminary interview with the lady—we shall just call her Adele. She is a good hypnotic subject. She has a very strong and illogical fear of water that can be explained by nothing that she can remember. I shall try to regress her, and it may be that we need go no farther than her own childhood to discover the cause." He walked thoughtfully back to his desk, glancing at his watch. "She is late, I fear. Sarah!" He called toward the side room from where they could hear the sound of a typewriter. It stopped and Sarah appeared in the doorway. "Call Mrs. Noble and make sure she has remembered her appointment."

He scowled at the blotter on his desk, tracing the ornate gold tooling of the leather with a neatly manicured finger. "This lady is both vague and a hysteric," he said almost to himself. "It would not entirely surprise me if she did not turn up." He picked up the file on his desk and turned back the cover.

Jo felt a sharp stab of disappointment. "Are people usually apprehensive about your treatment?" she asked after a moment's pause.

He looked at her thoughtfully. "It would be strange if they were not."

Sarah appeared in the doorway. "Sorry, Carl, she's not coming. She says her daughter is ill and she has to go to see her. I told her she'd have to pay for the appointment anyway—"

Bennet gave a sharp gesture of dismissal. He stood up abruptly. "I am sorry, Miss Clifford. I was looking forward to proving my case to you. I am afraid this visit has wasted your time."

"Not necessarily surely." Sarah had picked up the folder on the desk. "Have you ever considered undergoing hypnotic regression yourself, Joanna? After all, Carl now has an afternoon free—at your disposal."

Jo swallowed. "I suppose I should try it myself," she said hesitantly. "Do you think I could be regressed, Dr. Bennet?"

He spread his fingers in the air and shrugged. "We could try. People of strong personality tend to make good subjects, but of course they must allow themselves to be hypnotized. No one can be against their will, you know. If you are prepared to set aside your reservations completely I would be prepared to try."

"I have no phobias to speak of." She managed a little smile. "Hobby horses, yes. Of such are my columns made, but phobias, I don't think so."

"Then we could regard it merely as an interesting experiment." He bowed with old-fashioned courtesy.

Jo found she was breathing rather fast. The palms of her hands were sweating. "I'm afraid I would be a difficult subject even if I cooperate as hard as I can. I did take part in a survey at the university under Professor Cohen. He didn't manage to get anywhere with me."

Bennet sat down on the edge of the desk and looked at her thoughtfully. "Michael Cohen was one of the great authorities on the subject. I wish I had met him before he died," he said a little wistfully. "I'm surprised to find you so hostile to the theories behind hypnotic regression if you were involved in any of his clinical trials. When you say nothing happened, do you mean he was not able to regress you at all?"

Jo shook her head. "He couldn't hypnotize me. I didn't know why. I didn't fight it. I wanted it to happen."

Bells were ringing in her mind once more, full of warning. Almost in panic she turned away from him, not wanting him to see the struggle going on inside her; she crossed the carpet to look out of the window into the busy street below, shivering in spite of the humid warmth of the afternoon. The sun was reflecting on a window opposite, dazzling as she stared at it. She turned back to Bennet.

"I have a small tape recorder in my bag. Would you object if I used it while you try?"

He shook his head and gestured toward a table by the far wall. "As you see, I use one too, for various reasons. I also always insist that Miss Simmons is present to act as a chaperone." He did not smile. "I should explain, however, that often one needs a preliminary session to establish a rapport between hypnotist and patient. It is a far more delicate relationship than that implied by music-hall acts or sensational fiction. So you should not expect too much on this occasion." He grinned suddenly. "Or too little either, Miss Clifford. You may indeed be a hard subject—I'm sure with your cooperation, though, I can achieve something. And I have a feeling you would be an interesting case." He smiled boyishly. "Quite a challenge, in fact. But I don't wish to talk you into this if you still have any reservations. I think you should take a little time to consider—"

"No!" Jo surprised herself with the vehemence of her reply. "No, let's do it. I'd like to."

"You are quite sure?"

"Quite." She reached for her bag and pulled the recorder out of it. "What shall I do?"

He walked toward the window and half pulled one of the curtains across, shading the room. Above the roof of the opposite building a huge purple cloud had appeared, threatening the sun. He glanced at it as he went back to Jo.

"Just relax. You are very tense, my dear. Why don't we have a cup of tea or some more coffee perhaps while we talk about what is to happen."

Jo shook her head. "I'll be okay. I suppose it's natural to want to resist giving your mind to someone else." She bit her lip. "Can I just ask you to promise one thing? If anything happens, you'll do nothing to stop me remembering it later. That's important."

"Of course. It will all in any case be on tape." He watched as she set the tape recorder on the floor next to his couch.

"Shall I lie down?" she asked, eyeing it nervously.

"If you wish. Wherever you feel most comfortable and relaxed." He glanced at Sarah, who had quietly seated herself at the table in the corner before the tape deck. Then he turned back to Jo. "Now, Joanna—may I call you Joanna?"

"Jo," Jo whispered.

"Very well, Jo. I want you to relax completely and close your eyes."

Jo felt the panic overtaking her. Her eyes flew open and she sat upright. "Oh, God, I'm sorry. I don't think I can do it."

"Just as you like. Try leaning back against those cushions. Why don't we try a light trance first, just to make you feel more relaxed, shall we? There's nothing to worry about. Just something to make you feel good. You may have seen Bill Walton do it. It's a very usual way of testing people's reactions."

Behind him Sarah smiled grimly, recognizing the tone of his voice as she saw Jo make herself comfortable against the cushions, her ankles crossed on the soft hide of the sofa. Jo closed her eyes once more and visibly tried to make herself relax.

"That's fine." Bennet moved toward her on silent feet. "Now, the sun is filling the room once more, so I'm going to ask Sarah to pull down the blinds, but meanwhile I want you to keep your eyes tightly closed." He glanced at the window. The sun had gone. The narrow strip of sky visible from the room was a livid bruise of cloud. There was a low rumble of

38

thunder as he began speaking again. "That's right. You can feel the light burning your eyes. Keep them tightly closed. That's fine." He touched her face lightly. "Now you want to open them but you can't. The light is too bright."

Jo did not move. She could hear him clearly and she knew she could open her eyes if she wanted to, but she could sense the glare behind her lids. There seemed no point in moving until Sarah had shut out the sun, the dazzling white shape that had appeared over the rim of the house on the other side of Devonshire Place, shining directly into the room.

Bennet took her hand gently. "Jo, can you hear me? Good. Now I'm going to tickle your hand slightly, just enough to make you smile. Can you feel me do it?"

Sarah gasped. He had taken a small pin from his lapel and driven it deeply into her palm. Jo smiled, her eyes still closed, still wondering why he didn't shut out the sun.

Bennet glanced at Sarah. Then he turned back to Jo. "Now, my dear, I want you to go back to when you were a little girl . . ."

Some ten minutes later Sarah's whisper broke into his concentration. "Carl, she's the best subject I've ever seen."

He frowned at her, his whole attention fixed on the figure lying back against the cushions in front of him. "I had a feeling she might be," he replied in an undertone. "I can't understand why Cohen couldn't reach her, unless—" He broke off and looked at her thoughtfully.

"Unless what?"

"Unless he gave her a posthypnotic suggestion that she should not remember for some reason." He turned back to Jo. "Now, Jo, my dear, I want you to go back, back to the time before you were born, to the dark time, when you were floating free . . ."

Jo stirred uneasily, moving her head from side to side. Then she lay still again, completely relaxed as she listened to him.

"Now, Jo. Before the darkness. When you lived before. Do you remember? You are another person, in another time. Do you remember? Can you tell me? What do you see?"

Jo opened her eyes and stared hard in front of her at the arm of the sofa. "It's getting dark," she said uncertainly. "Dark and cold."

"Are you indoors or out, can you see?" Bennet frowned at the window, which showed that it was indeed getting dark and that a torrential summer rain had begun to fall, streaming down the windows, gurgling from a broken gutter. There was another deep roll of thunder.

Jo spoke hesitantly. "It's the trees. They're so thick here. I don't like the forest."

"Do you know which forest it is?" Bennet was watching her intently.

"No."

"Can you tell me your name?"

She frowned, puzzled. "I don't know. Some call me—they call me Matilda—No, Moll . . . I don't know."

"Can you tell me something about yourself, Matilda? Where do you live?"

Slowly Jo pushed herself up from the cushions till she was sitting bolt upright, staring into space. "I live," she said firmly. "I live far away from here. In the mountains." Then she shook her head, perplexed. "The mountains fill my eyes. Black and misty, not like at home." She began to rub her eyes with her knuckles, like a child. She looked bewildered. "I don't know. I don't remember. I want to sleep." She lay back and closed her eyes.

"Tell me something else then, Matilda," Bennet prompted gently. "What are you doing?"

There was no answer.

"Are you walking in the forest, or riding perhaps?"

Jo hunched her shoulders rebelliously and said nothing. Bennet sighed. "Come now, my dear. Tell me what are you wearing? Are you dressed in your prettiest clothes?" He was coaxing now. He glanced at his watch and then looked at Sarah. "Pity. I thought we were going to get something interesting. We might try again another time—" He broke off as Jo let out an exclamation.

"They told me to forget. How can I forget? It is happening now . . ."

Bennet had not taken his eyes off her face. He leaned forward, every nerve ending suddenly tense.

Slowly Jo was standing up. She took a couple of paces from the sofa and stood looking at the wall, her eyes wide open. "When is it going to stop snowing?" she asked distinctly. She wrapped her arms around herself as if trying to enfold herself more warmly in her thin linen dress and he saw her shiver violently.

"It is snowing hard," Bennet agreed cautiously.

She frowned. "I had hoped it would hold off until we reached the castle. I don't like the snow. It makes the forest so dark."

"Can you tell me what the date is, my dear?"

"It is nearly Yule." She smiled. "Time for feasting."

"And which year, do you know?" Bennet reached for a notepad and pen. He watched Jo's face carefully. Her eyes were normal and focusing, but not on him. Her hand, when he reached gently and touched it, was ice cold.

"It is the twentieth year of the reign of our lord King Henry," she said clearly. "What a foolish question." She took another step. "Oh, Holy Mother of God, we're nearly there." Her voice fell to a whisper. "I am going to William."

"Who is William?" Totally absorbed, Bennet stopped writing and looked up, waiting for an answer.

But Jo did not answer. Her whole attention was fixed on something she could see distinctly lying on the road in front of her in the snow. It was the bloody body of a man.

5

The melting snow was red with blood. Richard, the young Earl of Clare and Hertford, pulled his horse to a rearing halt, struggling to control the animal as it plunged sideways in fear, its ears flat against its head. It had smelled the carcass and the wolves at the same moment, and it snorted with terror as Richard tried to force it around the deserted kill at the edge of the track. A buzzard flew up at the riders' approach, leaving all that remained of the mangled corpse in the slush-threaded mud. A few rags of clothing were the only sign that it had once been human.

"What is it? What's happened?" The slim red-haired girl swathed in a fox fur mantle who had been cantering fast behind him was concentrating so hard on catching him up that his sudden halt nearly unseated her. Behind her, at a more sedate pace, rode a second young woman and Richard's twelve knights, wearing on their surcoats the gold and scarlet chevrons of Clare.

The riders formed a semicircle in the cold sleet and gazed down at the torn limbs. One or two of the men crossed themselves fervently and the red-haired girl found herself swallowing hard. She pulled her veil across her face hastily. "Poor man," she whispered. "Who could have done such a thing?"

"Wolves." Richard steadied his horse with difficulty. "Don't look, Matilda. There's nothing we can do for the miserable bastard. No doubt the men of the village will come and bury what the buzzards and kites leave." He turned his horse and kicked it on, forcing it past the body, and the other riders slowly followed him, averting their eyes. Two or three had their hands nervously on the hilts of their swords.

All around them the bleak Welsh forest seemed deserted. Oak and ash and silver-limbed beech, bare of leaves, their trunks wet and shining from the sleet, crowded to the edge of the track. Save for the ringing of the horses' hooves on the outcrops of rock and the squeak and chink of harness it was eerily silent.

Richard gazed around apprehensively. He had been shaken more than

42

he liked to admit by the sight of the slaughtered man. It was an ill omen so near the end of their journey. He noticed Matilda edging her horse surreptitiously closer to his and he grinned in sympathy, silently cursing the need for an armed escort, which prevented him from taking her before him on his saddle and holding her in the safety of his arms.

But escort there had to be. He scanned the lengthening shadows once more and tightened his grip on his sword.

Wales was a savage place; its dark glowering mountains, black forests, and wild people filled him with misgivings. That Matilda should want to come here of her own free will, to join William de Braose when she did not have to, filled him with perplexed anger.

"We should never have left Raglan," he said tersely. "Walter Bloet was right. These forests are no place for a woman without a proper escort."

"I have a proper escort!" He saw the angle of her chin rise a fraction. "You."

Far away, echoing from the lonely hills, came the cry of a wolf. The horses tensed, ears flat, and Matilda felt the small hairs on the back of her neck stir with fear.

"How much farther until we get there?" she whispered.

Richard shrugged. "A few miles. Pray God we reach there before dark." He turned in his saddle, standing up in the stirrups to see his men better. "Make all speed," he shouted, then spurred his horse on toward the north.

Matilda pounded after him, clinging low over her horse's neck, determined not to drop behind, and their thundering hooves threw up clods of mud where the ice-rimmed puddles were melting slowly in the rain. The track was growing increasingly treacherous and slippery.

She quickly drew level with him again, her white veil blowing for a moment across her face from beneath her fur hood. "Richard," she called, "wait. Slow down. This will be our last chance to talk. . . ."

He slowed fractionally, wiping the sleet from his eyes. "We have had time enough to talk," he said abruptly. "You have chosen to tell me very little. I have no idea, even, why you are here, which will make it hard for me to face your no doubt irate husband with a satisfactory explanation as to why I have brought you to him."

He saw her flush. "Just tell him the truth," she retaliated defensively.

"Very well." He lashed his reins across the horse's neck. "I shall tell him how I was quietly riding, minding my own business, from home in Tonbridge to Gloucester when I met his baggage of a wife, completely unescorted except for one trembling female, hell-bent on riding the breadth of England to his side in midwinter. I shall tell him that I saw it as my chivalrous duty to escort you myself. And I shall tell him that any man who leaves a young, beautiful, newlywed bride alone in Sussex with her mother-in-law, while he travels to his farthest lands, is a mutton-headed

43

goat." He managed a wry grin, ducking the wet slap of a low-hanging branch in his path. If Matilda had been his wife he would not have left her. He clenched the reins fiercely; no man would accuse Richard de Clare of lusting after another man's wife. He admired her daring and her humor and her spirit, so unusual in a woman, no more than that. He glanced across at her and saw that she was smiling. "Why did you choose to come to Wales?" he asked suddenly.

She looked down at her hands. "Because I have nowhere else to go but to my husband," she said simply. "With him I am a baron's lady, mistress of a dozen castles, a woman of some importance." Her mouth twitched imperceptibly. "At Bramber with his mother I am merely another female with the sole distinction of being hated by her twice as much as anyone else. Besides," she added disarmingly, "it's boring there."

He stared at her in disbelief. William de Braose was a vicious, ill-bred man at least twice her age, with a reputation few men would envy. Even the thought of the brute's hands touching her made the blood pound in Richard's temples. "And you would prefer your husband's company to being bored?" he echoed incredulously.

She raised her chin a fraction, a mannerism he was beginning to know well. "I did not ask your opinion of him, just as I did not ask you to escort me to him."

"No, I offered." He took a deep breath. "So—I shall tell him also," he went on, "that an invitation to this Christmas banquet we hear he is to give for Prince Seisyll tomorrow is the only reward I shall ask for all my trouble. I shall wave aside the gold and jewels he is bound to press on me for my services in escorting you. I shall nobly ignore his passionate outpourings of gratitude and praise."

Matilda made a small grimace, all too well aware of her husband's reputation for tight-fistedness. She frowned, glancing at Richard sideways. "Supposing he's furious with me for coming?"

"So you have considered that possibility at last!" Richard squinted into the wind. "He'll probably beat you and send you back to Bramber. It's what you deserve."

A racing shadow in the trees distracted him for a moment. He scanned the surrounding forest, his face set. They were passing through a clump of junipers, thick and impenetrable: the ideal hiding place for an ambush. Secretly he suspected that his men, however well armed, would be no match for the leaping, yelling Welsh should they choose to attack. He had heard that they could sweep down, cut a throat, rip open a horse's belly, and be away again before a man ever had the chance to draw his sword. He shuddered every time he thought of the dangers on the route that Matilda had so confidently decided she and Nell could ride on their own.

"Is that what you'd do to your wife?" She peered at him, wiping the rain from her eyes as they trotted on again, side by side.

44

"What?"

"Beat her and send her home."

"Of course. Especially if she turned up with a good-looking fellow like me." He forced a smile, his eyes still narrowed as he gazed through the icy sleet.

Matilda glanced at him, then changed the subject, turning in her saddle. "Poor Nell. She's still keeping up." The girl was white-faced and rode slumped in the saddle, her eyes fixed determinedly on her shiny knuckles as they clutched the cold, wet reins. She was obviously near to tears, oblivious to the halfhearted banter of the knights around her or the tired baggage animals who jostled her horse constantly with their cumbersome packs. Matilda grimaced ruefully. "She started this adventure so well with me, but she's regretting every step now. Ever since we crossed out of Sussex, even with you there to protect us, she's been scared and weepy. Seeing that poor man will be the last straw. She'll spend the night having the vapors."

"Don't tease her." Richard leaned forward to slap his horse's steaming neck. "She had a lot of courage to come with you. You didn't feel so brave yourself when you saw that corpse. And don't forget, no one else would come with you at all."

She frowned, and dug her mare indignantly with her heels, making it leap forward so that she had to cling to the saddle. "Most of the others were Lady Bertha's women anyway, not mine," she said defensively. "I didn't want them to come. I shall ask William for my own attendants as soon as we get to Abergavenny."

Richard suppressed a smile. "That's a good idea. Go and ride with Nell now. I'm going to scout ahead and check all is quiet." He did not give her the chance to argue, spurring his horse to a gallop.

The very stillness of the forest worried him. Where were the woodsmen, the charcoal burners, the swineherds, the usual people of the woods? And if not theirs, then whose were the eyes he could feel watching him from the undergrowth?

Sulkily Matilda reined in and waited for Nell to draw level. The girl's china-blue eyes were red-rimmed from the cold. "Are we nearly there, my lady?" She made an effort at smiling. "My hands are aching so from the cold, I'm drenched through to my shift, and I'm so exhausted. I never imagined it would be so many days' ride from Bramber." Her voice had taken on an unaccustomed whining note that immediately irritated her mistress.

"We're almost there, Nell." Matilda made no effort to hide her impatience. She was straining her eyes ahead up the track after Richard as the trees thinned and they crossed a windswept ridge covered in sodden bracken, flattened by the rain. There was a movement in some holly bushes on the hillside to the right of them, and she peered at them, trying to see through the glossy greenery. Her heart began to pound. Something was hidden there, waiting.

Two deer burst out of the thicket and raced away out of sight up the hill. Richard cantered back to her side. He was smiling, but there was a drawn sword in his hand. "I thought we were in for trouble for a moment," he called. "Did you see? Shall I send a couple of men after them? Then we can make our own contribution to the feast."

They plunged into the thickness of the forest again, their horses' feet padding in the soft wet leaf mold beneath the bare trunks of ash and beech. From time to time the cold waters of the Usk appeared in the distance on their left, pitted gray with raindrops. Sometimes the track ran straight, keeping to the line of the old Roman road, then it would wander away over the curving contours that followed, among the trees, the gently sloping hills. Slowly dusk was coming on them through the trees, up from the river valley, and with it came menace.

The escort closed more tightly around them and, at a command from Richard, the men drew their swords. Matilda saw his face was concentrated and grim and she felt a sudden shiver of fear.

They rode on in silence through the darkening forest until at last in the distance through the trees they glimpsed the tall white keep of Abergavenny Castle, swimming in the mist that had gathered over the river.

Richard's face grew more taut as he saw it. The castle meant sanctuary from the threatening forest. But it also meant facing de Braose and relinquishing to his care the beautiful child-woman who was his wife.

They rode as fast as they could through the half-light across the deserted fields that clustered around a small township, past the church, and up the track that led to the drawbridge and the high curtain walls of the castle. It seemed that they were expected, for the drawbridge was down and the guard stood to attention, allowing them to clatter through into the castle ward unchallenged. There, shadowed by the towering walls, darkness had already come and torches flared in high sconces, lighting the faces of the men of the garrison with a warm unreal glow.

As soon as they were across it the drawbridge began to move, the cumbersome clank of the rolling chains signaling the disappearance of the cold forest as the gates closed and the castle was sealed for the night.

William de Braose was waiting for them on the steps of the great hall. He was a short man of stocky build with a ruddy complexion set off by his tawny mantle, his dark-gold hair and beard catching fiery lights from the torches in the wall sconces behind him. He watched the men and horses milling round for a moment, then he slowly descended the steps and approached his wife, his hand outstretched to help her dismount. His face was thunderous.

Swinging off his own horse, Richard saw with a quick glance that for the first time Matilda looked afraid.

46

"In the name of Christ and all His saints, what are you doing here?" William roared. He reached up and pulled her violently from the saddle. When standing she was several inches taller than he, a fact of which he was obviously painfully conscious. "I couldn't believe it when my scouts said that you were coming through the forest. I thought I forbade you to leave Bramber till the spring."

"You did, my husband." Matilda tried to sound contrite as she pulled the furs more closely around her in the chill wind. "But the weather seemed so good this winter and the roads were passable, so I thought there wouldn't be any danger. I hoped you'd be glad to see me. . . ." Her voice trailed away to silence and she could feel her heart beginning to thump uncomfortably beneath her ribs. How could she have forgotten what he was like? The hostility with which he always treated her, the cruelty in which he took such pleasure, the rank smell of debauchery that hung over him? In spite of herself she shrank from him and abruptly he released her arm. He swung around on the circle of men that had formed around them, listening with open interest to the exchange. His face flushed a degree deeper in color. "What are you staring at?" he bellowed. "See to your horses and get out of my sight!"

Matilda turned, blindly searching for Richard among the men. He was standing immediately behind her. Gently he took her arm. "Let me help you in, Lady Matilda," he said quietly. "You must be tired."

William swung around, his head thrust forward, his fists clenched. "Leave her, Lord Clare," he shouted. "My God, you'd better have a good reason for bringing my wife here." He swung on his heel and strode toward the flight of steps that led up to the main door of the keep, his spurs clanking on the hollow wood. Halfway up he stopped and turned, looking down on them. "You are not welcome here, either of you." His face was puce in the flickering torchlight. "Why did you come?"

Matilda followed him, her cloak flying open in the wind to reveal her slim, tall figure in a deep-blue surcoat.

"I came because I wanted to be with my husband," she said, her voice clear above the hissing of the torch beside her. "My Lord de Clare was only going as far as Gloucester, but he insisted that it was his duty not to let me travel on my own. We owe him much thanks, my lord."

Her husband snorted. He turned back up the steps, walking into the great hall of the keep and throwing his cloak down on the rushes where a page ran to pick it up.

"His duty, was it?" He stared at Richard as he followed him in, his eyes stony with suspicion. "Then you will perform the double duty of escorting her back to Gloucester at first light."

Matilda gasped. "You're not going to let me stay?"

"Indeed I am not, madam."

"But . . . why? May we not at least stay for the feast tomorrow?" She had followed him toward the central hearth in the crowded hall. "Why shouldn't we attend? It is not my right as your wife to be there?"

"No, it is not your right," he roared. "And how in the name of Christ's bones did you learn of it anyway?" He turned on her and, catching her arms, gripped her with a sudden ferocity. "Who told you about it?"

"Walter Bloet at Raglan. Stop it, my lord, you're hurting me!" She struggled to free herself from his hold. "We stopped there to rest the horses and they told us all about it. He was very angry that you had not invited him."

She glanced around, suddenly conscious of the busy figures all around them. Only those closest to their lord and his lady seemed to realize that there was something amiss between them and had paused to eavesdrop with unashamed curiosity. The rest were too absorbed in their tasks. Smoke from the fire filtered upward to the blackened shadows of the high vaulted ceiling.

"Damn him for an interfering fool! If you had waited only another two days, all might have been well." He stood for a moment gazing at her. Then he smacked his fist into the palm of his hand. "Go on up." He turned away. "Go to my bedchamber and rest. You are leaving tomorrow at dawn. That is my last word on the subject."

Matilda looked around desperately. The evening meal was obviously not long over and the servants had only just started clearing away the trestles to make room for the sleepers around the fire. Two clerks had come forward, hovering with a roll of parchment, trying to catch William's eye, and the shoemaker, a pair of soft leather boots in his hand, was trying to attract his lord's attention behind them. Her husband's knights, men-at-arms, guests, servants, crowded around them. On the dais at the end of the hall a boy sprawled, his back against a pillar, softly playing on a viol.

Richard touched her softly on the arm. "Go up, my lady. You need to rest."

She nodded sadly. "What about you? Your welcome is as cold as mine."

"No matter." He smiled at her. "I'll take you back to Gloucester as he commands, first thing tomorrow. It is for the best."

He escorted her toward the flight of steps at the end of the hall that William had indicated, cut into the angle of the new stone wall, and at the bottom of the stair he kissed her hand.

A single rush taper burned weakly in the vaulted chamber above. A tapestry hung on one side of the shadowy room, and a fireplace was opposite. Matilda was trying to hold back her tears. "Go and find the women's quarters, Nell," she said sharply as the girl dragged in after her, still sniffing. "I suppose I'll"—she hesitated for only a second—"I'll be sleeping with Sir William in here tonight. I won't need you." She shivered suddenly and bit her lip. "I misjudged our welcome, it seems. I'm sorry."

She watched as Nell disappeared up the stairs that led to the upper stories of the tower, then with a sigh she turned to the fire. She stood for a long time before the glowing embers, warming her hands. All around her her husband's clothes spilled from the coffers against the walls, and on a perch set in the stonework a sleepy falcon, hooded against the dim light, shifted its weight from one foot to the other and cocked its head inquiringly in her direction as it heard the sound of her step. Wearily she began to unfasten her mantle.

In the hall below a Welsh boy slipped unnoticed to the kitchens and collected a cup of red Bordeaux wine from one of the casks that were mounted there. Onto a pewter platter he piled some of the pasties and cakes that were being prepared for the next day's feasting and, dark as a shadow, he slipped up the stairs to his lord's chamber. He was sorry for the beautiful girl in the blue dress. He too had been sworn at by de Braose and he too did not like it.

She was standing by the fire, the glowing embers reflecting the red glint in her massed dark hair. Her veil lay discarded on the bed with her wet mantle, and she was fingering an ivory comb.

The boy watched breathlessly from the shadows for a moment, but he must have moved, for she turned and saw him. He was surprised to see that there were no tears in her eyes. He had thought to find her crying.

"What is it, boy?" Her voice was very tired.

He stood still, abashed suddenly at what he had dared to do, forgetting the cup and plate in his hands.

"Have you brought me some food?" She smiled at him kindly.

Still he did not move, and, seeing his ragged clothes and dark face, she wondered suddenly if he had yet learned the tongue of his Norman masters.

"Beth yw eich enw?" she asked carefully, groping for the words Meredith, the steward at Raglan, had taught her, laughing at her quick interest. It meant, What is your name?

The boy came forward and shyly went down on one knee, set the wine and cakes on one of the chests beside the bed, then turned and fled back to the hall.

Matilda gazed after him for a moment, perplexed, and then, throwing back her hair, she sat down on the bed and began to eat. She was ravenously hungry and she had to think.

She sat for a long time over her cup of wine, as the rush burned lower. Then in the last flickering light she stood up and began to take off her clothes.

The sound of talk and laughter had begun to lessen in the hall below and now an occasional snore was beginning to echo up the stairs. To her relief there was no sign of William.

She slipped naked under the heavy bed coverings and, her plans quite made up for the morning, was soon asleep.

6

On the sofa Jo stirred uneasily. Beneath her lids her eyes moved rapidly from side to side and her breathing quickened.

"I was tired after the days of endless riding," she said slowly. "And I slept heavily. It is first light now. The room is gray and shadowy and the fire has sunk to a heap of white ash. I am sleepy . . . trying to remember where I am . . ." There was a long pause. "I am not alone anymore. . . . There is someone here with me in the room. . . ."

"So you are awake at last!" William leaned over the bed and dragged the covers down to her waist. His breath stank of stale wine. "My beautiful wife, so eager for her husband's company. I'm flattered, my dear, that you should have missed me so much." He laughed and Matilda felt herself shudder. She lay still for a moment, afraid to move, as his calloused hands gripped her breasts, then she reached down desperately for the bedcovers, trying to drag them over her once more, remembering the charm she had recited to herself in the dark, the charm that would protect her from him for months to come.

She forced herself to lie still and looked up at him, her clear eyes steady on his. He immediately looked away, as always uncomfortable beneath her gaze.

"You must not touch me, my lord."

His mouth widened into a sneer. "Oh, no? And why not, pray?" He grabbed her wrist, twisting it painfully until she wanted to scream, but she managed to keep her voice calm as she spoke. "Because I am with child. And my nurse Jeanne says if you lie with me again while he is in my belly he will be stillborn."

She held her breath, watching his face. Cruelty turned to anger, then disbelief, then to superstitious fear. Abruptly he released her and he crossed himself as he straightened, moving away from the bed.

"That witch! If she has put the evil eye on my child . . ."

"She casts no evil eye, my lord." Matilda sat up, drawing the fur

51

bedcover over her breasts and clutching it tightly. "She wants to protect him. That is why she sent me to you, while I was still able to travel. Your son must be born in Wales, in your lands in the Border March. You cannot send me back to Bramber."

She watched him, hugging herself in triumph as he stood with his back to her, staring down at the dead ash in the hearth. Then he swung around. "How does she know all this?"

Matilda shrugged. "She has the gift of seeing."

"And she sees that I will have a son?"

"A strong, brave son, my lord." She saw the look of triumph on his face as he stared at her.

"Very well," he said. "But you may not stay here. I shall order a litter to take you on to Brecknock. You will be safe there."

She lay back on the pillows and closed her eyes with a sigh. "You are kind, my lord. I will try to obey you. I just pray to the Blessed Virgin that the extra journey will not harm the child. I am so tired." She put her hand on her stomach dramatically. "Please. May I not rest a day or two more? For your son's sake?"

She glanced up through her eyelashes to see what reaction her words provoked. William seemed nonplussed. He strode back and forth across the room a couple of times, kicking viciously at the hay that was strewn on the floor, obviously struggling with himself. Seeing his preoccupation, she felt a wave of something that was almost affection for this stocky, broad-shouldered man, still almost a stranger to her. He looked so uncertain.

"Are you pleased, William?" she asked after a moment. "About the baby?"

"Of course I'm pleased." His voice was gruff. "But I don't want you here. Not today."

"But why not? I shan't be in your way, I promise." She raised herself on her elbow, her hair cascading about her bare shoulders, dark auburn in the pale sunlight. "You won't even know I'm here, and in a day or two when I'm rested I shall go to Brecknock if you think that's really best."

William straightened his shoulders, frowning reluctantly. "If I allow you to stay," he blustered, "and I'm only saying if, you would have to promise on no account to leave this room. Not for any reason. It would not be safe. You would have to give me your oath."

"I promise, my lord." She crossed her fingers beneath the covers.

"You do understand me. You are not to move from here all day, no matter what happens." He glared down at her. "In fact, you would have to stay in bed. The feast is not for you. It's no ordinary Christmas junketing but a gathering of local Welsh princes and dignitaries for political discussions. I have to read them an ordinance from King Henry. That's why the Bloets weren't asked. It's no place for them, and it's no place for women. Do you understand?"

He turned away from her and strode over to the perch where his falcon sat. Picking up the gauntlet that lay on the coffer nearby, he pulled it over his knuckles. Gently he freed the bird's jesses and eased it onto his fist, whispering affectionately as he slipped the hood from its head. The creature looked at him with baleful eyes. "If you are going to be here, I'll take this beauty back to the mews," he said grudgingly. "Remember, you are not to leave that bed. If you try, I shall have you locked up." He turned on his heel sharply and left the room.

Matilda waited until his footsteps had died away. Then she slipped triumphantly from the bed and pulled a fur-lined dressing gown around her shoulders. She ran to the high window and peered out, feeling the cold wind lift her hair, listening to the sounds of life that were beginning to stir in the bailey below. It was a gray morning. The watery sun above the hills to the east was so shrouded in mist and cloud that it gave off as little heat as the waning moon.

Shivering a little, she glanced around the room. It did not look so comfortable in the cold light but she hugged herself excitedly. Her plan had worked. She was free of Bertha, was mistress of her own large household, or would be very soon, and had ensured that she was free of her husband's loathsome attentions until her baby was born. She gave a wistful smile. She had never felt better nor stronger than in the last two months, and she knew there was no risk. She was strong and healthy and had had no premonitions for the baby or for herself. She frowned suddenly as she gazed from the window, for premonitions she had certainly had, strange formless terrors that had plagued her for the last three nights in her dreams. She shrugged away the thought. Whatever they meant, she was not going to let them spoil today's excitement.

She wondered where Richard was this morning, then abruptly she put him out of her mind. To think about Richard de Clare was dangerous. She must forget him and remember that she was another man's wife.

She dragged her thoughts back to the day's feasting. She had no intention of keeping her promise to William and staying in bed. She meant to be there at his side.

There were about five hours to wait until it began, she judged, squinting up at the sun. Many of the guests were probably already at the castle or camped around its walls, others would be riding down from the Welsh hills and from Prince Seisyll's court, wherever it was, with their attendants and their bards and their entertainers. She felt a tremor of excitement.

At the sound of a step on the stairs she turned from the draughty window and ran back to the bed, shivering. A small woman entered, her hair gray beneath a large white veil. She was bearing a tray and she smiled at Matilda a little shyly. "Good morning, my lady. I've brought you some milk and some bread."

53

"Milk!" Matilda was disgusted. "I never drink milk. I'd much rather have wine."

"Milk is better for you, madam." The older woman's voice with the gentle lilt of the hills was surprisingly firm. "You try it and see, why don't you?"

Matilda pulled herself up on the pillows and allowed the woman to feed her broken pieces of the fine wastel bread. She found she was very hungry.

"Did I see you in the hall last night?" she asked between mouthfuls.

The woman smiled, showing rotten teeth. "No, madam, I was in the kitchens most of yesterday, helping to prepare for the feasting."

Matilda sat up, her eyes shining with excitement. "Do you know how many people are coming? Was there much food being brought in? Are the guests already arriving?"

Laughing, the woman spread her strong, work-worn hands. Her nails were badly broken. "Oh, enough for two armies, madam, at least. They seem to have been at work for days, ever since Sir William even hinted at a feast. But yesterday and the day before, I have been helping too with a lot of the women, to see that all is ready in time."

Matilda lay back, stretching luxuriously beneath the rugs. "I wish I were coming," she commented cautiously. "Sir William feels that I should rest because of my condition, and not attend." She glanced at the other woman and saw with satisfaction that she looked astonished.

"Surely you'll feel better by then, madam, if you rest now." The woman smiled kindly and twitched one of the coverlets straight. "It would never do to miss such a fine occasion as this one, indeed."

Matilda smiled. "That's what I've been thinking. I feel much better already." She noticed that the plate was empty and smiled. It was no use pretending that she felt too ill to eat. She tried to compose her face. "Where's Nell, the lady I brought with me?" she demanded, suddenly remembering. "She should have come to look after me. I want her to arrange some maids. I brought no other attendants."

The woman concealed a smile. "Your lady, madam, is talking to Sybella, the constable's wife. I felt you needed food first, attendants later. I'm thinking you'd have waited all day indeed if it had been up to those two." Without comment she took the plate and cup and put them aside, then bent to pick up the mantle that Matilda had left trailing from the end of the bed.

"Tell me your name." Matilda was watching closely out of half-shut eyes.

"Megan, madam. My husband is one of Sir William's stewards."

"Well, Megan, I want you to see that my clothes chests are brought up here and then later, if I do feel better, will you help me to dress for the feast?"

"Of course I will, gladly indeed." Megan's face lit up with pleasure.

"And listen." Matilda raised herself on an elbow and put her finger to her lips. "We won't let Sir William know that I might be coming. I don't want him to forbid me, thinking I am more tired than I am."

She lay back on her pillows again after Megan had gone, well pleased with the little Welshwoman's conspiratorial smile of understanding.

Below in the courtyard the morning sounds were reaching a crescendo of excitement and down the winding stairs to the hall she could hear a hubbub of shouting and laughter and the crashing of the boards onto the trestles as the tables were set up. It was hard to lie idle with so much going on about her but she was content to rest for the moment. The time to get up would come later.

She watched as a boy staggered in with a basket of logs and proceeded to light a new fire, and then a man humped in her boxes of clothes. There was still no sign of Nell, but Megan was close on his heels. After throwing back the lids under Matilda's instructions, she began to pull out the gowns and surcoats, crying out with delight as she fingered the scarlets and greens of silks, fine linens and soft-dyed wools, laying them on the bed one by one.

Matilda looked at each garment critically, considering which she should wear. Ever since she had heard about the feast she had thought about the gold-embroidered surcoat brought to her from London by William for her name day. It had come from the east and smelled of sandalwood and allspice.

"Oh, my lady, you must wear this." Megan held up her green velvet gown trimmed with silver. "This is perfect for you. It is beautiful, so it is."

Matilda took it from her and rubbed her face in the soft stuff. "William thinks that green is unlucky," she said wistfully. She loved that dress and she knew it suited her coloring. It would go well below the gold.

Nell appeared at last, fully recovered from the journey and in high spirits, as Megan was hanging up the last of the gowns in the garderobe. She had brought a message.

"From one of Lord Clare's knights," she whispered, full of importance. "He wants to see you in the solar, now, while Sir William is out in the mews with his hawks."

She helped Megan dress Matilda hastily in a blue wool gown and wrapped her in a thick mantle against the drafts. Then, her finger to her lips, she led the way out of the bedchamber.

Richard was waiting in the deep window embrasure, half hidden behind a screen. He was dressed for traveling.

"Richard?" Matilda stared at him as Nell withdrew.

"I am leaving. Your husband demands it." He put out his hand toward her, then let it fall. He shrugged. "My men are waiting. I return to Gloucester."

"No," she whispered in anguish. "I thought he would change his mind and let you stay . . . I thought you would be here . . ."

He reached out and touched her hand. "This is your household, lady," he said sadly. "This is where you wished to be, at your husband's side. There is no place for me here. Better I go now."

"But I thought it would be different—I thought it would be all right." She looked away from him, her bravery and excitement forgotten. "I had forgotten what he is like." She put her hands to her face, trying not to cry. "And I have to stay with him for the rest of my life!"

Richard felt the sweat start on the palms of his hands. "You are his wife," he said harshly. "In God's eyes you belong to him."

They stood for a moment in silence. She wanted to cling to him. Firmly she put her hands behind her. "I am carrying his child," she said at last with an effort. "So he is going to let me stay. Not here, but at Brecknock. He is not going to send me back to Bramber after all." She gave a faint smile.

Richard stiffened. The pain in his face was hidden in a moment, but she had seen it. She clenched her fists in the folds of her long skirts. "Are you not going to congratulate me on fulfilling my wifely duty?"

He bowed slightly. "Why didn't you tell me before?"

"I couldn't . . ." she whispered. "I couldn't . . ."

Outside the wind was rising, funneling down the valley, turning the melted slush back to crisp whiteness. It rattled the shutters and screens and stirred the hay that covered the floors, releasing the smell of stale woodruff, tossing the firesmoke back down into the rooms.

"You said your men were waiting," she said at last. The words caught in her throat.

"So. God be with you." He took her hand and raised it to his lips. Then he left her. She heard him walk across the room and slowly down the long winding stairs, his sword catching on the stone wall as he went until the sound died away and she was alone.

She sat for a long time on the stone seat in the embrasure, then, stiff with cold, she returned to her room and crept back beneath the covers of the bed.

Some time later Megan reappeared. She was bubbling with excitement. Prince Seisyll had arrived with his eldest son, Geoffrey, and his retinue, his harper, and his chief councillors.

"Handsome he is," Megan reported breathlessly, her eyes sparkling. "A real prince to look at, and tall . . ."

Matilda dried her eyes, pushed back the covers, and slipped out of bed.

She was standing in the middle of the floor in her shift with Megan braiding her long hair to go beneath her veil when she heard William's unmistakable step on the stairs. She glanced around wildly, looking for somewhere to hide, not wanting him to see her preparations.

"Quick, madam." Megan threw a warm dressing gown around her shoulders. "Wait in the garderobe and I'll tell him you're busy." She giggled nervously as Matilda fled for the little archway in the corner of the room.

Standing motionless among the hanging clothes just inside the doorway behind the leather curtain, shivering in the draft from the open closet hole, Matilda held her breath and listened. There was a moment's silence, and then she heard William's irritated exclamation as he saw that the bed was empty.

"Your lady will be back in a moment." Megan's voice was as firm as ever, Matilda heard, and she imagined Megan gesturing modestly toward the doorway where she was hidden. To her surprise William made no comment. There was a pause as he fumbled with the lid of a coffer, then she heard his loud step as he left the bedchamber and the squeak and clatter of his chain mail as he ran down the spiral stairs again. She emerged to find Megan pulling her gown from beneath a cover on the bed.

"Lucky I thought to hide it, madam, isn't it?"

"What was my husband wearing, Megan?" Matilda was puzzled. "Surely he wasn't armed for a feast?" She held up her arms as the other woman slipped the fine green cloth over her head and began to lace it up the back.

"He was wearing a hauberk, madam, then he took his tunic and mantle from over there"—she indicated the rail on the far side of the room—"and put them on over it. I suppose he can't bring himself to trust his guest quite, even when by custom our people always leave their arms by the door when they accept a man's hospitality." She smiled a little ruefully. "And Prince Seisyll is the Lord Rhys's brother-in-law, and *he's* the ruler of all south Wales and at peace with your King Henry, so there would be no danger and, besides, I've always heard that Seisyll is a good man, and chivalrous, with honor better than many at King Henry's court." The color rose a little in her cheeks as she spoke.

Matilda smiled and touched her arm gently. "Of course he is, Megan. I expect William is just being careful, that's all, out of habit."

She bit her lips hard to bring out the red in them, and lifted a small coffer onto the table to find her jewelry and her rouge. "Are you going to attend at the back of the hall?"

"Oh, yes, indeed, as soon as you've gone down. I want to see all the finery and hear the music." Megan deftly twisted Matilda's hair up and around her head and helped Nell adjust the veil and the barbette that framed her face.

They were pulling the folds of her surcoat of scarlet and golden thread into place and tying the heavy girdle when they heard the trumpet summons to the banquet from the great hall below. Megan looked up in excitement as the notes rose to the high rafters and echoed around the castle. Matilda met her gaze for a moment, holding her breath, then impatiently she gestured at the woman to go down the stairs and peep at the scene. She wanted to time her entrance exactly.

Nell had secured herself a place at the feast by cajoling the chataleine, and she glanced at Matilda for permission to go as Megan returned, her soft shoes making no sound on the stone.

"They are seated, madam. They have washed their hands and wine has been called for. They're bringing in the boars' heads now. You must hurry." She was breathless with excitement.

Without a word Matilda crossed to the top of the stairs and, taking a deep breath, began to tiptoe down. She was scared now the moment had come, but she refused to let herself think about what would happen if William sent her away in front of everyone. She was too excited to turn back.

At the foot of the stairs she waited, her back pressed against the stone wall, just out of sight of the noisy hall. It was lit with torches and hundreds of candles, although it was full day outside, and a haze of smoky heat was already drifting in the rafters and up the stairs past her toward the cooler upper floors of the tower. The noise was deafening. Cautiously she edged a step or two farther and peered around the corner.

The archway where she stood was slightly behind her husband and his guests at the high table, and in the deep shadow she was satisfied that she would not be seen.

The prince, she could see, was seated at William's right hand. He was clean shaven and his dark hair was cut in a neat fringe across his eyes. He was finely arrayed in a sweeping yellow cloak and tunic and she could see a ring sparkling on his hand as he raised it for a moment. He had thrown back his head with laughter at some remark from a man on his right.

Then, as she was plucking up the courage to slip from her hiding place and go to his side, William rose to his feet, and she saw him produce a roll of parchment. He knocked on the table for silence with the jeweled handle of his dagger and then, with it still clutched in his hand, looked around at the expectant hall.

Matilda stayed hidden, scanning the crowded tables, trying to recognize faces she knew. There was Ranulph Poer, one of the king's advisers for the March, with his foxy face and drooping eye, who had visited them on numerous occasions in the summer at Bramber. And there too at the high table was plump, white-haired Philip de Braose, her husband's uncle, and between them a youth of about fifteen, not much younger than she. That must be the prince's son, she thought, and as he turned for a moment to lean back in his chair and look at his father she saw his sparkling eyes and flushed face. He is as excited as I am, she realized suddenly, and she envied the boy who was sitting there by right while she had to resort to subterfuge. To her surprise there were no other faces that she recognized. And there were no women at the high table at all, just as William had said. She had expected him to have invited many of the men whom she knew to be neighbors on the Welsh March, but as Walter Bloet had complained, none of them was present.

William was scrutinizing the parchment in his hand as if he had never seen it before. She could see the ugly blue vein in his neck beginning to throb above his high collar. His mail corselet was entirely hidden by his robe.

"My lords, gentlemen," William began, his voice unnaturally high. "I have asked you here that you may hear a command from the high and mighty King Henry regarding the Welshmen in Gwent." He paused and, raising his goblet, took a gulp of wine. Matilda could see his hand shaking. The attention of everyone in the hall was fixed on him now, and there was silence, except for some subdued chatter among the servants at the back and the growling of two dogs in anticipation of the shower of scraps that they knew was about to begin. Matilda thought she could see Megan leaning against one of the serving men at the far end of the hall, and briefly she wondered why the woman wasn't seated at one of the lower tables if her husband was a steward. Nell, she had seen at once, had found herself a place immediately below the dais.

Prince Seisyll had leaned back in his carved chair and was looking up at William beside him, a good-natured smile on his weathered face.

"This is an ordinance concerning the bearing of arms in this territory," William went on. "The king has decreed that in future this shall no longer be permitted to the Welsh peoples, under . . ." He broke off as Prince Seisyll sat abruptly upright, slamming his fist on the table.

"What!" he roared. "What does Henry of England dare to decree for Gwent?"

William paused for a moment, looking down at the other man, his face expressionless, and then slowly and deliberately he laid the parchment down on the table, raised the hand that still held his dagger, and brought the glinting blade down directly into the prince's throat.

Seisyll half rose, grasping feebly at William's fingers, gurgled horribly, and then collapsed across the table, blood spewing from his mouth over the white linen tablecloth. There was a moment's total silence and then the hall was in an uproar. From beneath their cloaks William's followers produced swords and daggers, and as Matilda stood motionless in the doorway, transfixed with horror, they proceeded to cut down the unarmed Welsh. She saw Philip de Braose lift his knife and stab the young prince in the back as the boy rose to try to reach his father, then Philip and Ranulph together left the table and ran for the door, hacking with their swords as they went. William was standing motionless as he watched the slaughter all around him, the blood of his victim spattered all over his sleeve. His face was stony.

Above the screams and yells a weird and somehow more terrible sound echoed suddenly through the vaulted wooden roof of the hall. A man-at-arms had plunged his sword through the heart of the old harper, who, seated with his instrument, had been waiting to serenade his prince's host. The old man fell forward, clutching wildly at the strings so that they sang in a frightening last chord and then, as he sprawled to the floor, Matilda saw the soldier slice through the strings of the harp, the blade of his sword still drenched with its owner's blood.

7

Slowly she became aware of the pain in her hands and, looking blindly away for the first time from the terror of the scene in front of her, she stared at them. For a moment she could not focus her eyes at all in the darkness, but then as the flickering torchlight played over the wall where she stood hidden she realized she was clinging to the rough-hewn architrave of the arch as though her life depended on it, and where her nails had clawed at the uneven surface her fingers were bleeding. There were smears of blood on the pale stone—her own blood.

It was the last thing she saw. In the grip of a numbing horror that mercifully blotted out the sound of the boy's desperate screams, she began to grope her way along the wall. Her gown and shift were drenched with sweat and she could feel the sour taste of vomit in her mouth as she dragged herself back up the spiral stairs, tripping on her long skirts in her haste to escape to the upper room before she collapsed.

The only sound she could hear was her own breath, coming in tight dry gasps that tore painfully at her ribs and caught in her throat, threatening to choke her and, once, the sob of agony that escaped her as she stumbled on her hem and fell heavily, flinging out her hands to save herself with a jar that seared through her wrists and into her injured fingers.

The bedchamber was deserted. The rushlights had died in a smoky smell of tallow and the only illumination came from the fire. After climbing dazed onto the bed she lay rigid, listening to the pine logs hissing and spluttering as they showered sparks onto the floor, where they glowed for a moment before going out. The distant sound of a shout echoed up the stairs and she turned over convulsively, pulling the covers over her head, trying to blot out the noise. Then all went black at last and she felt herself spinning down into silence.

Sometime later she stirred uneasily in her sleep, still hugging the pillow to her face. She half awakened and lay still, listening. A voice was calling her name in the distance, trying to rouse her and bring her back, calling a name again and again. She listened, half roused. But she resisted. She did not want to wake. She could not face the terror that consciousness would bring.

"Let her sleep. She will wake by herself in the end!"

The words echoed in her head for a moment, so clear they must have been spoken from beside the bed; then, as she turned her face away, they receded once more and she fell back into the dark.

When she next woke the room was absolutely silent. There were no voices, no sounds from below in the great hall. She lay for a while, her face still buried in the fur of the bedcover, too stiff and dazed to move, feeling its rancid hair scratchy against her mouth and nose, then at last she managed to raise herself a little and try to turn over. At once her head began to spin and she was overwhelmed with nausea. With a sob she fell back onto the bed.

A hand touched her shoulder and something cool and damp and comforting was pressed gently to the back of her neck.

"I'll help you, my lady, shall I?" Megan's voice was little more than a whisper.

At the sound of it Matilda forced herself to lift her head. Then reluctantly she pulled herself up onto one elbow and looked around.

"Megan? Megan, is it you? Tell me it's not true. It's not. It's not . . ." Her voice broke. "It must not be true."

The room was dark as she groped for the woman's hands and held them fast. Slowly as her sight adjusted to the gloom she could just see Megan's face in the dying glow of the fire. Her eyes were shut and tears streaked her cheeks as, wordlessly, Megan shook her head.

They remained unmoving for a long time, huddled together on the bed, their hands tightly clasped as they listened to the logs shifting on the hearth. Then at last Matilda pulled herself up against the pillows.

"How long have I been asleep?" she said. Her voice sounded strange and high to her ears. "Where is my . . . where is William?" She could not bring herself to call him her husband.

Megan opened her eyes wearily and sat motionless for a moment, staring in front of her. Then she shook her head, unable to speak.

"Is he still here, in the castle?"

"*Duw*, I don't know," Megan answered finally, her voice lifeless. "They took out the dead and cleaned the blood away. Then Lord de Braose sent a detachment of his men after the people who stayed behind at Castle Arnold. Prince Seisyll's wife, his babies . . ." She began to cry openly.

"His babies?" Matilda whispered. "William has ordered the death of Seisyll's babies?" She stared at Megan in disbelief. "But surely there are guards, there will be men there to protect them?"

"How? When all the prince's men came with him, thinking there is peace between King Henry and the men of Gwent, trusting the King of England's honor!" The gentle face had twisted with hatred.

"I must stop them." After pushing the covers aside, Matilda climbed shakily from the bed. Her feet were bare but she did not notice. Megan did not move as she made her way to the top of the stairs and listened for a moment to the silence that was broken only by the howl of the wind outside the walls. Steeling herself, Matilda began to tiptoe down, her feet aching from the cold stone.

The great hall was empty. The rushes on the floor had been swept away, leaving the flagstones glistening with water. The tables had been stacked and the chairs and benches removed. It was absolutely empty. Moving silently on her bare feet, Matilda crossed to the center of the floor and looked around. The echoing vault of the roof was quiet now and the fire had died. Two or three torches still burned low in their sconces, but there was no one to tend them and they flared and smoked by turns in the draft. The only smell that remained was the slight aroma of roasting beef.

"Sweet Jesus," she breathed. She crossed herself fearfully as her eyes searched the empty shadowy corners, but nothing stirred. There were no ghosts yet of the dead.

Forcing herself to move, she left the hall and went in search of her husband. The solar, the guardroom, the kitchens, and the stores were all empty. And the chapel, where the wax candles had burned almost to the stub. The whole keep was deserted. Reluctantly she turned at last to the entrance and, walking out, stood looking down into the dark bailey court-yard below.

It was full of silent people. Every man, woman, and child from the castle and the township appeared to be there, standing around the huge pile of dead. Behind them some of William's guards stood muttering quietly, looking uneasily around them into the shadows or toward the lowered drawbridge. They all appeared to be waiting for something—or someone. Nowhere was there a sign of the dark twisted face that belonged to her husband.

Matilda stepped out over the threshold and walked slowly down the flight of wooden steps. She was half-conscious of the inquiring faces turned toward her on every side, but her eyes were fixed on the bodies of the dead. The Welsh moved aside to let her pass and watched as she walked, head and shoulders taller than most of them, a stately slim figure in her gold and scarlet gown, to stand before her husband's victims. An icy wind had arisen. It whipped at her long hair, tearing it out of the loose braids that held it. Megan must have removed her headdress while she lay insensible and she had not noticed.

She stood there a long time, head bowed, her eyes fixed on the ground, only half seeing the flickering shadows thrown by the torches of the men-at-arms. Then at last she raised her eyes to look directly at the men her husband had killed. The body of Prince Seisyll lay slightly apart from the others and someone had crossed his hands across his breast. On his forefinger a dark red stone glittered coldly in the torchlight.

Slowly her gaze traveled back to the gory heap, searching for the body of his son, the boy whose excited happy mood had so matched her own. She saw him almost at once, lying sprawled beneath another man, his head thrown back, his mouth open in horror at what he had seen. A trickle of blood had dried on the downless chin. His fingers were still clutching the linen napkin that the page had handed him as William began his speech. A few feet from his head lay the harp with its severed strings. Its frame had been snapped in two.

Her feet no longer felt the cold as she walked across the cobbles to the gatehouse and out over the drawbridge. In fact, she felt nothing at all. No one tried to stop her. The guards moved aside to let her pass and regrouped beneath the gateway behind her.

She walked slowly down toward the shining sweep of the river, her hair quite loose now, lifting around her head in a cloud. The wind carried showers of icy raindrops off the iron whiteness of the desolate hills but she neither saw nor felt their sting on her face. Somehow she seemed to find a path as she moved unseeing through the darkness and avoided trees and bushes and the outcrops of rock in her way. The cold moon was glinting fitfully through the rushing clouds to reflect in the Usk beneath as she stood for a while on the bank gazing into the luminous water; then she walked on. Soon the castle was out of sight and she was quite alone in the whispering trees. There the snow had melted and clogged into soft slush beneath the network of roots and the path became muddy beneath her toes, dragging at the sodden train of her gown.

It was several minutes before she realized that there was someone speaking to her, the voice quietly insistent, urging her back, calming the unsteady thudding of the pulse in her head.

"I'm reaching her now," Carl Bennet murmured to the frantic woman at his side. He sat forward on the edge of his chair, staring intently at Jo as she lay restlessly on the sofa by the window. Outside the rain had begun again, sliding down the panes, forming little black pools in the soil of the dusty window box.

"Jo? Matilda? Can you hear me?"

His voice was professionally calm and reassuring again, only the beads of sweat on his forehead betraying the strain of the past hour.

On the sofa Jo stirred and half turned to face him. "Who is that?" she asked. "There is sleet in the moonlight. I cannot see properly." Her eyes opened and she stared blindly at Bennet. "Is it you? The Welsh boy who brought me my food? I did not know what was planned. You must believe me, I did not know . . ." With tears running down her cheeks again she struggled to sit up, clutching at Bennet's jacket.

Avoiding her desperate fingers, he leaned forward and put his hands gently on her shoulders, pushing her back against the cushions.

"Listen, my dear, I am going to wake you up now, I want you to come back to us. I am going to count to three. When I do so you will wake up as Joanna Clifford. You will remember all that has occurred but you will be relaxed and happy. Do you understand me?" For a moment he thought she had not heard him, but after a pause her hands dropped and she ceased struggling. He watched her face, waiting for the slight nod that came after a long perplexed silence.

"Good girl," he said softly. "Now . . . one—two—three."

He waited only a moment more, to be certain, then he leaned back in his chair and took off his glasses.

Jo lay still, staring from Bennet to his secretary and back. For a moment none of them spoke. Then, as Jo raised her hand and ran her fingers through her hair, Bennet stood up. "I think we could all do with some coffee," he said, his voice shaking. "Would you, Sarah, please?"

He walked across to the table and switched off the tape recorder with a sharp *click*. He took a deep breath. "Well, how do you feel, Jo?" he asked. His tone was light and conversational. His glasses polished to his satisfaction at last, he put them back on his nose. Then he turned to look at her.

"I don't know." Jo pushed herself up against the cushions. "Oh, God, I'm so cold. My feet are freezing." She leaned forward and rubbed them. "And my fingers are hurting— Oh, Christ, I don't believe it! Tell me it didn't happen!" She buried her face in her hands.

Bennet glanced at the open door through which came the sound of rattling cups from the kitchen.

"Do you remember everything?" he asked cautiously. After removing the reel from the recorder, he held it lightly between finger and thumb.

"Oh, yes, I remember. How could I forget!" Jo raised her face and stared at him. He recognized the same blind anguish he had seen as she acted out the role under hypnosis. "All that blood," she whispered. "To see those men die. To smell it! Did you know blood smelled? And fear? The stink of fear!" She stood up unsteadily and crossed to stare out of the window. "That boy, Doctor. He couldn't have been more than fifteen. He watched his father die and then—" Her voice cracked to a husky whisper and she fell silent, pressing her forehead against the window as a tear trickled down her cheek.

Quietly Sarah reappeared and put the tray on the desk. Bennet raised his fingers to his lips. He was watching Jo intently. Outside there was a flurry of angry hooting in the narrow street but none of them noticed it.

Jo turned back toward the room. Her face was white and strained. "Did you record everything I said?"

He nodded. Her own small tape recorder still sat on the floor beside the couch, the microphone lying where it had fallen on the rug.

"Come, have coffee now," he said quietly. "We can listen later."

"I still don't believe it," she said as she sat down and took the cup from him. It rattled slightly on the saucer as she tightened her grip. "You've set me up somehow. No, not intentionally, but somehow. There is no way all that was real, and yet I couldn't have dreamed that—that obscenity—that boy's death." She found herself blinking hard, and she steadied herself with an effort. There was a long silence.

She sipped the coffee slowly, then she looked up, forcing a smile. "So, tell me what you thought. How did I do as a subject?"

Bennet had taken his own cup back to his chair and Sarah, sitting at the side table, her own hands still shaking, turned to look at him. She had recognized his barely suppressed excitement.

He chewed his upper lip for a moment. "I think I can say in all honesty that you are the best subject I have ever worked with," he said at last. "As I told you, people's sensitivities vary enormously and it often takes several sessions before a deep enough trance is reached for any meaningful contact to be made with another personality." He took a gulp of coffee. "But this Matilda. She was so clear, so vivid." He stood up again. "And so powerful. Do you realize I lost control of you? That has never happened to me before in all my years of experience. I tried to break the trance and I couldn't!"

Jo stared at him. "I thought I had read that that couldn't happen."

He shrugged. "It was only temporary. There was nothing to be afraid of. But it was fascinating! Do you feel ready to discuss what you remember now?" He reached down to where a pile of notebooks lay beside his chair and selected one.

Jo frowned. Then slowly she shook her head, concentrating all her attention on the steaming black liquid in her cup, still fighting the unfamiliar emotions that overwhelmed her. "In a minute. I'm sorry, Dr. Bennet, but I feel rather odd."

He was watching her carefully. With a glance at Sarah he went over to collect the coffeepot from the desk in front of her and poured some more into Jo's cup. "I doubt if you have ever witnessed a massacre before, my dear," he said dryly. "It would be surprising if you were not upset."

"Upset! But I feel as though I had really lived through it, for God's sake!"

"You have. For you, every part of that experience was real."

"And not only for you," Sarah added softly behind him.

"It was a hallucination, some sort of dream." Slowly Jo put down her cup. "You must have put it all into my head. You are not trying to tell me that I am a reincarnation of that woman—"

"I am not trying to tell you anything," said Bennet with a sigh. "We are only just beginning to grope our way toward an explanation for this kind of phenomenon. All we can do is record what happens with meticulous

66

accuracy and consider the various hypotheses. I happen to believe in reincarnation, but, as you say, it may well be some kind of dream sequence, and it may come from nowhere but your own unconscious. The interest lies in trying to verify whether or not the events you appeared to live through really happened, and in recording every detail that you can remember." He took his glasses off again with a weary smile. "There is one thing I can assure you of, though. I did not put the idea into your head, telepathically or verbally. The tapes will bear me out on the latter and also my great ignorance of Welsh history. We did not study Wales, I regret to say, in Vienna before the war." He smiled. "We won't discuss anything further now, though, if you'd rather not. You are tired and we both need to evaluate what has occurred. But whatever the explanation, the fact remains that you are an amazingly responsive subject. You reached the deepest levels of trance, and next time—"

"Next time?" Jo interrupted him. "Oh, no, not again. I'm sorry, but I couldn't take it. I have enough material here to write my article and that is all I want."

For a moment he stared at her in dismay. Then he shrugged and resumed his seat. "Of course, I cannot compel you to return, but I do most ardently hope you will. Not only for your researches, but to help me with mine. This Matilda, she seems a remarkable girl. I should like to know more about her."

Jo hesitated. Then she stood up. "No, I'm sorry. It is interesting, I agree, but I don't like it. I was so much in your power, in your control. You could be levitating me next, or making me go stiff as a board, whatever you call it, for all I know." She shuddered.

"Cataleptic." He smiled again. "You were in a far deeper state of trance than is needed to induce catalepsis, my dear."

She had begun collecting her notebook from the table but at his words she swung to face him. "You mean you could have done that to me?"

"Of course."

"You didn't though."

"No, although it is still used by some practitioners as a method of gauging the depth of trance reached. I prefer to use a pin." His eyes twinkled behind his glasses.

"A pin?"

"Oh, yes. You'll hear it on the tape. I stuck a pin into the back of your hand. Had you not been in a sufficiently deep trance you would have shrieked at me and bled, of course."

Jo stared at both her hands in disbelief. "And I did neither?"

"You did neither."

She shivered. "It's horrible. You could end up having complete domination over people without them ever knowing it!"

Carl looked offended. "My dear, we have a professional code, I assure you, like all doctors, and, as I said, always a chaperone."

"In case you get your evil way with a woman patient?" The strain on Jo's face lessened as she smiled at last.

"Even hypnotherapists are human!" he responded.

"And as such are liable to be hurt by what I write about them in the magazine?" Serious again, Jo swung her shoulder bag onto her arm. She picked up her tape recorder and stood up, shocked to find her knees were still trembling.

Bennet made a deprecatory gesture with his hands. "I will admit I have read some of your work. I believe it to be well researched and objective. I can ask for no more from you in my case."

"Even though I'm not converted to your theories of reincarnation?"

"All I ask is an open mind." He went to the door ahead of her. "Are you sure you feel well enough to go? You wouldn't like to rest awhile longer?"

She shook her head, suddenly eager to be outside in the fresh air.

"Then I will say good-bye. But even if you feel you must leave us now, I beg you to consider returning for another session. It might help to clarify matters for both of us."

She shook her head. "No. I'm sorry."

"Well, then, can I ask you to note down every detail of what you re-member?" he begged. "While it is still fresh in your mind. I think you will find your memory clear and complete. Far, far more than you described to me. All kinds of details that you did not mention at the time but that you will remember later. You'll do it anyway for your article, I'm sure." He was standing in front of the door, barring the way. "And you'll check the history books to see if you can find out whether Matilda existed?"

She gave a tight smile. "I will. I'm going to check everything meticu-lously. That I promise you."

"And you will tell me if you find anything? Anything at all?" He took her hand and gripped it firmly. "Even if she is the heroine of a novel you read last year." He grinned.

"You don't believe that?"

He shook his head. "No, but I think you may. Perhaps you would come back, just to discuss what you have discovered," he went on hopefully as he opened the door for her at last. "Will you do that?"

"I'll certainly send you a copy of the article before it goes to press."

He sighed. "I'll look forward to that. But remember, you know where I am if you need me."

He watched as she walked along the carpeted hallway toward the stairs, then he closed the door and leaned against it.

Sarah was collecting the cups. "Do you think she will come back?" she

68

said over her shoulder. She twitched the blanket on the sofa straight and selected a new blank tape for the recorder.

Bennet had not moved from the door. "That girl is the best subject I've ever come across," he said slowly.

Sarah moved, the tray in her hand, toward the kitchen. "And yet you were dreading this appointment."

He nodded. "Pete Leveson had told me how anti she was. She had made up her mind before she ever met me that I was a charlatan." He chuckled. "But it is the strong willed, if they make up their minds to surrender to hypnosis, who are by far the best subjects. This one was amazing. The way she took it over. I couldn't reach her, Sarah! I could not reach her! She was out of my control."

"It was frightening," Sarah said vehemently. "I wouldn't have liked to be in her shoes. I bet she has nightmares about it. Did you notice? She wasn't half so confident and sure of herself afterward."

He had begun to pace the carpet restlessly. "I have to get her back here. It is imperative that we try it again."

Sarah glanced at him. "Weren't you afraid, Carl? Just for a moment?" she asked.

He nodded. "I didn't think it could happen. But it did. And that is why it is so important. She'll come though. She'll think about it and she'll come back." He smiled at Sarah vaguely, taking off his glasses once more and squinting through them at some imaginary speck on the lens. "If she's half the journalist I think she is, she'll come back."

8

As the cab drew away from the curb
Jo settled back on the broad, slippery seat and closed her eyes against the
glare of the sunlight reflected in the spray thrown up from the road by the
traffic. Then she opened them again and looked at her watch. It was barely
five. She had lived through twenty-four hours of fear and horror and it was
barely five o'clock. In front of her the folding seats blurred; above them
the tariff card in the window floated disembodied for a moment. Her
hands were shaking.

With a squeal of brakes the taxi stopped at the traffic lights and her bag
shot off the seat onto the floor. As she bent to retrieve it she found herself
wincing with pain. Her fingertips felt bruised and torn and yet, when she
examined them, they were unharmed. She frowned, remembering the way
she had clung to the stone arch to stop herself from fainting as she watched
the slaughter of William's guests, and she swallowed hard. She put her
hands deep into the pockets of her jacket as the taxi cut expertly through
the traffic toward Kensington, the driver thankfully taciturn, the glass slide
of his window tightly closed, leaving her alone with her thoughts. She felt
strangely disorientated, half her mind still clinging to the dream, alienated
from the roar of the rush hour around her. It was as if this were the unreal
world and that other cold past the place where she still belonged.

Her apartment was cool and shadowy, scented by some pinks in a bowl
by the bookcase. She threw open the tall balcony windows and stood for a
moment looking out at the trees in the square. Another shower was on its
way, the heavy cloud throwing racing shadows over the rooftops on the far
side of the gardens.

She turned toward the kitchen. After collecting a glass of apple juice
from the carton in the refrigerator, she carried it along to the bathroom,
set it carefully down on the edge of the bath, and turned on the shower.
She stepped out of her clothes, then stood beneath the tepid water, letting
it cascade down onto her upturned face, running it through her aching
fingers. She stood there a long time, not allowing herself to think, just
feeling the clean stream of the water wash over her. Soon she would slip

on her cool cotton bathrobe, sit down at her desk, and write up her notes, just as she always did after an interview, while it was still absolutely fresh in her mind. Except that this time she had very few notes, only the small tape recorder that was waiting for her now on the chair just inside the front door.

Slowly she toweled her hair dry, then, sipping from her glass, she wandered back into the living room. She ran her fingers across the buttons of the machine, but she did not switch it on. Instead she sat down and stared blankly at the carpet.

In the top drawer of her desk was the first rough typescript of her article. She could remember clearly the introduction she had drafted:

> Would you like to discover that in a previous life you had been a queen or an emperor; that, just as you had always suspected, you are not quite of this mundane world; that in your past there are secrets, glamour, and adventure, just waiting to be remembered? Of course you would. Hypnotists say that they can reveal this past to you by their regression techniques. But just how genuine are their claims? Joanna Clifford investigates . . .

Jo got up restlessly. Joanna Clifford investigates, and ends up getting her fingers burned, she thought ruefully. On medieval stone. She examined her nails again. They still felt raw and torn, but nowhere could she see any sign of damage; even the polish was unchipped. She had a vivid recollection suddenly of the small blue-painted office in Edinburgh. Her hands had been injured then too. She frowned, remembering with a shiver the streaks of blood on the rush matting. "Oh, Christ!" She fought back a sudden wave of nausea. Had Cohen hypnotized her after all? Had she seen that bloody massacre before, in his office? Was that what Sam had wanted to tell her? She rubbed her hands on the front of her bathrobe and looked at them hard. Then, taking a deep breath, she went over and picked up the tape recorder, setting it on the low coffee table. Kneeling on the carpet, she pressed the rewind button and listened to the whine of the spinning tape. She did not wait for the whole reel. Halfway through she stopped it and started to listen.

"William is reading the letter now and the prince is listening to him. But he is angry. He is interrupting. They are going to quarrel. William is looking down at him and putting down the parchment. He is raising his dagger. He is going to . . . Oh, no, *no NO!*" Her voice rose into a shriek.

Jo found she was shaking. She wanted to press her hands against her ears to cut out the sound of the anguished screaming on the tape, but she forced herself to go on listening as a second voice broke in. It was Sarah and she sounded frightened. "For God's sake, Carl, bring her out of it! What are you waiting for?"

71

"Listen to me, Jo. Listen!" Bennet tried to cut in, his patient, quiet voice taut. "Lady Matilda, can you hear me?" He was shouting now. "Listen to me. I am going to count to three. And you are going to wake up. *Listen to me. . . ."*

But her own voice, or the voice of that other woman speaking through her, ran on and on, sweeping his aside, not hearing his attempts to interrupt. Jo was breathing heavily, a pulse drumming in her forehead. She could hear all three of them now. Sarah sobbing, saying "Carl, stop her, stop her," Bennet repeating her name over and over again—both names—and above them her own hysterical voice running on out of control, describing the bloodshed and terror she was watching.

Then abruptly there was silence, save for the sound of panting, she was not sure whose. Jo heard a sharp rattle as something was knocked over, and then Bennet's voice very close now to the microphone. "Let me touch her face. Quickly! Perhaps with my fingers, like so. Matilda? Can you hear me? I want you to hear me. I am going to count to three and then you will wake up. One, two, three."

There was a long silence, then Sarah cried, "You've lost her, Carl. For God's sake, *you've lost her."*

Bennet was talking softly, reassuringly again, but Jo could hear the undertones of fear in his voice. "Matilda, can you hear me? I want you to answer me. Matilda? You must listen. You are Jo Clifford and soon you will wake up back in my consulting room in London. Can you hear me, my dear? I want you to forget about Matilda."

There was a long silence, then Sarah whispered, very near the microphone, "What do we do?"

Bennet sounded exhausted. "There is nothing we can do. Let her sleep. She will wake by herself in the end."

Jo started with shock. She distinctly remembered hearing him say that. His voice had reached her, lying half awake in the shadowy bedchamber at Abergavenny, but she—or Matilda—had pulled back, rejecting his call, and she had fallen once more into unconsciousness. She shivered at the memory.

The sharp clink of glass on glass came over the machine and she found herself once more giving a rueful smile. So he had had to have a drink at that point, as, locked in silence where he could not follow her, she had woken in the past and begun her search of the deserted windswept castle.

For several minutes more the tape ran quiet, then Sarah's voice rang out excitedly. "Carl, I think she's waking up. Her eyelids are flickering."

"Jo? Jo?" Bennet was back by the microphone in a second.

Jo heard her own voice moaning softly, then at last came a husky "There's someone there. Who is it?"

"We're reaching her now." Bennet's murmur was full of relief. "Jo? Can you hear me? Matilda? My lady?" There was a hiss on the tape and Jo strained forward to hear what followed. But there was nothing more. With a sharp *click* it switched itself off, the reel finished.

She leaned back against the legs of the chair. She was trembling all over and her hands were slippery with sweat. She rubbed them on her bathrobe. Strange that she had expected to hear it all again—the sound effects, the screams, the grunts, the clash of swords. But of course to the onlooker, as to the microphone, it was all reported, like hearing someone else's commentary on what they could see through a telescope. Only to her was it completely real. The others had been merely eavesdroppers on her dream.

Slowly she put her head in her hands and was aware suddenly that there were tears on her cheeks.

Nick swung out of the office and ran down the stairs to the street. The skies had cleared after the storm, but the gutters still ran with rain as he sprinted toward the parking lot.

Jo's door was on the latch. He pushed it open with a frown. It was unlike her to be careless.

"Jo? Where are you?" he called. He walked through to the living room and glanced in. She was sitting on the floor, her face white and strained, her hair still damp from the shower. He saw at once that she had been crying. She looked at him blankly.

"What is it? Are you all right?" He flung down the jacket he had been carrying slung over his shoulder and was beside her in two strides. Crouching, he put his arms around her. "You look terrible, love. Nothing is worth getting that worked up about. Ignore the damned article. It doesn't matter. No one cares what it said." He took her hand in his. "You're like ice! For God's sake, Jo. What have you been doing?"

She looked up at him at last, pushing him away from her. "Pour me a large drink, Nick, will you?"

He gave her a long, searching look. Then he stood up. He found the Scotch and two glasses in the kitchen. "It's not like you to fold, Jo," he called over his shoulder. "You're a fighter, remember?" He brought the drinks in and handed her one. "It's Tim's fault. He was supposed to warn you last night what might happen."

She took a deep gulp from her glass and put it on the table. "What are you talking about?" Her voice was slightly hoarse.

"The paragraph in the *Mail*. What did you think I was talking about?"

She shook her head wearily. "I haven't seen any papers today. I was here all morning, and then this afternoon I went . . . out." She fumbled with the glass again, lifting it with a shaking hand, concentrating with an effort. "They printed it, did they? The great quarrel between your past and present loves. That must have done a bit for your ego." With a faint smile she put out her hand. "Show me what it said."

"I didn't bring it." He sat down on the edge of the coffee table. "If you are not upset about that, Jo, then what's happened?"

"I went to see a hypnotherapist."

"You what?" Nick stood up abruptly.

She nodded, and fumbling for a cigarette, watched him in silence.

"You know, it isn't a fraud," she said at last. "I can't explain it, but whatever it was, it came from me, not from him." She balanced the cigarette on the edge of the ashtray and picked up her glass. "It was so real. So frightening. Like a nightmare, but I wasn't asleep."

Nick frowned. Then he glanced at his watch. "Jo, I'm going to phone Judy—I'll tell her I can't make it this evening." He paused, waiting for her to argue, but she said nothing.

She lay back limply, sipping her drink as he dialed, watching him, her eyes vague, as, one-handed, he slipped his tie over his head and unbuttoned his shirt. The whisky was beginning to warm her. For the first time in what seemed like hours she had stopped shaking.

Nick was brief to the point of curtness on the phone, then he put the receiver down and came back to sit beside her. "Right," he said, "let's hear it all from the beginning." Leaning forward, he stubbed out her abandoned cigarette. She did not protest. "I take it you've got it all on tape?" He nodded toward the machine.

"All but the last few minutes."

"Do you want me to hear it?"

She nodded. "The other side first. You'll have to wind it back." She watched as he removed the cassette and turned it over; then she stood up. "I'll go and get some clothes on while you listen."

Nick glanced at her. "Don't you want to hear it again?"

"I did. Just before you came home," she said quietly. "We'll talk when you've heard it."

It was a long time before Nick appeared. She was lying on the bed. She had not got dressed. She watched him quietly as he walked across the carpet and sat down beside her. He looked grim.

"How much of that do you remember?" he asked at last.

"All of it."

"And you weren't fooling?"

She sat up and swung her legs over the side of the bed. "Did I sound as if I were fooling? Did he?"

"All right, I'm sorry. I had to be sure. Do you want to talk about it now?"

"I don't know." She hugged her bathrobe around her. "Nick, this is crazy. I'm a journalist. I'm on a job. A routine, ordinary sort of job. I'm going about my research in the way I always do, methodically, and I am not allowing myself to become involved in any personal way. Part of me can see the whole thing objectively. But another part—" She hesitated. "I was sure that it was all some kind of a trick. But it was so real, so very real. I was a child again, Nick. Arrogant, uncertain, overwhelmed, and so proud of the fact that I was pregnant, because it made me a woman in my own right and the equal of William's mother! And I was going to be the mother of that boor's son!" She put her face in her hands. "That is what women have felt for thousands of years, Nick. Proud to be the vehicle for men's kids. And I felt it! Me!" She gave an unhappy laugh.

Nick raised an eyebrow. "Some women are still proud of that particular role, Jo. They're not all rabid feminists, thank God!" His voice was unusually gentle. "You remember all her feelings then? Even things you don't mention out loud?"

Jo frowned. "I don't know. I think so . . . I'm not sure. I remember that, though. Hugging myself in triumph because I carried his child—and because I had thought of a way to keep him from molesting me. He must have been a bastard in bed." Her voice shook. "The poor bloody cow!" She picked up a pot of face cream from the table and turned it over and over in her hands without seeing it. "She probably had a girl in the end, not the precious son she kept on about, or died in childbirth or something. Oh, God, Nick . . . It was me. I could feel it all, hear it, see it, smell it. Even taste the food that boy brought me. The wine was thin and sour— like nothing I've ever drunk, and the bread was coarse and gritty, with some strong flavor. It didn't seem odd at the time, but I can't place it at all, and I could swear I've still got bits of it stuck between my teeth."

Nick smiled, but she went on. "It was all so vivid. Almost too real. Like being on some kind of a 'trip.'"

"That follows," Nick said slowly. "You obviously have had some kind of vivid hallucination. But that is all it was, Jo. You must believe that. The question is, where did it come from? Where have all the stories come from that people have experienced under this kind of hypnosis? I suppose that is the basis of your article." He hesitated. "Do you think this massacre really did happen?"

She shrugged. "I gave a very clear date, didn't I? Twenty years of King Henry. There are eight of them to choose from!" She smiled. "And Abergavenny, of course. I've never been there, but I know it's somewhere in Wales."

"South Wales," he put in. "I went there once, as a child, but I don't remember there being a castle."

"Oh, Nick! It's all quite mad!"

"What did it feel like, being hypnotized?" he asked curiously.

She sighed. "That's the stupid thing. I'm not sure. I don't think I knew it was happening. I didn't seem to go to sleep or anything. Except real sleep when I slept in the castle. Only that wasn't real sleep because the time scale was different. I lived through two days, Nick, in less than two hours." She sat down on the bed again, looking at him. "This is what happened before, isn't it? When Sam was there. They did hypnotize me and they lost control of me that time too!"

Nick nodded. "Sam said you were told not to remember what happened, it would upset you too much. And he said I mustn't talk about it to you, Jo, that's why I couldn't explain—"

"I lived through those same scenes then," she went on, not hearing him. "I saw the massacre then too."

Nick looked away. "I don't know, Jo. You must speak to Sam—"

"It must have been the massacre, because I hurt my hands tearing at the stone archway. But I really bled in Edinburgh. My fingers were bruised and bleeding, not just painful!" Her voice was shaking. "Oh, God, it was all so real. Nick, I'm frightened." She stared at her hands, holding them out before her.

Nick took hold of them gently, standing up. "Come on," he said. "We need another drink. And something to eat. Is there any food in the apartment?"

She dragged her thoughts back to the present with difficulty. "In the freezer. I forgot to buy anything today." She gave a rueful smile. "I was going to go shopping on my way back from Devonshire Place but everything went out of my head."

Nick grinned. "I'm not surprised. Being a baron's lady with a castle full of serfs, you can hardly be expected to lower yourself to trundle around the supermarket with a shopping cart. You must try not to let it upset you too much, Jo. Try and see the amusing side. Think of it as a personalized horror film. You got front-row seats and no ice cream in the intermission. But, apart from that, thank God there's no harm done this time."

"That doesn't sound very scientific." She forced herself to smile. Standing up slowly, she pulled the belt of her robe more tightly around her. Then she headed toward the kitchen and pulled open the freezer door. "There's pizza in here or steak." The normality of her action calmed her. Her voice was steady again.

"Pizza's fine. What intrigues me is where you dredged all this information up from. The details all sounded so authentic."

"Dr. Bennet and Bill Walton both said that they usually are. That's one of their strongest arguments in favor of reincarnation, of course." She lit the oven and put two pizzas in. "Where it is possible to substantiate things apparently they are usually uncannily accurate. I'm going to check as much as I can. Is there any whisky left?"

"I'll get it."

She took down two plates and put them to warm. "Here, let me make a salad to go with these. Neither Bennet nor Walton was a fake, Nick. I was wrong to think it. They didn't ask any leading questions. Bennet didn't influence my 'dream' in any way. If he had, I'd have heard on the tape. Look, if there is any period of history I would say that I should like to

76

identify with at all it would be the Regency. If he'd been a fraud he would have found that out in two minutes." She poured vinegar and oil into a jar and reached for the pepper mill. "I daresay I could have reenacted a dozen Georgette Heyer novels. I read everything of hers I could lay my hands on when I was a teenager. But he didn't ask. He didn't guide me at all. Here, give this a shake. Instead I find myself in medieval Wales. With people talking Welsh all around me, for God's sake!"

Nick shook up the dressing and poured it over the salad. "If it was Welsh," he said quietly. "God knows what it was you said. If you had jumped up and down shouting *Cymru am byth* I might have been able to substantiate it!"

"Where did you learn that?" she laughed.

"Rugby. I don't mess about when I go to Twickenham, you know, it's very educational." He touched her cheek lightly. "Good to see you laughing. It's not like our Jo to get upset."

She pushed a plate at him. "As Dr. Bennet pointed out, it's not every day that 'our Jo' witnesses a full-dress massacre, even in a nightmare," she retorted.

They ate in the living room. "Bach to eat by," said Nick, putting his plate down and riffling through the stack of records. "To restore the equilibrium."

She did not argue. It meant they didn't have to talk; it meant she needn't even think. She let the music sweep over her, leaving her food almost untouched as she lay back on the sofa, her feet up, and closed her eyes.

When she opened them again the sky was dark outside the French windows onto the balcony. The music had finished and the room was silent. Nick was sitting watching her in the light of the single desk lamp.

"Why didn't you wake me?" she asked indignantly. "What time is it?"

"Eleven. Time you were in bed. You look exhausted."

"Don't dictate, Nick. It's time you went, for that matter," she said sharply.

"Wouldn't you like me to stay?"

She pushed herself up on her elbow. "No. You and I are finished, remember? You have to go back to your cozy love nest with the talented Miss Curzon. What was it you said on the phone, 'working late'—she won't believe it, you know, if you stay away all night!"

"I don't much care what she believes at the moment, Jo. I am more concerned about you," Nick said. He stood up and turned on the main light. "I don't think you should be alone tonight."

"In case I have nightmares?"

"Yes, in case you have nightmares. This has shaken you up more than you realize, and I think someone should be here. I'll sleep here on the sofa if the idea of me in your bed offends you, but I'm going to stay!"

She stood up furiously. "Like hell you are!" Then abruptly her shoulders slumped. "Oh, God, Nick, you're right. I do want you to stay. I want you to hold me."

He put his arms around her gently and caressed her hair. "The trouble with you, Jo, is that when you're nice, you're very, very nice, but—"

"I know, I know. And when I'm horrid you hate and detest me. And I'm usually horrid." She forced herself to smile. "Well, tonight I'm being nice. But it is only for one night, Nick. Everything will be back to normal tomorrow."

In bed they lay for a long time in silence. Then Nick raised himself on one elbow and looked down at her in the faint light that filtered through the blind from the streetlamp in the mews.

"Jo," he said softly. "You haven't told me yet about Richard."

She stiffened. "Richard?"

"Your lover in that castle. He was your lover, wasn't he?"

Restlessly she moved her head sideways so he could not see her face. "I don't know. It wasn't *me,* Nick! He left the castle. He wasn't there at the end. I don't know what happened next. I don't suppose I'll ever know." Agitated, she tried to push him away, but he caught her wrist, forcing it back against the pillow so that she had to face him.

"You're planning to see Bennet again, aren't you?"

She shook her head violently. "No, of course I'm not."

"Are you sure?"

Something in his voice made her stare up into his face, trying to see the expression in his eyes.

"For God's sake, don't do it. It's dangerous. Far more dangerous than you or Bennet realize. Your life could be in danger, Jo." His voice was harsh.

She smiled. "Now, that is melodramatic. Are you suggesting I could be locked in the past forever?" She reached up and tugged his hair playfully. "You idiot, it doesn't work that way. People always wake up in the end."

"Do they?" He lay back on the pillow. "Just make sure you've got your facts right, Jo. I know it's your proud boast that you always do, but just this once you could be wrong."

9

Early the next morning Sam paid off the taxi and stood for a moment on the pavement staring around him. Judy's address was scribbled on a scrap of paper in his hand.

He looked up at the house, then, slinging his suitcase over his shoulder, he ran easily up the long flights of steps until he reached the shadowy landing at the top of the stairs. It was some time before the door opened to his ring.

Judy stared at the rangy figure in the rumpled cord jacket and her eyes hardened. "What do you want?"

"Hello there." He grinned at her easily. "I'm Sam Franklyn."

"I guessed that. So—what do you want?" Her tone was icy. With paint-stained fingers she pushed back the scarf that covered her hair.

"May I come in?"

"Please yourself." She turned away and walked back into the studio. After picking up a rag, she began to scrub at her fingertips with some turpentine. "What have you come here for?" she asked after a minute. She did not bother to turn around.

Sam dropped his case in the corner and closed the door. "I rather hoped Nick would be here," he said mildly, "but I can see I've goofed. Where is he, do you know?"

"I don't." She flung down the rag. "But I can guess. He stood me up last night." She folded her arms and turned to face him. He could see now in the harsh revealing light of the studio windows that her eyes were red and puffy. There was a streak of viridian across her forehead.

"Any chance of some coffee while you tell me about it?" Sam said gently. "I've come straight from Heathrow and I'm parched."

"Help yourself. But don't expect me to make polite conversation, least of all about Nick. I'm busy." She turned her back on him again.

Sam frowned. He watched her for a moment as she picked up a brush and attacked the canvas in front of her. Every muscle in her body was tense, the angle of her shoulders set and defensive beneath the faded green denim of her smock.

"Do you know," she said suddenly, "I hate her. I have never actually hated anyone like that before."

Sam watched her thoughtfully. "It sounds pretty normal to me," he said evenly. "Do I gather we are talking about Jo?"

"Why don't you make me some coffee too, while you're at it," she returned sharply, "and let's not discuss Jo." Once again she pushed back the scarf that covered her hair.

Sam gave a small grimace. He found his way across to the kitchen by instinct and pushed open the door, then he stopped and surveyed the scene. There was broken glass all over the floor. Two saucepans of food had been left upside down in the sink. Staring down at the mess, he sniffed cautiously. One had contained asparagus soup, the other some kind of goulash. Sam frowned. In the pail below the sink were two china plates with the salad that had been on them. She had hurled out what appeared to him to have been a cordon bleu meal, complete with china.

Glancing over his shoulder, he watched for a moment in silence as she worked, then he began to hunt for some coffee and set the kettle on the gas.

"What do you call that picture?" he asked several minutes later when he handed her a mug.

She took it without looking at him. "What you mean is, what the hell is it?" she said slowly. She stepped closer to the painting, eyes narrowed, and added a small touch of red to the swirl of colors. "I had better not tell you. You'd have me taken away in a straitjacket." She gave a taut smile. "You're the psychiatrist. Why don't you tell me what it means?" She rubbed at the canvas with her little finger and stared thoughtfully at the smear of red it left on her skin. Then she swung around to face him again. "On second thought, why don't you drink your coffee and get out of here?"

Sam grinned. "I'm on my way."

"Good." She paused. "I told her, you know. In front of the whole bloody world."

"Told her what?" Sam was still studying the canvas.

"What Nick said to you on the phone. That she would crack if she were hypnotized again. That she is more or less out of her mind." She threw down the brush and crossed to the untidy desk by the window. After pulling open a drawer, she extracted a newspaper clipping. "This was in yesterday's *Mail*."

Sam took it. He read the paragraph, his face impassive, then he handed it back.

"You certainly made a good job of that bit of scandal."

Judy smiled. She turned back to her canvas. "So hadn't you better rush over to Cornwall Gardens and see if Nick can spare you one of her hands to hold?"

"That's what I've come for." Sam drank the last of his coffee, then put down his empty mug. "I take it," he added carefully, "that you think that Nick spent last night with her."

"Unless he got run over and is in the mortuary."

"And you were expecting him here to dinner."

"As you plainly saw."

"I am sorry." Sam's face was carefully controlled. "Nick's a fool. You deserve better."

She went back to the painting and stood staring at it. "That's right. And I mean to get it. Make no mistake about it, Dr. Franklyn, I mean to see that Nick leaves her for good. So if it's your mission in life to comfort Jo Clifford and see that she keeps calm and safe and sane, why don't you move in with her and send your brother to me."

Sam turned and picked up his case. "I'll bear that in mind," he said. He pulled open the door. "But if you'll take a piece of advice from me, I suggest you use a little more subtlety with Nick. If you behave like the proverbial fishwife he'll leave you for good. I know my brother. He likes his ladies sophisticated and in control. If he sees the mess in your kitchen he'll leave, and I wouldn't altogether blame him."

He didn't wait to hear the string of expletives that echoed after him as he began to run down the stairs.

Jo was sitting on the cold concrete steps outside the library watching a pigeon waddling along in the gutter. Its neck shimmered with iridescent purples and greens as it moved unconcerned between the wheels of the stationary cars intent on gathering specks of food from the tarmac. The roar of traffic in the High Street a few yards away distracted it not at all. Nor did the scream of an accelerating motorbike a few feet from it. Behind her the library doors were unlocked at last.

Standing up slowly, she brushed the dust off her skirt, watching as the pigeon, startled into sleek slimness by her sudden movement, took off and swept with graceful speed up and over the rooftops toward the park.

As she ran up the echoing staircase to the library she became aware suddenly that she could hear her own heartbeats drumming in her ears. The sound was disconcerting and she stopped outside the glass swing doors to try to steady herself. Her head ached violently and her eyes were heavy with lack of sleep.

Taking a deep breath, she pushed through the doors and turned toward the reference section, skirting the tables where already students and newspaper readers were establishing their base camps for the day. As she pulled the notebook from her bag she realized that her hands had begun to shake.

Begin with *The Dictionary of National Biography.*

It was unlikely she would find Matilda there, but it was a place to start.

She approached the shelf, her hand outstretched. Her fingers were trembling.

"Braos?" she murmured to herself. "Breos? I wonder how they spelled it." There was a rustle of paper beside her as a large bespectacled priest turned to the racing page. He looked up and caught her eye. His wink was comforting.

She walked slowly along the shelf, squinting at the gold-lettered spines of the books, then she heaved out a volume and carried it to a table, perching uncomfortably on the very edge of the chair as she began to leaf through the pages.

Don't let it have been real. . . . Please don't let it have been real. . . . I can't cope with that. . . . She shook her head angrily. The thick paper crackled a little, the small print blurring. A slightly musty smell floated from between the covers as the riffling pages stirred the hot air of the room.

. . . Bowen . . . Bradford . . . Branston . . . Braose, Philip de (fl. 1172) two inches of print, then Braose, William de (d. 1211). There were more than two pages.

She sat still for a moment, fighting her stomach. She could taste the bile in the back of her throat. Her forehead was damp and ice cold and her hands were burning hot. It was awhile before she became conscious that the priest was watching her closely and she realized suddenly that she had been staring at him hard, oblivious of everything but the need not to be sick. Somehow she forced herself to smile at him and she looked away.

She took a deep breath and stared down at the page. Was Matilda there, in the article that she could see at a glance was full of place names and dates? Had she lived long enough to make her mark on history and have her name recorded with her cruel, overbearing husband? Or had she flitted in and out of life like a shadow, leaving no trace at all, if she had ever existed?

The priest was still watching her, his kind face creased with concern. Jo knew that any minute he was going to stand up and come over to her. She looked away again hastily. She had to look up Richard de Clare, too, and Abergavenny, and make notes on them all. Then, perhaps, she would go and have a cup of coffee and accept the consolations of the Church if they were offered.

It was several minutes before the intercom on the doorstep below Jo's apartment crackled into life. Sam bent toward the display board.

"Nick? It's Sam. Let me come up."

Nick was waiting on the landing as Sam walked slowly up the carpeted stairs. "You're too late," he said brusquely. "She went to a hypnotist yesterday and let him regress her."

Sam followed him into the brightness of the apartment and stared around. "What happened? Where is she?" He faced his brother coldly, taking in the dark rings beneath Nick's eyes and the unshaven stubble.

"She had gone before I woke up." Nick ran his fingers through his hair. "I think she was okay. She was last night. Just shocked and rather frightened. She had a long session that seemed to get out of control. The hypnotist couldn't bring her back to consciousness. She seemed to get so involved in what was happening, it was so real to her."

"You were with her?" Sam turned on him sharply.

"Of course not! Do you think I'd have let her go! No, she brought back a tape of what happened and I heard it last night." Nick shook his head wearily. "She was in a terrible state—but not in danger as far as I could tell. She never stopped breathing or anything. I stayed the night with her and she spent most of it tossing and turning and pacing up and down the floor. She must have got up at dawn and gone out. She did say she'd go to the library first thing. Maybe she went there to see if she could find any of these people in a history book."

Sam took off his jacket and threw it on the back of the sofa. Then he sat down and drew the tape recorder toward him. "Right, Nick. May I suggest you return to your titian-haired artist friend and try to apologize for last night's ruined meal? Leave Jo to me."

"Like hell I will!" Nick glared at him.

"I mean it. Go back to Miss Curzon, Nick. She is your new love, is she not? I went there straight from the airport under the impression that you would be there. She is not pleased with you, little brother. If you value your relationship with her I suggest you make amends as fast as you can. Meanwhile I shall listen to the tape and talk to Jo when she returns. I don't want you here."

Nick took a deep breath. "Jo asked me to stay."

"And I am asking you to go." Sam turned his back on Nick, his shoulders hunched as he searched for the play button on the machine. "She is my patient, Nick."

Nick hesitated. "You'll call me after you've spoken to her?"

"I'll call you. Better still, do you still have your apartment in Mayfair?"

"You know I do."

"Give me the key then. I'll stay there for a night or two. And I'll see you there sometime, no doubt." He switched on the tape and sat back on the sofa thoughtfully as Jo's voice filled the room.

It was four hours before Jo came home. She stopped dead in the doorway, her keys still in her hand, staring at Sam. He had long ago finished playing the tape and was lying on the sofa, his eyes closed, listening to the soft strains of the Concierto de Aranjuez.

"How did you get on?" He did not immediately open his eyes.

Jo sighed. She dropped her shoulder bag on the floor and banged the door behind her.

"Where's Nick?"

Sam's eyes narrowed. "He felt he should return to make his peace with Judy. I'm sorry."

"I see." Jo's voice dropped. "And he's left you here to pick up the pieces. I suppose I should be grateful he stayed at all last night. I hope he told you I don't need you, Sam. Nothing awful happened. I'm perfectly all right. I did not become incurably insane, nor did I kill anyone as far as I know." She unbuttoned her jacket wearily. "When did he leave?"

"Soon after I arrived. He was worried about you, Jo." Sam was watching her closely. "Nick's a nice guy. Even if it is all over between you both, he wouldn't have left you alone, you know that."

Jo dropped her jacket on a chair and reached for the Scotch bottle on the table by the phone. "That's right. Good old St. Nicholas who never leaves a friend in the lurch. Want one?"

Sam shook his head. He watched as she poured; she did not dilute it.

"Have you heard it?" Her eyes had gone past him to the cassette lying on the coffee table.

"Twice." Her face was pale and drawn, he noted, her hair tied back into an uncompromising ponytail that showed new sharp angles to her cheekbones and shadows beneath her eyes.

"It all happened, Sam." She raised the glass to her lips. "I found it so easily. William de Braose, his wife—most books seem to call her Maude—I didn't even know it was the same name as Matilda—their children, the massacre of Abergavenny. It was all there for anyone to read. Not obscure at all." She swallowed a mouthful of whisky. "I must have read about it somewhere before, but I swear to God I don't remember it. I've never studied Welsh history, but all that detail in my mind! It doesn't seem possible. Christ, Sam! Where did it all come from?"

Sam had not taken his eyes from her face. "Where do you think it came from?"

She shrugged, flinging herself down on the sofa beside him, turning the glass around and around in her fingers.

Sam eyed the length of lightly tanned thigh exposed where her skirt caught on the edge of the cushions. He moved away from her slightly. "Where would you like it to have come from?"

Jo frowned. "That's a loaded question. Yesterday morning I wouldn't have hesitated to answer it. But now . . . Matilda was so real to me, Sam. She *was* me." She turned to face him. "Was it the same in Edinburgh? Did the same thing happen then too?"

He nodded slowly. "You certainly reacted dramatically under regression. A little too dramatically. That was why we decided it would be better if you remembered nothing of what happened afterward."

Jo jumped to her feet. "You admit it! So you told me to forget it, as if it had never happened. You took it upon yourselves to manipulate my mind! You thought it would be bad for me to know about it, so bang! You wiped it clean like a computer program!" Her eyes were blazing.

Sam smiled placatingly. "Jo, it was for your own good. No one was manipulating you. Nothing sinister happened. It was all taped, just as it was for you yesterday. It's all on the record."

"But you deliberately destroyed my memory of what happened!" She took a deep breath, trying to control her anger. "Was I the same person? Matilda de Braose?"

"As far as I remember you didn't tell us what your name was," Sam said quietly.

"Well, did I talk about the same events? The massacre?"

Sam shook his head. "You were much more vague with us." He stood up abruptly and walked over to the windows, looking up through the net curtains toward the sky. "You must not go back to this man, Jo. You do understand that, don't you?"

"Why not?" Her voice was defiant. "Nothing terrible happened. And he at least is honest with me. He has professional standards." She threw herself down on the sofa again, resting her head against the cushions. "Oh, sure, it was a bit nerve-racking for him, as it obviously was for you, but I was all right, wasn't I? I didn't seem hysterical, my personality didn't disintegrate. Nothing happened to me." She looked down at her hands suddenly, then abruptly she put them behind her.

"What's wrong?" Sam had seen her out of the corner of his eye. He went over to her, and, kneeling, he took both her hands in his. He studied the palms intently. Then he turned them over and looked at her nails.

She tried to pull away. "Sam—"

"Your hands aren't hurt?"

"No, of course they're not hurt. Why should they be?"

He let them go reluctantly, his eyes once more on her face. "They were injured last time, in Edinburgh," he said gently. "They started to bleed."

She stared at him. "There was blood on the floor, wasn't there?" she whispered after a moment. "I remembered that. And when I got home I found I was covered in bruises." She stood up, pushing past him. "I thought I'd had an accident. But somehow I never bothered to ask you about it, did I?" She bit her lip, staring at him. "That was your posthypnotic suggestion too, I suppose. 'You will not remember how you were injured, nor will you question why.' Is that what you said to me? God, it makes me so angry! All this has happened to me before and I did not know about it. You snatched an hour or so of my life, Sam, and I want it back." She looked down into her glass, her knuckles white as she kneaded it between her fingers. "It's the thought that these memories, this other life has been lying hidden in me, festering all these years, that frightens me.

85

. . . Wherever they come from, whatever they are, they must mean something special to me, mustn't they?" She paused, then she looked away from him. "Do you know how she died?"

Sam's jaw tightened. "Who?"

"Matilda, of course. They think she was starved to death." Jo drank the rest of her whisky quickly and put down the glass. She was suddenly shuddering violently.

Sam stood up. He caught her arm. "Jo—"

"No, Sam, it's all right. I know what you're going to say. I'm not about to get obsessive about her. It's me, remember. Level-headed Jo Clifford. I'm over the shock of it all now, anyway. Reading about it has put it in perspective. All those dry dates and facts. Ugh! Funny how history never seemed to be to do with real people, not to me anyway. At least not until now. . . ." Her voice trailed away. "When you and Professor Cohen finished your experiments, Sam, did you reach any conclusions?"

"We were able to float various hypotheses, shall we say." Sam smiled enigmatically.

"And they were?"

"Roughly? That different subjects reacted in different ways. We tabulated almost as many theories as there were regression sessions. You must read his book. Some people faked, there was no question about that. Some openly reenacted scenes from books and films. Some produced what they thought we hoped we would hear. And some were beyond explanation."

"And which was Joanna Clifford?"

"I think one of the latter." He gave a wry smile.

Jo eyed him thoughtfully. "I had a feeling you were going to say that. Tell me, Sam, do you believe in reincarnation?"

"No."

"Then what do you think happens?"

"I have one or two ill-formed and unscientific theories about, shall we say, radio waves trapped in the ether. Some people, when in a receptive state, tune into the right wavelengths and get a bit of playback."

"You mean I was actually seeing what happened in 1174?"

"An echo of it—a reverberation, shall we say. Don't quote me, Jo, for God's sake. I'd be drummed out of every professional body there is. But it does go some way to explain why more than one person gets the same playback on occasions. It explains ghosts as well, of course. A good all-around theory." He laughed.

"Have you seen a ghost?"

The strain, he noted with satisfaction, had lessened in her face; her neck muscles were no longer so prominent.

"Never! I'm not the receptive type, thank God!"

"Why not? Sam—" She paused in the doorway, running her fingernail up and down the cream-painted woodwork. "Can you hypnotize people?"

"I can. Yes."

"And regress them?"

"I haven't gone on with Cohen's experiments," he replied carefully. "There are others chasing that particular hare now. My field is rather different."

Jo grinned. "You didn't answer my question, Dr. Franklyn. Can you regress people?"

"I have, yes."

"And would you do it to me?"

"Under no circumstances. Jo—" He paused, groping for the right words. "Listen, love. You must not contemplate pursuing this matter. I meant it when I said you should not see Carl Bennet again. You must not allow anyone to try to regress you. I am not so concerned about the drama and the psychological stress that you are put under, although it is obviously not good for you. What worries me is the fact that you are prone to physiological reaction. You reflect physically what you are describing. That is very rare. It is also potentially dangerous."

"You mean if William beat me . . . her up, I'd wake up with bruises?"

"Exactly." Sam compressed his lips.

"And if she starved to death?" The question came out as a whisper.

There was a pause. Sam looked away. "I think that is unlikely." He forced himself to laugh. "Nevertheless, it would obviously be foolish to put yourself deliberately at risk."

For a moment Jo did not move, her eyes on his face. Then slowly she turned away.

It was dark when Dorothy Franklyn arrived at the apartment carrying an armful of roses. A tall, striking woman in her mid-sixties, she habitually wore tortoiseshell-rimmed glasses and immaculate Jaeger suits that made her look the epitome of efficiency. She was in fact always slightly disorganized and invariably late for whatever she was trying to do. Jo was enormously fond of her.

"Are you sure you don't mind me dropping in like this, Jo?" she said apologetically as she came in. "I came up for a matinée and then I had supper, but I wanted to leave you the flowers." She eyed Jo surreptitiously. "You look tired, my dear. Would you rather I just left them and went?"

Jo shook her head. She caught the other woman's arm and pulled her into the room. "Sit down and I'll put the kettle on. You've just missed your son. That's why I'm tired, he took me out to dinner."

Dorothy smiled, her whole face lighting with pleasure "Jo! I'm so glad. It broke my heart when you and he split up—"

"No—" Jo interrupted. "I meant Sam."

"Sam?" Dorothy frowned. "I thought he was in Switzerland."

"He was. He's stopped off in London for a few days—mainly to do a quick psychoanalysis of me, I think." Jo grinned wryly. "He's staying at Nick's apartment if you want to see him. Nick's not there, of course, so the flat is free."

She could feel the other woman's eyes on her face, bright with embarrassment and sympathy, and she forced herself to go on smiling somehow.

"How is Sam?" Dorothy asked after a long pause.

"Fine. He's been giving a paper on some terribly obscure subject. I was very impressed. He took me to tea at the zoo." She laughed.

Dorothy smiled. "He always says the zoo teaches one so much about people." She hesitated, eyeing Jo thoughtfully. "He has always been very fond of you, you know, Jo. I don't think you and Nick ever realized how much it hurt Sam when Nick walked off with you. Nick has always found it so easy to have any girl he wanted—I'm sorry, that sounds dreadful, and I know you were different—you were special to him. But you have been special to Sam too."

Jo looked down guiltily. "I think I did know. It's just that we met under such strange circumstances. I was a guinea pig in one of his experiments." She shivered. "Our relationship always seemed a little unreal after that. He was so concerned about me, but I always had the feeling it was a paternal concern, as if he were worried about my health." She paused abruptly. "He was, of course. I know that now. Anyway, he was twenty-six or seven and I was only nineteen when we first met. We belonged to different worlds. I did rather care for him—" She was staring at the roses lying on the table. "If I'm honest I suppose I still do. He's an attractive guy. But then Nick came along . . ." She stood up abruptly. "Let me put these in water or they'll die before our eyes."

"Is it serious, this thing with Judy Curzon?" Dorothy's voice was gentle.

"It sounds like it. She is much more his type than I ever was. She's domesticated and artistic and a redhead." Jo forced herself to laugh. "Perhaps I should cultivate old Sam now. Better late than never, and we seem to have quite a bit in common after all. It might even make Nick jealous!" Scooping up the flowers, she buried her face in the velvet blooms, then she carried them through to the kitchen and dropped them into the sink.

After turning the cold tap on full, she turned and saw that Dorothy had followed her. She was frowning.

"Jo. Please don't just amuse yourself with Sam. I know it must be tempting to try to hurt Nick, but that's not the way to do it. There's too much rivalry between those two already."

"Rivalry?" Jo looked astonished. "But they hardly see each other, so how could there be?"

"Sam has resented Nick since the day he was born." Dorothy absent-mindedly picked the petals off a dying rose and threw them into the trash. "I used to think it was normal sibling rivalry and he'd grow out of it. But it was more than that. He learned to hide it. He even managed to fool Nick and their father that he no longer felt it, but he never fooled me. As he grew up it didn't disappear. It hardened. I don't know why. They are both good-looking, they are both confident and bright. Sam is enormously successful in his own field. There is no reason for him to resent Nick at all. At least, there wasn't until you came along."

Jo stared at her. "I had no idea. None at all. I thought they liked each other. That's awful." Wearily she pushed the hair off her face. "I'm sure Nick likes Sam. He told me that he used to worship him when they were children, and I sometimes think that secretly he still does. Look at the way he turned to him when he was worried about me." She stopped. Had Nick really turned to Sam for help, or was he merely using him cynically to take her off his hands? She closed her eyes unhappily, trying to picture Sam's face as he kissed her good night. It had been a brotherly kiss, no more. Of that she was sure.

Dorothy had not noticed Jo's sudden silence. With a deep sigh she swept on after a minute. "I used to wonder if it was my fault. There was a six-year gap between them, you know, and we were so thrilled when Nick came along. Elder children sometimes think such funny things, that somehow they weren't enough, or that they have failed their parents in some way . . ."

"But Sam is a psychiatrist!" Jo burst out in spite of herself. "Even if he felt that when he was six, he must be well enough read by now to know it wasn't true. Oh, come on, Dorothy, this is all too Freudian for me at this time of night."

"Are you seeing Sam again?"

Jo nodded. "On Wednesday evening."

Dorothy frowned. "Jo, is it over between you and Nick? I mean, really over?"

Jo turned on her, exasperated. "Dorothy, stop it! They are grown men, not boys fighting over a toy, for God's sake! I don't know if it's over between me and Nick. Probably yes. But we are still fond of each other, nothing can change that. Who knows what will happen?"

After Dorothy had gone Jo sat staring into space for a long time. Then slowly she got up and poured herself a drink. She glanced down at the books and notes piled on the table, but she did not touch them. Instead, restlessly, she began to wander around the room. In front of the huge oval mirror that hung over the fireplace she stopped and stared at herself for a long time. Then solemnly she raised her glass. "To you, Matilda, wherever you are," she said sadly. "I'll bet you thought men were bastards too."

The answering machine was to the point:

"There is no one in the office at the moment. In a genuine emergency

89

Dr. Bennet may be reached at Lymington four seven three two zero. Otherwise please phone again on Monday morning.''

Jo slammed down the receiver. She eyed the Scotch bottle on the table, then she turned her back on it and went to stand instead on the balcony in the darkness, smelling the sweet honeyed air of the London garden, cleansed by night of the smell of traffic.

It was a long time before she turned and went back inside. Leaving the French windows open, she inserted her cassette back into the recorder and switched it on. Then, turning off the lights, she sat down alone in the dark to listen.

10

"**I**s he here?" Judy was standing in the darkened hallway outside Jo's door with her hands on her hips. She was wearing a loosely belted white dress and thonged sandals that made her look, Jo thought irrelevantly, like a Greek boy.

"Please, talk more quietly or you'll wake the whole house." Jo stood back to allow her to enter, as Judy's furious voice wafted up and down the stairwell outside the apartment door. It was barely nine o'clock on Sunday morning.

The apartment was untidy. Cassettes littered the table and the floor; there were empty glasses lying about and ashtrays full of half-smoked cigarettes. Jo stared around in distaste. Beside the typewriter on the coffee table there was a pile of papers and notes where she had been typing most of the night. Books were stacked on the carpet and overflowing onto the chairs. She threw open the French windows and took a deep breath of cool morning air. Then she turned to Judy.

"If you're looking for Nick, I'm afraid you're out of luck. He's not here. I haven't seen him since yesterday morning." She went through into the kitchen and reached into the refrigerator. "Do you want some coffee?" she called.

Judy looked taken aback. "He said he was coming back here." She followed Jo into the kitchen uncertainly.

"Well, he didn't come." Jo reached down a large vase from a cabinet and stuffed the roses from the sink into it. "Aren't these lovely? Nick's mother brought them up from Hampshire for me yesterday."

Judy's jaw tightened fractionally. "I have never met his mother."

"Oh, you will. She is already on your trail. Every girl friend has to be vetted and approved and then cultivated." Jo leaned against the counter and looked Judy straight in the eye.

"Do you still love him?" Judy tried hard to hold her gaze.

Jo snorted. "What kind of naive question is that? Do you really think I'd tell you if I did?" Behind her the coffee began to perk. She ignored it. "At this moment I wish both Sam and Nick Franklyn at the other end of the

91

earth, and if it makes you happy I will cordially wish you there with them. But I should like to say one thing before you go there. If you decide to make any more inventive little statements to the press about my sanity or lack of it, be very careful what you say, because I shall sue you for libel."

Judy retreated. "I don't want anything from you. I'm not surprised Nick couldn't wait to get away from here!" She turned to the front door and dragged it open. Behind them the phone in the living room began to ring. Jo ignored it as she unplugged the coffeepot. "Shut the door behind you," she called over her shoulder.

Judy stopped in her tracks. "Sam told me you're schizophrenic," she shouted, "did you know that? He said that you'll be locked up one of these days. And they'll throw away the key!" She paused as if hoping for a response. When none came she walked out into the hall and slammed the door. Jo could hear her footsteps as she ran down the stairs outside. Moments later she heard the porch door bang.

Behind her the phone was still ringing. Dazed, Jo moved toward it and picked up the receiver. Her hands were shaking.

"Jo? I thought you weren't there!" The voice on the other end was indignant. Jo swallowed. She was incapable of speaking for a moment. "Jo, dear? Are you all right?" The voice persisted. "It's me, Ceecliff!"

Jo managed to speak at last. "I know, Grandma. I'm sorry. My voice is a bit husky. Is that better?" She cleared her throat noisily. "How nice to hear you. How are you?"

"I am fine as always." The tones were clipped and direct. Celia Clifford was a vivacious and attractive woman of seventy-six who, in spite of the alternate cajoling and threats of her town-dwelling daughter-in-law and granddaughter, lived completely alone in a rambling Tudor farmhouse in the depths of Suffolk. Jo adored her. Ceecliff was her special property, her refuge, her hidden vice, the shoulder that tough, abrasive Jo Clifford could cry on and no one would ever know.

"You sound a bit odd, dear," Ceecliff went on briskly. "You're not smoking again are you?"

Jo looked ruefully at the ashtray beside the phone. "I'm trying not to," she said.

"Good. And nothing is wrong?"

Jo frowned. "Why should anything be wrong?"

There was a chuckle at the other end of the line. "There shouldn't. I just wanted to make sure that you didn't have any excuses up your sleeve. You're coming to lunch here, Jo, so you'd better get ready to leave within half an hour."

Jo laughed. "I can't come all the way to Suffolk for lunch," she protested.

"Of course you can. Take off those dreadful jeans and put on a pretty dress, then get in the car. You'll be here by one."

"How did you know I had jeans on?" Jo had begun to smile.

"I'm psychic." Ceecliff's tone was dry. "Now, no more talking. Just come." There was a click as she hung up and Jo was left staring down at the receiver in her hand.

Bet Gunning turned over in bed and ran a languid hand over Tim Heacham's chest. "Much drunker and you wouldn't have been able to make it, my friend."

Tim groaned. "If I had been much drunker, you could have been accused of necrophilia! If you have any sense of decency at all, Ms. Gunning, you'll fix me one of your magic prairie oysters in the kitchen and shut up."

Bet gave him an old-fashioned look as she padded out to the kitchen but she said nothing. She was too content. In a few moments she was back with a tray containing two coffee mugs and a glass. She watched as Tim drank down the mixture pulling a series of agonized faces, then she held out her hand for the glass. "Now. Coffee and then a cold shower. That will get you *compos mentis.*"

"Sadistic bitch." Tim patted her knee fondly as she sat down next to him. "Is this what makes you such a good editor? Rouse them, satisfy them, give them their medicine, kiss them better, and send them away!"

She laughed. "So you think I sleep with my staff as well?"

"It's the general word. And all your ancillary acolytes—like me. But only the men, of course, as far as I know."

Bet reached forward and tugged his hair. "Listen, Tim! If you want to talk shop, tell me how you are getting on with Jo's pictures. Have you started on them yet?"

"Of course. But I thought the deadline wasn't for months."

"It isn't." Bet inserted her legs beneath the sheet next to his and ran an exploratory finger across his solar plexus.

Tim flopped back against the pillows and pushed her hand away. "No go, love. Don't even hope. I've had it!" He grinned at her fondly. "I took some super pictures of a woman being hypnotized to think she was a nineteenth-century street girl. I'll show you the contacts. The only trouble with that article from my point of view is that however glamorous and exciting the stories these people are telling, basically they are still just Mr. and Mrs. Bloggs sitting there in a chair. But it is a tremendous challenge—to catch those faces and make your readers see in them the reflection of whatever character is inhabiting the person's mind at that moment."

"If anyone can do it, you can." Bet lay back on her elbow beside him and reached for her cup. "You know Jo was regressed herself once?"

"No. She told me about it. It was a failure. All that guff Judy sounded off was jealous rubbish."

Bet shook her head. "Not so. Nick talked to me about it a couple of weeks back. He begged me to kill the article. According to him Jo nearly died under hypnosis."

Tim sat up. "For Christ's sake—"

Bet smiled. "He overreacts. It would make a better article, you must admit, if Jo could say it had happened to her. Jo is nothing if not honest. If something strange happens to her she'll write about it."

"Even if it's published posthumously?" Tim swung his legs over the side of the bed and stood up. "My God, Bet! I thought you were Jo's friend! Would you really want something awful to happen to her just to make a good story?" He reached for his trousers and pulled them on. "Bloody hell!"

Bet laughed. "Don't be so dramatic. I want some action. I want to see Jo up against something she can't debunk, just for once. I want to see how she handles an article that really stirs her up. It'll do her good. I suspect Nick resents her success. He's jealous of her independence. That's why they split up, so a plea from him to call off the article comes over to me as very suspicious. She doesn't need his help—or his hindrance. Oh, yes, I am her friend, sweetie, probably her best friend."

"Then God help her." Tim tugged open a drawer and pulled out a black cashmere sweater, drawing it down awkwardly over his head. "With you and Judy Curzon for friends, who else does she need!"

"Well, there's always you, isn't there? You wouldn't be entertaining me so enthusiastically if you thought you could lay your sticky little hands on our Jo, would you, my love?"

Tim flushed a dusky red as he turned away. "Crap. Jo's never had eyes for anyone but Nick since I've known her." He stared into the mirror and ran his fingers through his hair.

"More fool her then, because Nick is playing the field. Where are you going?"

"Sunday or not, I have work to do. Are you going to cook my lunch?"

Bet stretched, snuggling back under the covers. "Why not? Who were you in your previous life, Tim, do you know?"

Tim turned and looked down at her. "Funnily enough, I think I do."

Bet's eyes grew round. "You are *joking?*"

"No."

"Well?" She sat up, the sheet pulled up tightly around her breasts. "Who were you?"

He grinned. "If I told you that, my love, I'd regret the indiscretion for the rest of my life. Now, you may go back to sleep for exactly forty-one minutes, then get up and put the roast on. I should be finished in the darkroom in an hour." With a wave he ducked out of the bedroom and ran down the spiral stairs to the studio below.

* * *

The north London traffic was heavy, and Jo was impatient, but she was so preoccupied she barely noticed the cars and the heavy pall of fumes under the brassy blue sky. It was not until the road finally widened and the cars began to thin that she started to relax and look around her. The air became lush with country summer: blossoms, thick and scented on the trees, rich new green leaves, hedgerows smothered in cow parsley and hawthorn while overhead the sky arched in an intensity of blue that never showed itself in London. Jo smiled to herself, turning off the main road to make her way through the lanes toward Long Melford. She always felt light-headed and free when she arrived in Suffolk. Perhaps it was the air or the thought of seeing Ceecliff, or perhaps it was only the fact that she was nearly always faint with hunger by the time she reached her grandmother's house.

She turned down the winding drive that led toward the mellow pink-washed house and drew up slowly outside the front door. Nick's Porsche was parked in the shade beneath the chestnut tree. She sat and stared at it for a moment, then angrily she threw open the car door and climbed out.

Nick must have heard the scrunch of her car tires on the gravel for he appeared almost at once around the corner of the house. He was in shirt sleeves, looking relaxed and rested as he grinned at her and raised his hand in greeting. "You're just in time for a drink."

"What are you doing here?" Her anger had evaporated as fast as it had come and there was a strange tightness in her throat as she looked at him. Hastily she turned away to pull her bag out of the car. She held it against her chest and wrapped her arms around it defensively.

"I needed to talk to your grandmother, so I called her up and came down last night." He stopped six feet from her, looking at her closely. She had unfastened her hair, letting it fall loosely over her shoulders in an informal style that suited her far better than her usual severe line, and she had changed into a soft clinging dress of peacock blue silk before leaving home. She looked, Nick thought suddenly, very fragile and very beautiful. He resisted the urge to reach out and touch her. "She's in the garden at the back with the sherry bottle. Come on around."

"What was so important you suddenly have to drive out to Suffolk to talk about it?" Jo asked mildly.

Nick was silent for a moment, still staring at her. Than he shook his head slowly. "I thought I'd do some research for you." He grinned. "Guess who came from Clare, just around the corner?" He began to lead the way across the gravel.

Jo followed him. "You came here to check on that?" she said in disbelief.

Nick shrugged. "Well, no, not exactly. I wanted to talk mainly. And I admit it, I told Ceecliff not to say anything about me when she called you.

I wanted to talk to you too and I thought you might not come if you knew I was here."

"It's a pity she didn't mention you," Jo retorted. "Your girl friend was with me when she called. You could have had a word with her and put her mind at rest. She clearly thought I had hidden you under my bed."

"Judy was at your apartment this morning?" Nick frowned.

Jo had begun to walk toward the garden at the back of the house. The grass was soft, scented beneath her sandals, with patches of damp velvety moss and strewn with daisies. "She was just telling me that your brother had confided to her that I was schizophrenic and would need to be locked up soon."

Nick laughed. "I hope you didn't believe her. I'm afraid you seem to bring out the worst in Judy." He was following her now, around the corner of the house. "Jo, I think there's something I should explain. Wait a minute, please." He caught her arm.

"There's no explaining to do, Nick." Jo turned on him, pulling herself free. "You and I have split up. You have a new woman in your life. The night before last you were kind enough to help me out for old times' sake, when I was feeling a bit frayed, but as soon as someone else turned up to sort me out, you went back to Judy. End of story. Lucky Judy. Only I wish you would explain to her she need not feel so insecure."

She could feel a sudden warm breeze stirring her hair as she walked on toward the walnut tree near the willow-shaded pond where her grandmother was sitting in a deck chair. On the horizon white cumulus was beginning to mass into tall thunderheads. She bent and kissed Ceecliff's cheek.

"That was unfair to trap me into coming here. Nick and I have nothing to talk about."

Ceecliff surveyed her from piercingly bright dark eyes. "I would have thought you had a great deal to talk about. And if he hasn't, I have! Nick has told me about your amazing experiences, Jo." She reached up and took her granddaughter's hand. "I want to hear all about them. You mustn't be frightened of what happened. You have been privileged."

Jo stared at her. "You sound as if you believe in reincarnation."

"I think I must. Of a kind." Ceecliff smiled. "Come on. Sit down and have a sherry and relax. You're as taut as a wire! Nicholas came up last night to talk to me about you. He was worried that you're trying to do too much, Jo. And I agree with him. From what he's told me, I think you need to rest. You must not try to venture into your past again."

"Oh, so that's it." Jo levered herself back out of the deck chair she had settled into. "He came here to get you to talk me out of going on with my researches. Part of the great Franklyn conspiracy. I wish you would all get it into your heads that this is no one's business but mine. What I do with my mind and my memory, or whatever it is, is my affair. I am a sober, consenting, rational adult. I make my own decisions."

Ceecliff was looking up at her as she talked. She grinned impishly. "There you are, Nicholas. I told you she'd say that."

Nick shrugged ruefully. "You did. But it was worth a try." He handed Jo a glass. "So come on, Jo. You haven't told us whether you found anything out in the library yesterday. We are all agog."

Jo stared at him in feigned astonishment. "Are you telling me now that you're interested? You amaze me! You weren't so interested yesterday when you couldn't wait to leave and go back to Judy!" She had forgotten her grandmother, seated between them.

"I only went because Sam said I had to, for God's sake!" Nick's face was flushed with anger. "Don't you think I wanted to stay? If he hadn't pulled rank and reminded me you were his patient I'd have waited all day to make sure you were all right."

Jo put her glass down on the tray so abruptly the sherry spilled onto the silver, spattering into amber droplets. "He said I was his patient?" she echoed. Her face had gone white.

Ceecliff had been watching them both intently. "I'm sure he didn't mean it literally, dear," she put in hastily. "I expect he meant that as you had both called him in for his advice he would like the opportunity of talking to Jo alone."

"I didn't call him in!" Jo glared at Nick repressively. "It was Nick's idea."

"Because he is obviously enormously concerned about you." Stiffly Ceecliff pulled herself to her feet. "Now, no more fighting, children. I wish to enjoy my lunch. Come inside and later Jo can tell us what she found out about her Matilda."

They took their coffee in the conservatory at the back of the house as huge clouds massed and foamed over the garden, blotting out a sky that had become brazen with heat. Ceecliff sent Nick out to bring in the garden chairs as the rain began to fall in huge sparse drops, pitting the surface of the pond. Then she turned to Jo.

"You're going to drive that young man straight into her arms, you know!"

Jo was pouring the coffee, frowning with concentration as she handled the tall silver pot. "It's where he wants to be."

"No, Jo, it isn't. Can't you see it?" Ceecliff leaned forward and helped herself to a cup from the tray. "You are being very stubborn. Especially as you obviously love him. You do, don't you?"

Jo sat down on the windowseat, her back to the garden. "I don't know," she said bleakly. Her hands were lying loosely in her lap. She stared blankly down at them, suddenly overwhelmingly tired. "I'm not sure what

I feel any more about anyone. I'm not sure I even know what I feel about myself."

"That's ridiculous." Ceecliff leaned forward and, picking up Jo's cup, put it into her hands. "Drink that and listen to me. You're getting things out of perspective."

"Am I?" Jo bit her lip. "Either Nick or Sam lied to me and I don't know which."

"All men are liars, Jo." Ceecliff smiled sadly. "Haven't you discovered that yet?"

The rain was growing stronger now, releasing the warm scents of wet earth that reached them even through the conservatory windows. Jo could see Nick hastily stacking the deck chairs in the summerhouse.

"That's a bit cynical, even for you, Grandma." She reached forward and touched the old woman's hand as Nick sprinted back toward them across the grass. Behind him the horizon flickered and shifted slightly before Jo's eyes. She blinked, watching as he opened the door and came in, shaking himself like a dog. He was laughing as she handed him a cup of coffee. "You're soaked, Nick," she said sharply. "You'd better take off your shirt or you'll get pneumonia or something."

He spooned some sugar into the cup and sat down beside her. "It'll soon dry off, it's so hot. Go on with what you were telling us at lunch, Ceecliff, about Jo's grandfather."

Ceecliff leaned back against the cushions on her chair. "I wish you remembered him better, Jo, but you were only a little girl when he died. He used to love talking about his ancestors and the Clifford family tree, which was more of a forest, he used to say. The trouble is, I never used to listen all that carefully. It bored me. It was about yesterday and I wanted to live today." She paused as another zigzag of lightning flickered behind the walnut tree. "I didn't realize how soon the present becomes the past. Perhaps I'd have listened more if I had." She laughed ruefully. "Sorry. You'll have to allow for an old lady's maudlin tendencies. Now, what I was saying was that hearing you talking about your William de Braose being a baron on the Welsh borders reminded me that of course that is where the Clifford family originally came from. I'll find Reggie's papers and give them to you, Jo. You might as well have them, and you may find them interesting now you have decided the past could have something to recommend it, even if it is only a handsome son of the Clares." Again the impish twinkle. She sighed. "But now you are going to have to excuse me because I am going to lie down for a couple of hours. One of the compensations of old age is being able to admit to being tired and then do something about it." With Nick's help she pulled herself out of the low chair in which she had been sitting and walked back slowly into the house.

"She's not tired," Jo said as soon as she was out of hearing. "She has ten times more energy than I have."

98

"She thinks she is being tactful." Nick stooped over the tray and poured himself another cup of coffee. "She thinks we should be given the chance to be alone."

"How wrong she is then," Jo said quickly. She flinched as another shaft of lightning crossed the sky. It was followed by a distant rumble of thunder. "There's nothing we need to talk about that she wouldn't be welcome to join in." The heaviness of the afternoon was closing over her, dragging her down. Her eyelids were leaden. She forced them open.

Nick was standing with his back to her, looking at the rain sweeping in across the garden. "I do have to talk to you alone," he said slowly. "And I think you know it."

Jo moved across to her grandmother's vacated chair and threw herself into it. "Well, now is not the moment. Oh, God, how I hate thunder! It's thundered practically every day this week!"

Nick turned and looked at her. "You never used to mind it."

"Oh, I don't mean I'm afraid of it. It just makes me feel so headachy and tense. Perhaps I'm just tired. I was working all last night." She closed her eyes.

Nick put down his cup. He moved to stand behind her chair, and, gently resting his hands on her shoulders, he began to massage the back of her neck with his thumbs.

Jo relaxed, feeling the warmth of his fingers through the thin silk of her dress, the circling motion easing the pain in her head as a squall of wind beneath the storm center sent a flurry of rain against the glass of the conservatory.

Suddenly she stiffened. For a moment she could not breathe. She tried to open her eyes but the hands on her shoulders had slipped forward, encircling her throat, pressing her windpipe till she was choking. She half rose, grasping at his wrists, fighting him in panic, clawing at his face and arms, then, as another rumble of thunder cut through the heat of the afternoon, she felt herself falling.

Frantically she tried to catch her breath, but it was no use. Her arms were growing heavy and there was a strange buzzing in her ears.

Why, Nick, why?

Her lips framed the words, but no sound came as slowly she began the long spiral down into suffocating blackness.

11

Two faces swam before her gaze. Absently she tried to focus on them, her mind groping with amorphous images as first one pair of eyes and then the other floated toward her, merged, then drifted apart once more. The mouths beneath the eyes were moving. They were speaking, but she couldn't hear them; she couldn't think. All she could feel was the dull pain of the contusions that fogged her throat.

Experimentally she tried to speak, but nothing happened as she raised a hand toward one of the faces—the blue eyes, the red-gold moustache, the deep furrowed lines across the forehead coming sharply into focus. It drew back out of reach and she groped toward the other. It was younger, smoother, the eyes lighter.

"I've phoned Dr. Graham." A woman's voice spoke near her, the diction clear, echoing in the hollow spaces of her head. "He was at home, thank God, not on that damn golf course! He'll be here in five minutes. How is she?"

Jo frowned. Ceecliff. That was Ceecliff, standing close to her, behind the two men.

She breathed in slowly and saw her grandmother's face near hers. Swallowing painfully, she tried once more to speak. "What happened?" she managed to murmur after a moment.

As Ceecliff sat down beside her Jo realized she was lying on the sofa in the dimly lit living room. Her grandmother's cool, dry hand took hers.

"You fainted, you silly girl. Just like a Victorian miss!"

"Who's there?" Jo looked past her into the shadows.

"It's me, Jo." Nick's voice was taut.

"Why is it so dark?" Jo levered herself up against the cushions, her head spinning.

"There's the mother and father of a storm going on, dear," Ceecliff said after a moment. "It's dark as doomsday in here. Put the lights on, Nick." Her voice sharpened.

The three table lamps threw a warm, wintry light in the humid bleakness

100

of the room. Through the windowpanes the sound of the rain was deafening on the broad leaves of the hostas in the bed outside.

"Where's the doctor?" Jo stared around.

"He's not here yet, Jo." Ceecliff smiled at her gravely.

"But I saw him—"

"No, dear." Ceecliff glanced at Nick. "Listen. That must be his car now." Above the sound of the rain they could all hear the scrunch of tires on the gravel. Moments later the glass door of the entrance hall opened and a stout figure let himself into the hall.

Ceecliff stood up. She met David Graham in the dim, heavily beamed dining room, which smelled of pot pourri and roses, and put her finger to her lips.

"It's my granddaughter, David," she murmured as he shook himself like a dog and shed his raincoat on the mellow oak boards.

David Graham was a fair-haired man of about sixty, dressed, despite the heat, in a tweed jacket and woolen tie. He kissed her fondly. "It's probably the storm, Celia. They affect some people like this, you know. Unless it's your cooking. You haven't been giving her that curry you gave Jocelyn and me, have you?" He did not wait to see her mock indignation. His bag in his hand, he was already moving toward the door of the living room.

Nick smiled down at Jo uncertainly. "I'll leave you both to it, shall I?"

"Please." David Graham looked at him searchingly for a moment, noting the tension of Nick's face—tension and exhaustion, and something else. Putting down his bag beside Jo, he waited until Nick had closed the door behind him. Guilt, that was it; Nick Franklyn had looked guilty.

He sat down beside Jo and grinned at her, picking up her wrist.

"Do you make a habit of this sort of thing, my dear?" he asked quietly.

Jo shook her head. "It's never happened before. I'm beginning to feel such a fraud. It's just the storm, I'm sure. They always make me feel strung up and headachy."

"And you're not pregnant as far as you know?" He smiled.

"Certainly not! And before you ask, I've given up smoking. Nearly."

"There's something wrong with your throat?"

She moved away from him slightly on the sofa. "A bit painful, that's all. I expect I'm getting a cold."

"Humph." The doctor bent to open his bag. He withdrew a wooden tongue depressor. "Open up. Let's have a look, shall we?"

Her throat was agony. Not sore. Not raw, but bruised and aching. Without registering any emotion at all the doctor put down the tongue depressor and reached for a thermometer. When it was in her mouth he brought his hands up gently to her neck, and, brushing aside her hair, he felt beneath her ears and under her chin with cool, impersonal fingers.

Jo could feel her hands shaking. "What is it?" she said as soon as she could speak.

101

He held the thermometer up to the green-shaded table lamp and squinted viciously as he tried to see the mercury. "I'm always telling Celia to get some proper lights in this damn room. In the evening you can't tell your gin from the goldfish water. It is ninety-eight point four, which is exactly what it ought to be. Your pulse is a bit above average for a Sunday afternoon, even in a storm, though. Let's try some blood pressure, shall we?"

"But my throat?" Jo said. "What's wrong with my throat?"

"Nothing that I can see." He was rummaging in his bag. "Where does it hurt?"

"It aches. Here." She raised her hand to her neck while her eyes focused on the little pump in his hand as he inflated the cuff around her arm.

It was all coming back to her. She had been in the conservatory with Nick. He had stood behind her, his hands on her shoulders, then slowly he —or somebody—had slid them up around her throat and begun to squeeze . . . She could remember what happened quite clearly now. It was Nick. It had to have been Nick. No one else was there. Nick had tried to kill her! She felt sick. Nick wouldn't hurt her. It wasn't possible. It must have all been some hideous nightmare. She swallowed painfully. But it was too real for a nightmare.

She realized suddenly that the doctor was watching her face and turned away sharply. "Is it high?" she asked as he folded away his equipment.

"A little, perhaps. Nothing to get excited about." He paused. "Something is wrong, my dear, isn't it? You look worried. Is there something you ought to be telling me?"

She shook her head. "Nothing, Dr. Graham. Except that perhaps I should own up to a few late nights, working. I expect that could make me feel a bit odd, couldn't it?"

He frowned. "I expect it could." He waited as though he expected her to say more. When she didn't he went on. "I can't explain the throat. Perhaps you're getting one of these summer viruses. Gargle. That will help, and I suggest you take it easy for a bit. Spend a few days here, perhaps." Smiling, he stood up. "Not that Celia is my idea of a peaceful companion, but this is a good house to rest in. It's a happy house. Better than London, I'll be bound. If it happens again, go to see your own doctor."

"Thank you." After pushing herself up, Jo managed to stand. Outside the window there was another pale flicker of lightning. "I'm sorry my grandmother called you out in this."

He laughed as he picked up his bag. "If she hadn't I'd have slept through it and kicked myself for not closing the vents in the greenhouse, so she did me a favor! Now, remember what I said. Take it easy for a bit. And do see your own doctor if you go on feeling at all unwell. . . ." He gave her a piercing glance, then with a nod he turned to the door.

As soon as he had stepped out into the hall Jo turned to the sideboard. The lamp shed a green, muted light behind it toward the mirror, and, tipping the shade violently so that the naked light of the bulb shone into her face, Jo stood on tiptoe, peering at the glass. Her reflection was white and stark, her eyes shadowed and huge in the uncompromising light. Leaning forward, she held her hair up away from her neck and peered at it. Her skin looked normal. There were no marks there.

"Jo! You're burning the silk on that shade!" Ceecliff's cry made her jump. Hastily she put it straight, noticing guiltily the brown mark already showing on the lining. She could smell the scorched fabric.

"What on earth were you doing?"

"Just looking at my throat." Jo glanced behind her grandmother. "Where is Nick?"

"He's holding an umbrella over David while he gets in the car. I suppose you won't do what David suggests and stay here for a few days?"

Jo sighed. "You know I can't. I'm too busy."

"Then you'll have some tea before you let Nick drive you home—"

"No!"

Ceecliff stared at her in astonishment. "Jo, dear—"

"I'm sorry. I didn't mean to sound so abrupt." Jo swallowed. "It's just that I don't want Nick to drive me."

"Well, you can't drive yourself, Joey. David was quite clear about that." Ceecliff's tone was surprisingly firm. "You stay here or you go with Nick."

Jo glanced toward the door. Her lips had gone dry. She took a deep breath. "Who was the man in here as I came round?"

Ceecliff had turned away, patting her injured lampshade with a proprietorial hand. "There was no one else in here, Jo. Only Nick and I."

Jo crossed to the door, steadying herself with her hand on the back of a chair. Swiftly she closed it. Leaning against it, she looked at Ceecliff.

"Someone tried to strangle me this afternoon."

Her grandmother pursed her lips. "Jo, dear—"

"I am not imagining it. Out there in the conservatory. Nick was massaging my shoulders. Then—" She shrugged wildly. "Someone tried to kill me!"

"Nick was the only person there, Jo." Ceecliff came toward her slowly and put her hands on Jo's arms. "Are you accusing Nick?" She was scandalized.

"No, of course not." Jo's voice had fallen to a whisper.

"Did you tell David all this?"

"I said my neck hurt." Jo shook her head.

"I think he would have been able to tell, Jo, if anyone had tried to kill you. There would have been bruises on your throat for one thing." Ceecliff moved toward the sofa and sat down on the edge of it. "I think Nick was right to be worried about this hypnosis, Jo. You are too susceptible—"

Jo flung herself away from the door. "This has nothing to do with the hypnosis! I wasn't imagining it! You would know if someone had tried to kill you!" She put her hands to her throat. "There was someone else there. Someone else, Ceecliff. It can't have been Nick. He wouldn't . . . He wouldn't want to kill me. Besides, there was someone else in the room when I woke up. You must have seen him. You must! For God's sake, he was standing right behind Nick!"

"Joey, there was no one there," Ceecliff said gently. "If there had been, I would have seen him."

"You think I'm imagining it?"

"I think you're tired, emotionally upset, and what we as children used to call thunder-strung." Ceecliff smiled.

She turned as Nick pushed open the door. He went straight to Jo, who had tensed nervously as he came into the room. "How are you?" he asked.

"I'm fine, thanks." She forced herself to smile at him.

"But she is going to let you drive her back, Nick, after you've both had some tea," Ceecliff said firmly. "She can come and pick up her car another time."

Jo swallowed. Her eyes had gone automatically to Nick's hands, resting on the back of the chair. They were firm, strong hands, tanned from sailing, slightly stained now, with lichen from the rain-soaked wood of the summerhouse door.

As if feeling her gaze on them, Nick slipped them into the pockets of his jeans. "Are you sure you're okay?" he asked. "I've never had a woman faint at my feet before. It was all very dramatic. And you still look very pale."

Ceecliff stood up. "She's fine," she said firmly. "You know where the kitchen is, Nick? Go and put the kettle on for me, there's a dear. I'll be out in a minute."

As he left the room, Jo caught her hand. "Don't tell Nick what I said, will you? He'll think it is something to do with the hypnosis too, and I'm not going to fight with him all the way back to London."

Ceecliff smiled. "I shan't tell him, Jo. But I think you should," she said slowly. "I really think you should."

The storm crackled viciously across Hyde Park, highlighting the lush green of the trees against the bruised sky. Sam stood looking out of the window of Nick's apartment in South Audley Street, feeling the claustrophobia of London all around him. He sighed. If it weren't for that keyhole glimpse of the park up the narrow street in front of the apartment, he would not be able to stay here. It calmed and restored the quiet sanity of self-perception. He spared a moment's regretful thought for his high-ceilinged apartment in Edinburgh with its glorious view across the Queen's Park toward the Salisbury Crags, then, turning from the window, he drew the curtains against the storm and switched on the light. After throwing himself down on the sofa, he picked up his third glass of Scotch and reached for the pile of books stacked on the coffee table.

The first that came to hand was *A History of Wales* by John Edward Lloyd, M.A., volume two. After turning to the index, he began to look for William de Braose.

"What the hell is wrong, Jo?" Nick glanced across at her as he swung the car at last onto the M11. The windshield wipers were cutting great arcs in the wet carpets of rain that swept toward them off the road. For the second time, as he reached forward to insert a new cassette in place, he had noticed her shrink away from his hand. And she was obviously having trouble with her throat.

With an effort she smiled. "Sorry. I'm still feeling rather odd. My head is splitting." She closed her eyes as the car filled with the bright cold notes of Vivaldi. Don't talk. Don't let him see you're afraid. It did not happen. It was a hallucination—or imagination. Nick is no killer and the other . . . the face with the hard, angry blue eyes and the beard. It was not a face she knew. Not from this world, nor from that other time of wind and snow and spinning distances. It was not William, nor the young and handsome Richard. It was a double vision, a dream. Part of the dream where someone had tried to kill her. Something out of her own imagination, like the pain.

"The traffic is building." Nick's voice hung for a moment in the silence, coming from a long way away as the tape came to an end. He leaned forward and switched it off before it had a chance to start playing again. "You should have stayed with Celia. You're worn out, you know."

She forced her eyes open, realizing that the engine was idling. Cars were around them on every side; the end-of-weekend rush back to London, earlier than usual because of the bad weather, had brought the traffic to a standstill.

"You've been asleep." He glanced across at her. "Do you feel any better?" The light in the sky was already fading.

Jo eased her position slightly in the seat. "I'll be okay. I'm sorry I'm being such a nuisance. I can't think what came over me."

"That damn hypnosis came over you." Nick eased the car forward a few yards behind the car in front and braked. His elbow out of the open window, he drummed his fingers in irritation on the roof above his head. "I hope this has finally convinced you, Jo, of the idiocy of persisting with this research. Sam must have spelled out the risks for you."

Jo colored angrily. "What the devil has my fainting to do with the fact that I was hypnotized a couple of days ago? Oh, Nick, drop the subject, please!"

She hunched her shoulders defensively. How was it possible to feel so many conflicting emotions for the man sitting next to her? Love. Anger. Despair. And now fear. Real fear, which would not listen to the reason that told her it was groundless. She knew Nick had not tried to kill her. The thought was farcical. But if not his, then whose were the hands that had encircled her neck? And if they had been imaginary, then why had she imagined them? Perhaps he was right. Perhaps being hypnotized had some delayed effect. Some dangerous, delayed effect. She shuddered violently.

Half of her wanted to beg Nick to pull onto the hard shoulder and put his arms around her and hold her safe, but even as she glanced toward him she felt again that shiver of fear.

It was another hour before they turned into Cornwall Gardens. She had already extricated her key from her bag and was clutching it tightly in her hand as the car drew to a halt and she swung the door open. "Please, Nick, don't come in."

She almost threw herself onto the pavement. "I'm going to take an aspirin and go to bed. I'll call you, okay?" She slammed the door and ran toward the steps, not looking to see if he followed. She had banged the front door shut behind her before he had levered himself out of the car.

Nick shrugged. He stood where he was in the middle of the road, his hand resting on the car's roof, waiting until he saw the lights go on in the room behind the second-floor balcony doors, then he climbed back in and drove away. He was very worried.

Wrapped in her bathrobe, Jo pulled the heavy sash windows up. Outside, the night was very warm and still. Darkness had come early with the heavy cloud and there was an almost tropical humidity about the air. She could hear the sound of flamenco coming from the mews and, suddenly, a roar of laughter out of the dark.

After half drawing the curtains, she switched on her bedside light with a sigh and untied her bathrobe, slipping it from her bare shoulders.

The light was dim and the small antique mirror that stood on her low chest was on the other side of the room, but even from where she stood she could see. Her body was evenly tanned save for the slight bikini mark, but now there were other marks, marks that had not been there before. Her neck was swollen and covered with angry bruises. For a moment she could not move. She could not breathe. She stood transfixed, her eyes on the mirror, then she ran naked to the bathroom, dragging the main light-pull on, flooding the room with harsh cold light from the fluorescent strip in the ceiling. She grabbed her bath towel and frantically scrubbed at the condensation that still clung to the large mirror, then she looked at herself again. Her neck was violently bruised. She could even make out the individual fingermarks in the contusions on the front of her throat.

She stared at herself for a long time before walking slowly to the living room. Kneeling down beside the phone that still lay on the coffee table, she did not even realize she had memorized Carl Bennet's number until she had dialed it.

There was a series of clicks, then the answering machine spoke. Jo slammed the receiver down and glanced up at the clock on her desk. It was nearly midnight.

Slowly she made her way back toward her bedroom. She was shaking violently, beads of perspiration standing out on her forehead. Somewhere in the distance she heard a rumble of thunder. The storm was coming back. She walked to the window and stood looking out at the London night. It was only at the sound of a soft appreciative whistle from somewhere in the banks of dark windows behind the mews that she realized she was standing there naked in the lamplight.

With a wry smile she turned away and switched off the light, then she climbed into bed and lay staring up at the darkness.

It was very early when she woke, and the room was cold and fresh from the wide-open windows. Shivering, Jo got up and put on her robe. For a moment she did not dare look at her reflection in the mirror. The pain in her throat had gone as had her headache, and all she felt now was an overwhelming longing for coffee.

In the bathroom she dashed cold water over her face and reached for her toothbrush. Only then did she raise her eyes to the mirror. There wasn't a single mark on her throat.

At the apartment in South Audley Street the following evening Nick threw himself down into the armchair facing the windows and held out his hand for the drink Sam had poured for him.

"I see it didn't take you long to find my booze," he said with weary good humor.

"You can afford it." Sam looked at him inquiringly. "So, what did you want to see me about? It must be important if it brings you here from the lovely Miss Curzon."

Nick sat forward, clasping his glass loosely between his fingers. He sighed. "I haven't seen Judy for two days, Sam. If you want to know, I spent last night in a hotel. I went to Judy's, then I couldn't face going in." He paused. "I want to talk to you about Jo. How did you find her on Saturday?"

"Tense. Excitable. Hostile." Sam was thoughtful. "But not, I think, in any danger. She was thrown by what happened at Dr. Bennet's, but quite capable of handling it, as far as it went on that occasion."

"But you are worried about her being hypnotized again?"

Sam swirled the ice cubes around in his glass. "I am worried, yes, and I spoke to Bennet this morning about it." He glanced at Nick. "Unfortunately the man was on the defensive. He seemed to think I was trying to interfere and spouted a whole bag of crap about medical ethics at me.

107

However, I shall persevere with him in case Jo goes back to him. Tell me, why are you still so interested? I should have thought Judy took up most of your time these days, and if she doesn't, she ought to!"

Nick stood up. "I still care for Jo, Sam, and there is something wrong. On Sunday she and I went to Suffolk. She was taken ill—" He stood staring out of the window toward the park as he drained his glass. "There was something very strange about what happened. We were talking during a violent thunderstorm and she had some kind of fit. The local quack said it was exhaustion, but I'm not so sure he was right." He put his glass down, then held his hands out in front of him, flexing the fingers one by one. "I think it was in some way related to what happened at Bennet's on Friday."

Slowly Sam shook his head. "I doubt it. What were you doing in Suffolk anyway?" He was watching Nick carefully.

"Just visiting Jo's grandmother."

"I see." Sam stood up abruptly. "So, you're still in with the family, are you? Nice, rich, respectable Nick! Does Grandma know you're living with someone else?"

"I expect so." Nick stared at him, astonished at his sudden vehemence. "Jo tells her most things. Sam, about Jo's illness—"

"I'll go over and see her."

"You can't. She's taken the phone off the hook and she's not answering the door."

"You tried?"

"Earlier this evening."

"She wasn't ill—"

Nick laughed wryly. "Not too ill to tell me to bugger off over the intercom."

Sam smiled. "In that case I'd stop worrying. The whole thing will have blown over in another few days. She'll write her article and forget all about it. And I'll have a word with Bennet to make sure he won't see her again, just in case she does take it into her head to try. But I'm not taking any of this regression bit too seriously and neither should you. As to the fainting fit, it probably was heat exhaustion. A day's rest and she will be right as rain."

Nick did not look particularly convinced as he turned his back on the sunset and held out his glass for a refill. "That's what she said when I dropped her off on Sunday night."

"Then she's a sensible girl. Hold on, I'll get some more ice." Sam disappeared toward the kitchen.

With a sigh Nick walked over to the coffee table and picked up the top book on the pile there. It was a biography of King John, borrowed from the London Library. Surprised, he flipped it open at the place at the back, marked by an envelope. There, in the voluminous index, underlined in red pencil, was the name Briouse, Matilda of.

He put the book down and glanced curiously at the others. A two-volume history of Wales, the everyman edition of Gerald of Wales's *Itinerary,* and Poole's volume of *The Oxford History of England.*

"Phew!" Nick let out a quiet whistle. Gently he put the books back in place and moved away from the table. "So you're not taking it seriously, brother mine," he whispered thoughtfully. "Like hell you're not!"

It was Tuesday morning before Carl Bennet could see Jo. Sarah Simmons was waiting, as before, at the head of the stairs, her restrained manner barely hiding her excitement as she led Jo through into Bennet's consulting room. He was waiting for her by the open window, his glasses in his hand.

"Joanna! I am so glad you came back." He eyed her as she walked toward him, noting the paleness of her face beneath her tan. Her smile, however, was cheerful as she shook hands with him.

"I explained what happened on the phone," she said. "I had to come and find out why. If it had anything to do with the past, that is."

He nodded. "Your throat was bruised, you said." He put on his glasses then tipped her chin gently sideways and peered at her neck. "No one else saw this phenomenon?"

"No. It was gone by yesterday morning."

"And there has been no recurrence of pain or any of the other symptoms?"

"None." She threw her canvas bag down on the couch. "I'm beginning to wonder if I imagined the whole thing."

He looked at her thoughtfully. "We can't be sure that it had anything at all to do with your regression, Joanna. It is, to be honest, so unlikely as to be almost impossible. It presupposes a degree of self-hypnosis on your part that I find hard to credit, and even if that were possible, we had no intimations that anyone tried to strangle you in your previous existence. However,"—he drew his breath in with a hiss—"what I suggest is that we try another regression, but very differently this time. I propose to regress you to an earlier period. Your Matilda was scarcely more than a child when we met her last. Let us try to find her again when she is even younger, and when, hopefully"—he grinned disarmingly—"the personality is less strong and more malleable. I intend to keep a tight control of the session this time." He laughed in suppressed excitement. "I suggest that you and I draw up a list of questions that I can ask her. Knowing who she is and the period to which she belongs makes everything so much easier."

He picked up a volume from his desk and held it out. "See." He was as pleased as a child. "I have brought a history book. Last night I read up the chapter on the reign of King Henry II and there are pictures, so I even know roughly about her clothes."

Jo laughed. "You've done more research than I, then. Once I knew she was real, and what happened to her—" She shivered. "I suppose I was more interested with the technicalities of regression originally and I never considered that it would really happen to me. Or how I would feel if it did. But now that it has, it's so strange. It's an invasion of my privacy, and I'm conscious all the time that there is someone else there in my head. Or was. I'm not sure I like the feeling."

"I can't say I'm surprised. People react in different ways: interest, fear, resentment, complete disbelief, mild amusement. By far the most common reaction is to refuse to have anything more to do with regression."

"For fear of becoming involved." Jo nodded almost absently. "But I *am* involved. Not only professionally, but, somehow, inside myself. Because I've shared such intimate emotions with her. Fear . . . pain . . . horror . . . love." She shook her head deprecatingly. "Am I being very gullible?"

"No." Bennet smiled. "You are sensitive. You empathize with the personality."

"To the extent where I develop the symptoms I'm describing." Jo bit her lip. "But then while it's happening I *am* Matilda, aren't I?" She paused again. "I don't understand about my throat, but after Friday's regression . . ." She stopped in midsentence. If she told Bennet about Sam's warning, he might refuse to risk hypnotizing her again, and she did want very much to go back to Matilda's life. She wanted to know what happened.

"You've had other symptoms?" Bennet persisted quietly.

She looked away. "My fingers were very bruised. I hurt them on the stones of the castle wall, watching William kill those men. . . ." Her voice died away. "But they only felt bruised. There was nothing to see."

He nodded. "Anything else?" She could feel his eyes on her face. Did the ability to hypnotize her mean he could read her thoughts as well? She bit her lip, deliberately trying to focus her attention elsewhere. "Only stray shivers and echoes. Nothing to worry about." She grinned at him sheepishly. "Nothing to put me off, I assure you. I would like to go back. Among other things, I want to find out how she met Richard de Clare. Is it possible to be that specific in your questions?" Had he guessed, she wondered, just how much, secretly, she longed to see Richard again?

Bennet shrugged. "We'll see. Why don't we start to find out?"

He watched as she took out her tape recorder and set it on the ground beside her as she had done before, the microphone in her lap. She switched on the recorder then at last lay back on the long leather sofa and closed her eyes. Every muscle was tense.

She was hiding something from him. He knew that much. And more than that understandable desire to see Richard again. But what? He

110

thought once again about the phone call he had had from Samuel Franklyn and he frowned. The call had come on Monday morning before Sarah had arrived and Sarah knew nothing about it. He had not allowed Franklyn to say much, but there had been enough to know that there was some kind of problem.

He looked at his secretary, who had seated herself quietly once more in her corner, then he turned back to Jo. He licked his lips in concentration, and, taking a deep breath, he began to talk.

Jo listened intently. He was talking about the sun again. Today it was shining and the sky was clear and uncomplicated after the weekend of storms. But there was no light behind her eyelids now. Nothing.

Her eyes flew open in a panic. "Nothing is happening," she said. "It isn't going to work again. You're not going to be able to do it!"

She pushed herself up against the slippery leather back of the sofa. The palms of her hands were damp.

Bennet smiled calmly. "You're trying too hard, Jo. You mustn't try at all, my dear. Come, why not sit over here by the window?" He pulled a chair forward from the wall and twisted it so that it had its back to the light. "Fine, now, we'll do some little experiments on you to see how quick your eyes are. There's no hurry. We have plenty of time. We might even decide to leave the regression until another day." He smiled as he felt under his desk for a switch that turned on a spotlight in the corner of the room. Automatically Jo's eyes went toward it, but he had seen already that her knuckles on the arm of the chair were less white.

"Is she as deeply under as before?" Sarah's cautious question some ten minutes later broke into a long silence.

Bennet nodded. "She was afraid this time. She was subconsciously fighting me, every inch of the way. I wish I knew why." He looked at the list of questions in his hand, then he put it down on his desk. "Perhaps we'll discover eventually. But now it just remains to find out if we can reestablish contact with the same personality at all! So often one can't, the second time around." He chewed his lip for a second, eyeing Jo's face. Then he took a deep breath.

"Matilda," he said softly. "Matilda, my child. There are some things I want you to tell me about yourself."

12

The candle on the table beside his bed was guttering as Reginald de St. Valerie lay back against his pillow and began to cough again. His eyes, sunk in the pallid hollow of his face, were fixed anxiously on the door as he pulled another blanket around his thin shoulders. But it made no difference. He knew it was only a matter of time now before the creeping chill in his bones reached his heart, and then he would shiver no more.

His face lightened a little as the door was pushed open and a girl peered around it.

"Are you asleep, Father?"

"No, my darling. Come in." Cursing the weakness that seemed to have spread even to his voice, Reginald watched her close the heavy door carefully and come toward him. Involuntarily he smiled. She was so lovely, this daughter of his; his only child. She was tall, taller than average. She had grown this last year, until she was a span at least higher even than he, with her dark auburn hair spread thickly on her shoulders and down her back and the strange green eyes flecked with gold that she had from her dead mother. She was all he had left, this tall graceful girl. And he was all she had, and soon . . . He shrugged. He had made provision long ago for the future when he had betrothed her to William de Braose. And now the time had come.

"Sit here, Matilda. I must talk to you." Feebly he patted the blankets that covered him, and the lines of his face softened as she took his hand, curling up beside him, tucking her long legs under her.

"Will you eat something today, Father? If I prepare it myself and help you with the spoon?" she coaxed, nestling close. "Please?" She could feel the new inexorable cold in his hand and it frightened her. Gently she pressed it to her cheek.

"I'll try, Matilda, I'll try." He pushed himself a little farther up on the pillows with an effort. "But listen, sweetheart, there is something I must tell you first." He swallowed, trying to collect his thoughts as he gazed sadly into her anxious face. So often he had hoped this moment would never come. That somehow, something would happen to prevent it.

"I have written to Bramber, Matilda. Sir William de Braose has agreed that it is time the marriage took place. His son could have married long since, but he has waited until you were of age. You must go to him now." He tried not to see the sudden anguish on her face.

"But, Father, I can't leave you, I won't." She sat up straight, her eyes bright with tears. "Nothing will make me leave you. Ever."

He groped for her hand again and held it gently. "Sweetheart. It is I who must leave you, don't you see? And I couldn't die happy without knowing that you were wed. Please. To please me, go to him. Make him an obedient wife."

He was seized by another fit of coughing and Matilda slipped from the end of the bed and ran to the pillow, cradling his head on her breast. Her eyes were full of tears as she clutched him, desperately clinging to him. "You can't die, Father, you can't. You'll get well. You will. You always have before."

The tears spilled over and dropped onto her father's gray head. He looked up, trying to smile, and raised a shaky hand to brush her cheek. "Don't cry, darling. Think. When you marry William you will be a great lady. And his mother will take care of you. Come, please don't be so unhappy."

"But I want to stay with you." She still clung to him stubbornly. "I hate William, you know that. He's ugly and he's old and he smells."

Reginald sighed. So often he had given her her way, this girl of his, and he longed to do so again. But this time he had to stand firm. For her own sake. He closed his eyes, smelling the lavender of her gown, remembering. She was so like her mother had been: willful, beautiful, wild . . .

Sleep came so suddenly these days. He could feel his lids drooping. There was no way to fight it. He supposed death would come like that and he welcomed the thought. He was too old now, too racked with pain to regret the young man's dream of death on the field of battle. Smiling a little, he relaxed against her, feeling the soft warmth of her body, the gentle brush of her lips on his hair. Yes. She was very like her mother. . . .

Instinctively Matilda ran first to the chapel for comfort. She pushed open a heavy door and peered in. It was empty. She could see the statue of Our Lady, lit by the single flickering candle that stood on the altar. After running to it, she crossed herself and knelt. "Please, Holy Mother, don't let him die. You mustn't let my father die. I won't marry William de Braose, so there's no point in trying to make me." She gazed up at the serene stone face of the statue. It was cold in the chapel. A stray draft coming from the slit window high in the stone vault above the altar sent a shiver of cold down her spine and she wondered suddenly with a tremor of fear if any-one was listening to her at all, if there was anyone there to care. She pushed away the thought and, ashamed, she crossed herself again. "You must help me, Holy Mother, you must." Her tears were blinding her again and the candlelight hazed and flickered. "There is no one else. If you don't help me, I'll never pray to you again. Never." She bit her lip, scared by what she had said. She shouldn't have done it, but the chapel held such echoing emptiness . . .

She scrambled to her feet then crept out, closing the door softly behind her. If she could find no comfort there, there was only one other thing to do. Ride. When you galloped fast into the wind you could forget every-thing but the speed and the cold and the power of the horse between your legs. She ran to the chamber she shared with her nurse and the two maidens who were supposed to be her friends, and rummaged through the rail, looking for her heaviest mantle.

"Matilda, come to your embroidery now, *ma p'tite.*" She could hear her nurse Jeanne's voice from the garderobe, where she was sorting clothes. "Tilda?" The tone sharpened.

After grabbing a fur-lined cloak, Matilda threw it around her shoulders and tiptoed to the door. Then, deaf to Jeanne's indignant shouts, she pelted down the spiral stairs.

"Shall I come with you, young mistress?" The groom who held her excited horse knew as well as she that her father had forbidden her to ride alone.

She flung herself into the saddle. "Not this time, John. Blame me if anyone's angry." She raised her whip and set the horse across the high slippery cobbles of the courtyard at a canter. Once beyond the crowded muddy village she pushed the animal into a gallop, feeling her hair stream behind her in the cold wind. Galloping like this, fast, she didn't have time to think. Not about her poor, sick father, or about the squat, red-haired man at Bramber who was destined to become her husband. Nothing mat-tered out here. Here she was free and happy and alone.

At the top of the hill she reined in breathlessly, pushing her tangled hair back as the wind tugged it across her eyes. She turned to look back at the village far away in the valley, and her father's castle behind it. I need never go back, she thought suddenly. If I don't want to, I need never go back. I could ride and ride and ride and they would never find me. Then she thought of Reginald lying so pale in his chamber, and imperceptibly she straightened her shoulders. For his sake she would go back. For his sake she would marry William de Braose. For his sake she would go to the end of the world if he asked it of her.

Sadly she turned the horse and began to pick her way back down the steep track.

For two days before the wedding the attendants of the de Braose household crowded them out, overspilling from the small castle and its walls into tents and marquees on the edge of the village. Old Sir William, a wiry hawklike man with piercing gray eyes, spent much of his time closeted with Matilda's father while his son hunted across the hills, sparing no time for his betrothed. Matilda was extremely glad. She had been horrified by her glimpse of the younger William, whom she had barely remembered from their introduction at their betrothal years before. She had forgotten, or perhaps then he had been different. His reddish hair and beard now framed a coarse, heavily veined face with an uncompromisingly cruel mouth. He had kissed her hand once, running his eye expertly up her body, judging her, Matilda thought furiously, as if she had been a filly he was contemplating buying for his stable, then he turned away, more interested in his host's hunting dogs than in his bride.

Reginald was too ill even to be carried in a litter to the wedding ceremony, so he summoned his daughter and new son-in-law to his room as soon as they returned from the parish church. Matilda had spent the first part of the day in a frozen daze. She allowed herself to be dressed in her finest gown and mantle without interest. She followed Jeanne down to the hall and gave her arm to old Sir William without a flicker of emotion on her face. Then she walked with him to the church without any sign that she heard or even saw the gay procession of men and women who followed them. But her fists were bunched so tightly into her skirt that her nails had bitten into her palms. "Please, Holy Mother, don't let it happen. Please, Holy Mother, don't let it happen." She was murmuring the phrase over and over again under her breath like a magic charm. If she kept on saying it, without stopping, it would work. It must work.

She scarcely saw when Sir William left her side in the church porch and his son took his place. She didn't hear a word of the service as the old half-blind priest gabbled the form, shivering in his surplice as the autumn leaves tossed around them and a few drops of icy rain splattered in under the porch roof. Even later, as she knelt to kiss her father's hand, she was dazed. It was not until he put gentle fingers beneath her chin and tilted it a little to look into her face, murmuring "Be happy, sweetheart, and pray for your old father" that her control broke. She flung herself at him, clinging to him, her fingers wound into the wool of the blankets. "Please, please don't die. Darling, darling Papa, don't make me go with him, please—"

Hastily William stepped forward, his hands on her arms, and he dragged her off the bed. "Control yourself, madam," he hissed at her sharply. "Come away. Can't you see your father's upset? Don't make it worse. Come quickly." His voice was rough.

Tearing herself free of his grip, Matilda rounded on him. "Don't touch me!'' she almost spat at him, her eyes blazing. "I'll stay with my father as long as I please, sir!''

William was taken aback. He stepped forward awkwardly, frowning. "You must do as I say, Matilda. You're my wife now.''

"Yes, I'm your wife, God pity me," she whispered in anguish, "but I'm his daughter first.'' She was shaking with fear and anger.

"Matilda, please.'' Reginald stretched out painfully to lay his fingers on her arm. "Obey your husband, sweetheart. Leave me to sleep now.'' He tried to smile, but his lids were falling. The familiar blackness was closing around him. "Go, sweetheart,'' he mumbled. "Please go.''

With one longing agonized look at him Matilda turned away. She glanced at William as he reached forward to take her arm and then dodged past him, gathering her skirts in her hands and, blind with tears, ran toward the door.

The wedding feast was interminable. She only nibbled at the food on the platter in front of her that she shared with her husband. He was drinking vast quantities of wine, roaring with laughter at the bawdy jokes of the men near him, rocking toward her every so often, trying to plant a kiss on her cheek or her shoulder.

She gritted her teeth and reached for her own goblet. Trying not to let the tiny seed of panic inside her grow, she kept thinking of the peaceful warm glow of the candle in her father's room and of the gentle, lined face on the pillow and the loving reassuring touch of his hands.

The bed was strewn with flowers. Matilda stood, clutching her embroidered bedgown tightly around her, not daring to look at her husband as he chased the last of the giggling women out of the room. His face was blurred with wine and lust as he turned triumphantly to her at last.

"So. My wife.'' He leered a little, his own fur-trimmed gown held around his waist by a gilded leather girdle. She stood transfixed, her back to the high shuttered window, her hands once more tight fists at her sides. She was much taller than he, but so slight he could have snapped her in half with one blow from his enormous fist.

Her heart was beating very fast as he raised his hands to her shoulders. She wanted to push him away, to run, to scream, but somehow she forced herself to stand still as he loosed her girdle and thrust the gown back from her shoulders. She made no attempt to hold it as it fell, sliding from her unresponsive arms to the floor, billowing out in blues and silvers around her knees, leaving her standing before him, naked. Almost wonderingly he raised a hand and touched her shoulder, drawing his calloused fingers down across her breast. Then he seized her, crushing her to him, running his hand down her back, over her buttocks, fondling, caressing. Her hair fell in a dark auburn curtain across her face as he lifted her onto the bed, and she made no attempt to push it away. She lay limp after a first involun-

116

tary struggle of protest at what he did, biting her lips in pain, trying not to cry out as the agony of his thrusting tore through her and the first dark drops of blood stained the bridal sheets. Then at last with a grunt he rolled off her and lay still.

She remained dry-eyed in the dark and tried to ease her aching body on the hot mattress, not seeing the embroidered canopy that hung over the bed. Some of the flowers had been caught beneath them and crushed, and their sweet scent mingled with the reek of sweat and drying blood.

Reginald de St. Valerie died at dawn. Lying sleepless in her chamber watching the light pale in the stuffy room, Matilda had ceased to hear the regular snores of her husband. It was as if some part of her had slipped away to hover over the deathbed, watching her father, seeing his face relax without struggle at last into peace. "He waited to see me married," she whispered into the dark. "He waited only for that." And then she turned at last to her pillow and began to cry despairingly.

The day after the funeral the long procession of horses and wagons set off across a bleak autumnal southern England toward Sussex. Matilda rode, upright and proud, beside her husband, her face set. She was determined not to weep now, not to show any emotion to her husband or his followers. Somewhere behind her in the train of riders was Jeanne, her nurse. Jeanne had understood, had cradled her head and rocked her as she watched beside her father's body. Jeanne had mixed her wine and herbs to drink, *"pour le courage, ma p'tite,"* and muttered magic words over the bed in which Matilda and William had slept, to help ease the girl's troubles. Each night had been the same. He had not spared her for her father's sake, nor had she expected it. The pain, after the first time, had not been so bad.

The elder William rode in front of them, the chestnut rump of his horse glistening beneath its gay caparison in the pale autumn sunlight. They were nearing a wayside chapel when Matilda, keeping her eyes fixed resolutely on her father-in-law's broad back, was surprised to see him raise his hand, bringing the long procession to a halt. Then he turned in the high saddle. "I'll wait, my son," he announced curtly. Matilda glanced at her husband, who was dismounting. He ducked under his horse's head and came to her side. "I always pray at holy places," he announced self-righteously. "I should like you to accompany me." He helped her down from the horse and, taking her arm, ushered her into the chapel. Puzzled, she glanced over her shoulder. No one else had made a move to join them. The entire cortège stood in the settling dust, disinterested, bored, as their lord's eldest son and his bride ducked into the dark chapel. For some reason Matilda suddenly felt afraid.

She knelt reluctantly beside her husband as he prayed. No words came to her own lips; her throat was dry. The Virgin had not heeded her supplications when her help had been needed so much. Now it was too late. What was the point of praying?

She glanced sideways at William. His eyes were closed, the short sandy lashes veiling the pale irises, the coarse folded flesh of his chin resting on the thick wool of his blue mantle. On his shoulder there was a large circular brooch, at its center a purple amethyst. The stone caught a little spark of light from the candle at the shrine.

They stopped a dozen times like this on the long journey and each time Matilda, too afraid to refuse, alone dismounted with her husband. But not once did she try to pray.

Bramber Castle was built high on a hill overlooking the marshes that flanked the River Adur. From far away they could see the tall keep rising against the burnished blue sky while gulls circled the towers, their laughing cries echoing across the salty reed beds.

Bertha, daughter of Milo of Gloucester, heiress of Brecknock and Upper Gwent, the wife of Sir William de Braose and Matilda's mother-in-law, was waiting for her husband and son in the lofty great hall. She was a stout woman of middle height, some years older than her husband, with white hair falling in long plaits to her waist. Her eyes were brown as hazelnuts and very shrewd. She kissed Matilda coolly and then held her at arms' length, scrutinizing her closely until the girl felt herself blushing uncomfortably beneath the uncompromising gaze.

"So, my son's bride," Bertha announced at last. "Welcome to Bramber, child." The words were not softened by a smile.

Then Bertha turned aside, drawing her son with her, and Matilda was left standing alone. After a moment, William's father joined her. He smiled. "I hope it won't seem too strange, my dear," he murmured. "My son is a good man. Harsh sometimes, but good."

Matilda lifted her green eyes to his and forced herself to return his smile, which was friendly enough. "Thank you, sir," she whispered. "I am sure I shall do very well with William." Happiness, they both knew, was not part of the marriage contract.

She became conscious slowly that Sir William's eyes had strayed beyond her. Someone was standing behind her near the hearth.

"Lord de Clare! My wife told me you were here. Greetings." The old man stretched out his hands with sudden warmth. Turning, Matilda saw he was addressing a slim young man, dressed in a scarlet mantle caught at the shoulder with gold. He had laughing hazel eyes and a shock of wheat-color hair.

"Sir William, I was persuaded by Lady Bertha to wait for you." Lord de Clare stepped forward to clasp his host's hands. Then he turned to Matilda. He bowed, smiling. "Madam?"

"This is my daughter-in-law," Sir William put in hastily. "Matilda, Lord de Clare has threatened this long time to ride over from his castle at Tonbridge to see my mews, haven't you, my boy?" The old man was plainly delighted to see his visitor.

"Lord de Clare." Matilda curtseyed and her heart inexplicably began to beat a little faster as she surveyed the young man's handsome face.

He grinned. "Do you enjoy hawking, madam? It should be an exciting day. I'm told there is good sport on these marshes."

"Indeed there is!" Sir William put in good-naturedly. "You must join us, Matilda. Watch my birds trounce this young fellow's, eh?" He chuckled broadly.

Matilda didn't hear him. She was drowning in the young man's gaze.

"So it was too late even when they first met," Sarah whispered softly. "She was already married to that boor! See if she and Richard ever managed to meet alone. Please, Carl. Ask her."

Bennet frowned. Nevertheless he leaned forward a little as he put the question. "Did you go hawking with Lord de Clare, Matilda? Did you manage to speak to him again?"

Jo smiled. Her eyes, open and dancing, were the eyes of a carefree girl.

"We rode away from the others, south toward Sompting. The forest over the Downs is thick with oak trees there and their leaves were gold and brown with autumn. Richard flew his peregrine when we got to the chalk fields and I pretended to fall from my horse. I knew he would dismount and come to me. I wanted him to hold me in his arms so much. . . ."

"My lady! My lady, are you hurt?" Richard's face was near hers as she lay still on the ground. He glanced behind him for help, then gently he cradled her head on his knees. "My lady?" His voice was sharper now. "For the love of Christ, speak to me!"

She moved slightly, letting out a small moan. His face was close to hers. She could see, through scarcely opened eyes, the fine hairs growing again on his chin where he had been shaved that morning, and feel the warmth of his breath on her cheek. He smelled of leather and horsesweat, quite unlike the musty reek her husband habitually exuded. She nestled a little closer in his lap and felt suddenly his hands inside her mantle. Was he feeling for her heart, or for her breast beneath the pale linen? She stiffened imperceptibly and at once he straightened, moving his hand.

"My lady?" he said again. "Speak to me. Tell me if you are hurt."

She opened her eyes and smiled at him, her breath catching in her throat as she found his face so very close to her own. "I must have fallen," she whispered.

"Can you rise?" He was trying to push her up as, behind them, the sound of horses' hooves thundering on the hollow chalk announced the rest of the party.

"I can manage! Thank you." Crossly she jumped to her feet, brushing leaves from her mantle, then she turned from him in a flurry of skirts and ran to scramble back onto her horse alone.

"Why didn't you let me go on longer?" Jo asked when Bennet woke her from her trance. She glanced down at the spool on her tape recorder, which was barely a quarter used. "I want to know what happened. I wanted to see Richard again."

Bennet frowned. "It was going well, Jo, and we have learned a lot from this session. I don't want you to grow tired."

She intercepted the worried look he cast in her direction. "Did you find out if someone tried to strangle me?" she asked. She was watching his face closely.

He shook his head. "At the period you described today you were scarcely more than a child—you didn't seem to know quite how old you were yourself. But if anyone tried to strangle Matilda it was at some time far in her future, Jo. Not when she was riding on the Downs with Richard de Clare."

"But something did go wrong. Something worried you?"

"Nothing at all. Nothing." He smiled reassuringly. "In fact, I would like to pursue our experiment further with you, if you agree."

"Of course I agree. I want to know more about Matilda and Richard. And what happened after the massacre . . . just a bit more." Jo grinned as she picked up her recorder and stuffed it into her bag. "But I warn you now, I'm not going to chase her story endlessly. There's no point in that and I have no intention of getting obsessive about all this. But just one or two more sessions as soon as you can fit me in."

Sarah rose and went to get the diary. As she did so Bennet came around the desk. He was frowning again. "Joanna. I must tell you that I had a phone call yesterday from a colleague who says he is treating you, a Dr. Franklyn."

Jo straightened abruptly, swinging her bag onto her shoulder. She tightened her lips. "Oh?" she said suspiciously.

"He has asked me for a meeting to discuss your case."

"No!" Jo threw the bag down on the sofa. "No, Dr. Bennet. Sam Franklyn is not 'treating' me, as you put it. He is interested in this business because he worked for Michael Cohen years ago. He wants me to stop the regressions because he doesn't want me to write about them. Believe me, he is not treating me for anything."

Bennet took a step backward. "I see." He glanced at her beneath his eyebrows. "Well, I told him I had to ask your permission, of course."

"And I will not give it. I have already told him to leave me alone. I am sorry he rang you, I really am. He should not have bothered you."

"That is all right, Jo." Bennet took the diary from Sarah and frowned at it through his glasses. "Friday afternoon at three o'clock. Would that suit you? I shall make it my last appointment and then we need not be hurried. And I shall tell Dr. Franklyn if he calls again that you would rather I did not speak to him."

After she had gone Sarah turned to Bennet. "She is hiding something, isn't she?"

He shrugged. "I suspect so."

Sarah raised an eyebrow. "So. Will you talk to this Dr. Franklyn?"

"I'm sure that in the course of events he and I will meet. It is unthinkable that I should not run into him, because a colleague of Cohen's would be an invaluable person with whom to discuss my work." He closed the diary and handed it back to Sarah. "I would not discuss Joanna with him, of course, unless I thought it to be in her best interests."

Sarah smiled thinly. "Which it would be, of course. Tell me. What do you really think about the bruises she told us about? Do you think they were real? No one else saw them."

"I'm sure they were real." He walked to the window and glanced down into the street.

"But you think they were of hysterical origin?" Sarah's voice was hushed. "She's not the type, surely?"

"Who can tell who is the type?" he replied thoughtfully. "Who can ever tell? And if she isn't the type, and the bruises were there . . ." He paused.

"If she isn't," Sarah echoed quietly, "then the man she was with really did try to strangle her."

As arranged, Jo met Sam on Wednesday evening at Luigi's. He took one look at her and grinned across the table. "Let's order before you hit me with your handbag, Jo."

"I'll hit you with more than a handbag if you try a trick like that again," Jo said. Her voice was cool as she glanced at him over the menu. "I absolutely forbid you to talk to Carl Bennet about me. What I do is none of your damn business. I am not your patient. I have never been your patient, and I don't intend to be. What I do and what I write is my own affair. And the people I consult in the course of my research have a right to privacy. I do not expect you to harass them, or me. Is that quite clear?"

"Okay. I surrender. I've said I apologize." He raised his hands. "What more can I do?"

"Don't ever go behind my back again."

"You must trust me, Jo. I've said I'm sorry. But I am interested. And I do have a right to worry about you. I have more right than you'll ever know." He paused for a moment. "So you decided to see him again. You'd better tell me what happened. Did you learn anything more about your alter ego?"

"A bit." Jo relented. "About her marriage to William . . ." She was watching his face in the candlelight. The restaurant was dark, crowded now at the peak evening hour, and very hot. Sam was sweating slightly as he looked at her, his eyes fixed on her face. The pupils were very small. Without knowing why, she felt herself shiver slightly. "Nothing dramatic happened. It was all rather low key after the first session." Her voice trailed away suddenly. Low key? The violence! The rape! The agony of that man thrusting his way into her child's resisting body, silencing her desperate screams with a coarse, unclean hand across her mouth, laughing at her terror. She realized that Sam was still watching her and looked away hastily.

"Jo?" He reached across and lightly ran his thumb across her wrist. "Are you all right?"

She nodded. "Of course. It's just a bit hot in here." She withdrew her hand a little too quickly. "Let's eat. I'm starving."

They waited in silence as the waiter brought their antipasto. As they were starting to eat, Sam said thoughtfully, "William was very close to King John, did you know that?"

Jo stared up at him. "You've been looking it up?"

"A bit. I have a feeling William was much maligned. Historians seem to doubt if the massacre was his idea at all. He was a useful pawn, the man at the sharp end, the one to carry it out and take the blame. But not quite as bad as you seemed to think."

"He enjoyed it." Jo's voice was full of icy condemnation. "He enjoyed every moment of that slaughter!" She shuddered violently and then she leaned forward. "Sam. I want you to do something for me. I want you to do whatever you have to do to lift that posthypnotic suggestion that I forget that first session in Edinburgh. I have to remember what happened!"

"No." Sam shook his head slowly. "No. I'm sorry. I can't do that."

"You can't, or you won't?" Jo put down her fork with a clatter.

"I won't. But I probably couldn't anyway. It would involve rehypnosis, and I'm not prepared to try to meddle with something Michael Cohen did."

"If you won't, I'll get Carl Bennet to do it." Jo's eyes were fixed on his. She saw his jaw muscles tighten.

"That wouldn't work, Jo."

"It would. I've been reading up about hypnosis. Believe me, I haven't been sitting around the last few days wondering what is happening to me. There are hundreds of books on the subject and—"

"I said no, Jo." Sam sat back slowly, moving sideways slightly to ease his long legs under the small table. "Remember what I told you. You are too suggestible a subject. And don't pretend that you are not reacting deeply again, because you have proved you are. Not only under hypnosis either. It is possible that you are susceptible to delayed reaction. For instance, Nick has told me what happened at your grandmother's house."

Jo looked up, stunned. "Nick doesn't know what happened," she said tightly. "At least—" She stopped abruptly.

"Supposing you tell me what you think happened." Sam did not look at her. He was staring at the candle flame as it flared sideways in the draft as someone stood at the next table and reached for her coat.

Jo hesitated. "Nothing," she said at last. "I fainted, that's all. It had nothing to do with anything. So are you going to help me?"

For a moment he did not answer, lost in contemplation of the candle, the shadows playing across his face. Then once more he shook his head. "Leave it alone, Jo," he said softly. "Otherwise you may start something you can't finish."

13

"May I have the Maclean file, *please?*" Nick's assistant's voice was becoming bored. "For Jim, if it isn't *too* much trouble!" Behind her the office door swung to and fro in the draft from the open window.

Nick focused on her suddenly. "Sorry, Jane. What did you say?"

"The Maclean file, Nick. I'll try to get Jo again, shall I?" Jane sighed exaggeratedly. She was a tall, willowy girl whose high cheekbones and upper class accent were at variance with the three parallel streaks of iridescent orange, pink, and green in her short-cropped hair. "Though why we go on trying when she is obviously out, I don't know."

"Don't bother!" Nick slammed his pen down on the desk. He bent to rummage for the file and threw it across to her. "Jim has remembered that I'm supposed to be going to Paris next Wednesday?"

"He's remembered." Jane put on her calming voice. It infuriated Nick.

"Good. Then from this moment I can leave the office in your hands, can I?"

"Why, where are you going until Wednesday?" Jane held the file clasped to her chest like a shield.

"Tomorrow the printers, then lunch with a friend, then I said I'd look in at Carters on my way to Hampshire." He smiled. "Then the blessed weekend. Then Monday and Tuesday I'm in Scotland." He closed his briefcase with a snap and picked it up. "And now I'm playing hooky for the rest of the afternoon. So if anyone should want me you can tell them to try again in ten days."

Each time Nick had phoned her Jo had put the phone down. The last time she slammed the receiver down she switched off her typewriter and walked slowly into the bathroom. After turning on the light, she gathered her long hair up from her neck and held it on top of her head. Then she studied her throat. There still wasn't a mark on it.

"So. That proves he did not touch me!" she said out loud. "If anyone really had tried to strangle me the bruises would have been there for days.

124

It was a dream. I was delirious. I was mad! It wasn't Nick, so why am I afraid of him?"

All she had to do was see him. Even his anger was better than this limbo without him, and once he was there in the flesh, and she reminded herself what he really looked like, surely this strange terror would go. The memory of those eerie, piercing eyes kept floating out of her subconscious, haunting her as she walked around the apartment. And they were not even Nick's eyes. She found she was shivering again as she stared at the half-typed sheet of paper in her typewriter. On impulse she leaned over and picked up the phone to dial Nick's office.

The phone rang four times before Jane picked it up.

"Hi, it's Jo. Can I speak to Nick?" Jo sipped her juice, feeling suddenly as if a great weight had been lifted off the top of her head.

"Sorry. You've just missed him." Jane sounded a little too cheerful.

"When will he be back?" Jo put down her glass and began to pluck gently at the curled cord of the phone.

"Hold on. I'll check." There was a moment's silence. "He'll be back on the twelfth."

"The twelfth," Jo repeated. She sat bolt upright. "Where has he gone?"

"Scotland on Monday and Tuesday, then back and straight over to France on Wednesday morning for a week."

"And today and tomorrow?" Jo could feel her voice turning prickly.

"Out. Sorry, I don't know where exactly."

Jo put down the phone thoughtfully. Then she picked it up again and dialed Judy Curzon.

"Listen, Judy, I need to see Nick. Will you give him a message please? Tell him I'm seeing Carl Bennet again tomorrow afternoon. That's Friday —at three. Tell him I'm going to find out what really happened on Sunday, come hell or high water, and if he wants to know he'd better be there. Have you got that?"

There was a long silence on the other end. "I'm not a message service," Judy replied eventually. Her tone was frosty. "I don't give a damn who you're going to see tomorrow afternoon, and obviously Nick doesn't either or you wouldn't have to call him here, would you!"

Jo sat looking at the phone for several minutes after Judy hung up, then she smiled. "Hoist with your own petard, Miss Clifford. You walked right into that one!"

"Pidwch cael ofon." The voice spoke to Matilda again as she stood once more outside the moon-silvered walls of Abergavenny. Then it tried in words she understood. "Do not be afraid, my lady. I am your friend." His French was halting but dimly she recognized before her the dark Welsh boy who had brought her food the night before. But he was no longer afraid; it was her turn for terror.

125

She did not speak. She felt the hot wetness on her face and she felt him brush the tears away with a gentle hand.

"You did not know then?" he stammered. "You did not know what was planned at the feast?"

Wordlessly she shook her head.

"It is not safe for you here, whatever." The boy spoke earnestly. "My people will seek revenge for the massacre. You must go back into your castle."

Taking her elbow, he tried to turn her back but she found her feet scrabbling agonizingly on the sharp stones of the river path as she fought against him on the slippery ground.

"No, no. I can't go back there. I'll never go back there, never." She broke from him and ran a few steps farther on, toward the moon. Before it lay the mountains.

"Where will you go then?" The boy caught up with her in three strides and stood in front of her again.

"I don't know. I don't care." She looked around desperately.

"I will take you to Tretower." The boy spoke, suddenly making up his mind. "You will be safe there." He took her firmly by the hand and strode out along the river. In a daze, oblivious of her torn and bleeding feet, she followed him.

She never knew how long she stumbled on behind him. At one point her strength gave way and she sank onto the ground, unable to go farther along the steep rough bank of the river. The water ran mockingly pure and silver near her as though no blood had ever stained it. Bending, she scooped some of it, icy and clean, into her mouth, and then she lay back on the wet grass, her eyes closed.

The boy came back for her and coaxed and pleaded, but she was unable to rise. Her back pained spasmodically. She realized suddenly that she was going to lose her baby and she was glad.

The boy tugged at her hand, begging her to go with him, continually glancing over his shoulder, obviously worried that they were being followed. Then suddenly he seemed to give up the struggle and disappeared as quickly and silently as he had come.

He has left me to die, she thought, but she was past feeling any fear. She tried to recite the Paternoster, but the words would not come in the right order and she gave up. How would God ever find his way again to this country? she wondered bleakly, and she closed her eyes to shut out the silver trail of the moon in the water.

But the boy returned with a shaggy mountain pony and somehow he helped her onto it. They forded a narrow river, the pony picking its way sure-footed through water shadowed now by stark overhanging branches entangled with clinging ivy. They passed the dark shape of Crickhowell Castle in the night, but she did not see it, and the boy, apart from detouring slightly to avoid it, did not acknowledge its presence. Somewhere once a fox screamed and Matilda clutched the pony's mane as it shied. They left the river and traveled through black unfriendly forest and over hills where the country was silent except for the occasional lonely hoot of an owl and the wind in the branches of the trees. Closing her eyes, she rode in a daze of pain and fatigue, not caring where she went or what he intended doing with her. Beneath her the pony, confident even in the dark, followed the boy at a steady pace, slowly climbing through the misty rain.

Then she opened her weary eyes in the cold dawn and saw the keep of Tretower at last in the distance. She knew dimly that they must have been seen and been followed by the forest people, but for some reason she had been spared. The boy who held her bridle had been her talisman. He turned as they neared the tower and she studied his face in the colorless light.

He smiled up at her, a sad, fond smile. Then he pointed. "Go," he said. "There will be your friends. Go with God and be safe, *meistress.*" He released her bridle and he was gone, gliding back into the woods on silent feet.

The pony stumbled on some rocks as she guided it as fast as she dared along the winding track toward the castle in the broad valley. She fixed her eye on the tower and refused to look to left or right as her mount carried her at a shambling trot along the path. To her surprise the drawbridge was down and she rode across unchallenged. Had everyone gone mad? Did they not know that the warring Welsh must be everywhere?

There was a veil of blood before her eyes as she sat astride her mount in the courtyard of the castle. She didn't dare try to slip from the saddle. The beast hung its head, its flanks heaving, and nuzzled a blown wisp of hay. There appeared to be no one there.

Then, slowly, as though from a great distance, people came. She heard voices and saw lights and she recognized the clanking sound of a bridge being raised behind her. Hands pulled at her dress. People took the reins, gripped her arms, tried to ease her off the horse. The air was full of the sound of someone sobbing and dimly she realized it was her own voice she could hear.

"Do not distress yourself, my dear." Bennet sat down beside Jo and gently put his hand on hers. His foot touched the small microphone on the floor and it fell over with a rattle. He did not notice. He was staring down at her hand, which was ice-cold and covered in chilblains.

"Is she all right?" Sarah came over and knelt beside them.

After a moment's hesitation he nodded. "Go on, my lady. What happened next?"

Jo withdrew her hand gently from his, rubbing it painfully as she stared past him into the room, her eyes fixed somewhere in the middle distance, far away.

"I stayed there at Tretower with the Picards," she said slowly. "They put me to bed and cared for me and my pains stopped. I was not to lose the baby after all. William sent after me. I was too ill to be moved then, so Nell came with my baggage from Abergavenny. But William did not come."

Christmas came and was over. Thick snows fell and melted into the swift-running Rhian Goll. Ice locked its water, thawed, and it flowed again.

Slowly, almost unnoticeably, her belly began to swell. The child inside her was doubly cursed by its father's name and by the scene she had witnessed that terrible night, and she still wanted to lose it. But it grew and seemed to flourish. She wanted Jeanne, her old nurse, Jeanne who would have understood the need to be rid of the baby and who would have found for her the juniper berries, pennyroyal, and tansy that, with the right magic words, would produce a miscarriage. Matilda shuddered and crossed herself every time she thought about it, for she knew what she contemplated was mortal sin, but what else could she do when the child within her was blighted?

But blighted or not, the baby grew and her own health improved. Nell tended her as best she could, and with her a new maid, Elen, one of Dame Picard's women, an orphaned Welsh girl with a plump cheery face and an infectious smile who made Matilda laugh and stilled for a while with her stories and songs the deep restlessness within her. There was no word from William.

As the winter weather began to ease its iron grip Matilda longed more and more to leave Tretower. She wanted to travel on to Brecknock where at least she would be her own mistress in her husband's castle. But it was nearly Easter before the weather broke at last and the first chilly primroses began to force their way from the iron ground into the fitful sunshine. Matilda had long given up the idea of taking a horse and riding alone to Brecknock, trusting on speed and surprise to get her there safely. Such tomboy escapades were beyond her now, but she was still resolved to go. Anxiously she watched the trees bending low before the March gales, willing the winds to dry the earth and make the roads passable. For that she had to wait until the first day of April. It was a beautiful bright breezy day, the trees tossing their buds, the river peaceful, the sky a pure azure.

She dressed herself quietly before the women with whom she shared the chamber were awake and slipped silently down into the great hall, where she knew John Picard would be taking some ale and bread before going out with his dogs.

He gazed at her appalled when she faced him with her cool demand for

128

a litter and an escort to Brecknock, his eyes staring from beneath his heavy eyebrows, his mouth slightly open.

Then he turned to his wife, who had appeared at the door of the still-room, an apron tied over her gown.

"She wants to leave us. She wants to go to Brecknock."

"And will go, by your leave, John Picard." Matilda smiled coolly down at him.

She turned to her hostess. "My mind is made up. I can't impose on your kindness any longer."

"But the danger!" Anne Picard stepped down into the hall and came to take her hands. "My dear, think of the dangers. And in your condition."

Matilda flinched away and drew her mantle around her shoulders as though trying to conceal her thickened body. "There can be no danger if you will lend me a litter and an escort," she repeated stubbornly.

She stood looking down at the couple, a tall, lonely girl, her face and hands grown thin, her eyes weary but resolute, and both knew that they would have to do as she asked.

John Picard insisted that he should ride with her to Brecknock, and Anne pressed on her the services of two of her own women, Margaret and Welsh Elen.

"There will be hardly any household over there, beyond the garrison," she pointed out. "It's no place for a woman. Oh, please change your mind. Stay, at least till the babe is born." She gazed earnestly at Matilda's face, unable to hide her anxiety, but the girl was adamant. She refused even Anne's pleas that she postpone her start for a day or two to give them time to get ready. "No preparations are needed," she announced firmly, trying to keep the impatience out of her voice. "Nell and Margaret and Elen can pack my boxes in the time it takes to harness the horses." She was not prepared even to remove her cloak again while she waited. The restlessness of the past weeks had suddenly become unbearable.

She did feel a pang of sorrow as she hugged Anne before climbing into the waiting litter, but as she settled herself beneath the fur blankets excitement began to take over again. The women who were to go with her mounted their ponies, and John Picard, blowing a kiss toward his wife as she stood beneath the gateway, led the small cavalcade across the bridge.

Only a matter of minutes after they set out Matilda had begun to regret her impetuosity. She had not foreseen the horrors of traveling over the mountain tracks in a litter. She swayed and bumped inside the uncomfortable vehicle, unable to rest or balance, not knowing which way the next lurch would go.

John Picard rode close at her side, his hauberk over his linen shirt beneath a warm mantle, his helmet in place, his eyes ever searching the budding thickets and bramble scrub along the road. The day was bright and it seemed quiet, but he was certain that from the moment they clattered across the lowered drawbridge they were being watched.

Secretly he was very relieved to be seeing Matilda away from Tretower at last. He was genuinely concerned for her safety, but he had daily been expecting trouble from the Welshmen in the hills since the paths and tracks had reopened. They must know that the wife of de Braose was there and her life surely would be a fitting revenge for the death of their prince and his sons.

The castle of Brecknock was not prepared for its lady. The small garrison in the outer bailey lived in wooden lean-tos and small stone outbuildings within the outer wall. The private chambers inside the keep—the great hall and the solar above it—were bare.

Standing in the drafty, damp upper chamber, Matilda felt herself ready to weep. Never before had she arrived somewhere before it had been ready for occupation. Turning, she swept back down the newel stair into the main hall and confronted the constable of the castle.

"The place seems hardly prepared," she said to him with a forced smile. "However, have your men light a fire so at least we can be warm. What is your name, sir?"

"Sir Robert Mortimer, my lady." He gave a slight bow, turning to relay her orders to the men hovering in the doorway.

"Where is the chatelaine? Why isn't she here to greet me?"

Sir Robert seemed embarrassed. "My wife died eighteen months back, my lady. The village women have done their best . . ."

"I'm sorry." Matilda bit back the rude words that had been on the tip of her tongue. "Where, then, is the bailiff? I want him here by sundown."

With energy born of despair she set about directing the inhabitants of the castle to work. Torches blazed in the sconces, the fire burned up at last, and wooden shutters were found and fastened over the narrow windows. John Picard lounged on a bench in the great hall, holding out his hands to the fire. The lack of comfort made no difference to him but he watched with admiration the figure of his hostess, still swathed in her mantle against the cold, as she moved from place to place directing operations. He saw her pause and look toward the door as a group of new figures appeared from the dusk outside.

"Clerics," he muttered to himself. He had no time for the church but he was pleased to see them for her sake.

Matilda gazed at the senior among the black-robed figures and smiled uncertainly. He was a grave, thin man in his late twenties, dressed with restrained sumptuousness, his mantle trimmed with miniver that showed up the plain black habit of the monk at his side. His eyes, ranging around the hall, took in every detail of the place and of the lady standing in front of him. Then he bowed courteously and held out his hand in the gesture of benediction.

"I am Gerald, madam, Archdeacon of Brecknock." He spoke softly and yet with great presence.

Matilda bowed her head to accept his blessing.

"I was with Prior John when I heard of your plight, my lady," he went on. "Some of the lay brothers are bringing furnishings across for you and I have sent to my house at Llanddeu for other comforts that may help you. I am sorry you should find Brecknock so unready for you."

"It's my own fault." She found herself responding to his warm smile. "I brought no retinue, Archdeacon. No escort except for the one John Picard there could spare me, out of his kindness. I was foolish to come, I suppose."

He scrutinized her face for a moment and then grinned boyishly. "I can understand you wanting to come here. One's home is always the best place to be, and I believe women in your condition frequently conceive such fancies. After all, where else should your child be born but here?"

She felt herself blushing at his outspokenness and, drawing her mantle more closely around her, she retreated to the fire where she stood and watched as two sandaled lay brothers from the priory carried in a folding stool and set it down near her. They were followed by others with trestles and tabletops for the dais, benches, and candlesticks. Finally a linen cloth was produced and carefully laid on the table. Matilda waited in silence as the hall was transformed. Slowly, through Gerald's eyes, she was beginning to see the funny side of her undignified arrival. He had been watching her closely and he didn't drop his eyes when she caught his stare, but grinned pleasantly once more. "Better?" he inquired humorously.

She laughed. "Much better, Archdeacon. I don't know how to thank you."

"Don't bother. My own reading chair is on its way down to you from Llanddeu. You will find it easier sitting on a chair with a back, I should imagine. If there's anything you need, or any help wanted, send for me. I'm usually there when I'm not traveling around the diocese." He stepped forward and took her hand earnestly. "I'll take my leave now, I can see you're tired. But remember, I'm there if you need me."

John Picard raised an eyebrow as Gerald left. "An intense young man, that. But I'm glad he's here. He'll keep an eye on you till your husband comes." He leaned back, tucking his thumbs comfortably into his belt.

It was from Sir Robert Mortimer that she at last understood the full extent of the danger in which she stood and which the Picards had managed to keep from her throughout the winter. John Picard had left at dawn the next morning, bidding her a cheerful good-bye and leaving her with a smacking kiss on the cheek, then Sir Robert had found his way to Matilda's side.

"I've ordered a double guard, my lady, on the walls and on the gate, and I've told them to keep the townsfolk out for now," he reported.

"Why?" She stopped clearing a pile of linen from the table and turned to look at him, puzzled. Nell went on folding the material, but her eyes too were fixed on the constable's face.

"We cannot take any risks with you here at Brecknock, my lady. Things have been peaceful this winter. We've had no trouble, but now you're here I'd expect them to have a go at you." He clenched his fist over the hilt of his sword.

"Have a go? Who?" Matilda narrowed her eyes.

"The Welshies of course, my lady. An eye for an eye; a death for a death, all that. You've heard of the *galanas?*"

She looked puzzled and he shook his head. "The blood feud. They will seek revenge, my lady. It's the law of these hills. Then, no doubt, if they get it, your descendants and relatives will seek theirs in their turn and so on it will go. It's the way the Marches takes their justice."

Matilda shivered. "So Seisyll's wife died?"

He shrugged. "As to that, I haven't heard for sure. But we've got to assume you'll be a target, with Sir William away at Windsor or wherever. Did the Picards not warn you?"

Matilda licked her lips nervously. "Yes, they did mention it. Lady Picard told me of the feud, but I paid no attention—I was ill . . . I must have put them in great danger while I was there." She walked over toward the hearth, her light-green skirts sweeping the rushes. "They sheltered me all winter, Sir Robert, and never let me know that."

Sir Robert rubbed his forehead with the back of his hand. "Aye, they're good folk right enough."

"Let the townspeople come and go as usual. I don't want them to resent me from the start. Give me a bodyguard of some sort, that'll be enough. These are my husband's people after all, not Seisyll's. I'm sure they're not involved in any feud."

Sir Robert frowned. He shifted uncomfortably from one foot to the other. "There's something I think you should understand, my lady." He looked at the floor, embarrassed. "The thing is, your husband is not exactly well liked by the people. These lordships came to him from the family of his lady mother. They do not like de Braose." His voice trailed away into silence.

"All the more reason that I should make them like me, Sir Robert," she flashed back at him. Then she smiled. "Please. Help me make friends with them. I should hate to feel that I have enemies here. Perhaps we can win them over if we try."

He looked at her determined, eager face and grinned. "Well, my lady, if those are your orders, I'd be glad, for one. They're not a bad crowd in

Aberhonddu. We'll guard you well and hope they're not overconcerned with the doings in Gwent. Will you be sending messages to Sir William?"

She nodded. "I must. He should be told I'm here, and I want some of my servants from Bramber. Will you arrange for someone to go to find him? Meanwhile I'll choose some women to serve me and we'll make a start at trying to make this place comfortable." She grinned, and turned back to help Nell with her task.

The next few days passed in a bustle of activity. As word got out that Lady de Braose was there, people from the small township below the castle walls began to make their way to her presence. She was called upon to act as arbiter and judge among them. They seemed to be accepting her. She had scarcely any time at all to herself, and almost forgot the worries and torments of the long winter. She found the people ready with their tithes of provisions and supplies, all eager and curious to see Sir William's bride, all apparently prepared to be friendly.

She spent long mornings closeted with Hugh the bailiff, who had eventually turned up between two men-at-arms, so drunk he was unable to stand. She had curbed her initial desire to have him flogged and waited to see him when he was sober. And she was pleased she had done so. He was in his own way grateful for her restraint and proved himself a competent enough steward after his initial defensiveness had worn off. He took her on a tour of the barns, storerooms, pantries, and the cellar, proud that Brecknock should still be comparatively well stocked after the long winter.

She sat for many hours, however, pondering over his accounts, desperately trying to make sense of the squiggles on the pages before her, applying her limited knowledge of reading, knowing his taunting eyes were upon her, waiting for her to make a mistake.

At last, exasperated beyond measure, she summoned Father Hugo, the priest who had been sent by Gerald to take mass at the chapel each morning.

"Father, I need your help." She looked up at him from Gerald's elaborate chair by the fire. "I need to know how to read properly. Can you teach me?"

Together they pored over the account book for some time. Then Hugo straightened up and put his hand to his eyes. "I can hardly read this man's hand myself," he muttered at last. "Especially these last few pages. I'll bring the mass book from the chapel for you. That at least I know is legible."

Two days later Gerald was ushered into her presence. "I hear you want to learn to read," he said without preamble. "Hugo is not the man to teach you, my lady. His eyes are too old to see the letters himself. I shall do it."

"You, Archdeacon? But how will you spare the time?" She was a little nervous of the energetic, handsome young man and she glanced rather apprehensively at the volumes under his arm.

133

"I shall teach you to write as well," he went on. "It is unthinkable that a lady of your standing should be unable to read and write with fluency. Writing is one of the greatest arts."

She blushed. He made her feel suddenly inadequate. Secretly she had been proud of the way she was handling the situation at Brecknock. It was the first chance she had had of applying her skills in running a household without her mother-in-law breathing down her neck, and although the household was abbreviated and inadequate, she was pleased with the way she was managing with the people she was carefully recruiting to her service.

Each day while he was at Llanddeu Gerald rode down to the castle and spent an hour or two in her company. Sometimes they read from his own writings and from his poetry, which he proudly brought to show her, and sometimes from the books from his library. They also struggled together with the bailiff's account books, and Gerald, his eyes sparkling with amusement, pointed out that the handwriting had markedly worsened from the day that Matilda had arrived at Brecknock and shown her determination to supervise his activities.

Almost at once she discovered to her consternation that Gerald proudly claimed kinship through his grandmother with Lord Rhys himself and that he knew all about the happenings at Abergavenny.

Since John Picard had left to ride home across the mountains to Tretower she had tried to put the memory of that terrible day out of her mind completely. It was easier than she expected because of her busyness at Brecknock, but sometimes, still, at nights, in spite of her exhaustion, the noise and stench of that bloody scene would return to her in horrifying nightmares from which she would awaken screaming. Also there was the baby. Each time it kicked she would shudder in revulsion as though it joined her by a cord to the treachery she wanted to forget. And now here was Gerald, sitting opposite her, a cup of wine in his hand, his thin, intense face serious as he gazed at her, forcing her to confront that terrible memory once more.

"Your husband was the instrument of cruel excesses, but I haven't any doubt that others, more powerful even than he is, were the real instigators of the crime." He leaned forward and looked at her intently. "You must not judge him, my lady. You do, don't you?"

She nodded slightly. "I was there, Archdeacon. I saw it all. I tell myself that such acts occur. I know this part of the country is more liable to them than most; I know William is a cruel, hard man. I've been told enough about him, but still, I couldn't believe he would commit such treachery. And I saw him, with his own hand . . ." She broke off, trying to stifle the sob which rose in her throat. "It was so terrible. Even that child, Geoffrey, Seisyll's son, and later the baby." She bit her lip and sat silent, twisting the cloth of her skirt between her fingers. Then she looked up suddenly, swallowing hard, and faced him squarely, her eyes fixed unwavering on his.

"My child is cursed, Father, by what happened that day," she burst out. "I would rather it is never born at all." She waited defiantly, half expecting him to be shocked, but to her surprise he nodded understandingly.

"It's a natural feeling," he said slowly, his low voice soothing and considered. "But it is wrong. You must have faith. The child is as innocent as it is possible for a human creature to be. He will be washed and sanctified by baptism and by our prayers. You must not fear for him." He drank back the dregs of his wine suddenly and rose to his feet. "And now I have some news for you, my lady. Three nights ago your husband was at Hereford. From there I understand he plans to go to Hay and then he is coming on here to Brecknock, so you will be seeing him soon. You must prepare yourself for that."

Matilda pulled herself to her feet. Her hands were shaking, and nervously she tried to hide them in the folds of her skirt, but the all-seeing eyes of the archdeacon had spotted them instantly. He put his hand gently on her arm. "You have been a good and loyal wife to William de Braose. Don't be afraid of him. He is still the Christian man you married." He grinned suddenly, his unexpected boyish grin that she found so heartwarming. "Perhaps now I shall be able to have my chair back when he comes. I miss it, I must confess, perched on that high stool when I'm reading at Llanddeu. I must be getting old." He sighed and put his hand to his back with a mock grimace of pain.

In spite of herself, she laughed. She had grown very fond of Gerald in the few weeks she had known him. "Poor Archdeacon. I must give you a salve to rub on your back. When William comes, your chair will be my first thought, I promise you. It'll travel up that track to Llanddeu faster than lightning!"

But even the sound of his gay chuckle as he pulled on his mantle and swung out into the soft rain to find his horse did nothing to ease the sick fear that flooded through her at the thought of William's imminent arrival.

14

Nick sat back and smiled at Judy fondly. "I never did ask you where you learned to cook. That was the most superb lunch. Thank you." He eyed the empty casserole and then leaned forward to pour out the last of the wine.

"A woman should keep some secrets surely!" Judy grinned. She had changed from her paint-stained jeans and smock into a summer dress with vivid blue stripes, which suited her coloring remarkably well. As she leaned forward to take his plate Nick caught a faint breath of Miss Dior.

"Coffee would make it perfect," he said hopefully.

"First crème brûlée, then cheese. *Then* coffee." Judy disappeared into the kitchen.

Nick groaned. "Are you trying to kill me or something?"

"As long as you can beat me at squash a meal like this once in a while won't kill you." She stuck her head around the door. "Do you really have to go to your mother's this weekend, Nick?"

He nodded. "I'm afraid I must. I haven't seen her for ages, and as I'm going to be away so much over the next month I thought I'd get it over with. And while I'm down there, if the tides are right, I thought I'd bring *Moon Dancer* back from Shoreham and leave her at Lymington." He levered himself to his feet. "There will be time for a siesta though, before I leave." In the kitchen he put his arms around her slowly, savoring the feel of her body beneath the thin cotton voile of her dress. "Friday afternoon is the best time there is for making love."

Judy raised her lips to his eagerly. "Any time is the right time," she murmured, trying not to wonder why he had not suggested she go with him to Hampshire. "Why don't we leave the rest of the meal until later?" She ran her tongue gently along the line of his jaw and nipped his ear.

His hands slipped around to the zipper at the back of her dress. Expertly he slid it down, pushing the fabric off her shoulders. Beneath it she was naked.

Unembarrassed, she wriggled away from him and stepped out of the dress. "I'll turn off the coffee."

He was undoing his shirt, his eyes on her breasts as she unplugged the pot and walked past him into the studio. In the bedroom she drew the curtain, blocking out the sun, then she turned in the shadowy twilight and held out her arms.

Nick laughed. "No. No shadows. I want to see you properly." Kneeling on the bed, he reached across and switched on the bedside light.

On the notepad by the lamp was a page of whorls and faces and doodles and strange shapes and in the center of them all, framed with Gothic decoration, the name Carl Bennet and a curlicued three. Nick picked up the pad and stared at it.

"When did you write this?"

"What?" Judy slid onto the bed beside him and lay down, her arms above her head, her legs slim and tanned on the white candlewick cover.

"Carl Bennet. Why did you write his name here?"

She sat up. "To hell with him. You're supposed to be thinking about me!"

"I am thinking about you, Judy." Nick's voice was suddenly hard. He pushed her back, leaning over her, his face taut with anger. "I am wondering why you have written his name down. Where did you hear it?"

For a moment Judy contemplated lying. Her brain was moving like lightning. If he found out the truth later he would blame her. Better tell him. Softly she cursed herself for writing the name at all—a stupid absent-minded, automatic reaction to having a pencil in her hand. . . .

"Jo rang yesterday," she said softly. She smiled, reaching up to kiss him, winding her arms around his neck. "She thought you might be here, that's all. It didn't sound important."

"What did she say about Bennet?" Unmoving, he stared down at her and for a fleeting moment she felt a pang of fear.

"She said she was going to see him. Nick, forget her—"

"Did she say when?"

"Today. I told you, forget her—"

"When, Judy?" Nick caught her wrists and disengaged himself violently from her embrace. He sat up. "She must not go there alone!"

She grabbed the bedspread and pulled it around herself as Nick stood up. "You're too late. She'll be there by now."

Without a word Nick strode past her into the studio. He picked up his shirt and dragged it on, groping for his shoes. Behind him Judy stood in the doorway, still swathed in candlewick. "Nick, please. Don't go."

He turned. "I'm sorry, Judy. I have to be there. I have to stop her if I can!"

The long train of horses and carts that heralded the arrival of William de Braose and his retinue began to assemble in the outer bailey of Brecknock Castle on the first day of May. The serfs and townspeople, out from dawn

137

about their ancient rites, tending the Beltane fires on the moors despite the threats from the priests, returned to find the castle full of men.

Matilda sat in her solar listening with Margaret to the clatter of hooves and the rumble of wheels below, longing to hide. She dreaded the meeting with William, try as she might to remember Gerald's reassurances, and when her husband's arrival was at last announced she took a deep breath to still her wildly beating heart and walked slowly down into the brisk spring sunshine to greet him. Dismounting, William looked up at his wife as she stood on the steps above him, his face impassive. He was splendidly dressed in scarlet and green, his mantle clasped by a great cabochon ruby, his fringed beard neatly trimmed. He strode up the steps two at a time and kissed her hand ostentatiously, taking in with one quick, satisfied glance the swell of her belly beneath the flowing lines of her gown.

"How are you, my lady? I meant to be with you long before this but the king kept me with him."

She raised her eyes from the floor to look at him, expecting to see anger and resentment there, but his eyes, behind the sternness of his face, were indifferent.

She forced herself to smile. "I am glad to see you, my lord. Very glad." Her gaze met his for an instant. He straightened his back, pulling his cloak higher up on his shoulder, and when he followed her back into the hall it was with a confident swagger. The moment of nervousness he had felt under the scrutiny of his wife's cool green eyes with their strange amber flecks had passed. He stuck his fingers jauntily into his girdle. He owed her no explanations; nor any man, save the king.

She herself poured the mulled wine that was awaiting him and stood beside him in silence while he drank. When he handed her back the goblet with gruff words of thanks he stood awkwardly for a moment looking at her as though about to say something else. But whatever it was, he changed his mind abruptly. He turned away, shouting commands to his men, and left her alone by the fire.

It took only a day for the castle to be transformed by the comforts carried in William's baggage train. Hangings appeared on the walls of the great bedchamber and cushions and fine sheets and covers replaced the rougher wear lent by the Benedictines from the priory. Two men were sent at once with the archdeacon's best chair, up the winding track to his house at Llanddeu.

Matilda continued without interruption her running of the castle, calling before her determinedly one by one the officers of her husband's household and making it clear that, while they should all continue their duties, she intended to oversee their activities herself in future as the mistress of the household, and that the servants she had taken on were to be assimilated into it. To her intense disappointment Jeanne was not among the train, and she did not like to ask William why the old nurse had chosen to remain at Bramber. She couldn't prevent herself from crying about it in the secrecy of the great bed, however. She had so much wanted Jeanne to be there when the baby was born. Jeanne could comfort her and help her, and would know what to do if anything went wrong.

Of William she saw little. He was constantly busy, riding to outlying castles or closeted with his scribes, writing endless long-winded letters that, according to Hugh, kept the clerks so busy that William had to pay them extra money to finish them. At night William slept in an upper chamber above hers. She was heavy and lethargic now, with the baby so close, and had dreaded that he might try to force his attentions on her even though but two months remained until the baby was due, but he remained distantly polite. Of Abergavenny they never spoke at all, and all her tormented questions, so long suppressed, remained unanswered.

It wasn't long before she noticed the small blond serving wench so often at her husband's side, giggling as he pressed sweetmeats and baubles on her. "He'll not grow cold at night, that's for sure, madam, with that puss to keep him warm," Elen commented tartly, seeing her lady's eyes following the girl around the hall, and Matilda forced herself to smile.

Gerald continued to visit the castle but less frequently. He combined his visits with journeys through the diocese and seemed suddenly even more preoccupied than before with church affairs. Matilda missed his attention and the talks they used to have, but she was less inclined to make any effort now, and thankfully set aside her reading save where she had to go over the household accounts. Now William's steward Bernard was there to do it for her, and she had only to supervise him and soothe his occasional quarrels with Hugh.

The soft warmth of June succeeded the windy days of May at last. She began to spend long hours in the small garden she was making between the kitchen buildings and the chapel, tending the seedlings she had planted and pulling the ever-strangling weeds. Her three women were constantly with her, helping her to her feet after she had knelt too long on the grass and scolding her when she dirtied her fingers in the earth, never leaving her alone, crowding her till sometimes she wanted to scream. She dreamed often of her lonely hillside vigils as a girl, far from crowded castles, and fought to keep herself shouting out loud with frustration.

"Oh, God! When will this waiting be over!" She rounded on Margaret at last. "I shall go mad. How do women put up with it!"

Margaret looked shocked. "It's our place, my lady. We must be patient like the Holy Virgin."

"The Holy Virgin was a saint, I'm not," Matilda retorted. She pulled viciously at a string of bindweed. "If it wasn't for this garden I would throw myself off the top of the keep. I never dreamed childbearing could be so awful."

Margaret lowered her eyes, embarrassed. "My lady, it's not for much longer," she whispered soothingly.

"It's long enough. Every minute is too long. And we need rain for these godforsaken herbs. Why doesn't it rain?" She stared up, furious, at the clear blue sky, determined to be out of temper. Nearby Nell and Elen were sitting on the wall chatting quietly together, their veils pulled forward around their faces to keep off the sun.

Matilda put her hand up to Margaret's shoulder and pulled herself heavily from the ground, shaking out her skirts. From the forge on the far side of the bailey came the sound of hammering and the hiss of a horseshoe going into cold water. She looked around, vaguely soothed by the familiar sights, but only the promise she had made to herself that once she was free from the burden of the child she would ride up to see Gerald in his own house bolstered her in the long dreary days. She put her hand to her back wearily. The lying-in woman had been at the castle now for two weeks. The wet nurse had been chosen and sat this very moment on the steps of the chapel, suckling her child in the drowsy sun, oblivious of the horses that stamped around her, waiting their turn at the forge.

Throwing down her trowel, Matilda lowered herself onto the little wall beside Elen. She had had it built bounding the garden on the side that faced the bailey, and although it was designed to keep marauding dogs and animals out and keep the hooves of excited horses from the tender young plants, it made a useful seat. She turned to watch the activity in the bailey beyond. On the far side of the cobbled area beyond the kitchens a knot of Welshmen stood talking together urgently, their excitable lilt plainly audible above the noise of the horses. Then, as she listened idly to the unintelligible music of their speech, they suddenly fell silent, listening to one of their number who, with waving arms and much gesticulation, had moved into the center of the group. They all looked at each other and then to her surprise over their shoulders toward her, and she saw that they were crossing themselves and making the sign against the evil eye.

"What's the matter with those men?" she asked uneasily.

Elen, following her gaze, smiled a little ruefully. "They'll be talking about the green water, my lady. I heard in the hall this morning. It's magic, so they say, and a message from God."

"Green water?" Matilda turned to her with a little frown. "I've heard nothing of this. Tell me about it."

"It's nothing, my lady. Stupid gossip, that's all," Margaret interrupted hastily. "Don't be foolish, Elen, talking like that. It's serfs' talk." Her plump face flushed with anxiety.

"It's not indeed," Elen defended herself hotly. She put her hand up to the irrepressible curly hair that strayed from her veil no matter how hard she tried to restrain it. "Everyone was talking about it this morning. It happened before, a hundred years ago, so they say, and then it was a warning from God that he was displeased about a terrible murder there had been." The blue eyes in her freckled face were round with importance. "It's a warning so it is."

Matilda shivered as though the cold shadow of the mountains had reached out and fallen over her. "If it's a warning," she said quietly, "it must be meant for me. Where is this water, Elen?"

"It's Afon Llynfi, madam, and the Lake of Llangorse that it flows from, up in the Black Mountains yonder." She crossed herself hastily. "They say it is as green as emeralds and runs like the devil's blood the whole way down to the Wye."

Nell pushed a furious elbow into her companion's side. "Be quiet," she hissed. She had seen Matilda's face, chalk-white, and the expression of horror in her eyes. "It's stupid to talk like that, Elen. It's all nonsense. It's nothing more than pondweed. I heard Hugh the bailiff say so himself. He's been down to Glasbury to take a look at it."

Matilda did not seem to have heard. "It is a warning," she whispered. "It's a warning about my child. God is going to punish my husband for his cruelties through my son." She stood up, shivering.

"Nonsense, my lady. God would never think of such a thing." Margaret was crisply practical. "Elen had no business to repeat such stupid gossip to you. No business at all." She glared at Elen behind Matilda's back. "It's all a fantasy of these people. They're touched in the head." She looked disdainfully at the group of Welshmen still huddled near the kitchens. "Now, my lady, you come in and lie down before the evening meal. You've been too long out in the air."

Scolding and coaxing, Margaret and Nell led their mistress back into the cool dimness of the castle, with Elen following unrepentant behind. Matilda lay down as they insisted and closed her eyes wearily, but she was feverish and unsettled and she couldn't rest. She didn't go down to the crowded hall for the evening meal and at last as the shadows lengthened across the countryside to the west she sent for Gerald.

In spite of Margaret's soothing words she became more and more agitated waiting for him. Her hands had started shaking and she began to finger the beads of a rosary. "Holy Mary, Mother of God, spare my child, please, please, spare my child. Don't let him be blamed for William's wickedness." The half-formed prayers caught in her throat as she walked agitatedly up and down the room. When at last, out of sheer exhaustion, she was persuaded to sit down again by the empty hearth in her chamber with Margaret and Nell and two of her waiting women, she felt herself near to panic.

Then they heard the steady slap of sandals ascending the newel stair, and she pushed herself eagerly to her feet. "Archdeacon," she exclaimed, but she slumped back into her chair disappointed. By the light of the rushlight at the top of the stair she saw the bent figure of Father Hugo.

"A thousand apologies, my lady," he muttered, seeing her disappointment only too clearly. "The archdeacon is not at Llanddeu. He has ridden urgently to St. David's where his uncle, the bishop, has died. When I heard the messenger's news I came myself to tell you. I thought perhaps I might be able to help. . . ."

His voice trailed off as he stood anxiously before her, his face gentle and concerned as he took in the signs of distress in his mistress's eyes.

Matilda looked up and smiled faintly. "Good Father Hugo. You're always very kind to me." She hesitated. "Perhaps I'm stupid, it's just that I heard about the River Llynfi, and I was afraid." She lowered her eyes. "It is many months since my husband's trouble at Abergavenny, but still it haunts my dreams. I was frightened it was God's warning that my child will suffer." She looked up again, pitifully seeking reassurance.

Hugo stood staring for a moment, puzzled. He knew from her anguished confessions what she feared for the baby, and he had vaguely heard something about the river. The latter he had dismissed as Welsh talk. He drew his brows together trying to think what would be best to say to this distraught woman. He had had no experience before of females and their ways and groped for the words that would relieve the pained look in her eyes.

"Be at peace, my daughter. God would not punish an innocent babe. The archdeacon has told you as much."

"But is it not written that the father's sins shall be visited on the child?" she flashed back at him.

He was taken aback and did not answer for a minute. Then he bent and patted her hand awkwardly. "I will pray. I will pray for guidance and for your safe delivery, as I pray every day. God will spare your child in his mercy, I am certain of it." He bowed, and hesitated, waiting for her to say something else. When she made no response, he sighed and, backing away, turned and plodded back down the stairs.

She slept hardly at all that night, tossing on the hot mattress, her eyes fixed on the rectangle of starry sky visible through the unshuttered window. Then at last as the first light began to push back the darkness she got to her feet and went to sit in the embrasure of the window, gazing out over the misty valley, watching as the cool dawn crept across the forests reaching towards the foothills of the mountains. Behind her, as the room grew light, Margaret slept without stirring on her truckle bed.

She was sitting in the solar, alone save for Elen, stitching the hem of a small sheet for the empty cradle by the wall, when the chaplain once more padded up the stairs and stood bowing before her, out of breath from the climb. He was agitated and pale himself, but seeing her face with the great dark rings beneath her eyes as she looked up at him, he felt a new and unexpected wave of compassion.

142

"What is it, Father?" She smiled gently, the sewing falling into her lap.

He twisted his wrinkled old hands together uncomfortably. "I told you, my lady, that I would pray for guidance last night. I knelt for many hours in the chapel and prayed to Christ and St. Nicholas, our patron." He winced, remembering the draft on the cold stone, which in spite of the straw-filled hassock had left his old knees rheumaticky and swollen. "Then I slept, and I had a dream. I believe it was in answer to my prayer, my lady." He crossed himself and Matilda and Elen, glancing at one another nervously, followed suit.

"The dream told you the reason for the river being green?" Matilda's voice was awed.

"I believe so, madam. An old man came to me in my dream and said that Christ was greatly displeased." He paused and gulped nervously.

Matilda rose to her feet, ignoring the sewing, which fell to the rushes, her eyes wide, one hand straying involuntarily to her stomach. She felt suddenly sick. "Why?" she whispered. "Why is our Lord displeased?"

"It is something that Sir William has done, my lady." The old man spoke in a hushed voice, glancing over his shoulder as he did so. "But it is something he has done here. He has kept some property for himself that was granted to our chapel. It was to be used both for its upkeep and for works of charity, and Sir William has not allowed the money to come to us."

Matilda stared at him for a moment in silence. "You're telling me that Sir William is misappropriating church property?" she said at last.

The old man shrugged apologetically.

She felt like laughing hysterically. "And this is an offense great enough to cause the mountain waters to change their color?" She turned away from him so that he couldn't see her face. She wasn't sure whether to laugh or cry. It took a moment for her to get herself under control again. Then she turned back to him. "Have you told Sir William of this dream?" she inquired gently.

He shook his head vehemently.

"Then I shouldn't at the moment. I shall try to find out whether he is indeed withholding tithes due to the chapel, and whether he is doing it knowingly. I am sure there has been some mistake. He would never take something that was the church's."

She waited until he had gone before bursting into tearful laughter, then she shrugged, wiping her eyes, and looked at Elen in despair. "I wish the archdeacon were here, Elen. He would know what to do." She sighed. "He would know the truth about Father Hugo's dream, and about the river waters." She took up the sewing, which Elen had recovered from the rushes, and sat down wearily.

"They are saying, my lady," Elen began cautiously, "that is, the townsfolk in Aberhonddu and Hay are saying, that the river runs green for another reason. They say it is because of the king's great sin in taking Walter of Clifford's daughter Rosamund to be his mistress and casting off Queen Eleanor again.''

She glanced at Matilda shrewdly, her blue eyes merry in her freckled face. ''I think it is more likely to be for the sins of a king than of one of his subjects, however great, that the waters of Afon Llynfi should change color, don't you?''

''I suppose so.'' Matilda walked over to the narrow window and looked out across the valley. Sheets of fine rain were sweeping in from the mountains and the smell of sweet earth rose to her from her little garden in the bailey below. She leaned out and sniffed appreciatively. ''I pray your story is true, or Father Hugo's—I don't care which. As long as the warning is not for me. And who knows, perhaps Margaret was right. Perhaps it is just pondweed.''

''Smelly it is, madam, anyway, Hugh says,'' Elen put in briskly. ''He thinks it's because there's been no rain, simple as that it is. And now this morning the rain has come so we'll soon know if the green all goes away. And your plants will be pleased by it, so they will!''

''Rosamund Clifford,'' Sarah whispered. ''Do you think she was an ancestor of hers?''

Bennet looked away from Jo's face, suddenly thoughtful. ''Ancestral memory? Transferred genetically? I've read some interesting papers on the subject.'' He shrugged. ''I don't believe it myself, but we'll have to see what part this Rosamund plays in the story. I should wake her now.'' He glanced at his watch. ''She's getting tired. She has lived through six months in that world of hers.''

''Oh, wait, Carl. Can't we find out about the baby—I know she would want you to ask about it—'' Sarah broke off suddenly as the door behind her opened.

Nick stared into the room. For a moment none of them spoke, then, after catching sight of Jo sitting on the sofa, Nick stepped inside the room and closed the door.

''Jo! Thank God I'm in time!''

Carl Bennet stood up, taking his glasses off in agitation. ''You can't come in here. Please, leave at once! Who are you?'' He stepped toward Nick.

Nick was looking at Jo. ''Jo asked me to come,'' he said. He glanced at Bennet for the first time. ''My name is Franklyn. I'm a friend of hers.''

''I thought I told you, Dr. Franklyn, that Jo has asked you not to involve yourself in this matter!'' Bennet stood looking up at Nick, his face stern.

''Dr. Franklyn is my brother,'' Nick replied shortly. ''Jo, for God's sake, explain.''

''Jo does not know you're here.'' Anxiously Carl Bennet put his hand on

Nick's shoulder. "She is in a deep trance. Now, please, I must ask you to leave—"

"Jo? Dear God, what have you done to her? You bastard!" Nick knelt at Jo's side and took her hand gently in his.

"Shall I call the caretaker?" Sarah said in an undertone. She had her hand on a bell by the door. Bennet shook his head. He sighed. "Please, Mr. Franklyn. You must leave. I am sure you realize it would be dangerous for you to interfere at this stage."

"Dangerous?" Nick was staring at Jo's face. Her eyes were looking at him quite normally, but she did not see him. The scene she was watching was in another time, another place. "She swore this wasn't dangerous. And she asked me to come with her," Nick went on, controlling his temper with an effort. "I only got her message an hour ago. Please let me stay. She would want me to."

Her eyes had changed focus now. They no longer looked at him. They seemed to stray through him, unfocusing, the pupils dilating rapidly as though she were staring directly at the window. Slowly Nick released her hand. He backed away a few paces and sat down on the edge of a chair. "I am staying," he repeated. "I am not letting her out of my sight!"

Jo suddenly threw herself back against the sofa with a moan of agony. Her fingers convulsed and she clawed four parallel grooves in the soft hide of the upholstery.

"Holy Mother of God!" She screamed. "Where is Jeanne? Why doesn't she come?"

There was a moment's total silence in the room as the three looked at her, electrified. Nick had gone white.

"Make it stop." Jo moaned. "Please, someone make it stop." She arched her back again, catching up one of the velvet cushions and hugging it to her in despair.

"For God's sake, Carl, what's happened?" Sarah was rooted to the spot. "Bring her out of it. Wake her quickly!"

Bennet sat down beside her. "My dear, can you hear me? I want you to listen to me—" He broke off with a cry of pain as Jo grabbed his hand and clung to it. Her face was wet with perspiration and tears.

"For pity's sake, wake her," Nick cried. "What's wrong with her?"

"She's having a baby." Sarah's voice cut in as Jo let out another moan. "Women do it all the time."

"Pregnant women, perhaps," Nick snapped. His skin was crawling. "Wake her up, man, quickly. Do you want to kill her?" He clenched his fists as Jo screamed again.

"Jo? Jo? Can you hear me?" Bennet battled to catch her hands and hold them still. "The birth is over, Jo. There is no more pain. You are going to sleep, Jo. Sleep and rest. And when you are rested, you will wake gently. Can you hear me, Joanna? Now, close your eyes and rest . . ."

145

"It's taking too long!" Elen looked at Margaret, frightened. Gently she sponged Matilda's face with a cloth wrung out in rosewater. "For sweet Jesus' sake, isn't there anything we can do to help?"

They both looked pleadingly at the midwife, who was once more feeling Matilda's stomach beneath the bloodstained linen. The girl was practically unconscious now, propped against a dozen pillows, the deep straw litter of the childbed covered with sheets to make it soft and smooth. Between each pain black exhaustion took hold of her, drawing her down into blessed oblivion before another spasm of rending agony began inexorably to build, tearing her back to screaming wakefulness. Only the warmth of the blood in which she lay soothed her.

"There now. He's nearly here, the boyo." The birthing woman was fumbling beneath the sheet. "Another push or two, my lovely, and it'll all be over. There's brave, it is." She smiled imperturbably as Matilda arched her back in another agonized contortion and a further spurt of blood soaked into the bedding. The rosary they had put in her fingers broke and the beads rolled across the floor. Horrified, Margaret crossed herself and it was left to Elen to twist a towel into a rope and give it to Matilda to grip as, with a final desperate convulsion, the girl's body rid itself of its burden.

For a moment there was total silence. Then at last there was a feeble wail from the bloodstained scrap of life that lay between her legs. Matilda did not hear it. She was spinning away into exhausted sleep, her body still hunched against another pain.

"Is he all right?" Margaret peered fearfully at the baby as the woman produced her knife and severed the cord. None of them had even doubted Matilda's prediction that it would be a boy. The baby, wildly waving its little arms in the air, let out another scream. It was unblemished.

"There, my lady, see. He's beautiful." Gently Elen laid the child in Matilda's arms. "Look at him. He's smiling."

Fighting her exhaustion, Matilda pushed away the birthing woman, who had been trying roughly to massage her stomach. She dragged herself up onto her elbow, trying to gather her courage. The moment she had dreaded was here. Somehow she clawed her way back to wakefulness and with outward calm she received the baby and gazed down into the small puckered face. For a moment she could not breathe, then suddenly she felt a strange surge of love and protective joy for her firstborn. She forgot her fears. He was beautiful. She buried her face in the little shawl that had been wrapped around him and hugged him, holding him away from her again only to look long and lovingly at the deep blue-black eyes and tiny fringed lids, the button nose and pursed mouth, and the thatch of dark, bloodstained hair. But as she looked the child's face grew hazy and blackened. She watched paralyzed as the tiny features became contorted with agony and she heard the child begin to scream again and again. They were

146

not the screams of a child, but those of a grown man, ringing in her ears. In her arms she held a warm woven shawl no longer. She was clutching rags, and through the rags she could feel the bones of a living skeleton. After thrusting the body away from her with revulsion, she feverishly threw herself from the bed and collapsed weakly on her knees, retching, at the feet of the terrified women who had been tending her.

"Sweet Mary, Mother of God, save him and save me," she breathed, clutching at the coverlet convulsively. Slowly the world around her began to swim. She saw the great bed rocking before her then a deep roaring filled her ears, cutting out all the other sounds, and slowly, helplessly, she slipped to the floor.

"Jo!" Nick reached her first. "Jo! It's all right. Jo, please, Jo . . ." He gathered her limp form into his arms, cradling her head against his chest.

"Leave her, please." Bennet knelt beside them. "Let me see her. Jo!" He snapped his fingers in her face. "Listen to me, Joanna. You are going to wake up now. Do you hear me. Now!"

There was a moment of total silence. Outside the sound of a police siren wailing in the Marylebone Road brought the twentieth century back into the room.

Jo stirred. She opened her eyes and lay looking up at Nick. The strain and anguish were slowly clearing from her face as she eased herself upright.

"Jo? Are you all right?" Nick's voice was gentle. He still had his arm around her shoulders.

She frowned, staring around the room, looking first at Bennet and then at Sarah who was standing, whitefaced, by the desk. Then her gaze came back to Nick. She smiled weakly.

"He's dead, isn't he?" she said shakily.

"Jo, love—" Nick pulled her close, his face in her hair. "None of it happened. Nobody died—"

She stared at him. "Don't lie to me." Her voice was very weary. "I want to know the truth." Her gaze traveled past Nick suddenly. "Archdeacon?" The room in Devonshire Place faded slightly as she peered toward the end of the bed. She was once again lying beneath the covers but now they were cleansed. Darkness had come outside and the room was lighted with a dozen torches. Gerald held a crucifix in his hand and he was praying quietly, his eyes occasionally flitting up to her passive face.

"The child is dead." She heard her voice as a hollow whisper in the silence of the castle. Somewhere in the distance the police car still wailed. Her lips and tongue were dry as dust.

Gerald kissed the crucifix calmly and tucked it back into his girdle. Then he came to the side of her bed and put his cool hand on her brow. "Not at all," he said cheerfully. "The child is squalling manfully. I've seen it. A fine healthy boy, my lady, to set all your fears at rest." His grave eyes surveyed her carefully, taking in the disarrayed tangled hair all over the pillow, the pallid, damp skin, the quick, shallow breathing. "You have a touch of fever. Enough to cause some wandering of the mind in your overwrought condition, but there is nothing to fear, for the child or for yourself. I have ordered sleep-wort and poppy for you to take. A good night's rest will set you right."

She opened her mouth to speak, but sternly he put his fingers to his lips and pronounced a blessing over her. Then he stood by and watched as Margaret, looking pale and shaken, brought her the sleeping draught, after which she lay back, exhausted. Too tired to think, she let her mind go blessedly blank and drifted slowly into the welcome forgetfulness of sleep.

"Who was she talking to?" Nick found himself glancing over his shoulder as Jo settled once more into his arms, her eyes closed. His skin prickled uncomfortably.

Bennet shook his head. "She was still seeing her archdeacon," he said slowly. "He must have spoken to her, reassured her. Look at the flush on her cheeks almost as if she were asleep—" Gently he picked up Jo's wrist and felt her pulse.

Sarah covered her with a blanket and for a moment they all stood looking at her. Bennet took off his glasses. His hands were shaking. "The brandy, Sarah, if you please."

"I hope you're satisfied!" Nick rounded on him. "Didn't you realize after last time how vulnerable she is? Didn't it dawn on you it might be dangerous to play with this . . . this asinine previous time with Jo? She nearly died under hypnosis before in Edinburgh. Didn't my brother tell you? She stopped breathing then! *Christ!*" He struck his fist onto his open palm. "You're supposed to be a reputable practitioner! If Jo hasn't got the sense to stay away from you, then surely to God you can say no to her yourself!"

"Nick?" Jo's voice from the sofa was still very weak. "Nick. Don't shout. Please."

He swung around to look at her. Jo was struggling to sit up. "Please, don't be angry. It's not Carl's fault. Everything went fine before. It was just that . . . that having a baby . . ." Tears began to trickle down her face.

Sarah tiptoed forward. She crouched beside Jo. "Here, have some of this. It will steady you." She closed Jo's fingers around the glass and helped guide it to her lips.

"My baby really is all right, isn't he?" Jo asked after a moment as she pushed the glass away.

Nick and Bennet looked at each other.

"Jo." Bennet waved Sarah away and sat down on the sofa next to her. He took her hands in his.

"What's happened?" She glanced wildly from him to the others and back. "What's wrong? It was some sort of hallucination, wasn't it? That way he changed in my arms. That wasn't real. Why don't you tell me? My baby is all right?"

Bennet swallowed. He was still firmly holding her wrists. "Jo, my dear. There is no baby. That was all in the past. Another world. Another age. Another you. There is no baby here." His face was full of compassion.

"But I gave birth to him! I held him . . ." Jo was crying openly now. She stared around, bewildered. "He was here . . . in my arms."

Bennet held out his hand to Sarah for the glass. "Drink a little more of this, Jo. It will help to clear your mind. The experience was so real for you it is hard to imagine it did not happen, but you must try to put things in perspective."

Behind him Nick and Sarah exchanged glances. Without a word she poured two more measures of brandy. Taking one for herself, she handed the other to Nick. He sat down heavily on the edge of the desk, his hand shaking as he raised it to his lips.

Bennet beckoned Sarah over. He stood up. "Sit here with her for a minute," he said softly.

As Sarah took his place and put a comforting hand on Jo's arm, he spoke to Nick in an undertone.

"Is there someone at home to look after her?"

Nick nodded grimly. "I'll be there."

"Then I suggest the best thing is for you to take her back and put her to bed. All she needs is a good night's sleep. I'll prescribe something." He reached into his desk for his prescription pad. "You mentioned that she nearly died under hypnosis before. Do you know the circumstances? You must believe me, she did not tell me, and neither did your brother."

"She doesn't know." Nick glanced at Jo. He lowered his voice still further. "I think you should speak to Sam. He was there."

"Dr. Franklyn did try to contact me." Bennet frowned. "But Joanna said I was not to confer with him. I must confess I did intend to speak to him. I suspected something must have occurred before, in spite of her protestations, but nothing like this!" He ran his fingers through his hair. "Nothing."

Nick scowled. "It is obviously time you and Sam got together, whatever Jo says. I'll tell him to get in touch with you again. Meanwhile, can you be sure she is all right?"

Bennet glanced at Jo. "I'll give you my home number. If anything happens over the weekend to worry you, call me. On Monday I have to fly to Chicago for ten days. It can't be avoided—but I can give you the name of a colleague—"

"Don't bother." Nick stood up. "She won't need to see anyone else. I'll take care of her."

It was another hour before Jo was well enough to stand. Helped by Sarah, Nick half carried her out to the waiting taxi. Thankfully he climbed in beside her and sat back, putting his arm around her shoulders.

"Feeling okay now?"

She drew away slightly. "I'm fine. I'm sorry. I made a fool of myself in there."

"It was hardly your fault." He stared out of the window. "I've asked the driver to stop off at a late-opening drugstore."

"Why?"

"Bennet's prescribed something to help you sleep tonight." He felt in his pocket for the prescription.

Jo snatched it out of his hand. "You know what I think of sleeping pills, Nick. Tell the driver to go straight to Cornwall Gardens." She tore the paper into tiny pieces.

"You can drop me off and then go on back to Judy."

"Jo." Nick was reproachful.

"Well, that is where you were, presumably? She's the only person who knew what I was doing this afternoon. I don't know why I told her really." She closed her eyes wearily, letting the scraps of the prescription flutter unnoticed onto the floor of the cab.

"You told her because you wanted me with you," Nick said gently.

Jo did not reply.

Once they were back at her apartment, Nick guided Jo to the sofa and she collapsed onto it with a sigh. He frowned. "Shall I call Sam, Jo? He ought to come to look at you."

"No!" With an effort she sat upright again. "I'll be fine, Nick. I'm going to have a bath, then I'll go to bed. There is no need for you to stay. Really." She glanced at him. At Bennet's and in the taxi she had been glad he was there, been reassured by his touch, but something had happened as he put his arm around her to help her up the stairs. She had been consumed with panic. It had obliterated every other feeling in her for a moment, even making her forget the baby. She had felt herself go rigid, her breath caught in a spasm of fear. Then, as swiftly as it had come, the feeling had disappeared, leaving her shaking like a leaf. She swallowed hard. "Please, Nick. I'd like to be alone."

Nick frowned. "At least let me wait until you're in bed," he said at last. "I shan't come near you, if that's what is worrying you. But I ought to stay. Supposing you fainted in the bath or something?"

Jo hesitated. She had been on the point of protesting that she had never fainted in her life.

"Okay," she said at last unwillingly. "Thank you."

"Let me stay next door on the sofa." He tried once more when she was at last in bed.

"No, Nick. Thanks, but no." She took his hand.

150

"You won't play the tape of what happened?"

"No. I'm going to sleep. Don't worry about me, Nick."

Nick looked at her for a moment, then he shrugged. "Right. I'll be at my apartment. Promise you'll call if you need me?"

"I promise. Now, please go."

She sat unmoving until she finally heard the door bang behind him. Then at last she lay back on the pillows and allowed the tears to fall. How could she tell him how much she wanted him to stay? Or how much she was suddenly afraid of him?

She fell asleep at last with the bedside lamp on, unable to bring herself to face total darkness. Outside her window the night was hot and stuffy. Slowly the pubs in Gloucester Road emptied and the sound of talk and laughter echoed up from the mews as people strolled home, enjoying the heady magic of a London night. Restlessly she turned on her pillow, trying to find a cool spot for her head, half hearing the noise as she drifted further into sleep. Outside the street quietened. A stray breeze, carrying the scent of heliotrope from among the pleached limes of the sunken garden beside Kensington Palace, stirred the curtains, and somewhere a cat yowled and knocked over an empty milk bottle, which rolled down a flight of steps into the gutter.

Jo did not move. She was lying on her side, her hair loose across her face, her arms around the pillow.

It was just beginning to grow light when she woke suddenly. For a moment she did not know what had awakened her, as she stared around the shadowy room. The lamp was still on by her bed, but outside, between the curtains, she could see the pale light of dawn above the rooftops. Then she heard it again. The hungry cry of her baby. Sitting up, yawning, she flung back her hair and reached slowly toward the cradle on the far side of the bed.

15

It wasn't there. The room was silent. And empty. For a moment she sat quite still, completely bewildered, then, slowly, she remembered and with a sigh she flung herself back on the pillows. Tears trickled down her cheeks. Her arms felt empty, desolate; she ached with loneliness. It was as if part of her had been removed. The baby, with his downy hair, his tiny fringed eyelids, the fragments of caul still clinging behind his ears, the pale-blue swaddling bands that had imprisoned his little fists as he lay in her arms, staring up at her with so much love and trust. "Oh, God!" She turned over and buried her face in the pillows. "It was a dream. A stupid, bloody dream!" She groped on the bedside table for a box of tissues, then she pulled her clock to face her. It was half-past four.

She had begun to shiver violently. For a moment she lay back, huddled beneath the covers, trying to get warm, then, miserable, she sat up again. It was no good. She would not sleep again and she was getting colder by the minute. She wished fervently she had allowed Nick to stay now. She wanted someone to talk to. Her head was splitting and her breasts ached. She crossed her arms, trying to ease the discomfort, and suddenly felt a cold wetness on the front of her nightgown. She stared down at herself in horror, then she shot out of bed. After running into the bathroom, she turned on the light and slipped down the ribbon straps, letting the thin cotton slip to the floor, leaving her standing naked in front of the mirror. Her breasts were full and tight, laced with blue veins, and even as she stared in fascinated horror at her reflection she saw a drop of watery blue liquid forming on her left nipple.

Her heart was pounding violently. Desperately she tried to control her tears as she reached for her bathrobe from the back of the door and folded it around her. Knotting the belt, she groped her way into the living room and reached for the phone.

Her hand was shaking so much she could scarcely dial, but at last she could hear the tone. It was several seconds before the receiver was lifted.

"Nick. Oh, Nick, please come. Please." She struggled to keep her voice steady.

"Jo? Is that you?" The voice at the other end was so quiet it was almost a whisper. It was Sam. "What's wrong?"

Jo took a deep breath, trying to calm herself. "I'm sorry to wake you, Sam. Can I speak to Nick, please?"

There was a slight pause, then his voice, very gentle, came again. "He's not here, Jo. Is something wrong?"

"Not there?" she echoed bleakly.

"I'm afraid not. What is it? You sound frightened. Has something happened? Tell me, Jo."

Jo swallowed hard. For a moment she could not speak, then she managed to whisper, "Sam, can you come over?"

He asked no more questions. "I'll be there in fifteen minutes," he said at once, then he hung up.

After she had rung off, Jo didn't move. Slowly the milk was soaking into her robe. Her teeth were chattering in spite of the warmth of the room and she huddled on the edge of her chair, rocking herself gently back and forth, only dragging herself upright at last when she heard the sound of a taxi in the quiet street outside. She reached the intercom at the same moment that it buzzed.

Sam came up the stairs two at a time.

"What is it, Jo? Are you ill?" He closed the door behind him and stood staring at her. She saw with a quick pang of misery that he was wearing one of Nick's jackets over his dark turtleneck shirt.

She was looking, he thought irrelevantly, more beautiful than he had ever seen her, her long disheveled hair dark against the stark white of her robe, her face pale, her huge eyes accentuated by the shadows beneath them.

"Nick said he'd go back to the apartment," she stammered. "He said I could phone."

"I'm glad you did." Sam steered her into the living room and toward a chair. "Now, tell me about it slowly."

Hesitatingly she told him about her latest visit to Bennet. She glanced at his face, expecting an outburst of anger, but he said nothing and she forced herself to go on. "Perhaps he knew what would happen. He prescribed sleeping pills for me before I came home, but I never take them. Nick wanted to stay, but I wouldn't let him, so I suppose he went back to Judy after all." She glanced down at her hands.

Sam said nothing. He was watching her face closely.

"I woke up," she went on with a heavy sigh. "The baby woke me with his crying—William, he was to be called, like his father and his father's father—but he wasn't there." Her voice shook. "And then I found—" She stopped. "I found that I'm . . ." She hesitated again, suddenly embarrassed. Mutely her hands went to her breasts.

Sam had seated himself near her on the arm of another chair. "I am a doctor, Jo," he said softly. "You're producing a bit of milk, right?"

She nodded, blushing. He smiled. He got up to kneel before her. "May I see?" Softly he pulled her robe open and looked at her breasts. He touched one lightly. Then he closed the robe again. He smiled. "It's nothing to worry about, Jo. Spontaneous lactation is unusual but not unheard of. It'll be a bit uncomfortable for a day or two but it will ease off. Stick some tissues in your bra." He crossed over to the table and picked up the whisky bottle. "I'll get some glasses, shall I?"

She followed him into the kitchen, pulling the knot of her belt tighter. "But how is it possible?" she asked huskily. "Is this another of your physiological reactions, like my hands?" She took the glass from him and sipped the neat whisky.

"I suppose so, in a way. You obviously went through all the emotional trauma of childbirth yesterday and in some women that would be enough to stimulate the glands. The breast is far more of a machine than people realize. It doesn't necessarily always need a pregnancy and a birth to start it working. Adoptive mothers have been known to produce milk for their babies, you know. Anyway, you mustn't worry about it. It's perfectly natural. Just leave things well alone and it will calm down on its own in a day or two." He leaned forward and tipped some more whisky into her glass. His hand was shaking slightly.

"Our dog had a phantom pregnancy once, when I was a child. Is that what I've had?" She managed a grin.

He laughed. "Something like that. But I don't expect you to produce any puppies."

"You are sure Nick wasn't there?" Her smile had vanished already as she turned away from him. "You checked in his room?" She paced up the small kitchen and then back, her arms wrapped around herself to stop herself shaking, the glass still clutched in one hand. "I still love him, Sam. That's the stupid thing. I love the bastard." She stopped in front of the sink, staring at the pink geranium in its pot on the draining board. Absently she leaned forward to pick off a dead leaf and so she did not see Sam's face. The cords in his neck stood out violently as he stared at Jo's back.

With a little laugh she went on without turning. "You won't tell him I said that, will you?"

"No, Jo." Shaking his head, he recovered himself with an effort. "I won't tell him. That I promise you."

Sam was whistling softly to himself as he nodded to the janitor at Lynwood House, where Nick had his apartment, and let himself into the elevator. It was still not quite eight o'clock. He pushed open the apartment door and stood for a moment, listening.

"You've been out early." Nick appeared at the bathroom door, razor in hand. "Pour out some juice will you? I'll be there in a minute."

Sam smiled. "Whatever you say, little brother. I trust you slept well?" He pulled Nick's jacket off and hung it up.

Nick was looking at his watch. "I'm going to give Jo a ring to see if she is okay. I half expected her to phone last night, the state she was in—"

"No!" Sam said sharply. He withdrew the copy of the *Daily Telegraph* he had under his arm and held it up to scan the headlines. "Leave her in peace, Nicholas, for God's sake. If everything you told me last night about her session with Bennet is true the last thing she will want is to be wakened at this hour of the morning by the telephone."

Nick had turned back to the bathroom. He unplugged the razor. "I suppose you're right. . . ."

"I know I'm right." Sam raised his eyes for a moment from the paper to give his brother a penetrating look. "I suggest you go down to see our mother this morning as arranged and let Jo alone for a couple of days. In fact, leave her alone until you get back from your wanderings across Europe. She does know you are going away?"

Nick shrugged. He was buttoning his shirt. "Scotland I can't cancel, but the trip to France I could postpone."

"Don't." Sam walked into the kitchen and rummaged on the shelf for the jar of coffee. "It isn't worth it. Jo has made it clear enough it is over between you. Don't let a temporary wave of sentiment because you saw her unhappy and emotional undo all the good you achieved by walking out on her. You'll just make the poor girl more neurotic than she already is."

"Why did she ask me to go with her yesterday then, if she doesn't want to see me anymore?" Nick followed him into the kitchen, tucking his shirt into the waistband of his trousers.

"Did she, though?" Sam glanced at him.

He fished a loaf out of the bin and began to cut meticulously thin slices, which he tossed into the toaster. "Have you any marmalade? I haven't been able to find it."

Nick sat down at the kitchen table. He reached for the paper and stared at it unseeing. "She shouldn't be alone, though, Sam," he said at last.

"She won't be," Sam replied. "I'll call her later. Remember, I am a doctor as well as a friend. I'll give her a quick check over, if necessary, and make sure she's in good spirits and while I'm at it read her the riot act about ignoring our warnings."

"And you'll phone me if she wants me?"

"She won't want you, Nicholas." Sam looked at him solicitously. "Get that into your thick head before you are really hurt."

155

Judy stared morosely beyond the reflection of the dimly lit bar, through the indigo windows, at the rain-washed Pimlico Road. "I never thanked you for giving me such a good write-up," she said at last to Pete Leveson, who was sitting opposite her. She turned her back on the window. "I'm sure it was thanks to you that the exhibition went so well."

"Rubbish. You deserved success."

Pete was watching her closely, noting the taut lines between her nose and mouth, the dullness of her eyes. "It is a bit of an anticlimax, now that it's over, I suppose," he said tentatively.

Judy sighed. She picked up her glass, staring around the wine bar with apparent distaste. "That's probably it."

"And how is Nick?" His voice was deliberately casual.

She colored. "He's in Scotland, on business."

"And Jo? Is she still dabbling in the paranormal?"

Judy drank her Buck's Fizz, then with a grimace she asked, "Does the name Carl Bennet mean anything to you?"

Pete raised an eyebrow. "Possibly. Why?"

"Jo went to see him on Friday afternoon, and the thought that she was going there was enough to scare Nick to death. He shot off after her as if she had left a message that she was having tea with the devil himself. Can I have another of these?"

Pete raised his hand to beckon the waitress without taking his eyes off Judy's face. He gave the order and tossed a five-pound note on the table. "Bennet is a hypnotherapist," he said. "One of the best, I believe. And among other things he takes people back into their previous incarnations to treat them for otherwise incurable phobias."

Judy's mouth dropped open. "You mean that is what Jo is doing? Jesus! She doesn't believe in that sort of thing, does she?"

"You are not a believer, I take it?" Pete was looking amused.

"No, I am not! No wonder Nick is worried for her sanity. Anyone who believes that kind of thing is certifiable. No wonder she freaked out when I told her Sam thought she was schizoid."

Pete was sitting back, still watching her closely. "She is doing it for a story, Judy," he said tolerantly. "I think you should watch what you say, you know."

Judy laughed again. Her third Buck's Fizz on an empty stomach was going to her head. "I don't have to in front of you, do I?" she said archly. "Or do you think there is a gossip columnist under the table? But seriously, who needs one of those when I'm having a drink with one of the most prestigious reporters in Fleet Street." She glanced at him provocatively under her eyelashes. "You had a thing going with Jo once, didn't you?"

Pete leaned back in his chair. "I don't believe it was a secret."

"And you still like her. Everyone who has had an affair with Jo seems to still like her. What a likable person she must be!" she added sarcastically. "Well, why don't *you* find out exactly what it is she is doing? It would make a good story, surely?"

"Jo is researching her own story, Judy." His voice was carefully neutral.

"It sure as hell wouldn't be the same story if you told it, though, would it?" She ran her finger round the inside of her glass and sucked it pointedly. "Yours would be much more . . . sensational!"

She had huge eyes—light gray, with radiating streaks in the irises, fringed with dark-red lashes. Pete contemplated them for a moment as he thought over what she had said. Jo was a friend and yes, he was still fond of her, but the story, if there was a story, would not hurt her. On the contrary, it would counteract that bit in the *Mail*. In fact, why not sell this one to the *Mail?* Give the real version of what was going on. Sensational, Judy had said. It was a word Peter could not resist.

Leaning forward, he put his hand over Judy's and squeezed it gently. "Why don't I get you another of those," he said quietly. "Then you needn't lick the glass. Later I'll drop you back at your place and we'll talk about this some more."

Two days later Dorothy Franklyn rang the bell of the apartment in Lynwood House. "I hope you don't mind, Sam, dear. I did so want to see you before you went back to Scotland." She dropped three green-and-gold Harrods bags on the floor of the hall, then she straightened, looking at him for a moment. Reaching up to kiss him, she rumpled his hair affectionately before walking past him into the living room. "When are you going back?"

Sam followed her. "I've a few things to do in town and Nick said I could use the flat while he's in France, so I'll be here a week or so, I expect." He threw himself into a chair and looked up at her. "You're looking very spry, Ma."

She smiled. "Thank you, dear," she said. "Now tell me, how is Jo?"

Sam raised an eyebrow. "What did Nick tell you?"

"Enough to make me very worried. This reincarnation business, Sam, it is all rubbish, isn't it? I don't like the sound of it at all. I didn't like it when you were working on your thesis under that creepy man Cohen, and I don't like it any better now. I think it's dangerous. It's got nothing whatsoever to do with medicine, or science. And to think that Jo has got involved with mumbo jumbo like that!" She shuddered visibly. "Can't you do something, Sam?"

Sam turned away from her and looked out of the window. In the distance he could see a solid wedge of traffic sitting in the broad sweep of Park Lane. "I'm not sure that I can," he said slowly. "I think Jo has already become too involved to extricate herself even if she wanted to. I believe that we are dealing with a genuine case of total recall of a previous incarnation. There are too many facts, too many details." He sighed. "Too many things fit into the picture, Ma." He glanced down at the books on the table. "I've been thinking about all this very hard over the past week. When I heard the tapes of Jo's first regression a lot of things began to make sense." He ran his fingers through his hair. "It has forced me to change my views. I believe now that maybe, once in a while, if a person— or people—have left things undone, or perhaps made a terrible mistake in one life, it is possible that when they are reborn they are given a second chance."

"And you think Jo is being given a second chance?" Her face was inscrutable as she watched him.

Sam smiled. "Jo. Or someone else."

"You don't really believe that?" she said after a moment. "That there is some kind of karmic replay?" She frowned. "That is an Eastern philosophy, Sam, not one that sits easily on Western shoulders." She paused. "But how is Jo in herself, Sam? Nick was very worried about her. Especially when you called and said she didn't want to see him before he went off to France. She did say that?" She was watching him carefully again.

"She was badly shaken by what happened last Friday and a bit confused. I think she felt she had made rather a fool of herself in front of him. It will all have blown over by the time he gets back and they will both be glad they didn't meet again to prolong the embarrassment."

"This theory of yours." She went to stand near him. "Does Jo believe it too?"

"Jo is still fighting it." Sam frowned. "And until she accepts it she is unlikely to accept the wider implication that others must have been reincarnated with her, so that they can work out their destiny together with hers. It has to work like that."

"So you think now that Jo is not the only one." Thoughtfully she walked back into the living room. "Do you think Nick is involved?" She looked at him suddenly. "He wasn't someone in this past life of hers?"

"Oh, yes, Nick is involved." Sam's voice had suddenly lost its lightness.

"How do you know?" she asked sharply. She sat down, putting her cup on the coffee table. "And you?" she said after a moment's hesitation. "Are you involved too?"

"I rather think I am." Sam sat down opposite her. "Crazy, isn't it?" He gave her a disarming smile.

"And do you have any proof for this theory?"

"Proof?" He looked at her in astonishment. "How can there be proof? Don't be obtuse, Ma."

"I mean, have you or Nick had this hypnosis thing done to you, to find out?"

He shook his head. "Some things one knows. One remembers . . ."

She shuddered. "You're giving me the creeps, Sam! I have never heard such a load of nonsense in my life. You've let your imagination run away with you. I suggest you go back to Scotland and imbue yourself with a good dose of Scots common sense!" She looked at Sam. "Who do you think you are—or were—in her story?"

Sam grinned. "Never you mind, Ma. I think we should stop talking about this." His tone changed. "Now, what have you been buying? Are you going to show me?"

She refused to be distracted. "Did this Matilda have many men in her life?"

Sam grimaced. "At least two. Probably three."

Dorothy was watching him closely. "Were they brothers?" she asked bluntly.

He laughed. "No, they weren't brothers! Come on. Let's stop talking about this."

She continued, irritated. "Have you told Nick about this idea of yours?"

"No."

"Are you going to?"

Sam shrugged. "That depends. I think it would be better if Nick concentrated on his advertising at the moment—and the delectable redhead in Fulham. There is no point in stirring things up needlessly."

"I'm glad to hear that." Dorothy stood up briskly, trying to ignore her increasing panic. "Sam, I have to go. I've got one or two things to do before I catch my train." She reached up to kiss him on the cheek, then she hesitated. "But tell me one thing first. You said you thought you had remembered things from the past. That is such a strange, frightening idea. What have you remembered?"

"It was when I was listening to the tape of Jo's first regression," he replied slowly. "I remembered a ring. A ring on the finger of a man." He stared at the ceiling over her head. "I have remembered that ring for eight hundred years."

There was silence in the room.

Dorothy licked her lips uneasily. "Why?" she whispered at last.

"Because he was my guest. And I murdered him."

It was several days before Jo's breasts returned to normal. Grimly she worked, typing up her notes, using every ounce of willpower she possessed to put Carl Bennet and Matilda de Braose out of her mind. She springcleaned the apartment, filled the storage closets, arranged to go back to Suffolk by train on Saturday morning to collect the MG, and less and less often had to remove the soggy tissues from her bra. Sam had told her that Nick was in France and she was glad. Nick was a complication she could not handle at the moment. Dutifully each night she took the two sleeping pills Sam had prescribed, went to bed at eleven, and slept heavily. Unpleasantly heavily.

She saw Sam only once more. He checked her over with quiet professionalism, ruffled her hair as if she were a naughty child, and went. She wished he had stayed longer.

When Pete Leveson called out of the blue she accepted his invitation to dinner with alacrity. He took her to the Gasworks and they sat in the huge, dimly lit reception room idly playing with the ornate chess pieces laid out in front of them while they waited for their table. Pete watched her covertly as he sipped his gin and tonic. "You're looking great, Jo. Really great. How is work?"

She smiled. "It's going quite well actually."

"How did you get on with Carl Bennet? I hope the introduction was useful." He moved a king's pawn, not taking his eyes from her face, and saw her wary look at once.

"It was very interesting. Thank you, Pete."

He waited for her to say more as she leaned back, staring idly around the room.

"Did you find out anything revealing?" he prompted at last.

She reached for her glass. "The woman never turned up that first time."

"First time?" He picked her up at once. "So you've been again? Did he use hypnosis on you?" He moved one of her knights for her with a malicious grin.

"Three times now." Gently she took it back from him and replaced it. She moved a bishop instead.

"And?"

She laughed uneasily. "It appears I have an alter ego. I still don't believe I am her reincarnation—I can't bring myself to accept that—but this woman is living a life somewhere there inside my head and it is so real! More real in some ways than the life I'm leading here and now."

"Check." Pete drained his glass. "You always were useless at chess, Jo. Why didn't you let me help you? We could have made the game last at least ten minutes. Tell me about her, this lady who lives in your head."

Jo glanced at him. "You're not laughing?"

"No. I told you. I find it fascinating. I have always hankered after the idea of having a past life. It's romantic, and comforting. It means if you fuck this one up, you can have another go. It also means that there might be a reason why I'm so unreasonably terrified of water."

Jo smiled. "I expect your mother dropped you in the bath."

"She swears not." Pete raised his hand to the young man hovering in the background and ordered fresh drinks. "So shoot. Tell me about your other self."

It was a relief to talk about it again. Relaxed and reassured by Pete's quiet interest, Jo talked on. They finished their drinks and moved to their

160

table in the grotto dark of the restaurant and she went on with the story. She kept back only one thing. She could not bring herself to mention her baby, or what had happened after his birth. When at last she had finished Pete let out a long, low whistle. "My God! And you're telling me that you intend to let it go at that? You're not going back?"

Jo shook her head. "If I go back again, I'll go a thousand times. I've got to make myself drop it, Pete."

"Why? What's wrong with knowing what happened? For God's sake, Jo!" He grinned. "I wouldn't stop. I'd go back again and again till I had the whole story, whatever it cost. To hell with where she comes from. Whether she's a spirit from the past or a part of your own personality fragmenting for some reason, or you in a previous existence, she is a fascinating woman. Think of the people she might have known."

Jo smiled wryly. "She knew King John."

"Bad King John?" He rocked back on his seat. "What a story that would be, Jo. Think—if you could interview him, through her! You can't leave it there. You can't. You must see that. You have to go back and find out what happened next."

Judy was in the shower when Sam called the next morning. Wrapped in a towel, she picked up the phone, shaking her wet hair out of her eyes, watching the drops lying on the studio floor. The water was still running down her legs making pools around her feet. She dropped the towel and stood in the rectangle of stark sunshine from the window.

"Yes, Dr. Franklyn, of course I remember you," she said, grinning. "What can I possibly do for you?"

Sam heard the grin at the other end of the phone. "I want you to do something for Nick," he said slowly. "He was feeling pretty low last week —I expect you know. And now he is in France and he could use some company. Supposing I gave you his address. How soon could you be at Heathrow?"

"You mean he wants me to go to him?" Judy's eyes widened in surprise.

"Shall we say I am sure he would be pleased if you were to turn up unexpectedly. I owe Nick a favor. I'll even pay for your ticket. My present to you both."

Judy raised an eyebrow. "It's very kind of you, Dr. Franklyn, and I'd love to go." She was staring at her naked reflection in the full-length mirror on the wall in front of her. "I never need to be persuaded to go to Paris. Especially is there's a free ticket! But if I weren't such an innocent, I might just ask myself what the real reason behind this sudden philanthropy was."

He laughed out loud. "Then I'm glad you're an innocent, Miss Curzon. I wouldn't want you any other way."

161

Ceecliff met Jo at Sudbury on Saturday morning and bore her home in an elderly Land Rover. The old house was full of dappled sunlight, every door and window open onto the garden, and Jo looked around her with enormous pleasure and relief. Somewhere deep inside she had been afraid the tension of that weekend two weeks ago might return.

Triumphantly Ceecliff produced a bottle of Pimms. "Nick is in France, you say?" She poured out two glasses as they sat down beneath the willow. Jo nodded.

"And did you make it up before he went?"

"We parted friends, I suppose," Jo said cautiously. What was the point of telling Ceecliff that he had left her frightened and alone in her apartment and gone straight to Judy? That he hadn't been there when she needed him and that she hadn't seen him since? She felt her grandmother's eyes on her face and forced a smile. "I've decided to go back to the hypnotist again. No more hysteria, no more involvement. Just to find out, objectively, what happened."

Ceecliff pursed her lips. "That is madness, Jo. How can you possibly be objective? How could anyone?"

"Because Dr. Bennet can tell me to be. That is the beauty of hypnosis, one does what one is told. He can use my own mind to hold everything at arm's length."

Ceecliff raised an exasperated eyebrow. "I think you're being naive, Jo. Extraordinarily naive." She sighed. Then after heaving herself out of her chair, she turned toward the house. "But I know better than to argue with you. Wait there. I'm going to fetch Reggie's papers for you."

She returned with an attaché case. Inside was a mass of papers and notebooks.

"I think you should have all those, Jo. The Clifford papers. Not much compared with some families' archives, but better than nothing. Most of it is about the eighteenth and nineteenth centuries. You can look at that another time. Here. This is what I wanted to show you." She unfolded an old letter, the wax that had sealed it still attached to the back, the spidery scrawls of the address faded to brown.

Reverently Jo took it and screwed up her eyes to read the unfamiliar copperplate hand. It was dated 12 June 1812. Jo read aloud. " 'My dear Godfon and Nephew'—he's using long *s*'s!—'I was interested in your remarks about Clifford Castle, near Whitney-on-Wye, as I too visited the place some years back. I have been unable to trace a family connection with those Cliffords—Rosa Mundi, you will remember, was poisoned by the indomitable Eleanor, wife to King Henry II, and I should dearly have wished to find some link to so tragic and romantic a lady. There is a legend, however, which ties us with the land of Wales, so close to Clifford. I have been unable to substantiate it in any way, but the story has persisted for many generations that we are descended from Gruffydd, a prince of south Wales—though when and how, I know not. Let it suffice that perhaps somewhere in our veins there runs a strain of royal blood—' " Jo put down the letter, laughing. "Oh, no! That's beautiful!"

Ceecliff grimaced. "Don't go getting any ideas above your station, my girl. Come on, put it all away. You can look at it later. Let's eat now, before the food is spoiled."

While her grandmother rested, Jo drove to Clare. She parked near the huge, beautiful church with its buttresses and battlemented parapets and stood gazing at it, watching the clouds streaming behind the tall double rank of arched windows. Had Richard de Clare stood looking at the same church? She could picture him now, the last time she had seen him, in the solar at Abergavenny, his hazel eyes full of pain and love and courage, the deep-green mantle wrapped around him against the cold, clasped on the shoulder by a large round enameled brooch.

She shoved her hands deep into the pockets of her jeans and stared at it morosely, then, hitching her bag higher on her shoulder, she let herself in through the gate and began to walk toward the south porch.

Richard de Clare had never stood in this church. One look around the fluted pillars and high windows told her it had been built long after Richard's time. Disappointed, she began to walk up the broad aisle looking around her. There were several other people wandering around with guidebooks, talking in muted tones. Ignoring them, she made her way slowly up the chancel steps and stood staring at the altar, thinking of the last time she had stood before a shrine—was it at Brecknock?—with Gerald saying mass. She remembered the mingling of the incense and the candles, their acrid smoke blown by the cold wind off the mountains that filtered through every corner of the castle. She remembered looking up at a carved, painted statue of the Holy Virgin and praying for her unborn baby, praying with a faith suddenly so intense, so absolute, that it had filled her at the time with a calm certainty that her prayers would be heard. I wonder how long Matilda kept that faith, she thought grimly, her eyes on the cross that stood on the altar. Did she still have it when she died? She had not told Pete Leveson that she already knew the end of the story, nor Ceecliff.

She was conscious suddenly of someone watching her as she gazed at the cross and, embarrassed, she turned away. In this so Puritan, so Spartan, church, the memories of her Catholic past seemed almost indecent, and to the agnostic, twentieth-century Jo, the urge to go down on her knees and then cross herself as she turned away from the sanctuary was like a primeval hangover of some strange superstition.

Hastily she retraced her steps and let herself out into the churchyard. She drove slowly through Clare, savoring the beautiful medieval buildings

163

of the Suffolk town, and turned to follow the signs toward the country park and the castle.

After parking once more, she stood and stared around her. Where the huge castle of the Clares had once stood were now the hollow remains of a ruined railway station. The Great Eastern Railway had come, destroyed most of what remained of the castle, and in its turn had gone, leaving only the empty shell of the station, trimmed and manicured, with mown grass between the platforms where the track had been. Only a few fragments of wall remained of the castle that had stood for nine hundred years. But the motte was still there—the high, tree-covered mound on which the original keep had stood—and determinedly Jo climbed it, following the spiraling path to its summit. From there she could see the whole of Clare spread out in a shimmering panorama before her. The air was soft. It smelled of new-mown hay and honey. She stood there for a moment and rested her hands on the surviving chunk of flint-built wall, as if by touching the stones she could reach back over the years, but nothing happened. There were no vibrations from the past. Nothing at all.

That night Jo went through her grandfather's attaché case. Sitting in her bedroom, the windows thrown open to the scented garden, she felt absolutely at peace. The small table lamp was attracting the moths but she didn't notice as she pulled out the old letters and diaries and his notes. Never before had she felt even the remotest curiosity about her ancestors. Like Ceecliff, her interest was in the present, perhaps because her father had died while she was still too young to remember him properly. Her mother Jo rarely saw now. They met from time to time, felt a rush of warm emotion as they kissed, then slowly sank into mutual incomprehension as they tried to find some common ground. At present Julia Clifford was in San Tropez. A fond smile touched Jo's mouth for a moment as she thought of her mother. They would meet again in the autumn or at Christmas, probably here, at Ceecliff's, exchange gifts and a little bit of gossip, then their paths would once more diverge. Jo looked back at the letter in her hand wondering suddenly how much of her own tartness was a direct reaction against her mother's vapid fluttering. But Julia, she knew, would have no time for the past either. For her the past, like Jo's father, was dead.

There was only one mention of the distant past in the letters. The mysterious Gruffydd of Wales. Was Matilda somehow an ancestor of hers, through him? But how was that possible when William was so implacably the enemy of the Welsh? She wished she had noted the names of Matilda's children more closely now, and what had happened to them. Only one name lived in her memory. Little William. Her baby.

She got home very late on Sunday evening, exhausted by the long drive through the heavy traffic, and she slept soundly, untroubled by dreams, to be woken by the phone.

"Jo? Is that you?" It was Bet Gunning. "What the hell are you up to, giving that story to Pete Leveson?"

"What story?" Jo yawned. She looked at her clock sleepily. "God! Is it really nine? Sorry, Bet, I overslept."

"Then you haven't seen today's papers?"

"No." Jo could feel her stomach beginning to tighten. "You'd better tell me the worst."

"*Daily Mail* exclusive—a whole page—by Pete Leveson. Entitled *Jo Clifford's Secret Life*. It's all here, Jo. Your hypnosis. Matilda de whatever-her-name-is . . . bloody hell! I thought we had a deal. I thought this was one of your articles for *W I A.*" Bet was furious. "I know we're a monthly. I know Pete is a friend of yours, but you could at least have given me an option—"

"Bet." Jo interrupted. "I know nothing about this. That bastard took me out to dinner on Friday night. We talked off the record, as friends."

"Off the record?" Bet scoffed. "That's just what it's not. He's got you verbatim. 'Imagine my terror and confusion,' Jo said to me last night, 'when I found myself alone in an alien world . . .'"

Jo could feel herself shaking with anger. "I never said any such thing!" she said furiously. "I'll sue him, Bet. How dare he! I'll call him now, then I'll get back to you—"

She slammed down the phone and dialed Pete's number. It was several minutes before he answered.

"Jo, how nice. Have you seen it?" His voice was laconic.

"No, I haven't seen it, you turd!" Jo stamped her bare foot on the carpet like a child. "But I've heard about it. Bet Gunning is hopping mad —but not as mad as I am. Everything I said to you was in confidence—"

"You never said so, Jo," Pete put in gently. "Sorry, but not once did you ever mention the fact that you wanted all this kept secret. If I'd known that—"

"You could have guessed, Pete. You used our friendship. That was the most cynical piece of underhanded behavior I have ever witnessed. And the fact that you didn't tell me what you wanted to do proves that you knew it."

There was an exaggerated sigh on the other end of the line. "Cool it, Jo. It counteracts the item in the *Mail* Diary the other day. It establishes that you're into something interesting, and it keeps you in the headlines. Three plus factors, if you ask me. When your own story comes out they'll be out there baying to read it!"

"Did you use Carl Bennet's name?" Jo was not to be appeased.

"Of course—"

"He'll be furious! You had no right without asking him."

"So, if he wants, I'll apologize, but he won't object to some free advertising. The Great Public will beat a path to his door. Look, Jo, love, it's

165

super talking to you, but I've got to get dressed. When you've thought about it a bit you'll realize it's all good publicity. See you!" Blandly he hung up.

Still angry, Jo dragged on her jeans and a sweater. After catching her hair back from her face with a scarf, she grabbed her purse. Outside Gloucester Road subway station she bought a paper from the news vendor, then she sprinted back to the apartment.

As Bet had said, it was a whole-page feature. There were no less than three photos of her—one a glamorous, misty picture taken three years before at a ball with Nick. He had been blocked out. The picture made her look dreamy and romantic and very beautiful. It had been taken by Tim Heacham.

Jo had to dial three times before she got through.

"I am sorry, Jo, I really am. I didn't know what he wanted it for." Tim was contrite. "Hell, what was I to think? Pete was back in favor as far as I could see. I had no reason not to give it to him."

"But it is such a god-awful picture! It makes me look—" Words failed her.

"It makes you look quite lovely, Jo. I did try to call you, as it happened, to check, but you were away."

"I was in Suffolk. I went to look at Clare while I was there."

"Clare?" Tim's voice sharpened. "Why?"

"Didn't you read the article?" Jo was staring at it as she spoke. " 'The handsome man whose love had come too late . . . The passionate Richard who had to turn away and leave his lady to her fate . . .' " She grimaced. "He came from Clare. I went to see his castle."

"And did you find him there?" Tim's voice was curiously flat.

"No, of course not. Is something wrong, Tim?"

"No," he said quietly. "Why on earth should anything be wrong?"

That night the baby woke her again. She was deeply asleep, the sheet thrown back because of the warm humidity of the night, the curtains and the window wide open. She woke very suddenly and lay still, wondering what it was she had heard. Then it came again, the restless mewling cry of a hungry baby. She felt herself grow rigid, her eyes wide in the darkness, not daring to breathe as the sound filled the room. Slowly she forced herself to sit up and grope for the light switch. As the darkness shrank back into the corners she stared around. She could still hear him. Hear the intake of breath between each scream, thin pathetic yells as he grew more desperate. She pressed her hands against her ears, feeling her own eyes fill with hot tears, rocking backward and forward in misery as she tried to block out the sound. At last she could bear it no longer. She hurled herself out of bed, then ran to the door and dragged it open, closing it behind her with a slam. Then she ran to the kitchen. With the two doors closed she could no longer hear his anguished cries. Her hands shaking, she filled the kettle, banging it against the taps in her agitation. The Scotch was in the living room. To reach it she would have to open the kitchen door. She stood with her hand on the handle for a moment, then, taking a deep breath, she opened it. There was silence outside in the hallway. She ran to the living room, grabbed the bottle, then she hesitated, looking at the phone. Any time, Sam had said. Call any time. . . .

She knelt and drew it toward her, then she stopped. The apartment was completely silent, save for the sound of the kettle whining quietly in the kitchen. She could not ask Sam to come to her in the middle of the night a second time, because of another nightmare.

She made herself some tea, took a slug of Scotch and the last three sleeping pills, then she lay down on the sofa in the living room and pulled a blanket around her shoulders in spite of the hot night. There was no way she was going back into her bedroom until morning.

Tim was in his studio, staring at a copy of the photo of Jo and Nick. He had blown it up until it was almost four feet across and had pinned it to a display board. A spotlight picked out their faces with a cold, hard neutrality that removed personality, leaving only feature and technique behind.

Thoughtfully he moved across the darkened studio to the tape deck and flipped a switch, flooding the huge, empty room with the reedy piping of Gheorghe Zamfir, then he returned to the photograph. He stood before it, arms folded, on the very edge of the brilliant pool of light, the only focus in the huge vaulted darkness of the studio.

Beside him on the table lay a small piece of glass. As he tapped the powder onto it and methodically rolled up a piece of paper, his eyes were already dreamy. He sniffed, deeply and slowly, then he walked back to the picture.

It was some time later that, with a felt pen, working with infinite care, the tip of his tongue protruding between his teeth, he began to draw a veil and wimple over Jo's long, softly curling hair.

It was about ten o'clock the next morning that a knock came at the apartment door. Jo opened it to find Sheila Chandler, one of her upstairs neighbors, standing on the landing. She was a prim-looking woman in her late fifties, the intense unreal blackness of her iron-waved hair set off by a startling pink sleeveless chiffon dress. Jo barely knew her.

She gave Jo an embarrassed smile. "I am sorry to disturb you, Miss Clifford," she said. "I know you're busy. We can hear you typing. It's just that I thought I must look in and see if there is anything I can do to help."

Jo smiled vaguely. "Help?" she said.

"With the baby. I've had four of my own and I know how it can be if

167

you get one that cries all night. Staying with you, is it?" The woman was staring past Jo into the apartment.

Jo swallowed hard. "He . . . you heard him?" She clutched at the door.

"Oh, I'm not complaining!" Sheila Chandler said hastily. "It's just that on these hot nights, with all the windows open, the noise drifts up the well between the buildings. You know how it is, and my Harry, he's not sleeping too soundly these days. . . ."

Jo took a grip on herself. "There's no baby here," she said slowly. "The noise must be coming from somewhere else."

The woman stared. "But it was here. I came down—last night, about eleven, and I listened outside your door. I nearly knocked then. Look, my dear, I'm not making any judgment. I don't care whose baby it is or how it got there, it's just, well, perhaps you could close the window or something. Have you tried gripe water?"

Jo took a deep breath. "I'm sorry, Mrs. Chandler"—at last she had remembered the woman's name—"but whatever you think, there is no baby!"

There is no baby.

She repeated the words to herself as she closed the door. Last night at eleven she had sat there, in silence, listening, and there had been no sound . . .

She went straight to the phone and called Sam, then she walked through into the bedroom and looked around. The windows were wide open. The room was tidy—and empty. The only sound was the distant roar of traffic drifting between the houses from the Cromwell Road.

Sam arrived at ten to twelve. He kissed Jo on the cheek and presented her with a bottle of Liebfraumilch.

She had put on some makeup to try to hide the dark rings under her eyes and was wearing her peacock-blue silk dress. Her hair was tied back severely with a black velvet ribbon. He looked her up and down critically. "How are you feeling, Jo?" The makeup did not fool him, no more than had her cheerful voice and breezy invitation. She had sounded near the breaking point.

"I'm fine. My breasts are back to normal, thank God!" She managed a shaky smile. "Let's open that bottle. I've drunk all the Scotch. Sam—I think I'm going mad."

Sam raised an eyebrow as he rummaged in the drawer for a corkscrew. She found it for him. "It's the baby. I've heard him again."

"I see." Sam was concentrating on the bottle. "Last night?"

She nodded. "And, Sam, the woman upstairs has heard him too. She came down to complain." Her hands were shaking slightly as she reached for two wineglasses from the cabinet.

He took them from her, his hands covering hers for a moment. "Jo, if

168

the woman upstairs has heard it there has to be a logical explanation. There must be a baby in one of the other apartments and you've both heard it."

"No." Jo shook her head. "It was William."

"Jo—"

"The noise was in this apartment, Sam. She said so. Last night. She stood on the landing outside my door and listened, and heard him!"

Sam pressed a glass of wine into her hand. "May I wander around?"

Jo waited on the balcony, sipping her wine, staring across into the trees in the square. It was five minutes before Sam joined her.

"I admit it is a puzzle," he said at last. "But I'm not convinced there isn't a baby—a real baby—somewhere in the building, or perhaps next door." He had brought the bottle with him and topped up her glass. "Unless—I suppose there is a faint possibility that somewhere psychokinetic energy is being created, presumably by you—to project the sound of a child crying, but no, I don't think so. It is so unlikely as to be impossible. I suggest you put it out of your mind."

"I can't," Jo cried. "Can you imagine what it's like hearing little Will cry, knowing he's hungry, wanting to hold him? Wondering why, if I can't feed him, someone else doesn't? Someone who is there, in the past with him!"

"Jo, I did warn you," Sam said gently. "You should have stopped while you still could."

Jo stared at him. "You mean I can't stop now?" She snapped off a stem of honeysuckle. "No, of course I can't, you're right." Leaning on the balustrade, she sniffed at the delicate red and gold flower. "I tried to call Dr. Bennet but he's still away in the States. Sam, I've got to work this thing through, haven't I? I've got to get it out of my system. And the only way to do that is to go on with the story. Find out what happened next." She turned to face him. "Please, Sam, I want you to hypnotize me. I want you to regress me."

Sam was watching her closely. Thoughtfully he raised his glass and took a sip of wine. "I think that's a good idea, Jo," he said at last.

"You mean you will?" She had been prepared for a stand-up argument.

"Yes, I'll hypnotize you."

"When?"

"After lunch. If the mood seems right we'll have a go this afternoon."

To her surprise Jo wasn't nervous. She was relaxed in Sam's company, relieved not to be alone in the apartment anymore, and she enjoyed the lunch with him. Several times she found herself talking about Nick, as if she could not avoid the sound of his name, but each time she sensed Sam's disapproval and, not wanting to spoil the atmosphere between them, she changed the subject. They played music and drank the wine, and she lay back on the sofa, listening to the soft strains of the guitar.

169

She was almost asleep when she felt him sit down on the sofa beside her and gently take the empty wineglass from her hand.

"I think this is as good a moment as any to start, don't you?" he said. He raised his hand and lightly passed it over her face, closing her eyes as he began to talk.

She could feel herself drifting willingly under his spell. It was different from Carl Bennet. She could hear Sam's voice and she was aware of her surroundings, just as in Devonshire Place, but she could not move. She was conscious of him standing up and going over to the front door, where she heard him draw the bolt. Puzzled, she wanted to ask him why, but she could feel part of her mind detaching itself, roaming free, settling back into blackness. Suddenly she was afraid. She wanted to fight him but she could not move and she could not speak.

Sam sat beside her on the sofa. "No, Jo," he said softly. "There is nothing you can do about it, nothing at all. It never seems to have crossed your mind, Jo, that you might not be alone in your new incarnation, that others might have followed you. That old scores might have to be settled and old pains healed. In this life, Jo." He gazed down at her silently for several minutes. Then he raised his hands to her face again. "But for now, we'll meet in the past. You know your place there. You are still a young and obedient wife there, Jo, and you will do as I say. Now, you are going back . . . back to that previous existence, Jo, back to when you were Matilda, wife of William, Lord of Brecknock, Builth and Radnor, Hay, Upper Gwent and Gower, back to the time at Brecknock after Will's birth, back to the day when you must once again welcome your husband and lord into your bed."

170

16

The dining room in the hotel on the rue St. Honoré was beginning to empty. Nick was immersed in some sketches and Judy was bored. She got up and helped herself to some English newspapers discarded on the next table, then, pouring herself some coffee, she began to leaf through them.

"God! They're not even today's," she exclaimed in disgust after a moment.

Nick glanced up. "They get the new ones in the foyer. Here." He tossed some francs on the table. "Get me a *Times* while you're at it, will you?"

But Judy was staring down at the paper on the table in front of her, open-mouthed.

"So he went ahead and did it," she said softly. "He actually did it."

There was something in her voice that made Nick look up. Even upside-down he recognized Jo's photo.

"What the hell is that?" he said sharply. He snatched the paper from her.

"It's nothing, Nick. Nothing, don't bother to read it—"

She was suddenly afraid. After a week without a mention of her name, Jo's shadow had risen between them again. She stood up abruptly. "I'll get today's," she said, but he never heard her. He was staring down at yesterday's copy of the *Daily Mail*.

He read the article twice, then, glancing at his watch, he stood up, folded the paper under his arm, and strode toward the iron-gated elevator. He passed Judy in the foyer and never saw her.

Impatiently he allowed the elevator to carry him slowly up to his floor. He wrenched the doors open, then strode to their room. It was several minutes before the number in London was ringing. He sat impatiently on the bed, spreading the paper out beside him with his free hand, as he waited for someone to answer.

The tone rang on monotonously in Jo's empty apartment. Upstairs, Henry Chandler looked at his wife in exasperation. "Why doesn't she get

171

an answering machine if she's a journalist? If that phone doesn't stop ringing it'll wake that damn baby again."

"She's gone shopping," Sheila Chandler said slowly. "I saw her leave earlier."

"Did you see the kid?"

"No, she was alone."

They looked at each other significantly.

Downstairs the faint sound of the phone stopped. Seconds later they both heard the thin protesting wail.

"Who are you calling?" Judy threw back the bedroom door and stood in the doorway, staring at Nick.

"Jo."

"Why?"

Nick put the receiver down with a sigh. "I want to know why she did such an idiotic thing as to give that story to Pete Leveson. She'll lose every bit of credibility she has as a serious journalist if she allows crap like this to be published. Look at this. 'I was married to a violent, vicious man, but my heart belonged to the handsome earl who had escorted me through the mountains, protecting me from the wolves with his drawn sword.' Dear God!"

He picked up the phone and rattled it again. *"Mademoiselle? Essayez le numéro à Londres encore une fois, s'il vous plaît."*

"It is nothing to do with you, Nick," Judy said softly. "Jo has done it, for whatever reason, and it can't be undone now."

She saw his knuckles whiten on the phone. *"Eh bien, merci. Essayez un autre numéro, je vous en prie, mademoiselle."*

"You're making a fool of yourself, Nick."

"Very probably." He tightened his mouth grimly as he slammed the phone down at last. "Sam's not there either. Look, look at this last bit. 'I shall not rest, Jo told me, until I have learned the whole story . . .' Even you, Judy, know enough now to have guessed that that is dangerous for her."

Judy turned away. "I don't expect she really meant it."

Nick stood up slowly and walked across to her, spinning her around by the shoulders. "You knew about this article, didn't you? Down there, in the dining room, you weren't surprised. You were triumphant." His eyes narrowed as he held her facing him. "So what do you know about all this?"

Judy stood quite still, staring up at his face. "You tell me something first, Nick Franklyn! Are you still in love with Jo? Because if you are, I shall bow out of your life now. Perhaps I could write an article or two myself. 'How my lover challenged a man eight hundred years old to a duel over another woman.' That's it, isn't it? You can't bear to think of her in his

172

arms, this Richard de Clare. You watched her, didn't you? Last week when you rushed off and left me, you went to Dr. Bennet's and watched her dreaming about making love to another man. You had to see it!"

She broke off with a little cry as Nick raised his hand and gave her a stinging slap across the face. The impact of it threw her against the wall and she stood there, her hand pressed to her cheek, her eyes brimming with tears. "You bastard—"

"That's right." His face was hard and very white. "I've warned you before, Judy. Leave Jo alone." He turned to the bed and picked up his portfolio. "I have a meeting to go to now. I suggest it might be better for both of us if you pack your stuff and clear out before I get back."

"Nick!" She threw herself at him and clung to his arm. "Nick, please, I'm sorry. I really am. I won't mention her again."

"I am going back to London tomorrow anyway, Judy. To Jo." Nick's face softened slightly as he saw her stricken expression.

"But she doesn't want you. She keeps telling you she doesn't want you."

"Whether she wants me or not, I want her." He spoke with enormous force, his eyes hardening.

Judy felt a sudden shiver. He was looking not at her but through her. She backed away from him. "I believe you're as crazy as she is," she whispered. "You can't force a woman to love you."

He stared at her, his attention fully on her again now. "Force her?" he echoed. "I won't have to force her." He laughed grimly. "I must go. Don't worry about your bill, I'll settle it. I'll see you soon, Judy." Gently he touched her cheek—still reddened from his slap—then he turned and left her alone.

Judy did not move. She stared around the room. The crumpled copy of the *Daily Mail* was still lying on the pillow where Nick had left it. She sat down, smoothing the page, and began to read slowly and carefully, taking in every word.

Sam was standing with his back to the window, his arms folded, listening as, hesitantly, Jo began to talk. Matilda had regained her strength slowly after the birth, but the day came at last when, accompanied by Sir Robert and four armed horsemen, she mounted for the first time the little bay mare William had given her. They rode out of the castle and turned northeast, following the rocky bed of the Honddu through a field silver and green with ripening oats and plunging almost at once into the woods.

"Llanddeu is up there, my lady." Sir Robert pointed up a hill to their left. "About three miles, I reckon. We'll go there when you're stronger if you like." But Matilda shook her head. Gerald had gone to St. David's now, confident he was to be its new bishop, and Llanddeu had lost its interest.

She was amazed to find how stiff she had become, but she gritted her teeth and pushed the bay into a gallop behind Sir Robert as they followed a well-worn track through the heavy, dusty woods. They had slowed again to a trot when suddenly Sir Robert pulled to a rearing halt in front of her and drew his sword. "Stop," he shouted. The four men with them closed around Matilda protectively at once, their swords raised and ready. She could feel herself shaking with fear, and the mare plunged nervously away from the horse next to her, sensing the danger. But, straining her eyes, she could see nothing in the heavy greenery all around them. She could hear nothing but the thudding of her own heart.

"What? What is it?" She looked around wildly.

"See, a rope." Sir Robert had dismounted. With one slash of his sword he severed a rope that had been tied across the track at the height of a man's neck as he rode on a horse. It fell, green-stained and invisible, into the grass at their feet.

"If we'd been going any faster or if I'd been distracted, it would have had us all off our horses." Sir Robert hit the undergrowth with the flat of his sword. "See, here. The rogues have gone. They were hiding behind these bushes. They must have fled before we arrived. They could be anywhere in the woods by now." A broken area of trampled greenery showed where several people had been crouching behind the thick holly.

"Were they robbers?" Matilda was still trying to soothe her horse, stroking the sweating neck, wishing she herself weren't shaking quite so violently. She knew it was as much exhaustion as fear, but nevertheless she felt weak and frightened.

Sir Robert nodded silently. He had stopped to pick up the rope and was coiling it over his arm. "Outlaws of some kind, I'll be bound. I'll have a word with Sir William. I doubt if the Welsh would set up a trick like that if they were after reprisals. No one knew which way we were coming." He swung the rope over his saddle and remounted.

Matilda noticed he didn't sheathe his sword.

"Reprisals?" Her heart began to hammer again at the word.

"That's right. They're bound to come some time." He turned his horse. "We'll go straight back, my lady, with your permission. I was a fool to come out with so few men. In future when you ride, I will see to it that you have a full escort."

She followed, relieved to be cutting short the ride. The thought of Welsh reprisals had become remote in the months at Brecknock, distracted as she had been by the baby and by William's arrival with all his men. The Welsh she had met in the county of Brycheiniog were friendly toward her. None had seemed to bear any grudge. She shivered. Outlaws. They must have been outlaws of some kind, bent on robbery. She refused to let herself believe that they were men from Gwent.

Nevertheless, it was a relief to be back inside the castle. Although William sent search parties out to hunt for the men who had set up the rope, no trace of them was ever found. They had melted into the forest as silently and efficiently as if they had never been.

"That was foolish, to ride so far the first time out after the baby," Sam said softly. He had seated himself next to Jo again. "But if you are well enough to ride, you are well enough to resume your wifely duties."

Jo drew in her breath sharply. "It is too soon," she whispered.

"No," Sam said, "it is the right time. Look at me, my lady. Open your eyes and look at me."

Jo had been staring toward the far corner of the room. Now, slowly, she turned to him and her eyes focused on his face. He held her gaze unwaveringly. "I am your husband," he said. "You do recognize me, don't you, Matilde"—he pronounced her name lightly, in the French manner—"I am your husband. Come to claim you."

"Please. No!" Jo edged away from him. "My lord, I told you, it is too soon."

Sam smiled. He put his hand out and caught her chin, forcing her face to his. Then he bent over her and kissed her on the lips. She went completely rigid, but she did not struggle. Sitting up, he looked down at her and saw her eyes were closed. "Look at me," he said threateningly. "Look at me!"

Her eyes flew open. They were scornful and cold.

Sam felt a sudden surge of anger flow through him. Oh, yes, that had been the way she always looked at William. So superior, so dismissive, so beautiful and remote that her disdain had unmanned him, but not this time. This time he had absolute control of her body and her mind.

He levered himself off the sofa and stood looking down at her, forcing himself to be calm. She was watching him docilely enough, her eyes still mocking, but he thought he could see fear as well, hidden, but there, as she stared at her husband and waited.

He smiled grimly. "Stand up, Matilde," he said slowly.

Hesitantly she obeyed him and stood quite still. He looked at her for a moment, then he turned to the tape deck in the corner. From his pocket he produced a cassette, which he slotted into the machine. He switched it on and listened as the first strains of an unaccompanied flute began to play in the room, then he sat down on the chair facing Jo. She had not moved. Her head was held at a defiant angle, her eyes watching him with cool disdain as he sat back and folded his arms.

"Now, my lady," he said softly. "I want you to show me some wifely obedience."

Matilda stared at her husband in horror. Behind him the blind flute player was sitting cross-legged on the floor of the window embrasure. She could hear the everyday noises of the castle all around them; any second someone would walk into the solar. She heard feet pattering down the spiral stairs in the corner and the swish of skirts on the stone. They hesitated then ran on down toward the lower floors, the sound dying away into the distance.

"Take off your mantle and gown, wife." He repeated his order.

She glanced at the musician who played on as if he had heard nothing. "My lord, I can't—I need my maid. Please, this can wait until nightfall—"

"It cannot wait until nightfall." His eyes narrowed and she could see the vein beginning to throb in his neck. He drew the ornately decorated dagger from his girdle and tested the blade gently against his thumb. "If the fastenings of your gown defeat you, I shall cut them for you."

She swallowed. She had only to call for a servant, to scream, to turn and run. He could not force her, not here. Not now. Yet something held her. She could not tear her eyes from his. Obediently she felt herself unfasten her jeweled girdle and let it fall to the floor. Her scarlet surcoat followed it. She paused nervously. "My lord, not here, I beg you—"

"Here, Matilda." She felt his hands on her head, slipping off the gauze headdress, allowing her hair to fall loose over her shoulders, then he was unlacing her gown, pushing it down so that it too fell to the floor. She was left clad only in her shift. She shivered violently in spite of the warmth of the early-autumn afternoon.

Behind her the flute player shifted his position slightly as the trembling notes of his tune died away. There was a long silence, then, unbidden, he began to play again.

"Take it off." William stood back and folded his arms.

Matilda crossed her hands on her breast, clutching the embroidered neck of her shift. "Would you have me stand naked before the servants and before your men?" Her eyes blazed suddenly, her fear eclipsed by a wave of scorn and fury. She dodged away from him but he was too quick for her. He caught her wrist. "I'll have you stand naked at the whipping post, my lady, before the whole world, if you defy me," he said evenly. He tore the flimsy shift from her body, tossing it to the rush-strewn floor. Panic-stricken, she raised her hands toward his face, clawing at him frantically, and beneath her nails a bloody welt opened down his cheek. With a curse he caught her by the hair, jerking her head back as greedily he seized her mouth with his own, his hands catching hers and holding them still as she struggled frantically to escape him. Behind them the flute player played on.

William was breathing heavily, sweat pouring from his face, and with a shudder she stood still, sensing suddenly that part of his excitement came from the knowledge that she was afraid. Raising her chin slightly, she stared at him disdainfully. He released her wrists immediately and she took a step back, proud in her nakedness, feeling his eyes on her body that only weeks before had been swollen and misshapen, but now had slimmed back, with the resilience of youth, to a lithe tautness. Only the fullness of her breasts betrayed the recent childbirth, and as she moved her head the heavy curtain of her hair swung forward to hide them from him. He licked his lips and slowly he began to remove his mantle.

Once again she could hear steps on the spiral stairs at the corner of the chamber. They were coming closer. She could hear knocking—a loud insistent banging at a door. Near them someone was shouting. She ignored the sound, her eyes on her husband's face, a flicker of mocking amusement showing in her expression as she saw him glance over his shoulder toward the rounded arch covered with a curtain that led toward the stairs. Abruptly he threw his mantle around her shoulders.

"So," he breathed. "We are interrupted after all, but only for a while. You will forget this little incident until we have another opportunity to be alone, do you hear me?" He drew her to him, his hands locked in the embroidered border of his mantle, her body pressed against his, his eyes fixed on hers. "You will remember nothing about it, nothing at all, but when I order you to come to me again, you will come, Jo, do you hear me? You will come."

"Jo!" Nick was banging on the door again. He tried the key a second time and cursed. "Jo? I know you're in there. Open the door!"

Outside the apartment upstairs a face appeared, peering over the winding bannisters. "She's in there all right. I saw her earlier." Sheila Chandler came down a few steps. "It's Mr. Franklyn, isn't it?"

Nick gave her a brief smile. "She doesn't seem to be hearing me."

"Perhaps she's asleep. What with the baby keeping her awake and everything."

"Baby?" Nick stared up at her. He frowned with a sudden shiver of apprehension, mechanically taking in the immaculate wave of the woman's hair and her elegantly cut silk shirt, then he turned back to the door and thumped on it with his fist. "Jo, if you don't open this door I'm going to break it down!" His voice echoed up and down the silent stairwell and above him Sheila Chandler's eyes rounded. Silently her husband came to stand beside her, staring down.

When the door was unbolted at last they both craned forward. Only Sheila saw that it was opened by a man.

"Sam?" Nick stared at his brother. "What the hell is going on? Where's Jo?"

Sam stood back to let him in. He closed the door, and as he did so Nick caught sight of a long raw scratch on his brother's face. Sam was in shirt sleeves—two buttons from the front of the shirt were missing.

"What the hell has been going on here?" Nick repeated as he thrust Sam out of his way and strode into the living room. It was empty. From the stereo the lonely, monotonous sound of a flute wove a pattern into the silence.

"She went into some kind of spontaneous regression." Sam was leaning against the wall, watching his brother closely. "She asked me to come over after she'd been having a series of nightmares about the baby—"

"The woman upstairs talked about a baby." Nick frowned.

"That is the strange part." Sam threw himself down on the sofa. "Apparently they've heard it wailing. Assuming the noises do come from this apartment, I can only put forward the hypothesis that the sounds come from Jo herself."

"You mean *she's* crying?"

"Either that or the sounds are being created by the strength of her emotions. You've heard of poltergeists! Noises created by energy charges within an individual." Sam wiped his face with a handkerchief. Noticing the blood on it, he frowned. "She . . . she flew at me when I tried to restrain her," he said quietly, dabbing at the scratch. "No, don't worry. She's all right now. She's asleep."

Nick gave him a long, hard look. Then he strode down the hall toward the bedroom. Jo lay on the bed wearing her bathrobe, her hair loose around her shoulders.

"Jo—" Nick sat down beside her and took her hands gently in his. "Jo?"

"Don't touch her." Sam had followed him. His voice was sharp. "I was about to awaken her when you started trying to break the door down. May I suggest you go and pour us all a drink while I sort things out in here?"

Nick's eyes narrowed. "I'd rather stay."

"I am sure Jo would prefer it if you did not. She would be extremely embarrassed to think you had seen her like this." Sam walked to the bedroom door and held it open for him. "Wait next door, please. This won't take long."

Nick hesitated, then with a shrug he walked through to the living room. He reached for the bottle of Scotch. It was empty, and he began to rummage in the cabinet, unconsciously straining his ears for the sound of voices. In the distance he could hear Sam's gently monotonous tones, and on impulse he tiptoed back toward the bedroom door and listened.

"Can you hear me, Jo?" Sam was standing over her now, looking down. "When you wake up you will remember nothing of what happened while you were hypnotized today, do you understand? You will remember that you asked me to help you, that is all. You will awaken calm and happy, but you will remember that next time I wish to hypnotize you, for whatever reason, you will agree. You will hear my voice and you will obey me. Do you understand me, Jo?"

Nick pushed open the door. "What the hell are you saying to her, Sam?"

178

Sam did not look around. "Do you understand me, Jo?" he repeated. "Now, when I count three you will wake. One. Two. Three."

On the bed Jo lay quite still, then slowly she opened her eyes. She looked around her, completely dazed, her gaze going past Sam to Nick.

"You haven't answered my question, Sam," Nick said furiously.

Sam smiled coldly. "Nor do I intend to. My methods of professional practice are none of your business." He sat down on the bed next to Jo. "How are you feeling now? You had another little fainting spell," he said.

"Fainting?" Jo hoisted herself up on her elbow. "I don't understand. What time is it?" She tried to sit up but Sam pushed her gently back against the pillows.

"Rest a minute, Jo. You'll be all right in a short time, I promise." He pushed the hair back from her face with a cool hand.

Jo was staring at him. "You!" she said suddenly. "You made me take my clothes off! You stood and watched me while that man was playing the flute. You said he was blind, but he wasn't, he was watching too—"

A frown crossed Sam's face. "You've been dreaming, Jo," he said. There was an edge to his voice.

"Oh, no, I remember clearly. You ordered me to take off my clothes." Her voice shook. "You had given orders that no one come in, hadn't you? I expect everyone in the castle knew what you had planned for me. Did that make you feel big, my lord? Did it? Is that how you get your pleasure?"

Jo scrambled across the bed away from him and stood up. She tightened the belt of the bathrobe. "What a shame that someone came!"

"Dear God, she's still in the past," Nick murmured. "Sam, it's happened to her again. For God's sake, wake her up properly!"

"Jo?" Sam ignored him. "Jo, calm down. Don't you recognize me?"

"Of course I recognize you!" She pushed her hair back off her face. "You're—" She stopped short, groping for a name. A second later she put her face in her hands, shaking her head from side to side. "You're not William," she whispered between her fingers. "You're not William, you're not . . . you're not."

Sam caught her wrists and pulled her hands away from her face. "Who am I, Jo?" he said. His eyes held hers.

"Sam," she whispered. "You're Sam."

"And who is this with me?" He was still holding her wrists.

"Nick." Her reply was scarcely audible.

He released her. "Fine. I suggest we all have a cup of coffee. Nick, rather than snooping in here, perhaps you could do that much for us?" He rounded on his brother harshly as Jo walked slowly over to her mirror and stood before it, staring at her face. Numbly she picked up her comb and began to draw it through her hair.

With a shrug Nick went into the kitchen. His hands were shaking as he picked up the kettle and held it under the tap.

Behind him, he did not see Sam walk swiftly down the hall to the living room, where he slipped the cassette into his pocket and then picked up Jo's dress and her bra and panties from the carpet and stuffed them behind a cushion on the sofa. When Nick appeared he was standing at the open French window staring out across the square.

"How is she?" Nick slid the tray onto the low table.

"Confused and disoriented." Sam did not turn around. "Give her a little time and she'll be fine."

"She needs help, Sam. If this is going to happen spontaneously, for God's sake! She needs psychiatric help."

"You seem to forget, Nick, that that is what I'm here for," Sam said, turning at last to look at him. "I warned you both what might happen if she got involved in this. Now all I can do is help. And first I want to see to it she doesn't go near that quack Bennet again."

"He's in the States."

"Good." Sam smiled enigmatically. "Long may he remain there." He raised an eyebrow. "You haven't told me, incidentally, what you are doing here. I thought you were in Paris until the weekend."

"I changed my mind. That was a pretty damn fool trick to play, sending Judy after me. What was the idea exactly?"

Sam sat down. "It was her idea. I just gave her the name of the hotel. Where is she now?"

Nick shrugged. "I told her to get lost."

"I see." Sam's gaze narrowed. "And you thought Jo would be interested to hear all this?"

"I don't give a damn if she's interested or not. I was worried about her. I saw that article Pete Leveson wrote and I thought she must be going out of her mind to give him the story. You have seen it, I suppose?"

"I've seen it. And she didn't give, Nick. He took." Sam stretched his legs out in front of him slowly. "I must say I think it was singularly naive of her to talk to him at all, but she's not herself these days, as we can all see. I want you to leave her alone, Nick." He sat forward suddenly. "Do you understand me? I want you to keep away from her. She can't cope with any more hassle."

"I don't think that's for you to say, Sam." Behind them, Jo had appeared silently in the doorway. She was wearing jeans and a deep-red silk shirt, unbuttoned at the throat. Her face was still very white.

Sam climbed to his feet.

She looked from one to the other. "I keep getting the feeling you two are trying to run my life for me," she said. "I'm very grateful and all that, but I don't need it."

"You do need help, Jo." Sam's voice was gentle. "And I think you realize it. That was why you called me this morning."

Jo bit her lip. "I wanted someone to talk to. But full-scale analysis, no."

Sam grinned back amiably. "You couldn't afford me, love, not for full-scale analysis! But seriously, I do want to help you. I have to go home tomorrow. I'm giving a lecture on Friday and another on Monday at a postgraduate conference, but after that I can come back, and I want you to agree to see me then, just to talk things through."

She frowned. "I won't need to, Sam. Really."

"If you really don't need to, we'll forget it, but if you have any more dreams, any more crying babies, then you must call me. Promise?"

Jo sighed. "All right. I promise."

"I'll give you my number in Edinburgh so that you can reach me there as well. And I don't want you to go back to see Bennet. He's away anyway at the moment, I gather, but he's not competent to help you, Jo. He doesn't know how to cope with the reactions he's getting from you and, more to the point, neither do you. I know you'll do the sensible thing."

Jo grinned. "You're the first person who has ever said that to me," she said. She reached forward and kissed him on the cheek, then she frowned. "What is that awful mark on your face?"

Sam glanced at Nick. "I scratched it on some wire," he said quickly. "Don't worry. I'll live. And now, I must go and get on with some packing. I'll give you a lift back to the apartment, Nick, shall I? I've got your car. It's parked around the corner."

"Then I'll have the keys." Nick held out his hand. "Perhaps you'd grab a taxi, Sam, if you don't mind. I'll come on later. I want to talk to Jo."

"It will be easier if we drive back together." Sam's tone was insistent.

Stubbornly Nick shook his head. "I'll be along later."

"Jo—" Sam appealed to her. "You're tired. You don't want Nick here."

"That's all right, Sam, thanks. But I do want to talk to Nick, as it happens." Jo smiled almost apologetically. She stood on tiptoe and kissed him again. "You've been very sweet, Sam. Thanks for coming."

Nick closed the door behind his brother thankfully and stood for a moment staring at it. Mortice, Yale lock, chain and bolt. Why the bolt, in broad daylight when Sam was here? He shot it experimentally.

"What are you doing?" Jo was behind him; she looked apprehensive.

"I was wondering why Sam found it necessary to bolt the door. Unless it was you, of course?" He eyed her thoughtfully.

"I never bolt the door. What are you talking about?"

The particular shade of burgundy silk she was wearing suited her exceptionally well. His eyes traveled to her breasts, outlined beneath the low-buttoned blouse. They seemed more prominent than usual. She was looking very beautiful. "Then Sam must have done it," he said. "Did you ask him to hypnotize you, Jo?" He moved away from the door and picked up his empty cup. He stared at it absently.

She nodded. "I heard the baby crying again and Carl Bennet wasn't there and I didn't know what to do, so I called Sam. He was marvelous, Nick."

Nick put down the cup. "He is pretty good, so I've heard," he said cryptically.

Jo smiled. "You heard right." She raised an eyebrow. "So. How was France? I gather you had company while you were there."

"I thought Sam might just find it necessary to tell you she had come after me," Nick said cynically. "It was the end of us, if it's of any interest. As far as I know, she's still there." He glanced at her. "Jo—"

"The answer is no, Nick."

His face hardened.

She walked out onto the balcony and stood there for a moment with her back to him. Then she turned. "Nick, do you believe in reincarnation now, after what's happened?"

"No. I do not."

"Then what do you think is happening to me?"

"I think you are the victim of your own imagination. No more than that."

"You don't think it is possible that everyone lives again? You don't believe that we might have known each other before, when I was Matilda—"

"No, I don't." Nick joined her on the balcony. He put his hands on her shoulders. "Don't try and talk yourself into this, Jo. It's madness."

"It was when I fainted at Ceecliff's," she went on as if she hadn't heard him. "As I was coming around I saw someone else's face there, in the room. Someone who was you and wasn't you. Someone beside you—"

"Please, Jo. I don't want to hear any more—"

"That person tried to strangle me. I couldn't breathe. That was why I fainted. I thought it was you, but it wasn't. His eyes were different and he had a beard . . ." She pushed past him and went back inside. "Nick, you were part of that life. And it's catching up with me! The people from the past are following me into the present! They are here, in the shadows!" Her voice was rising. "William, my husband William was here, in my bedroom, and the baby, my baby, little Will. Nick, I started producing milk to feed him! That's why I called Sam. I didn't know what to do!" Tears began to roll down her cheeks. "And the man at Ceecliff's house reached out of the past to try and kill me, Nick. None of it was my imagination. They were real!"

Nick was staring at her in horror. "Jo, for God's sake, get a grip on yourself. You're talking rubbish."

"Am I?" She took a deep breath. "How come the Chandlers upstairs heard the baby crying?"

"You should be very glad they did, Jo. That proves absolutely, beyond a shadow of a doubt, that it was a real baby they heard." Nick sat down, still watching her. "You need to get away, Jo. Right away for a few days. Listen. I'm not due back in the office until Monday—"

"I know what you're going to say." She gave him a brittle smile. "Thanks, but no."

"You don't know what I'm going to say. I was going to suggest that you come down to the boat with me—"

"Nick! Don't you understand? I'm afraid of you! Afraid of that other person—"

"There *is* no other person, Jo!" Nick caught her arms. "You've been cooped up too long in this apartment with this story all around you—tapes, books, nightmares. You've got to get away before it sends you really insane. I'm going to take *Moon Dancer* back to Lymington—I never got around to it when I went to see Ma last. Come with me. You know you've always loved the boat, and the sea air will help get things straight for you. It always did, remember?"

Jo hesitated. He was right. She had to get away. "No strings? Separate bunks?"

Nick grinned. "Scout's honor. Why don't I ring the marina and ask them to get her ready? We'll call in at Lynwood House and pick up my gear and we could be at Shoreham in a couple of hours or so."

Jo sighed. She stared around the room, thinking of the night before, sitting all alone, waiting to hear if the baby was going to start crying again. Abruptly she capitulated. "Okay, I'll come. Thanks."

He smiled. "Pack a bag while I phone." He watched as she moved toward the bedroom, seeing already a new lightness about her. He made the call and then threw himself back on the cushions of the sofa. They slipped a little and a bundle of rolled-up clothing fell onto the floor. He picked them up and shook the garments out, puzzled, then his face darkened.

Standing up he strode toward the bedroom. "Did you do a striptease for Sam as the hors d'oeuvre or the encore?" he asked, dropping her panties on the bed.

She stared at them blankly. "I don't understand."

"You don't understand?" Nick threw her dress and bra down as well. "How strange. I should have thought it was obvious. It is no doubt part of that precious professional relationship Sam is so keen to preserve. He takes off your clothes perhaps to take your pulse, then hides them under the pillow for tidiness' sake! Or was it because I arrived unexpectedly? Not that it's any of my business, of course."

"No, it isn't any of your business!" Jo flared angrily. She picked up her dress and shook out the creases. She felt suddenly very sick. "I must have left them there earlier. I don't know . . . perhaps last night. I felt so strange last night. I was drinking, and I took the last of the pills—"

"Jo, for God's sake!"

"There is nothing between Sam and me, Nick. Nothing. If it's any of your business." Her eyes flashed. "I'm not so sure this boat thing is such a good idea after all!"

"We're going, Jo." Nick picked up her bag. "Forget Sam for now. We'll talk about him later. Get a jacket. It might be cold on the water."

She hesitated. "Nick, this is stupid. We can't do it. To go away together would be crazy."

"Then it's a kind of craziness we both need." His tone was becoming threatening. "I'm prepared to carry you to that car, Jo."

She was too tired to argue anymore. She swallowed the automatic flare-up of rebellion and followed him downstairs, thankful only when the front door was closed without her hearing again the echoing wail of baby William's hungry cries.

Two and a half hours later, Jo clutched Nick's arm. "Nick, stop! Go back!"

The Porsche screamed to a standstill on the dusty road. "For God's sake, what's wrong?"

"That signpost! Did you see it?"

"Jo, you could have caused an accident. Christ! What is wrong with you? What signpost?"

He turned in his seat and reversed up the empty road, past the narrow turning to which Jo had pointed.

"There." She was pale and excited. "Look. It points to Bramber!"

"So?" Nick glanced in the rearview mirror and waved a truck past, then he pulled the car onto the grass shoulder. "What's so special about Bramber, suddenly?"

"It was William's home. It was where I went after I was married!"

Nick's hand tightened on the wheel. "After Matilda was married, I suppose you mean?"

"That's what I said. Oh, Nick, can we go there? Please?"

A car slowed behind them, hooted and overtook, the driver gesturing rudely as he disappeared around the curve of the road.

"Jo, we've come to forget all that."

"Oh, please, Nick. I'll never rest until I've been there now. Just for a few minutes. It's research for the article, among other things. I can see how much it's changed. Nick, don't you see? I'll be able to compare. It might prove that everything has been in my imagination—" Sadness showed in her eyes suddenly. "If I recognize nothing at all, at least we'll know then. The Downs can't have changed all that much, or the river. Please, Nick?"

184

With a sigh Nick engaged gear. He turned up the narrow road, glancing at the countryside around them. "We've been around here half a hundred times before, Jo. Every time we've left the boat at Shoreham we've explored the Downs to find pubs and restaurants—"

"But we've never turned off here." She was peering through the windshield, her hand on the dash. "I don't recognize anything, Nick. Not the countryside, the Downs are so naked—so small." He could hear the disappointment in her voice.

"They are the same as they were the last time you and I came down to the boat," he said gently. "Look—" He slowed the car. "It says 'To the Castle.' Shall I turn up there?"

She nodded. Her mouth had gone dry.

Nick swung the car up the steep lane between two small modern flint turrets and into a muddy parking lot. Above them rose a wooded hill with a squat little church nestling into its side. Jo pushed the car door open and stood up, her eyes fixed on the church. Nick hadn't moved. He was leaning across, watching her.

She looked down at him unhappily. "Nick, I have to do this alone. Do you mind?"

"Are you sure?"

She nodded.

"And you'll be all right?"

She looked around. "I'll be all right. Go and find one of those pubs you were talking about. Come back in an hour." She pushed the door shut.

Nick watched her walk toward the church. Only when she had disappeared inside did he turn the car and drive back down the lane.

Jo opened the door into the nave and stared around. The church was completely empty. She stepped inside, pulling the door shut behind her, her eyes on the huge arch of pale stone that spanned the roof before the altar. In her hand was a copy of the little tenpenny guide. This was William's chapel—and before him the chapel of his father, and his grandfather. It had been dedicated, the guidebook said, in the year 1073.

Slowly she walked toward the altar. If it were anywhere, his ghost would be there, in the very walls where he had knelt and prayed. She felt the skin on the back of her neck prickle as she stood staring up at the simple wooden cross with the pale ochre curtain behind it. No lighted candles, no incense. The bell was silent. But there was a sense of prayer. A presence.

I should be praying for their souls, she thought. Their souls—our souls —which are not at rest. With a shiver of something like defiance she made the sign of the cross and knelt before the altar, but the prayers would not come. The faith and burning trust that Matilda had felt before the twelfth-century statue of the Virgin were not for the twentieth-century Jo Clifford, kneeling in her shirt and jeans on the cold soap-scented flagstones. She felt nothing.

She was suddenly conscious of how quiet the church was, and how empty. Raising her eyes to the three small arched windows above the altar, she felt very cold. The air around her had become oppressive; the silence so intense she could hear it beating inside her head. Overwhelmed with panic, she scrambled to her feet and fled down the aisle, letting herself out of the door to stand in the vestibule, breathing deeply. Two women walked in past her and she felt them staring at her. They too brought a copy of the little guide, then they disappeared inside the church.

She stood in the graveyard shivering, feeling the warmth of the evening sun sinking through her shirt and into her bones. The air was glorious. It smelled of honeysuckle and woodsmoke from a bonfire below the churchyard, and of wild thyme from the Downs that ringed Bramber, bare and dusty beneath the hot evening sky. Immediately below her around the foot of the hill clustered the uneven, ancient roofs of the village of Bramber. Above, like a reproving finger, stood a huge pillar of masonry—part of the now-ruined castle.

Taking a deep breath, Jo left the churchyard and began to walk up the shallow steps cut in the side of the castle hill, across the overgrown depths of the defensive ditch and on toward the ruins.

The top of the hill was a broad flat area of mown grass in the center of which rose another steep-sided hillock, the motte on which the first William de Braose's wooden keep had been raised in the days of the Conqueror. It was shrouded now by trees, guarded by ancient yews. Very little of the castle remained. A few areas of crumbling wall around the perimeter of the hill where the only invaders were ash and sycamore, hung with the greenish, scented flowers of wild clematis. Only the one tall finger of wall remained rearing into the sky to remind the visitor of the castle's former glory.

Jo stood staring round her, lost. She could recognize nothing. Slowly she began to walk, seeing her shadow running before her across the grass, looking south toward the sea. Somewhere out there in the forest she had gone hawking with Richard and fallen at his feet to lie with her head on his lap. The forest had gone. Trees climbed the castle hill now, which then had been bare. Only the gap in the Downs was the same. The river was quite different too. So small. Surely then it had been vastly wider and there had been a jetty right there beneath the hill with ships and bustle and noise. The only noise now was the roar of traffic from the broad sweep of the fast road south, carried on the still evening air.

"Are you all right, Jo?" Nick had been following her silently.

She smiled at him. "The only thing I can recognize is the gap where the Downs aren't." She laughed wryly. "And the church. I think the tower was the same, though there used to be something on top then. And there was water all around here." She waved her arm. "I thought I said an hour?" She looked at him closely.

186

"I didn't like to leave you, so I parked in the lane at the bottom of the hill. I was afraid . . ." He hesitated. "Well, that something might happen."

"So was I." She put her hands on a fragment of wall, lightly touching the flints and mortar. "I should be able to feel something. I know I've been here before—how often have you heard people say that, joking? I do know it, yet I feel nothing. Why?"

"Perhaps you don't need to." He touched the wall himself. "Besides, it's quite possible that you had no particular affinity with Bramber. You probably have no reason to remember it. Matilda spent most of her time in Wales, didn't she?"

Jo nodded. "You're right. I expect all her memories are there." She sighed. "There was something, though—just for a minute, in the church." She shivered again. "William was so obsessive about religious observance. Do you know, his clerks had to be paid extra because of all the flowery bits of religious pomposity he insisted on adding to all his correspondence—" She stopped abruptly. "I must have read that somewhere—"

Nick took her arm. "Come on, Jo. Let's get on to Shoreham."

She shook off his hand. "You were right. I took my clothes off for Sam." She was staring into the distance. "I thought he was William. He ordered me to do it, Nick."

"Are you sure?" Nick stared at her grimly.

"I was in the solar of the castle at Brecknock and he stood in front of me and ordered me to undress while the blind man played the flute."

"William may have ordered you in your dream, Jo. Not Sam, surely. Sam wouldn't do such a thing." Nick swallowed uncomfortably.

"Why did I take my clothes off then?" she cried. "Why? If it was just for William I would have described it, not actually done it!"

He frowned. "You're making a terrible accusation, Jo."

"There was no tape of what happened," she whispered. "No one else there. Just Sam and me. And a pile of crumpled clothes." She shivered again, looking down at the shadow of the castle wall on the grass. "People can't be forced to do anything against their will while under hypnosis, I know that. But I was Matilda, and I thought he was my husband—"

"No, that's crap! You're talking complete, unmitigated crap." Nick turned away sharply. "I can quite believe that *you* might do anything. I've seen you, remember? But Sam? He'd be crazy to try something like that. Besides, nothing happened, did it? Your husband didn't rape you?" His voice was harsh.

Jo colored. "No, he didn't rape me, because someone—presumably you—came. But not before he had humiliated me and mocked me and set out to browbeat me like the sexist pig he was. He threatened to whip me, naked, before everyone in the castle, and no doubt if there had been time he would have had me on my knees before he put me on my back."

187

She began to walk swiftly down the way they had come.

Nick followed her. "Well, that proves it wasn't Sam at any rate," he said grimly. "I don't see him as kinky."

"Don't you?" Jo flashed back. "You surprise me."

Nick glanced at Jo from the phone. She was sitting in the corner of the pub nursing a Scotch and ginger. The noise level in the bar was fairly high. After taking out his diary, he found the number he was looking for and dialed it, leaning against the wall so that he could watch her while he waited, change in hand, for the call to connect. He was thinking about Sam.

Carl Bennet had come in from Gatwick Airport only three-quarters of an hour before. He cursed quietly as his wife came to get him out of the bath.

"Nick Franklyn? What the hell does Nick Franklyn want?" he muttered, wrapping a towel around his middle.

"I don't know, dear, but he's in a pay phone." Melissa Bennet smiled fondly at her husband as he tried to clean the steam off his glasses. "Get rid of him, darling, then come down and eat."

"Eat, she says." Bennet snorted as his wife ran down the stairs. "What the hell else does she think I did on that plane?" He picked up the receiver. "Yes?" he barked. His glasses had steamed over again.

Within seconds he was reaching for his notepad. "You are right. I should see her as soon as possible. I could fit her in tomorrow here." He listened again for a few minutes, frowning with irritation as Nick paused to slot more money into the phone.

"Very well, Mr. Franklyn. Monday at ten. I agree a break would do her good. But should this happen again—anything that worries you—I want you to promise to call me, here, at once."

He hung up at last and sat still, chewing the inside of his cheek. He sighed. Posthypnotic suggestion was always a dangerous field. To do as Nick Franklyn asked and wipe out the girl's memory of Matilda forever— that was a sad request. But the man was right. The past had to be controlled. It had to be relegated to where it belonged, otherwise it threatened to take Jo Clifford over and, in so doing, destroy her.

17

Sam opened the front door of the apartment to Judy that evening with a scowl. "I'm packing to go to Edinburgh," he said curtly. "I'm afraid I can't spare you much time."

"You can't?" Judy threw herself down on a chair. "That's good, because I don't require much time. You know of course that by now Nick and Jo are back together."

"I know they've gone down to the boat." He was watching her closely as he sat down opposite her.

"She doesn't want him. She is using him. You know that as well as I do, I expect."

Judy was wearing a pink flying suit that clashed violently with the bitter orange of the upholstery in Nick's apartment. She threw herself back in the chair, pushing her hands deep into her pockets. "I want Nick back and you want Jo."

She studied his face under her eyelashes, but his expression gave nothing away. "I think we should pool our resources, don't you?" she went on after a moment.

Sam got up and went to the drinks tray. "Assuming you are even remotely right," he said slowly, "exactly what resources, as you call them, do you have?" He poured out a stiff gin for each of them and began carefully to slice up a lemon.

Judy smiled. "Information. And a suggestion. You have a clinic or something in Edinburgh, don't you?"

Sam handed her a glass. "You mean I should whisk Jo off and hospitalize her somewhere, preferably behind locked doors, no doubt, thus leaving the field free for you?"

"Something like that, yes."

"I'm afraid I don't have a clinic, Judy. Nor am I attached to one." He took a sip from his glass reflectively and went to stand in his favorite position by the window. "Besides, Jo doesn't need hospitalizing."

"Yet."

He turned. "What does that mean exactly?"

189

"She's going crazy."

Laughing, he turned away again. "No, not crazy. A little confused, perhaps. A little frightened. But that is all." He picked the lemon out of his glass and sucked it. "There is no need for Jo to leave London to aid your plans." He paused. "I can drive a wedge between her and Nick that will put them farther than four hundred miles apart, I can assure you. I can make Jo hate him. I can make her afraid of him." He hadn't raised his voice, but Judy stared at him. His tone had been full of venom.

"You don't like your brother very much, do you?" she said cautiously. He grinned. "What makes you think that? I would be doing it for you!"

There was a long pause as they looked warily at one another. "I don't think so," Judy said at last. "I don't think you're even doing it because you like Jo. I think you're doing it to hurt Nick."

Sam laughed out loud. "Maybe. Maybe not. But you'll be there to pick up the pieces and kiss him better, won't you!"

Nick was sitting in the cockpit of the *Moon Dancer,* the tiller tucked beneath his arm, the sun full on his face as he squinted up at the spread of cream canvas.

"Happy?" He glanced at Jo, who was lying on the cabin roof. She was wearing white jeans, rolled up above the knees, and a striped bikini top. She rested her chin on her hands and grinned at him, her hair blowing across her face. "Happy. Better. Sane. Thanks!"

"And hungry?"

She nodded. "Are we going to stop at Bosham?"

"I don't see why not. Lunch at the Anchor Bleu and back out on the tide. Or we can spend the rest of the day there. Leave tomorrow. Whichever."

He adjusted the sheet a little, watching the mainsail wing out before the wind as the huge orange spinnaker flapped for a moment, then ballooned full once more.

Jo licked her lips, tasting the salt from the spray. "Let's wait and see." Already she could see the little pointed roof on the tower of Bosham church at the head of the creek. The tide was nearly high, brimming to the edge of the saltings, where a cloud of terns danced over the sparkling ripples. She turned to watch a huge ocean racer draw smoothly past them under power. "I haven't thanked you for last night," she said suddenly.

"For what? As I remember, nothing happened."

"Exactly." She pushed her sunglasses up into her hair. "You gave me space, Nick. It was what I needed. A super meal, enough Scotch to float the *Titanic,* and oblivion."

He laughed. "You certainly look a little less tense."

"I am. Once out of that apartment I seem to be able to think straight. I've behaved like an emotional idiot, allowing myself to be influenced by

190

all this business. Can you imagine? Jo Clifford, cool, businesslike, imper-turbable Jo Clifford, allowing herself to be so affected that my body re-acted psychosomatically. I shall write the story next week and get it out of my system completely, then I intend to forget all about it."

Nick glanced at her. "I'm glad to hear it," he said quietly. "Welcome back, Jo Clifford."

They anchored in Bosham creek and paddled ashore in the inflatable dinghy. After walking across the long lush grass of the quay meadow, they strolled past the church, breathing in the air heady with honeysuckle and roses, intoxicatingly sweet after the sharp salt of the sea wind, laughing as they dusted aside drifts of white petals from the hedge. They ate a ploughman's lunch sitting outside the pub in the sun, then walked on slowly through the village hand in hand, watching the tide lap up over the road and slowly draw back, leaving a shining trail of mud and weed. They hardly spoke at all as they walked along the point then back across the causeway to lie for a while side by side on the grass, dozing in the sun.

It was dark before they once more found their dinghy and paddled out beneath the stars to find *Moon Dancer* swinging at her buoy. Jo lay back against the rounded rubber sides of the little boat and stared up at the sky. "Do you know the names of all the constellations?" she asked lazily in the silence.

Nick looked up. "I used to. I'm always meaning to brush up on my astral navigation in case *Dancer* and I decide to head for deep water."

"Seriously?" She raised her head and looked at him.

"Why not? I can think of worse things to do for a year. Let Jim take over the business."

She bit her lip silently, watching as he came alongside the boat and reached up to knot the painter to a stanchion. They climbed on board and Nick opened the hatchway to the cabin. Jo did not follow him below. She stood for a moment quite still in the cockpit, staring across the darkly gleaming water. Then she shivered.

Nick had turned on the lights. "A nightcap before bed?" he called.

She did not answer. She was watching the line of orange lights strung like beads along the main A27 at the end of the creek in the distance. With the wind off the sea she couldn't hear the traffic. All she could hear was the occasional dull slap of water against the planking and a splash as a fish jumped in the darkness. Once more she looked up at the glitter of stars above them, with the broad swathe of the Milky Way like an untidy scarf of samite dragged across the midnight velvet of the sky.

A cold breath of air touched her cheek and she heard the immediate chatter of the halyards against the mast and the chuckle of rippling water beneath the bow. As the wind came around, *Moon Dancer* turned a little across the tide. Somewhere in the dark a nightbird screamed.

Jo climbed down into the cabin. Nick had put the kettle onto the little stove and was sitting on the bunk in the cramped cabin studying a chart of the Solent.

"Would you like to dig out a couple of mugs?" He didn't look up.

She didn't move for a moment then slowly she began to unbutton her shirt. She reached for the light switch and flipped it off.

Nick looked up startled. "Hey!" He stopped.

She took off her shirt and then her bra. He could see her breasts by the tiny light from the gas flame beneath the kettle. Holding his breath, he watched as she slipped off her jeans. Then she came and knelt in front of him.

"I'm frightened, Nick," she whispered. "It's not all over. It all happened, all those years ago, and the echo of it is still out there." She nodded toward the sky beyond the open hatch. "My destiny is somehow linked with a woman who lived and died eight hundred years before I was born. I can't turn my back on her."

Nick was slowly unbuttoning his own shirt. Gently he reached out and touched her breasts.

"I think you must, Jo. And I think you can."

He drew her between his knees, the angles of his face harsh in the blue light of the gas. "I'll make you forget. If it's the last thing I do, I shall make you forget."

"Are you sure you don't mind being hypnotized with Mr. Franklyn present?" Carl Bennet looked at Jo closely. Outwardly she was more relaxed than he had yet seen her. She was tanned and smiling, and yet he could sense a tension deep inside her that worried him.

She nodded as she sat down. "I want Nick here, and you do understand I don't want to be regressed anymore, Dr. Bennet. I want you to blot the whole thing out. Make me forget."

He nodded slowly. "It is the best thing, I think, my dear, although I must admit I am sorry in many ways. I had wanted an American colleague of mine to see you. I was talking to him in the States and he was hoping to fly over and see you himself—"

"No!" Jo clenched her fists. "I'm sorry too, in a lot of ways. I wanted to know what happened, but I can't take any more. I really can't." She looked at him earnestly. "It's affecting my health and my work and, for all I know, my sanity as well, so please, put a stop to it now."

Bennet nodded. "Very well. I agree. So let us begin. I should like you to close your eyes, Joanna, and relax." He was watching her hands, fisted in her lap. "Completely relax, beginning with your toes . . ."

"It takes longer each time," Sarah commented when Jo was at last in a deep trance.

Carl nodded. "She is becoming more and more afraid of what might happen and fighting it. I doubt if we could have progressed much further with her in this state of mind anyway."

Jo was lying back in her chair passively, her eyes closed, her hands hanging loosely over the armrests. Nick had seated himself unobtrusively in a corner of the room, his eyes fixed on Jo's face.

"Do you think this will work?" he asked softly.

Bennet shrugged. "It will if it is what she really wants."

He pulled up a chair next to Jo's and took her hand gently. "Joanna, can you hear me?"

Jo moved her head slightly. It might have been a nod.

"And you are relaxed and comfortable, still thinking about your weekend at sea?"

She smiled. This time the nod was more definite.

"Good. Now I want you to listen to me, Jo. It is twenty-five days since I first saw you here and you were first regressed. Since then the regressions have caused you much unhappiness and pain. I want you to forget them now, because you yourself want to forget them. When you wake up you will remember only that you had a few strange unimportant dreams and in time even that memory will fade. Do you understand me, Joanna?"

He paused, watching her closely. Jo was motionless but he could see the tension had returned to her hands. Abruptly she opened her eyes and looked at him. "I can't forget them," she said softly but distinctly.

Bennet swallowed. "You must forget, Joanna. Matilda is dead. Let her rest."

Jo smiled sadly. "She cannot rest. I cannot rest. . . . The story has to be told. . . ." Her gaze slipped past him. "Don't you see, I have to go back, to find out why it all happened. I have to remember. I have to live again that first meeting with John . . ."

"Stop her!" Nick had jumped to his feet. "Stop her! She's regressing on her own. Can't you see?" He grabbed Jo by the shoulders. "Jo! Wake up! For God's sake, wake up. Don't do it!"

"Leave her alone!" Bennet's peremptory order cut through his shout. Jo had gone rigid in her chair, looking straight through him.

"Jo." It was Bennet who took hold of her now, forcing her to turn her head toward him. "Jo, I want you to listen to me. . . ."

"Listen to me! Listen!" William de Braose was standing in front of her, furious. "You will say nothing to the king of what happened on our journey, nothing, do you understand me?"

For a moment Matilda felt the familiar surge of defiance. She met his gaze squarely, mocking his fear, then she looked away. If she fought with him now he would refuse to take her to the king's presence, and that, above all, she wanted. Meekly she lowered her eyes. "I shall say nothing, my lord," she whispered.

Gloucester was crowded. The encampment of the king's followers was laid out between the royal castle and the king's palace north of the city where King Henry habitually held his Christmas courts, a colorful array of tents with the leopards of the king's standard rippling from the flagstaff on the great central keep.

As they had arrived they had glimpsed the gleaming Severn River with the fleet of royal galleys moored in lines to the quays, but it was evening before they reached it and the castle, and the de Braose tents were raised next to those of their Marcher neighbors, who had come to attend the betrothal of the king's youngest son, John, to the Earl of Gloucester's daughter, Isabella; and it was even later before William, arrayed in his finest clothes, took Matilda at last to wait upon the king.

They found him in one of the upper rooms of the palace, seated at a large table on which were unrolled several maps. Beside him stood William Fitzherbert, Earl of Gloucester, who had arrived from his castle at Cardiff only two days previously, escorting his wife and small daughter, and several other nobles. Wine goblets had been used to hold maps flat as together they pored over the rough-drawn lines in the light of a cluster of great wax candles. There was no sign of Richard de Clare, she saw at a glance as she curtseyed low before the king, her heart thumping nervously. She had so desperately hoped he would be there.

"Glad to see you made it, Sir William." Henry acknowledged his bow. "My son is to be your neighbor in the Marches if our plans work out and we get a dispensation for this marriage." He peered at Matilda, half hidden behind her husband. "Your wife, Sir William? She can wait on young Isabella tomorrow. See if she can stop the wench blubbering." He snorted, holding his hand out to Matilda, who came forward eagerly.

"Your Grace," she murmured, bowing low. She glanced up at the heavy lined face and wiry red hair dusted with white, and found the king surveying her closely with brilliant blue eyes. She sensed at once the appreciation in his gaze and uncertainly drew closer to her husband.

"Your father, Sir Reginald, was a good man, my dear." The king held on to her hand. "The best steward I've had to attend me. And you've the look of him about you." He grinned at William. "Lucky man. She's a lovely girl."

Matilda blushed and stepped back as the king released his grasp, glancing nervously up at him from lowered eyes, but already his attention was on the maps before him once more. William was drawn immediately into the discussion around the table, so she moved quietly to the hearth, where the king's two great sable dogs lay basking in the heat, and she stood gazing down into the flames, wondering whether she should withdraw.

A moment later a door near her was flung open and a boy came striding into the room. He stopped short and looked her up and down arrogantly. "I saw you this afternoon with Sir William's party," he announced, coming to stand near her. His sandy hair was disarrayed and damp from riding in the rain. "Your mare was lame. You should have dismounted and led her."

"I beg your pardon." Matilda blushed hotly. "She was *not* lame."

"She was." He made a face at her. "I saw her. She was stumbling badly."

"She was tired." Matilda was furiously indignant. "There was nothing whatsoever wrong with her. I should never have ridden her if there was." She looked at the boy with dislike, noting his torn tunic and the scuffed shoes. "Anyway, it's got nothing to do with you. You've no business to tell me what I should or should not do." Her voice had risen slightly and she was conscious suddenly of a silence at the table behind her.

She turned, embarrassed, and met the king's cool gaze as he surveyed her, one eyebrow raised, over the maps.

"I hope my son is not being a nuisance, Lady de Braose," he commented quietly. And then, louder: "Come here, John."

Matilda gasped and, blushing, looked back at the prince, but already he had turned his back on her and gone to stand beside his father. From the safety of his position at the king's side he stuck out his tongue defiantly.

His father may not have seen, but one or two of the others at the table certainly had, including William. She saw him glare sharply at the boy, raising his hand as if he wanted to clout him, then, obviously remembering where he was, he too bent once again to the map before him. The king, suppressing with difficulty the amusement in his face, bowed slightly toward Matilda and once more lowered his own eyes. Her cheeks flaming, she turned back to the fire, wishing she could run from the room.

"He's an odious, precocious little prig," she burst out later to Elen when she was at last back in her tent. She turned so that the woman could begin to unlace her gown. "Heaven help that poor child Isabella if they are to be wed. The boy needs a thrashing."

"Hush!" Elen, frightened, glanced around. "You can't tell who might be listening out there, my lady. It would do no good to speak ill of the prince. No good at all."

"Prince!" Matilda snorted, beginning to tug at the braid in her hair. "He behaves more like a stableboy, except that he knows nothing about horses. Nothing!"

"He rides very well though, so I've heard." Elen gathered up the rich folds of material as her mistress stepped out of the dress. "He's as daring as any of his brothers, although they're so much older."

"Daring may be." Matilda was not to be placated. The hidden smiles of the men at the table still rankled, as did the look of amusement in the cold eyes of Henry himself. "He has no business to accuse me of riding a lame horse and making me look a fool in front of William and the king." There was a suspicious prickling behind her eyes, and she rubbed them fretfully with the back of her hand. "It's humiliating."

"Hush, my lady, he's only a boy." Elen opened a coffer and rummaged through the contents, looking for a comb. "Forget it. Think about tomorrow instead, and the lovely ceremonies and the banquet after. It'll all be so beautiful, indeed it will. I've never seen so many people and so much grandeur in all my life."

Matilda threw her a fond smile in spite of her vexation and sat down abruptly on one of the folding chairs so that Elen could reach to comb her hair. The pink cheeks of the Welsh girl glowed with excitement in the cold air of the dimly lit tent, and she remembered suddenly that for her too tomorrow was to be a great day. It was the first time she had attended court, and it was foolish to let the boy's deliberate taunts spoil what was to be such an exciting day—even if that boy was also the king's youngest son, the afterthought child of Henry and his formidable queen, Eleanor. And if the boy was to be the hero of that day, well, as William pointed out, it was probably the most exciting day he would ever have, except for the wedding itself, as the center of attention. What chance had he of shining in his own right with three splendid and magnificent brothers so much older than himself?

Dismissing Elen at last, she stepped wearily out of her shift, gasping at the cold, and leaving it lying where it fell, she climbed naked into the low bed and curled up beneath the heap of furs, listening to the shouts and noise of the vast encampment. It was nearly the hour of curfew when the fires would be damped, and it would grow colder still. She longed to call Elen into her bed for warmth, but she did not dare. Her husband's lust had been roused by the king's obvious admiration for her, and his crude fumblings and explicit leers at the banqueting board had made it clear that she was to expect him in her bed again that night.

Sure enough, the fires were barely doused when William came stamping into the tent, already beginning to unfasten his mantle.

"The moon's riding in a ring tonight," he exclaimed loudly, unclasping his cloak. "It'll blow before morning." He waved his esquire away and sat down to pull off his boots himself. "Well, my lady, you certainly impressed his grace the king." He chortled. "Not many stand up to that spoiled brat of his, I gather, and come away to tell the tale without having their hair pulled."

He saw his wife's eyes flash angrily in the light of the dim rushlight and stopped hastily. "I'm glad you're to attend Isabella tomorrow, my dear." He tried to appease her gruffly. "That's a great honor. You'll be right in the forefront of everything."

He pulled off the other boot with a grunt and threw it to the floor. "By Christ, Matilda, the king was in a fine mood today. He plans a great hunt the day after tomorrow and I for one shall be there with him. There's

196

good sport to be had in the forests around here at the moment. We shall have a fine day." He threw off the rest of his clothes and, blowing out the rushlight, turned toward the bed.

She gritted her teeth as he fell on her, and she felt his hands closing on her breasts, his knee forcing her thighs apart in the dark. "The king liked you, Matilda," he murmured, his face nuzzling into her neck. "He said I was a lucky man and he knows a thing or two about women, does King Henry. I'll have to watch you, won't I?" And he laughed exultantly as he thrust his way inside her.

The morning dawned frosty and bright, and the wisps of mist that had drifted upriver from the estuary were soon spirited away by the sun.

Matilda stood in the chilly tent and allowed Elen and Nell to dress her. First the pleated shift, then the undertunic of blue-green, and last, over it, her gown of scarlet cloth, embroidered at the hem with gold stitching and crystals. Around her slim hips the girls placed the beautifully worked girdle that was saved for state occasions. She bade Elen pin up her long braids under her veil and then she surveyed herself critically in the polished metal hand mirror Nell held for her. She saw herself pale, her auburn hair neat beneath the snowy veil, the gilt fillet that held it in place sparkling from a ray of sun which escaped the tent flap and strayed through the shadows to where she stood.

There was no hint on her face of the raw ache between her legs, nor the vicious marks on her breasts. She had been too proud to cry, but she had prayed for hours in the dark after William had at last fallen asleep that tonight he would be too drunk to leave the banqueting hall and that his grace the king would never look in her direction again.

The rooms occupied by the Countess of Gloucester were on the far side of the palace. Without William, who had left early to attend the king and the Earl of Gloucester for the signing of the formal betrothal documents, Matilda was lost. She stood in the center of the courtyard around which lay a huddle of buildings, surrounded by noise and bustle, feeling bewildered. Behind her, Elen stood wide-eyed, barely able in her excitement and nervousness to refrain from stretching out to catch her mistress's sleeve.

Eventually they had to find a boy to guide them to the countess's rooms. They followed him through a cluster of stone and wooden buildings, some new built, some already derelict, into the palace itself, and through dark passages and up stairs until at last they came to a heavy door hung with tapestry.

"She be in there, my lady." The boy jerked his thumb at the door. He sidled up to Elen and held out his hand. "I've brought 'e like 'e asked, mistress."

Elen looked at him, puzzled.

He wants you to give him a coin, Elen," Matilda commented abruptly, scarcely noticing as Elen, blushing, groped in the purse at her girdle for a quarter penny. She took a deep breath and, holding aside the hangings, opened the door.

The large solar behind it was full of women. Hawise Fitzherbert, Countess of Gloucester, large and florid, was surrounded by her tiring women, her voice, shrill with impatience and ill-humor, clearly floating above the subdued chatter around her. She turned as Matilda came in and, catching sight of her, raised her narrowly plucked eyebrows till they almost vanished into her hairline.

"Not another one. Has every woman in the country been sent to attend us?" She pursed her mouth sourly.

"The king, Lady Gloucester, asked me to attend your daughter today." Matilda, her cheeks burning, bobbed a small curtsey, conscious of the eyes that were all focused on her.

The woman snorted. "You and who else? Well, madam, and who might you be?"

"Matilda de Braose, Countess." Matilda took a deep breath, determined not to be put out.

"Never heard of you." The woman seemed determined to be ill-natured. She turned to take a brooch from an attendant and then paused as another lady stepped from the throng.

"Lady de Braose is the wife of Sir William, Countess, Lord of Brecknock in the middle March. It is a great honor that she should wait upon the little lady during her betrothal to Prince John." She spoke in a stage whisper, designed to be heard by everyone in the room, and Matilda saw the countess pause and frown, looking at her again, and she blessed her unknown champion.

She drew herself up. "Where is the Lady Isabella? May I offer her my greetings?"

The countess held herself upright, holding in her stomach as her gown was laced up, and then held out her arms for her girdle. "You can try," she said grudgingly. "She's sniveling in the garderobe."

With a swift glance at Elen, Matilda strode across the room. The women stepped back to let her pass and she could feel their eyes uncomfortably on her back, but her attention was fixed on the little side room from where she could hear the sound of heartbroken sobs.

In the corner, huddling on the floor beneath a rail of hanging clothes, a little girl was weeping as though her heart would break, clutching a rag doll. A large plump-faced nurse bent over her, coaxing, and behind, two maids hovered, clutching a selection of gowns and little mantles with which they were obviously hoping to dress her.

"What's the matter?" Matilda demanded, looking down at the child. She was horrified to see the little girl dirty and unkempt. Her hair was tangled with grass and there were dark smudges beneath her eyes.

198

"She tried to run away, madam, that's what's the matter." The nurse gave up coaxing and stood, her hands on her hips, looking down at the child in exasperation. "Here we are, with everyone nearly ready to go to the abbey, and the child refuses to dress. She says she wants none of the king's son. Imagine! How dare she, the little minx. You wait till her father gets wind of this. He'll take the strap to her buttocks until they're raw."

The little girl gave another sob and clutched her doll more tightly.

"Well, he won't get to hear of it," said Matilda quietly, trying resolutely to keep her temper with the insensitive woman. Her heart went out to the little girl. She had a sudden vivid picture of her own betrothal to William. She too had been a child, not much older than this one. She who had dreamed of a tall, radiant, chivalrous knight had been informed by her father with excitement of the great honor that had been done his family, that she had been chosen by the stocky, ill-tempered baron whose reputation even then was marred by cruelty and viciousness. Her first reaction too had been to run away. But then she sat down on her favorite spot on the hill and thought about her duty and, at heart a realist, about what chance she had of ever having a better offer of marriage. She had come home, apologized to her frightened mother, wheedled her angry father, and resigned herself to making the most of it, comforting herself with the thought that she was to be a great lady. But could she persuade this child to see the sense in that? This little girl whose real world was still peopled by dolls and puppies and her snow-white pony.

"Please, nurse, will you leave us for a while?" She turned and forced herself to give the agitated woman her most brilliant smile. "I'd like a little talk with Isabella."

The woman drew herself up to argue, but already Elen, who had followed close at her mistress's heels, was pushing her out, and the two protesting maids with her. Then she stood, her back to the doorway, panting.

"Silly women," she muttered. "Clucking like so many chickens, they are indeed. Poor *cariad bach.*"

Matilda knelt down in the rushes and held out her arms to the little girl. "Come here, Isabella, my love. Tell me what's wrong. Why are you so unhappy?"

Whether it was the sympathy in her voice, or the sight of a stranger, she couldn't tell, but Isabella, with another strangled sob, scrambled to her feet and rushed to her, throwing herself into Matilda's outstretched arms.

"There, there, child. There, there." Matilda rocked her gently for a while, touched by the feel of the tiny, frail body, so thin beneath the skimpy clothes. Then as the child's sobbing grew less, she pushed back the fair hair from her hot face and smiled gently at her. "Come on, sweeting, tell me what's wrong."

"I don't want to be betrothed." Isabella sniffed loudly. "I hate John. He's a bad, wicked boy. I don't want to be married to him, ever."

"Why, Isabella? Why not? Why do you think he's wicked?"

"He pulls the wings off sparrows." The ready tears spilled over again as the little girl buried her head in Matilda's shoulder. "He likes hurting things. He told me. And when I belong to him, he said he could hurt me. And he said he could make me cry."

"Christ blast that boy!" Matilda swore under her breath. She exchanged glances with Elen over the child's head. "Listen, Isabella. John only said that to tease. He would never hurt you. He couldn't. After mass in the abbey there will be a lovely party, and then you are to stay with your mother and father until you're grown up. John probably won't come near you again. And when you marry him, years and years from now, you'll be a princess. You'll be the most beautiful princess there ever was." She smiled down at the drawn, pale little face. "Come on, remember you're a great lady. Ladies must never be afraid." She dropped a kiss on the tangled hair. "Now, will you let your nurse comb you and wash you and get you ready?"

"But I saw him." The little girl was shaking still. "He pulled the wings till the bird screamed."

Matilda shivered. "I'll ask my husband to tell the king. John should be whipped for such cruelty."

"You promise?" Isabella rubbed her eyes with the back of her hand.

"I promise." Gently Matilda pushed her from her lap. "Now come on, there's not much time."

The nurse reappeared so swiftly it was obvious she had been listening outside the doorway. Half resentful of Matilda, half relieved that her charge had calmed down, she pushed her way to the child's side.

"Would you credit that boy," she muttered as she stripped the little girl and began rubbing the frail body with a cloth wrung out in a jug where the water had long since grown cold. "They sat there yesterday, side by side, when his grace the king brought them together, neat as two pins they were, both scrubbed and combed, and we saw John whispering to her. Then he took her by the hand and led her away. Lady Gloucester was that pleased, she was. Then the child comes racing in, screaming the place down. The earl was furious, *and* the king. Then young John came in all innocent. 'I don't know,' he says. 'I don't know what's making her cry.'" She pulled a clean shift over the little girl's head. Then the embroidered gown. Then she began to drag a brush through the delicate fair hair.

Outside in the solar the other women had been too preoccupied with the Countess of Gloucester's grumblings to pay much attention to what was going on in the garderobe, so when Matilda emerged, holding Isabella, now neat and clean and dry-eyed, by the hand, there was a moment's astonished silence.

"Well," her mother said at last. "About time too." Ignoring Matilda with calculated disdain, she went to take her daughter's hand. But Isabella snatched it away, clinging to Matilda and dodging behind her out of her mother's reach. Exasperated, the countess gave up without any further effort.

"Oh, for pity's sake, you go with the child if she cares for you so much," she snapped. "Stay with her and see she behaves. I want no more trouble."

Her heart beating with excitement, Matilda took Isabella's hand again and led the way out of the room. Outside she could hear the trumpet calls as the procession lined up to await the king.

St. Peter's Abbey was packed. They walked slowly up the nave between the lofty columns that vanished into smoky darkness high overhead, where the painted colors were still blackened and tarnished by the disastrous fire that had swept the church fifty years earlier. Matilda caught her breath with excitement and unconsciously clutched Isabella's hand even tighter. The abbey blazed with candles, and every light was reflected a dozen times in the finery of those who had crowded in to hear high mass. The air was giddy with incense.

The king was waiting for them in the choir with Prince John, splendidly dressed, beside him. With them was the tall figure of the king's justiciar, Ranulf Glanville, who supervised John's education, and the Earl of Gloucester, Isabella's father, with the bishops and clergy ranked on either side. The boy, John, stood quietly, his eyes resting on the tomb of Robert, Duke of Normandy. He looked as if butter wouldn't melt in his mouth. Never once did he raise his eyes to look at the trembling little girl who stood at his side as the blessing was pronounced. Nor did he look up as the choir burst into a joyful hymn of praise.

Once, though, he looked at Matilda. And she was surprised to see a direct challenge in his blue eyes. Amazed, she stared at him for a moment, not believing she had seen aright. The look had been so quickly veiled. I imagined it, she thought, bringing her attention sternly back to her charge and to the sacred mass, but somewhere a shadow had moved in the back of her mind, and she felt a flicker of warning.

The celebrations with endless hunting and feasting lasted several days, and then at last it was time once more to move on. Richard de Clare had not come after all, to Matilda's intense disappointment.

She had seen the king only twice since the banquet that followed the betrothal formalities and the mass in St. Peter's. On each occasion he was setting out in the cold dawn on a day's hunting, surrounded by his barons and knights, William among them.

Once Prince John was at his side and again she felt the boy's gaze on her. This time he was thoughtful, even calculating in his stare, and with a shiver she pulled her cloak around her and turned away to her tent. But not before she had seen that strange challenge again flickering in the depths of those cold blue eyes.

The next morning she was standing watching a ship being unloaded at the wharf, clutching her squirrel fur mantle around her against the icy wind from the Welsh mountains, when she heard her name called. She spun around. "Richard!" She let out a little cry of pleasure, hastily cut off as she glanced around her to see if anyone had heard. A few yards away Elen was bargaining with a packman in whose bundle she had spotted some bauble she wanted. "I had given up all hope of seeing you here!"

Richard glanced down at her. "How could I not come, knowing you would be here?" He was breathing deeply, trying to contain the emotions that threatened to overwhelm him as he stared at her, seeing her so much more beautiful, or so he thought, than when they had parted almost a year before. She had matured—turned from a coltish child into a lovely woman, her hair glossy beneath the fur hood, her cheeks whipped to color by the icy wind. He clenched his fist on the hilt of his sword.

"I hear you were delivered of a fine son, my lady," he said slowly at last. "My congratulations."

She smiled at him. She could think of nothing to say. Her heart was beating too quickly. She could hardly breathe. He had not touched her— not even kissed her glove—but she could feel his touch, feel the longing that stretched like a thong between them.

"There, my lady!" Elen returned triumphant with her purchase. "Shall we go on to the king's hall?" She glared at the tall, fair-haired knight with the chevrons on his surcoat who was staring with such naked longing at her mistress, and she shivered. There was danger in that look. "My lady." She pulled at Matilda's sleeve. "We should go on."

"I'll see you again?" Matilda could not take her eyes off Richard's face.

He nodded helplessly, half reaching out toward her with his hand. It fell back without touching her and, with a curt bow, he turned away.

All day Matilda waited to see him again, but he did not come. Nor was he to be seen at the high table in the king's great hall.

Disappointed and worn out with longing, she retired early, her head throbbing from the smoke and noise of the dinner, which had gone on for hours. She had unstopped a vial of poppy syrup and was mixing a little with some wine when she looked up and caught sight of a movement against the tent wall. Her heart leapt.

"Richard?" she breathed. But only silence answered her, and after a moment she turned away. It was her overwrought imagination. He would never dare come to her tent. She picked up the cup and sipped the tincture, feeling it run soothing through her veins, and as she slipped quietly out of her gown she had already begun to feel drowsy. She was too tired to call Elen or one of the maids. All she wanted was to sink into the bed and sleep the pain in her head away. Then suddenly she saw a shadow, clearly,

202

on the tent wall between the blowing hangings, silhouetted against a campfire outside. It paused and then moved silently toward the entrance flap. She caught her breath. That was not Richard. The shadow was too squat. Something about the stealth of the movement frightened her, and she sat up abruptly, pulling up the covers beneath her chin, holding her breath. There was a tiny *click*, like two stones being rubbed together, and then silence.

The shadow moved quickly to the entrance and paused again, then it shrank strangely and thickened as the prowler, whoever it was, stopped momentarily as though dropping something. Then it vanished.

Matilda sat for a moment, her heart in her mouth, wondering whether to call the guard. Then she slipped out of bed and, pulling the coverlet around her shoulders, tiptoed to the entrance of the tent and looked out. There was no one there. A fine starlit sky lit the dark encampment where here and there a damped fire glowed red beneath its turves. She caught her breath in the cold air, looking left and right and then glancing down at the ground, which was already white with icy dew.

A bundle lay at her feet. Puzzled, she bent and picked it up, still thinking of Richard. It was heavy and already the frosty night had worked its way into the rough cloth, leaving it stiff and frozen. She carried it into the tent and, lighting a candle from the rushlight that burned before the portable prie-dieu, examined it more closely. The material was tied with a leather thong.

Curious, she pulled at the knot, working at the tight leather until it came free. She unwrapped the sacking, then pulled out another bundle of cloth. It was multicolored, in the flickering light half gray, half scarlet. She unwrapped it.

Lying in the folds before her, heavy and stiff, were three severed hands. The scarlet of the cloth was the blood that had soaked through it, dyeing it into a gaudy, cheerful mockery of color. She gazed at them in horror for fully a minute, her eyes unconsciously taking in the details of the grimy nails, the whitened fingers, the beaten copper ring on one of the knuckles, unable to comprehend the full horror of what she saw, and then she turned, retching, and ran for the entrance to the tent.

"Someone come! Help me! Help me!"

Her screams echoed in the frosty air and within seconds the camp watch was mustering and a knight had ducked into the tent beside her, his face white beneath his chain-mail hood as he unsheathed his heavy sword. Horrified, he stared down at the tent floor, then helplessly he touched Matilda's arm.

"Hush, my lady, hush. There is no danger now. Look, my lady—your maids are here, and Sir William has been called." He pulled an embroidered length of tapestry from a table and threw it over the bloodstained bundle, hiding it from sight. But she could not stop screaming. It was as if something inside her head had snapped. She was outside herself, watching herself standing there, barefoot, wrapped in a fur cloak in the streaming light of the torch that one of the watchmen carried. But she could not stop screaming.

"Hush, Jo. Hush, there is no danger. It's all over. You're quite safe." Hands were shaking her and she could feel something cold on her face. Agitated voices surrounded her.
"Can't you do something, for God's sake—"
"Here, catch her hands. Hold her still."
She felt people clutching at her, struggling with her, holding her.
There was a prick in her arm—then she knew no more.

18

The room was small, shaded by a white Venetian blind against the sun. She blinked slowly, trying to clear away the fog in her mind. Her mouth tasted unpleasantly chemical.

"Jo?" A man was sitting by the bed. He stood up, bending over her.

"Nick?" Her tongue was so dry the word would not come.

"You're all right, Jo. Look, I've got a cup of tea here for you. Would you like a sip?" His voice was more gentle than she had ever heard it.

Jo rubbed her eyes. "Where is this? What happened?"

She managed to sit up, and drank a little from the cup Nick gave her. Her head was spinning.

"We are still at Dr. Bennet's, Jo. Do you remember? This is a recovery room. You've been asleep."

"Asleep? I thought . . . I thought he was going to hypnotize me again." She fell silent, leaning back against the pillows, discovering suddenly that there was a soft blanket over her legs. "He was going to see if he could make me forget," she repeated slowly.

"Has it worked?" Nick sat down on the chair beside the bed once more.

"I . . . I don't know." She pushed her hair off her face with both hands. "I feel so strange. I can't think straight. . . ." Through the blind she could see horizontal lines of brightness shimmering slightly, casting shadows on the cool olive of the walls around her. The room smelled of antiseptic. It was claustrophobically small.

Behind Nick the door opened quietly and Sarah peered in. She smiled with obvious relief as she saw Jo sitting up. "How are you feeling?"

"A bit peculiar." Jo managed to grin.

"Carl is very sorry but he is involved with his afternoon appointment now. He was wondering if you could both come back on Wednesday morning. It would probably be better anyway to leave things for a couple of days to see how you are feeling."

Jo frowned. "Afternoon appointment? I don't understand. What time is it?"

"It's teatime, Jo." Nick stood up. "You've been asleep for several hours. She'll be here on Wednesday," he said quietly, "I'll see to that."

"What do you mean, several hours?" Jo repeated in bewilderment as he closed the door behind Sarah and turned back to her. "What's happened? Did I faint again?"

"You got a bit upset and Dr. Bennet had to give you a shot of Valium to calm you down, that's all."

"Upset? Why was I upset?"

Nick gave the ghost of a grin. "I'm hardly going to tell you that, Jo. The idea was that you forget everything that has been worrying you. If the suggestion has worked, then it would be madness for me to tell you what happened, wouldn't it?"

It was ten past five before Nick finally paid off the taxi and followed Jo upstairs to her apartment. The phone was ringing as she opened the door.

"It's for you." She handed him the receiver with a weary grin. "The office."

She walked as always first to the French doors and threw them open, smelling the rich scent from the flowers on her balcony. It was strange how few of the balconies had flowers. In Germany or Switzerland they would all be a riot of tumbling color, but here in London hers stood out almost alone with its tubs and pots of pinks and geraniums, the honeysuckle, and the exotic passion flower that clambered around the stone balustrade. She smiled faintly. Nick had always teased her that she must be a country girl at heart because of her love of flowers.

She leaned on the balustrade. Her mind felt drugged. She could not focus her thoughts. Carl Bennet's face, and Sarah's, floated in her head, but there were others there too she could not grasp. Someone had talked about a horse being lame . . . she could remember being very angry about that . . . and then, later, there had been a hand with a ring on the finger, a hand with filthy nails . . .

"That was Jim." Nick came out onto the balcony behind her. "It appears Desco has turned down our presentation out of hand and is threatening to go over to the opposition. God damn it to hell! That was going to be one of the best promotions we've planned. I've only been away from the office ten days—lord knows how they've managed to get it wrong!" He made an effort at a grin. "Will you be okay on your own for a bit, Jo? I hate to leave you, but I think I've got to get over there to stop Jim cutting his throat!"

She nodded. "Nick, I'm sorry. It's my fault—you'd have gone back last week if it wasn't for me—"

"Jo—I should be able to leave them." He took a deep breath, trying to steady his anger. "Look, I'll be back for a late supper. We'll talk then.

Don't go out. Rest till I get back and we'll make do with a can of soup or something."

She followed him to the door and closed it behind him. She felt tired and hot and sticky and slightly sick, and she didn't want him to go.

She was lying on the sofa dressed only in her bathrobe with her eyes closed after a long cool bath when she remembered what had happened. One minute she was gazing vaguely across the room, wondering whether she had the energy to fetch herself a cup of coffee, the next she sat bolt upright. It was as if a curtain had lifted. As clearly as if he were speaking in the room she heard Carl Bennet's voice, "You will remember that you had a few strange, but unimportant dreams . . ."

"Gloucester . . ." she murmured. "But it wasn't a dream. It was at Gloucester that I met John. . . ."

It was nearly ten by the time Nick got back from Berkeley Street, and he was in a foul temper. "Jim has screwed the whole thing up," he said, flinging himself down in a chair. He looked exhausted. "I doubt if I can sort things out. If I can't I'm going to have to go to the States and stay there till I get another account as big as Desco, otherwise it's the end of Franklyn-Greerson. Jim just doesn't have a clue when it comes to fighting the big boys. He's completely naive!" He closed his eyes wearily.

"But I thought Mike Desmond was a friend of yours." Jo sat down beside him.

Nick shrugged. "This is business, not friendship. But I'll have a damn good go at getting it back before I give up entirely, you can be sure of that." He held out his hand to Jo. "Hell, I'm sorry, you don't want to hear about all this. How are you feeling? Has the headache gone?"

"Your posthypnotic suggestion didn't work," she replied bleakly. "I've remembered everything. Going to Gloucester, meeting Prince John—seeing Richard again."

Nick swore softly. "We'll have to try again, that's all." He shook his head. "I wonder if Sam is right and Bennet doesn't have the experience to cope."

"I don't think it's that. I think it's probably that in my heart I don't really want to give up. I want to know what happens. Anyway, come on." She released Nick's hand. "You must be starving and I've defrosted some lamb cutlets. Is that a bottle of wine you brought in with you? If not, there are several in the wine rack. I've been stocking up."

He drew the cork and poured two glasses for them while Jo put the cutlets on the grill pan and ground black pepper over them. She was beginning to feel hungry at last.

Nick handed her a glass. "It's not getting any time to breathe, my need is too great at the moment!" He sighed. "Well, what do we do about you now?"

"Nothing. I'll handle it alone."

"Handle it alone? You were screaming so loud that people came running from all over the building. Bennet had to give you a shot to calm you down, for God's sake! How can you handle it alone?"

Jo frowned. "It was only finding those hands like that, knowing suddenly that the Welsh were there, even in the king's encampment. I hadn't realized how afraid I'd been when we were in Wales—always wondering when their revenge would start. I felt safe at last at Gloucester and I was alone in that tent, dreaming about Richard when suddenly, out of the night, in the middle of the King of England's men, they were there. They could have cut my throat!" She shuddered as she began slicing some tomatoes and sprinkling them with a few dried basil leaves before setting them beside the cutlets to cook. She stared down at the knife in her hand and dropped it hastily into the sink.

"Whose hands were they?" Nick asked quietly. "Do you know?"

She rinsed her fingers under the tap.

"Three of William's knights." She took the glass he offered her and sipped it thoughtfully. "I remember it quite clearly. We had been riding for some time, through mist, on the way to Gloucester when we saw a small wayside chapel, a shrine to a local saint. It was only a huddle of stones with a heather-covered roof, but as usual William went to kneel before the altar."

Nick felt a quick shiver of warning touch his skin as he watched her. Her eyes were staring into the distance as she began to describe the scene, and he found himself wondering suddenly if she even knew he was there anymore.

"Someone had left a garland of wild roses and honeysuckle on the stone slab and sweet herbs had been scattered around on the earth. I didn't dismount, but Will had begun to squeal and I turned in my saddle and watched as the nurse raised him to her breast, wishing I could hold him myself." She paused, biting her lip. "Her mule lowered its head looking for grass to nibble, and the boy at its head let it wander to a patch at the side of the road and stood there with the leading rein loose in his hand. It was silent, save for the champ of bits and the stamp of horses' hooves. I used to join William, but lately I had taken to waiting in the road like the others—sometimes with a whispered prayer of my own, sometimes not." She smiled at Nick, who was staring at her. "After a moment William rose and crossed himself. Then he stopped. He was listening. Then we all heard it in the early-morning silence, the sound of a woman singing somewhere on the hillside behind the shrine. Everyone's head turned and two of his knights wheeled their horses, closing up near him as he stood dusting off his blue mantle at the knees. I remember they both had their hands on the hilts of their swords.

"The deep, melodious singing was in Welsh, but I could not pick out the words. I pulled my cloak more closely around me, patting the neck of my horse, which was beginning to fidget, impatient to be moving. Still no one spoke. I think we were all frightened.

"Suddenly William turned to one of his knights. 'Take two men and find her. Be careful. It may be a trap.' He swung himself back up into his saddle. Although his face beneath its weatherbeaten ruddiness was pale, he sat erect, gazing after the three men.

"After a few minutes the singing grew more distant, as though the singer were walking away from us, up the hillside.

"I saw William swallow nervously, his eyes fixed on the track where his men had vanished. His horse shook its bit impatiently and pawed the ground, and he stilled it with an oath and a tug at the reins. Not a breath of wind stirred the trees, and the drift of mist obscured the track completely and the air grew chill.

"He waited a few more minutes, as usual unable to conceal his irritation, then he barked a command and four more riders, their swords drawn, cantered up the track into the mist.

"The skin at the back of my neck began to prickle and I looked around uneasily while the armed escort fingered their swords nervously. Only the nurse with the placidly suckling child at her breast seemed unconcerned.

"Suddenly the four knights reappeared, slithering down the track. They were alone. The rider of the leading horse drew his mount to a rearing halt at William's side and saluted with his sword.

" 'No sign of them, Sir William. The track divides in several places, but the mist is thick in the trees and we could see no hoof marks. It's so quiet up there. We tried shouting, but . . .' Then his voice trailed away and he glanced over his shoulder at his companions for support.

"William's face flushed. 'They can't be lost,' he shouted. 'Look again. Take more men—take twenty men—and scour the hillside! I want those men found, and I want the woman who was singing.' He drew his sword and held it ready across his saddle, then he gave me a grim smile. 'This is some trick of those damn Welsh,' he said.

"The hillside above us echoed to the shouts of the armed men as they forced their horses through the thick undergrowth, hacking with their swords. But they found no sign of the missing men. Eventually William had to give orders to continue without them.

"It was not until we had trekked over the pass at Bwlch that I ceased to feel that strange prickling sensation beneath my skin. It was then that I realized what it was. We were no longer being watched. The severed hands came from those three missing knights."

Jo came to herself suddenly with the realization that the kitchen was full of the smell of burning. She put down her glass with a little cry and grabbed the grill pan.

Nick was staring at her, a strange expression on his face. "You described none of that under hypnosis," he said quietly.

"Didn't I?" She glanced up as she turned the meat and tomatoes and lowered the flame. After putting them back, she poured some more wine. "No harm done, thank goodness. It was just the fat catching. A good thing we were standing here."

Nick hadn't moved. "How much else can you remember?" he asked after a moment.

She reached into the cupboard for two plates. "Everything, I suppose, until we left Gloucester. At least, it seems like everything. Come on, let's eat before this lot gets itself incinerated. I don't want to talk about Matilda anymore. Tell me what you're going to do to sink the opposition."

It was nearly midnight when Jo had tidied away their plates and made some coffee. Nick was sitting on the floor of the living room, leaning against the sofa, his head resting on the seat cushions, his eyes closed, as he listened to the last tape of the St. Matthew Passion. As the last notes of the final chorus died away, he raised his head and looked at her.

"What was that flute music you had on that day Sam came over?"

"Flute music?" She knelt beside him and reached for the orange coffee-pot. "I haven't any recordings of flute music."

"You must have." He frowned. "It was a strange, rather haunting, formless solo piece. I've never heard it before."

She shrugged. "Perhaps it was on the radio." She glanced at him uncomfortably. Nick had drunk most of the bottle of wine himself, quickly, without savoring it, which was unusual for him, and she could see that he was still tense and angry, the lines of his jaw taut as he lay back against the sofa cushions.

"Tell me," he went on after a moment, "if you remember everything about your visit to Gloucester so clearly, did you meet Richard de Clare again?"

"Nick. I don't want to talk about it." She was filling her cup and did not look at him.

"I want to know, Jo." His voice was quietly insistent.

She sighed. "I did see him, yes. He was a close adviser of the king's. Once he arrived at Gloucester he was constantly in attendance on him."

"But did you see him alone?"

Jo smiled reminiscently in spite of herself. "Yes, I saw him alone the day after the awful business with the hands. He came to my tent. William had announced that we were going back to Bramber before the weather closed in. He was unnerved by the whole affair and he had given orders that we were to set out the following day."

"And Richard came to your tent?"

Jo glanced up, hearing the undercurrent of anger in his voice. "We said good-bye, yes," she said cautiously.

"Did he kiss you?"

She saw his blue eyes narrow. "Nick. For goodness' sake—"

"Did he?" He sat up, watching her intently.

"Yes," she said defiantly. "If you must know, he did. It was the first time he had ever held me properly in his arms. The tent was flapping in the wind, the heavy hangings that lined the walls rippling as if they were going to be torn off their hooks—it was so cold. The boy hadn't kept the brazier outside the door fed properly, and it was smoking, not giving out much heat. Richard came in and I realized Nell must have let him pass. Elen would never have let him come to me alone. William was with the Earl of Gloucester—" She paused, sitting on the floor, hugging her knees, gazing at the table lamp. There was a long silence. Nick's eyes had not shifted from her face.

"Go on," he said at last. "Aren't you going to tell me what happened next?"

She glanced up. "He didn't say anything at all. He just strode in, dropped the heavy curtains across the tent doorway and laced them together, then he took me in his arms. It was the first time we had kissed properly and I remember, for a moment, I was afraid. Then I forgot everything—William, little Will in the next tent with his nurses, the fear that someone might come—everything. I had never known physical desire before, only hints of it whenever Richard came near me, but suddenly I was overwhelmed by it." She paused and then went on thoughtfully. "I think we had both imagined that the feeling we had for each other could be contained in some courtly flirtation, but suddenly it took fire. I didn't care what happened. I led him to the bed and he pushed me down on the furs—" She stopped abruptly, seeing Nick's face, and gave an embarrassed little laugh. "Sorry. I was getting carried away! Anyway, it was quite good, as I remember. Matilda's first orgasm—"

She broke off as he lunged forward and caught her wrist, pulling it viciously so that she fell toward him, knocking the tray off the low table. The coffeepot slid to the floor and cracked against the table leg, soaking the carpet with coffee.

"Nick, stop it!" she cried. She could feel her arm pressing on a sharp piece of broken china. Warm blood flowed over her wrist. "Nick, please—you're hurting me—*please,* look, I've cut myself—" The blind fury in his face frightened her. "It was only a dream, Nick. It wasn't real! For God's sake, what's the matter with you? Nick!" His hand was on her throat, his eyes murderous. Jo struggled frantically, feeling the pressure on her windpipe slowly increase. Then abruptly his mood seemed to change. He moved his hand from her throat, catching her wrists instead, clamping them above her head while with his free hand he began to pull open her bathrobe. Then he bent over her and began roughly caressing her breasts. He smiled coldly. "That's better. You like a little medieval violence, don't you? It reminds you of the good old days—"

"Please, Nick! *Nick*—" Jo was terrified by the blind savagery in his face.

211

She had never seen anyone look like that before, except once . . . For a moment she stopped struggling and lay still, frozen with fear as she remembered the face of the man who had tried to strangle her before—Nick's other face—then with a last desperate pull she managed to break free of him. She rolled away and staggered to her feet, clutching her robe around her. "Get out! Get out of here," she shouted. "Get out of this apartment, Nick, and never, ever come back!" Her eyes were blazing with anger. "Don't you dare lay a finger on me again! I don't know what the hell you think you're playing at, but you get out of here. I won't be treated like this. Not ever, do you hear!" She backed away from him toward the front door, knotting her belt around her waist. "Did you hear me?" she repeated desperately.

He was smiling as he stood up. A cool, arrogant smile, which turned her anger back to terror.

"Nick, please. What's wrong with you?" She had nearly reached the front door. Turning quickly, she scrabbled with the latch, frantically trying to drag the door open, but Nick was close behind her. He slammed the door shut and rammed the bolt home, then he caught her arm. As he swung her to face him Jo screamed. But the sound never came. It was cut off short as he clamped his hand across her mouth, pulling her hard against him. He half dragged, half carried her down the passage to the bedroom and, without turning on the light, flung her on the bed.

She lay there for a moment, winded, then as she turned, trying to struggle to her feet again, she felt a blinding blow across her face. Half stunned, she fell back as Nick's weight came down on top of her.

"Now, my lady," he breathed, his fingers feeling for the knot of her belt, his face so close to hers she could see the gleam of his eyes in the darkness. "Another sound and I shall have to take steps to silence you."

She tried to wriggle sideways as she felt his knee forcing her legs apart, but he held her easily. Eventually realizing that the more she fought him the more he was going to hurt her, she made herself go limp, biting her lip in pain as he forced his way inside her. His mouth ground into hers and she opened her lips helplessly beneath his probing tongue, and suddenly through her fear she felt a little stab of excitement. As if he sensed it, Nick laughed softly, and she felt his grip on her wrists tighten. "So, my lady, you do enjoy violence," he whispered. "I think in a lot of ways you'll find I can please you better than Richard de Clare." And his mouth left hers and traveled down her throat toward her breasts.

He fell asleep eventually, still spreadeagled over her numbed body, his head between her breasts, his hands, loosened at last, outstretched across the bedcover. Agonized, Jo tried to move. She was crying softly, afraid to wake him as she tried again to dislodge the dead weight that pinned her to the bed. In the end she gave up and lay still, staring toward the window where the heavy curtains cut out the first signs of a beautiful dawn.

212

Nick woke just before seven. For a long time he lay unmoving, feeling the woman's body limp beneath his, then slowly he eased himself off her and sat up. He grabbed his trousers and staggered to the window, throwing back the curtains with a groan. It was full daylight. He looked at his watch in surprise, and then back at the bed as the stark daylight fell across Jo. She was lying naked on the bedcover, her hair spread across the pillow, her legs apart. There were vivid bruises on her wrists and breasts, and he could see bloodstains on the bedspread. There was a long jagged cut encrusted with dried blood on her forearm, more blood on the inside of her thighs—

He felt suddenly violently sick. She had not stirred. She did not even seem to be breathing. He threw himself toward the bed. "Jo? *Jo!* For God's sake, are you all right?"

For a moment she did not move, then, slowly and painfully, she opened her eyes, dazzled by the light, and stared around the room. It was a few moments before she began to remember. He saw the fear flicker behind her eyes as she looked up at him and a wave of nausea shook him again. She still had not moved but he saw her lick her lips experimentally, trying to speak. He reached for her bathrobe, thrown across a chair, and laid it gently over her.

"I'll make some tea," he said softly.

In the bathroom he tugged at the light pull and stared at himself in the cold, uncompromising electric light. His face looked the same as usual. Tired perhaps, and a little gray, but nothing strange. There was a scratch across his shoulder, otherwise nothing to show for Jo's fight for her life.

He walked slowly to the kitchen and made the tea, comforting himself with the familiar sounds as he filled the kettle and fished in the jar for two teabags. Then he walked through to the living room. It was cold; the French doors had been open all night. The grass in the square was still silvered with dew. He pulled the doors closed, then he turned and picked up his shirt. There were coffee stains on the sleeve. And blood. Pulling it on, he went back to the kitchen. He was numb.

Slowly he carried the two mugs back to the bedroom. Jo had not moved. Sitting on the bed beside her, he proffered one of the mugs tentatively.

"Jo—"

She turned her head away and closed her eyes.

"Jo, please. Let me explain."

"There is nothing to explain." She did not look at him. "Please, just go."

He stood up. "All right." He leaned forward as if to touch her shoulder, but he changed his mind. "I'll come back this evening, Jo. I'll make it up to you somehow," he whispered.

213

Leaving the two cups of tea untouched beside the bed, he walked slowly to the door. After unbolting it, he let himself out onto the quiet landing.

As he tiptoed down the stairs toward the street he heard the distant sickly wailing of a baby.

For a long time after he had gone Jo did not move. She lay rigid, listening to Will crying. Her fists clenched, her eyes dry, she stared at the wall, feeling the ache of her body where Nick had bruised her. Suddenly she sat up. She threw herself out of bed and ran to the bathroom, turning both bath taps on full, then she went to find her address book. She fumbled in her canvas bag in her haste, then pulled the book out and began flipping through the pages with a shaking hand, trying not to notice the mess of bloodstains that had soaked into the pale carpet in the middle of the room.

She stopped at Leigh Delamere service station on the M4, pulling into the crowded parking lot and resting her head for a moment on the rim of the wheel. She had thrown in her bags, typewriter, and camera barely fifteen minutes after calling Janet Pugh.

She pulled the rearview mirror toward her and studied her face. Her lips were still swollen and her eyes were puffy from crying so much in the night. She had dabbed makeup over her white skin and used lipstick and eyeshadow. It made her feel better. The long sleeves and high neck of her Victorian blouse covered the worst of her bruises.

She pulled herself painfully out of the car and swung her bag over her shoulder. It was only another twenty miles, if that, to the Severn Bridge. Then she would be in Wales.

Tim stood for a long time outside the house in Church Road, staring up at the gray slate roof with its dentillation of wrought-iron decoration. The house was identical to its neighbors, save for the front door, which was cream with a brightly polished knocker. The windows were hung with fresh, plain net curtains, like old-fashioned muslin, he thought, as at last he raised his hand to the knocker.

Sylvia Walton opened the door at his second knock. She had plaited her hair and wound it around her head in a silvery braid. It made her look like an Austrian peasant. His fingers itched for his camera, but he had not brought it with him. He grinned at her. "It was very good of you and Bill to let me come back and talk to you."

Sylvia smiled as she led him up the long flight of stairs. "He was pleased to hear from you again. Miss Clifford isn't with you this time?"

Tim shook his head. He followed her into the room they had been in before, but this time the lines of chairs were missing. Instead a small wheeled table that had been set for three was standing near the fireplace. Bill Walton was writing at his desk. He rose as his wife ushered Tim into

214

the room and held out his hand. The prominent green eyes surveyed Tim shrewdly. "So, Mr. Heacham, you want to try a little regression yourself," he said with a smile. "I'm glad you found your previous visit so interesting."

Jo drew the car up in a narrow lane and stared ahead of her through a stone arch. Her stomach muscles knotted. Abergavenny Castle. After climbing out of the MG, she walked slowly through the arch and stared around her.

The sleepless night and the long drive from London were catching up with her fast now and she ached all over with exhaustion. Her mind was mercifully blank whenever she thought about Nick. All she knew was that she did not want to be in London and that if anyone could comfort her it would not be Nick but Richard—a Richard she might never see again but for whom she longed with an almost physical ache. She drew a deep painful breath of air into her lungs and walked on.

This castle too was a ruin but there was far more of it left than at Bramber. She stepped onto a grass lawn strewn with daisies and stared up at a mock-Gothic stone keep, somehow garishly out of place on the motte at the center of the bailey where the Norman tower had stood. Around her rose high pinkish-gray ruined walls while below the hillside the river elbowed in a lazy curve through the valley. Beyond it lay the soft Welsh hills, shrouded in heat haze. One of the massive walls was covered in scaffolding and she could hear the soft lilt of conversation from high on the ladders near the top of the masonry, where a tree cast its shade over the stone.

Shivering, she began to walk around the perimeter path. Somewhere here, in the bailey below the motte, the Welsh dead had lain in terrible disarray, and in their midst Seisyll and his son. She stood still again, staring around. Surely something of the horror must remain? The stench of blood? The screams? She felt the warm wind from the south lift her hair slightly on her neck. A patch of red valerian in the wall near her stirred, but nothing more. The echoes were still. William de Braose was dead and Seisyll long ago avenged.

She parked her car outside Janet and David Pugh's neat white-painted house and rang the doorbell, staring back up the empty street, as she listened to the sound of footsteps running down the stairs and toward the door. For a moment after the door opened she and Janet stood staring at each other incredulously. Janet saw a tall, elegant young woman with long, dark hair wearing a high-necked, long-sleeved blouse and well-cut slacks, most of her face obscured by dark glasses. Jo saw a very pregnant, fair-haired woman in a sleeveless summer dress and Scholl sandals. She grinned. "My God, you've changed since school!"

"So have you." Janet reached forward tentatively and kissed her cheek. "Come in. You must have had a hell of a drive from London."

From her bedroom at the top of the house Jo could see the castle ruins. She stood staring out across the low huddle of rooftops, her hand on the curtain, before turning to her hostess, who was hovering in the doorway. "It was good of you to let me come like this, with no warning," she said. "I had forgotten you lived in Abergavenny, then when I knew I had to come here something clicked in my mind and I remembered your Christmas card."

"I'm glad you did. You're working on an article, you said?" Janet's eyes went to the typewriter standing in its case at the foot of the bed. "David was very impressed when I called the school and told him you were coming here. You're famous!"

Jo laughed. "Infamous is a better word these days, I fear." She took a brush out of her bag and ran it down her hair, which crackled with static. "You really don't mind my coming?"

Janet shook her head. Her eyes sparkled with sudden irrepressible giggles. "I'm thrilled. *Really.* You're the most exciting thing that's happened to us for months!" She sat down on the end of the bed with a groan, her hand to her back. "Well, what do you think of Wales, then?"

Jo sat down beside her. "I haven't seen much so far, but what I've seen is beautiful. I think I'm going to love it here." How could she explain that already it felt like coming home? Impatiently she pushed the sentimental phrase aside and pulled off her dark glasses at last, throwing them on the bed. Beneath them her face was very pale.

David Pugh came home at about six. He was a squat, florid, sandy-haired man with twinkling eyes. "So you've come to see where it all happened," he said cheerfully as he handed Jo a glass of sherry. "We were intrigued when we read the article about you in the paper." He stood staring at her for a moment, the bottle still in his hand. "You're not like her, are you? Not how I imagined her, anyway."

"Who?" Jo was looking around the small living room curiously. Books and records overflowed from every shelf and flat surface onto the floor.

"Our Moll Walbee." He was watching her closely. "You know who that is, surely?"

Jo frowned. She took a sip of sherry. Out of the back window across the small garden there was a hedge and more roofs and behind them she could still see the pink-gray stone of the strange Gothic keep in the castle grounds. "Moll Walbee," she repeated. "It's strange. I seem to know the name, but I can't place it."

"It is what the Marcher people called Maude de Braose. You seem to prefer the name Matilda, which is, I grant, more euphonious, but nevertheless she was, I think, more often known as Maude."

He poured a glass of sherry for his wife, and pushing open the hatch

216

into the kitchen, passed it through to her. Janet, a plastic apron over her dress, was chopping parsley. She looked slightly flustered as she dropped the knife and took the glass from him. "Shut up about that now, David," she said in an undertone, glancing at Jo.

"No." Jo had seen the challenge in David's eyes. "No, don't shut up. I'm interested. If you know about her I want to hear it. I can see you're skeptical, and I don't blame you. You're a historian, I believe?"

He snorted. "I teach history at a local school. That doesn't make me a historian, but I have read a bit about the history of the Welsh Marches. The Braose family made a name for themselves around here. And Maude is something of a legend. Moll is a corruption of Mallt, the Welsh for Maude, of course. Walbee, I surmise, comes from St. Valerie, which was her father's name."

Jo grinned. "That at least I know. Reginald."

He nodded. "Or it could, I suppose, be a corruption of de la Haie—from her association with Hay-on-Wye, but there must be dozens of parishes up and down the borders that claim stories about her. She was reputed to be a witch, you know."

Jo raised an eyebrow. "I didn't know." She leaned forward and took the bottle out of his hand, refilling his glass and then her own. "I'm not a historian, David. I know nothing about her save what I remember from my"—she hesitated, seeing the disbelief in his face—"my dreams, if you like to call them that. I looked her up in the *Dictionary of National Biography,* but I didn't look at any books on Welsh history. Perhaps I should."

Janet appeared with a saucer of peanuts, which she put on the arm of David's chair. "My husband is a bit of an expert on local legend," she said almost apologetically. "We must shut him up about it, because if he starts, he'll go on all night."

"No, I won't." He frowned at her. "All I said was that Joanna does not look like her. She was reputed to have been a giant. She is said to have stood in the churchyard at Hay and, finding a stone in her shoe, thrown it across the Wye, where it landed at Llowes." He grinned. "The stone is about ten feet long! And of course she built Hay Castle singlehanded in a night. And she was Mallt y Nos, who you can see riding across the mountains with the hounds of hell in the wild of a storm." He laughed out loud at the expression on Jo's face. "She must have been a fearsome lady, Jo. Overpowering, Amazonian even, who kept old William in terror of his life. Or that is the way the story goes."

Jo said nothing for a moment. Then slowly she began to pace up and down the carpet. "I don't think she was especially tall," she said reflectively. "Taller than William, yes. And taller than a lot of the Welsh, but then they are a short people—" She broke off in embarrassment, looking at her host.

217

He roared with laughter. "I'm five foot four, girl, and proud of it. It's power not height that counts in the rugby scrum, and don't you forget it!"

Smiling, Jo helped herself to peanuts. "It's hard to explain what it's like being someone else, even if only as a vivid dream. She doesn't inhabit my skin. I find myself in hers. I think and speak and feel as her. But I don't know her future any more than she would have known it. Now, talking to you, I know roughly what happened to her, but in the regressions I know no more than we know now what will happen to us tomorrow. If in later life she was called Moll Walbee, I don't know it yet. If later she came to dominate William, I have no clue. As a young woman only a year or so married she was afraid of him. And her only defense against him was disdain."

There was a moment's silence. Janet had seated herself on the arm of a chair near the kitchen door. "Do you really believe you are her reincarnation?" she asked at last, awed. "Really, in your heart of hearts?"

Jo nodded slowly. "I think I am beginning to wonder, yes."

"And are you going to go on being hypnotized to see what happened?"

This time Jo shrugged. "I'm not too happy about being hypnotized, to be honest. Sometimes I think I must, other times I'm too scared and I swear I'll never go back. I tried to get the hypnotherapist to make me forget her, but it didn't work, so now I don't know what I'll do."

"Well, that's honest at least." David had wandered across to his bookshelves. He picked out a heavy tome. "People who are capable of regression usually, if not invariably, regress into several previous lives," he said thoughtfully. "I don't think I've ever read of a case where just one life was picked out like this." He smiled at her quizzically. "It is most intriguing. Do you think that anyone else from Maude's lifetime has returned with her?"

Jo hesitated. "It is as much as I can do to believe in myself," she said slowly, "but sometimes I wonder . . ." Nick's face suddenly rose before her eyes. A Nick she had never known. A Nick, his face contorted with jealousy and anger, who had pinned her to the bed and raped her, and behind his face another, a face with red-gold hair and beard—the man who had tried to strangle her.

"Jo, what is it?" Janet's whisper brought her back abruptly to the room where she was sitting.

She smiled and gave another shrug. "Just something I thought of, someone who's been behaving rather strangely." She bit her knuckles for a moment. "But if he is the reincarnation of someone from my—from Matilda's past—who is he?"

David let out a little chuckle. "Don't worry about it too much, girl. I'm sure it will come to you. Either that, or you'll regain your wits. Now, why don't I find a bottle of wine so we can celebrate your visit, then while we eat I'll help you plan an itinerary so you can follow Matilda's footsteps, starting at Hay, where most of her legend is centered. That is why you've come to Wales, isn't it? To follow her footsteps?"

"I suppose it must be," Jo said after a moment.

"You know," he said, his hand to his cheek. "You could be like her, at that. I suspect you're a very determined lady when you want to be!"

Jo laughed. "I have that reputation, I believe."

"And you're not superstitious or anything?" he went on, almost as an afterthought.

"Not in the slightest."

"Good." He handed her the book. "Some bedtime reading for you, Jo. I think you'll find it interesting.

Nick let himself into his apartment with a sigh. He dropped his case to the floor and picked up the mail from inside the door, then he stopped and looked around, listening. "Is someone there?" he called.

An inner door opened and Sam appeared, lifting his hand in a laconic greeting.

"Sam!" Nick threw down the letter.

Sam raised a cynical eyebrow. "I don't think I've had so ecstatic a welcome for years!"

"Shut up and listen!" Nick pushed past him and went through into the living room. "I hurt Jo."

Sam had followed him and was about to help himself to a drink. He swung around and stared at Nick. "You did what?" he said.

"I hurt her, Sam. Last night. We were talking about the regressions and she began to tell me about things that had happened to her in that life— things she hadn't mentioned under hypnosis. She began talking about de Clare—describing how they had made love. . . ." He went to the tray of drinks. "I grabbed her, Sam. I saw red and grabbed her. I wanted to punish her. I wanted to hurt her. I might have killed her."

Sam was very still. "Where is she?"

Nick shrugged. "I don't know. I called a dozen times this morning and went back at lunchtime. Her car had gone. I went up to the apartment and looked around. She'd taken her typewriter and a suitcase. There wasn't a note or anything."

Sam pushed him aside and poured out two glasses of Scotch. He handed his brother one, then stood watching him thoughtfully. "How badly did you hurt her?"

Nick shrugged. "She knocked the tray off the coffee table and cut her arm. That was an accident, but I was pretty rough with her—"

"Did you rape her?"

Nick could feel Sam's eyes on him. He straightened defiantly. "Technically, I suppose I did."

"Technically?"

There was something in the coldness of Sam's voice that made Nick step back. "She and I have been living together on and off for years, for God's sake!"

"That is hardly the point." Sam sat down slowly. "So you forced her. Did you beat her up?"

"I hit her. She was covered in bruises. I don't know what came over me, Sam. It was as if I wasn't me anymore. I couldn't control myself. I knew I was hurting her, and I didn't want to stop!" He fumbled in the pocket of his jacket for a pack of cigarettes, extracted one, then threw it down with a curse. *"Christ!* This is all such a mess. I was jealous, Sam, of a man who died God knows how many hundreds of years ago. I thought for a while it was Jo going out of her mind. Now I think it's me!" He threw himself down opposite his brother. "You've got to help me. What the hell do I do?"

Sam leaned back in his chair. He was gently swirling his Scotch around in his glass. "You really want me to help you?" His voice had softened slightly. "I can, Nick. But you'll have to trust me. Have you ever considered," he said thoughtfully, "that Jo might not be the only one among us who is living again?"

Nick snorted. "You're not suggesting I am the reincarnation of her husband, or something?"

"No," I am not suggesting that. But I think it possible that you were perhaps someone close to her in the past."

Nick stared at him. "Are you serious?"

"Perfectly."

"Oh, come on! Don't hand me that crap. Jo might have been persuaded by all this. In fact, she actually asked me if I thought I'd lived before—"

"Perhaps she recognized you."

"No! Oh, no, I don't believe it. I've got enough problems in this life, and I'd have thought you'd have more sense than to encourage her. You of all people who saw the danger right from the start!"

"I saw the danger." Sam swung his feet up onto the coffee table. "But as Jo would not sidestep it, neither can we."

Nick glanced at him sharply. "What do you mean exactly?"

Sam had closed his eyes. "There is one easy way of finding out whether you were involved in her past, Nick," he said.

"How?" Nick paused. "Oh, no! You think I'm going to Bennet to let him try his regression on me?"

"There's no need." Sam took a sip from his glass. "I can do it if you'll let me."

Nick's mouth dropped open. "Are you suggesting that I let you hypnotize me?" he said incredulously.

"Why not? I can do it, Nick. And I have a feeling you might be surprised by what we find out." Sam smiled gently. "Have you ever won-

220

dered why Jo and you were so instantly attracted when you first met? Could it not have been that you were lovers once before? Is it not possible that the Richard she loved so much was your alter ego, eight hundred years ago?" He was watching Nick's expression closely. "It might be fun to find out," he went on persuasively. "It couldn't do any harm, and it might explain a lot of your ambivalence toward Jo now."

Nick sat down on the edge of a table, one foot on the carpet, the other swinging slowly back and forth. "I don't believe I'm hearing this. You actually think I am the reincarnation of Richard de Clare?"

Sam shrugged. "When dealing with anything like this, Nick, I keep an open mind. I think for Jo's sake you ought to as well. You owe it to her, if only to find out why you attacked her." His eyes narrowed.

"But why," Nick said slowly, "if I was Richard de Clare, would I be so jealous of him?"

Sam smiled. "Good question. Shall we find out?"

"You are serious?"

"Perfectly. If you don't regress, fair enough. Not everyone does by any means. At least we will have tried. If you do, it will be interesting."

"I don't know that I do trust you!" Nick looked at him suspiciously. "After what happened to Jo."

"What happened to Jo? She is a deep trance subject, Nick; you are not. The experience would not be the same for you."

"I'm glad to hear it," Nick said coolly. "There are one or two things you never explained, Sam." His knuckles tightened on his glass. "Like why it was necessary for Jo to take off her clothes the other night when you regressed her."

Sam raised an eyebrow. "Is that what she said happened?"

"That is what she said." Nick was watching him closely.

Sam smiled. "She experiences the trances so vividly she finds it hard to differentiate between that state and reality, at least for a time, as I told you."

"It was reality, Sam, that I found her clothes that night, hidden in the living room—"

"Perhaps she put them there before I came." Sam crossed one knee over the other, his whole body relaxed. "I'm not sure what you are implying, Nicholas, but may I remind you that it is you who raped Jo, not I. It is you who asked for help, and I can give it because I'm a doctor. And I think you need to try hypnosis."

Still uncertain, Nick hesitated. "I suppose it would do no harm to try. And I'd rather you did it than Bennet," he said at last, reluctantly. "But I hate the idea. And I doubt if it would work on me, anyway."

"Why don't we try?" Sam sat up slowly. "In fact, why don't we have a go now? You're worried. You're tired. If nothing else, I can help you to relax." He smiled. "Come and sit down over here, little brother. That's

221

right, facing the window. Now. Relax. Put the glass down, please. You're clutching it like a lifebelt! Now, let's see whether you can do one or two little experiments for me. We'll start with the lamp." Sam leaned forward and switched on the lamp at Nick's elbow. "No, don't look at the light. I want you to look past it, into the corner of the room."

Nick laughed suddenly. "It's like having the 'fluence' put on you by someone at school. Why don't you use a watch and chain?"

"It may have escaped your notice, Nicholas, but I don't wear a watch and chain." Sam moved silently from his chair and gently put his thumb and forefinger on Nick's eyelids. "Now, look toward the lamp again and start counting slowly backward from one hundred."

Several minutes later Sam stood up. He was smiling. He walked toward the window and threw it open, staring out for a minute up the narrow street opposite toward the traffic in Park Lane. Then he turned to Nick, who was lying back in his chair, his eyes closed.

"Comfortable, little brother?" he said softly. "No, don't try to answer me. You can't. I don't want you to speak at all. I want you to listen."

19

Janet knocked on Jo's door as she was undressing late that night. Pushing it open, she hovered for a moment, staring at Jo, who, wearing only her bra and briefs, was sitting on the edge of her bed.

"God, I'm sorry! I didn't think—shall I come back?" Flustered, Janet backed away. "I brought us some cocoa. I thought you might like to chat a bit. Old Welsh custom!"

Jo laughed. "Come in." She reached for her thin silk bathrobe hastily and drew it around her.

Janet sat down on the stool in front of the kidney-shaped dressing table, maneuvering her heavy body with difficulty. "Jo, I wanted to apologize for David. He can be a bit belligerent at times. He shouldn't have given you the third degree like that. He tends to think all Welsh history is his special province and he almost resents anyone else who is interested in it, besides which, as you can't have failed to gather, he is a rabid nationalist—"

"Quite apart from thinking that I am completely mad anyway." Jo smiled wearily. "He could be right at that. I'm glad he didn't order me out of your house. I really did want to know about Matilda, though—his Moll Walbee." She reached for the mug and sipped it slowly. "It was so odd to hear him talk about her with such knowledge. He knew so much more about her than I do, and yet at the same time he didn't know her at all."

Janet gave a rueful laugh. "That could apply to David on a lot of subjects." She was silent a moment, watching as Jo sipped again from her mug. The pale-blue silk of Jo's sleeve had slipped back to her elbow, showing clearly the livid bruising around her wrist and the long curved gash on her arm. "Jo," she said tentatively. "I couldn't help noticing—the bruises and that awful cut—" She colored slightly. "Tell me if it's none of my business, but, well . . . you sounded in such a state when you called this morning." She groaned slightly, her hand to her back. "There is more to this sudden trip than just research, isn't there?"

Jo set down the mug and pulled her sash more tightly around her waist.

"A bit of man trouble," she admitted reluctantly at last.

"And he did that to you?"

Jo sighed. "He was drunk—far more I think than I realized. I've never seen Nick like that before."

"Nick?"

Jo laughed wryly. "The man in my life. Correction, the man who was in my life. We'd been having lots of fights and we split up a couple of times, then we got back together and I thought everything was going to be all right. Then suddenly—" She paused in midsentence. "It was to do with my regressions. He doesn't approve of my doing it and he became a bit uptight about a lover I—Matilda—had had in the past. . . ."

"Richard de Clare?" Janet nodded. "I remember him from the article. He sounded really rather a dish. Every woman's fantasy man!" She broke off with an exclamation. "You mean this Nick knocked you about because you talked about a lover in a previous life while you were being hypnotized?"

Jo lay back on the bed, her arm across her face. "I think that was what it was about. The awful thing was, I think I wanted to tell him about Richard. I wanted him to know."

"And this is the man you mentioned earlier, the one you said had been behaving so strangely you wondered if he had lived before too?"

Jo nodded. She rolled over so that she could see Janet's face. "Isn't it strange? You and I used to talk in school about how it would be. You were the one who was never going to marry or have kids. Now look at you. Elephantine! And I was going to be a woman alone, without men."

"I always thought that was a stupid idea," Janet put in humorously. "One has to have men. Lovers."

Jo stared at the ceiling thoughtfully. "We were so idealistic, so naive! Do you know, I found out through Matilda what it was like to be forced to marry a man you hated. Forced, by a father who doted on you yet who, by custom, because you were a mere woman, had to hand you and your inheritance on to another man. I became a man's property, Janet. He could do what he wanted with me. Threaten me, lock me up, treat me like a slave, and order me into his bed and expect me to obey him. It's been like that for women for centuries and only now are we fighting for liberation. It's unbelievable." She sat up. "The only way I—I mean Matilda—could keep him out of her bed was to tell him when she was pregnant that a witch had foretold doom for the baby if he touched her."

Janet chuckled. "I'd like to see Dave's face if I tried that one. Mind you, I like him to touch me. Imagine, in my condition!" She patted her stomach affectionately, then she glanced up. "Did you—did Matilda have the baby?"

Jo nodded. "Do you want to hear the gory details of medieval obstetrics? Perhaps it's not tactful at the moment. The entire range of facilities were available to me—no expense spared. A pile of straw to soak up the

224

blood, a midwife who stank of ale and had all her front teeth missing—I imagine kicked out by a previous client—and I was given a rosary to hold. I broke it, which was considered an ill omen, and I had a magic stone tied on a thong around my neck. I was naked, of course, and the labor went on for a day and a night and most of the next day."

Janet shuddered. "Spare me. I'm going to have an epidural. Did it hurt terribly?"

Jo nodded. "I was too tired by the end to know what was going on properly. Then afterward, in real life, I began to produce milk for that poor scrap of a baby who was only a dream!"

"You're not serious." Janet looked shocked.

"Oh, it only lasted a day or two, thank God, but it was rather disgusting at the time."

Janet was staring at her. "It doesn't seem possible."

"No."

"And your Nick. Did he know about all this?"

"Oh, yes. He was, you might say, present at the birth. He was watching while I was describing it all under hypnosis."

"Then I'm not surprised he's a bit rattled." Janet shivered again. "The poor man must really feel weird. I'll tell you one thing. If all that had happened to me, I'd never let myself be hypnotized again as long as I lived. Never!" She shuddered theatrically.

"You wouldn't want to know what happened?"

"But you do know what happened, Jo. David showed you, in that book. She died. Horribly."

Jo drew her knees up to her chin and hugged them. "She died in about 1211. The events I am describing happened around 1176. That's thirty-five years later."

"And you're going to relive thirty-five years of her life?" Janet's expression dissolved suddenly into her irrepressible smile. "I take it this is a fairly long project, Jo?" The smile faded abruptly. "I think you're mad. Nothing on earth would make me go through with that deliberately. Didn't Dave say she had six children? Are you going to go through another five pregnancies and deliveries like that first one? I'm prepared to bet real money they still hadn't even invented morphine by the turn of the thirteenth century."

Jo grinned tolerantly. "Perhaps you're right. And it is a pretty thankless task, with no baby at the end of it . . ." She blinked rapidly, aware of a sudden lump in her throat.

Janet heaved herself to her feet and came and put her arm around her shoulders. "I'm sorry, Jo. I didn't mean to upset you—"

"You haven't." Jo pulled away from her and stood up. "Besides, if I'm honest I have a particular reason for wanting to go back. Not just to see Will, though I want to hold him so much sometimes it hurts." She gave an

225

embarrassed smile. "I have to go back to see Richard again. I need him, Janet. He's gotten under my skin. To me he is completely real."

"Supposing Matilda never saw him again?" Janet said thoughtfully after a moment.

"Then I'll have to learn to live without him. But until I know for sure, I have a feeling I shall go back. Come on." She reached for the bedcover and pulled it down. "I need my beauty sleep, even if you don't. Tomorrow I am going to Hay and Brecon and places to see if I can lay Matilda's ghost. If I can, then there will be no more regressions. No more Richard. Just an article in *Women in Action* that will be of passing interest to some and total boredom to others and then it will all be forgotten."

She climbed into bed and lay back tensely after Janet had gone, staring up at the ceiling in the dark, half afraid that all the talk of babies might once more conjure up the sound of crying in the echoing chambers of that distant castle, but she heard nothing but the gentle sighing of the wind.

Outside the window the clouds streamed across the moon and shadowed silver played over the ruins. If Seisyll's ghost walked, she did not see him. Within minutes she was asleep.

The breezes of Sussex were gentle after the frosty mornings of the west and the trees were still heavy with leaves as yet untouched by frost. As Matilda's long procession slowly traveled the last miles to Bramber, she could see from far away the tall keep of the castle, standing sentinel on its height above the River Adur. They rode slowly down the long causeway into the small village that clung among the saltings around the foot of the castle hill. The parish church and the castle looked out across the marshes and the deep angle of the river toward the sea. The tide was in and the deep moat full of water as they clattered across the drawbridge, with gulls swooping and wheeling around them and diving into the slate-colored ripples below.

Her beloved nurse Jeanne greeted them outside the towering gatehouse with tears of joy, but she had news of death.

"What is it, Jeanne, dear? Is it the old lord?" Matilda gazed around as she slipped from her horse, dreading suddenly any visitation of sickness that might come near her son. He was so little and vulnerable. She ached sometimes with love for the little boy and with the terrible fear of what might become of him.

"It's Sir William's mother, the Lady Bertha." Jeanne's wrinkled old face was suddenly solemn. "She slipped on the stairs and broke her thigh two months since. She lived on for weeks in terrible pain, poor soul, and then she died at last a week ago, God rest her. The bones were too old to knot properly." The old woman crossed herself and then looked up shrewdly under her heavy eyelids. "I wonder you didn't meet the messengers we

226

sent after Sir William. You'll be mistress of your own now, *ma p'tite*. I'm glad for you."

Secretly Matilda felt no sorrow for the domineering old woman, but she felt a moment's regret for William, who had cared for his mother in an embarrassed way.

William had left Gloucester with the king, taking with him most of his fighting men, save her escort, after a brief, futile inquiry into the murder of the three missing knights. It would be some time before he returned to Bramber.

Matilda suppressed the smile of relief that kept wanting to come. It might not be seemly, but a great weight had been lifted from her mind. She had dreaded her meeting with Bertha. The old woman's bitter tongue would not have spared her a lashing for her impropriety and disobedience in leaving Bramber the year before, nor would she have allowed Matilda to continue ordering her husband's household. She glanced around at Bernard, who was sitting slackly on his roan gelding behind her, apparently lost in thought. He would have lost all his respect for her if he'd heard Bertha. Now there was no danger. Bramber was hers. Breathing a silent prayer of gratitude, she raised her arm in a signal and the tired procession of horses and wagons moved slowly under the gatehouse into the steeply cobbled bailey within.

After dismounting once more, Matilda followed Jeanne into the cool dimness of the great hall and looked around with a quiet sigh of satisfaction at the beautiful arched windows, trimmed with delicately carved flintstone borders, and the intricate carving that adorned pillars and doorways. Bramber was beautiful compared with Brecknock. Beautiful, civilized, and safe.

She forced herself to go at once to look at the recumbent body of her father-in-law. It was because he still lived that Bertha had remained mistress of Bramber. Had he died as God, she was sure, had intended, Bertha would have gone to her dower lands and left Matilda in charge of the castle. It was because he still lived too that William was in such a strange position, a baron in all but title. She looked down at old William's face. He had changed not at all since she had left Bramber. The skin was perhaps more shrunken, the eye sockets more hollow as his dimmed eyes still gazed sightlessly at the ceiling. The only sign of life was the clawed hand that grasped incessantly at the sheet drawn up over the old man's chest. Dutifully she dropped a light kiss on the papery skin of his brown cheek. He gave no sign of recognition, and after a moment she left his bedside.

In the privacy of her own solar she hugged Jeanne again. After taking Will from his nurse, she unwrapped him herself and presented him for the old woman's inspection. Jeanne examined the baby's sleeping face. Then to Matilda's relief she nodded and smiled. "A fine boy," she commented. "He does you credit, *ma p'tite,* but then I'd expect you to have bonny children." She glanced sideways at Matilda. "I can see you're going to have another too. That is good. This time I shall be near to watch over you."

Matilda smiled. She had suspected that she was pregnant again, though outwardly her slim waist hadn't thickened an inch, so she wondered how Jeanne could tell so easily. But she was happy. This time she would stay at Bramber. Nothing would induce her to travel after William as she had done before. There was to be no possibility of the evil eye being directed at her unborn child. She took Jeanne's hands and kissed the old woman again on the cheek. The black mist-covered mountains of Wales and their unhappy memories seemed very far away.

Giles, her second son, was born in April the following year, as the heavy scented air of Sussex drifted like balm through the open windows of Bramber Castle, bringing with it the slight tang of salt from the hazy channel, floating in from the saltings below, and, from the fields and Downs, the heady perfume of apple blossom and bluebells. As the child was laid, sleeping peacefully, in its crib, Jeanne slipped silently to the glowing hearthstone and there laid wine and water and fresh towels for the fairies. With their blessing the child would grow strong and lucky. Matilda felt a sudden shiver of fear. There had been no such magic for baby Will. Dimly she remembered as a bad dream from the past the vision she had had at her eldest son's birth and she crossed herself, afraid for him. Then, even as she tried to recall the meaning of the vision, it blurred and slipped from her and she saw that Jeanne was watching her with strangely narrowed eyes. Matilda fought to look away but somehow she could not move. The memory grew dim and she saw only the reflection of the sunlight glinting on the ewer of water by the fire, and then again she slept.

In her bed at Abergavenny Jo stirred in her sleep as the dream faded. The moonlight touched her face with cold fingers and she flung her arm across her closed eyes and shivered before lying still again.

"I want you to listen to me carefully." Sam sat down on the edge of the coffee table in front of Nick, his eyes on his brother's face. "You trust me, don't you?"

Imperceptibly Nick nodded.

"Good. And you know I would do nothing to harm you—and I think it would harm you, Nick, to take you back into the past too soon. First I must prepare you. I must warn you who you were in that life, long ago. . . ." Sam paused, a flicker of grim humor straying across his face. "You were not Richard de Clare, Nick, and you have good reason to be jealous of him. He was your friend and your adviser. And he was your rival. You and he both loved Matilda de Braose. But Richard won her. It was to him that

228

she turned. She despised you. She feared you and hated you. She was your enemy, Nick. Do you remember?" He paused, watching Nick's face closely as his brother shifted uncomfortably in his seat, his face somber. His gaze had strayed from Sam toward the lamp once more, his eyes fixed on it, the pupils pin-size in the brilliant blue of the floodlit irises. Hanging down toward the carpet at his side, one of his hands twitched involuntarily as he clenched and unclenched his fist.

Sam smiled, wondering for a brief second if what he was saying had a grain of possibility behind it. Where had the violence in his brother come from? One day he would find out for sure, but not today. Today he was setting the scene.

"I think perhaps you do remember, Nick," he went on quietly. "You were a prince when you first saw her. She was beautiful and tall and charming. A lady. And you were a snotty boy. Do you remember? You were born too late. She was the first woman you ever desired and she was already another man's wife and the mother of his child, and you were too young still even to screw the serving wenches you caught in the dark corners of the palace. You made do then with pinching their breasts and thrusting your hand up their skirts, but later it was different. Later you could have any woman you wanted. And you took them. Peasant or lady. Willing or not. Your reputation has echoed down through the centuries. You took them all. All save Lady de Braose. Her scorn unmanned you. When she looked at you, you knew she still saw you as a sniveling child. And your love began to sour. You determined to bring her to her knees, do you remember, Nick? You told her husband to control her better, but he was weak." His jaw tightened momentarily. "She needed William's help and he failed her. When he should have whipped her and bridled her shrewish tongue, he let her speak. He let her walk into your trap, when he could have saved her." He stopped, unable to go on for a moment, sweat standing out on his forehead as he watched Nick's face. "You hated her by then, and you determined she would pay for her scorn with her life."

He sat forward on the edge of the table, hooking his forefinger into the knot of his tie and pulling it loose while behind him the sky was losing its color, the sunset fading as the glare of streetlights took over outside the open window.

"And now, Nick," he went on after a pause, "you and she have been born in another century and in another world, and this time you are not a child. This time she sees you as a man, a man she finds attractive, a man to whom she has submitted. But you cannot trust her. Your hate remains. You have not forgotten, Nick. And you have not forgiven. You swore vengeance against Matilda de Braose eight hundred years ago and you are pursuing it still."

He stood up abruptly and turned away from his brother. "And this time, my friend," he murmured, "when she calls on her husband for help, it will be there. I shall not let her down again. I have waited for the chance to make amends, and now at last I have it. Now at last we are all once more on the stage together." He turned. "You will love the role I've given you, Nick. You always were a conceited little bastard—so self-assured. So clever. So sure every woman will fall for you. And they all do, don't they? But Jo is beginning to see through you. She has tasted your violence now. She no longer trusts you, and if you hit her again, Nick, she will come to me. She will always come to me, I shall see to that. And I shall comfort her. She'll return to you for more because there is something of the masochist in Jo. Violence excites her. She may even tempt you to kill her, Nick. But I shall be there." He smiled evenly. "And this time I shall be the one in charge. This time I shall have men to help me. And you will crawl away, *my liege.* You will lick your wounds and beg for forgiveness as William did to his king, and I shall have you sent away, not to hide in France to die a whimpering shameful death like William had to, no, I shall have you committed, brother mine, to an asylum. The sort of place they put people who live in a world of make-believe and pretend that they are kings. And Jo will come to me. Jo will be mine. She will repent that she slighted me and beg for forgiveness and I will console her as a husband should."

He walked toward the tray and poured himself half a tumbler of whisky. He drank it down at a gulp and then poured another.

"Have you been listening to me, Nick?" He turned slowly.

For a moment Nick gave no sign of having heard, then slowly he nodded.

"And have you understood what I have told you?"

Nick licked his lips. "I understand," he said at last.

Sam smiled. "Good," he said softly. "So, tell me what your name was, Nicholas, in this past life of yours."

"John." Nick looked at Sam with alarming directness.

"And you know what you must do?"

Nick shifted in his chair. He was still staring at Sam but there was a clouded, puzzled look on his face.

Sam frowned. He put down his glass. "Enough now," he said slowly. "You are tired. I am going to wake you soon. You must ask me to hypnotize you again, little brother. You find that hypnosis is soothing. It makes you feel good. You are going to forget all that I have told you today with your conscious mind, but underneath, slowly, you will remember, so that when you are next with Jo you will know how to act. Do you understand me?" His tone was peremptory.

Nick nodded.

"And one other thing." Sam picked up his shirt and began carefully to straighten the sleeves. "A favor for a friend. Before Jo comes back you must go and see Miss Curzon. Make your peace with her, Nick. You like

Judy, remember? She's good in bed. She makes you feel calm and happy. Not like Jo, who makes you angry. Go and see Judy, Nick. Soon." He smiled. "Now I want you to relax. You are feeling happy now and at ease. You are feeling rested. That's good. Now, slowly I want you to count from one to ten. When you reach ten you will awake."

Slowly Nick began to count.

"Abergavenny, Crickhowell, Tretower," Jo murmured as she swung the MG onto the A40 next morning. She glanced up at the line of hills and then at the gleam of the broad Usk on her left, and she shivered, remembering the icy feel of the water, the snow beneath her bare feet, and the silence of the hills. Thankfully she concentrated as a tractor swung out onto the narrow road ahead of her. She leaned forward and turned on the car radio. She could not look at the hills now, not as well as hold the car on the road. She turned the station up loud and, hooting at the tractor, tore past him north toward Hay, refusing to let herself think about the vast empty area of moor and mountain far away on her right.

The approach from Talgarth was along the foot of the small foothills that hid the huge shoulders of Pen y Beacon and Twmpa—the Black Mountains that David had showed her on his map—but she could smell them through the open roof of the car, the sweet indefinable smell of the mountains of Wales, which she remembered from her dream.

The town of Hay, nestling in a curve of the Wye, was a maze of little narrow streets, crowded and busy, which clustered around the gaunt imposing half ruin that was the castle. As she drew into a parking space in the market square immediately below the castle, Jo sat staring up at it in awe. In front of her, to the left, was a cluster of ancient ruins, while at the right-hand end of the edifice was a portion that looked far more recent and appeared to be in the midst of rebuilding and restoration. That part looked as if it might have been recently inhabited. She climbed out of the car feeling strangely disoriented; this time yesterday she had been standing in the London apartment, phoning Janet Pugh. Now she was standing within a stone's throw of the building Matilda had built. She took a deep breath and made herself turn away toward the crowded streets behind her. First she must find a guidebook.

Bookshops throng the narrow streets of Hay-on-Wye. Shelves overflow onto the pavements. Fivepenny paperbacks rub shoulders with priceless esoterica and antiquarian treasures. Fascinated, Jo wandered around, resisting the urge to stop and browse, drawn constantly back to the brooding gray ruin. She bought her guide, a history of the town, and a little street map, then, with a pasty, an apple, and a can of lager she walked slowly down the hill toward the Wye, away from the castle. It was too soon to look at the castle. First she wanted to get her bearings.

Beyond the high modern bridge that spanned the river she found a footpath leading down through the trees to a shingle bank at the edge of the broad expanse of peat-stained water, carpeted so thickly in places with the tiny white flowers of water crowfoot that the water was almost hidden. She stood for a moment staring down at the river as it rippled swiftly eastward toward Herefordshire, pouring over the smoothed, sculpted boulders and rocks through flat water meadows and away from the mountains; then she found a deserted piece of sun-baked shingle and sat down. Opening the lager, she propped her back against a bent birch tree as she watched the water. Out of the corner of her eye she saw a flash of jeweled colors and recognized her first sight of a kingfisher. Enchanted, she stared after it, but it had vanished as quickly as it had come.

She rummaged in her bag for her books and sat eating as she looked through them, every now and then glancing up at the town beyond the river to glimpse the castle at its center or the church nestling beyond the bridge in the trees. Each time she found her gaze drawn back to the water, watching it as ripples formed patterns and swirls in the reflections of the clouds. A feather danced past, curled white in the sun, and far out in the middle of the current a fish jumped, silver-bellied, and plunged back in a circle of ripples.

The afternoon was very hot and still. Jo nodded, and her book fell into her lap. Forcing her eyes open, she made herself stare at the water again, trying to concentrate on staying awake, but the reflections danced in her eyes, dazzling, forcing her to close them again, and slowly, imperceptibly, the sound of the water dulled and grew muffled. It was only after a long while that she realized she could hear the sound of horses' hooves.

England lay beneath a pall of dust. The summer sun burning down beneath a coppery sky smelled acrid and the hot breeze that occasionally fanned the travelers' faces was dust-laden and gritty.

Wearily Matilda pulled up her horse at last. The groom who had been walking at its head raised his hand and the whole tired procession halted. Behind them the forests and rolling hills of Herefordshire shimmered in a haze. The Border March, a vast, wild area of forest and mountain and desolate moorland, lay before them to the west. At their feet they could see at last the River Wye, which had shrunk in places to a narrow ribbon of water flowing between broad strips of whitened stones. There were deep pools, shadowed from the beating overhead sunlight by the crowding alders and hazels, which in places overhung the water, and by great black rocks brought down by the spring floods. They alone were cool and green, the last refuge of salmon and grayling.

William was once again in attendance on the king, this time in Normandy. Matilda had received a message from him shortly before she left Bramber. The household had stayed there too long, overtaxing the facilities, running its supplies down to nothing, but still she had been reluctant

232

to obey William's instructions to set off once more for Wales. He planned to join her there, the message said, by Martinmas, so that he could enjoy some of the late season's hunting in the Hay forest.

One by one the horses and men picked their way almost dryshod across the silvery shallows. Before them lay the small township of Hay. It clustered around the church of St. Mary and the neighboring wooden castle on its mound securely surrounded by a thick high hawthorn hedge, trailing with honeysuckle and brambles. Outside the hedge the small fields, red-gold with brittle wheat, showed up in the heavy green of the encroaching forest. Somewhere nearby were the black brooding mountains, but they had withdrawn beneath a haze that hid all but the lowest wooded slopes of the foothills.

They rode slowly through the gap in the hedge and turned up the beaten earth track toward the castle. It was little more than a wooden tower, built upon a motte thrown up on the bank overlooking the river. Below it lay the still, deep waters of the church pool, the surface streaked with fronds of green weed. To the west of the castle flowed the Login Brook, shallow and stagnant in the heat of the sun.

Matilda halted the procession again just outside the castle wall and looked wearily around. The steward of the manor was waiting for her beside the church and, next to him, sunburned in homespun, the vicar and the castellan. She tried to smile at them. She was bored with the fawning servants who lived in these outlying castles and manors; she had wanted to go on to Brecknock, which at least she knew and where the faithful Robert and Hugh still served, but Hay it had to be, only eleven miles to the northeast. William had insisted on it.

She was conscious of eyes peering at her from dark doorways and around corners. An old man, his limbs wasted and immobile, lay propped up against the wall of an outhouse nearby, and he smiled toothlessly and nodded as he saw her gaze rest on him. Several children ran giggling behind her horse. One of them had a clubfoot, which dragged horribly as he tried to keep up with his friends.

"Lady Matilda, you are welcome to the Hay." The steward hastened forward as she slipped from the saddle and bowed low, his long hair falling across the bare crown of his head to reveal an ancient scar. He introduced himself as Madoc, the castellan as Tom the Wolf, and the thin cadaverous vicar as Philip. They bowed in unison. Then Madoc straightened up. He looked Matilda in the eye, no trace of servility in his manner. "The castle is prepared for you, my lady, if your servants will bring in the furnishings, and the kitchens are ready for your cook. We've had the fires burning since dawn. You have a visitor, my lady." His eyes narrowed in the sunlight. "The Earl of Clare rode in yesterday. He is in the castle waiting for you."

"The Earl of Clare?" Matilda's heart stood still for a moment. It was months since she had allowed herself to think of him. And now, suddenly, unannounced and unexpected, he was here! She did not bother to remount her exhausted horse. With the rein over her arm, she picked her way over the dry turf, rank with thistles, and made her way excitedly toward the gate in the castle wall.

Richard had just returned from a hawking expedition. He was standing, stripped to the waist, at the foot of the stairs that led up the side of the steep motte to the castle tower, while one of his men poured buckets of cold water over his head. He was quite unembarrassed when he saw her. "My lady!" He took another bucket of water full in the face and, spluttering, turned to chase the man away. The long line of pack animals, wagons, and attendants was crowding into the bailey around them, milling in the dust as they halted and began to dismount and unload, before making their way toward the stables and lodgings around the inside of the high wall. Matilda stood unnoticing in the middle of them all, smiling, watching as Richard toweled himself dry and wriggled into his tunic. Her heart was beating very fast.

He fastened his belt and ran his fingers through his wet hair. "Where's Sir William, my lady? I see he isn't with you." He ran ahead of her two at a time up the stairs to the keep. It was hot and stuffy inside and full of acrid smoke from the small fire in the hearth. Matilda followed him more slowly and stopped abruptly, her eyes smarting as she tried to accustom them to the dark after the bright sun outside. When she could see at last she saw Richard gather up his sword and gird it on.

"William is in attendance on the king. What are you doing here at Hay, Richard?" Suddenly she felt shy and ill at ease.

"Waiting for you, of course." He raised his eyebrow slightly, stepping close to her to kiss her hand. "I'm returning from Gloucester, so I sent most of my people ahead and stayed to do a little hawking in your beautiful valley. I heard you were on your way. It's been so long." He was still holding her hand.

She tried to pull it away without success. "Lord de Clare . . ." She glanced behind her at the doorway.

"I've tried again and again to visit you," he went on in a whisper, "but events have always stood in the way. I've been in France with the king or up north or in the Marches, but never when you've been here, or in far away Suffolk." He still held her hands, looking into her eyes solemnly. "Dear sweet God, but I've missed you so."

"No, Richard, please." She interrupted him, pulling her hands away at last. "Please don't talk like that." She hesitated, letting her light traveling cloak slip from her shoulders to the rushes, looking uncertainly into his face. He had not changed at all from the carefree youth who had escorted her across England. He was a tall young man, fractionally taller than she,

234

broad-shouldered and painfully slim, with merry hazel eyes. She bit her lip and half turned.

"Hey, what's wrong?" He swung his sword comfortably onto his hip. "Why do you look so sad? I thought you might be glad to see me!"

"Oh, I am, Richard." She swallowed, and smiled at him with an effort. "You'll never know how glad. It's just that . . . I'm tired, that's all. We've ridden such a long way today."

"My lady . . ."

She turned to find Jeanne pulling at her sleeve. The old woman's face was disapproving. "The little ones are asleep already, my lady. You should be the same." The old woman stooped slowly to pick up the fallen cloak, which lay forgotten on the ground. "Your room is prepared. I'm sure Lord de Clare will excuse you after your long journey."

"That I won't, old dame." Richard reached for Matilda's hand again. "Come, my lady, call for food and wine and music! We'll celebrate your arrival. I'm not letting you slip away to sleep with children tonight. You need cheering up, not sleep."

His high spirits were infectious, and Matilda could not help laughing with him, her eyes on his smiling face. It would be good to celebrate her arrival. Her weariness and depression began to slip away. She turned to Jeanne.

"Go to the children. They need you now, I don't. I can rest later."

"My lady, you're most unwise. You must rest." Stubbornly Jeanne remained at her elbow.

"I said you can go, Jeanne," Matilda rounded on her. "Lord de Clare and I have much to talk about."

Jeanne hesitated, her hands braced stubbornly at the front of her full black skirts, then reluctantly, muttering to herself, she left them, vanishing behind the screens at the end of the hall.

"She watches you closely, that one," he whispered as she left.

Matilda turned to follow his gaze. Then she laughed. "She was *my* nurse before she was my children's. Sometimes I think she forgets I'm grown up now. Now, my lord, tell me all the news, and cheer me up. I command it." She clapped her hands to summon her page. "Bring lights, and food and seats, Simon. Let's see what kind of food those Hay fires can provide."

Richard, one foot on a stool near the fire, gazed at her for a moment, head to one side. "We'll have music and poetry and good wine and conversation in that order. Will that cheer you?" He raised an eyebrow and grinned. "If it doesn't, I'm sure I can think of one or two other things that might appeal." He looked down at the rushes for a moment. When he looked up she could see that the color in his cheeks had risen a little. He caught her eye and for a moment, as they stood together in the center of the bustle of preparation, they gazed at each other without speaking. She felt a stab of excitement running up her body, and swallowed nervously.

235

He feels the same, she thought, and she felt herself beginning to tremble. She looked away first.

"William joins me here soon for the autumn hunting." Her voice was barely more than a whisper.

"Autumn is a long way away, my lady." He took her hand and raised it almost to his lips. Then he let it fall. "Come, where is that music? We must have music while we eat."

Matilda lay awake a long time that night, listening to the owls hooting in the yew trees below the Login Brook. She could feel the touch of Richard's hand on hers and sense the message in his eyes as, sitting next to her, he had shared her dish as they ate and listened to the boy who piped one dance tune after another for them. The firelight had played on his face as he leaned back in his chair and she had seen him watching her, his eyes never leaving her face. She lay still and fought back the longing that overwhelmed her, trying to think instead of her two baby sons, asleep with their nurses.

The river was lapping gently over its stones, murmuring peacefully beyond the bailey wall. The castle was silent. She gazed up at the ceiling over her head and the rail from which her bed curtains hung, and stared, near to tears, into the darkness.

Somewhere in the blackness of the room beyond the curtains a board creaked. She moved her head slightly, trying to see between the heavy folds of material. Perhaps one of her women had stirred in her sleep? Not a breath of wind moved in the trees outside. She stiffened. A slight scraping noise caught her ear, followed by profound silence. It was as though someone else too were listening in the dark.

She swallowed nervously, trying to forget the sudden awful memory of the shadow outside the walls of her tent at Gloucester. The entire garrison was within earshot if she screamed, and there could be no enemies within the castle. She shut her eyes, her fingers clutching the thin sheet up around her face.

Then distinctly she heard the slight rattle of a curtain ring. Someone was touching the curtains of her bed. Her mind flew to Richard. Surely he would not be so stupidly reckless? She lay tense, waiting, not daring to open her eyes.

The curtains were eased back a little more and she felt a slight pressure on the bed as someone leaned over her. Little prickles of panic were beginning to chase up and down her back and she fought desperately to remain still. Something wet fell on her hair, then on her face and her shoulder. A light mist like spring rain. Then she heard whispered words. She strained her ears trying to hear, wondering what prevented her still from crying out. It was a woman's voice, intoning softly. It sounded like a prayer. Or a spell. She felt herself grow cold. It was Jeanne; Jeanne was casting a spell on her. She tried to sit up, to shout at the old woman, to scream for Elen or the guards, but a black silken web seemed to be holding her down. She opened her mouth, but no sound would come. The voice was silent and she heard the curtains being closed gently once more. The old woman had gone. Whatever her spell had been, it was complete. It was too late to fight it. Matilda tried to raise her hand to make the signs against evil and the sign of the cross but her hands were too heavy to raise. Surely, she told herself sleepily, Jeanne could mean her no harm. Slowly her eyelids dropped. Her sleeplessness had gone. Relaxed and at peace, she turned over and was instantly asleep.

She rose at dawn and Elen dressed her in her gown of pale green; she twisted her heavy hair up beneath a simple veil, held in place by a woven fillet. It was too hot for a wimple or barbette, or even a mantle, and she did not send for Jeanne. There had been no sign of the old woman. Richard was already in the bailey surrounded by men and horses and dogs. "I hope you're coming hawking?" he called cheerfully when he saw her. "The birds are ready." The sky was limpid and clear. It was going to be another hot day.

She forgot the fears of the night as she gathered up her skirts and ran down the steps to her horse. They were no more to her now than some uneasy nightmare about which, though she remembered having been frightened, she could recall no details.

They rode out of Hay away from the sweeping escarpment of Pen y Beacon, which rose sharp as a knife against the sky, back across the shallow Wye, this time turning north toward the meadows that bounded Clyro Hill; the grooms and austringers with the precious hawks, Richard's chief falconer—some dozen horsemen altogether—clattered after them along the stony track, and another dozen or so men on foot. In the distance a curlew called.

All at once from a bed of reeds nearby they put up a heron. With an exclamation Richard pulled the hood from the bird on his wrist and tossed her into the air. They reined their horses in and watched as the humped figure of the heron flew low and lumbering for the river, but it was too late. The hawk struck it down within seconds. Excited, Matilda turned and called for her own bird, a small but swift and deadly brown merlin. She grinned at Richard. "I'll match you kill for kill." She pulled on the heavy gauntlet and reached down for the bird, feeling the power of its talons as it settled itself, bells jingling, onto the leather on her fist. She gripped the jesses and kicked her pony on.

Gradually the path began to climb, and after a while it plunged into the dry woods that cloaked the southern side of Elfael. Then the trees cleared and the moors rose bare before them. They waited as the beaters with their dogs scattered into the tall bracken. Richard's horse shifted restlessly beneath him as he turned to Matilda with a smile, soothing the glossy peregrine on his wrist. "We should have some good sport up here. It's early yet, and not too hot." He tensed suddenly as the beaters flushed a snipe from a marshy cwm. After slipping the hood from the bird's head again, Richard flew her and they waited, eyes narrowed against the glare, as she climbed high into the blue, towering above the quarry, ready for the deadly swoop.

His eyes gleamed with excitement as the bird plummeted down. "A kill," he murmured exultantly under his breath. He urged his horse forward into the breast-high bracken, the winged lure dangling from his fingers.

Matilda followed him, her eyes fixed on his broad shoulders, and she breathed deeply and exultantly in the sharp air, almost laughing out loud as she kicked her pony on and felt the wind lifting her veil, teasing, trying to dislodge her hair.

It was a good morning's sport. When they drew rein at midday the party was tired and hot. Richard slid from his saddle, then threw the rein to a groom and went to lie facedown on the grass beside a tiny upland brook. He grinned up at her, shaking the water from his eyes. "Come and bathe your face. It's gloriously cool."

Their attendants drew back into the shadow of a group of trees with the birds and Matilda, who had been watching as her horse was led away, dropped on her knees beside him and let her fingers play for a moment in the water. The mountain stream was very cold and within minutes her hands were aching with it. He laughed at her. "How improper! My Lady de Braose, paddling in the water like a child!"

She laughed a little guiltily. "I wish I could throw all my clothes off and jump in like a boy."

"Please do, madam. I should not object." He grinned shamelessly. She could not be angry with him. "God, Matilda," he went on, suddenly serious. "Would that you were not de Braose's wife." His voice took on a new note that frightened her. She glanced up apprehensively and found him gazing at her, the message in his eyes plain. "Let's walk in the woods a little way away from this rabble that always follows us. I must talk to you freely. Alone."

"No!" Her voice was firm, although her heart was beating fast. She wanted so much to throw caution aside and do as he asked. "No, not again, we mustn't. We mustn't as long as my husband lives." She rose, brushing the loose grass from her kirtle. "Please, don't ever speak of it again. Many things I would dare in this world, but I must not dishonor William again." She turned toward the trees, biting her lips miserably, wishing he had not spoken, but he had scrambled after her. He seized her hand.

"It is too late to speak of dishonor, Matilda. You are mine in your heart, and in your eyes when you look at me, and in your dreams. I know it."

238

Careless of who might still be able to see them, he pulled her to him, seeking her mouth with his own, caressing her shoulders gently as he pressed her against him.

She gave a little shudder of longing. "We must not," she murmured, her lips against his. "Such love will be cursed."

"Rubbish." His grip was more insistent now. He bent and, flinging his arm behind her knees, he scooped her off her feet. She gave a little cry of protest, but he ignored it, carrying her down the bank of the brook and wading across the gurgling water to the shelter of some gorse bushes on the far side. There he laid her on the ground. He reached for his belt and unbuckled it, laying his sword aside, then he bent over her once more, covering her face with kisses, his hands feeling for her breasts in the low neckline of her gown. She gasped with pleasure, her arms encircling his neck, drawing him down toward her as she felt him fumbling with her long skirts. All sense of caution was gone. She did not care who saw them as he took her swiftly, bringing her again and again to the giddy climax of excitement. Once, as her back arched against him, her hips moving with his, she opened her eyes, dazzled by the brilliant blue sky above them. For a moment she stiffened as something moved—a shadow against the sun—then the thrusting excitement within her claimed her whole attention once more and she fell helplessly into the tide of her passion.

When at last Richard raised his head he was smiling. "So, my lady, you are mine." He dropped his head to nuzzle her throat.

She stroked his hair gently, still trembling. "If I am discovered, William will kill me," she whispered.

"William is in France. He'll not find out," he said, sitting up slowly. "No one has noticed our departure. If they have, we'll say we were scouting for cover later in the day. Come." He stood up and held out his hand to help her rise. "Let us go and eat, my lady. Love gives a man an appetite!"

They walked slowly toward the clearing. By the trees Matilda halted and beckoned the food baskets forward with an imperious wave of her hand, aware that many eyes had been watching them and had probably missed nothing of their disappearance. Aware too that Richard was looking at her with eyes that made her shiver with desire. Only the slightly heightened color in her cheeks betrayed her inner turmoil as she stood haughtily by as the cloth was laid on the ground.

She glanced at Richard again. Outwardly at least he was calm now. He sat on a rocky outcrop of the bank, his tunic unlaced at the throat, his hand held out carelessly for the wine his page brought him. Catching her eye, suddenly he grinned again and raised the cup in half salute. "To the afternoon's sport, my lady."

She turned away abruptly and watched as the austringers settled their frames beneath the shade. The hawks huddled disconsolately on their perches, sleepy in the heat. Around them the grooms sprawled, shading their eyes from the light that pierced the high branches of the Scots pines, chewing on their pasties. The air was heavy with the scent of pine needles and dry grass.

The riders were upon them before anyone knew it. A party of a dozen or so, wearing the light arms of the Welsh, bows strung around their shoulders, their drawn blades glinting in the sun. Their leader drew to a halt before Matilda and Richard, the hooves of his sturdy pony dancing only inches from the edge of the white cloth on the grass. He saluted and sheathed his sword with a grave smile. Behind them their startled attendants stood helpless, guarded by drawn swords.

"*Henpych gwell, arglwyddes. Yd oedd gennwch y hela da? Balch iawn yw dy hebogeu.*" The man was swarthy. He had wavy hair and was dressed in glowing purple. "Greetings, lady; has your hunting been good?" he went on in flawless French. "I trust the sport of my mountains does me credit. I see your kill has been substantial." He nodded in the direction of the birds that lay trussed for carrying beside one of the grooms.

He eyed Matilda slowly, taking in the tall, slim figure with the bronze hair beneath the veil. "My Lady de Braose, if I'm not mistaken? I am Einion ap Einion Clud, Prince of Elfael." He bowed gravely in the saddle. "I was told you were in residence in Hay. May I ask when your husband is to join you there?" His eyes, green as the sunlight in the moss below the waters of the brook, were suddenly amused.

Matilda colored violently. This man had seen them. She knew it without a doubt. He had seen them make love. A quick glance at Richard showed her that he still sat, unarmed, wine cup in hand, on his rock. The set of his lips and the dangerous gleam in his eyes were the only signs that he was angered by the interruption.

"It was good of you to ride to greet us, Prince Einion," she said, keeping her voice steady with an iron effort of will. "My husband is at present in service with the king. May I ask what you want of him? Perhaps a message could be sent." Her face was haughty as she gazed at the man. The amusement in his face had gone. It was replaced by something hard and frightening. She refused to allow the suspicion of terror that gnawed suddenly at the back of her mind to show as stubbornly she held his gaze.

"It is a matter of a small debt, my lady. The kin of Seisyll of Gwent are unavenged. Do not think that the matter, of however little consequence, is forgotten." His voice was level and light in spite of the irony in his words. "Think about it when you roam about my hills, and bid your men keep watch over their shoulders. I doubt if any of them could willingly lose a hand even in the defense of your gracious person." He bowed again, mocking. She swallowed, clenching her fists to stop her hands from shaking. The moor was uncannily silent for a moment, then suddenly, close by, came the harsh grating call of a corncrake. Einion's horse threw up its head and whinnied. Instantly his mood seemed to change. He smiled a warm smile and raised his hand. "Good hunting, my lady," he murmured, inclining his head. "I trust your sport is as rewarding this afternoon! Farewell. *Duw a ro da it!*" He threw back his head and laughed, then with a wave of his arm he called his men to him and they turned as one and galloped up the hill in a cloud of dust and vanished over the skyline, leaving the moorlands empty.

Richard sprang for his sword, which had been resting only feet from his hand against a rock. "My God, I thought we were done for." He wiped his forehead with the back of his hand. "I'd heard that he had succeeded his father. He's a firebrand, that young man. Out for trouble. I doubt if Rhys will keep him in check for long. He honors the blood feud, it seems."

"The *galanas*, they call it," Matilda repeated softly. She gazed down into the swiftly running water for a moment. "He saw us, Richard. He saw us making love."

Richard glanced at her, his face grim. "Come, I'll take you back. Mount up. We return to Hay at once." He flung instructions over his shoulder at the frightened huddle of followers who waited beneath the trees. "It appears that you are not included in his particular feud," he said quietly, eyeing her gravely as a groom ran up with their horses.

"I was there when Seisyll died, but I knew nothing of William's plans," she said wearily. "A Welsh boy guided me over the hill to Tretower. He said they had no quarrel with me then, but . . ." She shivered. "Richard, you heard what he said about the hands. It must have been his men who brought that dreadful burden to Gloucester."

He shrugged. "As likely one as another. They are all related, these Welsh princes. They all remember the blood feud when it suits them."

He helped her into the saddle and then swung himself onto his own horse. "But it's a warning. Peace there may be officially, but never again should you venture into these hills without a full escort. Remember that."

They rode swiftly and uneasily back across the moor through the bracken and the woods into the village of Clyro and down across the low hill toward the ford, the lazy good humor of the morning completely gone.

The heat haze had again obscured the mountains and a heavy thundery cloud mass was building up beyond the closer hills.

Matilda rode into the outer ward of Hay castle with relief. She slid from her horse, ignoring Richard, who had sprung forward to help her, and ran toward the children's lodging. A terrible thought had come to her as they rode home. The children. William's children for Seisyll's. Would that be a fair exchange?

The elder little boy was playing in the dust with two companions at Jeanne's feet.

241

"Is Will all right?" It was many months since she had felt that terrible throat-constricting fear for her eldest son.

"Of course, my lady, why not?" The old woman looked up with a peaceful smile.

Matilda gave a sigh of relief. She might be spared from the *galanas* as Gwladys, Seisyll's wife, had been spared. But two of Seisyll's children had died, and she knew the Welsh would be scrupulous in their revenge.

She heard Richard's quick step behind her. "What is it? Is anything wrong?"

"Nothing." She shook her head. "They're fine." She smiled at him. "A foolish mother's sudden fears, that is all." She fell to her knees and hugged Will close to her, feeling the softness of his hair against her mouth.

The little boy wriggled free almost at once and staggered a few steps away from her before sitting down and running the dust once more delightedly through his fingers. Matilda looked up smiling. Her smile faded as she noticed Jeanne's calculating eye on Richard. The old woman's face had contracted into a passive mask and Matilda recognized suspicion and hatred in her eyes. Abruptly she remembered the strange events of the night before. She had been inclined to dismiss them that morning as a dream. But it had not been a dream at all. It had been Jeanne. She sighed. If the magic the old woman had woven was a spell to prevent her mistress feeling the pangs of love for this tall, handsome man, it hadn't worked, she thought sadly. For once, Jeanne, my old friend, your magic is not strong enough to save me.

She picked herself up wearily from the dust, and, shaking out her pale green skirts, she turned and walked toward her own lodgings, leaving Richard standing in the sun.

Behind her she could hear a voice calling suddenly. She stopped and hesitated, wanting to turn, but she was afraid that if she looked at Richard he would follow her inside. The voice was insistent. Someone was running after her. She felt a hand touch her shoulder and heard the soft lilt of a Welsh voice calling her. . . .

"Are you all right? Come on there, wake up, my lovely. Come on." The voice swam up again out of the shadows then receded. "You'd best go and find a doctor, Alan."

Someone was bending over her. Jo opened her eyes slowly. She was lying on the shingle near the river. With an exclamation of fright she sat up, her head swimming. The afternoon had gone. The sun was setting in a sea of golden cloud and two complete strangers were kneeling beside her at the river's edge.

242

20

The blank canvas beckoned. Judy was standing in front of it, eating a hunk of cheese, the structure of the painting floating in her head, ready to be trapped and laid on the naked background. She had changed her position slightly, studying the fall of light, when something distracted her and she turned toward the door of the studio, frowning. There was someone standing on the landing outside, his weight on the creaky board.

"Who is it?" she called. She put the last piece of cheese into her mouth and wiped her fingers on the seat of her jeans.

There was no reply. Frowning, she moved toward the door. "Is there someone there?" she said. She pulled it open, irritated at the interruption.

Nick was standing, looking out of the high landing window at the sloping rooftops of the house backs. He turned slowly and looked at her without a word. "Oh, no, it's you. What do you want?" Judy glared at him, determined he would not see the hurt and longing that rose to the surface at the sight of him.

"I thought I would see if you had got back from France safely," he said. He did not smile at her.

"As you see, I did." She put her hands on her hips.

"Judy—" He came toward her suddenly. "I'm sorry. I shouldn't have left you like that. It was a lousy thing to do after you had come out to join me. We'd had a good time."

"Until someone mentioned Joanna." Judy stood by the door holding it open as he walked past her into the studio. "How *is* Jo?"

Nick shrugged. "She's gone off somewhere. Is this going to be the new painting?" He was standing in front of the blank canvas.

"No. It's going to be a sculpture in bronze." Her voice was sharp with sarcasm. "So Jo is missing and you decided to visit the first reserve. Dear old unfussy Judy, always there to pat your head and make a man of you again." She was still standing by the door. "I'm sorry, Nick, but I'd like you to leave."

He walked back toward her. "Can I have a drink first?" There was a new harshness in his voice as he pulled her hand from the door latch abruptly and hurled the door shut. "A drink, Judy."

She took a step back in astonishment. "All right! Steady. How much have you had already?"

"Nothing. I've been in the office all morning trying to sort out the screw-up Jim Greerson's made of our best account and I'm going back there this afternoon. This visit"—he waved his arm around the studio—"is lunch."

"Then I'll get you some food."

"I said a drink." His eyes were hard.

"Okay. A drink." Judy was staring at him as she groped behind her in a cabinet and found a whisky bottle. "I'll fetch some glasses."

"Do that." Nick had not moved. He was looking at the blank canvas with the same intensity he would normally have given to a painting. His head ached, and he knew he was tense and irritable and that it had been a mistake to come. He wasn't sure why he had. His desire for Judy had gone and yet he had found himself hailing a taxi and giving her address automatically, compelled by a need to be with her that he could not define or understand.

"So what's wrong? Apart from the office, I mean?" Judy poured half an inch into the glass and handed it to him.

He drank it quickly and held it out to her again. As she was pouring he caught her wrist, forcing her to slop the whisky until the glass was almost full.

"Careful! Look what you've done!" she cried.

"Shut up, Judy," he said, bored. "One tumblerful is the same as the sum of all the prissy little doses you're going to give me one by one."

"I am not going to hand you little doses one by one. If you drink that lot on an empty stomach you'll be flat on your back!"

"Fine. With you in my arms?"

"No!" She took the glass out of his hand and put it down with a bang on the table. "Please leave now, Nick."

"Oh, come on!"

"I mean it!" She bit back sudden angry tears. "Please get out of here. Go back to your office and sort out your problems there, not in my studio."

She pulled the door open and stood by it. "I mean it!"

For a moment he hesitated, then he picked up the whisky glass, took a couple of gulps from it, put it down, and strode past her to the door.

"I thought you wanted me back," he said softly as he stood for a moment looking down at her.

"Out, Nick," she repeated.

He shrugged, then, with a strangely grating laugh, he walked past her and out onto the landing.

244

She slammed the door. For a moment she listened to the sound of his footsteps running down the long flights of stairs, then she turned back into the studio.

"Oh, yes, I want you back, Nick Franklyn," she said to herself softly. "But on my terms. Not yours."

As she picked up his glass and began to pour the whisky carefully back into the bottle, she found she was shaking.

They took Jo to a nearby boardinghouse, the two kind strangers who had found her on the riverbank. And there she was shown to a spotless room with a mansard window, overlooking the common beyond the river. Alone at last, she lay down wearily on the bed. Her last thought as she drifted into sleep was of little Will. As he played in the dirt of the castle bailey he had fallen on the ground and grazed his knees. She had to see that someone cleaned them properly and smeared on some antiseptic; the whole place was so filthy . . .

She awoke the next morning to the smell of frying bacon. Puzzled, she lay staring around her room, looking at the pink chintz curtains blowing at the open window and the pink drapes of an unfamiliar dressing table. Her mind was fuddled with sleep. Slowly she pulled herself into a sitting position and rubbed her eyes. She was still fully dressed. Someone had put a tartan blanket over her while she slept. Her bag and typewriter stood on the floor by the door and she could see her car keys on the dressing table. Vaguely she remembered giving her keys to the strangers; they must have collected her things.

The rest of it was coming back to her now too. Sitting by the River Wye, looking up at the broken silhouette of the castle, she had somehow gone into a regression; on her own and, without wanting to, she had slipped back to the time of Matilda and for two or three hours had lain on the white shingle in a trance, oblivious of the world around her. She hugged her knees with a shiver, wishing suddenly that Nick was there. Then she put her head in her hands. Had she even forgotten that? That she could never see Nick again? She bit her lip, trying to hold back the tears. Nick and she were finished and Richard was far away beyond her reach. She was alone.

Standing up shakily, she glanced at her watch. It was ten past nine. She went to the window and stared out at the low hills beyond the trees. It was somewhere up there that she and Richard had ridden with their hawks.

She found she was clenching her fists violently, suddenly overcome by fear. Was it her need to see Richard that had made her regress alone and unprompted, or was it something else? Was Matilda beginning to take her over? She took a deep breath. She had been mad to come to Wales, mad to think she could handle this alone. She did need Carl Bennet's help. He had started all this off and somehow he had to help her to get free of it again. She had to go back to him, had to persuade him to try again to make her forget, and as soon as possible.

Margiad Griffiths was in the kitchen when Jo, showered and in a fresh dark-blue cotton dress, went down. She turned from the stove and smiled. "Better, are you?" she said. "I've just made some coffee, or would you prefer tea?"

"I'd love some coffee, please." Jo sat down at the kitchen table. "I didn't realize I was so tired. I am sorry, I've put you to a lot of trouble."

"Not at all." Margiad reached down two earthenware cups from the cabinet. "The Peterses have gone, though. Sorry not to see you again, they were. They sent their best wishes."

"I wish I could have thanked them. I still don't know quite what happened to me by the river yesterday."

"Exhaustion, I expect." Margiad poured the coffee. "I usually put my guests at the tables in the sitting room, through there, if you'd rather . . ."

Jo grimaced. "No, I'd rather stay here, if I may. I expect all your other guests went out ages ago, it's so late."

Shrugging, Margiad passed her a bowl of sugar. "I've only the three rooms. The Peterses had one, and there was a nice young teacher in the other. Walking Offa's Dyke, he was, but he stopped here for the books. Everyone comes to Hay for the books."

Jo smiled. "I was here doing some research into the history of the town." The coffee was strong and fragrant. She could feel the heat of it seeping into her veins.

"Oh, it's an old town. The castle's very ancient. That's Richard Booth's now, of course. Did you see it?"

Jo shrugged. "I'm more interested at the moment in the old castle. The first one. It was near the church."

"Down here?" Margiad stared at her. "Well, now. I never knew that! Fancy there being another castle. You'll be off to see it later, I suppose?"

Jo sighed regretfully. "I can't today. I've got to go back to London." She stared down with some distaste as Margiad put a plate of eggs and bacon down on the table in front of her. "I didn't realize that was for me—"

"Go on, girl. Eat it up while I make you some toast. You could do with some good solid food in you." Margiad was watching her carefully while behind her the frying pan sputtered gently on the stove. "Will you be coming back this way then, or have you finished all your research?"

Jo picked up the knife and fork. She cut into the top of the egg and watched the yolk flow across the plate.

"I don't know," she said after a moment. "I think it's a case of whether it has finished with me."

Her walk back toward the town took her past the site of the old castle. All that remained was the motte, grass-covered and sown with wildflowers. There was no sign of the wooden keep or the bailey that she remembered, nor of the thick hedge. She stood and stared for a moment, half afraid that something would happen, but there were no ghosts, no shadows, just a cheerful black-and-white collie that loped across the grass, cocked its leg against the wall, and disappeared into the trees near the church.

It was market day and she stared in confusion at the clustered colorful stalls that had appeared around her car overnight, wondering how on earth she was going to move it. Catching the eye of the woman selling farm produce from the stall beside the MG, she shrugged and grinned apologetically. "I'm sorry. I didn't realize it would be market day. I wasn't feeling well yesterday, so I left the car here."

The woman grinned back. "So. It's not something you'll do again, is it?" she said cheerfully, and she turned away.

Jo stuck out her tongue at the woman's back. She threw her cases into the car and climbed into the driver's seat. It would take some careful maneuvering to extricate herself from the crowded, noisy square.

Slowly she wound down the window and leaned forward to insert her key into the ignition. In front of her the castle walls rose high and gray against the brilliant blue of the sky. When had it been built? she wondered idly as she turned on the engine. Would she ever know now? Her eyes traversed the high walls with the empty gaping spaces where the stone arches of the windows had fallen. In one of them a white dove was bobbing to and fro in the sunlight, its throat puffed into a snowy lace cravat as it cooed. Without knowing why she found herself staring at it with total concentration as behind her the noise of the market died away. She shivered. The silence was uncanny in the midst of so many people. Uncanny and suddenly frightening.

William arrived unannounced one blustery autumn night. He appeared with his men and horses, exhausted, mud-splashed, and wet with rain, before the gates of Hay, angrily demanding entrance to the castle. "The ford will soon be too deep to cross," he growled as his wife came forward to greet him. "By Christ's bones I'm glad to be here safe and sound. It's not the weather for traveling." He unclasped the brooch that held his cloak and flung the soaked garment to the floor. "How is the hunting, my lady?" His ruddy cheeks were a shade more deeply lined, she thought, and his paunch a trifle more pronounced, but he looked as fit and well as ever. "Will we kill tomorrow?"

She laughed. "So short a rest, my lord? Yes, the hunting's good. But we have been warned out of Elfael." She scrutinized his face closely. "Old feuds are remembered by the new prince."

William threw back his head and laughed. "Are they indeed? Well, I've plans for that young man and his territory." He threw a boisterous arm around Matilda's shoulder, pulling her down to plant a smacking kiss on her cheek. "He splits my lands in two, does our Einion. If I held Elfael, I'd hold the middle March from Radnor to Abergavenny. But let be for now. King Henry wants peace with Rhys ap Gruffydd at present. I'm content to bide my time. There are more amusing things to do in winter than plan a mud campaign. Like hunting and bedding my beautiful wife." He laughed again.

He was true to his word. By Yule the larders were hung with boar and venison, and Matilda knew herself to be pregnant once more. But it was not with William's child. Her monthly courses had stopped before William came back to her bed.

Gritting her teeth in disgust and pain, she allowed him to maul her night after night, praying he would never suspect the truth. That Jeanne had guessed she was certain, but the old woman kept an enigmatic silence on the subject of her lady's prematurely swelling belly. Of Richard she stubbornly allowed herself to think not at all. News had come that he was on his way to Ireland, and after that nothing.

Jeanne watched over her now with increasingly jealous care as the time passed, fending off even the faithful Elen, who had drawn apart, resentful and hurt, spitefully hinting that the old woman was a witch. Matilda was sure of it, and one day, bored with being kept indoors by the weather, she sought Jeanne out in the walled herb garden.

"Teach me some of your art, Jeanne," she whispered as she caught the old woman, muffled in a fur cloak, scraping snow into a bowl with a muttered incantation.

Jeanne jumped guiltily, then she turned, a crafty smile on her lips. She had lost the last of her front teeth and it gave her an expression of cunning. Matilda caught her breath at the sight, but she steadied herself and smiled, excited.

"I should like to know. Please tell me some spells."

Jeanne's eyes shifted sideways. "I know no spells, Lady Matilda. 'Tis healing I practice, that's all, with herbs and prayers. Those I'll teach you gladly."

Matilda nodded. "And I would gladly learn them, but the other things, Jeanne—" She looked the old woman in the eye. "What was it you whispered over my bed the night Lord Clare came to Hay?" Clutching her fists in her skirts, she was suddenly afraid as she waited for the answer.

Jeanne did not move for a moment, then slowly the hooded eyes fell to gaze at Matilda's stomach. "My power was not strong enough to save you," she murmured. "Now it is too late. Events are already in train. I can do nothing."

Matilda shivered. "There is nothing to do, Jeanne. My husband will never guess," she whispered. "We were discreet. We were never alone together again."

Jeanne shrugged. "The truth has a way of finding daylight, *ma p'tite.* One day Sir William will know. One day Lord Clare must pay the price."

"No!" Matilda clutched her arm. "No, I don't believe you. How could William find out? No one knows. No one. You would not tell him—"

Jeanne shook her head. "Not me, *ma p'tite,* nor the prince of the Welsh who saw you in Lord Clare's arms—" She ignored the look of terror that crossed Matilda's face as she hobbled stiffly away from her, pulling her furs more closely around her. "It is the child herself who will betray your secret. I have seen it in my dreams. And all for *nothing!*" She turned suddenly, spitting with vehemence. "Lord Clare is not for you, Matilda! You belong to another!" She spread her knotted hands expressively, then she shook her head.

Matilda shuddered. "I know," she whispered, her voice barely audible above the sighing of the wind. Snowflakes were beginning to drift down out of the sky, catching in the women's furs.

Jeanne pursed her lips over her toothless gums. "You don't know, *ma p'tite,*" she said softly. "And I pray that I have seen falsely and you never will. It is not your husband I have seen."

"Not my husband?" Matilda echoed. "Who then?" She ran after Jeanne, clutching at her arm. "What have you seen? Tell me!"

Jeanne stopped. "I saw a king," she whispered, and she glanced nervously over her shoulder. *"He* is your destiny. And I shall not be there to save you."

Matilda stared at her. "What do you mean?" Her mouth had gone dry with fear. "You must tell me!" She almost shook the old woman in her impatience. "Tell me!" But Jeanne shook her head, holding her finger to her lips. "Perhaps, one day, *ma p'tite"* was all she would say, and no matter how hard Matilda tried to persuade her she would not speak of the matter again. But she did take her mistress to her stillroom, and there she showed her the dried herbs and flowers, salves, and creams she kept locked in a chest. There were also stones, and branches of aromatic trees from faraway lands, and scraps of parchment covered with strange symbols. Those Jeanne whisked out of sight beneath a napkin, and when Matilda went again to look in the chest, they had gone. She had to be content with the arts Jeanne showed her, the simple spell of words to induce sleep in a fretful child, the way to consult the stars about the humors of the body, and how to prepare feverfew and gromel for when the labor pains came on her in the summer. But always she refused to speak more of what she had seen in her dreams.

Matilda was sitting one evening, listening idly to the singing of a wandering minstrel who had floundered in out of the snowdrifts, his gittern swathed in rags slung across his back, when she saw William poring over some parchments on the table, his forehead wrinkled with the effort of reading the close writing in the flickering light of the streaming candles. Outside the wind roared up the broad Wye Valley, slamming against the walls and rattling the loose wooden shutters. Once she thought she heard the howl of a wolf and she shivered.

He looked up at her suddenly, grinning. "A good haul today, my dear, eh?" He rubbed his leg, stiff from the saddle, and stood up slowly, coming to stand close to her chair. "There's some of the best hunting I know around here and I like the Hay. I'll be pleased when we have a more solid keep here, though. What do you say? Shall we pull it down and build in stone? That would make you feel safer, wouldn't it?" He looked up at her, cocking an eyebrow, then he reached for one of the parchments on the table. "I've been working out the moneys with Madoc and Bernard. The tithes are good, but the area should be better defended." He stabbed at the parchment with a grimy finger. "We're strategically placed here. I should make better use of the position. The Welsh may be quiet at the moment, but one never knows when they're going to plan a surprise attack. We could never hold them off here for long, and we have been as good as warned by your friend Einion." He rubbed his chin thoughtfully.

An extra blast of wind whistled through the shutters and one of the candles blew out, scattering wax over the table. William swore quietly as a page ran to the fire for a brand to relight it and he lowered his voice suddenly. "There is plenty of labor and it would be a good jumping-off place should one ever have plans to move into Elfael." He looked at her and raised his eyebrow again. "Well, woman, what do you say to the idea?"

She smiled. "It seems good. I won't deny I'd feel safer with a sound stone keep if we must stay at Hay."

He nodded. "We'll return to Brecknock for a while, then you can come back to supervise the building when I rejoin the king in the spring. Give you something to do, eh, while you're waiting to spawn that brat?" He laughed loudly and turned to pour himself more wine.

And so it was at Hay that Richard's daughter Matilda was born, on a cool, crystal-clear midsummer night, bright with stars that seemed to have been borrowed from the frosts of winter. Jeanne delivered the child, a flaxen-haired scrap, then laid the offerings on the hearth. The baby was tiny—more like a seven-month child than either of Matilda's lusty full-term boys, and William accepted her as such without a word of doubt, crossing himself as he caught sight of Jeanne muttering protective spells above the cradle, hastily turning away to his horses and his falcons. Alone again but for Jeanne, Matilda held out her arms for the child and took her, staring down at the delicate, perfect features. She had expected to feel an especial love for this child of her love. She felt nothing at all.

250

She shook her head and smiled. "Nothing. Just a superstitious fear of the unknown, I suppose. But I never thought you would do it. You used to be afraid even of falling asleep when you were a little boy—"

"It wasn't like falling asleep. I remember every word he said—" He hesitated. "At least, I think I do—"

Her eyes shot up to meet his. "Oh, Nick—"

"It's okay. There's nothing to worry about. Sam knows what he's doing."

She turned away. "That is what I'm afraid of," she said, so quietly he did not hear her.

Absentmindedly she picked up her sandwich again and stood staring at the wall on which hung a steel-framed silhouette of two children playing ball. It was several minutes before she could bring herself to speak again. "And did he find out who you were in Matilda's past," she asked at last, "or did he say you were not there at all?" She turned back slowly to look at his face. "Well, Nick? What did he let you remember?"

21

Jo did not want to stop. She wanted to drive on. She wanted to get as far away as possible from the Welsh Marches, where the name of every town and village seemed to beckon her back into the past. She was afraid that if she stopped it would happen again. The past was still there, floating on the edge of her consciousness, and with it the shadow of Matilda's fear.

Driving blindly southward, bypassing Abergavenny, she realized suddenly she must have taken a different road from the one she intended. She pulled up at last, grabbing her road map, trying to force herself to concentrate on the network of roads on the page in front of her, tracing a route back toward London with her forefinger as the sun blazed down on the car.

She stopped for a late lunch in the end at Monmouth, drawing the car onto the side of the road, too tired to drive farther without a break. The garden outside the pub was cool and shady, and she found herself relaxing as she ate a fresh crusty roll and a plate of Stilton salad, and sipped a glass of cider. Her panic was retreating. She had come, after all, to find Matilda. What had happened by the Wye and outside Hay Castle was no more than she had hoped might happen at Bramber or as she ran her hands across the ancient walls at Clare. Somehow she had triggered off some sort of trance and the place had done the rest.

So why had she been afraid? She leaned back in her chair, staring with half-closed eyes up at the underside of the striped umbrella that shaded her table. What she ought to do was face this strange talent she had found within herself and bend it to her will, summon it once more and with it discover whether Matilda had heeded Jeanne's warning.

Slowly she stood up and stretched catlike in the sun. Had Matilda ever come to Monmouth? she wondered. And if so, did she have the courage deliberately to try and find out?

Undecided, she walked slowly out of the garden and into the quiet road. She glanced with distaste at her car parked at the curbside; the thought of another four hours in the sweltering heat did not appeal to her, so she turned her back on it and walked on. The sun was now shrouded in haze, but it was still very hot as she followed a footpath between some old stone-built houses and made her way down to the Usk, where she sat down on a crumbling wall and watched a small lizard skitter over some dry moss and disappear into a crack in the stone.

After kicking off her shoes, she dabbled her feet in the icy water. A few minutes' rest was what she needed. Then she would decide whether to move on or wait to try to summon back the past.

The water was sucking at the moss-covered stones on the old bridge, combing tresses of brown weed into the streaming current. Now and then a stray glimmer of sunshine would escape the haze and turn the oily smooth surface into a sparkling pool that would shimmer and move and slide back into the brown oneness of the river.

Suddenly she found she was clutching her hands together, trying to force herself to look away as she felt a strange shimmer of unreality flicker before her eyes. She blinked and the scene steadied, then once again it seemed to move. She pulled her feet out of the river and made as if to scramble up the bank. "No," she whispered. "No. I didn't mean it. Not yet. I'm not ready. I don't want it to happen again yet. . . ."

The nausea had returned. Wearily Matilda rested her head against the pillow and waited for it to pass. Gently Elen placed a cloth against her forehead after wringing it out in the pitcher of ice-cold water. The girl's fingers were blue but she uncomplainingly dipped the cloth in again, soothing her mistress's fevered trembling with gentle hands.

"You'll not be able to leave Monmouth today, my lady. You must tell Sir William." She ran for the basin as Matilda began to retch again.

"No!" After pushing the bowl away, Matilda struggled to her feet. "I will go with Sir William. I have a feeling, a strange feeling here." She pressed her hand to her stomach. "There is danger somewhere, Elen. I'm sure I'm needed at Hay. We should not have allowed the children to travel on with the household without us."

"But, my lady, you're ill." Elen's eyes were soft with sympathy.

"I am not ill," Matilda snapped at her. "I told you. I am with child again."

"But you never have morning sickness, madam. Never in all the years I've known you—" She stopped abruptly at the sight of Matilda's face.

"Well, I have now, so be quiet about it." Matilda forced herself to climb out of the bed and reached for her gown. "Something's wrong, Elen. I can't explain it, but I have the feeling something awful is going to happen, and my feelings are always right. I must be with the children. I must—"

It had happened again the night before as she lay half waking in the firelight. A shadow hovering near her, something she could not grasp or see. "There's death here, Elen," she whispered. "Death near us." She doubled up again and Elen, her eyes enormous with fear, ran to hold her. For a moment the two women clung together. Then, slowly, Matilda straightened up, pushing tendrils of hair back from her damp forehead.

The realization that she was again pregnant had come as a bitter disappointment to Matilda. It was two years since she had given birth to her third son, Reginald, and she had dared to hope that God was sparing her the burden of further children.

Not realizing that this pregnancy would make her tired and ill within a few weeks, she had reluctantly agreed, while they were at Gloucester, to allow the children and their nurses and attendants to go with the main baggage train to Hereford and then on to the newly built castle of Hay, on its hill above the old site near St. Mary's, while she accompanied William on a tour of his castles in Gwent; and she had braced herself to visit Abergavenny once again, should he require it, although he had as yet made no mention of going there.

It was seven years since that terrible night, but she was certain that he too remembered it sometimes, with horror, in his dreams. And ever since they had waved the children away, she had been afraid. She pictured them. There was Will, tall and thin, riding very upright behind a groom, his delicate features solemn beneath the unruly mouse-color hair; Giles, so different from his brother, confident, with shiny copper-color hair, immaculately combed and brighter by far than her own. Then came Matilda, a delicate silvery waif of a child, strangely reserved, giving no love and expecting none in return; and last little Reginald, a sturdy two-year-old, fair like his sister, but as different from her as from the other two boys. They had all turned and waved back at her and shouted as the long procession of horsemen and wagons lumbered into motion. With them rode Nell. Poor Nell. Married and widowed within a few months, she had returned broken-hearted to Matilda, and, grateful to have been put in charge of the nurseries now that old Jeanne was at last dead, she ruled them with a gentle, eager love that had won the affection of nurses and boys alike. With the little girl she had no more success than Matilda.

Matilda had watched them ride off into the forest together until they were out of sight, then had turned sadly away.

Now, painfully, she began to dress, easing her aching limbs into the shift Elen held ready for her, then her gown and tunic. Last of all she held out her arms for her thick fur-lined cloak. The damp autumn winds had been cutting through to the bone as they hurled leaves, rain-sodden and brown, across their horses' paths on the long rides between castles. She shivered at the thought of it. But on the whole she was glad that William had decided they should winter in Hay this year. Hay was hers. In spite of everything Bramber still belonged to the ghosts of Bertha and old Sir William. And at Hay she would never meet the king.

She had pondered often on old Jeanne's prophecy, picturing again the harsh face of King Henry. He held every man's destiny in his hand, but why hers especially? She shivered—she had made the sign against evil again and again in recent months, sometimes feeling the huge eyes of little Matilda fixed on her face.

"I still think you should tell Sir William you're not well, my lady." Elen's chin was beginning to stick out in the way Matilda knew so well. "At least order a litter to carry you."

"No." Matilda rounded on her. "Be quiet, Elen. I will not have the litter. And I will not have Sir William told yet. I feel better as soon as I'm riding. Send for some hot broth for now, before I go down."

Elen signaled to the plump serving maid who had been squatting on her heels before the blazing fire and the girl disappeared. Elen snorted. "There's a lazy wench. She wouldn't lift a finger if she didn't have to. I'll be bound she sends someone else up with it." She began to busy herself packing away the last of the clothes and strapping the small coffer that stood at the end of the bed. Sure enough, when the broth arrived, it was not carried by the same girl. Elen went to meet the woman who held it. "I'll give it to my lady. You can go."

The woman handed it over without a word. She seemed about to turn, then she hesitated, her eyes going to the tall figure standing huddled in the heavy mantle by the end of the bed.

"*Arglwyddes!* My lady!" The woman's voice was low and lilting.

"I said you can go." Elen turned, her eyes flashing. "My lady does not want to be disturbed. Leave her in peace."

The other woman half raised her hand as though waving Elen aside. To the girl's indignation she took a step nearer. "Be silent, *bach*. I must talk with Lady Matilda. I must." She sounded troubled.

Matilda swung around suddenly, letting her cloak fall behind her. "Who's that?" She peered at the woman, her heart suddenly hammering in her chest at the sound of a voice that stirred a chord in her memory. "What do you want?" As the woman looked up at her at last she recognized her with a violent sense of shock. "Megan," she whispered. "Is it you?"

"So you remember me, my lady?" Megan stood for a moment, her hands clasped in front of her, looking steadily at Matilda's face.

Matilda looked down at the carpet of rushes, gently rustling in the draft. "I tried to forget, Megan. I tried to forget everything that happened at Abergavenny. Even you."

Megan nodded. "I knew you would."

"What is it?" Elen suddenly stepped forward. "What is it, my lady? Who is this . . . this person?" She looked Megan up and down haughtily.

"This person, *cariad,* has come to have words with your mistress." Megan turned on her sharply. "Now you, girl, go about your business. Put the broth down before you spill it. *Oy a Duw!*" She shook her hands in

257

agitation as Elen slopped the broth on the rushes. "Now go, I said. And you too, boy." She turned to the page who had come in behind her and leaned against the wall, watching the proceedings with interest while he chewed a straw.

Matilda raised an eyebrow. "Elen is my friend, Megan. Only I tell her to go."

"Well, then, tell her, my lady, now and quickly. If she's so high and mighty, why's she waiting on you then? She should be in the hall."

Matilda hid a smile. The two Welshwomen were alike in height and build, although Elen's hair was fiery and Megan's white beneath her veil. They were eyeing each other like two bantam cocks.

"Do as she says, please, Elen." She spoke firmly. "I'll take my broth while Megan is with me." She held out her hand for the bowl.

Elen cast a furious glance at her rival, then, pushing the now half-empty bowl of soup into her mistress's hands, she turned and flounced out.

Once she had gone, Megan seemed to lose her confidence once more. She stood, her eyes on the floor, twisting her fingers nervously together as Matilda sank thankfully into her chair and picked up the carved bone spoon. The room was silent for a while as she drank. Then at last, stifling the nausea that had returned as soon as the soup was finished, she looked up and forced a smile.

"I'm glad to see you again, Megan."

"Well, that's as may be." The older woman stood erect before the fire. Then suddenly she seemed to make up her mind to speak. She went to crouch beside Matilda's chair, her voice lowered.

"I've come to tell you not to go to Abergavenny again, my lady. That's all I can be saying about it. Don't go there."

Matilda shivered. "I don't want to, Megan, believe me. But if my husband says we must . . ."

To her amazement Megan rose and turned away to spit viciously into the hot embers.

"If your husband says he must, Lady Matilda, well and good. Let him go. But not you."

"Why, Megan?" Matilda glanced sideways at her, suddenly suspicious, as the other woman's pleasant, round face became stony and defiant.

"Maybe I know a good reason, maybe I don't," she announced. "Just remember, I'm telling you. Now I must away back to my people before they find I'm gone." She rose to leave but Matilda was too quick for her. Forgetting her sickness, she jumped up and grabbed Megan's wrist.

"I forbid you to go yet. Tell me what you know."

Megan glanced half fearfully over her shoulder. "Indeed I won't, for I shall say nothing, my lady. I've already said too much. I should not have come to you indeed." She wrenched her arm free of Matilda's grasp and fled through the door, her leather shoes pattering down the broad stairs.

Matilda moved to follow her, then she stopped and went back to her chair with a shrug. If the woman refused to say anything, there was no more to be done. She stood for a moment, thinking. Megan had braved a great deal perhaps to come and warn her, for the sake of their day of friendship so many years before. She put her hand to her aching back, then bent to pick up her fallen cloak from the rushes and warily wrapped it around her. William had to be warned, of course. She picked up the silver handbell by her chair and rang it for Elen. He must be told without delay. She breathed a fervent prayer that Megan, if she still wanted to guard her silence, had already left the castle. She didn't like to think of Megan, however stubborn, being subjected to the full brunt of William's anger in one of the dungeons below the keep if she refused to tell him the source of her information.

William's men, however, when they fanned out in their exhaustive search of the castle, found no trace of Megan, nor had anyone been able to think how she had come to be there. She was not known by anyone at Monmouth, nor had anyone seen her come or go, save the trembling girl who had willingly given up to her the chore of carrying up the hot soup.

"I've already sent messengers to Abergavenny," William announced, stamping into Matilda's chamber an hour later. "You and I will ride on as far as Dingestow to see how Ranulf Poer fares with the rebuilding of the fabric of the castle there. It may be that I shall wait there with him till the building season is over. You can ride on to Hay." He rubbed his hands ruefully. "Winter is coming early this year. There won't be many more weeks before the snows arrive if it goes on like this. What ails you, Moll?" He suddenly rounded on her irritably. "Has this wretched woman upset you?" He seemed to have noticed for the first time her pinched pale face and stooping back.

She forced a smile. "No, William, it's not that. I'm afraid I'm breeding again. I'm feeling sick with it, that's all."

He looked relieved. Not wanting to believe that Megan's warning might have any substance himself, he had resented the thought that Matilda might be frightened by it. "The ride'll soon perk you up! I was afraid for a moment you were ill," he said gruffly, and he rested his hand awkwardly for a moment on her shoulder. From time to time there were moments almost of tenderness between them now. "It'll be good to have another baby to keep you occupied, eh?" He gave a gruff laugh. "Now, the horses are waiting. This business with the Welshwoman has delayed us long enough. Let's ride." He swung on his heel and, slowly, clutching her cloak around her, she followed him down the stairs.

The extensive alterations on the remains of the old castle of Dingestow were nearly completed. As they rode along the newly cleared track toward it at the head of their troop of horsemen, Matilda saw the low curtain walls

259

swarming with men. Obviously Poer was trying to finish the outer defenses before the weather put a stop to the season's building. A thin film of ice turned the moat a milky blue beneath the frosted sky as they clattered across the bridge, which was still supported by a framework of scaffolding.

Ranulf Poer was seated by a blazing fire in the echoing keep, the plans for the castle spread before him on the table. He pulled himself painfully to his feet at their approach, his foxlike features sharper and more prominent than ever, his hair snow-white. He greeted them distantly, his mind obviously still half on the plans before him.

"We haven't long to finish the walls," he commented, showing William the outline on one of the pieces of parchment. "The Welsh are restless. I don't like it. We've had reports that trouble is coming. I'll be glad to have your men here while we finish. I can spare very few of mine for guard duty." He glanced almost distastefully at Matilda. "Is your wife staying here?"

"Thank you, no," she replied, stiffly, conscious of all her old dislike for the man flooding back. "I plan to travel on to Tretower, if you can spare me an escort." She tried to keep the edge of sarcasm out of her voice. It was wasted on Poer, though.

"Spare her the minimum, de Braose. We need those men here." He stabbed the table once more with his finger, before turning on his heel. "I can smell trouble, and I want to be prepared."

"It seems he's worried too." William threw down his riding gloves after Poer had stamped out, and held his hands to the fire, glancing around at the bare stone walls and the piles of unshaped stones still lying in heaps in the far corner below the dais. "You'd be best out of here, Moll. It'll not be comfortable anyway. Make your way as quickly as you can out of Gwent and into Brycheiniog." He thought for a moment, scratching his head. "I think you must give up your idea of going to Tretower. It takes you too close to Abergavenny, just in case that woman spoke the truth. Ride the direct route through the mountains from Llantilio to Llanthony. The good fathers will give you shelter for the night. From there to the Hay should be only a day's ride, even in this weather." He glanced over his shoulder. "Poer always was as nervous as a cat in these mountains. He doesn't believe Rhys can keep the peace in Gwent as he does in the rest of south Wales. Personally I think he still does. Just."

Matilda shivered. She had a strong suspicion that Poer was correct in his doubts, but she kept her fear to herself. William seemed confident, and her concern was to reach her children as fast as she could. If he became too worried, he might begrudge her even the small escort he had promised and insist she remain with him. They spent the night, fully dressed, huddled on straw pallets around the fire, and Matilda left Dingestow the next morning at first light. The wind had changed as night drove in from the western hills and with it came a wet windy warmth that loosed the ice in the hard earth and turned the winding tracks to running mud. With Matilda went Elen and her two women, Gwenny and Nan, and an escort of twelve men-at-arms. She rode fast, forgetful of her sickness, half exhilarated by the strong wind, half frightened by the brooding deserted country as their horses' hooves splashed through the shallow puddles on the hill tracks and through the deeper mud of the still, shadowy woods. In her girdle she carried a knife and, as they cantered on, she loosed it nervously in its sheath.

They paused early at the square-built tower of Llantilio, secure in its commanding position on the top of the hill, and, in spite of her eagerness to go on, Matilda reluctantly agreed that they spend the night there. She hardly slept. The sickness had passed, but her mind was in a turmoil of fear and impatience, and at first light they rode on.

They followed the old road north to where it plunged between the mountains and followed the River Honddu up the vale of Ewias toward Llanthony Abbey, the horses slipping and stumbling in the heavy rain. At midday the rain stopped at last and Matilda pushed the horses as fast as she dared beneath the threatening sky.

They passed the little church of Cwmyoy, the track leading up to it marked by one of the stone crosses that signposted the pilgrims' way through the mountains. Out of habit Matilda reined in her horse as so often she did when William was there. Then she remembered and, contenting herself with a quick prayer as they walked past, she spurred her horse onward again. The heavy clouds threatened more rain, which would make the road across the mountains impassable. Constantly before her was the image of her children alone with their attendants at Hay, with only a small garrison to guard them and the gates trustingly open so that the townsfolk could come and go.

Once Elen begged her to stop, if not for her own sake, then for the sake of their sweating horses and for Gwenny, who was sobbing with the pain of a stitch in her side, but she ignored her pleas. Silent drifting clouds obscured the still, silent mountains either side of the River Honddu. Even the buzzards had deserted the valley. The moaning of the wind in the trees was the only sound save the creaking of the leather and the occasional sucking squelch of a horse's hoof coming out of the mud. She glanced over her shoulder and saw that the men escorting her had drawn their swords. The sight gave her very little comfort.

It was early dusk when the exhausted horses filed into the wind-blown orchards that lay in the deep valley south of Llanthony Priory. There were signs of much activity and building. Llanthony, so long nearly deserted during the early wars, lying as it did so close to the border, had received substantial grants for its rebuilding from old Hugh de Lacy, the Lord of Ewias, and already a magnificent central tower and the presbytery had risen nearly to their full height in nests of wooden scaffolding.

Matilda breathed a sigh of relief as she slipped from her horse. Here at least, amid the orchards, gardens, and vineyards, they were safe and might pass the night in the canons' guesthouse without fear of attack.

"So, Elen, we are halfway home. I'm sorry I made you all ride so fast. I had no feeling of being watched, yet I was afraid, out there, on the road."

Elen snorted. "You afraid, my lady! And how is your sickness now, may I ask? Quite better, I'll be bound, while we're all as exhausted as kittens." She gestured toward the two wilting women who had dismounted behind them.

Matilda smiled. "Poor Elen. Perhaps my illness was all in my head. Perhaps I'm not even with child." She pressed her hand hopefully to her stomach.

"Indeed I think you are, madam." Elen smiled grimly. "But it'll be a miracle if you don't lose it, riding like that." She flounced indignantly ahead of her mistress into the newly built guesthouse.

With fire, and light, and succulent meat from the prior's kitchens washed down with raw wine from the vineyards along the Honddu, Matilda felt better.

"Only a few hours' ride till we reach the children." She smiled at Gwenny, who was helping her off with her gown. It was the first time she had undressed for three days.

Gwenny nodded shyly. "They're safe enough, madam. Mistress Nell would never let anything happen to them."

"Could Mistress Nell do anything against an army?" Matilda replied more sharply than she meant. She repented as she saw Gwenny's chin tremble. "Oh, I'm sorry, Gwenny. I know I could probably do no more than she could, but we are bringing twelve more men with us." She sat down heavily on the bed and took her brush from Gwenny's hand. "You go and sleep. Tell Nan and Elen too as well." She looked around the tiny cell-like room, so unlike the great chambers she was used to. "But you'll hear me if I call, from next door. Go on, girl, get some sleep."

She sighed as the door closed and she was left alone. Perhaps tonight she too would be able to sleep, lulled by the safety and serenity of the great priory, soothed and protected by the chanting of the monks in the choir of their beautiful new church.

She had only just dozed off, or so it seemed, when she was awakened by a furious knocking on the guesthouse door. It took a moment to remember where she was, then she was out of bed, groping in the dark for her fur-lined bedgown, trying to find the latch of the door to her room in the impenetrable blackness. She cursed herself for blowing out the light before she went to sleep. She ached with exhaustion.

The main door had been opened by one of her young men-at-arms, his eyes still bleary with sleep, his fingers fumbling to buckle on his sword belt as he dragged the heavy oak back and let in the cold night air.

It was the prior himself who hurried in, followed by two of his black-robed canons. His pale face was drawn and anxious. "Forgive me waking you so early, my lady." He motioned the man to shut the door as one of the canons put a lantern on the table and filled the dark room with leaping shadows. The man-at-arms went to the fire and, kicking off the turves on the embers, squatted down to feed it dried apple twigs from the basket near it. Soon it was blazing up. The prior sat down heavily on the stool by the table, his white hands twisting nervously together. "I had just come from celebrating prime when a messenger arrived." He gulped nervously. "He had galloped over the hills from Abergavenny, my lady. The castle has fallen. As far as is known no one has escaped."

Matilda felt Elen's steadying arm around her as she gazed appalled at the old man's face. She was conscious of Gwenny and Nan hovering behind her.

"Your husband, madam." The prior's voice was gentle. "Was he at the castle?"

She shook her head numbly. "He's at Dingestow, Father Prior. We were warned not to go to Abergavenny, and messengers were sent to the garrison there." She shook her head, anguished. "They should have been prepared."

"No messenger can have reached them." The prior made a wry face. "The boy who came to warn us said the Welsh hid in the underbrush that has overgrown the moat. They surprised them yesterday at dawn." He crossed himself. "The castle is burned. Apparently a Welshman spoke to the constable the night before and actually taunted him that they were going to take the castle, and for a while the garrison took the threat seriously and waited up. Then they gave up and went to bed. I can't believe it, but they did! How can they have been so foolish?" He wrung his hands. "They left the usual minimum guard on the battlements of course, but . . . The Welsh put up their scaling ladders and went straight in over the walls. The constable and his wife are captured with many others. A lot of men died. No one escaped. I can't think how it happened. When the Welsh themselves warned them." He sat there, shaking his head in distress, his narrow, lined face a picture of grief.

"Has someone sent messengers to Sir William? He must be warned in case they go on to find him at Dingestow." Anguished, Matilda was standing in front of the old man, not noticing how her bedgown had fallen open to reveal her full breasts, half swathed in her long copper hair. The prior, swallowing, averted his eyes. "I will send my fastest horses, my lady." He fingered the heavy silver cross that hung from a chain around his neck. "I feel sure he will have heard at once though. Dingestow is no more than a few miles from Abergavenny, but I will send, if you wish it."

"Please do, Father, he must be warned." Matilda shivered. "Is it known who led this raid?"

263

"The sons of Seisyll of Gwent, Lady Matilda. Two died at your husband's orders, but others lived and they're grown men now. They have waited a long time to avenge their father's death. We in Ewias and Gwent have heard often of their vows for revenge in spite of Lord Rhys's orders that peace is all-important. They only waited for their manhood and then —for de Braose." He shrugged and again Matilda felt a shiver run across her shoulders.

When the prior had gone she paced up and down, nervously chewing her thumbnail. Then suddenly she made up her mind. "Dress," she ordered Elen and the two women. "See that the horses are at the door at once," she flung at the guard. "We ride to Hay now. The Welsh could have attacked it already. They could be on the way there now. Don't wait for food, we must go."

She fled into her little room and began to pull on her clothes, bundling up her hair with pins inside the hood of her mantle, pricking her fingers in her haste on the brooch at its shoulder.

The deep Honddu Valley still lay in darkness, and the morning light touched only the tops of the western slopes of the Black Mountains as they set off up the long climb through the thickly wooded valley toward the bleak, silent moors, past the tiny chapel on the border and so into Brycheiniog and up toward the high pass between the mountains. Their horses were still tired from the previous day's ride but Matilda relentlessly pushed them on, her eyes fixed on the gap in the mountains ahead. Once there they paused for a moment to scan the countryside around them, bathed now in the warm russet of a watery dawn sun. Nothing moved in the bracken and grass. Even birds and sheep seemed to have deserted the high road. They pushed their gasping horses to a heavy gallop in the thick mud and began the long slow descent from the hills.

As the exhausted party trekked the last mile into Hay the sun disappeared and rain began once more to fall, a steady blanketing downpour that shut off the mountains and the valley and blinded the riders, soaking into their clothes and streaming from the horses' manes. The town of Hay seemed deserted, only the flattened puffs of smoke escaping from the streaming cottage roofs showing where the women were sheltering inside their dwellings. The castle was quiet. The guards on the main gate in the curtain wall stood to attention as their lady walked her steaming horse into the outer bailey and drew to a halt. All was well. There had been no attack. She breathed a silent prayer that it had been the same at Dingestow.

264

22

The shadow on the bridge had moved. Jo stared at it, puzzled, then she looked around her. The riverside was deserted; the backs of the houses that overlooked it had changed subtly—gray stone relieved here and there by boxes of geraniums and trailing lobelia now deeply textured by brilliant sunlight. The heat haze had dissipated, leaving the air quite clear.

She moved cautiously, and winced. Her foot had gone to sleep. Bending to rub it gently, she found her feet were bare—her shoes lying several feet away on the pebbles at the edge of the river. She glanced at her watch, then, horrified, stared at it again. She had been sitting there for an hour.

Slowly she stood up and hobbled painfully over the stones to reach her shoes. She remembered nothing from the moment she had kicked them off to cool her feet in the swift-running, brown water. Had she dozed off as she sat on the wall, or had she once more gone back into the past? Her mind was a complete blank. Dazed, she made her way back up the narrow lane toward her car. Somewhere at the back of her consciousness something was nagging; a memory trying to get out, but a memory of what? Had an episode of Matilda's life taken place in her dreams as she sat on the wall, just as it had at Hay—but if so, why could she not remember it? She felt a shiver of unease stir deep down inside her as she unlocked the MG and climbed in stiffly. Why should Matilda want to hide from her now? Biting her lip, she sat for a while, deep in thought, but nothing came, nothing but a vague feeling of unease.

Nick was waiting for her in her apartment.

He stood up as she came in. "Where have you been?"

"Away."

"And you don't intend to tell me where, I suppose," he said wearily.

"No."

"You missed your appointment, Jo." His eyes narrowed. "You were supposed to see Bennet yesterday and you didn't turn up."

265

"I'll call him and apologize." She felt a quick flash of anger. "You didn't have to wait to tell me that."

"We lost the Desco contract this afternoon."

"I'm sorry—that's tough. But this is not the place to think out your future."

Nick sat down on the Victorian chair by the fireplace and stretched out his legs in front of him. "I'll go," he said wearily, "when I'm ready. But I want some answers from you first." He paused momentarily. "Have you been seeing Richard de Clare again?"

Jo froze, staring at him. "You're out of your mind! You're talking as if he's a real man, which he isn't. And even if he were, it would be none of your business! You and I are through, Nick. Finished. How many more times do I have to say it?" She flung herself toward the front door and dragged it as far open as it would go. "Please, will you go now?"

Nick did not move. "Have you seen him again?"

"You really are going mad!" She stared at him in frightened despair. "As you just pointed out, I missed my appointment with Carl, so of course I haven't seen him. How could I?" There was no way she was going to tell Nick what had happened in Hay. "Look. If you won't go, then I shall—"

She broke off with a little frightened cry as he moved toward her with astounding swiftness and, putting his hand against the front door, pushed it closed. He gave a tired smile. "Don't worry, Jo, I'm not going to touch you."

Staring up at him, she was overwhelmed suddenly by pity as she recognized the deep unhappiness in his eyes behind the closed, hard mask.

"Nick," she said, trying to keep the ache of longing out of her voice. "What has happened to you? Where are you? You never used to be like this."

"Maybe you weren't two-timing me before." He turned away from her and stood in the middle of the room, his back to her, his arms folded across his chest. "And maybe I hadn't just lost my biggest client before. Losing that account could mean we fold. Desco more or less carried the firm."

"I told you, I'm sorry," she whispered. "But you'll find other clients. Look, I'm tired out. Can we talk tomorrow perhaps? I could meet you for lunch or something."

"I'll take you out to dinner this evening. Please come, Jo."

She hesitated, then shrugged. "Okay. Give me a few minutes to change."

When she emerged at last Nick was sitting waiting for her, a book in his hands. Recognizing it, she glanced at her bag, still lying where she had dropped it in the doorway. Sure enough it was open and a pile of guidebooks and maps had spilled across the floor.

266

"You've been to Hay-on-Wye?" Nick asked, slowly flipping the book shut and letting it fall onto the coffee table.

She nodded mutely.

"Why on earth didn't you say so? What happened?"

She shrugged. "Nothing much. I went to Abergavenny first, where"— she hesitated—"where Matilda spent so much time, to stay with an old school friend, and then they sent me on to Hay. I wanted to make notes for the article."

"And did you recognize anything?"

"Not even vaguely familiar. It had all changed so much." She was watching him while she was talking. The tension in his face had eased.

He walked across to the French windows. After drawing back the curtains, he threw them open and walked out onto the balcony. "I'm going to have to go to the States in a week or two," he said over his shoulder, "to see if I can win that other account we've been angling for. If I could get that, it would more than make up for losing Desco. And I haven't totally given up on Mike Desmond yet—if I can only concentrate." He frowned. "Oh, God, Jo. What is the matter with me? I know I'm behaving crazily." He ran his fingers through his hair.

Jo followed him outside. "You're tired, I expect," she said at last.

He shook his head. "It's more than that. It's as if—" He tightened his lips angrily. "No, no excuses. It's me. Some foul-tempered, vicious part of me. A part of me I don't understand." Absently he picked a bloom from the passion flower that trailed from an ornamental urn across the stone railings around the balcony. He scrutinized it carefully. "There is something rather horrible about these," he said after a moment, thoughtfully. "They're like wax. So perfect; so symmetrical, they don't look real. And all that symbolism. Nails, whips, blood, and wounds." He flicked it with his finger. Then he looked up suddenly with another lightning change of subject. "You remember your meeting with Prince John?"

Jo nodded, trying to ignore the sudden tightening of her stomach muscles at the mention of John's name. She watched as Nick leaned over the balcony and let the flower drop. It spun crazily as it fell, hit the railings below, and disappeared into the dark basement area.

"You didn't like him much, as I recall."

"Not me, Nick. Matilda," Jo corrected him gently. "No, she didn't. He was an utterly obnoxious child."

Nick picked off another flower-head. "Look, they're beginning to close for the evening." He held it in his palm for a moment before dropping it after the first. "Have you come across him again yet?"

"Who?"

"John."

Jo shook her head. "Don't let's talk about Matilda anymore, please. She

267

doesn't bring out the best in either of us." Jo glanced at her watch. "Why don't we walk up the road slowly? I'm ravenous."

She was very tired. She glanced at Nick across the table in the dim candlelight, watching the shadows playing on his face as he ate. He reached for his glass and raised it so that the candle reflected ruby glints off the Valpolicella. "Shall we drink to new beginnings?" he said, looking at her at last.

She smiled. "To your new account. May it be so huge you can afford two more Porsches!"

He laughed. "To that also. But I really meant to us. I didn't mean to hurt you the other night, Jo."

She looked away abruptly. "You damn well did, though."

"Will you give me another chance?" His eyes sought and held hers. They were almost transparent in their clarity in the candlelight. Unwillingly she put down her fork and almost without realizing she had done it, she moved her hand slowly across the table. He grasped it, his eyes still fixed on hers. "Can you forgive me, Jo?"

The touch of his fingers sent little tingles of excitement up and down her spine. With an effort she tore her gaze away. Between them the candle guttered violently above its strangely shaped sculpture of dripped wax. "I don't know," she said after a moment. "Nick, I don't know what to do."

"I'll make it up to you, Jo. I make no excuses. I don't know what happened." He moved his thumb slowly across her palm toward her wrist. "But I will make it up to you, if you will let me."

She was shaken by the wave of longing that flooded through her as his hand moved on lightly up the inside of her forearm, touching the rough scab that had formed over the gash there.

Slowly she shook her head. "It won't work, Nick. We don't belong together," she whispered. Her hand still lay beneath his on the table. "It was never meant to be." Tearing her eyes away from his face, she looked back at the candle, concentrating on the white heat at the center of the flame.

"It was meant to be, Jo." His words floated almost silently into her consciousness. "You are fighting your destiny, don't you see?"

She didn't answer. Unblinking, she went on staring at the flame. The silence stretched between them.

"What are you seeing, Jo?" Nick's voice came to her at last from a great distance. "Perhaps it's John. Why don't you spare a few dreams from Richard de Clare and think about Prince John. . . ."

The outer bailey of Winchester Castle, below the squat tower of the new cathedral, was busy with horses and grooms. Beside Matilda, William pulled up his horse and threw his leg stiffly over the pommel. It would be

268

good to have a few days' rest before going on to Bramber, where the old baron, his father, had at long last died.

"Whose men are those?" he inquired curtly, seeing some of the crowd without livery as his page ran to help him.

"Prince John's, my lord," the boy whispered hoarsely. "The king's son has come to hunt the New Forest."

William snorted. "That young hound. It's time he went to hunt himself some bigger game in France." He gave his arm to his wife and led her toward the hall. "But if it's to mean some good hunting in the king's forest, then I'll forgive him his presence here." And, chuckling, he went to greet his host.

Prince John had grown considerably since his betrothal three years before. He was still stocky and short for his age, but his face had fined down, losing the puppy fat that had marred his features, and his hair was the red-gold of his father's. He seemed pleased to see the newcomers at the evening meal in the great hall that night.

"Sir William, it's good to have you here," he exclaimed, leaning across his neighbor and gazing intently into the older man's face. "I trust you are fully recovered from your wounds? That was a sorry business, when the men of Gwent attacked Dingestow and killed Poer." He smiled grimly. "God rot them! You were lucky to escape.

"You will join us, I hope, for the hunt tomorrow? Then we'll have the chance to see your prowess." He selected a piece of meat from the plate and chewed it thoughtfully, the rings on his fingers winking in the candlelight. Beyond her husband, who seemed flattered by the boy's attention, Matilda could see little of the prince, and she sat back, not wanting to attract his attention. Her memories of him were not particularly pleasant. She had often thought of young Isabella as she heard of the king's youngest son traveling around England, enjoying himself in one great castle after another, sometimes in the company of Ranulf Glanville, who was acting as his tutor, sometimes with only his attendants and his favored groom, William Franceis. Her husband, who had met him often, liked the boy and spoke well of his promise, but she could not help thinking of the heart-rending scenes before the betrothal ceremony had taken place. She knew the child was safe at home in Cardiff, still with her mother, but the poignancy of the memory had been aggravated by the rumor that had reached her at Hay that the Earl of Clare was negotiating to marry Isabella's elder sister, Amicia. Desperately she tried to dismiss the thought of Richard from her mind, and, pushing aside her dish, she concentrated on the activity in the center of the smoky hall below the dais, where a singer with a harp was being ushered forward to entertain the guests. Her vow to think no more of Richard had been often and badly broken, but somehow through the years she had avoided seeing him alone.

The glittering crowd of nobles and their attendants gathered outside the castle at sunup the next morning. The air was full of excitement shared by the nervously curveting horses and the barking hounds. Matilda reined in her black mare tightly; the horse was already frothing at the mouth, her hooves beating rhythmically on the slippery cobblestones.

Prince John, dressed splendidly in brocade trimmed with ermine, was mounted on a tall raw-boned chestnut stallion two hands too high for him, but he reined it in savagely as it plunged beside the other horses. Already William was there beside the prince, and she saw John turn and grin at her husband and shout some good-humored jest when he was not preoccupied with staying on his horse. It seemed the boy had taken a fancy to William, and she saw scowls among the prince's friends as de Braose took the coveted position at John's side.

Then they were off, horses, hounds, riders, and foot followers pounding out of the gates and across the bare ground to the west of the town that separated the castle from the outskirts of the forest. The pace increased to a gallop. Matilda bent low over the mare's neck, excited at the prospect of the chase, intent on keeping up with the leaders as they plunged into the cool leafiness of the trees. Almost at once the hounds found a scent and their excited yelping turned to a full-throated roar. The huntsmen picked up the notes on their horns and the horsemen thundered after them down the grassy ride.

It was the first day of the season and they killed plentifully before turning their tired horses at last for home. The main party of riders split up into small groups as they walked back through the leafy glades dappled with the evening sunlight. Matilda was exhausted, and she had allowed her mare to drop behind the others a little and pick her own way quietly over the soft paths between the trees, when there was a thunder of hooves behind her. As she turned to draw out of the way of the hurrying rider, she found Prince John at her side. He reined in and grinned at her.

"A good start to the season, my lady. I trust you enjoyed your day?" His surcoat was stained with blood and the blade of his knife sheathed carelessly in his girdle showed an encrustation of gore.

She returned his smile cautiously. "It was a good day's hunting, Your Highness. I'm glad you were at Winchester. William always says there is some of the finest hunting in the land here."

"Ah, yes, the good Sir William." The boy eyed her thoughtfully. "He's a fine man and good with his bow, and he's a lucky man too, to have so beautiful a wife." He glanced at her sideways.

The ride narrowed and as the horses jostled for position his thigh for a moment brushed against hers. She felt a surge of repugnance. Was the silly boy trying to flirt with her? She forced herself to smile. "You are very flattering, Your Highness, thank you."

After a few paces, to her relief, the path broadened and she was able to guide the mare away from him a little.

270

"Sir William keeps you too much in those border lands of his," John went on thoughtfully. "You should come to my father's court with him."

"Oh, I stay on the estates because I want to. I hate court." Matilda was thinking wistfully of the times she had chosen not to go rather than risk meeting Richard; not wanting to see the king. She paused abruptly, seeing the prince scowling furiously, and cursed herself for her tactlessness. "But of course," she hurried on, trying to cover her mistake hastily, "I am much honored when I have a special invitation . . ."

"Honored but not pleased, it seems," he interrupted, his tone sarcastic. He stood up in his stirrups, reaching for a leafy branch and pulling it down as he rode under it. His horse shied, and John laughed. He seemed to make up his mind to try a different tack. "You're a lady who knows her own mind, I think." He reined his horse close to hers once more, "And too young and beautiful to be content with so coarse a husband. I wonder if perhaps a lusty prince would be more to your liking?" He leaned across and put his hand on her thigh.

Matilda was overcome with anger. Not stopping to think, she raised her whip and thwacked him smartly across the wrist with the handle. "I don't think you realize what you're suggesting, my lord," she flashed at him. "Do you wish to dishonor the wife of one of your father's most loyal subjects?"

Her fury dissolved suddenly at the sight of his red, discomfited face, and she tried to suppress a gurgle of laughter. He was, after all, but a boy. "I am sorry, my lord prince. It is just that you were only a child when last I saw you, and now—" Her words died on her lips at the sight of his face.

It was white with fury as he groped blindly for his reins, spluttering as he tried to speak. "God's teeth," he managed at last. "Not so much of a child, madam, that I don't know how to deflower a woman or father a brat, I assure you."

He pulled his horse to a savage halt, which sent it rearing and plunging sideways against the bushes at the edge of the path, and, giving her one murderous glance as he turned, he sent his horse galloping back down the ride.

Matilda let her mare stand for a moment as she realized, with a shock, that she was shaking from head to foot. She knew she had been a fool. She could have put him off tactfully without making an enemy of him. "An enemy for life." She murmured the words to herself, watching the mare's ears twitch at the sound of her voice, and she shook her head, trying to throw off an irrational feeling of fear. How stupid, to let a little incident ruin a beautiful and exciting day. Taking a deep breath, she gathered up her reins and turned once more to follow the sounds of the other riders, slowly making their way back toward Winchester.

She told William what had happened when they were alone together in their guest chamber that night. To her surprise he threw back his head and laughed.

"The young puppy!" he said. "The runt of the litter and he fancies his chances with my wife. You should be very flattered, my dear. Prince John has an eye for a pretty woman."

"But he's only a child," she burst out. "If it wasn't so funny, it would be disgusting."

"I'd bedded women and plenty by his age." William unfastened his mantle and threw it down. "Take no notice, Moll. Think of it as a compliment. He's spoiled and, as the king's son, few women refuse him. It's about the only benefit he does get from his position, poor lad. He's not yet learned enough discretion to know whose wife he can wheedle and whose he can't. He'll know next time." He laughed again.

For the remainder of their stay at Winchester John ostentatiously ignored Matilda and as obviously courted the attention of her husband. The sturdy baron was constantly required by his side, instructing, joking, even lecturing the boy, clapping him on his shoulders and laughing uproariously at his comments. Matilda watched silently as John listened and smiled, never totally unbending, but always allowing William to feel he had his confidence and his friendship, and she found herself wondering if the boy was quite as naive as William thought.

On the next hunting expedition she took care to remain in the center of a crowd of women followers, not once allowing her weary horse to drop back alone. She need not have worried. John went out of his way to avoid her, remaining constantly with his lords and William and the leading huntsmen.

When they left for Bramber Castle John bade William an almost affectionate good-bye. To Matilda he extended a cold, hostile hand, and when she curtseyed and murmured the appropriate words of farewell he turned away without a word.

"Has madam finished?"

Jo stared up with a start. The waiter was standing beside her, his hand on her plate. The food on it was practically untouched.

"I'm sorry," she said. "It was very good. I'm just not hungry."

She looked across at Nick. He was watching her through narrowed eyes, twisting his empty glass thoughtfully between his fingers.

"You hypnotized me!" She gasped.

He shook his head. "I did nothing. I merely sat here and listened. Two coffees, please, and the bill." He looked up at the waiter. Then he turned his attention back to Jo. He smiled faintly. "You were what I believe is called scrying, seeing pictures in the candle flame. No doubt you could see them in a crystal ball as well. You must be psychic!"

Jo had gone white. "That's nonsense—"

272

"Is it? It's more common to see the future than the past, I suppose, but either way, three hundred years ago you would have been burned at the stake for less."

"And today I could make my living telling fortunes. Oh, God!" She put her head in her hands. "I'm frightened, Nick."

"Why?" He picked up the bottle and poured the last of the wine into her glass. "You obviously have a gift. And if you are going to persist with researching into the past, the ability to do it yourself will at least save you Bennet's no doubt exorbitant fees." He pursed his lips. "Do you remember what you said?"

She took a sip from her glass, glancing around at the other diners. No one was staring. No one seemed to have noticed anything amiss. "It must have been you asking about Prince John earlier," she said slowly. "I saw him again. Only he was older this time. A teenager."

"But you found him as obnoxious as before." Nick was still twisting his glass between his fingers.

Jo nodded thoughtfully. "He seemed to think me attractive, but his methods of showing it were pretty crass. Thank you." She looked up and smiled as the waiter put a cup down in front of her.

"Perhaps your reactions were tactless and high-handed." A nervous tic had begun at the corner of Nick's eye.

She stared at it. "We are talking about me again," she said softly. "It was not me. It was Matilda."

"Whichever one of you it was, you should have had the sensitivity to handle the situation more discreetly." Nick took the bill and began methodically to check it.

"Why are you so angry?" Jo said suddenly. "It's as if you're taking it personally. I didn't mention Richard, did I? Or is it just because I talked about the past? Or because I wasted this beautiful meal? Or did I shout and yell and make an exhibition of myself?"

He shook his head, reaching into his pocket for his wallet. "None of them. Come on. Let's go." He pushed his chair back and stood up.

It was a glorious night, warm and balmy. They walked slowly back up Victoria Road. Most of the houses were in darkness. Here and there a window was still lighted, shadows moving behind the curtains.

Nick did not touch her. He strode ahead in silence. Only when they reached the step beneath the pillared porch did he speak.

"Are you going to let me come in?"

She stared up at his face in the light of the streetlamp. "No, Nick."

"Please, I won't hurt you, I promise." He put his hands on her shoulders and gently pulled her against him.

She wanted him badly. She could feel her heart beginning to beat faster as his mouth moved gently against hers, and she felt her resistance weakening as he moved his hands slowly from her shoulders toward her breasts,

273

massaging them sensuously through the thin material of her shirt, pressing her spine against the door. He felt in his pocket for his key, silencing her feeble protest with another kiss as he slotted it into the lock behind her and pushed it open. The hall inside was pitch-black. He did not bother to try to find the light switch. His arm pinioning hers, he kissed her more fiercely as the heavy door swung shut behind them, leaving them in darkness.

"Nick." Jo gasped. "Please, don't—"

"Why?" She could hear the strange exultance in his voice as he tore her shirt open and dropped his head to nuzzle her breasts.

"Please, I asked you not to come in—"

"But you want me, Jo," he breathed. "You want me." Catching her wrist, he pulled her with him up the stairs, unlocking the door to her apartment and pulling her inside. Only then did he release her. Jo groped for the light switch, trying to refasten her shirt and tuck it back inside her skirt. "Nick, please, I'm tired—" She backed away from him uncertainly. "Will you go if I make some coffee—"

"No coffee. It sobers you up too fast." He strode into the room, pulling the curtains shut and turning on the table lamp in the corner. "What we need is some more wine and some music." Leaving her standing by the door, he disappeared into the kitchen and returned with a bottle. "I see you've replenished your cellar." He smiled at her. "Put some music on, Jo. And relax." She was standing by the door, her hand on the latch. "Turn off the main lights and put on something quiet and sexy," he went on, his voice suddenly gentle. "I said I wouldn't hurt you. Come on. Relax." He turned away from her to find the corkscrew and set about drawing the cork and pouring out the wine.

Still hesitating, Jo moved to the shelf and shuffled through a pile of cassettes. Her hands were shaking as she picked one up. "Piaf?" she asked, conscious that he had put down the bottle and walked across toward the door. She spun around, afraid that he was moving to lock it, but he merely went to the switch and turned off the main lights, leaving only the soft glow from the one small lamp in the corner.

Trying to steady her nerves, she turned back to the tape, putting it on very low.

"Your wine." He was immediately behind her.

She faced him and took the glass from him. "You won't hurt me again, Nick. You promise," she whispered as he reached up to touch her face.

Nick smiled. "Why should I hurt you?" He took the glass back from her and set it down on the shelf behind her, then gently he drew her to him. With a frown he began to unbutton her shirt once more. He pulled it off then reached up to unfasten her bra. "That's better," he murmured as he dropped it on the floor. "Now, why have you still got your shoes on?"

He stood back and folded his arms once more, watching as Jo kicked off her high-heeled sandals, embarrassed at his sudden cold detachment.

She gave a nervous laugh as she turned away from him to pick up her glass. "Aren't you going to take off your shirt too?"

"Of course." He watched her drink. "You enjoyed it when I raped you the other night," he said suddenly.

"I did not," she flared.

"I think you did. I could feel it. A woman can't hide it when she's excited."

Jo stopped and picked up her shirt hastily, clutching it against her. "I hope you haven't got the idea that I like being knocked around, because I don't. Please, Nick, stop teasing me . . ."

Nick took a step nearer her. He dragged the shirt out of her hand and threw it down behind him, then he caught her by the elbows, pulling her hard against him. "Beautiful, independent, oh so liberated Miss Clifford! I doubt if any man has dared to tell you what to do before, has he? One look from those flashing eyes and men cower back into their corners. What was Pete Leveson like in bed, Jo? He looks like a teddy bear to me. I doubt if he ever beat you. Perhaps that's why you had such a short affair."

"Nick—"

"Or Sam. Sam has always wanted you, hasn't he? My mother came and told me as much today. Has he ever dared to touch you? I doubt it! My brother is scared of clever women!"

"Please, Nick!" She tried to pull away from him. "You're hurting me. You promised you wouldn't—"

"I'll do what the hell I like with you, Jo." He smiled at her. "Violence excites you. You like powerful men. You like a man who can bring you to your knees."

She struggled frantically. "You're drunk, Nick—"

"I don't think so. In fact, I've not drunk nearly enough." He let go of her so suddenly she nearly fell. "Let's have some more wine."

"You've had enough." She dodged away from him, then stooped and grabbed her crumpled shirt. "If you don't get out of here in ten seconds, Nick, I'm calling the police!"

He had picked up the wine bottle, and, holding it up to the lamplight for a moment, he poured some into his glass. He moved toward her, sipping it. "This is a good year," he murmured. "I'm glad you care about good wine. Many women don't—"

Jo was backing away from him toward the phone. As she reached it he lunged toward her and caught the phone cord, jerking it out of the socket. His wine spilled over her arm as, with a cry of fright, she dodged past him.

"You know, I quite enjoy your show of resistance, Jo," he said lazily. "I can see why men always prefer—what is it they call them—women of spirit!"

"Just stop all the chauvinist crap and get out of here!" Jo was shaking violently. She put the sofa between herself and Nick as she pulled on her shirt.

"We were talking about the men who told you what to do, weren't we?" he went on conversationally. "What about those men of Matilda's? William de Braose, now. He never asked permission before he screwed his wife, I'll bet. Did it thrill you? Being forced to obey him? You had to obey your husband, didn't you?" He was moving toward her again slowly, his handsome face set.

Jo backed toward the French doors. "Please, Nick, go away."

"You haven't told me yet. Did William turn you on?"

She shook her head. "Never. He was repellent."

"Yet you bore him six children."

"Not me, Nick. It wasn't me, for Christ's sake! Look, why don't we go out? It's a glorious night. Why don't we go for a drive? A long drive. Do you remember once we drove down to Brighton. We could have a swim at dawn and then have breakfast down there—"

"Tell me about Richard de Clare," Nick went on as if she hadn't spoken. "Tell me about the handsome Richard. He turned you on, now, didn't he?"

"Yes!"

Suddenly her fear and anger overflowed and she was yelling at him. "Yes, he bloody well did. He turned me on, as you put it. He was fun. He was humorous and good to be with. He wasn't intense and competitive. He wasn't a bloody chauvinist even though he was a medieval knight and an earl! He was a gentleman, Nick. Something you wouldn't know how to be, if they exist these days, which I don't think they do. And yes, he was good in bed. And in the bracken and anywhere else he happened to be! Very, very good. A hell of a lot better than you will ever be!" She stopped, panting.

In the silence between them the brown, spiced voice of Edith Piaf had begun to sing "Milord."

Suddenly Nick began to laugh. "So we have the truth at last." He went to the stereo and turned up the volume.

"Allez, dancez, milord! My only consolation, *milord,* is that you are dead, *milord!* Dead for eight hundred years! Poor Jo. Being screwed by a ghost! A fucking, imaginary ghost!"

He turned up the volume full, then gave her a mock bow. The sound blazed around the flat, reverberating off the walls, distorted almost out of recognition by the vibration of the bass notes. Jo clapped her hands to her ears.

After snatching his jacket off the chair, Nick slung it over his shoulder and walked to the front door, then he turned. "And you, Jo," he shouted.

"Are you a ghost as well? Think about it, my lady! Think about it!" He opened the door then strolled out onto the landing.

Jo hurled herself at the door and banged it shut, shooting the bolt and putting on the chain. She was shaking from head to foot. Then she staggered to the stereo and switched it off. Only then, in the sudden echoing silence, did she hear the furious hammering on the ceiling from the apartment upstairs.

23

The desk in Bet's office was covered with slides. She looked up as Jo came in and grinned maliciously as she switched off the viewing box. "God! You look as if you've had a hard night. Coffee or medicinal brandy?"

"Coffee, please." Jo flung herself down in the ocher armchair by the window, letting her bag fall to the floor.

There was a pot perking permanently in the corner of the office, slotted between the bookshelves and piles of magazines. Bet reached for a cup from the tray, filled it with black, unsweetened coffee, and handed it to Jo. "Are you going to tell me?"

"Nick and I had a fight last night."

"So what's new?"

Jo raised the cup to her mouth with a shaking hand. "He's behaving so oddly, Bet. Not like himself at all."

"I can't say I'm surprised. You heard about the screw-up Jim Greerson made of the new Desco campaign? He commissioned some unknown to do the artwork, then I gather Nick wasn't interested enough even to look at it, so Jim went ahead and approved it to show to Mike Desmond. Mike had fifty fits it was so lousy and ran screaming off to Franklyn-Greerson's nearest competitor and had hysterics in their lap." Bet scrutinized Jo's face with cool amber eyes. "But you knew all that."

Jo smiled wearily. "I knew the gist of it. Can I have some brandy in this coffee?"

Bet walked to her desk, opened the right-hand bottom drawer, and took out a full bottle of Courvoisier. "He didn't knock you around did he, Jo?" Her eyes were resting on the fading bruise on Jo's wrist.

Jo shrugged. "Only verbally last night."

"You mean he has before?" Bet was vastly intrigued.

Jo smiled. "Not really, I suppose. Sorry to disappoint you, Bet. But he did frighten me. It was as if he'd changed personality completely. It can't have just been business worries. Hell, I was around when he and Jim first went into partnership. They weathered all sorts of crises then and Nick

278

just took them as a challenge. He wouldn't let one thing like this change his whole personality!" She gave a little shiver. "He's acting like someone possessed."

Bet sat down on the chair behind her desk. She crossed her elegantly trousered legs.

"Do you still love him?"

Jo sipped her coffee. "God knows!"

"Then I suggest you leave the relationship to God for the time being." Bet scrutinized the soft red leather of her ankle-length boots. "What about thinking about work instead? I haven't seen your byline on the newsstands for weeks. You only appear to feature as the subject of other people's articles these days."

"Bet, I said I was sorry about that—"

"Forget it." Bet put her elbows on the desk. "I want this story for *W I A*, Jo. The whole story, as it happens. Matilda's life story. Not the romantic crap Pete Leveson was spooning out. I want the real version. The blood-and-guts reality. I want exclusive rights from now on. And I'll pay. I want to serialize more or less as it happens. Right to the bitter end."

"I don't know if I'm going on with it, Bet." Jo reached for the brandy bottle and slowly unscrewed it. "It frightens me so much. I was thinking of going back to Bennet and asking him again to help me forget all about Matilda. I went to Wales, to the places Matilda knew. When I got there I went into a regression spontaneously, without anyone there to hypnotize me. It was as if I were being taken over by her. I couldn't stop myself." She bit her lip. "I panicked and came home. It was terrifying, Bet. I couldn't handle it. I could suddenly see the whole thing getting out of hand, see her life unrolling hour after hour, day after day, taking over my own existence—"

Bet's eyes were shining. "Exactly! Jo, you've got to let it happen. Come on, don't tell me you don't want to do it. It's the scoop of the year. I want to know what it feels like for a twentieth-century woman to go through the time barrier into the dark ages—"

"It's hardly the dark ages, Bet. The twelfth century was a time of renaissance." Jo smiled wearily. "And it's not *me* who goes back. I am not conscious of myself as having any identity other than that of Matilda at the time. I only make comparisons afterward."

"Then make them afterward!" Bet picked up a pen and held it in front of her with both hands. "Come on, Jo, it's not like you to duck out of a challenge. Throw yourself into it. You said you had been to Wales?"

Jo nodded.

"Then go back. Go back now. Concentrate on the story. Don't fight it. Take this hypnotist man with you if you want to. *W I A* will pay. I'll draw you up a contract giving us exclusive rights. You can have three consecutive months. Maximum publicity, TV advertising—cover line, of course.

It's possible a TV series might come out of it—who knows? I'll talk to one or two people I know at the B.B.C. and see what they think. Come on, Jo. We're talking about a lot of money apart from anything else." She paused, giving her a sideways glance. "It'll get you away from Nick for a bit. That can't be bad either."

Jo took a deep breath. "True," she said. She was torn. The journalist half of her wanted to do it; it was the other half, the deep-rooted private half, which resented Bet's intrusion, and that half of her was still afraid. She looked thoughtfully past Bet out of the windows toward the river. "What about the rest of my series if I agree?"

"We'll do one of your other articles on its own if you've finished it. Drop the rest of the series for the time being. We can go back to them later." Bet stood up. She walked around the desk and took the brandy bottle out of Jo's hand. "Come on, I'll take you out to lunch. You have to admit it, Jo, it's a bloody good story. You're too experienced a journalist not to see that. You once told me you'd like to have been a war correspondent, remember? Now is your chance to prove it. Okay, so you're taking some risks, but think of the experiences you'll be having. There is a book in this, Jo. You can base it on our series." She scooped the strap of her tote bag onto her shoulder. Then she paused. "Listen, why not see if Tim Heacham will meet you down in Wales?" She dropped the bag and turned the phone on her desk to face her. "I'll call him now."

"I haven't agreed yet, Bet." Jo stood up.

"Yes you have." Bet grinned as she dialed. "You wouldn't have come to see me this morning if you'd really wanted to stop. You would have gone straight to your hypnotist. Here"—she held out the phone—"the number is ringing."

Bet met Pete Leveson for lunch at Langan's the following Monday. They sat downstairs, both greeting other diners for a few moments before they turned to one another. Pete grinned. "Perrier with a slice of lemon at this time of day, right?"

Bet raised an eyebrow. "That will do for starters." She sat back in her chair and looked him straight in the eye. "I'm prepared to bet you know why I asked you to meet me here."

"Hands off Jo Clifford?" Pete leaned back and crossed one long leg over the other. He stared up at the ceiling. "Do you intend to make it worth my while?"

"You mean you want me to trade stories?" Bet glanced at him quizzically.

"Possibly. *If* you know anything exciting that I don't."

Bet laughed out loud. "Touché. Supposing I promise to keep my ear to the ground?" She took up the menu and began to look at it thoughtfully. "There is one favor you might do for me, though, Pete," she said, not taking her eyes from the list of hors d'oeuvres. "Spend a little time with *la petite* Curzon. I think you'll find her grateful."

"You mean Jo will be grateful if Judy has less time for Nick."

Bet concealed a smile. "No, that's not what I meant," she said. She raised a languid hand to greet a colleague who had appeared in the doorway.

Peter gave her a sharp look. Then he grinned. "I see—and while the cat's away . . . She's gone to Wales, you said?"

Bet nodded. "Tim has gone with her. He's going to photograph the locations—ruins and mountains and things, and also try and catch Jo while she's in a trance. You'd be amazed how quickly he agreed to go. He dropped everything—left his entire diary to that dishy George chappie and whatever his other assistant is called, packed his knapsack and went."

Pete gave a silent whistle. "So that's the way the wind blows. Does Nick know what is happening?"

She shrugged. "I don't know and I don't care. Nick Franklyn is Jo's worst enemy in some ways. He distracts her from her work. He turns her neurotic when I want her incisive and militant. He blunts that acerbic edge that makes Jo Jo."

"Besides which, you've fancied him yourself for years."

Bet gave an enigmatic smile. "Have you tried the nest of quails' eggs they do here?" she said innocently. "If not, I'd recommend it."

There was a knock on Jo's bedroom door. She stood back from her suitcase and stared for a moment out of the dormer window toward the trees that screened the River Wye from her view. "Come in, Tim. I'm just about ready."

Tim appeared, stooping beneath the low sloping ceiling. "You were right about Mrs. Griffiths," he said in an undertone. "What a gem. I'm glad she had rooms for us." He wore an open-necked checked shirt and jeans. There was a camera case slung from his shoulder. "Shall we walk up into Hay?"

Jo nodded. She slipped her notebook into her tote bag and followed Tim down the creaking staircase and out onto the sun-baked pavement.

They walked slowly up the road past the church, stopping to stare at the grass-covered tump where once the first castle of Hay had stood, then they made their way toward the bridge that spanned the river. Leaning on the blue-painted railings, they stared down into the water far below.

"You say it happened here the first time?" Tim asked.

Jo nodded. "I was sitting on the shingle down there."

"And it happened completely spontaneously?"

"I think I knew something was wrong. Things went strange—a bit jerky, as if I were starting a migraine. Then, quite suddenly, I was somewhere else."

"You want to try again?"

Jo swallowed. "Of course. That's what we've come for. Actually"—she gave Tim a wry smile—"I'd rather have someone there. I think I'll feel safer somehow. Waking up and finding those people bending over me . . . I felt as if they had seen me naked."

Tim nodded soberly. "I do understand. Come on." He was about to turn away from the rail when he stiffened and leaned farther over, looking down into the bright glitter of the water. "Look. By those streamers of weed."

Jo felt a shiver touch her shoulders. She clutched the rail, peering down, half expecting to see some shadow from the long-ago past.

"There. See it?" Tim leaned over in excitement. "A huge fish."

Jo relaxed. She smiled at him in relief. "This is a famous fishing river. You should have brought your rods, if you fish."

"No way." Tim followed her toward the far side of the bridge. "I'd hate to kill anything for fun, that's a sport for the gods. Besides, I shoot as much as I want with my camera."

She turned in at the swinging gate that led off the road and onto the footpath. "That sounds very philosophical."

"Perhaps." He was grinning as he followed her down the footpath through the trees and onto the shingle strip along the river. Slowly Jo led the way to the spot where she had sat before, picking her way over the smooth rocks that lined the bank of the river. She stopped at last on the edge of the shingle once again.

"It was here," she said.

Tim was watching her. "You don't have to try to do it now, Jo. We can wait."

"No. I want to."

She put her bag down and sat nervously on one of the boulders. She swallowed, staring at the water, not blinking, allowing her eyes to be dazzled, deliberately trying to make her mind a blank.

Beside her Tim squatted silently, his eyes on her face. He was completely relaxed, his long limbs folded with the motionless ease of someone accustomed to the role of watcher. Jo, in contrast, was rigid with tension. He saw her swallow again. She was frowning. "It isn't going to happen," she said at last.

"You're trying too hard," Tim said easily. "Try to relax."

"I can't." She tore her eyes away from the water to look at him. "I suppose, deep down, I don't want it to happen. I'm afraid. Last time, sitting here, I was completely relaxed. It was the last thing I expected. Besides, I think I was so exhausted that my mind went a complete blank and that is when it happened."

"Were you afraid with Dr. Bennet?" Tim smiled easily.

282

She nodded. "I was afraid but I couldn't fight his hypnosis. He knew how to approach it obliquely to put me at my ease."

"You were telling me you read a book on self-hypnosis. What did that tell you to do?"

She grinned wryly. "It was incredibly complicated. To do with separating the two halves of the brain. You have to keep one half distracted while the other half is stimulated. I didn't read the instructions too carefully at the time, I must confess. It sounded awfully like hard work."

Tim laughed. "You should have brought it with you. I could have read out the instructions as we went along. I find it hard enough to cope with my brain even when I think it's working in unison." He stretched his arms above his head lazily. "Tell me the point Matilda's story has reached now."

"Well, here it was rather exciting." Jo smiled. "She met Richard again. They flew their falcons on the moors somewhere up there behind us, beyond Clyro, and they managed to go off on their own. They made love on the grass, by a mountain stream. Tim? What is it?"

Tim had scrambled to his feet. He walked to the edge of the river, kicking at the ripples with the toe of his shoe. "Nothing." He stooped, and picking up a small stone, skimmed it across the water. "Come on. Let's walk up and see your castle. We can always try again another time for a trance."

"All right. If you want to." Jo frowned, puzzled by his reaction.

Turning, he smiled at her, extending his hand to pull her to her feet. "I'd like to take some shots with the sun low like this, then why don't we find a nice pub and grab an early meal?"

"That would be nice." She picked up her bag and followed him over the stones. "Tim. Do you think I'm mad to pursue this?"

He shrugged. "Who knows? If you are driven to do it, then you must."

"Driven? By Bet, you mean?"

Laughing, he shook his head. "Driven by something inside you. Matilda herself perhaps, seeking to tell her story."

Jo shivered. "Do you think she is forcing herself on me? I don't feel possessed, not even obsessed. I think I'm just curious."

"Then you can choose."

"Would you go on if you were me?"

There was a moment's silence. Tim was looking up at the high bridge, his eyes narrowed. "I'm not sure. I believe in karma, you see."

"Destiny?"

"Something like that. To know what has gone before won't alter what is to come. Perhaps it is better not to know."

"But I do know." The words came out as a whisper. "I know what happened from books."

Tim shook his head. "You don't know the truth, Jo. You know a few disparate facts. Suppositions. It was too long ago, the characters too poorly documented, to know the truth. The only way you will find that out is to live Matilda's life again with her."

"Right up to the bitter end?" Jo thought for a moment. "I don't think I have the courage. I think I am afraid of death."

"Even when you are living proof of the fact that death isn't the end?"

She smiled. "That is begging the question. You are assuming that Matilda was a previous incarnation."

"I know she was," Tim said softly.

She stared at him. "You know? Or you would like to think so?"

"I know."

"Why are you so sure?"

For a moment she thought he was going to tell her, then he shook his head. "One day I'll explain, Jo. Not yet. Come on, the light's changing. Let's get to work."

They did a complete circle of the castle, photographing it from every angle, in some places close beneath the wall, in others viewing it beyond rooftops and trees, always at a distance.

"Aren't you going to try to go in?" Tim said, putting one camera away and taking a second one out of his bag.

Jo shook her head. "I don't think so. At least, not yet. It is so changed, Tim. Even if some of those walls are Matilda's own, even if she did lay some of the stones with her bare hands, it's not the same. I found that out at Bramber and Abergavenny. And so much of this is of a later date. No, I don't want to go inside."

Tim nodded. "Shall we go and look for a nice pub then?"

Jo had walked a few paces from him, staring up at the high stone wall. They were in Castle Lane, a narrow street where the buildings on the northeast side were overshadowed by the high walls of the ruin that faced them. She was staring up, her eyes focused on an empty arched window high in the crumbling walls.

Quietly Tim raised his camera. She did not notice, her attention riveted to the graying stone.

"Jo?" Tim said quietly after a moment. At first she did not appear to have heard him, then she turned. She smiled uncertainly. "I thought for a minute . . ."

He was putting his camera away. "Don't worry about it. It will come if it's going to. Bill Walton says self-hypnosis is often more effective than the other sort, but you can't force it, Jo. You will learn or it will come by itself—"

"It's not self-hypnosis, Tim. I told you, I never tried to do it deliberately except just now by the river." She stopped abruptly. "When did you talk to Bill Walton about it?"

"A few days ago." He led the way around the foot of the wall. "I . . . ." He glanced back at her sheepishly. "I had a go myself."

284

Jo stared at him. "You mean you were regressed?"

He nodded.

"And?"

"It didn't work." He lifted his camera bag on his shoulder. "Come on, I want food."

How could he tell her about what had happened in that shadowed upstairs room in Richmond? The whirling blackness, the despair, the fear and anger that had possessed him, the sense of overpowering frustration and, at last, the realization of failure that had pursued him through life after life, as he spun, without identity, down through the centuries.

He shook his head wearily, following Jo back down the steep pavement that led from the High Town down toward the river. He had gone back. Twice. And on neither occasion had he been coherent or cooperative. The second time he had cried. He knew he would not try again.

The church was very cool after the heat of the morning. After letting themselves in, Jo and Tim stared around.

"There she is," Jo whispered. Near the west wall lay the remains of a huge, worn stone effigy, barely recognizable as human. They approached it slowly and Jo stooped and rested her hand on the stone. "Moll Walbee," she said quietly. "I wonder if it is her."

Tim was looking at the leaflet he had picked up by the church door. "It says not here," he said. "It says it is the figure of an unknown monk."

They both stood in silence looking at the almost featureless figure before them, its worn head resting on a pillow of stone. Tim chuckled. "If it was her you can see why she was reputed to have been a giant. That bit alone must be over four feet long and it's only half of her—or him." He raised his camera and took a shot of Jo as she crouched down over the figure, her hands resting on the smooth stone, her eyes lowered, her long dark hair hanging loose over her shoulders.

She closed her eyes, trying to will some kind of warmth into the cold hardness beneath her hands. The church was completely silent. Tim did not move, watching the woman who, in her cool green linen dress, was as unmoving as the recumbent figure beside her, her tanned skin taking on the tones from the shadows of the nave. He found he was shivering and he fingered the top buttons of his shirt, drawing them together almost defensively.

Jo's eyes were still closed. He stared at the dark lashes lying on her cheeks and fought the sudden urge to touch her shoulder.

"Oh, Christ! Why won't it happen!" Jo cried suddenly. She slammed her fists down on the effigy. "I've got to know, Tim. I've got to. If it won't happen here, where will it?" She stared around the church. "I'll have to go back to Carl Bennet. I thought I could manage without him—I wanted to do it alone—"

"Perhaps that's it, Jo," Tim said quietly. "Perhaps you need to be alone. Perhaps its because I'm here."

"Perhaps it is." She swung to face him. "Perhaps it's because I want to cash in on it. I wanted to follow Bet's advice and do the articles for her. When she mentioned a book and even TV the idea excited me. I wanted to use all this, Tim. And it has spoiled it. It has made it contrived. Like you and your camera. You have no place here, Tim!"

"I have, Jo." He turned away from her and sat down in one of the pews, staring up toward the dark triple-arched chancel, with his back to her. "I do have a place here."

"I don't believe you." She glared at him. "I should never have asked you to come!" She scrambled to her feet and ran toward the door, pulling it open and disappearing out into the sunshine.

Behind her, Tim sat unmoving, listening to the echoing silence as the sound of the falling latch died beneath the church's vaulted roof.

Jo walked swiftly across the grass, swinging her bag, seeing it scattering the seedheads of the dandelions as she headed toward the overgrown untended half of the churchyard that sloped down steeply around the north side of the church. Somewhere nearby she could hear the gurgling of a brook. It was very hot indeed. The morning haze had cleared away and the full heat of the sun beat down on the top of her head.

She could feel the sudden perspiration on her back and between her breasts as she stopped and looked around. The churchyard was deserted. There was no sign of Tim. With a sigh she pushed her way through knee-high wild grasses, threaded with meadowsweet and campion and butter-cups, and sat down on one of the ancient lichen-covered tombs, beneath a yew tree, dropping her bag on the grass. She opened the top buttons of her shirtwaist and turned back the collar, lifting the hair off her neck as she stared up through the thick green of the tree toward the metallic blue of the sky. It was here, or somewhere very close to this spot, that Jeanne was buried. She could hear the drowsy cooing of a woodpigeon in a tree nearby.

Closing her eyes, she leaned back, letting the dappled sunlight play across her face.

The hall of the castle was crowded, wisped with smoke from the fires as the diners sat at the long tables. It was the autumn of 1187.

Matilda was seated at the high table, next to her husband, and on her right was Gerald, Archdeacon of Brecknock. Beyond William was Baldwin, the Archbishop of Canterbury.

Gerald leaned toward her with a cheerful grin. "His Grace looks tired. He did not expect his preaching of the Third Crusade in Hay to be greeted by a riot!"

Matilda smiled. "The men of Hay so eager to follow the cross, their wives so eager to stop them! It was ever so, I fear." She broke off, biting her lip. William had been conspicuous among the men of the Border March in not volunteering to go to rescue the Holy City from Saladin.

Gerald noticed her silence at once and guessed the reason for it. "The king has need of Sir William at home, my lady," he said gently. "Your husband will give money to the cause, which is as welcome as his sword."

"Even Lord Rhys and Einion of Elfael pledged their swords!" Matilda retorted. "And William dares to call them savages—" She broke off, glancing at William to see if he had heard, and hastily changed the subject. "Tell me about yourself, Archdeacon. Are you content? You seem to be high in the archbishop's favor."

His piercing eyes had lost none of their alertness and never ceased probing the men around him, but now they confronted her quietly as he wiped his lips on his napkin and reached for his wine. "I am never content, Lady Matilda. You should know that by now. I serve the king and I serve the archbishop, but I will confess to you a certain restlessness, a lack of fulfillment." He put down his goblet so abruptly it slopped on the linen cloth. "God needs me as bishop of St. David's!" he said vehemently. "Wales needs me there. And yet, still I wait!" He took a deep breath, steadying himself with an effort. "But I have continued with my work. And always I write. That has brought me much solace." He glanced past her at the archbishop. "Tomorrow we go on to my house at Llanddeu. The archbishop has graciously consented to spend the night there before going on to Brecknock and I have decided to present him with my work on the topography of Ireland. Did you know I was there with Prince John three years ago?" He shook his head wearily. "A fiasco that expedition turned out and no mistake, but it showed me Ireland again. And my book has been well received."

"You sound as though you dislike the king's youngest son," Matilda said cautiously, lowering her voice again.

Gerald shrugged. "One does not like or dislike. He offered me two bishoprics there. But I want St. David's, so I declined them." He smiled ruefully. "He is young yet, but he is spoiled. I think he is intelligent and shrewd, but he showed himself no campaigner in Ireland. Perhaps Normandy will teach him something."

He turned and waved a page forward, holding out his cup to be refilled with wine. "But now, with two of his elder brothers dead, John becomes a man of importance. He is nearer the throne now than he might ever have hoped. His father is old, Geoffrey's son is a child." He shook his head mournfully. "And Prince Richard is not yet married, in spite of all. John may yet come to be a force to be reckoned with."

Matilda shivered. "I don't trust him."

Gerald smiled at her shrewdly. "Nor I, my dear. We shall just have to hope that maturity will bring better counsel." He folded his napkin and

287

placed it on the table. "Now let us speak of pleasanter things. Tell me how your family are. What is the news here?"

Matilda frowned, troubled again. "There I need your advice. You spoke with the Prince Rhys ap Gruffydd yesterday. Is he a good man, do you think?"

Gerald frowned. "A strange question. As you said, he vowed to take up the cross." He smiled at her. "And his son-in-law, Einion, too. I remember you feared him once, for your children's sake." He put his hand on hers as it lay on the table. "But it's not just that, I can see. What troubles you, my lady?"

"He and William have been discussing an alliance." She looked down at the white cloth, her mouth set in a hard line. "He wants my little Matilda as wife for his son Gruffydd. William has told me that whatever he thinks of the Welsh he will agree. It is the king's wish."

Gerald shrugged. "Gruffydd," he mused, "is named his father's heir. He's not as handsome as his brother Cwnwrig, but he's tall and strong and he's able to cope with the quarrels with his brothers. They fight endlessly, you know, the sons of Rhys. They turn the poor man white-haired with worry. He'd probably make the child a good husband."

"I'm afraid for her, Gerald. I have kept my children safe from Einion and from the rest of Seisyll's kinsmen and now I'm to be asked to give her to Rhys with my own hands." She turned to him, suddenly passionate. "Swear to me, Archdeacon. Will she be safe?"

Gerald raised his hand placatingly. "How can I swear? I know Rhys to be a man of excellent wit. He's honest, discreet, I believe him to be sincere in his quest for peace. More than that I can't say, although he is my cousin. He wants this marriage obviously to seal this uneasy peace we have on the borders, to make sure the *galanas* never reappears between your houses. I suspect the power of de Braose is the nearest challenge to his, so he is anxious to secure a peace with you. What better way than by marriage? But all you can have is his promise. It is more than many mothers get."

He glanced down the hall to where ten-year-old Matilda ate at one of the lower tables with her nurse. Her two eldest brothers, William and Giles, were pages now in neighboring households, as was the custom, while Reginald, her third brother, hovered at a high table proudly serving the archbishop. Matilda's two youngest children, Isobel and Margaret, were in the nursery lodgings in the west tower. They were a happy, healthy brood of children, some of whom Gerald himself had baptized. He glanced fondly at their mother. She was a young woman, still no more than twenty-six or seven, he guessed, as erect and slim as ever in spite of all the children. He watched her for a moment as she too gazed down the hall at Matilda. It was a miracle that she had not as yet had to bear the grief of the death of a child. He sent up a brief prayer that she would never be broken by such a loss.

Matilda's gaze went down through the smoky torch-lit hall to fix on her daughter's face and, as if feeling her mother's scrutiny, little Tilly raised her eyes. They were clear, almost colorless gray. For a long moment mother and daughter looked at one another. Then Tilly turned away.

Matilda felt her heart tighten beneath her ribs. Always that indifference, that unspoken rejection.

Her thoughts spiraled back to Jeanne, all those years before. *It is the child herself who will betray your secret.* But how could she, when she didn't know?

Matilda bit her lip. In the last ten long years she had seen to it that she and Richard had never again been alone together. She had ignored the longing in his eyes and fiercely resisted the anguished burning of her own body. There was no way that Tilly could ever have guessed how much her mother loved the courteous, handsome visitor who from time to time came to see them at one or other of their castles.

"You sigh, my lady." Gerald brought her attention gently back to himself. "There is no need. I feel sure Gruffydd will be kind to her."

Matilda forced herself to smile. She nodded. "You are right, of course, Archdeacon." She felt his eyes probing hers and immediately her wary fear returned that he could read her thoughts; that he might even suspect that Tilly wasn't William's child. Desperately she tried to distract him, suddenly very afraid.

"Tell me, Archdeacon, do you intend to write a book about your trip around Wales with His Grace, the Archbishop?" she asked quietly. "It would make a fascinating account, I feel sure. You could include that shameful scene in the churchyard at St. Mary's this afternoon." She smiled and saw at once that the bait was taken. His eyes lit up and he was leaning toward her, his face intense with excitement.

Surreptitiously she glanced back toward her eldest daughter's table. Sure enough, the huge gray eyes were once more focused on her mother's face. This time Matilda saw not indifference in the child's face, but fear and—was it longing?

The candlelight was flickering in her eyes. Angrily she raised her hand to her face, shielding it as she turned back to Gerald, but he wasn't there. A figure was kneeling before her in the sunlight, camera raised. She blinked.

"Tim?"

"Welcome back." He took another picture and then reluctantly lowered the camera.

"How long have I been sitting here?"

"About an hour."

"I was at dinner . . ."

"With Giraldus Cambrensis. I am very impressed with your friends."

Jo stared at him. "How do you know?"

"I asked you where you were. You seemed to hear me quite clearly. You talked very logically, describing what happened here in the churchyard—the riot and the way the archbishop had to race back to the castle, and the incident where a man tried to get through the gate to give his oath to take up the cross and only made it at the cost of losing his trousers—" He chuckled. "You know of course that Gerald took your advice. He wrote an account of his trip through Wales—the *Itinerary,* it's called. It is still in print today." He grinned.

"And you photographed me?"

"That is what I'm here for, Jo."

She bit her lip. "It makes me feel so vulnerable."

"Only your expression."

"Did I talk about my daughter?"

"You did." Tim stood up abruptly, dusting the grass from his knees. "The child who made a cuckold of de Braose."

Jo started visibly. "I said that?"

"You must have, love, mustn't you?" His voice was very dry. "Imagine little Tilly going to marry a Welsh prince."

"If she did." Jo rose stiffly from her uncomfortable seat on the old tombstone. "My grandfather reckoned the Cliffords were descended from a Welsh prince, Tim. Perhaps that is how it happened. Perhaps after all, Matilda was an ancestor of mine. Matilda and Richard de Clare!" She paused for a moment, savoring the thought.

Tim smiled almost wistfully. "And you are pleased that you can still go back into the past?"

She nodded. "I have to find out what happened. Whether Tilly married Rhys's son. In a way I hope she did. I'm beginning to feel rather pro-Welsh —I like the idea that I could be descended from a prince. Perhaps I could call David Pugh and ask him to look it up in his books. I promised I would call them while we were down here. But dear God! To sacrifice such a child to dynastic ambition. It was cruel."

"You said she was a strange little girl?"

Jo nodded. "She was distant. Cold. Self-possessed. Not like the boys who romped around like puppies. Yet not like Richard either." She glanced up at him with a rueful little smile.

"Did William ever find out she wasn't his?"

Jo shrugged. "I can't see into the future, Tim. It doesn't say so in the books that I know of, but I can't believe that he didn't guess. She was so different from the others. So fair."

"And Richard was fair?"

Jo nodded. "Fairish."

"And you are still fond of him?"

"Matilda, you mean? She still loved him." Her voice betrayed sudden pain. "That was why Tilly was so special." She picked a stem of soft creamy meadowsweet from the long grass near her, twisting it between her fingers.

Tim was watching her with half-closed eyes. "Where does Nick fit into all this, Jo?" he asked suddenly.

She stared at him. "Nick? He has nothing to do with it."

"Are you sure?" He began to lead the way slowly through the grass toward the wrought-iron gates that led out of the churchyard into the road. "I think he is involved—I think he is also living again. As I am, Jo."

She stopped dead. "Is that why you went to see Bill Walton? To see if you had lived at the same time as me?"

Tim nodded slowly.

"But you said it didn't work."

"That wasn't quite true, Jo. I didn't go into a full-blown regression like you, but something did happen. It's not the first time, you see. I've had a feeling for a long time that I've lived before. Not just once, but many times. I've read a lot about it—particularly about Buddhism—and I've been taught to meditate and to try to contact my past incarnations through meditation. The Tim Heacham no one knows!" His smile did not quite reach his eyes. "I thought it might help me to come to terms with the present if I could find myself in the past. I went to see Bill to see if he could make things a bit clearer."

"And did he?" Jo whispered.

He shook his head. "I went back twice after I went with you, hoping he could sort me out. But my alter egos or whatever you like to call them were too angry, too unforgiving, to emerge peacefully." He snapped off a frond from a sweeping branch of yew as they walked slowly past it. "My previous incarnations were full of anguish, Jo. Full of failure and betrayal."

"But who were you?" Jo was staring at him. "Why don't I recognize you?"

Tim grinned bitterly. "Perhaps because we were not destined to play a part together. Then or now."

"And you think Nick is?"

Tim eyed her silently. Then he nodded.

Jo swallowed nervously. "Nick's been behaving very strangely. I wonder if he suspects."

"He would have to be very unimaginative not to."

"Who was he, Tim?"

Tim shrugged. "You have the cast list, not me. The only thing we both know is that you don't seem to resemble Matilda physically all that much. You're not her double or anything—at least, not as far as you know, are you?"

Jo smiled. "Well, I'm not eight feet tall, as David said she was!"

291

"But your hair, your eyes. If you were in a film, would you and she be played by the same actress?"

"I don't know. I'm darker, I think. Matilda's hair was much brighter—almost auburn. I don't know about her eyes. I don't remember ever staring at myself in a mirror for long—the mirrors weren't very good, anyway. They were metal, not glass. You'd have to ask someone."

"Richard de Clare?" He smiled gravely.

She laughed. "Well, not William, that's for sure. Oh, Tim, I'm not the right person for this to happen to! I've no sense of destiny. I think karma and kismet and things like that are a load of bullshit. Easy ways out. 'If it's destiny, then there's nothing I can do about it.' That's a copout. Not for me."

"And, of course, you have never had the feeling that you've been here before."

"Never! I don't believe in sentiment and woolly romanticism, Tim. I'm Jo Clifford, remember?"

"How could I forget?" He rumpled her hair affectionately. "So you mean to fight destiny if it dares to rear its woolly romantic head in your direction?"

Jo nodded emphatically. Then she frowned. "You think it will?"

He nodded, not smiling. "I think it already has, Jo. I think the cast is assembling. We know that something pretty grim happened to Matilda. She was betrayed by her husband and by her friends and she was murdered, probably at the king's orders. Maybe—just maybe—her soul has been crying out for justice."

"Tim!" Jo stared at him, appalled. She shuddered. "You're not serious!"

For a moment he said nothing, his eyes fixed on the road ahead of them as they turned out of the churchyard and followed the wall toward the town center, then he grinned. "It's a hell of a dramatic theme for your book!"

"It's horrible. It's grotesque. You think you're here for me to get my revenge on you? You and who else, for God's sake? Who do you think Nick was?"

"I told you, I don't know. Forget it, Jo! Calm down. I was only joking."

"You weren't. You were damn serious. So tell me. Who else is involved?"

He shrugged. "I really can't even guess. Perhaps Judy? Perhaps Bet? People you know. Pete Leveson?"

"And Nick."

He nodded. "And Nick."

"And you think Matilda is out for revenge, through me?"

Tim stopped. He caught her arms and spun her around so the sun was shining directly into her face. For several seconds he stared at her intently, then released her. "No. No, I don't think she is. I think you are as helpless in this as the rest of us." He touched her cheek gently with his finger.

"I was sorry to hear about the Desco account." Bet met Nick's gaze challengingly in the dim light of the saloon bar. Behind him along the edge of the canopy over the beer pumps a line of pewter tankards gleamed softly. They swung gently in unison as a tall head brushed against one and the burnished surfaces winked and rippled.

Nick inclined his head slightly. "I hope to be replacing it almost at once."

Bet smiled. "I've no doubt you will. But you must keep a tighter rein on that partner of yours."

Nick frowned. There were taut lines of strain around his eyes. He looked pale and tired. "It was bad luck, Bet. No more."

"There's no room for bad luck in this game, Nick. You know that as well as I do. Tell me." She changed the subject almost too abruptly. "How is Jo?"

She was watching him closely but his expression gave nothing away. He raised his glass slowly. "As far as I know she is well."

"Some time ago you asked me to suppress an article she wanted to write."

Nick swallowed his drink and put the glass down, fitting it meticulously into the wet ring it had left on the table. He smiled coldly. "A request you saw fit to ignore."

"I am Jo's editor, Nick. Not her wet nurse. If she wants to write something and I think it is good, I'll publish it. It is good. Damn good. And you know it."

"Good for the circulation of *W I A* maybe." Nick's eyes narrowed suddenly, and, meeting his gaze, Bet felt herself shiver. "You're a selfish bitch, Bet Gunning," Nick went on. There was no venom in his voice, but nevertheless she shifted uneasily in her seat.

"No. I'm a damn good editor."

"Maybe. I'm glad I'm not one of your writers."

"You could be." She held his gaze steadily. "Your version of what's happening to Jo."

For a moment she thought he hadn't heard her. His eyes seemed to be looking straight through her, then abruptly he beckoned the bartender. He ordered new drinks for them both.

"Where is Jo?" he said at last.

She drew her new glass toward her. "Out of London."

"Did she tell you what happened?"

"Between you? Yes."

"And you believed her, of course."

"Of course."

"Are you going to tell me where she is?"

"No."

"I'll try to find her, you know."

"She's working, Nick. Give her a break. She's a first-rate journalist and her work is important to her. So is finding out about this Lady Matilda. You can't stop her. She is going to the top and either you've got to learn to live with it, or you've got to find yourself another woman."

Nick was watching her thoughtfully. "And you are available?"

She smiled. "I could be."

"What about Tim Heacham? I thought you and he were living together."

She shook her head. "I've cooked him Saturday supper and Sunday lunch from time to time. It amused us both, but he's got other arrangements at the moment." She smiled knowingly. Then she leaned forward and put her hand on his knee. "Shall I cook you dinner this evening?"

"Not this evening, Bet." He smiled faintly. "I'm flattered and of course I'm tempted, but just at the moment I have other plans. And they involve Jo."

Bet moved away from him slightly. "So. Do you love her?"

He didn't reply immediately.

"She's with Tim. But of course you'd guessed that," she said softly. She watched for his reaction through narrowed eyes.

He gave a half smile. "She's not interested in Tim. If he's with her it's for work. Are they in Hay?"

"You're not thinking of going down there?" Bet was watching his eyes. The harshness had returned and it made her uneasy.

"I may." He pushed away his glass. The drink was barely touched. "I don't know what I'm going to do." He stood up. Gently he put his hand on Bet's wrist as she toyed with the stem of her glass. "I nearly killed Jo the other night. Did she tell you that, Ms. Gunning? We weren't playing your sophisticated games. She wasn't enjoying what I did to her, but she had mocked me. She slept around, then taunted me with what she had done. She's playing a dangerous game. So if you see her before I do, you had better warn her of the fact." He turned toward the door, then he stopped and looked back at her. "Did she tell you she had been playing the field?"

Bet shook her head. "She hasn't, Nick, I'm sure—"

"You're sure?" He took a step back toward her. "You've sent her off with Tim Heacham, knowing he'd give his right arm to sleep with her."

Bet kept a tight rein on her anger. "Jo doesn't sleep around and you know it."

"She told me about it, Bet." He gave her a look of withering contempt. "She bragged about it."

Bet stared at him. "Who is it?" she whispered.

294

His knuckles went white as he clenched his fists. "Richard," he said softly. "His name is Richard."

She stared after him as he turned away out of the gilded swinging doors. Already the seat next to hers had been taken and someone was hovering waiting for hers. "Richard?" she repeated in a whisper. "Christ Almighty, Nick! Richard is a ghost!"

She took a cab back to the office, paying the driver with shaking hands, then she caught the elevator up to her office, not even hearing the cheerful banter of one of her colleagues as he got in beside her.

In her office she slammed the door and reached for the phone. The number Jo had given her was scribbled in the back of her address binder.

She bit her lip as the phone rang, hitching herself up onto the desk. "Mrs. Griffiths?" she said at last as the number was answered. "Please, I must speak to Miss Clifford. Is she there?"

"I'm sorry. She and the gentleman have left." The Welsh voice rang out loud and clear in the quiet office. "Going on to Raglan, they were."

"Raglan?" After putting down the receiver, Bet stared at it blankly. "Dear God, I hope it's a long way away."

She stood up and walked across to the window, gnawing her thumbnail as she stared down at the broad glitter of the Thames. In spite of the heat of the afternoon she was feeling very cold.

Tim was gazing up at the massive gray ruins of Raglan Castle. "I'm glad your friend Pugh told us to come here," he said in awe. "It's magnificent." Then he glanced at her sideways. "But you don't have to tell me. It's not your castle."

Jo laughed softly. "It was too long ago, Tim. Of course everything has changed. Let's stay out here on the grass—just for now."

He looked longingly over his shoulder at the castle. "Why don't I go away? I could leave you to it, while I explore."

She nodded. "Good idea."

He looked down at her fondly as she knelt on the mossy grass, then, camera in hand, he turned away and strode up the steep bank toward the enormous walls.

Jo closed her eyes. Her hands were shaking slightly as she tried deliberately to empty her mind. The castle grounds were silent. The air was heavy, the sky soft with deep black cloud. It was very hot. She forced her eyes open slowly, staring down at the grass, feeling the heat and her exhaustion overtake her, suddenly fighting sleep.

Tim was coming back. Out of the corner of her eyes she saw him walking toward her, tall, loose-limbed. She frowned. It was too soon; it should

295

have taken him hours to go around the castle and she wasn't ready. Behind him she saw a flicker of lightning dance for a moment behind the majestic walls of the castle, lighting up the windows as though candles still burned there against the black of the sky. Then she heard the music of a harp.

24

Matilda was standing resting her hand on the stones of the new high wall of Radnor Castle. It seemed strange that she could look out at the Welsh tents all around the castle, a sight she dreamed of with dread for so long, and yet know them to be friends. The red prancing lion flag of Prince Rhys flew gaily in the cold wind near them, as she looked down at her small daughter, who stood shivering at her side, her fur-lined mantle whipped open by the wind.

"Well." She smiled. "To think my little girl is to be a princess."

Tilly uncharacteristically groped for her mother's hand, giving rather than seeking comfort. "I like Lord Rhys. He sent me a necklace of crystals." The child gazed out toward the tents and pavilions encamped around them in the valley, her eyes shining. "And I'm to have a white pony with scarlet harness and John Spang, the prince's fool, has promised me two puppies from his own bitch. I like him."

Matilda was staring at the heavy cloud that hung over the encircling mountains, her heart heavy as Tilly prattled on. Then she stooped and kissed the top of her little girl's head. "You'll be happy in your new home, Tilda. Lord Rhys will be a kind father." Her voice broke at the word, and she fiercely blinked back her tears, turning her face away.

"Can I go and play with 'Sbel and Margaret now?" The child was itching to run off, uncomfortable as she sensed her mother's tightly controlled misery, not understanding.

Matilda forced herself to smile. "Of course, darling. Run along. Ill come and kiss you good night later."

She did not let herself watch the small head as it darted from her side and ran down the stairs inside the thick wall. Instead she turned back to watching the bleak hills beneath the threatening sky.

It was not until very late that she took a candle and climbed slowly, her heavy blue kirtle gathered in her hand, to the little girls' bedroom high beneath the stone roof of the main keep. Tilly was already asleep, worn out with excitement, in the big bed that she shared with her sisters. Matilda tiptoed toward the bed and saw Eleanor, the children's nurse, sitting

297

in the shadows beside the dying fire. The girl was sobbing quietly into her apron.

Matilda stopped, her heart beating fast. "What is it, girl? Why are you crying?" Her voice was sharper than she intended.

Eleanor jumped and raised a reddened face from her lap. "Oh, my lady!" She screwed up her kerchief and rubbed her eyes with it. "My lady. I don't want to leave you all and go to them heathens." She hugged herself as the tears began to fall again.

Matilda felt her heart sink, the tears rising unbidden behind her own lids. She swallowed hard. "Don't talk such nonsense, Eleanor. Rhys is a good Christian prince. And he is a kind man. I should never let a child of mine go to him otherwise." She dropped her voice suddenly. "I hoped you didn't let Tilda see you cry like that."

"Of course not, my lady." Eleanor sniffed indignantly. "I would never let her, she's so happy about going." She dissolved into tears again.

Matilda crossed to the bed, looking at the three sleeping heads: Tilda serene and pale; Margaret with her shock of copper hair tossed on the pillow, so like her mother in miniature; and little frail Isobel, no more than a baby, so happy to be promoted to her sisters' bed, not realizing she had come so that Margaret should not suddenly be alone. Margaret had her arm protectively around the little girl's shoulders. But Tilly slept apart, her back to the others. Matilda wondered if she even realized that tomorrow she was to leave them. She sank slowly to her knees beside the bed, swallowing hard, and, crossing herself quietly, she began to pray, suppressing the sudden treacherous thought that far away in Deheubarth Tilly would be able to betray neither her mother nor her true father.

The wedding ceremonies were over and the feast had already lasted an age. Matilda looked anxiously at her little daughter sitting in the place of honor next to her husband. Gruffydd was a good-looking young man, rather florid, with tightly curling golden hair. He drank often and deeply and ate hungrily from the platter he shared with his new wife. Tilly had touched almost nothing. She looked around her with unnaturally brilliant eyes, a deep flush on her usually pallid cheeks. The crystals at her throat gleamed and reflected from the candelabra on the table and the pure gold band in her hair glowed on the silk veil. She looked, among the solid men and robust women at the high table, like a delicate little fairy. Matilda eyed the Princess Gwenllian, Gruffydd's mother, a raw-boned woman with eyes rather too close together over the high-bridged nose, with unease. But she saw the woman lean over and pat Tilda kindly on the shoulder, her eyes smiling, and she felt a little reassured.

The wedding celebrations continued for several days, and then at last came the morning when the Welsh party began to pack their tents and shelters. Matilda and William in Rhys's great pavilion gravely kissed their solemn little daughter and her tall groom and watched as with Prince Rhys and his glittering throng of followers they mounted and prepared for the ride to Rhys's palace of Llandovery in Cantref Bychan.

"So that seals the peace as long as King Henry lives, at least," William commented tersely as they rode away.

Matilda turned to him, her heart growing suddenly cold at his tone. "And if the king should die, what then?"

William shrugged. "Who knows? We'll pray he lives long and heartily. If he should die and Rhys and his sons do not acknowledge his heir, then I will have played my hand badly." He frowned. "Tilda will be all right, whatever happens. They will keep her away from the fighting if there is any. But, by God, if they try to use her against me . . ." He left his threat unspoken.

Matilda found herself gazing at him in blank despair. Had he then washed his hands of the child the day she went to another man's table? Was she nothing to him any longer other than a pawn that he might have carelessly let slip in a chess game of far more important pieces? She gazed into William's eyes and shuddered. If his eldest daughter could look to no mercy from him, who could? She silently prayed that none of the rest of her children should find themselves dependent on his mercy one day; nor she herself.

Miserably she looked over her shoulder, back toward the west, where the sun was sinking in a blaze of gold behind Lord Rhys's mountains. Somewhere there, Tilda was alone.

"Jo, don't cry, love." The voice was gentle. She felt an arm around her shoulders. Tim was bringing her back, but she didn't want to come. Frantically she resisted him, fighting to regain the world from which he was dragging her. She could still see the countryside wrapped in forest below the castle wall on which she stood, while superimposed on it, like a shadow, were the ruined masses of another castle. The sky flickered with lightning and she felt the scene shift gear before her eyes. The wall beneath her hand had gone; she found she was clawing at the grass.

"I want to know how Tilly is," she cried miserably. "I must know. I must find out what happened to her—"

"Jo, you will find out." Tim pulled her against him gently. "But later. Not now. Get up, love. It's beginning to rain. We'll go back to the car and find somewhere to stay, all right?" Carefully he pulled her to her feet.

Still dazed, she clung to him as her knees threatened to give way. She had begun to shake violently.

Tim almost carried her back to her car, pushing her into the passenger seat as the rain began to fall in earnest, then he let himself in on the driver's side. "I'll find a hotel for us, shall I?" he said gently. "A hot bath and a good dinner is what you need."

299

He glanced at her as he leaned forward to turn on the ignition. She was lying back in her seat, her eyes closed, her face pale with exhaustion. "No more, Jo," he said softly. "It's taking too much out of you."

She smiled faintly. "I'll be okay. After a good night's sleep. I'm just so very, very tired."

He drove for about twenty minutes through narrow lanes in the teeming rain before drawing up outside a long white-painted, stone-built inn. He peered through the windshield wipers at it and grinned. "It looks nice. I can almost smell that dinner."

Jo smiled. "Lead on then," she said. But it was with an effort that she climbed out of the car after him.

The landlord was a tall, florid man of about fifty, who greeted them like long-lost friends. "The best dinner in Gwent, I can give you," he said to Tim with confidential modesty as Jo sank onto the settle in the dark hallway. "And I've a cellar here would make some of your London hotels green with envy, man. There's only one problem. I've just got the one room free, see? A double it is. But just the one."

Tim glanced at Jo. Then he nodded. "We'll take it."

She did not protest.

A hot bath and a change of clothes in the low-ceilinged whitewashed bedroom and Jo was beginning to feel herself again. She grinned at Tim. "I'll toss you for that sofa thing later."

He grimaced. "You won't have to. I'll do the gentlemanly thing and volunteer."

They both looked at the small two-seater settle by the window with its worn toile de jouet cover. Jo laughed. "And you over six feet tall. Perhaps we can put a bolster down the bed in the best tradition."

"No need. I shall take a temporary oath of abstinence. Anything that would be more comfortable than this bed of Procrustes." He slapped the arm of the sofa.

"I'll trust you then." She laughed. "Come on. Let's eat."

The meal was all they had been promised and more. Looking around the small dining room, Tim let out a contented groan. "I shall recommend this place to Egon Ronay."

Jo leaned forward to top up his wineglass. "Don't. It will be swamped with horrible townees and spoiled. This must stay a secret. Just ours." She yawned. "But, nice as it is, Tim, I think I'm going to have to go to bed. I'm completely exhausted."

He nodded. "I think you should. You still look shattered. Go on up, Jo. As it's stopped raining I shall go for a bit of a walk."

Jo stumbled up the narrow twisting staircase to their room. Snapping on the light, she stared around it. There was little furniture. The large old-fashioned bed, with a candlewick bedspread, an Edwardian dressing table and chair, and the settee by the window. On the polished floor there was a rush mat. With a sigh she slipped off her clothes and put on her thin silk bathrobe. She brushed her hair slowly, then, after pulling one of the books from her tote bag, she flung herself down by the window.

The casement was open, looking out over a small back garden. Beyond the drystone wall the hillside stretched downward into the shadows of the valley. In the silence she thought she could hear the sound of a stream out of sight in the darkness. Slowly she opened the book, frowning as a moth dived in through the window and blundered toward the lamp at her elbow. The volume was a biography of King John. She looked at the picture of him on the cover. It showed an elegant stone effigy, wearing a crown. She turned slowly to the illustrations in the book, staring at statues, sketches, illuminations, even coins. One thing they all seemed to agree about. John had been a good-looking man. A straight nose, a firm mouth—frequently bearded—and deep-set arrogant eyes. She half closed her eyes with a shiver. This was the man who had ordered Matilda's death.

She glanced up at the window again, staring at the raindrops as they fell, huge and wet, onto the sill. Then with an effort she tore her gaze away. She forced her eyes open as slowly the book slid from her hands to the floor. She did not try to pick it up. She stared around the room. The walls appeared to be moving slightly in the shadows; the floor rippled. She pushed herself up on the sofa, clutching at its back, and put her hands over her eyes, rubbing them violently, trying to swing her feet to the mat, but somehow they would not obey her. They felt heavy, as if they no longer belonged to her. Her head was hammering and once again she was conscious of a strange flickering behind her eyes. Exhausted, she fell back, her head on the shiny material of the sofa arm, and, defeated, she closed her eyes.

The borders shimmered beneath the burnished August sky as Matilda and William and their attendants rode toward Marlborough for the royal wedding. It was a long time since Matilda had thought about the girl who was soon to become John's wife. It pained her to think of the child she remembered—small, frail, and very frightened—being linked forever with the volatile prince, a prince who was now heir to the throne after his father's death and the succession of his brother, Richard.

The Downs reflected the beating sunlight as the horses wearily made their way toward the encampment around the abbey outside the walls of Marlborough. The pennants and the flags hung limp and unmoving from the tents and flagstaffs. Everywhere horses and men stood dejected and exhausted in the heat. In the center of the encampment the royal pavilion stood open and empty. Prince John had taken a few companions and gone into the forests, seeking the cool of the shade.

In the Countess of Gloucester's quarters, late at night, after William had gone off to roister with the prince and his cronies, Matilda found Isabella, seated quiet and pale before a polished mirror, looking in something like wonder as a lady combed out her pale silver hair, fingering her silky tresses as though she had never seen them before. Beside her on the stool sat another girl, almost as fair, almost as delicate; a little taller, with watchful dark eyes. She was patting her sister's arm reassuringly when Matilda was shown in, and Matilda saw her eyes at once seek her own in the mirror, hostile and suspicious. This then was Amicia, Isabella's sister, the girl who, she now knew for sure, was to marry Richard de Clare.

Refusing to meet the glance in the mirror, Matilda went to put her arm around Isabella's thin shoulders and dropped a kiss on the fair head.

Isabella looked up and smiled weakly. "I'm glad you've come."

"I promised, didn't I?" Matilda took the comb from the maid and gently continued combing, drawing the fair hair back from the girl's hot face.

"And you'll attend me tomorrow, in the abbey?"

"Of course." Matilda tried to smile at Amicia. "Do you attend your sister too?" she asked quietly.

At once the eyelids were lowered. Amicia nodded meekly. "I do my duty, madam, as my mother demands of me."

"Where is Lady Gloucester?" Matilda couldn't help wondering why the woman wasn't with her daughter at a time like this.

Amicia shrugged. "We see little of our lady mother, madam. Since our father died, she prefers the company of men and, of course, of the prince." Her voice was heavy suddenly with innuendo. In the mirror Matilda saw the younger sister blanch. The girl's hands, clasped in her lap, were white at the knuckles, and she felt a rush of sympathetic anger. It was insufferable that this small delicate girl should be linked with someone as insensitive and boorish as Prince John.

"I hope, Lady Matilda," Amicia went on, not taking her eyes from Matilda's face in the mirror, "that you will do me the honor of attending me at *my* wedding. I know Sir Richard would be pleased. You are, I believe, such an *old* friend."

Matilda could feel a flush of anger mounting in her cheeks, and she instantly wanted to give hurt for hurt. "I shall be pleased to, my dear. It will after all be rather an anticlimax for you—after your sister has wed a prince." She was sorry instantly that she had said it. Isabella gave a little gasp, looking up at her sister pleadingly, while Amicia, white with fury, rose to her feet and swung for the first time to look Matilda in the face.

"Prince John is a brute, madam, and a cruel man with women, as everyone knows." She looked coldly at her trembling sister. "I wish Isabella joy of him. I shall have a kind and gentle husband. But then"—she almost spat the words—"you would know all about the qualities of Sir Richard, madam." After gathering her rich green skirts about her, she swept out through the curtained doorway, leaving the other two to gaze at each

302

other in horror. Isabella's eyes were filled with tears. "I don't know what's happened to Amicia. She used to love me."

"She's jealous of you, child." Matilda took the elder sister's place on the stool and put her arm around Isabella. "Can't you see? Her younger sister is marrying a royal prince. It is more than she can bear."

"And she's jealous of you because you're so beautiful and the world says Sir Richard loved you once."

Once.

Matilda's arm fell away from the girl's shoulders. Yes, he had loved her once. She had thought he loved her still. It had been that knowledge which had bolstered her during the long lonely nights when she had had to submit to William's rough attentions, and which had somehow comforted her against all his abuses when he was drunk. She shivered suddenly. She had not realized that anyone else had ever guessed their love. But these two people knew. Isabella, who would be the wife of the prince, and Amicia, who was to marry Richard. And if they knew her secret, how was it possible that the rest of the world did not know it too?

Above the camp the stars were enormous in the bronze-black arch of the sky. She stopped for a moment on her way back to the de Braose tents to gaze up at it, feeling the immensity of it above her, quietly soothing her. A slight breath of hot air, almost a breeze, stirred the skirt of her gown for a moment, then the night was still again.

"Do you find it hard to sleep, Lady Matilda?" She started at the deep voice at her elbow, and then, recognizing with a guilty shock the figure of Prince John in the shadows, she curtseyed low.

"I was returning to our tents, sir, after visiting your bride."

John frowned. She could see his face quite clearly in the luminous starlight, strong and clean-cut, with the arched brows and heavy high-bridged nose of the Plantagenets. His shoulders had broadened with manhood and the hot Normandy sun had tanned his face to a uniform darkness. He smiled at her, showing white, even teeth. "How is my little bride? Still shaking at the thought of the ogre she must marry?"

Matilda clenched her fists at his mocking tone. "She is very young, Your Highness, and very shy. You must give her time."

"She has had time. Ten years to get used to the idea."

"She has also had ten years to brood over the cruelty you showed her at Gloucester."

John threw back his head and laughed. "I had no idea I had made any impression on her at all at Gloucester. So much the better. I see you are sorry for her, Lady Matilda. I think you should spare me some sympathy. Imagine being married to that little milksop. Can you see her in bed? Can you see her the mother of strapping sons?" John laughed bitterly. "I'll wager the good Sir William had no such fears about you on the eve of his wedding!" He glanced at her sideways, "But then," he went on, following

303

his own train of thought, "I *must* have sons. It is imperative that I secure my own line . . ." He stopped abruptly. "Are you coming to my brother's coronation, madam?"

She smiled, relieved by the sudden change of mood. "You must know, surely, that women are not invited, Your Highness. It appears the king does not share your appreciation of the female sex."

John snorted. "True. The king wants it to be a sacred occasion. I would have women if it were *my* coronation. Women everywhere! If ever I am crowned, Matilda, you shall attend me. I swear it." He threw his arm around her shoulders roughly and reached across to kiss her cheek. Then before she had a chance to struggle he released her abruptly and with another lightning change of mood turned away from her. "You know that my brother is to marry at last? It was agreed before my father died. He and Alice, the daughter of the King of France, are to marry." He gave a cynical laugh. "My father no longer needs the lovely Alice to comfort him, so he felt he could at last spare the lady to her rightful betrothed and honor the agreement with King Louis."

"Sir!" Matilda was shocked. "I can't believe that there was any truth in the rumors that your father loved Alice. Why, that's almost incestuous, his own son's betrothed. I'm sure you don't really believe it either."

John merely shrugged. "My father was a passionate man. A great man in many ways." He was thoughtful for a moment, gazing up at the burning heavens. "He was a good king, my father."

Matilda stirred uncomfortably. She wanted to return to her tent. The prince's moody company made her nervous; the camp seemed totally deserted. She wondered too what he was doing out here by her tents quite unattended, and almost as though he had read her thoughts he smiled at her again, throwing off his reverie. "The banqueting hall was too hot for me. A stag-night roister is all very well, but if the groom melts clean away before he gets to his bride it defeats its purpose, so I came out. Half the good fellows in there were asleep, your husband among them. The others are too hot to care, and if they do, they suspect me of going to find a final friendly bed for the night." He laughed again, a dry mirthless laugh. "My last night with a real woman, before I have to commit adultery to gain satisfaction from my bed."

Another slight breeze stirred the pennants hanging above the tents and gently moved the skirts of Matilda's kirtle over the ground, which was beginning to gather dew. She felt herself grow suddenly cold. Taking a step away from him, she quietly closed her fingers on the folds of her kirtle, holding it clear, ready to run. She took a deep breath. "It is late, Your Highness, and I attend your bride early in the morning. If you will excuse me. . . ."

"I have not yet thanked you for your wedding gift," he went on, as if she had not spoken. "Three hundred cows and a fine Hereford bull, they

304

tell me." He smiled, his eyes blue slits, catlike, in the dark face, one eyebrow slightly raised. "I'll wager that was your choice, Lady Matilda. I sense a touch of irony there. No, my lady, I'll not excuse you, not yet."

His hand reached out, touching the shoulder of her gown. "Why do you fear me?" he said softly. "I've not harmed you." His hands were on her shoulders, gently pulling her toward him. They were strong hands, the hands of a man.

She raised her eyes to look into his face. There was no sign there of the boy she had so disliked, nor the importunate adolescent who had accosted her at Winchester. These thin, arrogant features were those of an adult, and, she suddenly realized, alarmingly attractive.

"Your Highness." She tried to draw back, but he was holding her too hard, his fingers digging into the flesh of her arm. His face was close to hers.

"I have not dismissed you, my lady," he breathed. "Nor do I intend to, yet."

Mesmerized by the intense blue of his eyes, she felt her lips meet his at last with a shock of recognition. For a moment her body seemed to cleave to his, then abruptly his strange spell was broken as a voice rang out cool and loud from the dark near them. "Good evening, Your Highness, my lady."

John released her with an oath and whirled around, his hand flying to the hilt of his dagger.

A figure had stepped out of the shadow of one of the pavilions and, coming nearer, bowed low. As he stood up again, tall and slim beside the figure of the prince, Matilda saw with a sudden gasp that it was Richard de Clare.

Richard bowed to her formally and distantly, and then turned again to the prince, grinning. "We missed you in the hall, sir, and some were growing worried."

"Indeed, Lord de Clare." John's voice was low-pitched and very cold. "It was good of you to volunteer to find me. As we are so soon to be brothers-in-law perhaps you felt a family feeling of protection?"

Richard colored a little at the note of sarcasm, but he bowed amiably enough. "Shall I walk with you, sir? Lady Matilda looks tired. I'm sure she's anxious to get some rest."

Recovering herself as best she could, Matilda swept a deep curtsy to the prince, then she turned toward her own quarters, picking up her skirts as soon as she was out of sight, and careless of her dignity, ran toward the safety of her tent.

It was already growing dark, and the wedding celebrations were all but over the next day when at last Richard sought out Matilda from the thronging guests and guided her toward the shelter of a tall hedge threaded with honeysuckle and dog roses. His face was grim. "You're playing with fire when you flirt with John, surely you know that," he began furiously.

Matilda blushed. "I did not flirt with him! He followed me. I had no wish even to talk with him, believe me. I dislike that young man."

Richard glanced over his shoulder. "Don't talk so loud," he said anxiously. "Well, he certainly likes you, and it wouldn't do to make an enemy of him by showing you don't return his feelings." He glanced at her obliquely.

"Are you suggesting that I—"

"I am suggesting nothing, Matilda. Just take care. Please." He put his hand gently on her arm.

Matilda pressed her own fingers miserably over his, swallowing the lump that came to her throat. "I will take care, Richard. I know he's dangerous."

"I leave tomorrow to attend the coronation." His voice dropped almost to a whisper. "Then I go to Cardiff. I am to marry Amicia of Gloucester within the month."

She felt rather than saw his eyes on her and blinked back her sudden tears. "I know, Richard. I wish you every happiness." She took a deep breath and turned away for a moment, trying to regain control over the misery that had welled up until it was almost too great to bear. When she faced him again she was smiling. She broke off the delicate pink shell of a dog rose and pushed it gently into the clasp of his mantle. "Let us still be friends, Richard dear." She was almost as tall as he, and gazing at him for a long, last moment, she leaned forward suddenly and gave him a quick kiss on the lips, then she turned and fled.

She sent her maids away early that night and, blowing out the candles, lay dry-eyed in the dark, listening to the distant shouts and music that floated across the encampment. William, she knew, was with the prince. Richard too, she supposed; the three men with whom her life seemed inextricably bound, drinking together at the banqueting board, toasting each other into the night.

She lay for a long time listening to the giggles of the two girls who attended her as they prepared for bed beyond the thin canvas partition in the tent, then gradually as they grew quieter her eyelids became heavier and eventually she dozed.

It was Gwenny, the elder of the two, who wakened her, roughly shaking her shoulder in the dark. The camp was silent, and the coals in the brazier beyond the tent flaps were long dead. "My lady, you're to come quickly." The girl was shaking with fear.

Matilda sat up. "What is it? What has happened?" She reached for her bedgown and wrapped it around her naked shoulders as the girl lit the candle by her bed.

306

"You're wanted, my lady. In the Countess of Gloucester's tent. Quickly." Gwenny was panting slightly, still shocked from her own awakening by the countess's terrified maid, and the candlelight showed her round face plump and perspiring as she searched by the bed for the discarded leather slippers. "Oh, my lady, there is such trouble there, I hear."

"What trouble, girl, tell me?" Matilda pushed her feet into the slippers and stood up, reaching for the candle. "What's happening?"

But Gwenny only shook her head dumbly, too terrified by the threats that the maid had passed on to anyone who might speak of the night's happenings. Seeing her mistress was ready, she led the way out into the still night.

In the Countess of Gloucester's tent, rich with silks and lit with myriad candles, an anxious group of whispering women were clustered around the countess. As Matilda ran in, clutching her robe around her, they stopped and stood back, revealing Hawise of Gloucester, dressed still, but disheveled and tearstained, standing over a kneeling girl. She had a firm hold of the girl's hair and was shaking the unresisting head back and forth with pitiless violence.

"Dear God!" Matilda stopped in amazement. "What's happening? What are you doing?" Her eyes blazing, she flew toward Hawise, knocking the woman's hands away, and found herself looking down at the figure on the rugs at her feet. It was Isabella.

Matilda took a step back. She felt herself go cold as, now that the pressure on her hair had been released, the girl crouched lower, cowering away, her hands pressed desperately to her face. Behind her Amicia was standing, her own expression blank with horror, her eyes fixed on her sister with a desperate fascination.

Forgetting the other women, Matilda dropped on her knees and threw her arms around the girl, cradling the fair head on her breast.

"You must go back to him, Isabella. Now." Her mother's voice, cracked with emotion, cut through the silence.

Matilda tightened her grip on Isabella's shoulders. The girl was completely silent; not tearful, not sobbing; her stillness somehow more appalling than crying and shouting would have been. At her mother's voice, there was no reaction at all. Only a numb despairing rigidity.

"Will you ask these ladies to leave?" Matilda gestured impatiently, looking up at Hawise through the curtain of hair that had fallen loose from her plait. "Amicia, fetch your sister a warm mantle." The girl's skin was like cold alabaster in the heat of the night.

She saw Amicia turn into the depths of the tent, and slowly, one by one, the other women began to move away, although Hawise had not yet spoken. Then at last she seemed to find her voice again. "No one must know of this shame," she whispered harshly. "No one must ever hear what has happened tonight. If any of you ever speak of it, I'll have your tongues cut out, do you hear?" Her voice rang up the scale and cracked hysterically. "There's nothing wrong with my daughter. Nothing wrong between her and the prince; just wedding-night nerves. She's going back to her husband directly. Lady Matilda will take her back to the royal tent."

Whispering uncomfortably, the women slipped one by one into the darkness, leaving Matilda and the countess looking at each other. Quietly Amicia brought a sable rug and placed it gently over her sister's shoulders with shaking hands. Then she too crept away.

Hawise stood looking down at her daughter and suddenly her tears began to fall again. "The disgrace. The humiliation! She has betrayed us before the whole world by running away from him." She groped for a lace kerchief and pressed it to her streaming eyes. "How can the silly chit have done such a thing? What was he thinking of to let her?"

"What happened?" Matilda spoke gently in the girl's ear. "Can you tell your mother or me?"

But Isabella shook her head. As she pressed closer to her Matilda could feel the warmth slowly coming back to the girl's taut body.

"Your mother is right. You must go back to your husband. It is not so bad, what happens, you know. You will grow accustomed to it." She smiled sadly. "You may even grow to like it, my dear. But whatever happens it is your duty to go to him. Come." She took the girl's hand and raised her gently to her feet. Isabella stood submissively before her, her eyes on the ground, her sumptuous bedgown bordered with golden embroidery falling in full pleats around her. It was, Matilda noted with a strange feeling of relief, untorn and unsullied.

Gently she led the unresisting girl out toward the royal pavilion, skirting the damped fires and the rows of sleeping tents. The guards at the entrance came to a salute as they passed through, their eyes curiously taking in the details of the two women in their nightclothes, and Matilda, her arm firmly around Isabella's shoulders, escorted her quickly from their gaze. John's servants, bowing, held back the heavy tapestry hangings that covered the entrance to the sleeping area.

"Go to him," Matilda whispered. She glanced around nervously, not wanting the prince to see her, but as she spoke a small plump woman appeared from the inner room and curtsied. "There you are, Your Highness," she addressed Isabella, who stared at her blankly. "The prince your husband told me to come to keep you company and fetch you a hot posset." She held out her hand and guided Isabella through the curtains. "His Highness has gone for a ride. He said he doubted if he'd be back by morning, so you may sleep undisturbed tonight." The woman was careful to keep any expression out of her voice, but she glanced over Isabella's head at Matilda and made a wry face that Matilda guessed was intended to mean that the prince had in fact said a great deal more than that and at some length. She sighed, and gave the girl a gentle push. "Good night, Isabella. Sleep well, love."

She watched for a moment as the woman hustled about fetching a jug of steaming, fragrant liquid and a goblet and then as Isabella climbed, still moving as in a dream, into the high bed, Matilda turned and pushed her way out of the room, suddenly stifled by its oppressive heat.

She made her way quickly and nervously back to the de Braose tents, half afraid she would be once more waylaid by the prince, conscious suddenly of the black shadows behind the circled tents, of the grove of trees, the leaves unstirring in the windless air, and of the motionless encampment guards half dozing as they leaned on their swords.

But it was Richard who waylaid her. He stepped from the shadows, his finger to his lips, and beckoned her after him into the shelter of the trees. "I could not leave like that," he whispered. "Not without just one more moment alone with you. Dear God! Why did we not meet each other in time!" The wind teased the streaming torch on the edge of the encampment near them and she saw the shadows playing on his face.

"It was not to be, love." She put her hands on his shoulders. "Maybe, one day—"

He seized her hands, enfolding them in his own, holding them pressed against his chest. "One day!" he echoed bitterly. "When you belong to de Braose and when the prince has already marked you for his own!"

"That's not true!" She pulled away from him violently. "John is nothing to me and I am nothing to him. Nothing!"

He was looking down at her, his eyes gleaming strangely in the torch light.

"Nothing?" he echoed.

"Nothing. I swear by all I hold sacred!"

He shook his head. "Don't swear. You don't know what may happen. The prince has power, Matilde." He touched her hair gently. "Dear God! I want to throw you on my horse and gallop away with you. Take you for my own!"

For a moment she felt a blind excitement as the power of the passion in his voice flooded through her. If he had asked her then she would have gone, but his hands fell slowly to his sides and he shrugged. "I am to be brother-in-law to the prince, it seems."

Her eyes filled with tears. "As befits a great earl," she whispered. Forcing herself to smile, she looked away. "I must go in, Richard."

"Of course." He took her hand and raised it to his lips. "I'll see you again. Soon."

She nodded dumbly, then she turned away, pulling her cloak around her as she dodged past the flare and into the darkness.

When Tim came upstairs it was already dark. He had walked some four miles down the valley and back, shrugging off the heavy warm spots of rain, and he was tired. He pushed open the door quietly and glanced into the bedroom. Jo was asleep on the sofa, by the window. Her book had fallen to the floor. With a fond grin he picked it up and put it on the table without looking at the title, then he turned and, pulling a blanket from the bed, he tucked it gently around her. Then he paused, frowning, as he looked down at her face. An expression of anguish had crossed her features momentarily and as he took her hand, gently slipping it beneath the blanket, he found her fists were clenched.

"Jo?" he whispered. "Jo? Can you hear me?"

She did not respond. She was breathing in tight, almost imperceptible gasps.

"Where are you, Jo?" he murmured, but she did not answer. He touched her face lightly, then reached over to turn out the lamp.

He undressed quickly in the dark and slid into bed, and lay listening, but Jo was completely silent. Not so much as a sigh came from her as she lay locked in that different world on the far side of the room.

He must have dozed off after a while, for a slim moon had appeared at the window when he woke suddenly. He gazed at the luminous dial on his wrist. It was ten past three. Then he realized what had disturbed him. Jo was moving restlessly on the sofa. She moaned softly and he saw her sit up. The blanket slid to the floor and she swung her bare feet off the seat and stood, staring around the room.

"Don't tell me it's your turn for the bed," he said quietly into the shadows.

She did not reply. She moved toward him slowly, staring down at him in the watery moonlight.

"I thought you'd gone," she whispered at last.

"Only for a walk." He propped himself up on one elbow.

"Weren't you going after the prince?"

Tim froze. "Jo?" he said softly. "Jo, can you hear me?"

She was half smiling, her eyes on his face. "There's no one here," she whispered. "Oh, Richard, please. Make love to me just once more. Surely it's no sin when we love each other so much. Tomorrow you can go. You'll be brother-in-law to the prince. You'll be Amicia's forever. Give me just a few hours more." She was fumbling with the sash of her bathrobe.

Tim ran his tongue over his dry lips. "Jo," he said hoarsely. "Jo, I think you'd better wake up—"

She opened the gown and let it fall to the floor. Beneath it she was naked. He stared at her body, silvered in the thin moonlight, and felt himself tense all over as she threw herself toward the bed and wriggled into his arms beneath the sheet.

"Richard! Oh, Richard!" Her mouth sought his as his arms closed around her. "Dear God, please hold me!"

With a groan Tim lay back, gathering her against him, feeling the silky weight of her hair slide over her shoulders onto his face and neck, blotting out the moonlight.

He kissed her again and again, threading his fingers through her hair, holding her face still as her slim, warm body lay on his. He kissed her mouth and her eyes, her neck and her breasts, then, catching her shoulders, he turned her onto her back, lying on top of her, his tongue probing between her lips, feeling her legs fall willingly apart to receive him.

It was daylight when he fell asleep at last, his arms still around her, one thigh lying possessively across hers.

He slept heavily, barely stirring when Jo slipped from the bed and, grabbing her bathrobe, fled into the bathroom.

She was fully dressed when he woke to the sound of a knock at the bedroom door. He watched sleepily as she took a tray from their host and slid it onto the bedside table, then she sat down on the bed beside him. She smiled wanly.

"So you're awake."

Tim grinned. "Barely. Is that early-morning tea I see?" He sat up slowly then he looked at her remorsefully. "Jo, it was my fault. I took advantage of you last night. I should have said no. I should have tried to wake you somehow—"

"I was awake." Her face was drawn and tense. "But I thought you were Richard. I wasn't in a trance, Tim. I knew I was in this room. I knew we were in a pub. I knew this was the twentieth century." Her hands were shaking suddenly and she clutched them together. "But I was still Matilda. And you—you were Richard."

Tim gave a tight smile. "Matilda was one hell of an uninhibited lady. I'm not surprised Richard could never get her out of his system." He smiled gently.

Jo colored violently. After reaching for the teapot, she managed to pour out two cups, using both hands on the china handle. He took his cup from her hastily and sat leaning against the pillows, staring down into the tea. "That was the last time they made love," he went on quietly.

She looked up. "How do you know?"

"I just know. They weren't meant for each other." He gave a rueful grin. "Shame, isn't it?"

She was staring at him. "*You* were Richard de Clare," she whispered at last. "It did work with Bill Walton!"

For a moment she thought he wasn't going to answer, then he nodded reluctantly. "It's not as simple as that, though, Jo—Jo? What is it?"

311

She was crying suddenly; soundless, exhausted weeping, the tears falling remorselessly down her cheeks.

"I thought it was Nick," she said brokenly. "Oh, Tim, I'm sorry, but I so wanted it to be Nick."

25

Nick was lying on the sofa in his apartment with his eyes closed, listening to the quiet strains of Debussy, when Sam let himself in through the front door and pulled off his raincoat, shaking it in the hall before hanging it up. He appeared in the doorway and stared down at his brother in surprise.

"I thought you were off to New York today?"

"I've postponed the trip until the second." Nick did not open his eyes. "That way I can see all the top men in one go. There's no point in going twice."

Sam raised an eyebrow as he crossed to the tray of drinks. "That doesn't sound like you. Do you want a Scotch?"

Nick shook his head. "I'm energetic when I need to be," he said. "It's just that there are a few things I want to sort out before I go." He sounded depressed.

Sam was pouring himself a large gin. "Would one of those things be Jo?" he said softly.

Nick altered the position of his head slightly so that he could watch Sam as his brother walked to the window. Another summer storm was brewing and the light outside was sulfurous as the cloud billowed up over London from the west. "I used to think you were quite fond of her," he said reflectively. "But you're not, are you?"

Sam stiffened. "What makes you think that?"

"Observation."

"Then your powers of observation must be sadly awry. I am very fond of her." Sam was staring out at the thunder clouds. A flicker of lightning lit the sky above the park, turning the trees fluorescent for a fraction of a second in front of the bruised purple of the storm. "It's you who seem to be having trouble working out your feelings for her. You still need my help, I think." He turned at last and looked at Nick. "All that hostility is still there, isn't it?"

"The hostility your hypnotism was supposed to cure? It didn't work, did

313

it? I never thought you'd be able to do it. I doubt if I was even properly under."

Sam smiled. "Oh, you were properly 'under,' as you put it. You just don't remember. Perhaps I should do it again." Sam perched on the edge of the coffee table, looking at him. "Why don't we try and see what happens?"

Nick glanced at him suspiciously, suddenly remembering his mother's anxiety. "Why are you so eager to hypnotize me, Sam?" he asked after a moment.

"I'm not eager," Sam said. "I'm merely offering."

Nick put his glass down. To his own surprise he found himself putting his misgivings firmly aside. "Perhaps a bit of mental massage is just what I need one way and another."

Nick sat back in the chair and settled his shoulders against the deep-orange cushions. Only a few moments later Sam was smiling in triumph. "Well done, Nicholas," he murmured. "That's it. Now you are completely relaxed. Completely asleep. But you can still hear me, can't you?"

Nick nodded.

"Good. Open your eyes and look at me. That's it. Now, I want you to remember who I told you you were, once before, eight hundred years ago. Who was it, Nick?"

His brother's eyes were steady. They narrowed slightly. "John," he said.

Sam smiled again. "Good." He took a deep draught from his glass. "Now, Your Royal Highness." He emphasized the words mockingly. "We discussed Matilda de Braose, did we not?"

Nick nodded. A frown appeared between his eyes.

"The woman you loved, sir," Sam went on relentlessly. "The woman who rejected your advances and spurned you. The woman who accused you of murder before the world."

Abruptly Nick stood up, almost knocking into Sam as he strode across the room, his face angry, his fists clenched. "She taunted me about my nephew, Arthur—"

"And that was when you first decided that she must die," Sam said softly. "But now she has returned to taunt you again. And even in this life she still despises you. She still thinks herself superior to you—to you! You will punish her again, won't you, sir?" he whispered. "But before you do it, you will tell me what you intend."

"I will tell you."

Sam smiled. "I wonder who you really were in that previous life," he said reflectively. "If you were anyone at all. Come, little brother. Why don't we find out, just for the hell of it." Standing up, he took Nick's shoulder and steered him back to the chair. "I want you to think back to when you were a child. Back to when you were a baby. Back even before

314

you lay in the womb, back to the time before the darkness, back to the late twelfth century when Richard Lion Heart was on the throne of England. Tell me, did you have a life then too? Did you know me as William de Braose?" Nick had not moved. His face was like carved stone.

"Well?" Sam leaned over Nick and, taking a handful of his hair, pulled his head back so that his brother was forced to look up at him. "Who were you?"

Nick's eyes were cold. His mouth moved into a half smile as for the first time he looked at Sam directly. "Can you have forgotten so soon?" he said slowly.

Sam drew back abruptly. "So." He swore under his breath. "The trance wasn't deep enough. You've been fooling me. Yet I could have sworn—" He took several steps back. "Nick? Nick, can you hear me?"

Nick nodded slowly. He was watching Sam with the half smile still on his face.

"I see." Sam reached into the pocket of his cords and pulled out a clasp knife. "Well, let's put it to the test, shall we? I am going to tap your hand with my finger. It is not going to hurt and I doubt if you will feel it at all." He unfolded the knife. After grabbing Nick's hand he held it a moment, staring at the palm, the blade poised. Nick did not seem to have noticed. Slowly Sam turned the hand over and deliberately he stroked the blade across the back of Nick's wrist. A thin line of blood welled up, but Nick had not flinched.

"So. A deep trance still exists," Sam murmured as he put the knife away. "And your wit comes from another time. Yes, brother, I have forgotten who you are. Why don't you tell me?"

Nick straightened his shoulders. Slowly he stood once more. "You dare call me brother?" he said.

"Your name?" Sam said. "Tell me your name, then I shall know what to call you?"

"I am John Plantagenet," Nick shouted suddenly. "I am the king's brother! I stand in England now in my brother's stead," he said slowly. "And one day, de Braose, I shall make you kneel to me. You, and that witch you call your wife." He smiled coldly. "Are you deranged, man? Can it be that you do not know your prince?" He strode toward Sam suddenly and took hold of the front of Sam's shirt. The blood from the cut on the back of his wrist was trickling across his palm and a smear of it transferred itself to the blue cotton as Sam tried to pull himself free. "Look at me!" Nick shouted suddenly. "And look well, de Braose! Remember the face of your future king!"

For a moment neither of them reacted to the sound of the front door buzzer. Nick had not heard it, but Sam, as he wrenched himself away, turned angrily and glanced toward the hall.

It buzzed again. Sam cursed. He had to get rid of whoever it was. He

315

backed away from Nick cautiously. "I shall return in a moment, sir," he said, trying to contain the anger and impatience that had swept through him. "Sit down, sir," he added forcefully. "We shall continue this conversation in a moment." He paused, reluctant to move, but Nick, after a second's annoyed hesitation, had swung away from him and was standing in the middle of the room, his arms folded across his chest.

Sam hurried into the hall, closing the door behind him, as the buzzer sounded for a third time, and he dragged open the front door. A bedraggled figure was standing on the dimly lit landing, dressed in a fawn raincoat. It was Judy Curzon.

"Thank God!" she said, pushing past him. "I thought you were out. I'm half drowned."

"Judy!" Sam was still holding the door. "Wait! You can't come in! Why didn't the janitor ring through to say you were here?"

She had unknotted her belt and dropped the soaked raincoat on a chair. "He wasn't in his cubbyhole, so I dodged past and grabbed the elevator. I hate being interrogated by your janitor. It makes me feel like a burglar. What do you mean I can't come in, for Christ's sake? Why not?"

"I have a patient here, Judy—"

"Crap! You don't have patients. You do experiments on poor, bloody animals." Judy pushed open the drawing-room door. "Get me a drink and a towel and let me wait until the storm is over, then I'll go—" She stopped dead in the doorway. "Nick?" Her good humor vanished. "I thought you were supposed to be in the States."

Nick turned slightly toward her but he said nothing, and after a moment he turned back to the window where the lightning was almost continuous behind the streaming rain.

Judy scowled. "And hello to you too, Nicholas, sweetie!" She walked across to the table and picked up the gin bottle, holding it up to the light. "You said you were with a patient, Sam. Do I gather you meant your benighted brother?"

Sam had followed her into the room. He closed the door firmly. "Sit down, Judy, and please be quiet." His voice was quietly threatening. "Nick is deeply hypnotized. He doesn't know you are here."

She stared at Sam, then, stunned, she turned to Nick. "You mean it? He can't see me? Have you made him go back into the past, like Jo?" Judy raised her hand as if to touch Nick's face, then abruptly she moved away from him again.

Sam nodded. "I've been trying to do that, but he is not so good a subject as Jo. He doesn't go deeply enough into the trance."

Judy poured herself out an inch of gin. "But he's deeply enough in a trance for me to come into the room and him not know it! What has he done to his hand?"

Sam smiled enigmatically. "I cut him."

Judy stared, aghast. "Why?" she breathed.

"To see if the trance was deep enough."

Judy had begun to feel a little sick. After staring at the blood on Nick's hand, she turned to look at Sam. "You're sure you didn't have a fight?" she asked faintly.

Sam shook his head. "Of course not."

"Wake him up, please." She was suddenly frightened.

"I was about to when you arrived." Sam helped himself to another drink. He was watching Judy closely, noticing the conflict of emotions as they followed one another in quick succession across her face. Fear, disgust, interest, excitement, and then something like calculation betrayed themselves in her eyes. But no affection that he could see.

"Can't he hear us talking at all?" she said after a moment. Nick was staring out of the window at the rain.

"He can. But he's not listening. He's in a world of his own, aren't you, my liege?" He walked up to Nick and slapped him playfully on the shoulder.

Nick turned. His expression was icy. "You display the manners of a peasant, de Braose," he said.

Sam colored. "Peasant or not, brother," he replied smoothly, "I am the one who holds the power now. I can free you or leave you locked in the past. Do you know what would happen to a man who thinks he is King John? He would be put away somewhere where he could harm no one for the rest of his days!"

"Sam!" Judy cried. She ran to him and grabbed him by the arm. "Sam, for Christ's sake, wake him up. Stop it!"

Sam smiled at her. "Afraid of losing your handsome Nicholas to the men in white coats?"

She clung to him. "Wake him up! What you're doing is evil. It's vile! You're manipulating him!"

"No, no." Sam gently drew away from her. "He'll be okay. I've done nothing to harm him."

"What about posthypnotic suggestion?" Judy was watching Nick's face in anguish. "What have you told him to do when he wakes up?"

"Ah, yes, the one thing every layman—or woman—has heard of." Sam folded his arms. "Perhaps you have some good ideas for one or two posthypnotic suggestions yourself?" He stared at her, one eyebrow raised, his eyes full of amusement.

Judy glared at him. "Well, you could tell him to leave Jo alone for a start," she snapped. "If you'd like to do something for me."

They both flinched as another flash of lightning lit the room.

Sam was watching Nick's profile. "I am not prepared to do that," he said.

"I thought we were on the same side! You said you could split them up. You sent me after him to France to get him away from her!"

"And obviously it was a lousy idea." He turned to her finally, his voice heavy with dislike. "I can't force him to like you." He smiled faintly. "Though he obviously does, in spite of the fact that, as I told you before, I believe you have certain habits which put my brother off. Pursuing him is obviously one of them." He threw himself down on the sofa, pulling one ankle up to rest on his knee as he looked up at her. "Though as I recall you did not expect to see him when you came here this evening. You therefore came to see me, I presume, or was your visit really merely an excuse to get out of the rain?"

Judy scowled. "Whatever I came for, it was obviously a big mistake!"

Sam ignored the indignant words. "So. You came to discuss Nick."

"I may have." Judy looked at Nick uncomfortably. "But I can't talk about him like this as if he's not here! It's not fair. It's grotesque!"

"Then I shall awaken him and you can tell him your problem to his face."

Sam stood up. He strode over to Nick and swung him around. "You remember what I told you, brother?" he said quietly. "You remember what you must do. But the rest you will forget. Whatever you have been experiencing there, in your head, you will forget for now. You will forget everything, save the fact that you are rested and relaxed and ready to receive your visitor, when I count to three. Now. One—two, three."

Judy held her breath as she watched them. Slowly Nick's face became reanimated and suddenly he was looking straight at her.

"Judy? When did you arrive?"

She forced herself to smile. "Only a few minutes ago. I wanted to get out of the storm."

Nick turned to the window, puzzled, then he put his hand to his head. "What happened? Was I asleep?"

Sam grinned. "You asked me to hypnotize you, remember? I was hard at it when Judy arrived."

Nick groaned. "Did I say anything odd?"

Judy looked away. "Of course not."

She looked up into his face. For a long moment they stared at each other, then Judy smiled. "I'm very good at keeping secrets. Sam," she said, "tell me, who was I in this past life you are all living so cozily together? I'd like to know."

He shook his head. "I don't run sideshows, and I'm not a therapist."

"But you regressed Nick!" She colored indignantly.

"For a reason. And because he is my brother. I'm sorry, Judy. It would not be ethical for me to do it to you. But, for what it's worth, I wouldn't bother."

Her mouth dropped open. "What do you mean?"

318

"I mean I don't believe you've lived before."

Judy laughed. "I see. Keep it in the family, eh? All nice and cozy. How convenient. Just like the way you've been priming Nick!"

"What do you mean?" Nick sat up suddenly.

"I mean the whole thing is a great hoax! You weren't regressed. He told you who you were and then he told you what to do! Some past life!"

"Judy." Sam's voice was low and threatening. "You heard and saw nothing but the end of our session."

"What does she mean, Sam?" Nick stood up.

"She means I was telling you to forget your worries and relax. For some reason she found that sinister."

"You told him—"

"I told him nothing." Sam interrupted forcefully. *"Nothing,* Judy, that need be of the least concern. But in one thing you were right. It was not a proper regression. As I told Nick before, he is too tense yet to attempt it."

The ringing of the phone punctuated the end of his sentence. Sam, who was standing right beside it, picked it up. For a moment he stood listening, a frown on his face, then suddenly he was smiling.

"Why, Jo! How nice to hear from you. How are you?" He waved Nick away as the latter tried to reach for the phone. "No, he hasn't, as a matter of fact. He's not going until the second now . . . I see. Poor Jo, where are you, then? . . . No, I won't tell him. Of course I won't." He smiled sweetly at Nick. "Yes. Yes, I'm glad you called. Keep in touch."

He put the receiver down gently. "That was Jo," he said unnecessarily. "She's at the Black Lamb Hotel near a place called Talgarth."

Judy's eyes blazed. "You bastard!" she said. "I distinctly heard you promise Jo you wouldn't tell Nick where she was!"

Tim had caught a taxi from Paddington back to Covent Garden. He walked heavily up the stairs to the studio and stared around. The place was blazing with lights, the small dais surrounded by floods and spots, a wind machine playing on the girl who stood there dressed only in the finest wisps of chiffon amid a litter of straw bales.

George Chippen, his assistant, was busy with his camera, snapping the laughing girl, but he stopped as Tim appeared and walked over toward them. Tim altered the position of one of the spotlights a little and winked at George. "I'll get hay fever if I hang around here," he commented with a heavy attempt at a smile. "You carry on, George, you're doing a great job. *Ciao,* kids. I'll see you all later." After humping his heavy bag into the corner of the studio he dropped it, then he climbed the spiral staircase to his bedroom, oblivious of the glances of curiosity that followed him from the studio floor. He locked the door, then flung himself on the bed, staring up at the ceiling.

It had been his idea to leave. She had not argued. Subdued, scarcely speaking, she had driven him to Newport Station. There she had kissed him once, a long wistful kiss, full of kindness, but without passion.

"I'm so sorry, Tim," she whispered. "I wish it could have been for real."

"So do I, honey." He had stroked her hair lightly, trying to memorize the touch of it beneath his hand. "So do I."

With a groan he turned his face to the pillows to hide the wetness on his cheeks and he began to sob quietly, like a child.

Sometime later he heard George run up the spiral stairs and tap on the door. "Tim? Tim, can I come in?" The boy sounded excited and cheerful.

Tim did not answer. He pulled the pillows over his head and after a while he heard the patter of running shoes on the wrought-iron steps as George went down once more. Tim sighed. Sitting up, he blew his nose loudly, then he reached for the phone.

"Mrs. Griffiths? It's Tim Heacham. Tell me, did Miss Clifford get back safely?"

At the other end of the line Margiad Griffiths untied her apron with her free hand and stretched to hang it on the back of the kitchen door. "Why, Mr. Heacham, I'm so sorry, but I wasn't here when she came back. It was my daughter who saw her. Miss Clifford never said she'd be wanting the room again, you see, and it had gone. So sorry, I was. I'm afraid I don't know where she went. And I had another message here to give her too. . . ."

Tim closed his eyes wearily. "It doesn't matter," he said. "Thanks anyway. I'll hope to see you again one day." He hung up and threw himself back on the bed as, far below, the clang of the street door closing echoed up through the empty studio. George had gone.

Tim lay for a couple of hours staring out of the high windows that showed nothing but rooftops silhouetted against the purple storm clouds. At least it had stopped raining. His head ached and his throat was sore. He felt unbearably lonely.

Slowly he sat up at last. He leaned across the bed and unlocked a drawer in the nightstand next to it then drew out a box. He sat and looked at it for a long time, then slowly he opened the lid and pulled out the hypodermic, the narrow tourniquet, and a packet of powder.

To lose a woman twice, be it to destiny or to another man—what kind of man did that make him? What was it she had said once? That he reminded her of an Afghan hound! He laughed out loud, the bitter sound ringing around the empty room. At least he had one night to remember, one night she could never take away from him.

Methodically he went about his preparations, meticulously sterilizing the needle. It wasn't often he resorted to this; not yet. Snorting was usually enough; that and the cigarettes. Anything to keep the shadows at bay. But tonight he wanted to crash out all the way. Out into the whirling spaces beyond his mind.

The office was full of strange noises at night. Nick lay on the long, elegant couch, staring at the Venetian blind drawn down across the curtainless window. The streetlamps outside sent weird horizontal shadows tumbling through the slats and across the white carpet toward him like the rungs of a ladder. For the fiftieth time he closed his eyes and tried to sleep. His head was spinning, but Judy's words kept coming back to him. *It's all a hoax . . . He told you who you were . . . He told you what to do . . .* Judy and her stupid redheaded temper! She had stormed at Sam and then at him, angry with them both for some reason, then she had grabbed her wet coat and run out into the rain.

When she had gone, he and Sam had had a furious argument.

Nick sighed and sat up slowly. It hadn't just been Judy. In this very room his mother had warned him; his gentle, loving mother, who worshiped Sam, had tried to tell him something; as good as said that Sam was dangerous. Nick shook his head wearily. Why should Sam want to harm him? It didn't make sense.

What had their quarrel been about? He couldn't even remember that now. He had asked Sam about the hypnosis but his brother had refused to be drawn, saying Judy was neurotic and sex-starved, and it was then that Nick had decided to go out for a walk. He had strolled slowly down Constitution Hill, staring up at the harsh light of the electric lanterns in the streaking rain, smelling the wet flowers and earth beyond the high walls of Buckingham Palace, then on around the Victoria Memorial, the palace huge and dark behind him, down Birdcage Walk, conscious of the lightning flickering now in the distance behind Big Ben. The roads were empty; Horseguards, bare and swept with rain, the lighted windows in the Haymarket, eerie in the empty street. He made his way slowly back up Piccadilly, and then, unable to face speaking to Sam again that night, he had come back to Berkeley Street and opened the locked office.

He paced up and down the carpet. Bet had told him that Jo was in Wales with Tim Heacham. The last person on earth she would want to see was him, but now that he had her address he knew he had to go to her.

With a sigh he switched on the light, and, reaching for the percolator, he gave it an experimental shake. There was still some coffee in it and he plugged it in.

He had to see Jo; he had to make things all right with her somehow. He stared down at the glass of the pot with a frown, watching the condensation forming on its sides as the coffee began to warm. He was being torn apart. Half of him wanted to see Jo, to hold her, to comfort her and beg her to forgive him for ever hurting her. He didn't understand even now why he had done it, or what had made him so angry. But he was angry still, and part of him still seethed quietly inside; part of him was still fanatically jealous. Part of him wanted to hurt her again.

He paced up and down the carpet a few times, listening to the occasional car roaring up the street outside, then he glanced at his watch. It was nearly three. Sitting down at his desk, he flicked on the desk light and pulled out a map. It would do no harm to work out the route to Wales. In the morning he would make the final decision as to what he should do.

When Jim walked into the office at eight, Nick was hard at work.

"Good God, Nick! Now you're making me feel doubly guilty! What time did you get here, for chrissake?" Jim said, flinging down his briefcase.

Nick glanced up. "I've been here all night." Giving a wry smile, he stretched his arms above his head. "But don't go on with the martyr act, you've done your penance—and I came here for peace as much as anything else. Look, Jim, I want to be here for the meeting with Mike Desmond, then I have to go away for a couple of days."

Jim groaned. "Nick, for God's sake. You're needed in the office!"

"Not if you're here. You can handle things."

"You still believe that?" Jim's tone was bitter.

"We've all screwed things up once in a while." Nick stood up and picked up the coffeepot. It was empty. "The secret is to get back out there fighting. Otherwise you're dead." He turned back to Jim. "I have a feeling you'll handle this meeting like a master, that's why I want to sit in on it. And, let's face it, we've got nothing to lose. In fact, if we get Desco back and I win the New York accounts we'll have to expand!" He walked to the window and pulled up the blind, then he turned to Jim and grinned. "And I'm just in the mood to build an empire at the moment, so you've been warned!"

It was seven-twenty that evening when at last he walked into the bar of the Black Lamb near Talgarth. He glanced around. It was empty.

"What can I get you, sir?" The bartender appeared through a bead curtain at the back as Nick hauled himself wearily onto a stool. He ordered a Scotch and soda, looking around with some curiosity. There was no sign of Jo. "You seem very quiet, landlord."

The man shrugged. "They'll all be in later. Friday, see. Tarting themselves up, they are, then come eight, they'll all be here." He pushed the glass across the bar.

"Have something yourself." Nick flipped a five-pound note onto the counter. "Tell me, do you still have a Miss Clifford staying here?" He picked up his glass.

The man grinned. "Thank you very much. One more night, she said. She's out now though—going to Radnor, I think she said she was, this morning." He drew himself a pint before opening the till to look for the change. "Friend of hers, are you?"

Nick nodded. "You haven't another room, I suppose?"

"Just for the one night is it?"

"Just the one."

"Well, if you don't mind somewhere a bit shabby like, maybe I could fit you in. It's bad time of the year, see, with all the visitors."

"I don't mind as long as I can sleep." Nick finished his drink and pushed the glass back toward the man. "Tell me, do you expect Jo—Miss Clifford —back for dinner?"

"Well, now, we don't exactly serve dinner, sir. Chicken in a basket we can do you, or a nice scampi." He leaned forward suddenly, staring past Nick out of the window. "Isn't that her car now?"

Nick swung around. His jaw tightened as he watched Jo back the MG into the corner of the parking lot behind the pub. She climbed out of her car and he saw her stand for a moment staring at his Porsche, then she glanced over her shoulder toward the pub. Even from that distance he could see the sudden anxiety on her face. She was wearing a deep rose-color blouse with jeans, and he found himself staring at her hungrily as she stooped into the car to find her bag, then she slammed the door and walked almost reluctantly toward them.

She pushed the door open. "What are you doing here, Nick?" she cried. "Didn't I make myself clear? I never want to see you again!"

Behind them the barman folded his arms and leaned with interest against the till.

"I told Sam not to tell you where I was," she went on, flinging her bag down on a chair. "A gin and tonic, please, Mr. Vaughan."

"Coming up." He reached up to the gin bottle with a grin. "The gentleman is paying for it, is he?"

"He is."

Nick noticed that her hand was shaking as she reached for the glass and to his surprise he felt a quick surge of pleasure.

"You should know better than to trust Sam," he said softly. "You should know better by now than to trust Sam with anything at all."

She did not smile. "It's over, Nick. Finished." She tried to drag her eyes away from his face. His handsome features were shadowed with fatigue. She looked down abruptly at her glass. "Please, Nick. Don't make a scene here."

"I'm not going to make a scene. All I want is to talk." Nick made a despairing grimace at their host, who was listening with undisguised attention. "Where, by the way, is the talented Mr. Heacham? I thought he was supposed to be with you?"

She tensed suddenly and he saw the color in her cheeks. "He had to go back to town. He only came to take some pictures."

Nick tried to hide his elation. "All the better. We can talk in peace. Look, Jo. I'm going back to London tomorrow, so you needn't panic. Why don't we have something to eat and a bottle of wine, then we'll talk later. That's all I want to do. Please—" he added as an afterthought.

Jo hesitated, then she stood up, forcing a smile. "All right. I'll go and change out of these jeans and join you in ten minutes. But just for a meal." She picked up her bag. "Do I gather you intend to stay here tonight?"

He nodded. "Mr. Vaughan has a closet for me, I believe."

"That's just as well." She gave him a tight smile. "Because my room is single."

"Ouch!" Vaughan said quietly as Jo swung out of the room. "Would I be right in thinking you've offended the lady?"

Nick gave a dry laugh. "Something like that," he said.

In her room at the top of the steep stairs Jo shut the door and leaned against it. She closed her eyes and took a deep breath, then slowly she walked to the small table, which sported a square mirror, and stared at her reflection as she began to unbutton her blouse. She had known when she called Sam that he would tell Nick where she was. Was that why she had done it? She pulled off the blouse and threw it on the bed then wearily she slipped out of her jeans. As she pulled on her bathrobe, she went to the door. There would be time for a shower and a few minutes flat on her back with her eyes closed before she need go back downstairs.

"Have you gone back into the past again since you've been here?" Nick looked up at her across the small table. The room was noisy now, crowded and full of cigarette smoke.

She was toying listlessly with her french fries. After a minute she nodded. "You know, when I wanted to go into a trance with Tim there so that he could photograph me—nothing happened. I couldn't do it—but then later I did."

"And it frightened you, didn't it?"

"It frightened me that I couldn't control it." She glanced up at him under her eyelashes. "I was going to Radnor today, then halfway there I stopped. I panicked. I didn't want it to happen again; suddenly I didn't dare go anywhere Matilda might have been. I didn't want anything to trigger off another regression, not alone."

Their eyes met. Nick's face was harsh. "So your past doesn't please you. Do you intend to forget about Matilda now?"

"How can I? I'm trapped." She gave up all pretense of eating and reached for her wineglass. "Are you going to say I told you so?"

He ignored the question. "You need not have come back to Wales."

"Oh, but I did have to. I'm working on a story, and I want to finish it."

"Even though you're afraid?"

"Even though I'm afraid," she repeated slowly, with a rueful smile. "Remember the war correspondent."

He was watching her closely. She had let her hair fall loosely on her shoulders and was wearing now a tan linen dress, unadorned save for a thin gold chain around her neck. As she spoke a heavy lock of her hair slipped forward onto her breast. She put down her glass. "Have you come up here to apologize, Nick?"

"For what?" He narrowed his eyes.

"For what?" she echoed. "For bloody well nearly killing me once, then last time for scaring me silly." She stared at him. "Don't tell me you don't remember what happened!"

He smiled grimly. "I remember clearly. Tell me, did Tim photograph you while you were making love to one of your phantoms? Will there be pictures of you writhing in ecstasy all over the gutter press?"

Jo's eyes hardened. "You know bloody well there won't. Nick, if you've come up here to make trouble again—"

"Trouble?" He raised an eyebrow. "I'm not going to make trouble."

She stared at him. He was watching her with a strange look on his face, half wry amusement, half something harder—and more calculating, and she felt a prickle of apprehension. "Nick, you behaved like a madman," she whispered. "I was scared."

"With reason." He picked up the wine bottle and filled his glass.

"You're not even sorry, are you!" She was incredulous.

"I didn't want to hurt you, Jo."

"Then why did you do it? Were you drunk?"

"Perhaps." A half smile flickered behind his eyes.

She swallowed hard. "I don't understand you anymore, Nick. You've changed."

He laughed uneasily. "Obviously for the worse as far as you're concerned."

"Yes, for the worse." Her eyes sparkled angrily. "Judy Curzon may like your new macho image, Nick, but I don't. I find it boorish. What the hell is happening to you?" She stood up abruptly. "I'm tired. I think I'll go to bed now. I'll see you in the morning, no doubt, before you leave."

For a moment he thought she was going to say something else, then she changed her mind and threaded her way swiftly out of the bar without a backward glance. Nick did not move. He picked up the bottle again, refilling his glass, and sat staring out of the window at the twilit garden, his back to the crowded drinkers. What the hell was happening to him? He had no idea either, and he was beginning to feel afraid himself.

Jo lay in bed, staring at the ceiling. It wasn't yet fully dark. She could hear the low rumble of conversation from the bar downstairs, the occasional

325

shout of laughter, the banging of the door to the parking lot. Outside the window a bat was flitting back and forth against the yellow twilight.

She clenched her fists suddenly. "Oh, God, no. Not here. Don't let it happen here." She sat bolt upright. There was perspiration on her face as she pushed back the sheet, her breath coming in quick shallow gasps, and swung her feet to the polished floorboards, feeling their cool solidity with thankfulness, as she gripped the headboard and stood there for a moment, staring down at the pillows, trying to steady her breathing.

Outside there was a shout beneath her window. She half turned, trembling, not relinquishing her hold on the bed, and raised her eyes cautiously toward the evening light. It was greener now, less bright. Laughter and a scuffle in the shrubs outside was followed by the sound of car doors slamming. Somewhere an engine roared. With a sigh of relief she staggered across to the window and leaned out, feeling the cool air on her face. She could smell the sweet-scented stock in the bed beneath the window.

It had not happened after all; there were no cars in the past. Behind her the sound of someone climbing the narrow creaking stairs made her turn wearily from the window. She glanced at her watch. It was ten-fifteen.

The steps stopped outside her door.

"Jo? Are you there?"

She froze. *Nick.* Her lips formed the word soundlessly as her eyes flew to the key standing in the lock. Had she turned it before she climbed into bed?

She ran to the door and put her hands against the panels.

"Jo?" He sounded impatient this time. "For God's sake, open up!" The handle rattled, and she felt the wood move slightly as he pushed, but the key held. "Jo! Stop being so bloody childish!"

She bit her lip, saying nothing as once again the handle turned.

"All right, have it your own way, Joanna mine." His voice was slightly slurred. "I'll see you in the morning."

She heard him stumble as he began to climb the ladderlike attic staircase at the end of the dark landing, then there was silence.

Her eyes filled with tears. "Nick. Oh, Nick, what's happened to you?" she murmured as she threw herself onto the bed. "What has happened to us both?"

"You didn't mind me coming over, Tim?" Judy was standing uncertainly in the middle of the darkened studio. "I know it's late, but I was up at an exhibition at the Barbican and I didn't feel much like going home. Not yet." She glanced up at him. "Life's being a bit of a bitch." There was despair in her voice.

Tim gave a rueful scowl. "I'm sure I can find something here to keep the bitch at bay for another few hours. Booze. Dope." He threw himself down on a canvas chair. "Me, if you want me."

Judy sat down on the edge of the dais, her arms wrapped around her knees. "I wouldn't mind a drink," she said. She was trembling slightly.

He laughed. "What else?" Hauling himself to his feet, he went into the kitchen and took a bottle of champagne out of the refrigerator.

She stood up and followed him. "Were you really in Wales?"

He swung around. "Who told you that?"

"Nick. He's followed Jo down there, you know."

Tim had been rummaging in a cabinet for two champagne glasses and he straightened abruptly, his face contorted with pain.

"They belong to each other, Judy," he said after a moment, controlling himself with an effort.

She took the glasses out of his hands. "Oh, I know I've lost him. For now. But one day I'll get him back. I have to get him back, Tim."

He shook his head. "Jo and Nick have a date with destiny, Judy."

She threw back her head and laughed. "Crap! You're stoned already. You didn't even wait for me."

He picked up the bottle and tore the foil off the neck. "As a newt, my love. It helps." After tossing the wire into the sink, he flipped the cork.

Judy picked up her foaming glass and walked thoughtfully back into his studio. "It was here I told Nigel Dempster she was going mad," she said over her shoulder. "I thought I had won then. I really thought Nick had finished with her for good." She ran her hand down the bank of switches by the door, flooding the huge bare room with stark light, and let out a small cry of surprise as the sudden illumination revealed a large easel in the corner of the studio, covered by a sheet. "Have you taken up painting?" She moved toward it purposefully.

"Don't touch it, Judy!" Tim was standing in the kitchen doorway, swaying slightly, his glass in his hand.

"Why? Are you shy?" She laughed harshly.

"I said, don't touch it!" He moved with sudden speed toward her. "If you touch that cover, I'll strangle you."

Judy dodged out of reach. "Tim. You're embarrassed!" Champagne slopped onto the floor from her glass as she ducked past him and caught the corner of the sheet, pulling it from the huge board and throwing it onto the ground.

She stared at the tinted life-size photograph in silence, her eyes traveling up the tall, slim body of the woman she saw there, taking in the pale-green gown falling in heavy folds to the floor, the fur-trimmed surcoat, the wimple and veil.

"It's Jo," she breathed at last.

"Top marks for observation!" He picked up the sheet.

"But how—how did you get her to let you take a picture like that?"

Tim laughed heavily. "I didn't exactly take it like that."

"You mean it's a mockup? But it's so real—"

"That's a naive remark, coming from you."

She ignored the retort. "Her eyes are a different color. And her hair," she went on, touching the photograph lightly. "It's Jo, but it isn't Jo at all. You've caught someone else. Someone as real as you or me. It's not just the clothes . . ." There was a long silence as they both stood staring at the picture, then she turned back to him. "You're in love with her too." She made the statement in a flat, unhappy voice that made him glance at her sharply.

"Quite a pair, aren't we?" he replied. He covered the picture again, meticulously pulling the sheet straight. "You love Nick and I love Jo. And they love each other."

"Did she tell you what she looked like in the past?" Judy asked suddenly.

He shook his head. "No need. I can see her clearly in my mind as she was." With a sigh he walked to the wall and began to turn off the lights one by one.

"I wonder if Nick can too." Her voice was very husky.

Tim picked up the champagne bottle. "I wonder," he echoed.

"She was very beautiful, Matilda de Braose," Judy said as she held out her glass.

Tim filled it until it overflowed onto the floor and slopped over her shoes. "The most beautiful woman in the world," he agreed unsteadily. "The most beautiful woman in the world!"

Nick was reading the papers at a small round table at the open French windows of the pub dining room when Jo came down for breakfast. She was wearing jeans again, with a loose white silk blouse.

He stood up as she appeared. "Coffee is on its way. How did you sleep?"

"Not too well. And you?" She surveyed him cautiously as she slipped into the chair opposite him.

Nick grinned. "It was very hot up in that attic." He grinned suddenly with something like his old humor as behind them the door opened and Dai Vaughan appeared with a tray of coffee and cereal and toast. He slid it between them onto the table.

"Will you be wanting to stay tonight after all?" he asked Nick as he began to set their places. "Just so that I know. The room is empty if you want it."

Nick shook his head slowly. "I have to go back to London," he said.

Jo glanced at him sharply. "Do you have to go this morning?" she said in spite of herself.

He nodded. "I think it would be best, don't you?"

"I suppose so." The magnetism between them was still as strong as ever. She longed to reach across the table and touch him. But somehow she resisted.

"Perhaps—" Nick hesitated. "Perhaps I could stay until this afternoon, then we could go for a drive or something? I'd like to see a little of this Wales of yours before I leave." He held his breath, waiting for her response.

Dai Vaughan straightened as he set the coffeepot in front of Jo. "Now there's an idea," he said cheerfully. "Why don't I put up a picnic for the both of you. It'll stay fine awhile yet, with luck!" He squinted out of the window. "Where would you like to go? I can lend you a map. Llangorse Lake? The waterfalls? Castles? Or why not go up to the mountains by here —Castel Dinas perhaps. There's a fine view and lovely country, and it's not too far."

Jo frowned. She had been watching Nick's face. "I don't want to go anywhere that might remind me," she said quietly. "Not today. I can't cope with that. Castles make me nervous."

Dai laughed. "Oh, it's not a castle like Bronllys or Hay. It's an earthwork, see. Celtic, I think it is." He picked up the tray. "Will you be leaving this afternoon too, Miss Clifford?"

Jo nodded.

Nick raised an eyebrow. "Are you coming back to London?" He tried to keep the triumph out of his voice.

She watched Dai Vaughan until he was out of the room. "No. I'm going back to Hay."

"You're continuing with your research, then?"

She rested her chin on her hands. "I've got to, Nick. I told you, I can't let it go. Not yet."

He scowled. "But you will let it go today?"

She nodded. "I'd like that. Let's go and see this Castel Dinas. I doubt if the de Braoses were into archaeology." She smiled at him suddenly, the wariness lifting from her face. "Truce for today, Nick?"

"Truce." He leaned forward and put his hand on hers.

A haze had formed over the mountaintops as they parked the Porsche in a narrow lane and climbed out. Nick was holding the ordnance survey map in his hand. "I don't think there's much point in taking the food with us," he said. "It may be nice now, but the weather's closing in fast. Do you still want to go up there?"

She nodded, staring up at the gaunt shoulders of the Black Mountains rising above them, clear and sharply defined in the brilliant sunlight, save where wisps of cloud and mist touched them and drifted down into the folded cwms.

Nick shuddered. "God, what a lonely place! That must be"—he glanced down at the map—"Waun Fach. Heaven knows how it's pronounced!"

"It's beautiful." Jo was staring around her. "Quite beautiful. Smell that air. Hundreds of miles of grass and wild thyme and bilberries—and just look at the hedges down here. Honeysuckle, dog roses, chamomile, foxgloves—and a thousand flowers I don't even know the name of. . . . *Nick!*"

After dropping his map on the car hood, he had put his hands on her shoulders, drawing her to him, feeling the warmth of her flesh beneath the thin silk of her shirt as he folded his arms around her and pressed her against him, his mouth nuzzling into her hair. Jo closed her eyes. For a moment she stood still, feeling the tide of longing rising in her as she clung to him, overwhelmed with happiness suddenly, her doubts dissolving as she raised her mouth to his for a long passionate kiss, her hands automatically reaching for the buttons of his shirt, slipping inside to caress his chest.

With a smile she drew back a little and looked up at him at last.

Then she froze. The face of the man who stood staring down at her did not belong to Nick. Her stomach turned over in icy shock as recognition hit her and she remembered the blue eyes, the arrogant brow, the imperious touch, and her own body's helpless response as this man had drawn her, long ago, against his hard body.

"No!" Jo's eyes were dilated with fear as she pulled away from him. "Oh, no! No! Please God, no!"

She tore herself out of his arms and began to run up the lane away from him.

"Jo!" Nick called angrily. "Come back here! What's the matter?"

But she took no notice. After hurling herself at the gate, she scrambled over it, staring up the steep grass slope in front of her. Far above their heads she could hear the lonely scream of a circling buzzard.

Nick vaulted over behind her. "Jo, wait!"

But she had begun to run, shaking her hair out of her eyes, her heart thumping in her chest as she forced herself as fast as she could up the steep ridged grass with its scattering of sheep droppings.

Nick stood for a moment watching her. His good humor vanished, he made himself take a deep breath, trying to steady the sudden wave of anger that had gripped him. In front of him Jo had stopped again. She turned, gasping for breath, staring down at him from the slope, and he could see the fear in her eyes.

Behind her the mist was drifting down across the mountain. A patch of sunlight dimmed and disappeared. It was becoming oppressively hot again. There was no breath of wind.

Slowly he began to follow her upward.

Jo reached the earthworks first and stood panting, staring around her at the piles of fallen abandoned stones and the ditch and ramparts of the Celtic fortress, high on its hill amid the encircling mountains. The mist was growing thicker. Blind with panic, she whirled as a quiet rumble of thunder echoed round the Wye Valley in the distance.

Nick had stopped several feet from her, breathing heavily from the climb. He was watching her with a strange half smile.

"Don't run anymore, Jo," he said quietly. "There's no point."

She could feel the blood pounding in her temples as she took a few staggering steps backward, her hands held out in front of her.

Nick . . . help . . . me . . .

She wanted to call out to him. To Nick. Not the other man, to Nick. But the words would not come, trapped ringing in her head by the mist and the silence and by Nick's strange implacable smile as he began to follow her again.

Turning, she started to run once more, stumbling down the steep bank of a ditch. Around her the hills closed in; the mist lapped against the grass and once more there was a rumble of thunder in the east.

Dear God, she had been here before. This place she recognized; it came into her story and was indelibly etched upon her memory.

It must not happen here. Not in front of Nick—not now, not bring her helplessly to her knees alone here, with a man who hated her—

"Jo! Stop, for God's sake—" His voice was irritated now. *"Jo—Jo, come back . . ."* It was echoing slightly in the eerie silence of the hills. "Jo . . ."

26

A visitor was announced as Matilda stood running her eyes down a list of accounts. She was alarmed and astonished to see the king's brother, whom she thought to be at Gloucester with William. John was bare-headed, his color heightened from the gallop through the chilly morning.

"How is the gracious Lady Matilda this fine day?" the prince inquired with a mocking bow.

"I am honored that you should come to Hay, Your Highness. I am well." Her voice was guarded and her hands, clasped before her, were unconsciously plaiting her girdle. She saw his eyes running down the line of her body, ever insolent, the pupils hooded by lazy eyelids.

"Good. I've come, my lady, from Hereford. No doubt you are aware that my brother, the king, commanded me to demand homage from the princes in Wales." He stopped. "But of course, your daughter is married to one of them, is she not?" He smiled coolly. "Have you news of her, perhaps?"

Matilda paled and looked away. Since her worst nightmares had been realized and Gruffyd had joined his father in revolt against King Richard, there had been no news of Tilda.

"Nothing, Your Highness," she replied firmly.

John frowned, as if suddenly aware of her distress. "She is safe, I am sure, Lady Matilda," he said more gently. "I shall, if you wish, send messengers to inquire." He smiled amiably as she turned to face him, her eyes alive with hope. "But for now, my lady, I had in mind to visit one of the castles in your husband's holding, Dinas, somewhere to the west in the Black Mountains." John took a cup of wine handed to him by a servant and drank it in a gulp. "I hear too that it has a magic spring, blessed with powers of healing."

Matilda thought rapidly. "The building there is finished, I believe. I haven't been there yet, my lord, and I have heard the spring has certain wonderful properties. Surely you do not need such magic, Your High-

332

ness?" She couldn't resist the last question, but immediately regretted it, as his good humor vanished and his face became surly.

"I am interested in such places." He was silent for a moment, the empty goblet dangling from his fingers, his eyes fixed on the wall somewhere behind her. "You have heard, I suppose," he went on suddenly, "that my brother, the king, refuses to come and meet Lord Rhys at Oxford? I pacify the Welsh princes for him, they agree not to fight while the king is away on his crusade, and I get Rhys to come with me to pay homage to Richard. But Richard is too high and mighty to come halfway to meet him at Oxford as our father would have done." He held out his goblet for more wine. "Lord Rhys, with all the exquisite touchiness of the Welsh, has decided now that he has been mortally insulted and he refuses to meet my brother or his envoys at all." John drew his hand impatiently across his brow. "God's teeth, you can't say I haven't tried." He was silent again for a moment, then, his black mood passing as swiftly as it had come, he grinned at her again. "So you see, I have given myself a few hours to rid myself of my frustrations, madam."

Matilda tried to force a smile. "I am sure I can find men to guide you into the mountains, my lord, and an escort."

"I have an escort." He gestured impatiently. "I need a guide and I should like *you* to accompany me, Lady Matilda. It is unthinkable that you have not yet visited the castle yourself. It is a duty I am sure Sir William would expect of his wife. He sends you greetings, by the way. He chose to visit Wigmore on his return to his estates. He will be back soon enough, no doubt." He threw himself into a chair and rested his ankle casually across his knee, his mocking look once more upon her. "I hear you ride with the courage of a man, madam, so I am sure you wouldn't refuse to come with me on such a small adventure."

He threw his challenge so lightly she had risen to it without even realizing, the memory of his boyhood insults about her horsemanship suddenly surfacing in her mind. "Of course! It's not more than a dozen miles. . . ." Too late she sensed danger, and his next words filled her with foreboding.

"A small party, well mounted, could do it in an hour or so, no doubt. Just you and I, madam. The guide and my men. This will be no trip for a bevy of lady's maids."

She glanced at him warily, but he was intent on tracing the chased pattern of the goblet with his thumbnail and refused to meet her eye.

"Find fresh mounts for Prince John and his followers," she commanded suddenly, her mind made up. The waiting servant bowed and turned toward the door. "Saddle my chestnut and tell Ifor the huntsman to be there to guide us to Castel Dinas. We leave at once, then we will be back by dark. Does that satisfy you, my lord?"

He jumped to his feet, grinning like a boy, as he swept up his gauntlets and adjusted the sword belt at his waist. "Indeed it does, my lady."

The wind freshened as they rode out of Hay toward the west. Ifor, a small curly-headed figure on his raw-boned cob, trotted ahead, a bow slung across his shoulders, while behind followed the four knights who had accompanied John from Hereford. Matilda felt a momentary pang of anxiety when she saw the escort was so small but her pride would not let her press more men on the prince. If he thought four men sufficient for the king's brother, then so be it.

They rode swiftly, following the narrow but well-marked track that wound around the foot of the hill toward the little trading borough of Talgarth, the horses' hooves kicking up great clods of the soft red earth. John rode in silence, his mouth set, but she thought she saw a gleam of triumph in his eyes as he turned once to look at her. She whipped her horse to keep up with him. "Ifor is a good man, Your Highness. He will take us by the most direct route. Are you familiar with Brycheiniog?"

"I am not." He glanced up at the thickly wooded shoulder of hillside to their left. "But I thought I would improve my acquaintance with the de Braose possessions." Was that innuendo in his voice and in the sidelong glance he sent her? She felt another tremor of warning.

The road was rough and muddy from the recent rain, and the ride took longer than she expected. Parts of the track had been washed away, and Ifor had to lead them away from the smoother ways into the thick woods, where they bent low over their horses' necks, avoiding the sweeping branches of the trees. Although they had left Hay before noon, the light was already beginning to fail as they trotted into Talgarth. Again she felt the warning prickle under her skin. How were they to return by nightfall if the road was so slow?

She noticed John draw his dark cloak over his hauberk, concealing the intricate details of his brooch and belt. Curious eyes followed them down the main street of the town, and she was glad they had Ifor with them, calling out friendly greetings in Welsh as they passed toward the bridge over the angry red waters of the swift-flowing Enig Brook. The prince's exasperated report of the failure of the negotiations with Lord Rhys had filled her, once she had overcome the accustomed pang of worry about Tilda, with a sense of foreboding. She knew, as perhaps John did not, just how quickly the vengeance of the Welsh could make itself felt in the valleys of the wild country round them.

The horses climbed slowly out of Talgarth away from the square peel tower that guarded the bridge. Before them lay the mountains. Matilda cursed herself for allowing them to come at all. It was growing late and the slowness of the ride meant that, with the heavy clouds hanging so low over the peaks, it was growing dark, and this was no place to be benighted. Shivering, she pulled her cloak more closely around her shoulders and kicked her mount close up behind John's. The escort closed tightly about them and they rode in silence save for the occasional clink of harness or the click of hoof on stone. Matilda could see John's hand on the hilt of his sword as he looked about him. At last he too seemed to be growing nervous. Before them the *mynydd-dir* rose in a high barrier, misty and black. Behind, the broad Wye Valley was lost to sight behind the band of woods.

They rode hard, not sparing the horses on the rugged path which followed the wandering of the tumbling Rhian Goll, running angry and muddy red with flood waters from the mountains. A cold drizzle was beginning to fall. To their left the great triangular hill of Mynydd Troed rose in a massive shoulder in front of the clouds.

Castel Dinas stood sentinel over the pass. It was an awesome, lonely place. Matilda could feel her horse beginning to tremble, perhaps sensing her own fear. Its ears pressed flat on its head, its eyes staring, it followed its companions as their guides wheeled off the track and turned up a steep turf ramp that led to the walls of the castle itself.

"Open up there," John shouted into the gale. "Lady de Braose demands entry." But there was no answer; the gatehouse was deserted.

The horses had come to a rearing halt outside the north entrance. On either side a deep dry ditch encircled the high escarpments of the castle. Before them the gatehouses flanked a strong nail-studded gate. The builders had obeyed William's orders well so far.

John forced his frightened horse near enough to the gate to allow him to beat on it with the hilt of his sword. "Ho there! Entry!" he shouted, but the wind whipped the words from his lips. Behind them the clouds were flying up the pass, gray, thick, hiding trees, mountains, perhaps men . . . From the corner of her eye Matilda thought she saw something move below, on the side of the hill. The palms of her hands were sweating with fear and the horse, sensing it, plunged suddenly sideways fighting the bit, poised to bolt back the way it had come.

Then at last a small gleam of light showed in one of the high slit windows of a gatehouse.

"Open up, you lazy clods." John put every ounce of strength he had left into his shout. "Lady de Braose wants entry to her castle."

At last they heard the bars being slid back and the great slabs of oak swung open to reveal half a dozen men, drawn swords in their hands, streaming torches held above their heads for light. Piles of dressed stone and mortar, weird white shapes in the gloom, lay all around in the shelter of the bailey's walls. At the far side the lower part of the new keep showed pale and square, obviously unfinished, in the darkness.

"Who is the constable here?" demanded Matilda. "Why was there no lookout posted? Prince John and I have ridden far and fast. We do not expect to be kept waiting outside like serfs." Her fear had turned to fury. Gripping her whip, she wheeled the horse. "Shut the gates now, you oafs,

335

before half the countryside wanders in at your invitation. Where is the captain of the guard?"

Four of the men ran to push the gates shut and slid the bars across into the sockets. One of the soldiers came forward and dropped on one knee. "The constable is sick, like many in the garrison, my lady. Forgive him. He did not know anyone was coming." The man hesitated and looked quickly over his shoulder at his companions. "It is hard to keep a full lookout up here."

Matilda was not to be appeased. "Hard! Hard to keep a lookout! Then post some more men, sir. I don't care if you have to carry them up, but do it. You could be attacked and overrun and have the enemy sitting before your fire before you knew he was at the gate."

"May I ask the nature of the illness that strikes down so many of this garrison?" John's lazy voice broke in suddenly.

"I don't . . . I don't know, sir. 'Tis very common . . ."

"They're all dead drunk, Your Highness." One of the other soldiers stepped forward suddenly, his face lit by the torchlight showing a scar from eyebrow to chin. "That's the illness of Castel Dinas. If you'd been an hour or so later I'd have been down with it myself, and probably my fine companions as well. There's not a man will stay sober the night through here and keep his sanity."

John looked at Matilda and raised an eyebrow sardonically. "Perhaps we should join them in their merrymaking, my lady. God's teeth! It doesn't look as though there'll be much service here tonight. You, fellow." He nudged the kneeling man with his foot. "Show Lady de Braose and myself the splendors of your new tower. We need food and wine and warmth."

The man scrambled up, and bowing, ran ahead of them toward the keep. It was Spartan indeed. A hearth had been built into one wall in the new fashion but it lay empty. Instead a pile of logs burned low in the middle of the floor, the smoke straying through the room and escaping at last through the doorway from which they had entered. Around it were the snoring sleeping figures of a dozen or so men. Goblets and jars of wine had fallen to the floor, and the room stank of stale wine and vomit.

Matilda pulled her cloak to her nose in disgust. "Get them out," she ordered, her mouth set.

"But, my lady—" The man looked at her aghast.

"Get them out." She had raised her voice only a little. "Is the hall of my lord and husband going to be used as a pigsty? Get them out and swill the floor. *Now.*" She shouted the last word, stamping her foot. The soldier, with one look at her blazing eyes and set chin, bowed and ran to the sleeping forms, setting about them with the flat of his sword.

John looked around and then strode to the staircase in the wall. "Perhaps there is a solar that would be more habitable," he commented sourly, and ran up, his spurs ringing on the stone. There was a moment's silence and then she heard him call. "It's clean and dry here. We'll make this our headquarters. Fire and lights!" The last words were bellowed in a voice meant to be obeyed.

Her exhaustion and fear and the anger and shame that followed it when she found the condition of the castle had preoccupied her so much that she had for a moment not fully realized her predicament. But now it became obvious there was no chatelaine here, no maids; whatever womenfolk there were attached to the garrison, washerwomen or followers, must, she supposed, return to some local village or encampment at night. There was no sign of them. She paused at the foot of the stairway, the stones still dusty from cutting, and glanced up at the racing shadows thrown on the stark walls by the torch as the man ran up ahead of her. Up there John was waiting. His maneuver, if maneuver it was, of getting her alone to Dinas had worked better than he could have hoped. Her heart thumping with fear, she began to climb the stairs.

With the help of several of the least drunken of the garrison, the solar was made more habitable. There were only planks on boxes provided by the carpenter to sit on, but hay was brought to warm the floor and piles of furs and fleeces, and the wine was good. Cold mutton and rye bread proved the only food, but there was plenty of it, eaten from tin plates on the plank bench.

"I can understand why these men have to get drunk," John commented, elbows on knees, as he sat chewing a mutton bone. "Sweet Lord, but this is a wild place. What made you think it was complete?" He gave her a mocking smile as he raised his goblet to his lips, and she felt herself blushing.

"We were informed it was finished and garrisoned, sir. The accounts called for no more money for stone." She sipped her wine, grateful for the warmth it spread through her veins.

"The stone's all here, I can see that. It's stacked in the bailey. But the castle's less than half built." John threw a bit of gristle into the fire. "No chapel, no stores, no inner wall, no other building save the keep. Only the foundations. I saw them in the dark."

Matilda shrugged. "Sir William will be furious when he finds out. And as for them all being drunk, they should all be flogged. They shall all be flogged."

John raised an eyebrow. He was drinking hard, the heavy wine bringing a flush of color to his cheekbones. "You'd enjoy that, would you, madam? We'll see what we can arrange for you. I intend to hold an inquiry myself as soon as it's light and they've slept it off sufficiently to stand. Don't worry. They'll be punished." He stood up abruptly and hurled the bone across the floor. "Now. For our sleeping arrangements."

Matilda clenched her fists. "I shall not sleep tonight, my lord. I

337

couldn't." She could hardly order the king's son to go and sleep below in the hall amid the stench and filth. She could only rely on his sense of chivalry. "Our escort will attend you. I shall sit here by the fire." She stood up and, turning her back to him determinedly, held out her hands to the flames.

"Oh, come, Matilda, that's hardly friendly." He was behind her and she felt his hands on her shoulders. "The warmest thing would be for us to lie together, surely." His fingers moved forward and down until they closed over her breasts.

She caught her breath. "That would not be right, Your Highness." She gasped desperately. He was turning her to face him, his lips reaching for hers, cutting off her protest as he pulled her against him.

His body was young, lean and strong, and in spite of her instant repugnance as he pressed her against him, Matilda felt her own flesh respond, yearning suddenly for the confident, clean touch of a young man after so long with only William to maul her. In spite of herself she hesitated, yielding slightly, her body torn with longing.

John laughed triumphantly. "So, we make progress at last, my lady. Come." He caught her hand, pulling her toward the pile of rugs and furs that had been heaped on the floor in the corner. "We shall find this journey was, after all, not wasted—"

"No!" Matilda tore herself away from him. "I think, sire, you cannot know what you're suggesting." She spoke as repressively as she could, hoping he could not feel her violent trembling as he caught her arms and pulled her against him again. He was immensely strong. His hands gripped her cruelly tight and his face was only inches now from hers. "I am the wife of Sir William de Braose, not a common whore," she hissed, her momentary weakness gone. She flung his hands from her arms and stood rigid, her eyes flaming. "And I think, sir, you forget your new wife. Perhaps you should reserve your attentions for her and getting that son you were so anxious for."

There was a long silence. Then John gave a little laugh. She did not dare to look at his face as, suddenly terrified by the audacity of what she had said, she backed away from him. He was breathing fast, his eyes narrowed, his fist clenched on the hilt of his dagger as he watched her, and she felt her bones dissolve in an icy trickle of terror as, slowly, he began to unbuckle his belt. He laid his dagger aside, on the improvised table, then he turned to her again. "You may be no whore yet, my lady," he snarled, "though some would beg to question your innocence when they speak of your friendship with Lord de Clare. Oh, yes!" He laughed again. "You color and look away. So modest and so shy, madam. Yet your tongue betrays you for a shrew and, by God's bones, I'll make a whore of you as well! Sir William would not begrudge me a night with his lady, I'll warrant. He follows my star closely. You should do the same. When I'm king I shall remember my friends." He moved purposefully toward her. "And I shall also remember my enemies, madam."

She tried to dodge away around the blocks of stone toward the archway that led to the spiral stairs and to escape, but John was there, barring her way.

"Which are you, Matilda?" he whispered, breathing heavily. "My friend or my enemy?"

"Neither, Your Highness. I am the wife of one of your brother Richard's most loyal subjects—" She broke off, biting her lip, seeing the blind fury in his face as she mentioned the king's name, cursing herself for her tactlessness. "And we shall be yours too, sire, should you succeed him," she rushed on, backing away again. "Your friends—your loyal friends—" She gave a little cry as he lunged forward and caught her arm and pushed her, stumbling, toward the pile of blankets.

He threw her down and stood for a moment over her, staring down in cold triumph. "Then prove your loyalty, madam," he breathed.

"No!" She tried to crawl away, dragging herself across the piled furs, hampered by her heavy skirts. "Your Highness, please! Think of Isabella. You break your vows of knighthood, sire—"

Her anguished cry turned to a scream as, with an oath, he threw himself on her, pushing her violently over onto her back, one hand clamped over her mouth as she tried to scream again, the other groping for her throat.

"Silence, woman!" he hissed. "Do you want the entire garrison here as spectators to our lust?"

She was struggling desperately against him, afraid now only of the pitiless fingers tightening around her throat as she fought for breath, clawing frantically at his hands, hearing nothing but the roaring in her ears as her struggles grew weaker. Then everything grew dark and she lay still.

She felt herself moved, her kirtle stripped from her, her gown unlaced and pulled from her body, and she was lying naked on the furs before the fire, struggling for breath through a swollen half-closed throat. Through the darkness she saw his face above her, his eyes intense, blue as the unfathomable sky, his hair and beard gold in the flickering light of the flames. Then all went black once more.

His lips took hers, his tongue moistening her dry mouth, his hands crushing her breasts before moving on to caress her body and push demandingly between her thighs. She did not struggle, scarcely conscious anymore of what he did to her, seeing the arched vaults of the roof, smoky and dark above his shoulders, spin and recede into the darkness, flicker in the firelight, and grow dark once more. He took her again and again, seemingly unconcerned whether she lived or died, venting his fury and his lust on her acquiescent body, then he pulled her roughly over onto her face and threw himself on her again. Her single agonized scream, dragged in pain and humiliation from her bruised throat as he drove deep inside her, was lost in the rancid sheep's wool of the fleece that filled her mouth and nose.

It was a long time before she realized that he had at last moved away from her. Her bruised body, spreadeagled over the untidy heap of blankets, refused for a moment to respond as she tried to ease her position, wanting to curl up against the cold that hit her now the sweating body of the man left her uncovered. With a groan she rolled onto her side and managed to drag the fleece over her, then she lay still, her eyes still closed, her body a mass of aching bruises.

John had pulled on his tunic and mantle. Buckling on his belt with its jeweled dagger, he turned to her at last and stood looking down at her for several moments. Then he smiled. "If you will excuse me, Lady Matilda," he said softly, "I will go and see that the horses are comfortable and fed." She heard him cross the room and run down the steps. He did not come back.

She did not move for a long time, then, driven by cold as the fire died, she dragged herself to her feet and, still dizzy and confused, groped wearily for her clothes before taking wood from the basket and dropping it on the cooling embers.

For ages she stood rigid by the fire as it blazed up again, then at last, weary beyond endurance, she sank to her knees and, wrapping herself in her cloak, rested her head on her arms on one of the upturned boxes.

She slept fitfully, half listening for John's returning footsteps, but they did not come. Toward dawn she fell more deeply asleep for a while and then awoke abruptly when somewhere just outside the window of the keep a cock crowed. She was painfully stiff and very cold. The fire had died to white ashes and through the badly improvised shutters in the windows the cold morning light stretched across the floor. A pool of dull light showed in the hearth beneath the broad chimney.

Climbing numbly to her feet, Matilda crossed to the window and pulled down the shutter. A mist swam outside, lapping the mountains, condensing like rain on the sill of the embrasure. She shivered.

The great hall had been cleaned. A fire had been lit in the fireplace and a makeshift table was already standing on the dais. At it sat John, finishing his breakfast. He half rose when she appeared, giving her a mocking bow, then he continued eating. His eyes were cold and uncompromising.

Matilda stood for a moment watching him, fighting her revulsion and terror as she pulled the hood of her cloak more closely around her bruised throat.

"Come, join me for breakfast, my lady," he called, not looking up. "You must be hungry after so disturbed a night." He beckoned a servant from the shadows and indicated his empty goblet.

Summoning every shred of dignity to her aid, Matilda walked toward him across the floor. By the dais she dropped him a haughty curtsy. The castle seemed full of people this morning as, reluctantly, she took her place beside the prince. A shame-faced servant brought her bread and mulled wine, while another scattered fresh rushes on the floor. From somewhere in the bailey came the sound of hammering. John looked up again.

"Where is the castellan?" he snapped to the man with the rushes. "Now that Lady de Braose is here, bring him at once—let us hear the reasons for the state of this place."

The servant bowed and ran out, returning almost at once with a tall man dressed in his hauberk and fully armed. He fell on his knees before Matilda. John, seemingly uninterested, continued eating.

Matilda swallowed painfully. "Well," she said with an effort, "what have you to say?"

The man's face was gray. "I am Bernard, my lady. Forgive us." He clasped his hands pleadingly. "This castle is a terrible place. No man can stay here and keep sane. I've begged for a transfer, but no one comes to relieve us." He glanced at the prince. "My lord, have pity."

John snorted. "Pity. When you can't take a little discomfort!"

"It's not the discomfort, sir, no indeed." The man leaned forward earnestly.

"What, then?" John looked scornful. "Have the Welsh prince's men been frightening you, then?" He put on a singsong voice full of sarcasm and scorn.

"No, sir. We're not afraid of the Welsh." Bernard was indignant. "No, my lady, it's something else." He dropped his eyes suddenly and shifted his weight uncomfortably from one knee to the other.

"What?" John demanded unsympathetically.

"It's the old ones of the castle, Your Highness." His voice had fallen to a whisper. "They walk the ramparts beside our men. They tramp the ditch, they ride on the hill. They are everywhere in the dark." He crossed himself fervently and they saw him finger the amulet that hung at his throat.

Matilda glanced at John, shivering in spite of herself.

"What nonsense is this you talk?" he asked. "What old ones of the castle? There's no one in these hills but shepherds and warring Welsh tribes."

Beside him, Matilda's fingers were pressing white on the goblet in her hand. A little hot wine slopped on her wrist.

"They're shadows, Your Highness. Castel Dinas was theirs a thousand years ago. Maybe more. Before Our Lord was born this land belonged to them. We find their belongings in the foundations. The ditches and ramparts were dug by them. Their gods still rule, my lord. Christ is not welcome here. The walls of the chapel fall each time we begin to build. . . ." He was speaking quickly now, his hands pressed together, beads of sweat standing out on his brow.

John stood up and leaned toward him across the table. "God's teeth!

341

Are you telling me that this garrison is reduced to total terror by a pack of ghosts?" His voice was icy.

The man lowered his eyes. "They're real, my lord. I've seen them. Spirits, maybe, from the old days, but they're real. My lady, please release us. The only way is to abandon the castle to them." He turned to Matilda at last, his hands pressed together in supplication.

"How dare you suggest such a thing?" John's voice cut through the man's pleading like a whiplash. "The punishment for desertion is known to you, no doubt. I think you had better consider well before you suggest abandoning a strategic point such as this."

"That is enough." Matilda rose painfully to her feet and tried to clear her throat. "You may go for now," she said wearily. "There will be no punishments until messages have been sent to Sir William. You will see to it meanwhile that the building goes on and that there is no more drunkenness."

The man scrambled to his feet and, bowing low, fled from the hall.

John turned to her. "What, no floggings, Lady Matilda? Do you feel that they're justified being lazy good-for-nothing hounds because they can tell a good ghost story?"

She colored. "Perhaps they're right, my lord," she said defiantly. "There is something evil about this place."

"Apart from me, you mean?" His voice was heavy as her clear green eyes sought his and held his stare for a moment. He looked away first.

"It's lonely here certainly," he said at last, rising to his feet, goblet in hand still, and walking over toward the hearth, "and it's eerie in all this mist."

She watched him as he stood looking down into the glowing ash. His handsome face was pale and drawn, and there was an almost feline tautness about his muscles as he flexed his fingers slowly around the stem of the earthenware cup. She shuddered violently.

"The mountains are often eerie to the sensitive, Your Highness," she said softly. "I believe the men here are right. The old gods still walk these hills. This place is theirs and they will protect their own."

He swung around and gave her a searching look. "And are you their own too, my lady?" he said mockingly. "I think not. These gods or ghosts or men did not leap to your defense, as I recall, last night."

Ignoring the impotent fury that showed for an instant in her eyes, he took another thoughtful sip from the goblet. "No, this is rubbish. I'm prepared to swear that a few floggings and perhaps a hanging or two would ensure that no more gods or ghosts were ever seen here. You cross yourself, my lady? Can it be you are afraid of ghosts?" His eyes glittered once more. "Surely not, with me here to protect you even if your gods will not!" He took a step toward her.

Matilda felt the blood drain from her face. "You are no protection, my lord prince," she said. "God help the people of this country if ever you should become its king!"

She turned her back on him sharply, trying to steady her shaking hands.

Behind her there was a moment's silence, then she felt his fingers lightly touch her shoulders. "You presume too far, my lady," he said softly in her ear.

"As you did, Your Highness," she whispered. "God forgive you."

His hands fell away, but for a moment he did not move. "We were meant for each other, Matilda," he said quietly. "You cannot fight what God intended."

"*God!*" She faced him abruptly. "You think *God* intended you to take me as you did last night?"

He gave a half smile. "He was perhaps the source more of the inspiration than the method, madam. The result is the same. You are mine."

For a moment she stared at him in silence, her eyes huge as they held his, searching for some trace of gentleness behind the stark words. There was none.

He held out his hand suddenly and, taking hers, raised it to his lips. "You have to accept the inevitable, my lady," he said softly. "The stars themselves have spelled out our destinies—"

"No!" She pulled her hand away from him violently. "No, I don't believe you."

He smiled faintly. "As you wish, but it will be the harder lesson for you to learn. Come, let us inspect the holy well that graces this unholy place. Then perhaps we can return to the Hay. Your hospitality on this occasion does not overwhelm me, madam!"

Brushing past her, he pulled his cloak from the stool where he had flung it and ran down the steps into the misty cold sunshine. For a moment she did not move, overcome with fear and disgust, then reluctantly she forced herself to follow him outside.

The cold windswept valley was swathed in feeble sunshine as the heavy clouds streamed past, while all around them the mountains rose like evil presences, brooding, guarding Dinas and its secrets. She found she was shivering violently once more.

Dinas Well lay outside the north gate, a small bubbling spring surrounded by sharp rushes where a low wall of loose stone had been raised to protect it. There were signs that offerings had been left to the guardians of the well, whoever they might be, and garlands of wilted michaelmas daisies decorated the stone.

For a moment John stood staring down at it, then slowly he pulled off his heavy mantle and began to unlace the russet cotte beneath it, baring his breast to the teeth of the gale. Matilda caught her breath in horror. On his breast was an angry suppurating wound in the shape of a crescent moon.

He knelt, hesitating for a moment at the edge of the bubbling spring, then, clenching his teeth, he bent toward it and began to splash the icy mountain water over the wound. It was as she watched that somewhere the memory stirred at the back of her mind of Jeanne's voice talking about the holy well of Dinas. It was this water alone that could heal the incurable wounds procured by witchcraft; and this man was a descendant of Melusine—the daughter of the devil. Crossing herself, Matilda turned quickly away, her fear and revulsion doubled. It was a long time before she dared turn back as for the last time he bent and scooped some water into the palm of his hand and splashed it over his throat. And when she did turn she saw him toss a gold coin into the opaque green waters of the pool.

At last he rose to his feet, the water still glistening on his neck. "Let's see what magic this can perform," he said as he shrugged his mantle back on. "Perhaps it will redeem my good opinion of this Godforsaken place! Shall we call the horses and get out of here? I feel we've done all we can. I've seen the splendors of your defenses." He smiled amiably enough, but she flinched at the double-edged cut to his meaning. "Come," he went on. "We've seen the well. I wish to return to Hay. The day is several hours old, and I don't relish the thought of another night here."

There had been no storm in London. Above the high dome of the Reading Room at the British Museum the sky was relentlessly blue and harsh. Sam Franklyn stretched and sat back in his seat, staring thoughtfully upward. Making up his mind abruptly, he began to shut the books in front of him. He closed his slim notebook and twisted around to tuck it into the pocket of the jacket hanging on the back of his chair, then he stood up. He was smiling as he handed in the armful of textbooks at the circular central counter.

He made his way out of the museum through the crowds of visitors, pushed out of the swing doors, and ran down the broad flight of steps. The heat hit him like a hammer as he headed for the shade of the plane trees in Great Russell Street and began to walk briskly southwest, threading his way purposefully toward Long Acre.

Tim was peering through the viewfinder of his camera at the brilliantly lit dais in his studio. Nearby George was altering the positioning of the spots trained on a young man holding the leash of a tall, elegantly bored Dalmatian.

Sam stood in the doorway, surveying the scene over the shoulder of Tim's other assistant, Caroline, who had run down the long flight of stairs in answer to his ring. His gaze rested on Tim and he frowned.

The young man on the dais stretched ostentatiously. "I'll have to take the dog out for a crap soon, Tim, old son. Hurry it up a bit, for Christ's sake."

Tim ignored him. He waved George a few feet to the left and bent once more over the camera.

Sam slid into a chair at the back of the studio and sat watching the scene. It was half an hour before Tim had completed the session to his satisfaction and the young man and his dog dispatched out into the street. Caroline whispered at last in Tim's ear and he turned, seeing Sam for the first time as he sat in the shadows.

"I'm sorry, Dr. Franklyn, I didn't realize there was anyone here."

They surveyed one another warily as George and Caroline plunged the dais into darkness and slowly began to tidy away the props. Tim moved toward Sam slowly. He was suddenly feeling very tired. "What can I do for you?"

Sam stood up and extended a hand with a relaxed smile. "I wanted to talk to you about Joanna. You were with her in Wales, I gather."

Tim headed for the kitchen. He found two cans of beer in the refrigerator and handed one to Sam. "Jo is an old friend and a colleague of mine, Dr. Franklyn. I don't talk about my friends behind their backs."

A look of veiled amusement crossed Sam's face for a split second. Almost instantly the expression was bland once more. "All I wanted to know was whether she seemed well and happy. As you may know, I have been helping her with her problems."

"She told me," Tim said shortly.

"So. How was she?" Sam's eyes were suddenly probing as they sought and held the other man's.

Tim ripped the ring off his can of beer and flicked it into the corner. He looked away. "She was all right."

"Did she have any regressions while you were there?"

"That was what we went for."

"Of course. How many did she have?"

Tim walked to the side of the studio and pulled at the lever that slid the blinds back from the huge skylights, flooding the whole area with sunlight. "Two or three."

Sam narrowed his eyes. "Did they distress her?"

"The whole thing distresses her, Dr. Franklyn. The fact that she could not at first regress under self-hypnosis frightened her, then when it did happen, the experience itself frightened her. Waking up and having to leave that other world behind to come back to this one frightens her too."

"So. She was frightened. But she displayed no physical symptoms afterward. Bruises? Cuts, aches and pains that were inexplicable?"

Tim thought for a moment. "No."

"Do you have the photographs you took of her?"

Tim frowned. "I don't know that I should show them to you without her permission."

"I'm her doctor, man. I'm in charge of her case."

"Her case?" Tim glanced at him sharply. "I wasn't aware that Jo was a case."

345

"Tim?" George appeared behind them. "Shall I start on the film?" He glanced curiously at Sam, who ignored him.

Tim nodded impatiently. "Let Caroline help you." He waited as the two of them collected the cameras and left the studio, then he turned back to Sam. "Is she still in Wales?" he asked.

Sam nodded. "My brother has gone to her."

A wave of near physical pain swept over Tim and he turned away sharply, trying to hide his face, conscious that Sam was watching him closely. He had a feeling that this man could read his mind.

"I'll get the photos," he said. He moved hastily across the studio and, unlocking a cabinet, produced a portfolio. He laid it on a large table and snapped on the harsh overhead light that hung low over the table, then pushed the folio toward Sam.

Slowly Sam opened it. His face was impassive as he turned over each successive photo. The pictures of scenery, the castles, the mountains, he barely glanced at. His attention was fixed solely on Jo.

Tim walked away miserably. He threw the empty beer can into a bin and went back into the kitchen for another. His guest, he noticed, had barely touched his own. The kitchen seemed suddenly very stark and bare; the white fittings had a surrealist glow in the slanting light from the sun filled studio. It was like a morgue.

He stood in the doorway drinking his beer fast, watching Sam's face, which was floodlit by the working lights. Like a Rembrandt painting, he thought suddenly, the one of the doctors leaning over the table staring at the corpse. He shuddered violently at the analogy. "She said it made her feel naked," he said, joining Sam by the table. "Me, photographing her like that."

Sam did not look up. "Her expression is certainly very revealing," he said guardedly. "Photographs can tell you so much about the subject." He paused. "And about the photographer." He glanced at Tim and Tim stepped abruptly backward, shocked at the open dislike, even hatred, he saw in the other man's eyes.

For a moment they held one another's gaze, then Sam looked away. He laughed. "Perhaps I'm wrong, but I don't think so." He closed the portfolio and pushed it aside. "Are these all you have?"

"That's all." Tim's voice was very dry. He did not allow his eyes to wander toward the portrait on the easel beneath its cover.

Sam folded his arms, straightening. "I knew there was someone else," he said softly. "I didn't know who it was until now. Have you been regressed?"

Tim did not reply for a moment. His instinct told him to be very careful. Sam was dangerous. He wished, as so often these days, that his head was clearer. "Yes," he said at last. "I've been regressed."

346

Sam nodded slowly. "So," he said, almost to himself. "Now there are three."

"Three?" Tim echoed.

Sam smiled. "The three men who loved the Lady Matilda."

Tim stared at him. "And you are one of the three," he said thoughtfully after a moment.

"Me?" Sam said. "Let us say I'm an observer. Just an observer." He picked up his beer can and raised it to his lips. "For now, anyway."

27

Jo had fallen first to her knees, then slowly down until she was sprawled on the grass, her head near a lump of roughly shaped stone. Nick knelt beside her. "Jo!" he called urgently. "Jo, for God's sake, can you hear me?"

His anger had vanished, the sudden unsought surge of antagonism gone. He took off his shirt and rolled it up, gently pushing it beneath her head, and, worried by her stillness, felt for the pulse in her wrist. It was there, quick and light, but steady, her breathing shallow. As he knelt, helplessly watching her, she flung out her arm with a little painful cry.

"Jo?" he whispered. "Jo, where are you? Can you hear me?" There was no response. Her eyes did not open; her face was still.

He chafed her hand gently as the thunder rumbled closer behind them and he saw a flicker of lightning in the valley. "Jo, love, you must wake up. We can't stay up here in the rain. Jo!" He spoke more loudly, taking her by the shoulders and shaking her. She groaned and her eyes opened, but she did not see him. Her gaze went past him to the distant hills.

"Please, no," she whispered. "Please."

"Jo! You must wake up." Nick shook her again, more roughly this time. "Jo. Come on! Listen to me." He let her fall back with a sigh, and touched her face lightly with the tip of his finger. "Are you with him again, Jo? Is Lord de Clare there?" His jaw tightened. "Are you lying in his arms at this very moment?" He clenched his fists. "Why here, Jo? What happened here? What triggered it off?"

She didn't answer. Far away in the mists of that other storm, Matilda was staring at the streaming torches of the frightened soldiers.

A heavy drop of rain fell on Nick's naked back. He glanced up, aware suddenly of how close the storm had come. The sky overhead was indigo above the soft weight of the slate-bellied clouds. Two more drops fell on Jo's white blouse as he stared down at her trying to control the conflict of strange emotions inside himself. "Christ!" he cried out loud suddenly. "Oh, Jesus Christ!"

He bent over her and kissed her fiercely, his eyes closed as he felt the complex web of anger and frustration and desire ride over him. Then it was gone as fast as it had come and he was aware only of the fact that he was kneeling on the bleak mountainside with an unconscious woman and that it was about to pour with rain. He scrambled to his feet and, gently extricating the shirt from beneath her head, shrugged it on. Then he stooped and lifted her from the ground. Slowly he began to descend back toward the car, holding Jo in his arms, wary of the steep ground that was slippery now beneath the rain. He had gone perhaps half the distance back toward the lane when he heard a shout. The rain was falling harder now. He shook his head to clear it from his eyes, conscious of the sweat standing on his forehead. His heart was pounding. Jo was slim, but she was tall, and already her weight was exhausting him, tearing at the muscles of his arms and shoulders.

"Wait, man, wait! I'll help you!" The figure was gesticulating now as it appeared out of the rain, a black-and-white collie at his heels. "An accident, was it?" He was beside Nick now, a small man in plus fours, incongruous with shirt sleeves and a flat cap against the rain. Nick gently lowered Jo's feet to the ground, supporting her weight on his shoulder, gasping for breath.

"She fainted," he said after a moment, noting with relief the broad shoulders and sinewy arms of his rescuer. "I had to try to get her out of this rain."

"Put her arm around my neck, here. I'll give you a hand." The man spoke with calm authority. "We'll get her to my car, see. It's only down there." He gestured to a stony track leading up from the lane. In the dancing lightning Nick could see a silver Range Rover drawn up on the grass immediately below them.

Between them they lifted Jo into the back, her head cushioned on a blanket. Then Nick climbed in beside her as their rescuer vaulted into the driver's seat, the dog beside him. Outside the rain became heavier every second, drumming on the roof, surrounding them in a wall of streaming water as it poured down the windshield and slammed against the windows.

The man turned, his elbow over the back of his seat. "They're the devil, these storms. They come so fast then in ten minutes the sun is out again. Is that your Porsche I saw a couple of miles back?"

Nick nodded. "We walked farther than I realized."

The man was staring down at Jo. He nodded. "Easy to do in the mountains. And in this funny old weather too. Will we take the lady to the hospital? It'll be easier in this, I reckon."

Nick stared down at Jo. She was deathly pale, her head rolling sideways as the man turned back to peer through the windshield, beginning to ease the car forward slowly up the rutted lane. Her hands were ice-cold, her breathing very shallow. Nick rubbed her hand gently. After finding another blanket covered in dog hairs, he laid it over her. With a sigh he

349

nodded at the man's back. "Yes, please," he said. "I'd be very grateful if you would take us to the hospital."

Jo awoke in the hospital, disoriented and afraid, and meekly she submitted to a barrage of tests before at last she was discharged by a puzzled doctor who could find nothing more wrong than a possible allergy to electrical storms. Deeply relieved that she appeared to be all right, Nick phoned Margiad Griffiths and told her to expect them back in Hay that evening.

"You poor child. Come on up. I'll help you to your room," Mrs. Griffiths met Jo at the door as Nick pulled their suitcases from the car. "I'm just so very sorry you couldn't come here on Wednesday when you asked, but we were so full up, we were." She took Jo's elbow in her hand and firmly guided her toward the stairs. "Your fiancé said you'd share a room. I hope that is all right?"

Jo nodded wearily. "That's fine, Mrs. Griffiths, thank you."

"And that nice Mr. Heacham?" Mrs. Griffiths asked curiously as she stopped on the landing, panting.

"Has gone back to London. He was a colleague, as I told you."

The other woman sniffed loudly. "Colleague he might have been, my dear. But he was very much in love with you. But you know that of course."

Jo gently removed her arm from Mrs. Griffiths's protective clutch. "Yes, I know," she said bleakly.

"May we see our room?"

Jo jumped visibly as Nick's voice came from immediately behind them on the stairs. He was carrying their suitcases.

Flustered, Mrs. Griffiths threw open the door opposite them. "There," she said. "I hope you like it." She shot a nervous glance at Nick.

The room was a large one. Two single beds with a foot space between them faced the windows that looked out onto the street. The bedspreads and curtains were of primrose yellow chintzy material and the carpet moss-green. Jo walked to the window and threw it open, staring out at the quiet houses opposite. She was trembling slightly. "This is a lovely room. Thank you."

Mrs. Griffiths preened herself visibly. "I wanted you to have the best this time, my dear. Now, Mr. Franklyn said you'd like supper in, so I've put on a nice piece of lamb. It'll be ready about eight, if that is all right with you." She smiled from one to the other. "My Ted, he loved my cooking when he was alive. He always said my lamb roasts were the best he'd ever tasted. Now"—she looked around with quick confident posses-siveness—"I think you'll find you've everything you need. But you've only to call downstairs if you can think of anything." She glanced ner-

350

vously at Nick once more as he opened the door for her and ushered her out, then he closed it firmly behind her.

He spun to face Jo. "So, even she could see that Tim Heacham is in love with you!"

Jo froze. Slowly she turned to face him. "Tim has gone back to London, Nick. He came here to take photographs. That was all."

"Did you sleep with him?"

She walked across to the nearest bed and pulled her suitcase up onto it. "I didn't sleep with Tim, no."

She had still been Matilda when she had slipped into Tim's arms, and he? Surely for a few hours he had been once again Richard, Earl of Clare. She looked up and met Nick's eye steadily for a moment before beginning to pull clothes from her bag. That hard suspicious face, the tightened jaw, the eyes cold with anger. He had changed again to that other Nick. The Nick who had made her so afraid because he reminded her of an arrogant Plantagenet prince. She swallowed hard, trying to put the thought out of her mind, shaking out her two dresses, hoping he would not see how her hands were trembling. "Are there any coat hangers in the closet, Nick?" She forced herself to sound normal. "I think I should change for this sumptuous dinner, don't you?" She gave him a hesitant smile. "I'll have a shower and get the smell of hospital out of my hair."

He picked up his own bag and flung it on the other bed. "Right, I'll have one after you." He grinned at her suddenly as he pulled out a fresh shirt. He was himself again.

Jo picked up her bathrobe and washing things and opened the door, glad to escape. She wanted to be alone, to think; to try to face the terrible suspicion that was becoming every second more real in her mind—that Nick had once been John, King of England, the man responsible for her death.

She closed the door behind her softly and took a deep breath. Below her Mrs. Griffiths was climbing the stairs once again. She came to an abrupt halt as she saw Jo with her hand on the handle of the door.

"Miss Clifford, I forgot to tell you. After you left here on Wednesday a Miss Gunning called from London. She said I was to tell you if I saw you again to call her urgently. You can use the phone in the parlor if you like."

Jo frowned. She glanced at her watch, then back at the bedroom door. "I might just catch her before she goes out. Thank you. I'll phone straight away." She followed Mrs. Griffiths down the stairs. "She's my boss, in a manner of speaking," she said apologetically as Mrs. Griffiths showed her the phone in what was obviously her private sitting room. "I'll pay for the call."

Bet was in the bath.

"Jo? Thank Christ you've called! Where are you?"

351

Jo looked around the small neat room with its deep armchairs with spotless antimacassars. She could smell the lamb cooking.

"Back in Hay. What is so urgent, Bet?"

"Jo, love, I'm not sure how to say this, but I had lunch with Nick on Wednesday. We talked quite a bit. Jo, listen, I think he's going to try to come after you. I know this sounds crazy, but I think he's dangerous. I think he's out of his mind. He really hates you, Jo. God knows what's got into him, but I think he is capable of trying to kill you!"

There was a moment's silence, then Bet's voice rang out again in the quiet room. "Jo? Jo, are you there? Did you hear what I said?"

"I heard," Jo said softly.

"And?"

"And I hope you're wrong." Jo's voice was bleak. "I hope to God you're wrong. . . ."

In London Judy Curzon was staring curiously around the small neat living room of the house in Gloucester Avenue. Everything was immaculately in place. The white sofa with two geometrically designed black-and-white cushions, the only furniture besides a white table and a phalanx of bookshelves down one wall, holding, besides hundreds of books, a stereo system, video recorder and television, and a rank of indexed filing boxes.

"A drink, Judy?" Pete Leveson followed her into the room after closing the front door.

"Thank you." She was still looking around with interest.

Noticing, he gave a rueful smile. "This is all the furniture left after my first two wives cleaned me out. It's all one needs. Something to sit on, books, and music."

She took the glass from him. "My philosophy too. Only I make my guests sit on hard stools, or the floor." She gingerly lowered herself onto the sofa. "Are you sure you don't mind my coming over?"

Pete walked over to the window. He threw up the lower sash and sat down on the white-painted window seat. "I'm glad you did. I needed some company. So, what's new in Fulham?"

"I'm preparing for a new exhibition."

"So soon?" He put his foot up on the seat and clasped his hands around his knee.

"Not so clever really. I had nearly enough material for two exhibitions anyway. This one is exciting though. It's going to be in Paris. But I didn't come to talk about that. Pete, I need your help."

"You don't need my help, Judy. But you'll have it, for what it's worth. I enjoyed writing up the last one, and the thought of a trip to Paris to write about the next is not entirely obnoxious to me." He grinned. "I might even buy a picture myself this time."

"I'm not talking about the exhibition!" Brushing aside his intended compliment, she jumped up restlessly and went to stand in front of his bookcase, staring up at the lines of titles. "I want you to . . . that is . . ." She turned awkwardly toward him. "You know Tim Heacham, don't you?"

Pete concealed a smile in his hand. "Of course."

"Did you know he was in love with Jo Clifford?"

"I had heard rumors to that effect, yes."

"He doesn't just fancy her, Pete. It is something much, much more. . . ." For a moment Pete saw an almost painful sympathy in her eyes and he looked at her with renewed interest. Her short red hair was becomingly tousled, her dark-green shirt and her jeans well cut and for once paint-free. She exuded an air of gamine charm that did not quite conceal the determination which directed all her movements. His eyes rested on her broad, almost masculine hands with their neatly trimmed nails. Scarlet talons were more to his taste, but she certainly had something, some underlying current of sexuality that appealed to him enormously. He stood up and reached for her glass. "Let me get you another," he said gently. "I take it you feel that I can help their romance along somehow."

She narrowed her eyes. "Yes. And for a start you can tell the world what a mess Nick has made of his business affairs."

Pete's mouth fell open. "Hang on a minute. I had the impression that you were rather keen on Nick yourself."

The green eyes clouded. "No longer. The reason he has been ignoring the office more and more is because he has been hypnotized too, like Jo. And in his previous existence he knew her before. And he hated her enough to kill her." She took the refilled glass from him and gave him a knowing smile. "Surely you could use material like that, Pete, couldn't you?"

Jo stood for several minutes after she had hung up the telephone, staring out of the window at the roof of the tower of Hay Church, almost hidden among the trees. She was numb.

"Finished, then, dear?" Margiad Griffiths popped her head around the door. "Supper will be on the table in fifteen minutes, if you were going to have a quick bath."

Jo looked blankly at the bathrobe and sponge bag she had put down on one of the chairs. Slowly she picked them up. "I'll pay you for the call," she said huskily.

"Bad news, was it, dear?" Mrs. Griffiths came into the room properly. "That white, you are. Here." She gave a conspiratorial smile. "Why don't I give you a glass of sherry. That'll perk you up a bit, so it will. You can take it upstairs with you."

Gratefully Jo took the tiny thistle crystal glass of sweet sherry and made her way back upstairs. The bedroom door was still shut. She locked herself in the bathroom and, drawing the shower curtain around the bath, turned on the tepid water before she pulled off her mud-stained jeans and blouse and stepped under the shower attachment, letting the water stream over her face and breasts, soaking her hair until it turned to a jet curtain of wet silk on her back.

Supper was ten minutes late and Margiad Griffiths was flustered. "It's the wine, see. I sent my Doreen up the road to get you some from the Swan, but I don't know if it's any good. My late husband, he knew about wine, but I don't like the stuff myself!" She thrust the bottle at Nick shyly and then handed him the corkscrew.

Nick looked gravely at the label. "That's very nice, thank you. Will you thank your daughter for going to so much trouble," he said to her with a smile.

He grinned at Jo as their hostess withdrew. "Chambré it certainly is, after its voyage back from the Swan, wherever that is. The label says it was a good wine once. But it has been shaken to the point of shall we say sparkling, if not actually frothing."

Jo managed to laugh. "The way I feel now, I don't care how it comes as long as it's wet and alcoholic." She watched him draw the cork and gingerly sniff the neck of the bottle. "The food looks lovely," she said soberly after a minute.

"And so is the wine, in spite of its adventures. Here's to the intrepid Margiad—isn't that a lovely name?" Nick took a large mouthful. "And here's to you, Jo." He met her eye, suddenly sobering.

Jo sat back in her chair. "There was a phone message waiting for me to call Bet Gunning this evening," she said. Her gray-green eyes studied his face gravely. "I spoke to her just now."

"Oh?" Nick picked up his knife and fork.

"She said she had lunch with you last week."

"Nick smiled. "Is that why she called? To tell you what happened?"

"What did happen, Nick?"

"She told me to keep away from you. She said I was ruining your career prospects and spoiling your literary style. She then offered herself to me as compensation. When I declined her kind suggestion she was a little upset. Though not enough, I should have thought, to report back to you. What was her version?"

Jo gave a small smile. "Much the same. Bet is nothing if not honest. Perhaps she wouldn't have been if you had accepted her offer." She took a tentative mouthful of lamb. "She also told me she thought you hated me." She did not look up.

Nick said nothing for a moment.

"Hated me enough to want to kill me," she went on, so quietly he thought for a moment he had not heard aright.

"Jo." He reached across the table and took her hand. "Bet is a self-confessed troublemaker and bitch. She also had a vivid imagination. For God's sake—" His expression turned to one of incredulity. "You don't believe her?"

She shook off his fingers and put down her knife and fork. "No, of course not."

She reached for the wine bottle and poured some more into her glass. "But you have been rather odd, Nick. You admitted it yourself." Her hand was shaking as she looked up at him. She forced herself to smile.

He frowned. Then abruptly he stood up, pushing his chair back, his food hardly touched.

"Jo, we've got to have this out. I love you—" He gave her an embarrassed grin. "Not an easy thing for an Englishman to say in broad daylight, but, there, I've said it. I think I've loved you ever since I first met you."

There was a moment's tense silence as they both considered suddenly the deeper implications of what he had said. With a shiver Jo looked down at her plate. Her throat had constricted so tightly she could barely breathe.

"Then why did you go to Judy?" she whispered at last.

He groaned. "God knows! Because you told me to go to hell, I suppose." He paused. "Because sometimes you make me so angry—"

"Angry enough to want to hurt me—" She looked up at him.

"No!" he replied explosively. "It is as if—" He paused in midsentence, staring out of the window. "It is as if there is something in my mind that closes down like a shutter. When it happens I don't know what I'm doing for a while. That's not an excuse, Jo. There is no excuse for what I did to you. It's perhaps all the more frightening because it's like that. I don't understand it." He frowned. "But it will not—cannot happen again."

Jo ached suddenly to stand up with him and take him in her arms, but resolutely she sat still, staring down at her plate again. "Sit down, Nick, and eat your supper. Mrs. Griffiths will be so hurt if we don't at least make the effort," she said quietly. "I expect you've been overworking, what with the worry about Desco and everything," she added, as matter-of-factly as she could. "That might explain it all."

He sat down heavily opposite her. "It might, I suppose." He gave a weary smile.

"Why did you come here, Nick?"

"To Wales?" He paused. "To see you. To be with you."

"But why?" She clenched her fists in her lap, waiting for his reply.

"Because I was worried about you, I suppose," he replied after a moment.

"I see." She bit her lip. "And you're still going back tomorrow?"

"I have to. I'm due to fly to New York on Wednesday and I've got an awful lot to do first. But I'll wait and see how you are before I go. It worries me the way you are having these regressions spontaneously. Supposing there had been no one there. Supposing it had happened to you in the street, or driving, for God's sake!"

"There is no reason it should happen again, Nick." Jo gave up her attempt to eat and laid down her knife and fork. "I don't think what I had today was a regression anyway. I just fainted—like I did at Ceecliff's. As I told you, the doctor said it was probably something to do with the thunder we've been having so much. It happened before in a storm, remember? He thinks it's an allergic reaction to electric force fields, or something." She gave a little laugh. "He said I'd probably be the sort of person who pukes under pylons."

Nick managed a smile. "But you didn't tell them about the regressions, did you?"

She shook her head. "They'd have locked me up, Nick. And kept me in for a month for psychiatric tests. If anyone is going to do any tests on me, it's going to be Carl Bennet." She glanced up at him under her eyebrows. "Would you come with me, Nick, if I went back to him?"

Nick frowned. She saw his fingers clench and unclench around the handle of his knife. "As an observer, Jo," he asked quietly after a long pause, "or as another patient?"

She went up at about nine. Nick did not stop her. Nor did he suggest he go to bed too. Instead he let himself out into the street and began slowly to walk toward the church.

The churchyard was shadowy. It smelled of new-mown grass in the evening twilight as he sat down on the wall and lit a cigarette, feeling the dew soaking into his shoes. He could see the bats flitting in and out of the darkness of the yew trees around him and once or twice he heard their faint sonar squeaks. Slowly it grew dark. He knew he ought to go back. Mrs. Griffiths would probably be waiting to lock up, but somehow he did not want to leave the quiet velvet night. He ground out his third cigarette into the grass with his heel, conscious that the dew was striking chill all around him now. Moths had begun to crawl over the streetlight near by, fluttering desperately in its harshness. He watched as the bats swooped through the pool of light, taking the mesmerized insects in quick succession before wheeling out into the darkness again and circling for another swoop. In the distance he heard a clock chime eleven.

Reluctantly he stood up.

Jo was asleep. He clicked on the lamp beside his bed but she did not move and for a moment he stood looking down at her. He had described the strange thing in his mind as a shutter. It was more like a shadowy incubus, lying sleeping in his brain, that every now and then shook itself and stirred and murmured. And when it spoke he had to obey. He felt the prickle of fear touch the skin at the back of his neck as his mind skidded obliquely away from the lurking suspicion that had begun to haunt him. But there was one thing he had to face. Whatever it was, this alien part of him, Bet was right, it threatened Jo.

Gently he pulled the sheet up over her shoulders, touching a strand of her hair as he tucked it around her. Asleep she looked so vulnerable. Why should any part of him want to harm her? Bet had seen it. Her bantering and flirting had stopped the moment she had seen the other being in his eyes. And Judy. What was it she had said to him? *You weren't regressed. Sam told you who you were and then he told you what to do.* He sat down on his bed thoughtfully. But his first attack on Jo had been before Sam had hypnotized him. And Sam would never want him to hurt Jo. Angrily he pushed away the echo of his mother's voice. *You must never let Sam hypnotize you, Nick. . . . Did he find out who you were in Matilda's past? What did he let you remember?*

He remembered suddenly Judy's expression as he had moved toward her in the living room of his apartment, intending to take her glass and refill it. She had backed away from him, and he had seen in her eyes the same fear and uncertainty he had seen in Bet's; Judy too had glimpsed the stranger in him.

Jo stirred on her bed and flung out her arm, but she did not wake. Nick looked down at her, then he walked away to the other side of the room. He did not dare let himself touch her again.

She woke at dawn. Her eyes strayed sleepily around the unfamiliar room focusing on the open window for a moment, then she started to shake.

She sat up, clutching her pillow to her chest, burying her face in it as she tried to control the terror that flooded through her. The memory had returned all at once, just as it had before, the details three-dimensional in their clarity. Castel Dinas in the threatening storm, Prince John, the drunken men, and her own vulnerability and fear as the king's brother made his intentions clear.

She clutched the pillow tighter, seeing again the handsome, drunken face above her, feeling his brutal hands on her breasts, feeling her absolute powerlessness before his determination.

"Are you all right, Jo?"

She stifled a scream as Nick's hand closed over her wrist, and, tearing herself from his grasp, she threw herself to the far side of her bed. "Don't touch me!" She slid out of the bed, still holding the pillow, and backed away from him. She was trembling violently.

"I'm not going to touch you, Jo." Nick moved back. He sat on the side of his own bed, his eyes on her face. "You've had a bad dream, that's all."

"A dream!" Her face was white as she stared at herself in the dressing-table mirror. "Do you think a dream did this? And this?" She thrust her wrists at him and then her shoulder in the thin silk nightgown with its ribbon straps. Both were bruised and there was a long scratch on her neck near her collarbone. Her throat was bruised and swollen.

Nick stared at her in horror. He had become suddenly very cold. "Jo! I hope you don't think I did that, for Christ's sake. I didn't do it!"

"Didn't you?" She was like a trapped animal, her shoulders pressed against the wall. "How do I know it wasn't you?"

"It wasn't, Jo." Nick moistened his lips nervously with his tongue. "You were asleep last night when I came back from my walk. I didn't touch you. I slept here in this bed, until just now when you woke me. For God's sake, Jo! Do you think I could do that to you in your sleep and you not wake?" He was breathing heavily. "You've had a dream. Another regression in your sleep. It wasn't anything to do with me, Jo."

She was a little calmer now. He saw her arms still defensively clutching the pillow, her face pinched and white. "No," she breathed at last. "It was at Castel Dinas, I remember now." She took a deep painful breath. "We rode there with the prince's men. There was a storm and the castle guard was terribly frightened—of the ancient gods. I don't know who they were. Celts, or Druids, I suppose, but they still walk the hills. John and I were there. Alone."

"John?" Nick whispered. He could feel the goose bumps rising on his skin.

Jo looked at him directly for the first time. "Prince John," she said. They stared at each other in silence.

Nick tried to swallow the sudden bile that had risen in his throat. "And he did that to you?" he said slowly.

She nodded. He could see the accusation in her eyes. "It *was* you, Nick—"

"No!" He launched himself from the bed. "Jo, get a grip on reality! It was not me! You were in a trance. No one touched you except inside your head. I took you to the hospital and they kept you there for hours while they examined you. There wasn't a mark on you. Not yesterday, not last night. It happened in your sleep, Jo!" Gently he took the pillow from her and put it back on the bed, then he caught her hands. They were ice-cold. "Jo. I think we should see Bennet. As soon as possible." He pushed her into a sitting position on her bed.

She was looking up at him. Tentatively she raised her hand and traced her fingers lightly over his eyes and nose. Suddenly her eyes filled with tears and she threw her arms around his neck. "Oh, Nick, don't let it be true. Please," she cried desperately. "Don't let it be true."

After-dinner cigar smoke wove around fluted silver candlesticks and drifted up to the high ceiling, curling beneath the plastered moldings. Ponderously Sam stood up, a glass of port in one hand, and walked down the long table to a vacant chair near its head. He put down his glass and extended his hand. "Dr. Bennet? My name is Samuel Franklyn."

Bennet looked up and surveyed him briefly, then he indicated the empty place beside him. "Please, sit down, Dr. Franklyn. I hoped we might meet here this evening," he said. He reached for the decanter. "We have a patient in common, I believe." He glanced up once more, his eyes narrowed. "One of the most interesting cases I have ever come across. Cigar?"

Sam shook his head. "She has finally changed her mind about our conferring—now that it is too late for me to stop your becoming involved—did she tell you?"

Bennet raised an eyebrow. "She did not. But I did intend to have a word with you anyway, I must confess." He was studying Sam's face with interest. "When did you last see her professionally?"

"On the twelfth. You were away, I believe."

Bennet nodded slowly. "I saw her the following week. We had a very disturbing session during which I tried, at her request, to suggest to her that her interest in her past life would lessen or be lost altogether. She rejected the suggestion and became very disturbed. It was necessary to sedate her. I have not spoken to her since then. She missed her next appointment." Thoughtfully he kept his eyes fixed on Sam's face.

"She went to Wales." Sam took a sip from his port. "She decided to try to check some of the facts and locations of these regressions for herself. And now, I gather, she has begun to regress spontaneously."

Bennet sighed. "Autohypnosis. I was afraid that might happen."

"And not entirely involuntary, I think. I gather you believe in this reincarnation?"

Bennet smiled warily. "I try to be objective about my patients. In fact I had contacted one or two people with whom I would like to have confronted Joanna. A medieval historian. A linguist who would question the Welsh she has begun to speak from time to time. A colleague, Stephen Thomson—you've probably come across him—all of whom would be better equipped to judge the material she is producing. They could tell us so much about where all this is coming from if she could only be persuaded to return."

Sam gave a slow smile. "She will return, I'm sure of it. My brother is with her in Wales at the moment, and I think he'll see to it, one way or another, that she comes back. You met my brother, I believe?" he added thoughtfully after a moment.

"On more than one occasion." Bennet laughed ruefully. "He does not trust me, nor my trade."

"No, he wouldn't." Sam fell cryptically silent. He helped himself to some more port and passed the decanter on around the table. "I would be interested myself in your experts' views. And so I think would Nick." He leaned forward, his elbows on the table. "He worries me sometimes, Nick," he said reflectively.

Bennet refrained from commenting. He was watching Sam closely.

"He is becoming more and more unstable," Sam went on. "With violently swinging moods. If he were a patient I would be a little concerned by now. As his brother I find it hard to be objective." He gave a disarming grin.

"There didn't seem much wrong with him to me." Bennet leaned sideways, his elbow on the back of his chair. "He is worrying about a woman with whom he is obviously deeply in love, that's all." He paused. "He also is, I think, a deep trance subject himself. I should like the chance to regress him. I sense a soul much troubled through the ages. I should hazard a guess that you think so too."

Sam's hand, lying on the table near his glass, had closed into a fist. "I am not sure I share your belief in reincarnation, Dr. Bennet."

"That surprises me." Bennet smiled faintly. "I pride myself in having a nose for these things, and I should say you have reason to believe you have much in common with your brother."

"Possibly." Sam gave him a cold glance. "If I were to persuade him to bring Jo to you again, will you assemble your experts? But no more suggestions that she forget Matilda. She has to follow the story through."

Bennet frowned. "Has to?"

"Oh, yes, she has to." Sam stood up. He held out his hand. "It's been very interesting meeting you, Dr. Bennet. I'll be in touch when Jo and Nick return to London. . . ." He gave a small bow and turned away, walking slowly back along the table toward his original seat.

Bennet watched him as he went, a preoccupied frown on his face. There was something about Dr. Sam Franklyn that disturbed him greatly.

Jo and Nick arrived in Carl Bennet's consulting room the following Tuesday. Besides Carl and Sam there were three strangers present.

Bennet took Jo's hand when she came in. "Let me introduce you to my colleagues, my dear. This is Stephen Thomson, a consulting physician at Barts. He is something of an expert on stigmata and other phenomena of that kind." He gave her an impudent grin. "And this is Jim Paxman, a medieval historian who knows a great deal about Wales, and this is Dr. Wendy Marshall, who is an expert on Celtic languages. She is going to try to interpret some of the Welsh words and phrases you come up with from time to time. She will know at once if they are real—and from the right period."

Jo swallowed. "Quite a barrage of experts to try to trip me up."

Bennet frowned. "If you object, I shall ask them all to leave, Jo." He was watching her anxiously. "I don't mean this to be an inquisition."

"No." Jo sat down resolutely. "No, if I'm a fake, no one wants to know

360

it more than I do." She gave Sam a tight smile. He was seated unobtrusively in the corner of the room, watching the others. He had nodded to her briefly, then his gaze had gone beyond her, to Nick.

Bennet glanced at Sarah, ready by her tape recorder, then he smiled. Around them the others were arranging themselves, leaving Jo alone, seated in the center of the room. "Shall we begin?" he said gently. He sat down next to her.

Jo nodded. She sat back, her hands loosely clasped in her lap, her eyes on Bennet's face.

"Good," he said after a moment. "You have learned to relax. That's fine. I heard you had been practicing."

Every eye in the room was on him as gently he talked Jo back into her trance. Within seconds he was content. He looked over his shoulder at Sam. "The self-hypnosis we were discussing has made her easier to regress. She doesn't really need me, save as a control." He straightened and looked at the others. "She is ready to be questioned. Who would like to have a go first? Dr. Marshall, what about you? Would you perhaps like to ask her something in Welsh? She has, as we all know, maintained that she has no knowledge at all of the language in this incarnation, and I suspect that would be very easy to prove one way or the other. Easier than questions of historical detail."

Wendy Marshall nodded. She was a tall, slim woman in her early forties. Her hair, an attractive brown, was drawn back into a clip at the nape of her neck, to fall in undisciplined curls down her back. Its exuberance contrasted sharply with her severe expression and the puritanical simplicity of her linen dress. Picking up the clipboard that had been resting on her knee, she stood up and walked toward Jo.

"Nawr te, arglwyddes Mallt." She launched at once into a torrent of words. "Fe faswn i'n hoffi gofyn ichwi ychydig cwestiynau, os ca i . . . I have told her that I'm going to ask her some questions," she said over her shoulder.

The silence in the room was electric. Nick found he was clenching his fists, as, like everyone else, he watched for Jo's reaction.

"A ydych chi'n fyn deall i? Pa rydw i'n dweud? Fyng arglwyddes?" Wendy went on after a moment.

There was a long pause. Jo gave no sign of having heard her. Her attention was fixed somewhere inside herself, far from the room in Devonshire Place. Wendy gave a shiver. She glanced at Bennet. "I just asked her if she understood me," she said in an undertone. "She looks completely blank. I am afraid it looks as though she has been fooling you."

Nick stood up abruptly. He walked toward the window and stared out, forcing himself to stay calm. Behind him, Sam's gaze followed him thoughtfully.

Nick spun around. "You think she's been lying?" he burst out. "You think the whole thing is a hoax? Some glorious charade we've all made up to amuse ourselves?"

"Nicholas, please." Carl Bennet stood up. "I am sure Dr. Marshall is implying no such thing." He turned to Jo. "Can you hear me, Lady Matilda?" His tone was suddenly peremptory.

Slowly Jo looked toward him. After a moment she nodded.

"You have told us that you speak the language of the hills," he said firmly. "I want you to answer the questions this lady asks you. You can see this lady with me, can't you, Matilda?"

Jo turned to Wendy, looking straight at her. Her eyes were strangely blank.

"Speak to her again now," Bennet whispered.

Wendy raised a disbelieving eyebrow.

"Fyng arglwyddes, dywedwch am y Cymry sy'n drigo o gwmpas y Gelli, os gwelych chi'n dda," she said slowly, speaking very distinctly. *"Ydych chi'n fyn deall i?"*

Jo frowned. She pushed herself forward in the chair, her eyes focused now intently on Wendy's face.

"Y . . . y Cymry o gwmpas y Gelli?" she echoed hesitantly.

"That's it! I've asked her to tell me something about the people of Hay-on-Wye," Wendy said quickly over her shoulder, her face suddenly tense with excitement.

"Eres ych araith," Jo said slowly, fumbling with the words. *"Eissoes, mi a wn dy veddwl di. Managaf wrthyt yr hynn a ovynny ditheu . . . pan kyrchu y Elfael a oruc Rhŷs . . ."*

"I will tell thee of what thou desirest . . . of Rhys's attack on Elfael," Wendy murmured, scribbling in her notebook. "Slowly. *Yn araf.*" She had forgotten her irritation with Bennet and with Nick as soon as Jo had started to speak. Sitting down close to her, she waited for a moment, her eyes intent on Jo's face. *"Siaradwch e, yn araf, os gwelych chi yn dda,"* she repeated at last. "Slowly, please. *Yn araf iawn.*"

Jo gave a little half smile. She was looking beyond Wendy now, toward the windows as if she were watching Nick.

"Rhys a dywawt y caffei ef castell Fallt a gyrrei ef Wilym gyt a'y veibion o Elfael a Brycheiniog megys ry-e yrrassei wynteu y ymdeith Maes-y-fed." She paused thoughtfully. There was silence in the room, broken only by a quiet rattle as Sarah dropped her pen on the table in the corner; it rolled unnoticed across the polished surface to fall silently onto the carpet.

"Don't tell me that's not real Welsh she's speaking," Bennet said triumphantly. "What is she saying now?"

Wendy shook her head. "It is Welsh," she said quietly, "but it's hard to understand. The pronunciation is unusual and the syntax . . . that use of the old perfect form *dywawt* is striking. It's an early Middle Welsh form that has disappeared. And also very odd is her use of the verbal particle *ry* with the pronoun *-e,* meaning 'them,' following it. Such usage is very early." She looked around at the others. "You would not expect to find it even in the Middle Welsh of the thirteenth or fourteenth century. It is very, very interesting."

"She is talking to you from the twelfth century, Dr. Marshall," Sam put in quietly. "You would not, I am sure, expect anything other than twelfth-century speech."

Wendy swung around to look at him. "She speaks modern English," she said sharply. "Using your criterion I would expect her to speak the language of Layamon, or even more likely Norman-French. But not the English of the 1980s."

Sam shrugged. "She has a twentieth-century brain, Dr. Marshall. The memories she is drawing on include the languages she would have spoken at the time. But they are being relayed through the medium of a twentieth-century woman who, until now, has been instructed to answer in the twentieth-century idiom. Why don't you address her in old French? Or even Latin. See what happens!"

"Pan dducpwyt chwedyl o'n orchyfygu vi bydwn yngastell Paen," Jo went on suddenly, completely oblivious of the exchange going on over her head. *"Gwybuum minheu yna ymladd a wnaem ninneu. Nyt oed bryd inni galw cymhorthiaid . . ."*

"What is she saying now?" Bennet leaned forward urgently.

"Wait! I am trying to understand her," Wendy snapped. She was frowning intently. "She said she would have to fight. There was no time to summon aid . . ."

"Where? Where is she?"

"Pain's Castle is it? She is going to defend Pain's Castle."

"Y glawr mawr—Y bu yn drwmm etto," Jo went on.

"The heavy rain, it was still heavy . . ." Wendy echoed under her breath.

"Oed goed twe ymhob cyfer—"

"There was thick forest all around—"

"Y clywssam fleiddyeu pellynnig—"

"We could hear distant wolves."

Jo was sitting bolt upright suddenly, and she had begun to talk very fast, growing more fluent by the second as her tongue became accustomed to the unfamiliar sounds she was uttering. Her eyes were wide open, the pupils dilated, and she was becoming more and more excited.

"Tell her to speak English!" Bennet interrupted sharply. "I think we've proved our point beyond any doubt. Tell her, quickly . . ."

"Dyna igud. Siaradwch Saesneg yn nawr, os fues dim ots gyda chi." Wendy leaned forward and touched Jo's arm almost reluctantly.

Jo drew away. She was staring beyond the people sitting around her in the room, into the far distance, where she could see an untended fire, burning low, the acrid smoke billowing around the castle hall as first one log and then another slipped from the dogs and fell into the ashes.

She was hearing the silence of that cold desolate night, torn by the ugly shouts and screams of men and the angry clash of swords as the first wave of attackers was beaten back from the scaling ladders they had flung up against the walls. She and she alone must take command. The lives of every man and woman in the castle depended on her now that the castellan was dead. Slowly she stood up and drew her cloak around her, then she turned toward the door. Somehow she must find the strength to take up his sword.

"Seasneg, fyng arglwyddes. Nid ydyn ni ddim i'n eich deall chi!" Wendy cried. "Speak English. We can't understand you!"

Jo stopped abruptly in the middle of her flow of words. *"Avynnwch chwi y dywettwyf i Saesneg?"* she repeated, puzzled. *"Saesneg . . .* English . . . I must talk English?" Then, haltingly, she began to speak once more in a language they all understood."

28

Bennet put his hand on Jo's forehead for a moment. "Quiet now. Lady, rest," he commanded gently. He looked at Nick. "So now you know about the siege of Painscastle. Your Matilda was a courageous lady, to hold the place until help came. She doesn't seem too tired. Shall we go on?"

Nick nodded. "Why not? She's not upset."

"Does anyone else want to question her?" He glanced at Jim Paxman, who shook his head. "For now I am intrigued. Later, perhaps, I'd like to cross-question her further." There was a pencil in his hand. "I'm making some notes of things I'll ask her. So far her detail is uncanny!"

"And accurate?" Sam's cold voice from the corner made them all glance round uncomfortably.

"I haven't faulted her on anything yet," Jim replied cautiously. "But there is so much more there than I or anyone else could verify, even with the minutest study of the chronicles. No, Carl, please get her to carry on. I want to hear more of her family. And more of the campaign. Rhys didn't leave it at that, you know. No way. He went back!"

Carl nodded. He turned back to Jo. "Matilda," he said softly. "Tell us what happened next."

It was nearly dark. Matilda sat in the window trying to match some final stitches into her embroidery, in the private solar she used as her own in the castle of Hereford, where William was now the sheriff. Impatiently she selected a length of golden thread and squinted up against the last flaming gold of the western sky to try to thread it. The knock at the door made her bend the thread and she cursed under her breath. She had been treasuring the hour of silence alone in the upper room, with even her daughters and her women chased away, and she longed to prolong the moment if she could. Her head ached a little and her eyes were sore, but as long as she could still see to sew she had the excuse to remain alone.

The knock sounded again, more urgently, and this time the heavy handle turned. "My lady?" Elen put her head round the door.

"Elen, I told you I want to be alone. For a while, just until full dark."

"I know, my lady." Elen grinned unrepentantly. "But you've a visitor, see, and I thought it was time I lit the sconces and saw about sorting a few things in the garderobe here. And look at you," she scolded suddenly. "Trying to work in the dark and ruining the sight of your eyes as you sit there, is it?" She pushed open the door and hurried across the room. Behind her, on the threshold, stood Richard de Clare. He was alone.

In spite of herself Matilda felt her heart give a lurch at the sight of him.

Seeing her, he bowed, his old grin unmistakable, lighting his face. He held out his hands.

Matilda glanced at Elen, who was fussing about with a lighted spill, going from sconce to sconce, but the woman kept her back ostentatiously turned and after a moment she disappeared behind the curtain into the garderobe.

"Richard!" She could hold back no longer. Her hands outstretched, Matilda ran to him and felt for a moment his strong arms around her, the touch of his lips on hers. Then gently, too soon, he was pushing her away with another light kiss on her forehead. "Oh, Richard, my dear, my love! It's been so long."

"It has indeed." He stood back, still holding her hands, and looked her up and down slowly, his eyes taking in every detail of her slender upright figure. Her hair seemed as burnished as ever beneath her headdress. His own, as he saw ruefully that she had noticed, was nearly white.

"Richard, what happened?" She reached to touch it with longing, wistful fingers.

He grinned. "Married life, sweetheart, and premature old age, combined with our East Anglian weather and the ministrations of your son. He is with me, by the way."

Behind them Elen cleared her throat loudly before appearing in the doorway. "My lady, Sir William has finished with the sheriff court sessions for the day. His brother-in-law Adam Porter is here and he is with him at present, but I'm thinking he was about to come up here." She was carrying an embroidered surcoat over her arm. "I'd best be here when he comes."

Matilda glanced helplessly at Richard, who merely smiled and shrugged. "He never forgave you, you know, for supporting William Longchamp against Prince John," she whispered. Then with her voice politely social again: "Are you pleased with Reginald? I was so glad when he became your esquire. You should have brought him up with you to see me, Richard. I suppose he's grown so large I'll not recognize him, like my other boys." She sighed. "It's hard to think of myself as mother to so many enormous children, Richard. I don't feel old."

He threw back his head and roared with laughter. "No one else would believe it either, sweetheart. Your waist isn't an inch wider than when I first saw you. Do you remember? Just after your wedding, when you came

366

to Bramber and I saw you riding across the saltings with William. So tall and stiff you were on your horse, with your hair newly put up beneath your veil and wanting to tumble down again, like a maiden's." He raised his hand gently to her temple and then almost guiltily let it fall. They had both heard the firm step on the stairs and they drew slightly apart.

William, when he appeared, was in jovial mood and seemed content to forget his political differences with Richard. He had never over the years by so much as a hint betrayed whether or not he had ever heard any of the rumors that she knew had abounded about her love for Richard, and now as always when she saw the two men together she could not help wondering, comparing, and guiltily moving to her husband's side. William, for his part, flung out his arms expansively at the sight of his visitor and embraced him.

"I heard you'd arrived. How is Reginald behaving in your service? Moll, help me with my tunic. Where are the pages?" He started to shrug the heavy garment off his shoulders. "My God, I'll be glad when this spell at Hereford is over. Being sheriff is all very well, but dispensing the king's justice becomes wearisome after a while, I can tell you. I need some fighting to loosen up my bones again."

Richard grinned. "I heard about your extra duties, William. My congratulations. I see you are a man to be reckoned with now throughout the land."

William beamed, holding his arms out for the new tunic that Elen had brought to him. "I think you might say so," he agreed. "I think you might say so."

When William returned to his duties in the court room the following morning, Matilda and Richard ordered their horses and their hawks and rode out of Hereford toward the southeast into the great forest of Aconbury. The leaves were everywhere turning to russet and gold and the horses' hooves brushed through the rustling carpet, stirring the bitter scents that teased the nostrils and caught at the back of Matilda's throat. Richard rode slightly ahead of her, his eyes screwed up in the frosty glare, but after a while he reined back alongside her.

"Tell me, how have things been, my dear?" he said quietly. "Have you heard any news of your little Tilda?"

Matilda's heart lurched. Did Richard know? Had he ever guessed that her strange silver-haired daughter was his? She swallowed the lump in her throat with an effort and, summoning a smile, she managed to nod. "Gerald saw her in the spring. I am a grandmother, Richard." Her eyes sparkled suspiciously for a moment and Richard found himself fighting the urge to touch her hand. "She has a little son," she went on. "Rhys Ieuanc, young Rhys, after his grandfather, God rot him!"

Richard searched her face for a moment. "Rhys took Mallt's castle in the end, of course."

Her face tightened with anger. "As you say, he returned after the last of the snow with no warning and with such a strong force there was no time for the constable to summon aid. William had gone to fight in Aberteifi with Will—Rhys agreed to spare the castle only if they abandoned the campaign in his lands and came back to Hay."

"And he agreed," Richard said quietly. "I could not understand why. It seemed unlike William."

She smiled ruefully. "Whoever understands William, my dear? He is a law unto himself."

There was a long silence as the horses walked slowly on, then Richard spoke again.

"I came to Hereford with a proposition which I hope will please you. I must put it to William, but I should like your views. It touches us very closely." His eyes were fixed on the gilded leather of the rein in his hand. She followed his gaze, noting absentmindedly how thin his hands had become, the joints slightly accentuated. "I should like my daughter, little Mattie, to marry one of your sons. If you agree I think William might find the match acceptable."

She didn't answer for a moment. The sun's rays breaking through the thick treetops of the copse into which they had ridden fell across the party, throwing a gold veneer onto the horses' coats. At the heels of her mare an excited dog suddenly began to bark, and was at once silenced by an angry command from a huntsman behind them. There was a lump in her throat when at last she spoke.

"I should like that, Richard. Above all I should like that." She paused again. "You were thinking of Reginald, I suppose? Have they formed an attachment to one another? That is good. Giles anyway plans to take Holy Orders after Oxford and then Paris. But Reginald—oh, yes, I am sure that William would approve of a link with the house of Clare for Reginald." She looked up at him and smiled. "Yes, it's what I had hoped for, Richard. We have plans for the two girls, of course. Margaret is to marry Walter de Lacy and William is hoping for an alliance with the Mortimers for little Isobel, but marriages for the other two boys have not yet presented themselves. I think"—she dropped her eyes, almost embarrassed—"I think William is becoming very ambitious, Richard. I think he has set his sights very high for the future."

Two days later Richard left. Matilda was standing in her solar, giving orders to her steward, when Elen brought him in. He was already dressed for the road.

"My lady," he said formally. "I come to take my leave."

Her hand clutched involuntarily at the quill with which she had been checking the lists before her. It was a moment before she could look up. "Must you leave so soon, Lord de Clare?" Behind her the steward bowed and left the room and she was conscious of Elen rounding up the ladies who had been at work with their sewing near the fire. In moments the place was empty but for themselves.

As the heavy door closed behind the last of them he caught her hands in his. The pen fell to the rushes as he raised them to his lips. "I don't know how long it will be before we see each other again."

"Richard!" she whispered in anguish. She clung to him blindly, raising her lips to find his as her eyes filled with tears. "I thought growing older would teach me sense," she murmured. "I thought at least it would be easier to bear as time went on."

He held her so tightly she could hardly breathe. "It will never grow easier, my darling, never. That is our punishment for a forbidden love." His lips touched her eyelids gently. "If two of our children can find love with one another, perhaps that will ease our own pain. At least William has agreed in principle to the idea."

She nodded, unable to speak, clinging to him desperately.

"I have to go," he said at last. Gently he tried to release himself from her arms.

"I know." She clung to him even harder. "Oh, Richard, take care of yourself, my dear." She reached up for a final kiss. Neither of them spoke for several minutes, then at last Richard straightened and firmly pushed her away.

"We will meet again." He forced himself to smile. "Who knows, maybe at Mattie and Reginald's wedding, God willing!" He caught her hand and kissed it quickly, then he turned and swung out of the tall, vaulted chamber and disappeared, his spurs ringing on the stone of the staircase as he ran down toward the entrance to the keep. Behind him Matilda began to cry.

"That's enough!" Nick crossed the room in two strides. His eyes were blazing. "Wake her up. Quickly!"

Tears were pouring down Jo's face as she spoke, her words almost unintelligible through the violence of her sobs.

He sat down beside her, his arm around her shoulders. "Wake her up, man. She's had enough!"

Sam pushed himself away from the wall against which he had been leaning. "Don't interfere, Nick. Grief is all part of life's rich pattern. She sinned. She has to suffer." His voice was heavy with irony. "Surely you of all people would agree with that."

Nick glared at him and, as Bennet and his colleagues watched, the concern and anguish vanished from his face to be replaced by cold anger. "She is weeping for Richard de Clare!" he said through clenched teeth. "One of John's advisers and even his friend! Dear God! She mocks me, even now! Flaunting her love of the man and rejecting me. Me! As if I were no one."

369

They stared in astonishment at the arrogant fury of his expression, so unlike anything that anyone who knew Nick had ever seen, and they saw the color run up his neck to suffuse his face.

Bennet stood up hastily. "Steady, my friend," he said, laying his hand on Nick's arm. "Jo was mocking no one. Couldn't you see how she was being torn?"

Nick shook off the hand and dragged his eyes away from Jo's face, visibly struggling within himself, his jaws clenched as he stared at Bennet. He was looking straight through him as if he weren't there, oblivious of the presence of anyone else in the room. The sweat was standing out on his forehead.

Bennet glanced at Sam. "What is wrong with him?" he said sharply. "This man is possessed in some way!"

Sam shook his head. "As I told you, I suspect my brother has an incipient mood disorder," he said quietly. "It is becoming less easy to hide—"

"Rubbish!" Bennet snapped. He clicked his fingers in front of Nick's face. "He is as much in a trance as Jo. He has been hypnotized—but not by me. I think this is a reversion of some kind. Has he been having hypnotherapy, do you know? Or trying regression himself?"

Sam raised an eyebrow. "Under the circumstances, would you be surprised if he had?"

"No." Bennet looked up at him and pushed his glasses onto the top of his head. "I am merely concerned in case he has entrusted himself to someone who is less than competent." The two men held one another's gaze for a long moment. It was Sam who looked away first.

"I am sure he wouldn't do that." Sam did not bother to hide his amusement. "Why don't you ask him what he's been up to?" He turned to Nick. "Nicholas, you are making a fool of yourself, brother," he said sharply. "Wake up! Look at all these keen scientific minds watching your performance!"

Nick glanced around. For a moment he looked bewildered. Then he gave a sheepish grin, the anger gone from his face. "I'm sorry. I don't know what came over me. I didn't know what I was saying—"

"That's all right," Bennet said slowly. He was scrutinizing Nick closely. "You didn't say anything to worry about. Now, let's see what we can do for Jo, shall we? It is, after all, she we have come to discuss." He glanced around at the others. "Does anyone want to question her further before I awaken her? No? Right, then."

Jo stared around the room blankly for a moment as she regained her awareness of the present day. Her nose was swollen, her eyes streaming. Unobtrusively Sarah picked up a box of tissues and put them down on the sofa beside her. Jo grabbed one. "Sorry," she said miserably. "It's so silly to be upset. I can't seem to stop crying."

370

"I'll make coffee," Sarah said softly. "For everyone. I think that should be the next priority before anyone asks any questions."

"But I want to know," Jo said. She blew her nose. "Did I speak real Welsh? Did you understand what I was saying?" She looked at Wendy.

Wendy nodded. "You spoke a version of real Middle Welsh. I don't think there is any possibility at all that you could have picked that up by accident, or without long and intensive study, so it would not have been cryptomnesia. Your pronunciation was fluent if unusual—I have no way of knowing if it was genuine, of course, but I suspect so. I am completely lost for an explanation as to how you could have done it."

Bennet smiled. "You are still not content with my explanation, then?"

Wendy laughed. "I'm reserving judgment. *A ydych chi'n fyn deall i? Pa rydw i'n dweud?*" She turned back to Jo suddenly.

Jo shook her head and shrugged. "It's no use. It's gone. I don't understand anymore." She put her hands to her head. "What did you say?"

"I only asked whether you still understood me." Wendy stood up and threw her notes down on the table. "It is extraordinary. Quite extraordinary!" She swung around to face Carl. "Could it be some kind of possession? Or even a case of multiple personality?"

"There is no question of it," Carl said swiftly. "Jo came to me with no history whatsoever of mental or personality problems. Whatever this is, I am certain in my own mind that it is from her own past."

"And it has now become part of her present," Sam put in quietly. "I suspect that the past was unresolved. Perhaps resolution can only come in this life."

Jo shivered violently. "Sam! That's horrible! What are you saying?"

"People are not reborn without a purpose, Jo. They return to progress or to expiate their sins."

"Rubbish, man!" Jim Paxman gave Sam a look of undisguised dislike. "I have never heard such arrant nonsense. If this is an echo from the past, then that is all it is, an echo. With no more meaning or purpose than the accidental replaying of an old record. This woman is in some way acting as an instrument, a . . . a . . . ." He groped for the right word.

"A medium?" Wendy put in thoughtfully.

"If you like, but that has psychic connotations which I don't accept. We are not dealing with ectoplasm or crystal balls here. That is not what we are talking about at all."

"Aren't we?" Nick said.

Everyone looked at him. There was an expectant silence.

Behind them Sarah pushed open the door. On her tray were eight cups of coffee.

* * *

Sam and Nick both went back to Cornwall Gardens with Jo. They were all silent in the taxi, and once they were in the apartment Nick went straight to the cabinet in search of the bottle of Scotch.

Jo threw herself down on the sofa. "I feel as if I've been through a mental mincer," she said. She put her arm across her eyes. "Isn't it funny? I thought today would prove something—either that I'm hallucinating or inventing things or that it is all real and I am the reincarnation of Matilda de Braose, and yet, with all that talk and all that argument and all those experts, it has proved nothing. In fact, now it is worse. All they have done is make me terribly aware of the fact that there are a whole lot more theories to account for my condition than I had ever thought of and I am more muddled than ever."

"Forget it all, Jo." Nick sat down near her with a sigh. "Why the hell should you turn yourself into a specimen under a microscope for that lot? Or me, for that matter." He frowned. "We know what we believe. That is what is important."

"And what do we believe?" Sam put in.

"That's the point!" Jo sat up. The Scotch had brought the color back to her cheeks. "I don't know anymore. Except that it's not just me. We are all three involved. We are, aren't we?" She looked from one to the other.

"Perhaps." Sam walked out onto the balcony and stood looking down at the square. A group of children were playing on the grass behind the railings with a huge striped plastic ball. He turned to lean on the balustrade. "We must all experience with an open mind and record meticulously and with unbiased comment what happens. Particularly you, Jo, if you still intend to write a book on all this. The book will be of enormous scientific—or occult or historical or linguistic or whatever—significance. Let those experts of Bennet's with their analytical minds tear that apart. From now on we'll leave them out of it. We don't need them. The man himself is, of course, a fool. You do realize that, don't you? For all his expensive offices and the panoply of medical props he is not a qualified psychiatrist."

Nick raised an eyebrow. "He couldn't call himself doctor, surely, if he weren't qualified."

"He qualified as a physician in Vienna just after the war, but he never practiced as far as I can see, either in general practice or as a specialist, until he came to England, when he did a minimal training in hypnotherapy and launched himself as an expert on some decidedly fringe activities."

Nick gave a lazy smile. "It struck me he didn't think much of you either."

"Shut up, both of you." Jo stood up. "Why don't I get us all a salad. I want to think about something else for a change. My mind is so tired, so terribly tired of all this—" Her voice trembled slightly.

With a glance at Sam, Nick followed her into the kitchen. "Jo, what happened to me at Bennet's?" he asked in an undertone. "Did I go into some sort of trance as well?"

She looked at him, astonished. "You?"

"Yes, me, Jo." He glanced over his shoulder hurriedly. "I am beginning to think Sam may have given me some sort of posthypnotic suggestion—"

"Sam?" Jo stared. "You haven't let Sam hypnotize you?"

"Now, who is taking my name in vain?" Sam had brought the bottle of Scotch with him into the kitchen.

"No one." Jo glanced at him uncomfortably. She turned hastily to the refrigerator and took out a plate of cold meats and a bowl of salad, then she reached into the door for a bottle of wine. "Sam, the corkscrew is in the drawer behind you. Leave my Scotch alone and pour us all some wine instead, will you? When did you say your plane was tomorrow, Nick?" she went on hastily.

Nick was watching his brother expertly insert the tip of the corkscrew into the center of the cork. He was frowning.

"Eleven. I'm going to have to go as soon as we've eaten, Jo. There are things I must do at the office before I go back to the apartment to pack."

Jo looked down at the bottle of olive oil in her hand. "You haven't said how long you will be away," she said. He must not know how lost she felt at the thought of his leaving.

"Ten days at least." His voice was gentle.

"Ten days for Jo to sort out her affairs with Richard de Clare," Sam put in as he poured out the three glasses of wine, meticulously stooping, his eye level with the worktop, to check that all contained identical amounts.

"Sam." Jo glanced at Nick, suddenly terrified that the mention of the name would change him again, back to the frightening travesty of the Nick she knew. His face had hardened, but he was still Nick. The stranger was not there behind his eyes.

"She's finished with de Clare," Nick said after a moment. He picked up one of the glasses. "And de Clare knows it."

"Knew it, Nick," Jo said quickly. "It was all a long time ago. Here, take the salad through, and the bottle."

Sam was watching her as she took the plates from the cabinet.

"You intend to follow this story through to the end, don't you, Jo?" he said softly as the door swung closed behind Nick.

She straightened abruptly. "Don't be absurd. You know damn well I'm not. And you know why."

"I think you will. I don't think you'll be able to stop when the time comes."

"Oh, believe me, I will, Sam." Jo clenched her fists. "Do you think I will want to go on when John turns against them? I don't want to know what happens then. Do you think I could bear to live through all that—the knowledge that Richard did not lift a finger to try to save her, for all his love. And William! William, after all their years of marriage, their children —William betrayed her!"

"She had betrayed William first," Sam said sharply. "She had driven him too far."

"He was a coward," she retorted. "A bully and a coward."

Sam flinched visibly beneath her scorn. "He paid for that last betrayal," he said. "He paid. Dear God, how he wanted to make reparation. Don't you think he wanted to return to save her?"

Nick pushed open the kitchen door behind them. "Come on, you two, what's happened to supper?"

"No!" Jo did not even hear him. "No, I don't think he did. He didn't give tuppence for anything but his own skin. Don't forget, he let his own son die too. His eldest son!"

Sam narrowed his eyes. "His son! Will wasn't his son. Will was the bastard of that weak fool, de Clare. An incestuous bastard!"

"Sam!" Nick shouted. "Stop it!"

Sam ignored him. He hadn't taken his eyes off Jo's face. "Do you know who little Matilda de Clare married? No, not Reginald. Not good, honest, upright Reginald, so like his father. No, you let her marry Will! You let her marry her own brother!"

"No!" shouted Jo. "No, that's a lie. Will was William's true-born son."

"I don't believe you. Matilda was a whore. She deserved to die the way she did."

"Sam, shut up!" Nick glared at his brother. "You bastard! Leave it alone, do you hear?"

Suddenly Sam smiled. "Of course. I'm sorry. How tactless of me." He was breathing hard. "Yes, why don't we have supper! It can't matter now, anyway, can it, what happened eight hundred years ago?"

It was a quiet meal. After leaving most of her food untouched, Jo pushed her plate aside and toyed instead with the glass of wine. It was only just after eight when Nick stood up.

"I must go, Jo." He took her hands as she rose too. "Take care, won't you."

She gave a watery smile. "Of course. Don't worry about me."

"If you want to speak to me, Jim will have the phone number in the office. And I'll be in touch with them just as soon as I hit New York. Do you want me to call you?"

She shook her head. "Forget me for ten days, Nick. Concentrate on your work. I'll see you when you get back."

He looked at her hard for a few moments, his blue eyes intense, then he kissed her gently on the forehead. "Sam will be here to take care of you, don't forget, if you need him."

374

Sam was still seated. He refilled his glass slowly, watching as Jo raised her arms suddenly and threw them around Nick's neck.

He frowned. "I'll see you back at the apartment later, Nick," he said.

"You're not coming with me now?" Nick disengaged himself gently. There was a hint of caution in his tone as he looked down at his brother. "There are one or two things I want to say to Jo first."

"No!" There was no reason for Jo's involuntary response; its violence surprised even her. "I mean, not now, Sam, please. I am so tired. I'd really rather be on my own this evening, if you don't mind."

"I won't keep you long." Sam did not move.

Nick put his hands on the back of Sam's chair. "Come on, you can see Jo wants us both to go."

"She'll change her mind." Sam glanced up at Jo with a smile. "A cup of coffee, then I'll leave if you still want me to. I promise."

She clung to Nick for a moment on the landing and stood watching him walk down the stairs, then slowly she turned back. "You really want coffee?"

"Please." Sam had collected the plates. He carried them through to the kitchen, then he leaned against the wall, watching as Jo set about making some instant coffee. "Not the real thing?" he inquired lazily. There was a slight smile at the corners of his mouth.

"It takes too long," Jo said over her shoulder. "I mean it, Sam. I really am too tired to talk." She turned suddenly and looked at him. "Sam—"

He raised an eyebrow.

"Is Nick—" She hesitated. "Have you ever hypnotized Nick?"

Sam smiled. "That's an odd thing to ask."

"Have you?"

"Put down the kettle for a moment and look at me."

"I'm making your coffee."

"Put it down, Jo."

She did so, slowly. Then she stared up at him. "Sam—"

"That's right, Jo. Close your eyes for a moment. Relax. You can't fight it. There is nothing you can do, is there? You are already asleep and traveling back into the past. That's it." Sam stood for a moment staring at her, then he moved forward and took her hand, leading her out into the apartment's short hall. A right turn would take him toward the front of the apartment, the living room with its open balcony doors. To the left was the bedroom and next to it the bathroom.

He turned left. In the bedroom he pushed Jo into a seated position on the end of her bed, then he moved to the windows and closed the heavy curtains. He switched on the lamp. It cast strange synthetic shadows in a room where the evening sunlight was still struggling through between the folds of the heavy material, lighting up a dazzling wedge of gold on the dusty rose of the carpet.

Sam folded his arms. "So, my lady, do you know who I am?"

Jo shook her head dully.

"I am your husband, madam!"

"William?" She moved her head slightly as though trying to avoid some dazzling light.

"William." He had not moved. "And you and I have a whole night, do we not, to remind you of your duties to your husband."

Jo stared up at him, her gaze alarmingly direct. "My duties? Of what duties do you intend to remind me, my lord?" Her tone was scornful.

Sam smiled. "All in good time. But first I want to ask you a question. Wait. There is something I must fetch. Wait here until I return."

Matilda stared at William's retreating back. He slammed the heavy oak door of the bedchamber and she heard the ring of his spurs on the stone as his footsteps retreated. She shivered. The narrow windows of the chamber faced north and the shutters braced across them did nothing to keep out the cold. She went to stand near the huge hearth, drawing her fur mantle around her. Her bones had begun to ache now in the winter and she could feel her soul crying out for the balm of spring sunshine. She must be beginning to feel old! What had William gone to find? Wearily she bent and picked a dry mossy apple bough from the basket and threw it on the fire. It scented the room immediately and she closed her eyes, trying to imagine herself warm.

William returned almost at once. He flung back the door and stood before her, his face closed, his eyes hiding some new anger. She sighed, and forced herself to smile.

"What is it you wish to ask me, William? Let us speak of it quickly, then we can go down to the great hall where it is so much warmer."

What was it he held behind his back? She stared at him curiously, feeling as she always did now for him a strange mixture of scorn and fear and tolerance and even perhaps a little affection. But he was so hard to like, this man to whom she had been married now for so many years.

William slowly held out the hand he had been keeping behind his back. In it was a carved ivory crucifix. She drew back, catching her breath, recognizing it as coming from a niche in the chapel, where it was kept in a jeweled reliquary. It was reputed to have been carved from the bone of some long-dead Celtic saint.

"Take it."

"Why?" She clutched her cloak more tightly around her.

"Take it in your hand."

Reluctantly she reached out and took the crucifix. It was unnaturally cold.

"Now," he breathed. "Now I want you to swear an oath."

She paled. "What oath?"

"An oath, madam, of the most sacred kind. I want you to swear on that crucifix in your hand that William, the eldest child of your body, is my son."

She stared at him. "Of course he is your son."

"Can you swear it?"

She stared down at the intricately carved ivory in her hand—the decorated cross, the tortured, twisted figure of the man hanging on it in his death agony. Slowly she raised it to her lips and kissed it.

"I swear it," she whispered.

William drew a deep breath. "So," he said. "You told the truth. He was not de Clare's bastard."

Her eyes flew to his face and he saw the paleness of her skin flood with color. For a moment only, then it was gone and she was as white as the crucifix she had pressed to her lips.

He narrowed his eyes. "You swore!"

"William is your son. I swear, before God and the Holy Virgin."

"And the others? What of the others?" He took a step toward her and grabbed her wrist. He held the crucifix up before her eyes. "Swear. Swear for the others!"

"Giles and Reginald, they are yours. Can you not see it in their coloring and their demeanor? They are both their father's sons."

"And the girls?" His voice was frozen.

"Margaret is yours. And Isobel." She looked down suddenly, unable to hold his gaze.

"But not Tilda?" His voice was barely audible. "My little Matilda is de Clare's child?" He pressed her fingers around the crucifix until the carving bit into her flesh. *"Is she?"* he screamed suddenly.

Desperately she tried to push him away. "Yes!" she cried. "Yes, she was Richard's child, God forgive me!"

Abruptly William let her go. She reeled back, and the crucifix fell between them in the dried herbs on the floor. They both stared at it in horror.

William laughed. It was a humorless, vicious sound. "So, the great alliance with Rhys is built on counterfeit goods! The descendants of Gruffydd ap Rhys will not be descendants of mine!"

"You must not tell him!" Matilda sprang forward and caught his arm. "For sweet Jesus' sake, William, you must not tell him!" She gave a little sob. Dropping his arm, she whirled around, scrabbling on the floor until she found the crucifix. She grabbed it and thrust it at him. "Promise me. Promise me you won't tell him! He would kill her!"

William smiled. "He would indeed—the fruit of your whoring with de Clare."

She was trembling. The fur cloak had fallen open. "Please, promise me you won't tell Lord Rhys, William! Promise!"

"At the moment it would be madness to tell him," William said thoughtfully, "and I shall keep silent for all our sakes. For now it shall remain a secret between me and my wife." He smiled coldly. "As for the future, we shall see."

He stretched out and took the crucifix out of her hand. After kissing it, he put it reverently on the table, then he turned back to her and lifted the fur from her shoulders. "It is so seldom we are alone, my lady. I think it would be a good time, don't you, to show me some of this passion you so readily give to others." He carefully removed her blue surcoat and threw it after the cloak before he turned her numb body around and set about unlacing her gown.

She was shivering violently. "Please, William! Not now. It is so cold."

"We shall warm each other soon enough." He turned and shouted over his shoulder. *"Emrys!* You remember Emrys," he said softly. "My blind musician?"

She did not turn. Clutching her gown to her breasts, she heard the door open behind her then close again quietly. After a few moments' silence the first breathy notes of the flute began to drift into the chamber, spiraling up into the dark, smoke-filled rafters.

She shuddered as William's cold hands pulled the gown out of her clutches and stripped it down to the floor.

"So," he whispered. "You stand, naked in body and naked in soul." He took a deep, shaky breath. "Let down your hair."

For some reason she could not disobey him. Unsteadily she raised her hands to her veil and pulled out the pins that held it. She uncoiled her braids, still long and richly auburn with only a few strands yet of silver, and began to unplait them slowly, conscious of the draft that swept under the door and toward the hearth, sending icy shivers over her skin. She still had not looked at the musician.

William watched in silence until her hair was free. It swung around her shoulders and over her pale breasts, rippled in the firelight into dancing bronzed life.

He took another deep breath and groped at last for the brooch that held his own mantle. "You have a girl's body still, for all the children you have carried," he said softly. "Trueborn or bastard, they haven't marked you." He put his hand on her belly.

She shrank back, her eyes silently spelling out her sudden hatred, and he laughed. "Oh, yes, you detest me—but you have to obey me, sweetheart! I am your husband." He dropped his cotte after his mantle. "You have to obey me, Matilda, because I have the key to your mind."

She swallowed. "You have gone mad, my lord!" As if breaking free of some spell, she found she could move suddenly. Turning, she picked up her fur cloak and swung it around her until she was covered in rich chestnut fur from chin to toe. "You hold no keys to my mind!"

378

"But I do." Abruptly the music stopped. William raised his hand in front of her face. "Drop the cloak, Matilda. That's right." He smiled as, unnerved, she found herself obeying him. "Now, kneel."

Furious, she opened her mouth to argue, but the argument did not come. Scarcely realizing she did it, she knelt on the rich fur and stared up at him, the firelight playing on her pale skin as slowly he began to undress himself. Watching, she saw the stocky naked body, the mat of graying chest hair, tapering down to his belly, the sturdy muscular thighs, the white ugly scars, one on his left thigh, the other on his left shoulder. She had seldom seen him naked. Though everyone customarily slept unclothed, wrapped in blankets and furs, or sprawled in summer on coarse linen sheets, she resolutely rolled herself in the covers whenever possible and kept her eyes tightly closed. Now there was no escape. Some force of will in him seemed to keep her eyes open, fixed on his body. Nervously her gaze traveled down to the rigid penis, then back to the corded muscular arms that could hold her so mercilessly as he used her. She clenched her fists defiantly, her eyes rising once more at last to meet his.

He smiled. "Lie down, wife. There on the floor."

"No," she breathed, summoning the last vestiges of her strength to defy him. "No, my lord, I will not. It pleases you to treat me like a whore but I am your true wife, faithful to you for many years. If I must submit to you it will be on our marriage bed!"

"Faithful?" He sneered suddenly. "You have betrayed me with de Clare. With who else, I wonder?" He looked at her, suddenly calculating.

She dropped her gaze and he laughed. "Your eyes spell out your guilt! Who was it? One man? Two? A hundred?"

"Only one other, my lord." Why was she answering him? It was as if some force compelled her to make the admission.

"And who was that one other?"

"One to whom you yourself would have given me, my lord," she burst out. "And I did not lie with him willingly. Before God, I swear it! He took me by force."

William raised an eyebrow. "And who was this so eager suitor, madam?"

"Prince John," she answered in a whisper.

"So!" The angry color rose in his cheeks. "So, you are a royal whore. And where did John take you? On a bed trimmed with cloth of gold? No matter. For me you lie on the floor where you belong."

He stooped and picked up the broad leather belt he had dropped with the rest of his clothes. "Lie down, Matilda, or I will give you the thrashing you deserve."

Behind them the music began again suddenly, thin and breathy, unrelated to the darkness of the chamber, the flaring smoky torches in the sconces, or the bittersweet smoke of the fire. Outside the wind had begun

379

to moan gently across the hills, an eerie, dismal sound, as lonely as the cry of the hungry wheeling buzzard, riding the currents below the streaming clouds.

Matilda did not move. Her eyes narrowed scornfully. "You resort so easily to violence. You are like an animal, my lord. What you cannot take by force you wish to destroy." She saw his hand tighten on the leather thong and she felt a quick pang of fear, but she did not move. "I have often wondered why you have never beaten me," she said half thoughtfully. "You have often wanted to." She smiled at him. "Perhaps you have never dared."

He stared down into the mocking amber eyes. The sorceress. The witch. Did she know then that he was afraid of her? He clenched his fist tighter on the belt, resisting the urge to cross himself with his free hand. He must take her now, while his desire was hot, while his anger sustained him. Whip her and mount her and by God's bones he was not too old to get her with child again. A trueborn child to replace the bastard girl he had given to the Welsh.

He stepped forward, his arm raised, and brought down the leather thong across her shoulders with every inch of strength he possessed.

He heard the air whistle out of her lungs as the blow fell, but apart from that she did not make a sound. For an instant he saw fear in her eyes, then hatred—then, as he raised his arm for the second blow, she threw back her head and laughed. The sound rang out, wild and mocking, and he felt his desire shrivel and die as he heard it. Goose pimples raised on the flesh across his shoulders. With an oath he dropped the belt and groped at his feet for his tunic.

"So be it," he breathed. "You may laugh now, my lady. You may call up whatever demons protect you and scorn me now, but mine shall be the last laugh. Stay here! Stay in your castle, my lady! Stay in the past and lick your wounds. *Stay there!*"

He swung his mantle over his shoulder and walked out of the chamber.

Dry-eyed, Matilda climbed to her feet. She picked up her cloak and wrapped it around her tightly, trying to stem the sudden, agonized shuddering that racked her body, then wearily she climbed onto the bed and pulled the covers over her.

Only then did she realise the music was still playing softly in a dark corner near the window.

29

There was a persistent knocking somewhere in the distance. Judy dragged herself up out of the fog of sleep and groped for her bedside clock. It was three-fifteen.

With a groan she sat up and reached for her bathrobe. Staggering slightly, she switched on the bedside lamp and pushed open the door into the studio. It was quite dark in there, the smell of turpentine and oil paint pleasingly overlaid with beeswax. She sniffed appreciatively; smells were always so much stronger and better defined in the darkness.

After snapping on a single spotlight in the corner, she made her way to the door. Behind her the new canvas, nearly finished, stood alone in the center of the floor, and she glanced at it possessively as she passed. Totally absorbed, she had been working on it, in spite of the lack of light, until nearly two.

"Who is it?" she called. She slipped the chain into place. "Stop making such a noise and tell me what you want."

"It's me, Sam Franklyn." The knocking stopped abruptly.

"Do you know what time it is?" Cautiously she opened the door and peered through the crack.

Sam was leaning against the wall. His shirt was unbuttoned and he carried his jacket over his shoulder, his finger hooked through the loop. Slightly bleary-eyed, obviously tired, he was, she realized for the first time with a sudden sense of shock, as handsome in his own way as his brother. With an obvious effort he stepped forward and pushed at the door, swearing violently as the chain caught it and held it fast, bruising his knuckles. "Open up, Judy, for God's sake. I need to talk to someone."

"Someone? Anyone?" She stared at him indignantly. "Are you drunk, Sam?" She reached for the light switch by the door and flooded the studio behind her with light as the fluorescent strips clicked on. After pushing the door almost shut, she slipped off the chain.

"No, I'm not drunk." Sam walked in past her. "But I would like to be. Do you have anything here to create the desired effect?"

Judy raised a sarcastic eyebrow. "If it were up to the Franklyns I

381

wouldn't have much left for anyone to get drunk on! Anyway, I thought you were a coffee addict."

He grinned at her, but there was no humor in his eyes. "Coffee up till two perhaps, but then Scotch."

She shrugged. "One. Then you can go home. I'm sick of you and Nick using this place as a railway station bar! What's the matter anyway?"

"The matter? Why should anything be the matter?"

Judy found the bottle of Scotch in the kitchen cabinet and brought it back into the studio. "People don't usually arrive here at three in the morning wanting a drink without something being the matter," she said curtly. "Is Nick still in Wales?"

Sam shook his head. "They came back at the weekend. Nick is flying to the States tomorrow." He emptied the glass and put it on the table. "I lie. This morning. He is going this morning."

"And does he still think he's King John?" Judy poured herself a small measure and sipped it without enjoyment. She had begun to shiver.

Sam smiled. He sat down and put his elbows on the table. "He *was* King John."

"Crap. You've been feeding him that stuff deliberately. What I want to know is why? You don't like your brother, do you, Sam?"

"How perspicacious of you to see it." Sam picked up his empty glass and thoughtfully held it level with his face, squinting through it sideways.

"And you are setting him up?"

"Possibly. Give me another wee dram and I shall reveal all."

Judy hesitated. He was not obviously drunk, but he was making her feel uncomfortable. There was something strange—even frightening—about him as he sat motionless at the table, a sense of latent power that could be unleashed at any moment. Still shivering, she reached for an old sweater that was hanging over the back of a wooden chair near the table and knotted it around her neck like a scarf. "Okay. It's a deal. One drink and you reveal all," she said.

She watched while he drank, then she sat down, arms folded, and waited.

He put down the glass. "I am a puppeteer, Judith. A Punch and Judy man. A kingmaker. Nicholas is dancing on the end of my string." He held out his hand, angled above the floor as though he held a puppet there before him, dancing at his feet.

"Even in the States?" she asked dryly.

"In the States, sweet girl, the king who lives in his head will sleep. He will wait until he returns to his native land and then he will strike."

"Strike?" Judy echoed. She looked at him apprehensively. "What do you mean, strike?"

"Who can tell?" Sam said. "He is a king." He laughed suddenly, then abruptly he looked back at her. "He seduced my wife, you know."

382

"Your wife?" Judy echoed in amazement. "I'm sorry, Sam. I didn't know you were married."

"Oh, yes." He balanced the chair on its two back legs, lolling in it comfortably, his fingertips resting on the edge of the table. "Because he is king he thinks he can do what he likes with other people's lives. He thinks he can take with impunity. He doesn't know how wrong he is."

Judy was watching him nervously. He was like Nick; he could be blind drunk and not show it at all. She eyed the bottle, which she had left on the table less than two feet from his hand. It was still half full.

Standing up, she edged away from him. "I don't know about you, but I need some coffee, however late it is."

"Not for me." He moved slightly in his chair to watch her. "I have just come from Joanna's apartment," he went on after a moment. "I walked around for a long time before coming down here."

"Oh?" She hid her surprise as she went back into the kitchen and switched on the light.

"She is a lying bitch." He said it reflectively, but without malice. "A beautiful, lying bitch."

"Do I gather you made a pass at her?" She jumped violently as she turned from the cabinet and found him standing immediately behind her. He had moved after her with extraordinary and silent speed.

He ignored the question. For a moment he stood staring at her, then he smiled again. "You too are a beautiful woman, Judith. One thing my brother has is an impeccable taste in women." He reached out and touched her arm. "Look at me."

Startled, she lifted her eyes to his and for a moment she found herself trapped, the clear, almost colorless irises holding her gaze, and she could feel her mind reaching out to meet his, eager for the fusion. For a brief second she remained absolutely still, then with an effort she tore her eyes away. "Oh, no you don't, Dr. Franklyn! You can't hypnotize me. I'm immune!" Her eyes narrowed with anger. "I wasn't good enough for you before, remember? There was no way you wanted to include me in your little happy family of medieval freaks. So, who have you decided I could be, now that you've changed your mind? Eleanor of Aquitaine? A serving wench to hitch up my skirts for you and bare my backside whenever you fancy a quick poke, now that Jo has rejected you! You realize you could lose your license for all this? And for what you're doing to Nick!" She backed away hastily as he took a step toward her. "Don't you touch me, Sam. I warn you. You'd better go!"

Sam grabbed her wrist. "Oh, come on, Judy." He pulled her toward him. "Don't play the shy virgin with me—you know what it's all about. I need you. Believe me, I need you."

There was no room for her to pull away from him in the small kitchen, trapped as she was between the worktop and a cabinet, and before she

383

knew what was happening he had seized her mouth, forcing his tongue between her teeth. For a moment she was too shocked to move, then, tearing herself away, leaning backward over the work surface, she gave him a stinging slap across the face. "I'll give you two minutes to get out of here!" she spluttered furiously. "Then I'm calling the police."

He laughed. "Just try it." He staggered very slightly as he moved toward her again.

Sam reached for her, but she had ducked past him, and, dodging his grasp, she ran through the studio and into her bedroom, where she slammed the door and locked it. Breathing in tight, angry gasps, she waited, listening. Sam was coming after her. She heard him knock into something in the studio and flinched. "Please, God, not the painting." Throwing herself on the bed, she grabbed the phone on the table on the far side of it, punched in 999, then she waited, holding her breath as the handle of her door rattled.

The police were there in four minutes.

When the doorbell rang she unlocked the door cautiously and came out, pulling the belt of her robe more tightly around her as she peered out into the studio. Two uniformed constables were already standing there, staring around, their caps held beneath their arms. Sam had opened the door to them.

"Are you the lady who phoned for assistance?" one of them asked as Judy appeared.

She nodded. "You bet I did. This bastard is as drunk as a lord and I want him out of here." She pushed her sleeves up to the elbows, unconsciously businesslike. "He tried to force his attentions on me."

"Right, sir." One of the policemen turned to Sam. "It sounds as if you'd outstayed your welcome. What about going home and sleeping it off, eh?"

Sam glared at him. "If you think I'm drunk, officer, you are a poor judge of men."

"I'm not saying you're drunk, sir," the constable said evenly. "Just that this lady would like you to go."

Sam swayed gently.

Judy caught her breath.

"She is a painter of pornographic filth," he went on thoughtfully. "She should be locked up for producing suggestive muck like this." He gestured at the broad canvas with its impasto of pale colors.

"Doesn't look pornographic to me, sir," the other police officer said slowly. "In fact it looks very pretty."

"*Pretty!*" Sam's scorn distracted them from Judy's indignation. "It is ugly! Ugly and twisted and tortured, like a woman's mind." Before anyone could stop him, he grabbed the canvas and wrenched it from the easel. Judy's scream of anguish did not stop him from bringing it down with a violent crack across his knee. He hurled it into the corner of the studio and

384

laughed, then he moved toward the wall. "More pictures. It hurts, doesn't it, Judith! It hurts when I destroy them. Are they a part of you, then? Children? Bastard children? Like Matilda gave me?"

The two officers closed on him before he got near the wall.

"That's enough, sir."

For a moment Sam hesitated and something that might have been regret showed in his eyes as he stared down at the ruined painting. Then it was gone. "Enough?" he yelled. "Enough! The day I hear my daughter is another man's bastard! *Christ Almighty!*" He tore his arm out of the policeman's grasp and took a furious swing at the man's face, splitting his lip so the blood spattered across his chin. "Don't you tell me that's enough!" he shouted again as they dived on him. "I haven't even begun!"

Pete typed the last line of his story, ripped the paper out of the machine, switched it off, and sat back with a contented sigh. He glanced at his watch. It was nearly four A.M.

He picked up his glass and sipped contentedly at a brandy and soda as he read through the piece. It was neat, snappy; not dream-factory stuff like the last one, but still very, very romantic. He grinned maliciously. This would show Bet Gunning what he thought of her claim to exclusive rights! And if it had the side effect of pushing Nick and Jo together once and for all, well and good. That would leave the sexy and informative Miss Curzon for him.

He leaned forward and switched off the desk lamp, then, stretching, he stood up and walked across to the open window. Staring out at the silent street, he took a deep breath of the warm fragrant air. At this time of night when the accursed traffic slept at last you could smell the flowers from Regent's Park.

The room was very cold. Jo shivered violently, curling up for a moment as tightly as she could to try to find some warmth, and she felt around, her eyes still shut, trying to pull the bedclothes over her again. There were none there. Puzzled, she opened her eyes and stared around.

She was lying on the carpet in her bedroom. For a moment she lay still, her mind a blank, then slowly she sat up. Outside the closed curtains she could hear the clatter of dustbins in the mews and the roar of traffic in the distance from the Cromwell Road. Overhead a broad-bellied jumbo jet was flying low across London, heading for Heathrow. Stiff and aching, she stood up slowly, and, still disoriented, she stood still for a moment. Then, suddenly realizing that she was cold because she had no clothes on, she moved awkwardly to the door and unhooked her bathrobe, wrapping it around her. Her shoulders ached and there was a raw streak of pain across her back.

Wearily she drew back the heavy curtains, letting the daylight flood into the room. Her bed was still made, the covers unrumpled. Her clothes were on the floor and she picked them up. Her dress was torn down the front, ripped almost in half. She stared at it, feeling the first stirrings of panic. She had been in the castle—which castle? She could not remember now, and William had been there—a furiously angry William who had forced her to undress and had struck her with his belt.

Her mouth went dry. She turned and fled into the bathroom, tugging on the light cord and throwing off the bathrobe as she turned to look at her back in the huge mirror. There was an angry bloody welt across it, reaching from her left shoulder blade across and around to her ribs on the other side. She swallowed hard, trying to control the urge to retch, her hands shaking so much she could barely turn on the tap and splash cold water over her face. It was now she needed Carl Bennet's expert's advice on hysterical and psychosomatic manifestations! Yesterday she had produced none, but now! She bit back a sob, burying her face in a towel. Now she had produced a beauty!

Painfully she dressed. Then she wandered, still feeling strangely disoriented, to the front of the apartment. The balcony doors were open, the remains of a meal spread on the coffee table. She must have gone into a trance quite suddenly after Nick had left. She picked up the three placemats—then she frowned again. Sam. Sam had been there too. When had he left? He had not gone with Nick—she had made him some coffee —or had she? Frowning, she carried the things through into the kitchen and stared around. All the paraphernalia for making coffee was spread around on the worktop, the jar of instant still open. She screwed the lid on automatically; she would never normally have left a coffee jar unsealed. Had it happened then, while she was busy? It didn't make sense. Nor did the spoonful of coffee in the bottom of each cup, the kettle unplugged, full, standing on the worktop, the milk—sour—out of the refrigerator. She sighed and plugged in the kettle again, then thoughtfully she made her way to the phone.

She dialed Nick's apartment.

There was no reply. She glanced at her watch. It was after nine. Nick could already be on his way to the airport and Sam must have gone out. As she slammed down the receiver, she winced at the pain in her shoulder.

After making herself a cup of coffee, she carried it back to the bedroom thoughtfully. At least there would be no baby crying today; he had gone, faded, like the strange discarnate dream he must have been, now that her children were all grown up.

She put the cup down on the mahogany chest of drawers in the corner, then she frowned. Her tape recorder was sitting there beside a pile of magazines and she distinctly remembered putting it in the drawer in the living room the day before, after they had come back from Devonshire Place. She clicked it open and looked down at the unfamiliar tape. Then, puzzled, she slotted it back into position and switched it on. For a moment there was silence, then the haunting, breathy sounds of a flute filled the room.

"No!" She clapped her hands to her ears. "No, it's not possible! It was in the castle, not here! No one could have recorded it! Not from my dream!"

The sound filled the room; the sound the old man had made, sitting in the corner of the bedchamber as William humiliated her; the sound that had gone on without ceasing even when he had raised the leather thong and brought it down across her shoulders. Shaking her head, she desperately tried to block out the sounds, then she grabbed the tape recorder and switched it off, ejecting the cassette and turning it over and over with trembling hands. It wasn't a commercial recording. On the blank label someone had written *perpetuum mobile.* Nothing else. There was no clue as to the player or the instrument. Dropping the tape as if it had burned her, she stared around the room, trying to calm herself. Was this some joke of Sam's? Some stupid trick to make her regress even when she had no wish to? Some way of hypnotizing her without the preliminaries—even without her knowledge? She pushed her hair out of her eyes with both hands and took a deep breath. But surely he wouldn't do such a thing! Why should he want to? And if he had, why hadn't he stayed with her and woken her himself? Her eyes fell suddenly on the torn dress in the corner where she had thrown it across the chair, and she felt the breath catch in her throat. "Oh, no," she whispered out loud. "No, Sam, no! You wanted to help me! Why should you want to hurt me, Sam? Why?"

For a moment she thought the sharp sound of knocking was from inside her head and she winced, putting her hands to her ears, then she realized suddenly that the noise came from the hall. There was someone knocking on her front door. For a moment she couldn't bring herself to move. Then slowly she turned.

It was Sheila Chandler from upstairs. The woman smiled tightly. "How are you, dear? We haven't heard the baby lately."

Jo forced herself to smile back. "The baby has gone," she said.

"I see. Look, I don't want always to seem to be complaining"—Sheila looked down sideways as if overcome with embarrassment—"and we never would on a weekend, of course, that would be different, but, well, it is only Wednesday, and it really was so terribly loud—and it was one in the morning!"

Jo swallowed. "I know. I'm terribly sorry. I don't quite know how it happened."

Sheila nodded. "I expect your boyfriend had had a bit too much to drink. He doesn't seem to have been himself lately, does he?" she said pointedly. Her eyes were busy, darting past Jo into the apartment. "Harry said he heard him leave. He must have missed his footing on the stairs, Harry said, because he swore so dreadfully! So it echoed up and down the stairwell. My dear, I know blasphemy doesn't mean anything to you younger people these days, but really, to swear by Christ's bones! What in the world is it, dear? Are you all right?"

Jo had grabbed at the door jamb for support as the blood drained from her head and a strange roaring filled her ears. She felt the other woman's fingers on her elbow, then an arm was around her shoulders as slowly Sheila helped her back inside the apartment and pushed her gently down onto the sofa. She realized Sheila was bending over her, her face full of concern. Her mouth was moving; she was still talking. With an enormous effort Jo tried to understand what she was saying. "Shall I get you some water, dear?" The words seemed to come from a huge distance away. Weakly Jo shook her head.

William! William had been there in the flat with her! Like the baby, other people had heard him. He had shown himself as a real presence.

She sat up with a terrific effort of will. "I am sorry." She took a deep steadying breath. "I—I saw a doctor yesterday about these dizzy spells. They're so silly. I'll—I'll try to make sure there isn't any noise in future. I am sorry you were disturbed, only William—" She bit off a hysterical laugh. "William doesn't understand about apartments. He's not used to them, you see. In fact, he's not really used to neighbors at all."

Sheila stood up and with a little automatic gesture twitched her skirt straight. "I see. He lives in the country, does he? Well, we'll say no more about it." She glanced around the room. "Do call upstairs, dear, if you are feeling poorly, won't you? I'm always in. Would you like me to make you a nice cup of tea now?"

Jo shook her head. "That's kind but I've some coffee, and I was just going to get dressed." She pulled herself upright. "Once again, I am sorry about the noise."

Obviously reluctant to leave, Sheila backed slowly toward the hall, but at last she was once more out on the landing and resolutely Jo closed the door behind her.

Slowly she walked back toward the bedroom and picked up her cold cup of coffee. Sipping it with a grimace, she sat down on the end of the bed; she hadn't even the energy suddenly to go and warm it up.

On the floor something touched her bare foot.

Looking down, she saw, half hidden by the folds of the bedspread, a broad leather belt.

"Look, Jo, I can only take a short break." Tim tucked the receiver closer to his ear as he looked over his shoulder at the two models on the dais. He sighed. "I tell you what. I'll meet you at Temple subway at twelve. We'll go for a quick walk along the Embankment. That really is all the time I can spare today. Are you sure you're okay, Jo?" he added. She sounded strangely tense and breathless.

"I'm fine, Tim. See you at twelve."

As he picked up his camera, he turned back to George with a grimace. "I'm going to have to go out in a couple of hours, so let's get this show on the road. Now," he said.

Jo was sitting on a bench in the Embankment Gardens near the statue of John Stuart Mill, staring reflectively at the pigeons pecking around her feet. She glanced up with a smile when she saw him. "Have you ever tried to photograph that incredible color in their necks? I'd love an evening dress like that."

"Try shot silk," Tim said dryly. He was looking down at her intently. "You look very tired. What's the matter, Jo?"

"Can we walk up through the Temple?" She stood up and he saw her flinch slightly as she hitched the strap of her bag onto her shoulder. "It'll help to keep moving."

"Anything you like." With a half-regretful glance at the roses in the beds behind them, he fell into step beside her in silence, from time to time glancing at her. He was puzzled and a little apprehensive.

"I had to talk to someone, Tim," she said at last as they climbed the steps up into Essex Street slowly. "I'm going to give it all up. The book, the articles, the whole idea. I'm not going to follow it through anymore." She hesitated. "I thought I might fly over to the States."

"With Nick, you mean?" His voice was carefully neutral as they walked slowly down Devereux Court and turned into the Temple.

"He left this morning—" She stopped, then she began again, fumbling for words. "I can't cope, Tim. Last night something happened." She eased her bag on her shoulder uncomfortably as they stood staring at the fountain. The high jet of water glittered in the sunlight, spattering slightly out of the circular base. Where they stood the grass had been walked away, save here and there where a few blades stuck up through the dusty soil, but in the shade of the trees the air smelled cool and fresh from the water. There was a yellow iris in the corner of the pool. She stared at it in silence for a moment.

"Sam came over."

Tim's eyes narrowed.

"Some strange things happened, Tim, and they frightened me." She began walking again and he followed her. "I had a regression, but I don't think it was spontaneous. And I don't think I was alone."

"You think Sam hypnotized you?"

"He's done it before. I asked him to. But this time I hadn't, and I wanted him to leave, but I don't think he did. I think he hypnotized me without my even knowing it. This morning I found—" She bit her lip. "I found a tape of music that I remember from the trance. Flute music, and I don't think they even had flutes at that period—or at least not that kind of flute. It's the only anachronistic thing that's happened. And there was

389

something else—" Again she stopped. This time she couldn't go on. Glancing at her, Tim saw her face was pale, the skin drawn tight with fatigue and worry. He drove his hands into the pockets of his trousers, his fists clenched.

"What else, Jo?" he said softly.

She shook her head. "Tim, I think Sam may have somehow been directing the whole thing. I don't think any of it was genuine after all. I think he's behind it all—even you and Nick. Somehow he's manipulated us all into believing that it was all real. Do you know, this morning when my nosy neighbor came down to complain about the music in the night, she said she'd heard someone leave the apartment and I thought it was William! I thought somehow he had manifested himself into a physical presence, like a ghost! Then I realized it must have been Sam they heard. It was Sam all the time. Sam still somehow pretending to be William . . ."

Slowly they had walked on toward the Temple Church, and on impulse Tim pushed open the door and gestured to Jo to go in ahead of him out of the hot brilliant sunlight into the cool of the interior.

"I have a feeling the whole thing is some sort of horrible hoax," she went on, scarcely noticing where they were going. "I think Sam might even somehow have initiated the whole thing all those years ago when I was a student. None of it is real, Tim." Her whispered words echoed around the silent church. "And I can't bear it. I wanted it to have happened." She took a deep breath, trying to steady the shakiness in her voice. "I know I'm not being objective! I know I'm being stupid and sentimental and I should have my head x-rayed again, but I can't bring myself to believe it's a hoax! I don't want to believe it's a hoax!"

"It's not a hoax, Jo," Tim said softly. "In some ways I wish to God it were. But you are right in one thing. Sam is involved. He came to see me last week and I knew it then. He is part of it, Jo."

She stared at him. "How?" she breathed.

"There were three of us, Jo, three men who all loved you as Matilda. And who all love you now."

In the silence that followed they looked up, startled, as a tourist, walking slowly around the church behind them, raised his camera and took a flash picture over Jo's shoulder. He grinned at them apologetically and moved on.

Jo stared down unseeing at the stone effigy of a knight lying before them on the ground. "Three men?" she echoed in a whisper. "Who?"

Tim shrugged. "The only one I know about is Richard," he said sadly. "Only Sam and Nick can tell you who they were, if you don't know yet."

There was a long silence.

"Sam hates Nick," Jo said softly. "I never realized it until Mrs. Franklyn told me, then suddenly it was so obvious, in everything he does and everything he says."

390

"How well do you know Sam?" Tim put his arm around her shoulder.

Gently Jo moved away from him. "I've known him about fifteen years. I like him. He's fun and he's kind and he's very attractive. If Nick hadn't come along I suppose I might have—" She stopped abruptly. "Oh, Tim—" Her voice shook.

Tim took a deep breath. "Don't let him hypnotize you again, Jo. Don't ever trust him."

"No," she whispered. "No. But it doesn't matter now, because it's all over. Whether it's real or not, it is over. And I wanted you to know because . . . because you are . . . were . . . involved."

Tim bowed slightly. "Thanks." He gave a rueful grin suddenly. "How strange! Do you see where we are, Jo?" He indicated the effigies at their feet.

She stared down.

One of the four stone effigies that lay with their feet toward the east was the carved figure of William Marshall, first Earl of Pembroke. On his left arm he carried a shield, in his right hand a sword. His face, moustached and bland, stared from his mail hood up past them toward the dome of the church, the eyes wide. One foot was broken, the other rested on a small snarling animal. A thin ray of sunlight straying through the clear glass of one of the south windows touched his face.

"We knew him, you and I," Tim said softly.

For a moment neither of them moved, then Jo turned and, with a little sob, she almost ran from the church.

Tim followed her slowly, closing the door behind him with a clatter that echoed in the silence of the building.

She was standing outside, staring up at the sky. "I am going, Tim," she said wildly. "I am going to the States. None of this will matter there."

Tim nodded slowly. "So. When will you leave?"

She shrugged. "I'm seeing Bet late this afternoon. There's a contract I've got to tear up." She gave a rueful laugh. "Once that is over I'll sort things out and leave as soon as I can." She shivered. "It's cold. Let's do what you first suggested and walk down along the river."

The tide was high, the moored ships riding up alongside the river wall, the thick Thames water deeply opaque as it slopped cheerfully against the gray stone. They leaned on the wall and stared over at the river boats chugging up the center of the tide. Tim's fingers itched suddenly for his camera as he stared south toward the opposite bank. The choppy water, sparkling in the breezy sunlight, threw a rippled haze of refracted light onto the black paintwork of the old Thames barge moored against the green piles.

He took a deep breath. If Jo could throw off the past, surely to God he could too!

Slowly they began to walk west toward Westminster. He glanced at his watch. "I have got to get back by two, Jo," he said gently. "I've got another session starting then."

She smiled. The wind had pushed the hair back from her face, bringing some color back to her cheeks. "You do think I'm right to go, Tim." She was almost pleading suddenly.

"One can't run away from destiny, Jo." He didn't look at her. "But then your destiny is tied up with Nick."

"Is it?" she said in a small voice. "All I know is, I want to be with him." She walked on, her eyes narrowed in the dazzle of light off the water, watching the gulls wheeling and diving in the wake of a police launch as it churned westward. "The trouble is, I have a feeling that in that previous life of ours he hated me."

"You do know who he was, then?"

Tim had almost to run to keep up with her as she began to walk faster and faster. Then she stopped dead, staring unseeing toward the Festival Hall across the glittering water.

"But it's not real, Tim," she said at last. "That part of it is not real."

Tim clenched his fists in his pockets as she began walking once more, but he said nothing. It wasn't until they reached Westminster that she stopped again.

She turned to him at last. "You'll have to take the subway back if you're going to make it by two. I'm sorry. I've made you late."

He nodded.

"Tim"—she caught his hands—"Tim, that night in Raglan. I'm glad it happened."

He smiled at her. "So am I, Jo." The smile broadened. "I owe destiny one now."

"Perhaps in our next life . . . ?"

He laughed out loud. "It's a date."

He stood watching as she dodged across the road and jumped on a bus as it moved up the road, then he turned toward the steps that led to the station near Westminster Pier. His smile had died as swiftly as it had come.

"No! No! No!" Bet slammed her fist on her desk, making the pens jump up in the air. "No, you can't tear up that contract! I won't let you! If you try to wriggle out of this I'll see your name is mud with every magazine in the country!"

Jo sat tight-lipped in front of her. "Look, for God's sake, be reasonable!"

"I am being reasonable! I have offered you as much time as you need. I've promised you a monumental fee. I've offered any research facilities you care to name. I arranged for one of London's top photographers to go with you to Wales. I will do any goddamn thing you like, Jo, but I want that series! What's wrong, anyway? Is it Nick? He's put you up to this, hasn't he, the bastard! Or is it that you are afraid of him?" Her eyes were probing suddenly. "You didn't tell me what happened in Wales."

Jo looked away. "Not much," she said guardedly. "Look, Bet, please. You won't get me to change my mind—"

"Then you've got to give me a good reason for your decision. Did Nick threaten you?"

Shaking her head, Jo sighed. "On the contrary. He told me he loved me."

"But! There has to be a but!"

Jo smiled. "You're right, of course. There are so many buts. Even so, I want to go to New York to be with him."

Bet groaned. "Jo, do you know what the temperature in New York was yesterday? It was ninety-four degrees with a humidity of ninety percent. Are you serious about going? You've only to touch another human being and you both die of nuclear fusion."

Jo laughed. "Isn't it fission? If I remember, they've got pretty efficient air-conditioning over there—"

"Passion flourishes on the streets," Bet said darkly. With her customary impatience she stood up and went to her favorite stance by the window. "If it's not Nick, then something else has happened to frighten you off," she said over her shoulder.

"Yes."

"Are you going to tell me what?"

"I don't think so, Bet. Let's just say that I'm worried about my sometimes tenuous grip on sanity."

Bet laughed. "Oh, that!"

"Yes, that. I'm not doing it, Bet. And you know you can't make me. That contract only bound me to exclusivity."

Bet threw herself back into her chair. She took a deep breath. "Okay, I tell you what. Let's both go away and think about it, and in the meantime you can do me a favor to put me in a good mood."

Jo relaxed a little, but even so she eyed Bet suspiciously. It was not like her to surrender so easily. "What favor?"

"I'm planning to run an article about a fellow called Ben Clements and his wife. He is one of these self-sufficiency buffs. The types you were about to try to discredit in your original series. Back to nature, nostalgia—everything modern and chemical and easy is bad. Everything old and muddy and difficult is good. How would you like to go and interview them for me? I want a nice three pages with pictures. But not Tim Heacham this time, please. I can't afford it."

"I've heard of Clements," Jo said thoughtfully. "He lives up in the Lake District somewhere, doesn't he?"

Bet looked vague. "I heard he's moved. I'll call up the file if you're interested."

Jo smiled. "Okay. If I can do it straight away I will, just to put you in that good mood. Then I'll go to New York."

Bet leaned forward and pressed the buzzer on her desk. "Sue? Get the Ben Clements file, would you?" She glanced over her glasses at Jo. "You won't back out of this?"

"I won't back out of it." Jo stood up. "You've got to try to understand about the other thing, Bet. It's not just a series of articles. It's *me*, and I can't be objective about what's happening anymore."

The door opened and Bet's secretary appeared with a manila folder. She grinned at Jo as she put it on Bet's desk.

Bet flipped open the file. In it were one or two cuttings, some notes, and a photograph. She passed the photo to Jo. "There he is, a nice old boy by the look of him."

Jo studied the face before her. Ben Clements looked as if he were in his early sixties, his hair and beard white, his face tanned and wrinkled, netted with a thousand laughter lines.

"I gather he has a young wife, and hers is the angle we want, of course. Here"—Bet thrust the file at her—"stick that in your bag and work on it when you get home. I am scheduling it for the December issue, so I'll want it by the sixteenth at the latest. Obviously I don't want you to make it too summery—but you needn't waffle on about Father Christmas on the farm. I've enough references to seasonal spirit in the rest of the issue. I'm trusting you, Jo. Normally I'd get one of our own feature writers on this."

Jo took the file. "Don't worry, Bet. You've made me feel so guilty already that I won't let you down. I promise. I wouldn't mind a trip up north actually."

"He's moved, I told you. But you'll find all the details in there." She looked at her watch. "God, I've got a meeting downstairs in three minutes. Good luck with the article."

Jo didn't open the file until she was home. She threw herself down on the sofa and, kicking off her sandals, put her feet on the coffee table before taking out Ben Clements's photo and studying it closely. As Bet had said, he looked a nice old boy.

She tipped the contents of the file out onto her lap and looked through it. His address and phone number were on a card by themselves, the last item to come to hand. Jo picked up the card and looked at it, then she put it down. For a moment she stared into space, then slowly she began to laugh. "You are seven kinds of no-good clever scheming cow, Bet Gunning," she said out loud to the empty room. "But it won't change my mind!"

The card read:

The headline in the morning paper in huge black letters was BAD KING
JOHN GOOD FOR JO. Judy stared at it in stunned silence as she stood on
the curb, not seeing the traffic as it streamed within inches of her along the
Fulham Road. Pete had done it! He had printed what she had told him,
word for word!

> Advertising executive Nick Franklyn can comfort himself after his
> latest big disappointment in the world of business. In the wake of live-
> in girl friend Jo Clifford's revelations about her previous life as a
> medieval femme fatale, Nick, not to be outdone, had himself hypno-
> tized by his psychiatrist brother. Imagine his surprise when he found
> out that in his previous life he had been, not Jo's lover, nor her
> husband, but her king!

Judy folded the paper abruptly and shoved it in the litter bin on the
lamppost beside her. She felt slightly sick. Turning, she began to walk
slowly up the road, pushing her hands deep into the pockets of her peacock-blue jeans. Pete had promised he would not tell anyone who had
given him the story, but would he keep his word? She bit her lip nervously. Nick was in the States, but someone was bound to tell him about
the article. Jo would see it too. And Sam. She shivered.

Sam had spent the rest of the night he had been arrested in jail. He had
appeared before the magistrates on Wednesday morning contrite and very
sober, accompanied by his impeccable character and his professional quali-
fications, to say nothing of Nick's solicitor, Alistair Laver. The outcome
had been a heavy fine, and he was bound over to keep the peace. When he
rang Judy later to apologize she hung up on him.

She bought a pint of milk and some bread and cheese, and on second
thoughts another copy of the paper, then she made her way back to the
studio.

Pete answered on the second ring. "Hi! Have you seen the article?"

Judy grimaced. "It's a bit sensationalized, isn't it?"

Pete laughed. "I thought you wanted it shouted from the rooftops. That
was the biggest print I could persuade the editor to use without being
considered vulgar! Has the victim screamed yet?"

"Pete! You're looking for trouble!"

"No. No. I was just doing a lady a favor."

Judy sighed. "I almost wish I hadn't told you now. It seems a cheap
thing to do. Nick's in the States. Jo is the only one who is likely to see it."

Pete chuckled. "And the redoubtable Ms. Gunning. I can't wait for her to spot it. I tell you what, sweetie. Why don't you and I have lunch? We'll split a bottle of bubbly and plan your next revelation. At this rate I shall have to pay you a retainer. What do you say? Joe Allen's at one?"

"Okay. Thanks, Pete, I'd like that." She hesitated suddenly. "But supposing someone sees us? They might guess it was me that told you!"

"Deny it." Pete was smiling to himself as he stirred milk into his cereal. "Deny everything, Judy. I always do. I'll see you at one o'clock!"

Bet rang Jo at four minutes past eight. "Have you seen what that unprincipled bastard Pete Leveson has done now?"

Jo sat down, pulling the phone onto her knee. "That's a good one, coming from you, Bet! What has he done?"

"He's printed the sequel to your story."

Jo froze. "The sequel?"

"About Nick. Dear God! No wonder I thought there was something odd about him last time I saw him. And to think I nearly—" She shut up abruptly.

"You nearly what, Bet?" Jo said sharply.

"Nothing, Sweetie." Bet swiftly turned on the charm. "Jo, love, you must have known all this for ages. You might have told me! It explains his crazy behavior, for God's sake. And it makes the story so much more exciting. And to have had a declaration of love from him too! You must go through with it, Jo. You must! You do see that, don't you?"

"Bet—" The muscles in her stomach were clenching nervously as Jo sat forward on the edge of her seat. "What exactly does Pete say?"

"Listen. I'll read it to you." Bet read the article aloud in a fast monotone. She paused expectantly when she had finished. "Well?"

For a moment Jo said nothing. Her hands were sweating. She could feel the receiver slipping as she held it to her ear. The room was spinning slowly around her.

"Jo? Jo, are you there?" Bet's insistent voice cut slowly through the pulsing in her head.

Jo managed to speak at last. "Where did he get the story from?"

"He doesn't say. Quote "Close friend of Nick's" unquote. He's timed it well with Nick abroad. It is true, I suppose?"

"I don't know," Jo said. "He never told me he'd been regressed. I asked him but he avoided telling me. It's . . . it's grotesque." Her voice sank to a whisper.

Her suspicions, her worst secret fears—they were true, then, and now the whole world knew. She suddenly felt sick.

"Are you going to call him?"

"No."

"But you must! You've got to ask him if it's true."

"Over the phone? When he's three and a half thousand miles away? If it's true and if he had wanted me to know, he'd have told me." Jo took a deep breath and closed her eyes. "Leave it, Bet. I can't cope with all this. Not now. Please, leave it alone—"

"But, Jo—"

"Bet, you told me Nick wanted to kill me. It wasn't Nick. It was John. It was John who ordered Matilda's death."

There was a long silence. At the other end of the phone Bet's eyes had begun to gleam. "Jo," she began cautiously.

"No," Jo said. "I don't want to talk about it." She changed the subject abruptly. "I called your Mr. Clements in Brecon."

"Oh, good." Bet contained her excitement about Nick with an effort. "When are you going to interview him?"

"On Tuesday. I'll drive down on Monday afternoon and stay with Mrs. Griffiths again. That'll give me a week to write and polish the article for you."

"I knew you'd do it, Jo. And then, if while you're there anything should happen—"

"It won't." Jo's voice was repressive. "Believe me, Bet, it won't. Especially now." Her last words were barely audible.

Bet bit her lip, trying to keep her voice casual. "When was Nick planning to come back?"

"He didn't know. It depended on how things were going in New York."

"And you'll still be going out there when you've finished the article?"

There was a long silence. "I don't know, Bet," Jo said at last. "I'll have to think about it now."

The lane was steep and very rutted when Jo finally arrived at Pen y Garth. Nervously she put the MG into first and crawled up it, waiting to hear the hard-crusted earth ripping out the bottom of the car. At the top of the hill the pitch debouched suddenly onto a mountainside ablaze with gorse and ended in front of a low, whitewashed farmhouse. After drawing up with relief, Jo climbed out and reached for her bag. The familiar smell of mountain grass and wild thyme and bracken filled her lungs, mixed with the acid sweetness of the pale-pink roses that clung and tumbled around the sentry-box porch at the front of the house. Above the white walls there was an uneven roof of thick Welsh slates, green with lichen and speckled with yellow stonecrop.

Jo stared around. The farm faced east toward the Wye Valley. She could see for miles.

"You like our view?" A figure had appeared in the doorway.

Jo smiled. "It's quite breathtaking."

Ben Clements laughed. "In every sense, if you'd walked up from the road. Come in."

She followed him into the single large room that made up the ground floor of the farmhouse. Half kitchen, half living room, the stone floor was scattered with brightly colored rag rugs and littered with toys, the walls crammed with books and pictures.

Jo looked around, startled by the color and the untidiness of it all. "I didn't realize you had small children!" she hazarded as she avoided a wooden train set.

He threw back his head and laughed. "One of the penalties of growing old is insanity in our family! I got married at the age of fifty-seven and, unequal to the horrors of family planning, found myself pregnant, as you might say. Have a drink. I never ask anyone up here before twelve and then I don't have all this silly social nonsense of poncing about with coffee and what not. You can have Scotch or beer."

Jo grinned. She could feel she was going to like this man. "Scotch. Please."

He nodded approval. "I hope you didn't want to see Ann and the kids particularly. She's taken them to Hereford for the day to see some cousin or other who's paying a flying visit."

Jo felt her heart sink. "It would have been nice. I'm writing for a woman's magazine. So the woman's angle is important."

"Ah." He grimaced. "I've screwed things up, haven't I? Conceited male thought it was me you would want to see. My usual interrogators are nearly always men, my dear. Forgive me." He handed her half a tumbler of Scotch, undiluted.

Jo laughed. "I wanted to see you both. Perhaps I could come back when Mrs. Clements is at home and interview her then, and interview you now?"

It would mean staying longer in Hay. Was that what she wanted really? Pushing away the thought, Jo concentrated on the gentle face of the man in front of her. He was still smiling. "Fair enough. So, do you want to see the farm at all?"

Jo reached into her bag for her notebook and camera. She nodded. "I'm going to take some snaps if I may, then we'll send down a proper photographer if mine aren't good enough!"

"Of course they'll be good enough." He led the way to the door. "You mustn't be defeatest, my dear. That won't do at all." He turned. "Ann told me you were a formidable lady, whose articles are nearly always very scathing. That true?"

"Often. Does it worry you?"

"Not a bit!" He ducked under the low doorway and preceded her around the farmhouse to the back, where a stone wall surrounded a large vegetable garden. "I've had everything thrown at me by the farming guys who think I'm crazy. Luckily more and more people are seeing it my way now, and I think people of the organic persuasion are slowly winning through."

Quickly and methodically he showed Jo around the smallholding, supervising her notes and taking most of her photographs for her. Then he led the way back inside and refilled her glass.

"Ann's left a cold lunch for us. Shall we eat outside?" He glanced at her. "I amuse you, don't I?"

Jo smiled. "No. I was just thinking you might as well have given me duplicated notes at the door. You are too used to giving these interviews."

"Okay, I stand reprimanded. Now, you interview me." He carried the plates out to a table outside the back door where the blazing sun was partially deflected from them by a trellis hung with honeysuckle. "Ask me all the questions I haven't answered yet."

Jo sat down. "Does your wife get lonely up here?"

"Shouldn't you ask her that?" His face lit with humor.

"I shall. I just wondered what you thought she felt about it."

"Well." He took a huge mouthful of food. "Ann is a remarkable woman. She has enormous inner resources. Of course, I am presupposing her genuine love of the country, but there is more to it than that. She loves the mountains and the rivers and the loneliness. She loves the soil, the joy of making things grow, just as I do. She likes the people, the villages, the towns—we're not antisocial just because we live up here alone, but neither do we miss people when we don't see them for a while. Like me, she came to Wales as a foreigner. I'm a north countryman; she, God help her, is American! But we have both been completely absorbed by this country with its people and its traditions, its history. These hills may look lonely to you, but they are full of life and dreams and memories. Fascinating. What is it? What have I said?" His shrewd blue eyes had noticed Jo's sudden tenseness.

She forced a smile. "Nothing. Go on."

"You're a skeptic? A townie?"

"No." Jo met his gaze. "I've lived up here too."

"Ah. I wondered why they'd sent *you* particularly. So you understand what I meant. Whereabouts did you live?"

Jo hesitated. Now she had said the words she could hardly retract them, and besides, she had an overwhelming urge to confide in him. After glancing across at his face briefly, she looked away across the falling mountainside toward the misty distance and took a deep breath.

"You'll probably think I am mad. It was a long time ago. In a previous existence." She paused, waiting for his laughter.

He said nothing, however, watching her intently, and after a minute she went on.

399

She told him everything. When she fell silent at last he did not speak for several minutes, gazing silently out across the panoramic view.

"That is a truly amazing story," he said at last. "Truly amazing. I had heard of Moll Walbee, of course. Who hasn't around here? But to have entered so completely into her life, that is extraordinary."

"You believe me, then?"

"I believe it has happened to you, yes. As for the explanation—" He shrugged. "I think I must seek for a more mundane explanation than reincarnation." He smiled enigmatically. "To do with the relativity of time perhaps. I would suggest that you have an area of your brain particularly sensitive to what one might call the echo of time. You have tuned in, as you might say, to Matilda's wavelength and can, when in a state of receptiveness, 'listen in.' " He put his head on one side. "How does that theory sound to you?"

Jo grinned. She leaned forward and pulled her plate toward her again, helping herself to a slice of Ann Clements's crumbling stoneground bread. "To be honest, my brain has given up asking how and why. The last few times it happened I wanted to fight it. I don't want it to happen again. And I think I know how to stop it now. One must not let one's brain be distracted into blankness. It is only receptive when it's idling, like a car engine out of gear."

"Fascinating," Ben said again. "You know, you must talk to Ann about this. She was a psychology major at UCLA and past life recall was a particular interest of hers. She wrote an article about it for one of your sister magazines some time ago. Your editor might even have seen it."

Jo stared at him. Then she gave a wry smile. "I think she may indeed," she said. "It would have been almost too great a coincidence, my coming here otherwise, I suppose." She sighed. "But I am glad I'm here now. Talking about it has helped. Perhaps Bet has done me a favor after all."

He glanced at her under his heavy eyebrows. "I'm not surprised that it has worried you, though. It would scare the pants off me!" He reached for some bread and applied a rich lump of cheese to the crust, then, munching thoughtfully, he sat back in his chair. "But from what you have said it's not your journeys into the past that have upset you and put you off repeating the exercise. It is the involvement of other people in the present. If you don't mind my saying so, it sounds to me as if you've allowed yourself to be too much used by people who seem to have points they all want to prove at your expense, from your journalist colleagues to your boyfriend."

"But they are all involved—"

"Perhaps." He reached forward and touched her hand. "It's a nice theory, but don't be too ready to believe what others say, my dear. Look in your own heart for the answer. That is the only place you'll find the truth. Now, let me get you some cheese. This is our own cream cheese from

Aphrodite and her daughters, or there is a curd cheese from Polyphema, the one-eyed goat." He twinkled at her mischievously. "You must keep your brain fully alert while you are here, Joanna. I am not sure I could cope with a visitation from a baron's lady as well as afternoon milking!"

30

Jo took the wrong road at the bottom of the hill and found herself heading northwest instead of back along the Wye Valley toward Hay. She almost stopped to turn, then on a sudden defiant impulse she drove on into the narrow busy streets of Brecon itself, slowing the car to a standstill in the knotted traffic. She found a place to park, then wandered slowly around the town before climbing to the cathedral with its squat tower. By the time she had reached it she had made up her mind.

After pushing open the door, she walked in, staring around. The guidebook was very informative. It was during the lifetime of Bishop Giles de Breos and his brother Reginald that the eastern part of the original Norman church of Bernard of Newmarch had been replaced by the chancel, tower, and transepts that exist today. Her eye traveled down the lines of close print. Reginald was the only Lord of Brecknock to be buried in the Priory Church. She bit her lip, staring around. Reginald was buried there. There, somewhere beneath the lovely arching vault of the chancel. . . . Suddenly she didn't want to know. Reginald, that sturdy, cheerful boy, her third son, whom she loved in such an uncomplicated way and who had loved her. Her eyes filled with tears, and it was only with an effort that she pulled herself together. After all, she had not needed to come into the cathedral. If she had really wanted no more to do with the de Braose family she should not have gone to Brecon at all. She stood staring up at the high altar with its carved reredos and its offering of flowers below the huge stained-glass window, then forced herself to look back at the guidebook that told about the church of the de Braoses.

There wasn't much left of the castle. A mound and an ivy-covered fragment of wall, that was all, but she was used to that now. She climbed the worn staircase carefully and stood staring out across the rooftops toward the vivid toothed outline of the Beacons. Yes, this view she did remember; the outline in the mist and the sunset behind that faraway bastion of mountains. She dug her nails into the stone blocks of the wall, then, taking a deep, relaxing breath, she deliberately began to empty her mind.

The room was dark and there was a pounding in her temples. She tried to raise her head, then, with a groan, let it fall back on the pillows, lights flashing and searing behind her eyelids. She lay, exhausted, for what seemed a long time, then dazedly she realized there were people in the room with her. Someone helped her to vomit and she lay back again, a cool wet cloth across her burning forehead. She heard Elen's voice, alternately scolding and soothing, and a man's voice intoning something. Was it prayers or a magic charm? She tried to concentrate, but her mind slipped away and wandered again.

Two men in Aberhonddu had died of the plague and one of William's clerks had succumbed, with suppurating boils beneath his armpits. She had visited him, holding a bunch of rue to her nose, and laid a gentle hand on his forehead, trying to ease his pain, before they realized what illness it was that had struck him down.

The summer was cursed. No rain had fallen. The harvest was failing. Heat shimmered and hung over the mountains like an oppressive cloud. Lord Rhys was dead. His sons still fought one another ceaselessly and Gruffydd was imprisoned now at Corfe. There was no news of Tilda, nor of the little son that Gerald had told them she had borne. No news . . . no news . . .

Desperately she called for her nurse, but Jeanne did not come, and Matilda could feel the tears wet on her cheek as the delirium swept her once more into darkness.

A cursed summer. A summer where William had quarreled with Trehearne Vaughan, her kind, scholarly friend, their neighbor at Hay, the man who had given her her Welsh bard, a kinsman of the Welsh princes. His face floated in and out of her dreams with William's. William who never came. William, who kept away from the plague-bound castle and left her to her fate.

It was a long while later that she woke and, for a time, looked around. The pain in her head seemed to have eased for a moment and then she became conscious of the terrible burning in her groin. She groaned and closed her eyes. It had been dark beyond the unshuttered window, but the flickering light from the sconce by her bed seared her eyes; the room was pungent with burning herbs from a brazier. She tried to call out and tell them all to go away—to leave her, to save her children, her babies—but her tongue was swollen and dry in her mouth and no words came. One or two angry tears squeezed out between her swollen eyelids and she slid once more into a half-sleeping dream. When she awoke again her bed was wet with sweat and vomit and there seemed to be no one there to help her. "They have left me to die." The whole of her left side pained her and there was an agonizing cutting pain beneath her arm now as well as on her side.

"Christ! Christ, be with me!" This time she managed a whisper, but at once someone was there, sponging her face. "Be brave, Mother dear. You will be well." It was Margaret's voice, shaking, pleading. "Please, Mother. You must get well." The girl was bending over her, trying to ease away the foul pillow. Matilda heard herself scream as the girl jarred her body and she saw the terror in Margaret's eyes. Then she saw nothing more.

When she next awoke it must have been dawn. The sconces had gone out and the brazier was cold. A pale light was beginning to filter through the unshuttered window opposite the bed, and she could hear the clear, joyful caroling of a thrush from the rowan tree outside in the bailey. She lay quite still, shivering beneath the damp covers, wondering where she was. The room smelled terrible. She tried to lick her lips, but her tongue was too dry. She could feel the sticky pus running down beneath her arm and shoulder. After closing her eyes, she drifted into an uneasy sleep. She did not know it yet, but her indomitable body had won the battle against the plague.

As soon as she was strong enough, she sat in the high arched window of her solar, looking down toward the town and out across the river to the mountains. It worried her that her legs were feeble and unsteady still, but it was pleasant to lose herself for a while in the broad view, resting from her study of the accounts and figures that she had had brought to her bedside. The people of Aberhonddu had suffered terribly from their losses in the plague and the poor harvest, and she knew that they and all her vast estates faced untold hardships, if not starvation, in the coming winter. With her hand pressed to her aching forehead she tried once again to calculate how the meager contents of the granaries within the castle and its farms could be made to stretch.

Her eye was caught suddenly by a flurry of activity near the Honddu Bridge and she sat forward with interest. A small group of horsemen seemed to be waiting there, stirring the dust on the roadway as their impatient animals pawed the ground. Then she saw for whom they were waiting. A party of men-at-arms were riding two by two up the track from the east. Before them, clearly recognizable under his banner, rode William, his surcoat emblazoned with the rising eagle, shimmering in the sun, the black horse on which he rode prancing slightly, resenting the firmly held rein.

The party on the bridge rode forward to meet him and for a moment the two groups of horsemen drew to a halt, facing each other in the dusty road.

Matilda passed her hands over her eyes again, sighing. Her sight had seemed weaker since her illness and all this peering into the glare gave her a headache. She thought at first the flashes of light catching her vision were from her own head but then, with a shock, she realized they came from the sunlight reflecting on drawn swords. She leaned forward suddenly, her heart thumping, and the accounts slid unheeded from her knees to the floor.

The smaller group of men were being beaten back toward the bridge and they seemed to be fighting for their lives. She tried to follow William, lost sight of him, then saw him again. He was determinedly fighting one man, the leader of the other group. Then suddenly it was all over. The man was disarmed. Matilda saw his sword fly, at William's savage stroke, in a great arc, flashing in the sunlight as it fell into the undergrowth by the side of the road. The man was dragged from his horse and his hands bound behind him. Then the victors remounted and at a yell from William set off at the gallop toward the bridge. The man tried desperately to run with them, lost his balance and fell, to be dragged mercilessly behind the horses of his captors. Matilda watched, sickened, until they were out of sight at the gates of the township, and then she turned from the window. So William had come back.

Elen dressed her in her scarlet surcoat as she asked and then went down to find Dai, a shepherd who had come in from the hills to sell his flocks to the drovers and had stayed, working for a while, in the stables of the castle. Somehow it had become his self-appointed task to carry Matilda up and down the steep, winding stairs to her solar and out into the herb garden whenever she required, handling her with such gentleness and ease that she had grown dependent on him in her weakness, although she knew he pined for his hills and would long since have been gone but for her pleas that he stay.

"I will wait for Sir William in the great hall, Dai bach," she said with a smile, and she was rewarded with a long slow grin as with a quiet *"Ie, fyng arglwyddes"* he bent over her.

But William did not come into the hall, although she waited for what seemed like an eternity. When she had almost given up, leaning with closed eyes against the narrow, high-backed carved chair by the hearth, she heard the clatter of hooves and the shouts of men in the bailey outside. Taking a deep breath to steady herself, she pushed herself up from the chair to be standing when William appeared.

"A hanging! There's to be a hanging!"

She heard the excited page call across the hall and saw him scamper out again into the sun. With a quick look over their shoulders in her direction the three men who had been sweeping out the old rushes cast aside their brooms and ran after the page, pushing each other in their haste to leap down the flight of steps outside the hall.

Matilda looked around for Dai but he had gone. The man she had seen must have been some felon William had encountered on his way from Hay and he was going to administer summary justice before bothering to come to greet her. She sighed, thinking of the poor scoundrel she had watched them drag away.

Slowly, with shaking steps, she made her way to the doorway and, clinging to the doorpost for support, looked out at the scene below her in the bailey. The open area between the walls of the keep and the outbuildings that clustered round the outer walls was full of men and horses. Her husband was the only man still mounted. She saw him at once, and near him a soldier on a ladder was easing a rope across a beam that jutted beyond the rough stones of the wall.

She could see no sign of the prisoner. William's face shocked her. It was cruelly twisted, full of hatred and malice, and though he looked straight at her, she knew that he hadn't seen her.

She glanced up, shuddering, at the serene sky and at the heavy fruit on the rowan tree growing in the bailey above the teeming, shouting men. The women of the castle had gathered together near the kitchens and gossiped quietly as they waited curiously, their eyes on the crowd of men. Matilda felt a touch on her arm. Margaret was standing behind her. "Come away, Mother. Don't watch."

Matilda shrugged her off. "I've seen hangings before, child. I was looking for your father."

A sudden noise, half shout, half sigh, made her turn back to the scene below. They had thrust the prisoner up onto the back of a raw-boned horse and were leading him beneath the noose. His face was covered in mud and blood, but as she glanced at him compassionately, Matilda suddenly gave a gasp.

"It's Trehearne Vaughan from Clyro! It's Trehearne," she cried desperately. "Dear God, is William out of his mind? We've got to stop him. Margaret, help me quickly!" She pushed forward, gripping her daughter's arm.

"William, for Christ's sake, stop!" she screamed. "Don't do it! At least take time to decide—" But her cry was lost in the roar of the crowd as, with a thwack on its rump, the horse was sent careering across the cobbles, leaving Trehearne hanging from the beam. His legs kicked violently.

"Cut him down, for God's sake!" she screamed again above the noise of the crowd. "Oh, God! Oh, God, stop it! Save him!" She never knew how she found the strength to cross the bailey, but at last she was by her husband. "William, you can't know what you're doing!" She grabbed at his bridle and his horse reared back, its eyes wild. "Cut him down, for the love of God." She groped at him frantically, her eyes blinded with tears.

William glanced down at her for a moment unseeing, his face a twisted mask, then suddenly he seemed to realize she was there as she pulled desperately at his mantle. He smiled, and abruptly she stepped back in fear. "Cut him down. A good idea." He forced his plunging horse toward the man and sliced through the rope with one stroke of his sword. Trehearne fell to the cobbles and lay there twitching, his face swollen and purple beneath the mask of drying blood.

406

Looking down at him for a moment, William, in the expectant hush around him, suddenly laughed. "I think we'll have his head," he said in a tone so quiet that Matilda scarcely heard it. He beckoned and two men-at-arms caught up the spasmodically jerking body and dragged it to the stone mounting block. There, at a nod from William, one of them struck off the man's head with one blow from his heavy two-edged sword. A great sigh ran round the bailey, followed by a yell and wild cheering.

All around her men and horses had begun to move again, the spectacle over. There was work to be done. Ignoring the fallen trunk of the man and the bloodied head that lay on the cobbles where it had fallen, William reined back his terror-stricken horse and rode past Matilda to the steps of the great hall. Dismounting, he flung his rein to a squire and stamped up into the doorway without a backward glance.

Matilda stood where she was in the middle of the bailey, holding Margaret's arm. The girl's face was white and Matilda could see the blue veins in her temples beating wildly. Swallowing with an effort the bitter bile that had risen in her throat, she began slowly to walk back toward the keep, consciously keeping her back straight, forcing her steps one by one as she leaned on Margaret's shoulder, feeling the curious glances being cast in her direction by the dispersing crowd.

Dai appeared as she reached the steps and, unceremoniously picking her up, carried her back to the chair by the hearth. William was pouring himself wine from the jug on the table.

"*Fyng arglwyddes,* may I have your permission to return to my hills?" She suddenly realized that Dai was kneeling before her, his face a pasty yellow. "I no longer wish to serve you. I'm sorry, *meistress bach. Dioer,* you were good to me indeed, you were, but I cannot stay."

"I understand, Dai." She sighed. Her hands were shaking uncontrollably. "God go with you, my friend."

She watched him stride toward the doorway, expecting him to turn, but he didn't. Neither did he so much as acknowledge William's presence standing behind them. He went out onto the steps without a backward glance and ran down out of sight.

Margaret pressed a goblet of wine into her hand. "Drink this, Mother, you look so pale." She glanced apprehensively over her shoulder toward her father, but he continued to ignore them, pouring himself another goblet and emptying it down in one gulp.

Matilda turned and looked at him at last. "Did Trehearne really merit such high-handed, barbaric treatment, William?" she asked, her voice trembling.

He set down the goblet with a bang on the trestle. "In my opinion, madam, he did."

"He seemed to be waiting for you at Aberhonddu."

"We had arranged to meet there, certainly." He strode down off the dais. "He seemed to think we could discuss our differences and part friends. Ha! He misjudged me!"

Matilda raised an eyebrow. "So, I think, do a lot of people, William," she murmured in disgust. "Have you thought of the repercussions that will follow? Trehearne was well liked by others as well as me, and he has powerful kinsmen."

"So he couldn't stop telling me. The man blabbed like a coward. He thought you could stop me. He thought Gwenwynwyn would avenge his death and that the Marches will be alight from Chester to Monmouth with revenge for his scrawny bones." He turned and spat viciously into the rushes. "I doubt if he's as important as he thinks.

"Page!" he yelled at the boy who was listening, open-mouthed, by the serving screens. "Help me off with my hauberk before I send you after Gwenwynwyn, you imp!" He threw back his head and laughed, then he hurled his goblet at the wall, where it struck and rolled away, dented, into a corner.

Lying taut and sleepless in bed that night next to her snoring husband, Matilda could not close her eyes.

The picture of Trehearne's pitiful death kept rising before her, and with it the sight of her husband's laughter. William seemed to care neither for the death of a neighbor and her friend nor for his broken word—for he had, it appeared, given Trehearne safe conduct to travel through his lands —nor for the revenge that would undoubtedly follow. His conceit and his overweening arrogance were complete.

And, though it didn't seem important anymore, she could not help but notice that he had not once inquired for her health or excused his own flight from Brecknock in the summer. When they had finally gone to bed he had been incapably drunk.

There were tears on her cheeks when Jo came to. She remained quite still, leaning against the wall, her eyes fixed on the mighty summit of Pen y Fan, and for a moment she did not dare move, wondering, with a shudder of disgust, if she still had the marks of the plague sores on her body. Then suddenly, below her in the street, she heard some children laughing. The sound acted like a charm, easing away the awful realities of the stench and filth and misery of her trance. She stood upright, feeling the sun beating down on her head. There was a throbbing in her temples and the perspiration trickling down between her shoulderblades was aggravating the raw whiplash across her back, but other than that there was no pain. She shuddered violently. William had indeed much to answer for.

Margiad Griffiths was in the kitchen when Jo arrived back at the house. She glanced at Jo in concern. "There, now, it's ill you're looking again, girl," she said. "Come you in and sit down. And have a glass of my sherry,

408

won't you? I'm all alone here. You're doing too much driving up and down, you are. Why don't you try and stay down here for a bit?"

Jo sat down gratefully on a kitchen chair. "I would like to," she said. "I'm doing two jobs at once, that's the trouble." She sipped the sherry and closed her eyes.

"Do you want to go and have a sleep, girl? I'll get you some supper later." Margiad eyed her closely. She could see the exhaustion on Jo's face, the gray pallor beneath her tanned skin, the lines of pain that had not been there two weeks before when she had first seen her.

Jo shook her head slowly. "Do you believe in destiny, Mrs. Griffiths?"

"Destiny, is it?" Margiad thought for a moment. She pulled out the chair opposite Jo and eased herself into it.

"Fate, you mean? No. I don't. Life is what you make of it yourself. We've no one to blame but ourselves in the end. It's depressed you are, isn't it?"

Jo nodded. "I suppose I am." She reached for the bottle unthinkingly and refilled her empty glass. Margiad, who had not yet sipped her own sherry, said nothing.

"I think I'm being haunted," Jo said softly.

Margiad raised a brisk eyebrow. "Who by?"

"A woman who died nearly eight hundred years ago."

"You mean you've seen her?"

Jo frowned. "She's not a ghost. Not an external thing at all. She's inside me. Somewhere in my mind—memories. . . ." She put down her glass and put her hands over her eyes. "I'm sorry. You must think I'm mad."

Margiad shook her head slowly. "I told my Doreen that you had a fey look about you when first I saw you. You've Welsh blood in you, haven't you, for all your English way of talking?"

Jo groped in her pocket for a tissue. Not finding one, she stood up and tore a paper towel from the roll over the sink. "I think I must have," she said slowly.

"It is like that with a lot of Celtic people," Margiad said comfortably. "They have the sight. It is not easy for those who cannot control it, but you must learn to live with it. Don't fight what's in you, girl. Accept it as a gift from God."

"But I'm not foreseeing the future," Jo said in anguish. "Though, God knows, perhaps that would be even worse. I'm seeing the past! In great detail."

"Then, there's a reason for it. A truth to be learned, an injustice to be righted—who knows?" Stiffly Margiad stood up. She disappeared into her sitting room and Jo could hear her rummaging around in a drawer. A moment later she returned. In her hands was an old leather-covered Bible. She thrust it at Jo. "Pray if you can, girl. If you can't, just put it under your pillows. It'll ward off the bad dreams. Now, I've a nice stew cooking. It'll

409

be ready in an hour, so you go up and have a hot bath and put all this out of your head!"

Nick lay back on his hotel bed and tore off his tie. His shirt was damp from the heat of the sidewalk outside and he was sweating and uncomfortable but, for the moment, he was too exhausted even to go and stand under the cold shower. He put his arm across his eyes. The presentation had gone well; he should be elated. He listened wearily to the wail of a police siren fifteen floors below on Lexington Avenue.

He was almost asleep when the phone rang beside him. He rolled over onto his elbows and picked up the receiver.

"Nick?" It was Jim Greerson. "How did it go?"

Nick lay back. "Okay. I think things are looking hopeful. How about your end?"

"I had dinner with Mike Desmond as arranged last night. I groveled a bit more, old boy, and then I told him what an ass he was, chucking the best up-and-coming firm in London just because we'd given a break to a new fellow. I told him we'd supervise a new campaign for him personally." He hesitated. "When I say we, I actually said you."

"And?" Nick crossed his ankle over his raised knee. He was gazing up at the ceiling.

"He's not too pleased with the service he's got so far from you know who. I gather he expected them to jump once they'd got a sniff of the account, instead of which, according to him, they send some teenybopper copywriter over. I saw him at a good psychological moment. Besides which, he said he couldn't pass up the opportunity of being serviced by royalty." Jim sniggered.

"Royalty?" Nick leaned over and reached for the jug of orange juice on the bedside table. "What royalty? Don't tell me Prince Edward has decided to become an adman?"

"No, old son. You."

"Me?"

"Your secret life. You mean you don't know it's blown? It's all over the papers here, for God's sake. The *Mail* had it on Thursday and the *Standard* on Friday."

Nick sat up. "What secret life? What the hell are you talking about?"

"Hang on, hang on. I'll find the page and read it to you. Bear with me, old boy. It's midnight here, and I've had a hard day."

Nick lay still, his eyes closed, as Jim read the piece to him over the transatlantic line. He felt completely detached, as if the person being talked about were someone else. He was not surprised, not even indignant. Merely very, very weary.

When Jim finished there was a brief silence. "Is it all true, old boy?" Jim said tentatively after a moment.

"It's true that I let my brother hypnotize me, yes," Nick said curtly. "As to what happened, you'll have to ask him. I remember nothing about it. It all seems very far-fetched." He heard himself laugh. "I suppose Judy Curzon is responsible for this. I'll wring her neck when I get back."

"Better send her to the Tower, old boy, it's more in character." Jim laughed uproariously. "You haven't heard from Jo about it, then?" he asked curiously after a moment.

"No," Nick said shortly. "Not a word."

There was a moment's silence, then Jim went on. "Listen, I've got a meeting at eight tomorrow, so I'd best go or I'll never wake up. I'll call you tomorrow, same time, okay?"

Nick replaced the receiver. Sitting up, he swung his legs to the floor. The air-conditioning had made the room very cold. He walked into the bathroom, stripped off his shirt, and turned the shower full on, then he went back to the phone.

"I want to call London," he said brusquely, and he gave his own number.

Margiad Griffiths woke Jo with a cup of tea. She sat down on the edge of Jo's bed. "How did you sleep, then?"

Jo stretched. "Very well. Your charm must have worked." She felt beneath the pillow for the old Bible and touched it lightly.

Margiad nodded. "I knew it would. There was a phone call for you earlier," she went on. She reached into the pocket of her skirt for a piece of paper. "Mr. Clements. He said would you go and have lunch with him and his wife tomorrow about twelve. He said don't call back unless you can't go."

Jo smiled. "That's nice of him. Mr. Clements is the reason I'm here. He's written lots of books on smallholdings and animals and the history of Northumberland. He's bought a place near Brecon."

Margiad stood up. "Famous, is he?" She smiled. "And you're writing about him, are you? Good. That'll take your mind off your other troubles." She hesitated in the doorway. "What will you do today, then?"

Jo sat up, pushing her heavy hair off her face. She glanced at the window where a thin layer of hazy cloud masked the blue of the sky. "I'll stay here another night or two if I may," she said. "I've some notes to write up about Ben Clements, and then—" She hesitated. "Then I think I'll explore Hay a little more."

Heavy swirling black clouds were building up in the western sky although as yet there was no breath of wind. Matilda reined in her horse and glanced up, then she signaled the horsemen around her to hurry as they cantered back down the track toward Hay, following the curving arm of the Wye through the flat dry meadows, throwing up clouds of powdery dust that stung the eyes and choked the throat. A zigzag of lightning lit up the purple sky and sent her horse shying across the path of her companion, Lady de Say, who swore like a man and grabbed at the pommel of her saddle to prevent herself from being thrown. It was unbearably hot.

"I'll wager a silver penny we can get back before the first raindrop falls," Matilda called over her shoulder. She was exhilarated suddenly by the threat of the storm.

It had been a bitter and unhappy year, and she had been preoccupied during much of the ride with dark thoughts of the events that had followed Trehearne's murder. His death had served, inevitably, as an excuse for more fighting in the hills and the intervention of his kinsman, the increasingly powerful Prince Gwenwynwyn, who had laid siege to Painscastle in his turn with a huge force of men. In a last attempt at mediation their son-in-law, Gruffydd, had, at Matilda's suggestion, been brought back to Hay from his imprisonment at Corfe. But his surly attempts as a peacemaker failed and on 13 August, the feast of Holy Hippolytas, hostilities had culminated in a major pitched battle in the hills behind Trehearne's home at Clyro, as the barons fought desperately to retain their ascendancy in the borders. They won, but with a terrible toll of Welsh lives.

Another flash of lightning ripped across the sky, followed by a distant rumble of thunder. Putting her dismal thoughts firmly behind her, she raised her whip and urged her horse into a gallop, her veil streaming in the wind, tendrils of hair tearing themselves loose from her wimple and whipping across her eyes.

She raced up the hill into Hay, scattering children and poultry, oblivious of the shaken heads and secret smiles of men and women who saw her pass into the great gates in the walls of her castle. The guards came to attention smartly and Matilda reined in her horse to a rearing, sweating halt. With a glance up at the huge, swollen clouds, she turned to claim her wager from the disheveled, unhappy lady who had tried to keep up with her ahead of their bodyguard, when all thoughts of it were driven suddenly from her head by the sight of a figure coming toward her across the bailey.

Dropping her horse's rein, she gave a short gasp, not daring to believe her eyes.

"Tilda?" she whispered at last as she slipped from the high wooden saddle. "Tilda, is it really you?" The girl had grown as tall as her mother, slim, with silver hair and a complexion as fair as the ivory of a carved crucifix.

"I hope you are well, Mother dear." Tilda smiled and curtsied formally before submitting coolly to her mother's ecstatic kiss. "I have come to be with Gruffydd."

"And your baby, Tilda? Did you bring him?" Matilda held the girl's

412

two hands in her own, gazing into her face. There was so much of Richard there—and so little.

Tilda lowered her lashes. "I have two children now, mother. Rhys who is two, and Owain. He is only seven months. They—" She hesitated, glancing away. "That is, we thought it better that they should remain with Gruffydd's mother and their nurses. I have come alone."

"You mean they wouldn't let you bring the children with you?" Matilda seized on the fact hotly. "The Welsh have kept them as hostages, two small babies!"

"No, Mother, do be calm. It wasn't safe or suitable to bring them, that's all. They are safe and happy where they are. I wouldn't have left them otherwise." Tilda glanced up as the first heavy drops of rain began. "Come, let's go in, Mother. I don't want to tell you my news in front of your entire escort, in a thunderstorm!"

She led the way to the door of the hall, her figure slim and erect like her mother's. But there the similarity ended. Where Matilda was auburn and high-colored, Tilda was pale and ethereal. The mother belonged to the sun, the daughter to the moon.

Since Margaret had gone at last, only a month before, to marry her Walter, the castle had seemed quiet. Of all her children Margaret was the most like her mother, and Matilda missed her support and companionship sorely and dreaded the fact that at any moment Walter would take her away to his earldom across the Irish Sea, in Meath. Isobel was soon to go too, to Roger Mortimer at Wigmore, whose first wife had died in the plague and whose eager suit William had indulgently agreed, so it was a double joy to have her eldest daughter home.

But Tilda proved a hurtful disappointment. She showed little warmth to her mother, answering her excited questions in a bored tone that effectively dampened Matilda's enthusiasm. She went to sit obediently at Gruffydd's side as soon as he returned with William to the castle and reduced Isobel to tears with her cutting, icy criticism.

Matilda, who had been going to beg her to come with her to Bramber for the Christmas celebration, bit back the invitation. "You've changed, Tilda. You used to be gentle and obedient to your family," she reproached her sadly.

Tilda drew a quick breath and turned on her mother, her eyes flashing. "I owe you no obedience, Mother. My duty is to my husband! And it is hard to be gentle when my father is called an ogre and a murderer throughout the principalities. He is known for his treachery and his double-dealing. And as for you." The girl paused, her nostrils pinched suddenly. "They call you a sorceress," she hissed. "I hear stories being told to my children of Mallt the witch who will come for them if they don't sleep, and it's their own grandmother who is being talked of!" Her voice had risen to a cry of anguish.

413

Matilda looked at her in horrified silence for a moment. "Why don't you stop them?" She turned away, not wanting the girl to see the indignant tears that threatened to come suddenly to her eyes.

"Because for all I know, it's true." There was no mistaking the hard note of dislike in Tilda's voice. "I remember you muttering spells when I was a child, you and that old nurse of yours. I remember the smoking concoctions you would brew up in your still room. And there are other things. They say you talk to spirits, that you called up a hundred thousand devils at Dinas, that you ride with the storm—as you did"—her eyes suddenly flashed—"the day I came here, Mother."

Matilda sat down on a carved joint stool and gazed into the glowing embers of the fire. "If you believe all that of me, Tilly, why did you come back to us?"

"I came to see Gruffydd. I didn't know if he would be allowed to come home. I had to come here."

"I see." Matilda's voice was flat. "Well, my dear. You'd better go to him, then." She shifted slightly on her stool, turning her back to Tilda, and sat in silence.

Her daughter stood for a moment, hesitating, half regretting her outburst, then with one backward glance at her mother's hunched figure she swept past her out of the door.

Matilda saw to it that they were never alone together after that, and although she spoke kindly to Tilda and treated her with every consideration, it was with relief that she saw her leave Hay at last with Gruffydd.

William, his elbows firmly spread upon the table, commented at the meal that evening. "That was a good marriage. I've had my doubts about the politics of it often enough: the link wasn't strong enough to hold old Rhys, but Gruffyd is a good enough man, for a Welshman. I could wish he were stronger, but I reckon he's made our daughter a good husband. She looked well and happy." He glanced at her, grinning. "I know you were never content to see her off into the Welsh hinterland, Moll. I hope this visit has at last put your worries at rest."

All Matilda could do was lower her eyes and nod.

"No! That's wrong!" Jo was shaking her head. "William knew! He knew she was not his daughter! He would not have said that! He would not have cared. . . ."

She staggered slightly, her hand against the cold, shadowed castle wall; her head was spinning and her mouth was dry. She felt slightly sick. She rubbed her eyes with her knuckles trying desperately to clear her head. "He would not have called her 'our' daughter. He knew. He knew about Richard by then. He had forced me to tell him. . . ."

But did he know? She could feel her heart beginning to pump uncomfortably beneath her ribs. Was it William who had questioned her about her unfaithfulness with Richard, or had it been Sam? Sam pursuing her into the past. A Sam who had taken upon himself the face of William de Braose. A Sam who had forced her to strip and then whipped her—something the real William had never dared to do.

She closed her eyes, breathing hard.

When she opened them again she was conscious suddenly that a man was staring at her. He had parked a Land Rover in the shadow of the wall near her, watching her closely as he climbed out and locked it. She smiled uncomfortably at him and forced herself to walk on slowly, aware suddenly that he probably thought she was drunk.

She stumbled again, and as her hand shot out to steady herself, she stared at her fingers braced against the stone. Make notes. That was the thing to do. With a pencil in her hand she felt real; she could fight Sam and William and the past and everything they threw at her.

Determinedly she groped in her bag for her notebook, trying to fend off the strange dislocation that still lingered as she stared up toward Pen y Beacon and the pearly mist that clung about its summit.

Three-quarters of the way across England, at Clare, Tim Heacham, a page meticulously cut from a newspaper in his pocket, was standing by the walls of what had once been a mighty castle. The taxi that had brought him out from Colchester had gone. He was alone. Slowly he walked over the grass, his hands in his pockets, his eyes on the ground a few yards in front of him. There had to be something he could do, but his mind was a blank.

Nick and Sam Franklyn. He should have known. He should have trusted his instincts. He should have warned Jo while there was still time. Now it was too late. Whatever was to happen was already in train, and there was nothing he could do. Nothing.

He looked up at the sky. "Oh, God, Jo, I'm sorry," he whispered. "I'm so very sorry."

31

Ann Clements was fifteen years younger than her husband, a plump, very blond woman with large teeth and a warm, irrepressible smile. She kissed Jo as if she had known her for years.

"Are you going to interview me or shall I interview you?" she said cheerfully as they picked their way into the house over the two small toddlers, a vast quantity of scattered Legos, and a large white rabbit with pink eyes.

Jo laughed as she patted one of the children on the head. "Perhaps we'd better toss for it."

"All right." Ann smiled at her. "That is Polly you're stroking. The other one is Bill and the rabbit is called Xerxes. Sit down. I'll make us some coffee. Once Ben comes in I'll start lunch." She turned to an immense heap of unwashed dishes, searching for two mugs. "Ben told me all about you, of course. Put that down, Polly." She had not turned around and Jo concluded with a grin that she had eyes in the back of her head as the little girl with her mop of blond curls guiltily put down the milk jug. "I've seen people being regressed back home in the States—it's practically a minor industry there—but your case sounds absolutely amazing. Ben tells me you intended to write a book about it."

Jo nodded.

"But you changed your mind?"

Jo shrugged. "I thought I had when I saw Ben. Now I'm undecided again. I went straight from here to Brecon on Tuesday after I'd seen him. I regressed there, and once again yesterday in Hay. Both times deliberately. But I just don't know what to think anymore. If it were just me, I'd go on. It is all so real to me, and someone has proved I was speaking real old Welsh, and that clinched it for me, but then some rather unpleasant things happened."

"And you found other people muscling in?" Ann rinsed out the two mugs.

"I found that, after all, the whole thing could have been orchestrated by someone else." Jo bit her lip "And if that's true, his motives terrify me."

Ann glanced up at her. "Can you tell me about it?"

Jo shrugged. "It's all so involved. There's one friend . . . a colleague really. Tim Heacham. He has been regressed—quite independently. He was one of the people in Matilda's story."

Ann raised an eyebrow. "Could be true, you know. Or it could be strong autosuggestion. Has he gone into the detail you were able to?"

Jo shrugged again. "I don't think so. The experience seems to have been very different for him, but he's afraid of getting any more involved. He wants nothing to do with it. And now I've found out there is someone else—a man I'm very fond of. He seems to have been regressed as well."

"Sounds as if the habit's catching." The dry comment was all but drowned by screams from Bill as his sister tugged a great handful of his hair. Ann calmly picked up a child under each arm.

"If you were to ask my advice I should say leave your friends out of this. Let them all work out their own problems. And you concentrate on yours."

"And go on doing it?"

Ann straightened, pushing her hair out of her eyes. "Do you think you can stop?"

Jo rescued the box of coffee filter papers from Bill, ruffled his hair absently, and handed the box to his mother. "No, I don't think I can." She gave a half-embarrassed smile.

"Then you must go on with the book idea." Ann put the pot on the stove. "It's a good way of approaching it. Writing is one of the best therapies there is, you must know that. And it gives you a justification for following the story on without being afraid it is becoming an obsession. It kind of justifies your actions, forces you to stop and analyze them, and gives you an excuse for doing it all in one. It also gives you a natural cutting-off point at the end." She looked at Jo closely. "That's kind of a safety valve. It's something I think you must have. But there are other precautions you must take—I'm surprised your therapist hasn't made them clear to you. You must stop either trying or allowing yourself to regress when you are alone. For two reasons. The brain enjoys excursions of this sort. They take on an almost narcotic compulsion and become easier and easier to do, and from what Ben tells me, you are finding that already. All you need now is some sort of trigger—a place, an association even, or, as you told Ben, an electrical storm to stimulate the brain cells. You don't want to end up finding the past is more compelling than the present! The other reason is self-evident. You are alone and unmonitored. That could be dangerous." She glanced at Jo and smiled. "If you go into a trance in the middle of the M4 you just might get run over!"

Jo gave a shaky laugh. "That had occurred to me. But I can't always stop it happening."

"I think I can teach you how. If you let me." Ann picked the pot off the stove and poured coffee into the two mugs. "I hope you don't mind me saying all this, but it's an area that interests me and I had a feeling you might just find it easier to talk to a complete stranger about it all. But if you want me to drop the subject, say so. I won't be offended——"

Jo glanced out of the window at the view across the mountains. "No," she said slowly. "You're right. I do need someone to talk to. And it's strange but I feel you know more about this than Dr. Bennet."

Ann shook her head. "I doubt it. I think it's more that I can put myself in your shoes better than he can. He's a man, after all. He's probably all excited about the mechanics of what is happening to you and has forgotten that there's a human being here, getting all screwed up in the process."

Jo gave a wry smile. "I haven't told you the worst yet. The newspapers got hold of the story—perhaps you saw them. If not I'll show you the cuttings. You might as well read them. Everyone else in England has."

"This is not England," Ann rebuked gently. "As you of all people should know! No, I haven't seen them. We get papers with the mail, but there never seems time to open them in the summer." She gave each of the children a glass of pressed apple juice and then threw herself down on a chintz armchair. "Now, sit down and show me before Ben comes in."

She found some glasses and read both Pete's articles without comment. Then she handed them back to Jo. "If this Pete Leveson was a friend of mine, I'd cross him off my Christmas card list," she said succinctly. "You can do without publicity like that. Your Nick Franklyn must be spitting blood."

"He's in the States." Jo smiled faintly. "He probably doesn't even know about it."

Ann gave her a long shrewd glance over her glasses. "Don't take this too seriously, Jo. Hysteria is one of the most catching conditions. These men—and it's unusual for men"—she interrupted herself thoughtfully—"they are fond of you. They see you deeply involved with something they cannot be part of, and they try, consciously or not, to join you in your past."

"So you don't think they've been reincarnated too?"

She shrugged. "I think it's unlikely. I haven't met them, so I can't form an opinion as to how genuine they are. But I still hold by my advice. Ignore them if you can. And work out your own destiny. And leave them to work out theirs."

"But supposing my dreams aren't real either!" Jo stood up restlessly. "This is where all my doubts come back. Supposing Nick's brother has implanted King John in Nick's mind. Supposing he has done the same to me with Matilda." She shook her head wearily. "There's something almost

418

evil about Sam these days. Something strange. He's very clever, Ann. He frightens me."

"Is he clever enough to have taught you ancient Welsh in three easy lessons?"

Jo looked down into her coffee mug. "I don't see how he could have."

"Neither do I." Ann relaxed back into her chair. "I believe you have tapped into another life somehow. Maybe this Sam Franklyn is trying to manipulate you and his brother for some reason of his own, but if he is, he's working on something that is already there, at least as far as you're concerned, believe me." She sat forward suddenly. "Can you hear the geese chattering? They've seen Ben. We'll talk about this some more after lunch, okay?"

Jo had all the notes she needed on Ann by four o'clock. They had walked the smallholding again, taken more pictures, and Jo had tried her hand at milking. It was in the cowshed that Ann turned to her, leaning against the angular rump of the pretty Jersey cow.

"Would you allow me to try some regression techniques on you later, when the kids are in bed?"

Jo hesitated. "I don't know. I think I'd be embarrassed—"

She glanced at Ben, who was gently rubbing some ointment into the eye of one of his calves.

"No need. You are concerned to find out about Matilda's children and grandchildren. You need to see some of the happy side of her life, if she had any, poor lady. Why not let me try and lead you there? Better than going back to Hay and violently hallucinating in the parking lot all alone."

Jo made a face. "Put like that—"

"You can't refuse. Good. Listen, go and call your landlady and tell her you are staying here tonight. We'd love to have you, and that way it won't matter if it gets late. We'll keep it happy and loose, I promise."

They drank homemade wine while Ann prepared the quiche for supper, then, when they had eaten, she led Jo to the sofa and sat her down.

Ben perched himself uncomfortably in the corner, his eyes on his wife's face as she talked Jo back into a trance.

"Hell, Annie, I didn't know you could do that," he murmured as Jo obediently raised her arm and held it suspended over her head.

Ann took off her glasses. "I have a lot of talents you don't know about, Benjamin," she retorted. "Now, to work." She knelt at Jo's feet. "Matilda de Braose, I want you to listen to me. I want you to talk to me about your son. Your eldest son, Will, the child who gave you so much pain at his birth. He is grown up now. Tell me about him. . . ."

"Will had been ill all winter again." Jo shook her head sadly. "So ill. He wanted to go with his father to fight with the king and Prince John against the French, but he had to stay with me at Bramber. Then, at the end of May, it happened. John came back to us."

419

Matilda was waiting in the great hall, arrayed in her finest gown, her hair netted in a filet of silver, with Will, gaunt still, but stronger, at her right hand, when a flurry of activity at the door announced the arrival of their new king.

King Richard had died on 6 April in the Limousin, to be succeeded, not by Arthur, his elder brother's child, the true heir, some said, by strict right of primogeniture, but by his younger brother, John. John, the grown man the country needed for its king.

William had been among the first to kneel to declare his allegiance before the new king set off for England, and Bramber had been their first stop on the road to Westminster after landing at Shoreham.

Staring at the doorway, Matilda felt a slight constriction in her throat as John appeared, surrounded by his followers; but with every ounce of courage she possessed, she stepped forward to greet him, curtsying to the ground over the hand that he held to be kissed.

His blue eyes, as she glanced up, were inscrutable, but he retained her fingers in his for a moment longer than necessary. "I trust you remember, my lady, that I invited you, many years ago, to be at my coronation."

"Thank you, Your Grace, I shall be there." Her glance shifted to William, who was beaming at the king's side. Behind him, the king's retinue were crowding into the great hall: nobles, officers, captains of his guard, all travel-stained and weary after the Channel crossing, but eager for the refreshment that Matilda's cooks and butlers had been preparing since dawn.

With the king ensconced on the high seat of honor, reaching out for the goblet of wine that Will, on one knee, passed him, Matilda gave a little sigh. This should have been a moment of great pride and happiness, with her husband so obviously high in the favor of the new king, so why was she uneasy? She glanced at John and found he was watching her over the rim of the goblet. In spite of herself she felt the heat rising in her face and she looked away again.

Then he was speaking and she knew that, over the hubbub of talk and the intervening crowds who fawned and crowded around him, John was talking to her.

"We look forward to our coronation and to services from our loyal and devoted subjects, as we know you all to be. We know there can be no treachery among those of you who stay our friends." He rose and flourished the cup and William, delighted, responded pledge for pledge.

Matilda thought of the coronation to come at Westminster Abbey, lit with a thousand candles, thick with incense, and then of the ceremonies that would follow, and tried to put her worries out of her mind. John was king now. He would almost at once, Will assured her, be returning to France. With William so high in favor the next years should be good.

420

Forcing herself to be calm and to share the excitement and good humor of the gathering, she at last took up her own cup and held it out to be filled.

"That's good," Ann put in softly, almost afraid to speak as the silence stretched out in the room. "But I don't want you to think about the king too much. Tell me about your children. About their marriages. Talk about Reginald and Giles and Will. Talk about the good times, if you can. . . ."

For a moment Jo stayed silent and Ben shifted uncomfortably in his seat, his eyes leaving her face at last to stare out of the window to where the last pale-green reflections of the sunset were slowly merging into true darkness. From the hillside he could hear the occasional contented exchange between his grazing sheep, and involuntarily he felt himself clutching at the arms of his chair as if to reassure himself of its solidity.

The Christmas celebrations had already begun when, in a flurry of lathered, muddy horses, William arrived at Hay and greeted his wife. He was in a high good mood as he kissed her. And, uncharacteristically, he had brought her a gift, a milk-white mare with a mane and tail like pure watered silk, trapped out in gilded harness.

"It's a horse such as the infidels ride in the Holy Land," he claimed proudly as he led Matilda out into the windswept bailey to see. "See how she carries her head, and the set of her tail? She will make a queen of you, my dear."

The mare nuzzled Matilda's hands, blowing gently as she stroked it and Matilda bent to kiss the silky nose. Her heart had sunk, as always, when her husband returned. But, for the horse, she felt instant and unqualified love.

William called for mulled wine to be sent up to their chamber that night. As his wife sat clad only in her loose, fur-lined bedgown, William, still dressed, perched on the high bed, sipping the steaming drink. He watched as she sent away her women and she herself started to unbraid the long copper hair. Now there were silver streaks in the tresses that reached to the floor.

Favor with King John had brought yet more power to William, and Matilda, as so often, found herself looking secretly at him as he sat preening himself, wondering apprehensively at the pride and confidence he displayed.

He was becoming increasingly unpopular in the country, and part of this unpopularity was, she knew, due to jealousy. The king had favored him, a border baron, above many another man of far higher birth and better claim to the monarch's favor, and she often asked herself secretly why John gave William so much trust. He had favored him from their first meetings when the king was but a boy, seeming to prefer the bluff, stocky baron to the more effete of his earls, and yet she wondered sometimes whether

John really liked him at all. She had seen those intense blue eyes studying William as the older man grew drunk and incautious at banquets and festivals; it was always after that that the cold gaze would stray to her and she would look quickly away, refusing to meet John eye to eye.

Shortly after his coronation, at which Isabella of Gloucester had not appeared, John had had his marriage annulled on the pretext that as he and his wife were second cousins and he had never had the papal dispensation required to marry her, the marriage was invalid. Matilda had at first been angry beyond all reason, but quickly she realized that such an end to the marriage could only bring relief and happiness to the poor, scared child. She had ridden to Cardiff to see Isabella, putting her arm around the girl, who had become as thin as a skeleton and was wearing a robe of penitential sackcloth. "Poor darling," she murmured. "The king has dishonored you most horribly. You should be our queen."

But Isabella shook her head. "I am happy now. It's what I always prayed might happen. That or the release of death." She lowered her eyes, toying with the rosary beads that hung at her girdle. "Be pleased for me. Pity the new wife, whoever she may be."

She, as it turned out, was another Isabella, Isabella of Angoulême, a lady well able to cope with John and his rages.

When John heard of Matilda's visit to Cardiff he was irrationally angry. "Your wife, Sir William," he hissed at the trembling baron, ignoring Matilda, who was standing calmly beside her husband, "takes it into her head to meddle in matters that do not concern her." His face was white with anger and his eyes glittering slits in the mask of his face. "The lady to whom I was formerly associated does not require her attentions."

"Isabella was and is my friend, Your Grace," Matilda interrupted before William could mumble an embarrassed apology. "I like to visit my friends when they are in need of comfort."

"And you found, I am sure, that she needed no comfort." John's voice dropped a fraction lower.

Matilda smiled. "Indeed she didn't. She was happy at last, Your Grace. Happier than she had been since the day of her betrothal. But I was not to know that. I did not realize you had spared Isabella what you did not spare me!" Incautiously she rushed on: "I have witnessed for myself, after all, the form Your Grace's attentions can take. I know the suffering they can cause." Her eyes held his for a moment, blazing with anger, before realizing suddenly the foolishness of betraying her feelings. She turned abruptly away. It was not before, however, she saw John's pale cheeks suffuse with blood until his face was nearly purple.

On that occasion, however, he had controlled himself with an effort, and William and Matilda were curtly dismissed from the royal presence without another word. It was only as she was leaving the room, curtsying one last time as they reached the doors, as protocol demanded, that Matilda raised her eyes again to the king's face. The expression that she saw there made her stomach turn over with fear.

Once outside, William had been beside himself with fury. "Do you want to jeopardize my position, you stupid woman!" He raised his hand as if to strike her, and then thought better of it. "Have you no idea how much rests on my friendship with the king? How much he may do for me—how much money I owe him!"

This last he added in an undertone. He was becoming increasingly worried by the vast debts he was building up. Starting with the five thousand marks he owed for the Honor of Limerick, which the king had granted him after his uncle Philip's death, and followed by other honors and the large feudal reliefs, a thousand pounds each, he would have to pay for the marriages of his two sons. Matilda could do much to maintain him in the king's favor, of that he was sure, and yet every time she was within earshot of her monarch she seemed determined to anger him.

William had often puzzled over the strange relationship between his wife and John. He knew John was attracted to her. He knew that he had once made an approach to her, out hunting in the New Forest, and he had, in spite of his laughter, been flattered and pleased by the prince's attentions to his wife. It had seemed harmless enough at the time, and it had occurred to William once or twice over the years to wonder if he owed his favor with King Henry to John's interest in Matilda. Then the interest seemed abruptly to have cooled, and William was, in spite of everything, relieved at the time; John had a reputation in some quarters for making very free with the wives of his followers. Now he was not so sure. The king's interest would have been all to the good. Hostility was the last thing William wanted, and now he found himself wondering increasingly if he maintained his friendship with the king in spite of Matilda, not because of her, and he resented her bitterly for it. And was it because of her antagonism John still withheld the most tantalizing prize of all, the gift of an earldom?

He had sent her back to the Brycheiniog estates then, while he himself had stayed hopefully at the king's side.

When Gwenwynwyn attacked the de Braose Marcher lands yet again, it had been thanks to her warnings that William was ready for him. He repelled the attack with energetic fury and was rewarded the following year with the lordships of Glamorgan, Gwynllwg, and Gower. He had seemed especially close to the king after that, but even so, some whispered that he had had to extract the rich lordship of Gower from John by threatening to leave the king when he was most in need of the baron's support.

Matilda glanced at him again, her comb lying motionless in her lap. He had followed John to Normandy, but how did he stand with the king now?

She watched him as he raised the goblet to his lips.

"We return to France in the spring," he commented abruptly, as if read-

423

ing her thoughts. "But by then it will be too late. Normandy will have fallen to the French king. Only Château Gaillard holds out for us now, and the coastal towns. Except that Philip Augustus has lost his best excuse for fighting."

Matilda glanced up again. "What do you mean, he's lost his excuse?" She eyed her husband distastefully.

"Arthur. Prince Arthur is dead." William tipped back the goblet and drained it.

"The king's young nephew?" She began to work at a tangle in her hair with the ivory comb even as she felt a muscle somewhere in her stomach start to tense.

"Yes, Arthur. We captured him at Mirabeau. The little runt was attempting to besiege his own grandmother! Eleanor sent word to John and we marched from Le Mans in two days—two days, mark you—and had them all in the bag in hours. John had the boy sent to Falaise." William fell silent for a moment, picking his teeth with the corner of his thumbnail.

"And?" she prompted him.

He shrugged. "Arthur hasn't been seen since."

"So you don't know that he's dead."

"It's fairly certain," he admitted guardedly.

"But the king must have confided in you. He always does. Surely you can tell me, your own wife." Matilda concentrated on her hair, carefully casual.

William was watching the rhythmic strokes of the brush, fascinated. He licked his lips, half astonished at himself to feel desire for her still after all these years.

"Oh, yes, the king confided in me." He could not resist rising to her remark, and he did not notice her secret smile as suddenly he sat forward on the edge of the bed, his voice low. "But I didn't need his confidence this time, Moll. I was there. I saw it all. He killed Arthur with his own hands and threw the body into the Seine!"

Matilda felt herself grow cold. "With his own hands?" she heard herself repeat the words, incredulous.

William slipped from the bed and came to squat near her, his fingers held out to the blaze. "We were at Rouen for Easter. John had been drinking. We all had! He decided he was going to interrogate the prisoners and he sent for Arthur. The boy stood there arrogantly and refused to recognize his uncle as king. John flew into a rage and went for him. But, God damn it, if the boy had had any spirit at all . . . He just stood there and allowed John to put his hands around his neck and shake him. We all had to swear on Christ's sacred bones we would tell no one of his death. The king wanted him alive." William stood up, rubbing his own neck ruefully. "He had given orders that the boy be blinded and gelded and kept a harmless hostage by Hubert de Burgh at Falaise, and Hubert refused like a whey-faced woman. It was Hubert's fault. The boy would have been a useful pawn, damn it!" He paused, his back to Matilda.

"I helped them tie the stones to the body and we heaved it over into the river, but as ill luck would have it, a fisherman found the wretched corpse some days later. Luckily by then it was unrecognizable. Nobody could be sure. But some guessed."

Matilda listened in silence, horrified, picturing John's sudden drunken rage and his assault on the frightened, lonely boy, remembering the night when he had put those same hands around her throat.

Why had William not lifted one finger to help him? Why had he not tried to restrain the king at least? She looked at her husband and shuddered.

William was incredulous. "The boy was a traitor! He deserved to die! It was only John's goodness that had kept him alive at all—"

"John has no goodness, William. He did what would have been best for his own cause—until he got drunk and lost his temper. It was Hubert among all of you, from what you say, who had goodness and compassion."

She climbed up into the bed, keeping her gown wrapped tightly around her. "Call the servants, William. Let them make up the fire and put out the sconces."

William crossed to the bed and laid a tentative hand on his wife's shoulder, but, clutching the fur even closer to her, she rolled away from him, her eyes closed, and William, shrugging, turned back to the fire.

He did not mention Arthur again, but the next morning he called for his clerks and stewards, and after several hours closeted with them before piles of parchments he sent for the prior from St. John's at Brecknock. "I intend to build you a fine new church on your hill, Father Prior," he said when the old man arrived, mudstained from his furious gallop at the heels of William's messenger.

When the astonished man, speechless with surprise and gratitude, had bowed his way out of the room, William sat back at the table and smiled at Matilda, who had been summoned with peremptory haste to the meeting.

"Do you remember, years ago I planned this, Moll? A beautiful new church, to the glory of God? It will be the greatest church in the land when I've finished." He swaggered across the room and poured himself a cup of wine. "People will remember me for hundreds of years for the beauty of the building, and my piety and generosity in paying for it." He sat down again, smiling. Matilda could see he was already very drunk.

Wearily she rubbed her hand across her eyes. She had slept little, the image of the boy prince in his terror and loneliness rising before her every time she had tried to sleep. She forced herself to give her husband a wan smile. Did William really think that he could atone for his complicity in the murder of a child by building a church? Watching him drink the last dregs from the goblet and turn once more to the parchment on his table, she realized that indeed he did.

32

Judy opened the door and stared.
"So, it's you. How was New York?"

Nick followed her to the studio. "Very hot." He walked over to her easel and looked at the sketch she had pinned there. "Would I be right in thinking you had been seeing something of Pete Leveson while I've been away?" Turning back toward her, he surveyed her grimly.

Judy looked defiant. "Is there any reason why I shouldn't?"

"None at all." He was tight-lipped. "I should say you were made for each other. Your idea of loyalty is strange, to say the least, Judy." Folding his arms, he waited for the outburst he knew would come. He was not disappointed.

Judy narrowed her eyes. "I owe you no loyalty, Nick. Nor allegiance! I'm not part of your jolly little charade. It is you and Sam and Tim. So fight it out between you. I've joined the spectators. Have you seen your brother yet?" she added suddenly.

Nick shook his head. "I'm on my way back to the apartment now."

"Well, he's been busy while you've been away, and he's damn lucky he's not in prison. He came here, drunk, and smashed up my studio. So I called the police and the bloody fool took a swing at one of them."

"Christ!" Nick stared at her. "What happened?"

"Your friend Alistair got him off with a fine and being bound over. But I'll tell you something right now. If you come here making trouble, you'll get the same treatment. I really was fond of you, Nick, do you know that? You and I could have been great together, but not now. I think you're mad, all of you. Jo's welcome to whichever one of you wins. If she's alive to find out!"

She walked across to the window and slammed it down, cutting out the noise of the traffic.

"What do you mean, if she's alive?" Nick's voice was sharp.

"Sam is setting you up, Nick, I told you, only you're such a blind fool you can't see it. He hates Jo, and he's jealous of you. He's been programming you to hurt her. He's been feeding you these stupid ideas—you

427

don't really believe you're King John, for God's sake? You'll end up in a funny farm if you do! Impulsively she clutched his arm. "Nick, I do still care about you—and I'd hate to see you get hurt, and whatever I feel about Jo, I don't want to see her end up Sam's victim. He's mad, Nick. I really believe he's mad. Do be careful. Please."

Stunned, Nick said nothing for a moment. Then: "Is Sam still at my apartment?"

She shrugged. "I didn't inquire—he called after he got out of court, but I told him to go to hell, so he's probably out to get me as well by now."

"And Jo? I tried to call her from New York but she never replied."

Judy raised an eyebrow. "Then let's hope he hasn't got at her already. He came from her apartment that night he came here, Nick. That's all I know."

It took Nick seven minutes to reach Cornwall Gardens. He sprinted up the stairs. Jo's apartment was empty. It had the feel of a place that had been deserted for several days. On the mantelpiece a bowl of roses had faded, their petals scattered up the carpet; otherwise the place was unnaturally tidy.

He wandered over to the balcony doors and glanced out, noticing that the plants in the tubs outside had wilted in the heat, then he turned away. The kitchen was spotless, everything in place. In the bedroom the curtains were half drawn. He noticed the tape recorder on the chest of drawers and idly switched it on, listening as the thin, haunting strains of the flute filled the room. For a moment he stood quite still, puzzled; he had heard that music before when Sam was here, alone with Jo. He snapped off the music and was about to leave the room when his eye was caught by the belt lying across the chair. He recognized the engraved buckle. It was Sam's.

His eyes suddenly murderous, he raced up the passage and dragged open the front door. After slamming it behind him, he descended the stairs two at a time and dived into his car. He pulled out into the traffic with only a perfunctory glance in his mirror, then tore up Gloucester Road and turned right toward Queen's Gate.

Sam was writing at Nick's desk. He looked up when he heard Nick's key in the lock.

"So, the wanderer returns. How did you enjoy your bite at the Big Apple?"

Nick strode across the room and confronted him across the desk. "Where is Jo?"

"Jo? I have no idea, Nicholas. At home perhaps?" Sam's breath smelled of Scotch.

"You know damn well she's not at home." Nick produced his hand from behind his back. In it was the belt. "Do you know where I found this?"

428

Sam stared at it. He gave a half smile. "The instrument of chastisement," he said almost thoughtfully.

"The what?" Nick froze. He leaned across the desk and gripped the front of Sam's shirt, half dragging him out of his chair. "What the hell are you trying to say, Sam? Have you gone crazy?"

Sam smiled. "Someone had to beat her, Nick. And it was less than she deserved. Many men would have killed their wife for what she did. She admitted it, you know, in the end, and she submitted to her punishment on her knees. She wanted it. It must have helped to ease her conscience."

Nick let go of him abruptly. He was staring at his brother in complete horror. "You are crazy," he whispered. "God in heaven, you are crazy! Where is she, man?" His blue eyes narrowed furiously. "If you've hurt her I swear to God I'll kill you!"

Sam laughed. He pushed his chair back slightly and shifted in it sideways, draping his arm across its back, totally relaxed.

"John," he said softly. "John, King of England. She betrayed you too. She scorned you. She mocked you publicly. Kings do not stand for treatment like that from anyone, never mind from the women they desire. You killed her before, brother mine, and you'll kill her again." He leaned forward suddenly. "Remember? You want her to suffer. And you want me to see her suffer. You are going to tell me what you intend to do to her, Nick, and you will beg me to come and watch you take your revenge."

"Stop that crap, Sam! I know what you're up to." Nick clenched his fists till the nails bit into his palms. "You get out of this apartment. Get out and go back to Scotland, and leave us alone." His voice had sunk to a hiss.

Sam stood up. "It's too late, Nick. I began to plant the seeds in your brain the first day I realized who I was. I remembered that massacre at Abergavenny, you see. I remembered stabbing that Welsh quisling till his warm blood ran up my arm. I remembered I was William de Braose and Matilda was mine. *Mine*, Nick. And she'll be mine again. This time I shall be ready when the trial comes." He moved away from behind the desk. "I prepared the ground too well." He laughed. "You are an arrogant fool. You played into my hands, trusting your mind to me."

Nick kept an icy grip on his temper. "You are talking pure melodrama, Sam. What you're implying is not possible and we both know it. Pack your things and get out."

Sam stood still for a moment staring at him, his face alight with malicious amusement. "She slept with Heacham, you know," he said suddenly. "In Wales. I recognized him at once. De Clare. He still has a hold over her, of course, but he knows he will lose her." He laughed. "He's weak. He was too weak to save her then, and he's too weak now." He picked a few books off the table and collected some loose change off the desk into his pocket. Then he looked up. "You don't believe me, do you, Nick? But it's true, you know. I really did regress you. You were—you are John Plantagenet," he said.

Nick did not move. The sweat was standing out on his forehead as Sam left the room. He steadied himself with an effort, then with deliberate slow movements, as if he were in a dream, he went to the pile of phone books and reached for A–H.

"Tim?" His mouth was dry. "This is Nick Franklyn."

"Hello, Nick." Tim sounded subdued.

"I have reason to believe you may know where Jo is." Nick controlled his voice with an effort. "She is not at her apartment."

There was a moment's silence. "She went to Wales. Bet Gunning talked her into doing an interview with some guy about organic farming."

"About what?" Nick exploded.

"I know it sounds unlikely," Tim responded. "It was obviously a ruse to get her back there. But I don't think it'll work. She wants to give it all up, you know. She tore up the contract to write the story for *W I A*. She has decided to have nothing more to do with Matilda or the past. Something frightened her very badly." He hesitated, and Nick heard the tremor in his voice. "Have you spoken to your brother since you came back?"

"I have indeed." Nick glanced at the door. He could hear the closets in the spare bedroom opening and closing as Sam took out his clothes and threw them on the bed. "I think you can take it that my brother will have no more say in Jo's affairs," he said grimly. "No more at all. And neither will you."

The sun had broken through the haze early and its heat baked the ground. Jo pushed her typewriter away on the table outside the back door and stood up. Ann was dyeing wool, pressing the loose skeins into the onion-skin water again and again. She pushed her fair hair back from her face with the back of her wrist. "Finished the article?"

Jo smiled. "The first draft. I'd like you and Ben to read it and make suggestions." She took a deep breath of the hot mountain air. "It's so peaceful up here, I'm even amenable to criticism today!"

Ann laughed. She hooked a skein out of the water and began to wring it out. "If your piece is too sweet and nice, won't your editor hurl it back at you and ask you to anoint it with vitriol?"

"You've obviously heard about me!" Jo sat down on the close-cropped grass and after a moment stretched out full length, her arms flopping above her head. "Don't worry. I'm rude enough to upset you both quite a bit if you take it the wrong way." She sat up again and shaded her eyes. "And I don't want you to take it the wrong way, Ann. You're living a pastoral idyll up here, but you just cannot claim it has any relevance to real life."

Ann raised an eyebrow as she pegged the skein on the line to drip.

"Says who? Why should real life be 'down there' and 'up here' be unreal?"

"Because real is what ninety-nine percent of the population have to live. Mass produced, mass packaged, and mass managed. It's the only way for there to be progress. It's sad, but it's true."

"So we should conform? Help to starve the land, poison the waterways, pollute the air? No, Jo. We are pioneers, prophets. Leading people back to common sense, health, and sanity." Ann gave a gurgle of laughter suddenly. "Go on. Write that down, too."

"What's it like in winter?" Ignoring the comment, Jo wrapped her arms around her knees.

"Lonely. Hard. Sometimes frightening."

"Like it was eight hundred years ago for everyone." Jo's voice was suddenly bleak. "The disease then. The squalor, the poverty of life! That is why we have to move on, Ann. To end all that. To make it less hard. You know, I . . . that is, Matilda, just accepted it. It made her unhappy—she was full of compassion and she used her medical knowledge such as it was, as best she could—but she never questioned. No one questioned anything. It was as God wished."

" 'The rich man in his castle, the poor man at his gate. God made the high and lowly, he ordered their estate,' " Ann recited quietly. "I can still remember singing that in church!"

"God!" Jo buried her head in her arms. "William did everything in the name of God."

"It is man's blessing that he does learn from his mistakes, Jo," Ann said gently. "Not all of them, and not fast, but he does learn. And he progresses, as you say. Did Will de Braose have TB? From what you told me it sounds like it. . . . We've learned to control that. And you talked about the plague in Aberhonddu. That doesn't haunt the people there anymore. I'd be the first person to praise that kind of progress, but in some things man has been too clever. He has rejected good things as well as bad. Now he has to swallow his pride and retrace a few steps, that's all. Learn to listen quietly to the beat of the universe as his ancestors did. Learn to listen to nature and take her in partnership, not try and make her a robot slave."

Jo looked up, squinting in the sun. "I stand rebuked," she said softly. "Write that down, Ann. I'll print it."

Ann grinned. "It's a deal." She turned to go into the house, then she stopped and glanced at Polly and Bill, who were playing in a sandpit near them. "If the kids have a sleep after lunch, Jo, I'll take you back again if you like."

Jo hesitated. "I think I'm going to have to go on, Ann," she agreed at last. "On to the end of the story. That is the only way I'll be free of her. And I'd like it to be with you there."

Ann frowned. "You don't mean you want to go on, until her death?"

431

"I think I have to."

"Are you sure?" Ann was looking doubtful. "I know it's often done, but you don't know how she died. Death scenes can be pretty traumatic, even under deep hypnosis."

"I do know how she died."

"How?" Ann sat down at the table near Jo, her elbows spread, her chin propped on her hands, her eyes fixed on Jo's face.

"John had her thrown into a dungeon and starved to death."

"Sweet Jesus!" Ann caught her breath.

Jo smiled bleakly. "It's knowing about it when she doesn't that is so terrible. I watch her with part of myself, antagonizing John, antagonizing him almost deliberately, from the first day they met." She clenched her fists suddenly. "He loved her, Ann. I really think he loved her, and she found him attractive once he had grown to manhood, and yet they never managed to communicate. They just seemed to knock sparks off each other all the time."

"None of this was in that article you showed me."

"Pete obviously doesn't know his history. He just thought it would be fun linking the name of a king to the story of Matilda. Linking Nick's name—" She bit her lip and turned abruptly away to study the view. "I just want to get it over with, Ann," she said after a moment over her shoulder, "so I can get on with my own life. Matilda is an intrusion! A parasite, feeding off me, sucking my . . . not my blood, exactly, but something."

"Your life force." Ann stood up again. "I've had an idea. Come and help me prepare the salad, then later we'll try a new approach. It may be that you've put your finger on something. I'd like to try an experiment. I'd like to see if Matilda really is a memory—or if she is a spirit, using you for some purpose. A spirit who is not at rest."

Jo gasped. "You're not serious? You mean I'm possessed?"

Ann laughed. "It's always a possibility. Come on. Don't worry about it. Later we'll try to find out what this poor lady wants from you."

Worn out by the heat, the two small children went to bed in their cool north-facing bedroom without their customary protest. Outside, Ben had moved the table into the shade of one of the ancient yew trees near the house. He sat down on the wooden chair and looked solemnly at his wife. "Take care, Annie. You are sure you know what you're doing?"

Ann sat down opposite Jo. "I know," she said. "You trust me, Jo, don't you?"

Jo nodded, her eyes on Ann's face.

Slowly Ann reached forward and put her cool hands over Jo's. The shadow moved slightly and Jo felt the sudden blaze of the sun in her eyes. She closed them involuntarily, conscious only of the heavy scented silence of the early afternoon.

"Matilda." Ann's voice was gently insistent. "Matilda, I command you speak. Matilda, if you are a spirit from the world beyond, tell us what it is you want in our world. Your time is past, your story is finished, so why do you speak through Joanna?"

There was a long silence. Jo's eyes remained closed, her whole body relaxed. Ann repeated her question twice more, then she glanced at Ben. "You were right. It's not a spirit, or if it is, I can't reach it. It just struck me that Jo could be a natural medium. But I don't think it is that. If she is possessed, it is not in the way people usually mean when they talk of possession."

"Bloody ridiculous, woman! Wake her up and let's have some of that foul coffee." Ben was looking distinctly uncomfortable.

"It's too hot for coffee." Ann stroked Jo's hand gently. "Lady Matilda. Tell me more about your children. Whom did they marry?"

Jo opened her eyes slowly. She drew back a little into the shade, looking past Ann and Ben across the grass toward the steep slope where the garden began to fall away into the valley. Beyond lay the hazy mountains.

The day of Will's wedding to Mattie de Clare dawned bright and showery. Bramber Castle was in high excitement, for not only was the eldest son of William de Braose at last being married, but the king himself was guest of honor.

Matilda stood staring out across the broad waters of the River Adur from the deserted solar, lost in thought. Below, her husband was with the king and the other guests, waiting while Mattie and her ladies made last-minute preparations for the ceremony.

Mattie had spent much time with Matilda over the past years, learning at her side the accomplishments of a great lady. She was a quiet, gentle girl who had shown signs of great beauty as, slowly, she began to turn into a mature young woman. Will had often been with them during that time, kept from the manly pursuits for which he longed, and from his father's side, by the debilitating cough and weakness that still plagued him constantly, and Mattie had grown to regard him with an almost blind adoration which half embarrassed, half pleased him. Matilda was overjoyed to see them marry, but the arrangement hadn't been without its problems. She thought suddenly of the scene when Reginald had first heard the news. "But I thought I was the one she would marry! You've always spoken of me being the one, Mother," he had appealed to her wildly. "I know her and I know her father from when I was serving with them. It's my right! It should be me!" But William, now Lord of the Three Castles in addition to his other titles, and deeper than ever in the king's debt, had been adamant. He wanted Reginald to marry Gracia de Burgh. "She's a red-blooded young woman. She needs a man. And now. Will is always ill.

I doubt sometimes he'll live out another winter," he had said with outspoken brutality. "Mattie is too young to marry yet, so they can wait. If Will is strong enough when she is old enough, then they can marry. But I need the de Burgh alliance now."

He needed, as they all knew, the de Burgh power behind him. But, in the event, the de Burgh marriage had been fraught with delay, and it had been only a short while before that Reginald had married his Irish heiress, with his brother Giles officiating at the ceremony.

Among the first favors John had granted after his accession had been the installation of Giles as Bishop of Hereford. She thought back to how William had watched so proudly his tall, copper-haired son, who now sported mitre and cross with much grave dignity. The young man's calling unnerved William, and filled him with superstitious awe that annoyed and puzzled him, even as he bathed in the glory that his son's position brought to him.

Matilda smiled quietly to herself. They had been so lucky, on the whole, in their children. Isobel and her husband, Roger Mortimer, had presented Matilda with two grandchildren. Margaret, married five years before, wrote long letters regularly from Ireland, where she now spent most of her time and she too seemed very happy, although the girl did have one sorrow, unskillfully hidden in her letters. This was that no child had as yet been born to her marriage with her beloved, handsome Walter, the Lord of Meath.

"I have vowed, Mother dear," her latest letter had said, "to found a nunnery to the blessed memory of the Virgin Mary, if she grants my great desire to have a son. And Walter too has made the same vow. He has expressed the longing to found an abbey somewhere in the shadow of Pen y Beacon, perhaps at Craswall, where he holds tenure. Pray for me, Mother dear, that my own prayers may be answered. I hope we may return to Ludlow soon, so that I can see you—"

Only the thought of Tilda brought real sadness. Widowed now for four years, after Gruffydd had died of some sudden, virulent fever, she had helped bury him in his father's abbey at Strata Florida, but when Matilda wrote to suggest she return to her family, she sent a snubbing reply that it was her intention to bring up her two boys as true sons of Wales and when that task was done she would be content to lie at the side of her husband. There had been no exchange of messages after that, and Matilda nursed her hurt in secret, showing that final letter to no one before she held the parchment in the flame of a candle and watched it blacken and curl in her fingers.

And now Will's wedding had arrived and with it a new honor for William, for King John, the threat of invasion by Philip of France at last over, had agreed to attend the marriage.

Matilda bit her lip. So once more they shared the same roof together, the three men who so ruled her life: William, the king, and Richard de Clare.

She had been shocked by Richard's appearance. He had grown thin and stooped since their last meeting, and his skin strangely sallow. His eyes were the same though—as searching and powerful in their hold over her as ever.

He had arrived alone at Bramber with Mattie and his son, Gilbert. It was five years since he had, at last, separated from the embittered Amicia, and she had chosen not to come to her daughter's wedding feast, a fact that had caused Matilda to send up a prayer of thanks.

Behind her, one of her women appeared and cleared her throat loudly. "My lady, Sir William has asked for you again. His Grace is impatient to proceed."

Slowly Matilda turned. She smiled. If her eldest son and Richard's daughter could be happy together, then perhaps, after all, there would have been some point to their own impossible love story.

Too soon the ceremony was over. The chapel was hot and stuffy from the candles and incense and the press of people. As she knelt for the mass following the nuptials Matilda glanced sideways at Richard, who was beside her, and he turned at once, instantly conscious of her gaze. At the altar Giles was the celebrant, attended by his own chaplain from Hereford and the castle chaplain and the priests from the neighboring church at Steyning, all clustered around him like so many highly colored butterflies.

"Are we now brother and sister, my love?" She heard Richard's whisper over the slow sound of the chanting. They were kneeling so close to one another she felt him stir and then his fingers feeling for hers hidden by the stiff folds of her kirtle.

A happy warmth filled her heart. "For always, Richard," she murmured back, and for a moment they looked at each other again. On her other side William, unaware of anything but the mystery before him, knelt, his eyes fixed to the altar. In front, the newlyweds shared a faldstool together, solemn-faced, intent on the words their brother was uttering, while the king also knelt on the purple velvet of a cushion to one side of the sanctuary steps.

Matilda's happiness was so complete it was a shock to find John's gaze not on the mass but fixed on the place where an embroidered fold of damask hid her hand as it lay still gently clasped in Richard's.

Slowly John raised his eyes to hers and she saw the hardness in them masked only by a slight speculative frown.

33

The Porsche turned cautiously up the steep lane following its bumpy twists and turns as Nick peered through the windshield and then down at the ordnance survey map on the seat beside him. He was very tired.

After drawing the car up next to Jo's at the top of the lane, he climbed out at last, staring at the view in silence. Then something made him turn.

Jo was standing behind him in the doorway to the farmhouse. She was far more tanned than he remembered, her face and arms burned like a gypsy, her long hair caught back on the nape of her neck. She was wearing a simple white dress and low-heeled sandals and looked, so he thought with a pang of strange fear, almost supernaturally beautiful. Slowly he swung the car door shut.

"How are you, Jo?"

She still had not smiled. "How did you know where I was?"

"Someone told me you were back in Wales so I drove to Hay. Margiad said you were up here." He had not moved.

She watched him warily. His face was thin and there were lines of fatigue beneath his eyes and around his mouth, but he was still in her eyes the most handsome man she had ever seen. He was wearing an open-necked blue shirt and cords. "You've seen the article?" she said softly.

He nodded.

"Is it true?"

For a moment he didn't reply, then slowly he nodded. "I think it probably is."

Behind her Ann had emerged from the low shadowed building. She looked at them in silence for a moment, then she held out her hand. "Hi. I'm Ann," she said.

"Nick Franklyn." Nick moved forward at last and gripped her fingers for a moment. "I'm sorry to arrive unannounced. I meant to call from Hay, then I thought perhaps I'd better surprise you—"

"In case I ran away?" Jo said.

436

"Under the circumstances I wouldn't have blamed you if you had." He forced himself to smile at Ann. "I'm sorry if I'm intruding—"

"You're not. I'm glad you're here. And you're in perfect time for a drink. Ben has promised we can resort to gin tonight after inflicting home brew on Jo all yesterday, so you picked your moment well." Ann turned. "Jo. You promised Bill and Polly you would build one more sandcastle before they went to bed."

She watched as Jo disappeared into the farmhouse. "She said she never used to like kids," she said reflectively, looking after her. "Till she had six of her own." She gave a wry little laugh. "Now she's great with them. Better than me." She linked arms with Nick and led him toward the stone wall that bounded the garden at the western end. They stopped and leaned on it, staring at the mountains in the distance. A smoky haze was beginning to shroud the valleys round their feet.

"Jo has told us something of her story," Ann said reflectively after a moment. "She has asked me to help her, and I want to."

"I gather she has decided to stop the whole thing."

"She can't stop, Nick."

Nick sighed. He said nothing, his eyes on the distant view.

"She showed me the article about your experiences," Ann went on after a minute.

Nick slammed the palm of his hand down on the top of the wall. "My 'experiences,' as you call them, were not genuine," he said forcibly. "Most of that article was a load of rubbish." He swung to face her. "It has to have been!"

Ann looked at him seriously, trying to read the expression in his eyes— the anger, the frustration, and, yes, the fear. It was all there for a moment before the shutters came down and she saw his face close.

"Most?" she said softly. "Then some of it was true?"

He leaned against the wall, facing her now. "I find it strange she should confide so completely in people she barely knows," he said with sudden harshness, ignoring her question.

Ann smiled. "There's a reason. I do know something about hypnosis— and about past life recall—but I hope it's more than that. I hope we have become her friends as well. I can't take the credit for it if we have, though. That's Ben. Everyone trusts Ben." She glanced away almost shyly. "I hope you will too."

As if on cue, Ben appeared from behind the house carrying a basket loaded with vegetables. He raised an earthy hand and disappeared in through the front door.

Ann stood up. "Come and meet him, then we'll get you that drink. Jo must be about ready for rescue from our kids by now."

437

They ate outside by candlelight beneath a luminous sky streaked with shooting stars. In the valley they could hear the yap of a hunting owl and, closer at hand, the thin whisper of upland crickets.

Ben pushed back his plate. "That was lovely, Annie. You excelled yourself, my dear."

She smiled at him dreamily. "And my reward? Will you fight the filter, just this once?"

Ben laughed. He leaned across and rumpled her hair. "Just this once, okay. Come on, Jo. You look like a competent sort of female. Help me."

Ann leaned back in her chair as Jo and Ben disappeared into the kitchen and the door swung shut behind them, shutting off the stream of light from the oil lamps.

"I suppose you don't feel like confiding in a couple of strangers too?" she said after a moment.

Nick was staring at the stars. "There must be a shower of meteorites going over," he said quietly. "That's about the sixth shooting star I've seen."

"They're supposed to be lucky," she said. "I'm a good listener, Nick."

He smiled in the darkness. "I don't know if there is anything to say."

"You're worried."

He nodded.

"And you're afraid."

He tensed and for a moment she thought he would deny it. "Yes, I'm afraid."

"For Jo."

"What would you say if I told you I think I may have been programmed to hurt her?"

"I would say it was impossible."

"But can you be sure of that?"

She could feel his eyes on her in the small dazzle of the candlelight. "Almost. Yes." She leaned forward. "What do you mean by programmed?"

"I allowed my brother to hypnotize me. I trusted him completely, I had no reservations. It turns out I was mistaken in doing that. He claims"—he hesitated—"he claims that he has already set me on a course from which I cannot draw back. One that involves Jo's destruction."

He had taken an unused spoon between his fingers, twisting it restlessly to and fro. It snapped suddenly under the pressure and Nick stared down at it in surprise. "I'm sorry—"

"It doesn't matter." Ann hadn't taken her eyes from his face. "Listen. Tell me honestly. How do you feel about Jo? Do you distrust her in any way? Do you dislike her? Resent her? Hate her?"

"No. God in heaven. No!"

"You say that without reservation?"

"Yes."

"Then I don't think you have anything to fear."

"But supposing Sam has planted some idea in my head that I don't remember? He has discovered—or tried to convince me—that I am—I was—John. He knows and I know that Jo is—was—Matilda. For God's sake, can't you see what's happening? He wants me to kill her again!"

Ann felt a whisper of cold air across her skin. She glanced at the candle flame, expecting it to flicker. "What you are suggesting, Nick, can't happen in real life. It's pure science fiction. If it were possible, people would have the perfect murder weapon, wouldn't they?"

"You're sure?"

"I'm sure. What kind of creep is your brother anyway? Jo told us she had always liked him."

Nick stood up abruptly. He walked to the edge of the terrace and stood looking out into the darkness. Far away in the valley car headlights showed for a moment on the main road as two tiny silent pinpoints of light, then as the road wound out of sight they disappeared.

"I think he is in love with Jo," he said softly.

"Then why would he want you to kill her, for God's sake?"

He shrugged. There was a long silence. "I've always worshipped Sam," he said at last. "But now I realize that he hates me. I expect he always has."

Ann stood up. She went and stood beside him. "That's tough."

"Yes." His voice was bleak. For a moment he said nothing more, then out of the silence he said, "Please, don't regress her anymore, Ann."

"If I don't she will do it on her own, Nick, spontaneously. The need to know what happens next is too strong in her. She can't fight it. Maybe that is something your brother has implanted in her. I don't know. But if Jo is going to regress with this violence it is much better that it happens in reasonably controlled conditions among friends than out in the streets or somewhere on the mountainside." She could see his face clearly in the starlight. "Are you afraid to see her as Matilda again in case it prompts you to try to hurt her?" she asked at last.

"I suppose I am."

"There is no need." She hesitated for a moment, then plunged on. "We had planned for another regression this evening. If Jo still wants to do it, Nick, I think we should. I think it's doubly important, now that you're here."

The ride through the hills was exhilarating. Matilda sat her white Arab mare, feeling the creature's grace and speed as it danced ahead of the more solid horses of her kinsmen Adam de Porter and Lord Ferrers. In spite of the fear that lurked at the back of her mind and the need for haste as they rode down the tracks softened by spring rain and everywhere budding with new green, she felt a strange, optimistic lightness of heart.

By the time they rode into Gloucester, though, her mood had changed. A damp white mist clung over the river, swirling up the narrow streets of the town and hiding the tower of the cathedral. The joyous spring day had been extinguished by a damp, cold evening, and her fear had returned fourfold. She and she alone must face the king and beg him to reinstate William in his favor.

William's fall had been sudden and unexplained. Only two days after John had left Bramber after Will's wedding, messengers came from the royal exchequer, abruptly demanding repayment of all the money that William owed the king.

"Christ's bones, how does he think I can pay?" William had fumed, waving the parchment under Giles's nose. "And why now? Why does he want the money now? He made no mention of it at the wedding! He seemed pleased to be there."

"Can you really owe the king so much, Father?" Giles had at last managed to take the parchment from his father's flailing hand. "How could you let your debts mount so?" His solemn face was anxious.

William rounded on him. "There isn't a nobleman in the kingdom who doesn't owe money to the king! Fees, fines, reliefs, taxes! Good God above, how could any of us pay so much? He knows he'll get it all in the end, or if he doesn't, his heirs will, from mine. Apart from anything else, I have had two lots of marriage relief to pay in six months—a thousand pounds each! That's what your brothers' wives cost me!"

Giles was reading the parchment slowly, his finger tracing the figures methodically down the page. "It says here, Father, that you still haven't paid any of the relief for your Honor of Limerick after Uncle Philip died. That dates back five yerars."

"Five years!" William exploded. "Some of the bastards haven't paid for fifty years! Why does John suddenly pick on me? What about some of his precious earls?"

"Have you displeased him at all, Father?" Giles looked up, his green eyes scanning his father's face seriously.

"Of course not." William smacked the palm of his hand with the rolled parchment. His jaw was working with agitation. "God damn it, Giles"— for a moment he forgot his son's exalted calling—"he came to Will's wedding. He gave him rubies and emeralds for a wedding gift. Would he have done that if I had displeased him?" He strode back and forth across the floor excitedly.

"Perhaps it is merely routine demand from the exchequer. The king may not even have realized from whom he was ordering the money." Giles hesitated. "I suppose our mother . . . ?"

"Oh, yes!" William whirled around. "Your mother! She might well have something to do with it! She was antagonizing the king deliberately. I've seen it coming. If she's said something else to make him angry . . ."

"No, Father." Giles's cool voice cut across William's outburst. "I was going to suggest you ask Mother whether the Welsh lands might not produce some of the money to pay off a little of the debt. She is renowned, in the March, you know, for her husbandry." He smiled. "She is your best steward, Father. I don't think sometimes you realize how hard she works."

William snorted. "Well, if she's hoarding my money—"

"Not hoarding, Father. She takes a pride in her herds and her lands. She loves the Welsh hills. I hear people speak of her with awe and respect and love." Seeing his father's expression, he hastily changed the subject. "I am sure you can have this demand postponed, Father, if you go to see the king again. Why not ask him directly? Take him a gift—a new book for his library is a sure way to win his favor back, you know that as well as I do. Wait on him as soon as you can."

William looked hopefully at his son, a little reassured by Giles's calm words. The demand had worried him. A year earlier he would have laughed it off and stuffed the parchment away among a hundred others in his own chancery office, confident in the king's total goodwill. Nothing obvious had happened to shake his confidence and yet there was something, an uneasy feeling gnawed at the back of his mind, a suspicion that the king was not quite as friendly as before; a hint here and there among his friends that he should tread warily. Nothing had been said; nothing done. But William had felt a sudden chill hover over him.

Matilda was appalled when she saw the size of William's debt. "Have you paid nothing to the king since his coronation?" She scanned the parchment and looked up from William to Giles to Will, who was leaning by the chancery window, his arms folded, a worried frown on his face; behind them the scribe and William's clerk sat at the high desk, their pens at the ready. Why? Why the sudden demand after all these years? She had a vision of John's face in the chapel and she closed her eyes, trying to steady the sudden irrational wave of fear that had filled her and the thought that the demand might not be unconnected with the fact that the king had seen her hand in that of Richard de Clare.

"We must pay something at once, William." She beckoned her own steward, who was waiting with an armload of rolled parchments. Then she stopped. "I thought you were told originally to pay the taxes for Limerick to the Dublin exchequer. Why does Westminster suddenly want them?"

William shrugged. His shoulders drooped a little.

She gave an exasperated sigh. "Here." She pulled a parchment from her steward's hands and scrutinized it closely. "I can find about seven hundred marks. Those will be sent to the exchequer straight away. See to it," she directed William's steward, who bowed and began to scribble as she felt for the keys at her girdle. "It is lucky, William, that we had so good a year

in the March. I was able to sell cattle and there is money in the coffers."
Giving one of the keys to her steward, she directed him to fetch the gold.
"It is not safe to be so much in the king's debt, William." She put her hand
on his arm gently. "We must pay it off."

William laughed. The whole episode had frightened and annoyed him,
and his family's reaction to the size of his debt had first worried and then
irritated him irrationally, but now that some money was to be returned,
and so easily, he felt completely happy again. "That'll be enough for the
king," he replied, shaking off her hand. "I'll have a word with him. I'm
sure it's all a mistake."

But it was not a mistake. The king had, it appeared, every intention of
holding William to the repayment of his debts. He accepted the carefully
chosen, exquisitely illuminated volume of Geoffrey of Monmouth's *History
of the British Kingdom* and within two weeks William had received a further
demand from the exchequer.

Early the following year the next blow had fallen. William was ordered
to give up his lordships of Glamorgan and Gwynllwg to one of the king's
new favorites, an adventurer named Fawkes de Breauté.

"Christ's bones, Moll. What will he want next?" William had ridden in
desperation to consult his kinsman William, Earl Ferrers, who remained
high in the king's favor, and he had returned with vague assurances of
friendship from the young man but with the same advice—pay up as much
as you can and keep a low profile until the king's displeasure was dissipated.

"He wants money, William. You've got to accept the fact and we've got
to find it." Matilda forced herself to continue studying the embroidery
before her, feeling the tightness of fear close across her chest like an iron
band. "You cannot get out of it. He will not be fobbed off any longer.
John is getting angry."

Again and again William begged and pleaded with the king to extend
the time he needed to repay his debts and reinstate him in favor, but to no
avail. The king remained deaf to his desperate demands to be granted
further audiences and turned to new friends. It was clear that the de
Braose family was to be ruined unless something or someone could be
prevailed upon to change the king's mind. So, after long and worried
consultations with Giles and Will, who had arrived with Mattie and their
baby son, John, diplomatically named for the king, it had been agreed that
Matilda should try alone, and try before the king heard that Giles had
obeyed his conscience in deciding to support the church in its quarrel with
the king over the election of the new Archbishop of Canterbury. Having
read, in Hereford Cathedral, the papal interdict suspending church services throughout the kingdom, Giles had prudently followed the example
of the other bishops, who had defied the king and fled to France.

The king was in council at Gloucester Castle, and it was with a profound

442

feeling of foreboding that Matilda relinquished her mare to the esquire who ran forward to help her dismount and preceded William Ferrers and Adam into the great hall. John was, it appeared, busy and could or would not receive them at once, so, her heart pounding nervously, Matilda took the carved oak chair to which John's chamberlain had shown her and sat down nervously, clutching her mantle around her and glancing up at Adam, who, resting an arm protectively on the back of the chair, stood close beside her. Ferrers, less in awe than the others, went off cheerfully in search of refreshment.

She closed her eyes and leaned her head back for a moment, feeling the heavily carved ornamental wood press into the back of her skull. Her courage, for the first time, was beginning to fail her. What if the king should refuse to grant her an audience? What if he refused her plea? What if he refused to see William and persevered with his plan to bring him, and thus the whole family with him, to ruin? She shivered a little in spite of the warm furs around her shoulders.

They waited a long, long time in the great hall, watching the busy throng who were gathered there. From time to time men passed into the presence chamber to see the king and reappeared again, but no one came to call the de Braose party.

Cold night had settled in outside. Through the ever-reopening outside door Matilda could see the swirling mist and the white haloes around the burning torches as men moved back and forth across her line of vision. More branches were heaped on the two huge fires, and aromatic smoke escaped now and then in puffs that hung beneath the high beams of the roof.

And then the door opened again and a party of men were hurried out. The usher approached the chamberlain and whispered, and the man turned and began to walk purposefully in Matilda's direction.

She sat without moving, watching his stately progress down the hall, only the whitening of her knuckles, as her fingers clutched unconsciously together, showing the turmoil inside her.

Then he was before her. He bowed. "His Grace will see the Lady of Hay," he stated gravely. "He does not wish to see you, sir, nor you, my lord." He nodded at Adam and Ferrers in turn and then, without looking to see if she followed, he slowly retraced his steps down the length of the great hall.

John surveyed her for a long while without speaking and then, with a snap of his fingers, dismissed the clerks and attendants crowding the room and watching the tall, graceful woman who curtsied before her king.

He waited until the door had closed behind the last bowing figure and then he leaned back in his chair and smiled. "I wonder if I can guess what brings the Lady Matilda to Gloucester?"

She lowered her eyes. "Your Grace is probably aware of my predicament. I would not presume on our long friendship if I had not thought you might grant my request." Glancing up, she saw something akin to amusement in his face and, taking courage, she smiled. "Please see William once more, Your Grace. Give him a chance to explain to you our temporary difficulties in raising so much money so fast. We will pay. But please, give us time, Your Grace. And please smile once again on William. He is so fond of you, so devoted to your service. You have broken his heart with your disfavor—" She broke off, seeing the black frown that, at the mention of William's name, succeeded the look of humor.

"William, my lady, is a fool," he snapped. "He preens and crows under my favor and amasses fortunes and lordships all on credit, and then when I seek to realize some of my debts, he fawns and whines like a kicked dog." He leaned forward in his chair, his blue eyes suddenly flashing. "God's teeth, Matilda. I made your Sir William. From a petty border baron I raised him to one of the greatest in this land. And I can reduce him again as quickly." He smashed his fist against the palm of his hand.

Matilda shuddered.

"Your husband, madam, was becoming too ambitious, too powerful," he went on. "I smell treachery there."

Matilda gasped indignantly. "Your Grace, that's not true! William is a loyal servant. And he is your friend."

Rising, John stepped off the low dais on which his chair was placed and, throwing one leg over the corner of the table, rested there, his arms folded.

"He sought alliance with the rebellious lords of Ireland, my lady. Lords who have defied my justiciar there. They complained when he took Limerick from your son-in-law. Do you know why I took it?" He stared at her intently. "I took it because no dues have been received from William. The Earl Marshall was at court this winter pleading the cause of the Irish lords. You did not know, perhaps, that I have reinstated them now in their land in exchange for a pledge of loyalty. Yes, Walter de Lacy too. But my benevolence does not extend to your Sir William. He has driven me too far with his greed. God's blood! He even covets an earldom!"

Matilda bit her lip and then nodded reluctantly. "There is no treachery in that, Your Grace."

"Perhaps not." John was thoughtful. "Nevertheless, I prefer men about me who serve me out of loyalty. I mistrust ambition." He snorted. "A quality you did not display when you had it in your power to take a prince for a lover, though you did feel able to give your favors to a mere earl." His eyes, deliberately insolent, slid up and down her body and she reddened violently.

"I am an elderly matron now, sire. Too old, I think, for such adventures," she stammered.

444

John laughed again and, pushing himself up from the table, came and stood close to her. Slowly he raised his hand and touched her cheek. "You scarcely look a day older, my dear, for all your little Welsh princeling grandchildren." He paused. "Is that what you have come for? Did you hope to seduce me into waiving your husband's debts?" For a moment their eyes met. She saw the challenge in his gaze and something else— something that was veiled so quickly behind the hard, enigmatic stare that she wondered if she had glimpsed it at all.

She took a step back, feeling the heat mount in her cheeks again. The interview was not going the way she had intended. "I came here to ask delay from Your Grace for the sake of the friendship you once had for us both, no more than that, sire," she said with quiet dignity.

John turned away abruptly. "Very well. I will give him another chance. For your sake. But I will require substantial proof of his intentions. Castles, hostages." He spoke curtly.

"Hostages!" Matilda repeated indignantly. "Why hostages? Is our word not good enough?"

"William's isn't." He threw the remark over his shoulder as he returned to his chair and lowered himself into it.

"Then mine, my lord. There should be no need of hostages."

"Oh, come, Matilda, it is customary. Are you afraid I might demand your own fair self?" He smiled. "I'm sure we can take someone you won't miss too much! Tell your husband to come to me the day after tomorrow at Hereford. I will hear his excuses then. But never again. This is his last chance to convince me he can work something out. His last chance."

With a gesture he dismissed her. Then as she curtsied and turned toward the door he called out. "By the way, my lady. I have no doubt you have heard that following the papal interdict I am confiscating all church property for the use of the crown. I understand there are substantial properties waiting for me in Hereford. Episcopal properties."

Matilda swallowed, nervously holding her breath.

"You must admit, my lady"—his voice was as smooth as a cat's purr— "that I have grounds for scenting treachery within the de Braose family. Very good grounds."

When William returned to the Hay from his meeting with the king three days later, it seemed that all had gone well. He strode into the hall, where most of the household were gathered for the noonday meal. At his side were two of the king's officers.

Matilda laid down her napkin and rose to her feet, anxiously scanning her husband's face for signs of worry or anger. He met her eyes and then glanced down, swallowing nervously.

"Father, what happened? What did the king say?" Will was around the table and off the dais in a moment, confronting his father. There was silence in the great hall. At the high table all eyes were fixed on William

445

and at the lower tables where other members of his household ate; men and women alike waited with bated breath for their lord to speak. The only sound came from the fires, where logs hissed and crackled between the great iron dogs and from behind the serving screens at the back of the hall, where a hastily suppressed giggle rang out in the silence.

"We have reached an agreement." William spoke at last. Matilda saw him swallow again and she felt a tremor of unease. Silently they waited for him to go on.

"The king has agreed that I can spread the payments of my debts over several years," he continued, and then, as if conscious for the first time of the watching eyes from the depths of the hall, he stepped onto the dais, lowering his voice. "The king has requested one or two guarantees that I will pay." He glanced over his shoulder at the waiting officers and then turned back, refusing to meet Matilda's gaze. Full of misgivings, she slowly seated herself once more, forcing herself to stay calm.

"What guarantee does the king demand, William?" She reached slowly for her goblet, keeping her voice slow and steady with an effort.

"I have agreed that he take all my Welsh lands and castles into the royal holding, just until I pay. He has already sent constables to take them over —all but Hay, which he said was more yours." He frowned. "And then . . ." Once more he looked at the floor, his voice trailing away uncertainly as a gasp of horror went around the high table.

"*And,* William?" Matilda could feel Reginald beside her holding his breath. She put her hand gently over his on the table. Before them the plate of meat congealed in a pool of cooling fat.

"And I agreed that we should give him hostages, Moll. Many, many other families have been asked to do the same. It's not just us." He hesitated. "He wants Will, and our two grandsons, little John, and Isobel's son, baby Ralph—"

"*No!*" Will sprang to face his father, his face white with fury. "You would dare to hand babes over to the king! Ralph is only three days old, for God's sake! How did the king know Isobel had come here from Wigmore? How did he know Ralph even existed?" He turned and glared accusingly at his mother, but William interrupted.

"No, Will, not your mother. I told him. I had to offer more surety. He would not give me the time to pay otherwise. I had to have time. I thought he was going to arrest me." His eyes were fixed at last on his wife's face.

Slowly she stood up. So John had been mocking her all along, lying when he said he would demand no one of importance to her. After pushing back her chair, she walked behind the others seated at the table and came around to the edge of the dais. Her eyes were hard as she turned to the king's officers standing side by side below the step. "If the king requires hostages he shall have them," she stated flatly. "I will give myself if necessary, but I would deliver none—*none* of my sons to the king, you can

446

tell him that. If he asks why, remind him of his promise to me and tell him that perhaps he should think of the *honorable* way he treated his brother's child, his own nephew Arthur, then he will know why I would not trust him with my sons!"

"Matilda!" William broke in, scandalized. "You mustn't mention that. It is not supposed to be known! I swore to keep it a secret!"

Matilda turned her blazing eyes on her husband. "I think it is as well that the king should know that his people realize what has been going on. I wouldn't trust him with *any* of my family. He let me believe he would ask for no hostages of importance and then he does this."

William hastily stepped from the dais. He put his hand on the shoulder of one of the king's officers. "Tell the king I'm sorry. Tell him I'm still ready to make good." He hesitated. "But without hostages. I'll go before his court and whichever barons he chooses. . . . Make no mention of anything my wife said. Please. She was overwrought."

The king was told, however, word for word, what Matilda had said.

He reacted with an outbreak of unprecedented fury, followed by the issue of orders that William and Matilda and their entire family should be arrested without delay. Appalled, Matilda listened to the breathless, garbled warnings as she stood with Earl Ferrers in the bailey at Hay as a messenger from Hereford flung himself off his lathered horse at her feet, gesticulating wildly behind him, tripping over his words in his haste.

Matilda went cold with terror as she understood at last that the king was sending men to arrest them. "You must leave," she said to the young earl urgently. "Leave quickly. This is our quarrel. You're not involved and there's no need for you to get on the wrong side of the king."

Ferrers had gone quite pale. He scrambled hastily onto the horse that his esquire had brought him ready for a hawking trip, and sat for a moment looking down at Matilda. "If there's anything I can do, I will. You know that."

"I know." She smiled tautly. "Now ride quickly. I want those gates closed."

She watched with a frown as the young man galloped out, not pausing even to summon his attendants, save for the astonished esquire who had time only to throw himself across his own unsaddled gelding and pelt after his young master. Then slowly—too slowly, it seemed to Matilda—the great gates swung to behind him. With a hammering heart she beckoned the messenger and sent to find her husband.

"What shall we do?" William looked from one to the other of his sons. "It's all your fault, you stupid woman." He turned on Matilda. "Why could you not have kept your mouth shut? Now the king will never forgive us! We are all doomed. It is the end."

"She did right, Father." Reginald's was the only calm voice among them. "You should not have allowed the king to demand our children. If

447

you had failed to pay, he might have—" Seeing Mattie's face as she held little John in her arms, he broke off abruptly. The whole family was congregated around the fire in the solar. Will stood behind his wife, his hands gently on her shoulders. Only Isobel was missing, still in bed after the birth of her baby. No one had told her that her little Ralph had been demanded as hostage.

"There's nothing left for it but to fight him." Reginald spoke again. "You've nothing to lose, Father, and a lot to gain if you win. That way you could demand exemption from the debt altogether, or at least time to pay on your own terms."

"No, Reginald!" Adam de Porter's quiet voice cut him short. "You must not fight the king. Your father must demand a fair hearing and I think your mother should ask the king's pardon for her rash remark. You must all throw yourselves on the king's mercy. To fight him would be treason."

It was Matilda's turn to be furious. She faced him. "Never. Never will we throw ourselves on John's mercy, nor appeal to his honor. He doesn't know the meaning of the word."

"Reginald is right, you know, Father." Will spoke at last. "We should fight. Things have gone too far now. You reclaim your rights and territories and repay the debt as and when you can and then the king will have no more complaint against you. And Mother must never apologize to the king. That would be unthinkable." His eyes strayed to his mother's face and for a moment they held one another's gaze. Matilda looked away first.

There was a knock outside. The door opened before anyone answered and Stephen the steward appeared, a worried frown on his lined face. "The king's men are at the gates, my lord, demanding entry. They have warrants."

"They are not to come in." William slammed his fist on the table. "Pour some slops on their heads if they dare to try. Tell them to go back to the king and tell him that William de Braose will fight him first."

"No! William!" Adam put his hand on his brother-in-law's arm but William shook it off angrily.

"Yes! I have had enough of going in fear, begging and cringing. Tell them that, steward. De Braose will fight!"

The king's messengers rode away without much argument, but it was obvious they would soon return with reinforcements.

Adam left as soon as the coast was clear. "I cannot agree with what you're doing, William. It's treason," he said before he rode away. "You must ask the king's pardon and submit to him." But William would not listen. The days of fear and pleading were over. With his family behind him at last, he felt confident he could repair his self-esteem. When a detachment of the king's troops arrived at Hay to try to carry out the arrests, he repelled them with something like a grim good humor, hurling insults after them when three days later they rode away to the east.

Nick jerked upright in his chair. So they thought they could fight him, the fools! How could de Braose be so arrogant; how could she be so proud, so stubborn . . .

He stared around, disoriented. The others were sitting in silence, each deep in his own thoughts, Jo gazing blankly out into the darkness.

"Are you all right, Nick?" Ben leaned forward and touched his arm.

Nick forced himself to smile. On the table, the candle had burned so low the wick floated in a small pool of liquid wax. "Sorry." He took a deep breath. "I must have been asleep. I'm a bit jet-lagged, I suppose."

"And tired. It is midnight, after all. Come on." Ben stood up. "I'll show you where you can sleep."

Nick rose to his feet unsteadily, still grasping for reality. He hesitated for a moment then he dropped a kiss on Jo's forehead. "Good night," he murmured.

Jo and Ann watched him follow Ben into the house. Then Ann got up. "We're putting him in the apple loft, Jo. It makes a lovely bedroom in the summer. Unless you want to sleep together?"

Sitting down on the edge of his bed, Ben wearily pulled off his socks. "I'll never be able to get up for milking." He groaned.

Ann grinned. "Go on. You always say you only need two hours' sleep."

"I do. But they've got to be the right two hours, and that's about ten o'clock." He stood up and began to take off his trousers. "What do you make of the boyfriend?"

Ann had been brushing her hair. Her hand stopped in midstroke. "He frightens me."

"Frightens you?" Ben repeated incredulously. "I thought he was a decent sort. Very decent. And they obviously love each other. Once they've got this peculiar business settled, they'll be fine."

Ann shook her head slowly. "It's not as easy as that, Ben. I told Nick there was no way he could have been given posthypnotic suggestions to make him hurt Jo or do anything he didn't want to, but that wasn't strictly true. If his brother is anything like as clever as I think he is, he will have found a way around Nick's natural inhibitions easily. Nick and Jo have reason to be afraid, Ben. I think he has planted posthypnotic suggestions in both their minds. I think he is playing them against each other for some reason I cannot even begin to guess, and he's so sure they'll work he can brag about them to Nick." She shivered suddenly. "The awful thing is, I think they might work all too well, whatever they are."

Ann couldn't sleep. For more than an hour she tossed and turned beside Ben, who always slept at once, flat on his back, relaxed and seemingly

449

dreamless, then she got up. She pulled on a silk kimono over her cotton nightgown and tiptoed out of the room. The children were sleeping soundlessly in their bedroom beneath the sloping roof. Bill, who still slept like a baby, on his back, his arms above his head; Polly curled in the fetal position, her thumb firmly plugged into her mouth, the two golden heads still and angelic. She crept out of the room and closed the door silently.

The kitchen was still hot from the woodburning stove. She lit a lamp then opened the door of the firebox quietly and threw in a log. It would be nice to have hot water for the morning. Often in the summer she didn't bother. . . .

"There wouldn't be a chance of a cup of tea, would there?" The voice from the end of the dark sitting room made her jump nearly out of her skin.

Nick rose from the shadows and came toward her.

"Of course." She glanced at him curiously. He was wearing a pair of faded jeans. His top was bare, as were his feet.

"Sorry if I frightened you. I think I'm too tired to sleep. My brain is whirling in ever-decreasing circles." He perched on a stool at the edge of the lamplight. "I took off my watch. Do you know what time it is?"

"After three." Ann filled the kettle and put it on the stove. "It'll take a while to boil. The fire was nearly down."

"I want you to hypnotize me, Ann." Nick leaned forward suddenly. He reached out a hand toward her. "I must find out the truth. Please."

"Are you sure you want to know the truth?" She surveyed him solemnly. Then almost without knowing she had done it she took his hand. She squeezed it lightly and then drew away.

He nodded. "If Sam has planted any ideas in my head I want you to find out what they are and kill them, do you understand?"

"Nick." She began to pace up and down the floor slowly, her arms folded, her bare feet kicking the silk of the kimono into a rhythmic billowing pattern over the stone flags. "There are things you must understand. Posthypnotic suggestion—if that is what we are discussing—is a strange and inexact science. I don't know what your brother might have suggested. Neither do I know what safeguards and conditions he may have imposed."

"He has suggested that I was King John of England in a previous life. He has suggested that as John I was in love with Matilda de Braose. I think he has suggested that I killed her—or ordered her death—because she rejected me, and I think he has suggested I kill Jo as some sort of crazy revenge." He took a deep breath. "Did Jo tell you that I have already hurt her? Twice."

Ann sucked in her breath. "No, she didn't tell me that." She stared at him: at the handsome, strong face, the determined chin, the firm blue eyes beneath straight brows, the broad muscular shoulders of a sportsman,

450

strong arms, slim hips. She closed her eyes. He was unquestionably a strong man. A man who could easily overpower any woman if he chose. And he was an attractive man. Very attractive. . . . She saw the slight smile on his lips and dragged her eyes away from him quickly. Christ! She was supposed to be the hypnotist! She shivered again.

She moistened her lips with the tip of her tongue. "Yes," she said, "I'll try."

Quietly Sam let himself back into Nick's apartment. He put his bag down in the hall and stood still, listening. There was no sound. Even the noise of traffic was silent at this hour, the occasional cars in Park Lane muffled by the closed windows. He walked quietly forward and peered into Nick's bedroom. It was empty, as he had known it would be. A quiet check on the other rooms proved Nick wasn't there either. Smiling to himself, he switched on the lamp in the living room and walked over to the windows. For a moment he stood still, staring at his own dark reflection in the glass, thrown into relief by the single bulb, then he reached up and drew the curtains together with a sharp rattle. He turned and looked around.

It was a large rectangular room, the polished wood floor carpeted with brightly colored rugs. The walls were covered with paintings and drawings —one of them a sketch of Jo. Sam stood in front of it for a moment, considering it. It wasn't good. It did not do her justice.

Behind him the phone rang. He turned and looked at it, then he glanced at his watch. It was four in the morning.

He picked up the receiver.

"Nick? Thank God, I thought you might have gone away for the weekend." Sam said nothing. He was smiling faintly.

"Nick? Nick, are you there?" Judy's voice rose hysterically. "Nick, did you find Jo? Pete and I have just been over at Tim Heacham's and he was saying the craziest things. He was doped up to the eyeballs, but he said Jo really was going to die and none of us could do anything about it—*Nick!*"

"Nick isn't here, my sweet." Sam sat down on the deep armchair and cradled the receiver against his left ear. "I'm sorry. You must have missed him."

There was a breathless silence. Then she whispered, "Sam?"

"The very same. How are you, Judith?"

"Where is Nick?" She ignored his question.

"I have no idea. I am not, as someone once said, my brother's keeper." He rested his feet on the coffee table.

"And Jo? Is Jo all right?"

"Do you really care?" His tone was scathing. "Stop being a hypocrite, Judith. It is only days since you were fulminating against Ms. Clifford with all the somewhat limited invective at your command. I have told you Jo

451

has nothing to do with you. Go back to your *paparazzi* boyfriend and mind your own business."

He put down the receiver with almost delicate care before standing up and strolling out to the hall. He picked up his bag and, dropping it on the bed in the spare room, threw back the lid. He had not turned on the lights. Outside the first tentative notes of a blackbird whistled over the rooftops, echoing in the silence of the huge courtyard at the back of the apartment block. Sam slipped his hand into the side pocket of the bag and drew something out. He carried it to the window and held it up to the gray dawn light. It was a carved ivory crucifix.

"I'm sorry, Nick." Ann threw herself back into the chair wearily and closed her eyes. "I've used every technique I know. It's not going to work."

"It's got to work!" Nick clenched his fists. "Please, try again."

"No. It's no use." She stood up. "Look, it's nearly dawn. We're both exhausted and, as you said, you're probably suffering from jet lag. Why don't we get some sleep? We can try again tomorrow."

"Tomorrow might be too late." Nick reached forward and caught Ann's wrist. "Don't you realize that? Please, just once more. Then, if it doesn't work, we'll give up."

Ann sat down on the edge of the coffee table facing him. "You're too tense, Nick. You're fighting me and I don't have the experience to get round that."

"Have you got some tranquilizers or something I could take?"

She laughed. "In this house? Ben would divorce me if I took anything stronger than feverfew tea for my migraine!" She sighed. "Look, I'll try once more. Sit back, put your feet up, and relax. I'll go and make that tea we've been waiting for and I'll put a slug of brandy in it. Try to unwind, Nick. Close your eyes. Let your mind go blank."

She stood looking down at him for a moment, surprised by the sudden surge of almost maternal affection she felt for the man lying so helplessly before her. Quickly she turned away.

She made two cups of tea and poured a double measure of brandy in each, then she carred them back to their chairs.

"There, that should do the trick." Sitting down opposite him again, she slid the cups onto the coffee table.

"Nick?"

His head had fallen sideways on the patchwork cushion. Gently she touched his hand. There was no response.

With a sigh she took the woven blanket from the sofa and drew it over him, then, after turning down the lamp, she blew out the flame. The room was no longer dark. The still, eerie, predawn light was filtering in between the curtains. She drew one back silently and stood, sipping her tea, looking

452

at the dim, colorless garden and the white cauldron of luminous mist beyond them in the valley. Suddenly she shivered violently.

She turned and looked at Nick.

Whatever devil he was going to have to fight inside himself, she was not going to be able to help him. He and Jo were going to have to face it on their own.

34

With the dawn came rain; heavy, soaking rain from gray clouds drawing their soft bellies over the mountain-tops, drenching the thirsty ground. Ben came in from the cows, dressed in a bright yellow sou'wester and cape, as the others were having their breakfast.

Nick was pale and drawn, watching moodily as Jo spooned cereal into the bowls of the two little ones. Feeling his eyes on her, she glanced up. "You look tired," she said gently.

"I didn't sleep too well." He glanced at Ann, presiding over the coffee-pot. The room was fragrant with toast and new coffee and the spitting apple logs Ben had thrown into the stove. It seemed very normal and safe.

"Are the kids going down the hill this morning?" Ben hung up his wet oilskins and began to wash his hands.

"I'm running them down in half an hour." Ann poured her husband his mug of coffee and pushed it over the table toward him. "I take turns with our neighbor at the bottom of the track on Saturday mornings to have each other's kids," she explained as she filled up Nick's cup. "That way every other weekend we can get into Brecon and do a bit of shopping or whatever on our own. Not this morning, though. I'll just be glad to get them out from under."

Ben laughed. "She doesn't mean that. Ten minutes after she gets back she starts to worry about them."

Ann smiled at him affectionately, then she looked at Jo and Nick. "What would you two like to do this morning?"

"Walk," Jo put in quickly. "Walk in the rain."

Ann raised an eyebrow. "That whim I think we can accommodate. And you, sir?" She turned to Nick.

"Why not? Some fresh air will do me good, and we don't want to get under your feet either."

"You're not!" Ann said sharply.

There was an awkward silence. Abruptly she pulled Bill off his chair and began to bundle him into his anorak, ignoring his vigorous protests that

454

his mouth was still full and he hadn't finished. "Are you sure one of you wouldn't rather come down with me?" She glanced from Jo to Nick and back. "You can't both want to go out in the rain." She saw Jo's knuckles whiten for a moment on the corner of the table.

"I think there are things Nick and I should talk about," Jo said after a moment. She bit her lip. "We'll be all right. We won't go far."

Ann was watching Nick's face again and she saw the tiny movement of the muscles at the corner of his jaw. She sighed. "Right. Well, help yourselves to mackintoshes or whatever on the door there, and when you get back we'll have coffee and cakes, okay?"

"And for Christ's sake, don't get lost!" Ben put in. "This is a real mountain, not Hyde Park. Stay within sight of the wall. It will lead on down the hill for about three miles if you want a decent walk and then bring you back past all the best views." He cocked an eye out of the window at the uniformly gray murk of the low cloud and gave his rumbling laugh. "See you when you get back."

The mist was cold and wet on their faces when they stepped out into the silent white world. Jo put her hands firmly in the pockets of her mac. "I'd forgotten what it was to feel cold. It's hard to believe the weather can change so much after last night."

"It's the cloud." Nick pulled up the collar of his jacket. "It's probably bright sunshine down in the valley."

Ten paces behind them the farmhouse was already barely in sight, dissolving and drifting, its gray slates and white walls the perfect blend of mist and cloud.

Jo stopped. "Where is the wall?"

"Here. Beside us. Ben was right, it would be easy to get lost." Nick touched her elbow, guiding her a little to the left.

Jo moved slightly away from him. Her heart had begun to beat in a quick, uneasy rhythm. She glanced back. The farmhouse had gone; they were completely alone.

She pushed her hands further into her pockets. "How did the trip to the States go? You haven't told me yet."

Nick was walking a couple of paces behind her, his eyes on her slim figure in the tightly belted raincoat and black rubber boots. Somewhere deep inside himself he felt a sudden awakening of anger.

She turned, pulling off the blue scarf Ann had lent her and shaking her hair free. "Do you think you'll get the new account? What is it, Nick?" She had seen it at once in his eyes. "What's wrong?"

He shook his head desperately. "Nothing. Nothing's wrong. I didn't sleep, that's all. Yes, I think there's a good chance. I'm flying a team out to New York next week to discuss things with the marketing director out there; then, if all goes well, we'll take over the launch of their product in the UK early next year." He stopped and picked up a loose stone from the ground beneath the wall, hurling it into the whiteness. "If we get the account I'll be taking on new staff because it looks as though Desco has had a change of heart."

"Oh, Nick, I am pleased." Unobtrusively Jo put several feet more between him and herself. "I knew it was just a temporary hiccup."

Nick gave a strained laugh. "Firms larger than mine have gone under through losing one account." He did not look at her. "Jo, I didn't come up here to discuss the problems or otherwise of Franklyn-Greerson."

"No." Jo glanced across at him. Now that the moment had come she didn't know what to say. She clenched her fists, aching to touch him and yet not daring to move. In anguish she turned away. "What do you think of the Clementses, Nick?" she asked softly.

"I like them." He grimaced. "And I think we need them. Dear God, we need someone."

Jo frowned. She could see the faint outline of a group of trees near them now and hear the distant bleating of a sheep. Below on the hillside the mist was graying but above their heads it seemed brighter and there was a hint of glare in the air. She tensed suddenly, realizing that Nick was standing beside her again.

"Listen, Jo—"

"No, please, Nick." She backed away. "Please—don't touch me—"

"Don't touch you!" His anger overflowed suddenly. "Always the same! You sleep with my brother, but I must not touch you!"

He reached out toward her, but she edged away from him, her boots slipping on the wet, muddy grass.

"I haven't slept with your brother! That's a lie!"

"How do you know?" Nick's voice was dangerously quiet.

She stared at him in horror. "What do you mean?"

"I mean, he hypnotized you. He told me all about it, Jo. William de Braose—my brother! How strange that he should choose to be a man like that!"

"Perhaps he had no choice," Jo cried.

Nick raised an eyebrow. "Or perhaps that identity gives him all the chances he wants to screw Matilda and by proxy her latter-day descendant!"

"He didn't—" She backed away from him until she felt the rough stones of the wall against her back. "He . . . he wanted to, but he couldn't manage it—"

"So he beat you instead? And I gather you thought you deserved it. Perhaps you even enjoyed it?"

"No, I damn well didn't!" Jo exploded. "If I ever set eyes on your brother again I'll kill him with my bare hands. He's a sadistic, twisted psychopath!"

456

Nick laughed coldly. "But you have to admit he had a point. You were unfaithful to your husband."

"You of all people should know about that," she retorted defiantly.

He smiled, his eyes hard. "I remember only one occasion," he said slowly, "when you lay with your prince."

"I was raped by my prince," Jo said forcibly. "He nearly killed me!"

"He loved you, Jo, but you made him angry. You kept on making him angry—"

"Not *me,*" Jo cried wildly. "It wasn't *me,* Nick! And what Matilda did was none of your business. Nor Sam's. Nor even mine, perhaps! Oh, God, this whole thing is a nightmare!" She pushed at him desperately. "Let me pass, please. I want to go back to the house."

Nick did not move. He caught her wrist and, forcing her arm backward, held it pressed for a moment on the top of the wall. Lichen streaked the white sleeve of the raincoat.

"You may or may not have slept with Sam, but you did sleep with Tim Heacham while you were in Raglan, I hear. You've been having quite a time, haven't you, Jo?"

She shrank back. "I can sleep with whom I damn well please, Nick Franklyn, you don't own me! Let me go—"

"Your husband was right. You do need to be punished—"

"I haven't got a husband!" Jo shouted. "For God's sake, you're mad as well! Don't you see, it's not real, none of it is real!" She stopped struggling as his grip on her wrist tightened and pain shot through her shoulder. "Nick, please, you're hurting me. Nick!"

For a moment he didn't move. Closing his eyes, he felt the sweat standing on his forehead. Then his stomach heaved and, dropping Jo's wrist, he staggered a couple of paces back, retching into the grass.

"Nick?" Jo was staring at him, frightened. His anger had gone as quickly as it had come and in its place was a blank, uncomprehending terror. "Nick, what's happened? What has Sam done to you? Oh, God, what are we going to do?"

Straightening, Nick wiped the back of his hand across his forehead. He was shaking violently as he turned back toward her. "I've hurt you." He gasped. "God, Jo, I've hurt you—" He caught her arm again, but gently this time, and looked down at it. There was blood on the back of her hand, welling between the streaks of green from the mossy stones.

"It's only a graze." She snatched it away from him.

Nick stood motionless. He felt dizzy. "He's manipulating me! He's made me believe I'm someone I'm not. Jo, he's turned me into a killer!" He leaned forward on the wall and put his head in his hands.

Jo was trembling so violently she could hardly stand. "Let's go back inside—"

"Ann can't help me." He didn't move. "She tried last night."

457

Jo had turned away toward the house. She stopped in her tracks. "When?"

"Neither of us could sleep. We had some tea, and I told her what I was afraid of. She tried to regress me, but she couldn't." Taking a deep breath, he grasped the top of the stone wall so tightly his nails splintered.

"I love you, Jo," he whispered suddenly, his voice husky with despair. "Whatever happens, I want you to know that."

The kitchen smelled of baking. "Well, you two weren't long," Ann said cheerfully. "I thought you'd wait till the sun came out at least." She glanced up and the smile faded from her lips. "What happened?"

Nick hung up his jacket on the back of the door and threw himself on the sofa. "You've got to help me, Ann. For pity's sake, help me!"

Ann glanced at Jo, who had walked to the sink and was running warm water over her hand, her back to them both. She took a deep breath. "I'll try again," she said. "Jo, will you leave us alone? Take a couple of mugs of coffee out for you and Ben. He's in the cowshed."

She waited until Jo had let herself out of the kitchen door, then she turned. "What happened?"

"Nothing. But it nearly did. I could feel him, Ann, inside me. Cold, calculating, angry, bitter. I knew that I—he—could do anything. Anything! I fought it this time but another time I might not be able to."

"Sit down. Here." She pointed to the kitchen table. "I'm going to light the oil lamp. You said Sam uses lights to induce hypnosis. There—now, look at the flame. Don't blink. Occupy your mind totally with that speck of fire. That's fine." Her voice had lost its tension as she gained confidence. "Good, now relax. Relax, Nick, and listen. Just listen to my voice. Don't shut your eyes—you can't shut your eyes. Good." She saw the strain on his face begin to fall away as he stared at the light. "Good, that's fine. Now, I want to go back in time, Nick, back to when you were a child . . ."

Ben looked up from the leg of the cow over which he had been bending. He ran his hand gently down it, then stood up and smacked the cow affectionately on the hindquarters.

"Is that my coffee? Bless you, my dear."

Jo sat down on a hay bale, her own mug cupped between her hands. "Ann is trying to hypnotize Nick."

"She told me she tried last night to no avail." Ben sat down comfortably next to her. "What have you done to your hand?" His sharp eyes had missed nothing.

"I caught it against the wall, that's all." She looked away from him. "Oh, Ben. What's happened to him?"

Ben patted her shoulder. "He confided in Annie last night, my dear, that he is very worried. If Ann cannot help him we both feel he should consult your hypnotherapist without delay. He is, after all, a professional,

458

and he knows the background to your case." He smiled. "I think it would be best if Nick went back to London, Jo."

She nodded slowly. "I suppose so." She was about to drink the last of her coffee when she lowered the mug again. "He thinks he's going to try to kill me, Ben. But why? Why should Sam do this to us? Why? He can't really believe he was Matilda's husband. And if he does, why should he want Nick to hurt me? It just doesn't make sense."

"Things that make sense to the insane mind are seldom obvious to others," Ben said soberly. "And it sounds to me as if Nicholas's brother must be insane."

He put down the mug at his feet. He was about to stand up when from the house they both heard the sound of a frightened scream.

Ben was on his feet first. With Jo close behind him he raced toward the kitchen door and flung it open.

Ann was lying on the floor; there was no sign of Nick.

Ben flung himself on his knees beside her as she struggled to sit up, her face white. "Ann, for God's sake, are you all right? What happened?"

"I-I annoyed him," she said shakily. She clung to the table leg for support. "It was my own fault. I shouldn't have attempted to regress him. I don't know enough about it—"

"What did he do, Ann?" Jo had gone cold all over. She stared at Ann for a moment, incapable of moving, then, galvanized into action, she found a cloth. After wringing it out under the tap, she knelt beside Ann, holding it gently to the bruise that was rising on her temple.

"He didn't attack me or anything. He just pushed me, that's all, and I slipped. I must have caught my head on the table or something. It was my own silly fault." Ann took the cloth from Jo's hand and pressed it more firmly against her head. "I shouldn't have interfered. It was crass stupidity. I should have known his brother would be too clever for us, but I still thought I could somehow cancel out the hypnotic suggestion. I had Nick under—he was responding well and I took him back to his childhood. I asked him one or two questions about when he was little. He seemed to realize Sam's hostility when he was a child and he steered clear of him—worshipping from afar. Then I took him back further. I wanted to find out if the idea of his being King John came from deep within his own unconscious or from his brother's suggestion." She shook her head. "He regressed easily. Once he was under he went into what seemed like total recall of a succession of lives. I wasn't prompting him. He was one man who lived around the turn of the century and who died at the age of twenty-four from typhoid." Ann, still sitting on the floor, hugged her knees. "Then he said he had lived in the reign of Queen Anne as a sailor, and he said . . . he said he's waited for Matilda, but the time was wrong." She glanced up as Jo caught her breath. "He said he waited again and again and then he produced another incarnation some one hundred and fifty years before that and he talked what sounded like French. That time he died of plague in Paris. Then there was a long gap." Ann paused. For a moment she didn't seem able to speak. "Then there was John, the youngest son of King Henry II of England."

Jo had gone white as a sheet. "You mean it is true?" she whispered. "He really was John? It wasn't Sam at all?" She closed her eyes, still kneeling at Ann's side. "He's followed me. Followed me from the past. But why? John hated Matilda. He—" Her voice broke. "He sentenced her to death." She looked up in despair. "Is that why he's here? To pursue me even beyond the grave? I knew, Ann. I recognized him. Weeks ago, I saw it in his eyes, but I didn't understand. I didn't realize what was happening—"

"No, Jo. That's rubbish. For God's sake, you are not the same people! You keep on emphasizing that yourself." Ann pulled herself to her feet. "And Nick loves you. He *loves* you, Jo." She went to the sink and wrung out the cloth beneath the cold tap once more. "It could still be that Sam initiated the idea. I just can't be sure. I don't know. I don't have enough experience to be able to tell. All I can say is, he seemed to know so much about John."

"What made him push you over, Annie?" Ben asked gently. His face was grim.

Ann gave a shaky smile. "I questioned his royal prerogative. I'm a republican, don't forget. I don't know how to handle kings. He didn't mean to knock me—he just didn't know I was there. I asked him about the de Braoses and why he had chosen to persecute them. He got angry—furiously angry—and began pacing up and down. Then he—well, I guess you'd say he flung out of the room, and it was just bad luck I was in the way. It was the year 1209. He told me that William had burned the town of Leominster in Herefordshire. One moment he was apoplectic—then suddenly he laughed. . . ."

Ben patted Jo on the shoulder, then he walked slowly to the door. "Did he go out this way?"

Ann nodded.

"You two stay here, I'll see if I can find him."

The kitchen was very silent. Neither Ann nor Jo said a word. In the stove a log fell, hitting the iron door with a rattle, and they both turned to look at it. Then Jo spoke in a whisper. "Ann, I must know what happened next. I have to know what the king did."

"You do know." Ann turned on her. "Jesus, Jo! Can't you leave it alone? You know what he did!" She sat down at the table and put her head in her hands. "Hell, I'm sorry. That's not fair. I guess I'm a bit rattled, that's all. I'll help you if I can. I said I would. But I'm no good at this, Jo. I'm in over my head."

"You don't have to do anything, Ann. Just be here with me."

"Now? But they'll come back any moment—"

"I don't care. I have to know what he's thinking. Don't you see?"

"No. I don't see. Jo, you're upset. It probably won't work anyway—"

"It will. All I need is a trigger, you said so yourself. So I'll find a trigger." Jo looked around wildly. "That lamp—that's fine—a lamp and a bowl of water. I'll look into the reflections."

She stood up and went to the sideboard, staring along the shelves. Her arm caught a glass, sweeping it to the floor with a crash. She didn't even notice. She reached up and took down one of Ann's black earthenware mixing bowls and turned back to the sink. "I have to do it, Ann. Don't you see? I have to look into the past so that I can go on living in the present!"

She filled the bowl with clear water and put it on the table, then she sat down opposite Ann, who reached out and gently touched her hand.

In silence they both looked down into the depths of the water.

Matilda had been staring out of the high window toward the shadowed distances of Radnor Forest. She turned and stared at her steward in frozen disbelief as he stood, shuffling his feet uncomfortably, in the center of the high, echoing stone chamber.

"But William left to try to recapture Radnor Castle from the king!"

"He failed, my lady." Stephen looked at her, his shoulders slumped with despair. "The king holds every de Braose Castle save Hay now. There was nowhere for Sir William to go after his assault was beaten back by the king's constable at Radnor—I suspect he did not care to come back here defeated, my lady—" Stephen glanced up at her under his eyelashes. "So he marched to Leominster and sacked the place. He burned it to the ground. The king will never forgive this, Lady Matilda," he went on gravely. "I fear your husband has now gone too far ever to turn back."

"We will be outlawed." She gasped. "What possessed him? To burn the town!" Putting her hands to her eyes, she tried to stifle the sobs that threatened to overwhelm her.

On 21 September the king proclaimed William de Braose a traitor and appointed Gerald of Athies to travel to the borders and declare all the baron's homagers free of any allegiance to their lord. William's followers left him almost to a man, to pay homage direct to the king.

At last only the faithful Stephen remained, riding with Matilda into the hills to hide what remained of their money and jewels in a deserted mountaintop shrine where the old gods, if they still dwelt there, would guard the hoard. Even William was not told of the location.

Once they were safely back at Hay Matilda took Stephen's hand. "You must stay here when we go," she said sadly. "Our quarrel is not yours, dear Stephen. Think of us and pray for us. You must hand over Hay Castle to the king and give him your unreserved homage."

"What will you do?" Stephen looked at her sadly.

She shrugged. "Try to get to my son Giles in France perhaps." She

461

looked around miserably. "We can't stay here. Thank you, Stephen, for all you've done. Thanks to you the gold at least is safe, and if we ever return it will be there."

"You will return, my lady." He raised her hand gently to his lips. "You will return."

William and Matilda rode out of Hay Castle at dawn the following day, their only companions Will and Reginald.

It was the beginning of a nightmare. King John's pursuit of them was relentless. His troops harried them unmercifully, always close behind. Several times they tried to leave the border, heading south, but each time they were forced to retreat into the icy woods, where, after weeks of rain, the last leaves were beginning to fall, leaving the tracks exposed and dangerous. Reginald was the only one who remained healthy and tried to humor the party. William had developed a pain in his side that worsened daily. Will, try as he might to hide it, was once more succumbing to his sore throat, and Matilda, though she fought it with all the willpower she possessed, could feel her tall, slim body beginning to stoop and thicken at the joints with the hateful, inflaming rheumatism brought on by the cold weather. Riding was painful for them all, and despair very close.

Here and there they found a few days' respite, lodged secretly by monks or relatives who still had sympathy for the homeless family, but always fear of discovery moved them on.

As Christmas approached they were once more on the border only a few miles north of Hay, almost back where they started. They had been galloping hard for two days, trying to avoid soldiers, who had come nearer to them than on any previous occasion. "It was treachery," Matilda could not help repeating over and over to herself as she bent low over her horse's mane, following close behind Will. Her fingers were swollen and reddened until she could no longer hold the reins. Will, not saying anything but noticing, had knotted them for her so that she could slip them over her wrist, but there was no need. The mare automatically followed the others now. "We have been betrayed," she repeated again, "by somebody we thought was our friend. They could not have found us otherwise." Only the strange hotness on her cheeks told her that she was crying. Then the wind and rain on her face froze the misery and her thoughts became numb again.

They followed the valley roads through the woods, trying to avoid the hills, where there was no shelter. She didn't know if Reginald knew where he was leading them anymore, and she no longer cared very much. All she wanted was to lie down somewhere and go to sleep and never wake again. Never to mount her horse and force her aching limbs to ride another mile. Never to feel another blast of wind.

The day was so stormy it was hard to tell if it was high noon or dusk, and when the armed figures stepped out on the waterlogged track in front of them, catching at Reginald's bridle and dragging his horse to a standstill, she felt only disbelief, thinking them part of the murk. Then at last, when she realized that they were real, all she felt was dull relief that at last the chase was over.

The wind whipped their words away before she could hear what the men said to Reginald and Will, who, coughing pitifully, had ridden up beside his brother. She only saw that her sons held their hands away from their swords in surrender and looked at one another apprehensively.

Their captors ignored William, armed though he was, and he sat unmoving as his horse stopped of its own accord, his head sunk between his shoulders, one hand still pressed to his side.

Then the trek began again, but walking this time, with a man at her horse's head. They were prisoners. She dropped the pretense of holding the reins and tried to warm her poor swollen hands by breathing on them and tucking them under her mantle.

After what seemed an eternity of frozen tracks they reached a clearing in a valley wood with, at its center, a long, low wooden building thatched with reeds. She felt herself helped somehow from the saddle and two men half carried, half dragged her toward a doorway. It was the last thing she knew.

The door latch rattled and Ann looked up. Her attention had been so completely on the bowl of shadowy reflections before her that she had forgotten the others. Ben walked slowly into the kitchen. Behind him came Nick, his face ashen. She saw at once that he was himself again. She held her finger to her lips and silently the two men sat down at the table. Both were staring at the bowl of water as Jo, unaware of their return, went on speaking slowly.

It took a long time for her to recover her senses before the fire. She was conscious of gentle hands removing her clothes, even her shift; of soft linen towels rubbing her icy skin and then of a long warm robe fastened at the waist by a girdle of spun flax. She was given flummery, a hot, spicy oatmeal gruel, from the cauldron on the fire, and meat from the spit, and mead, and then was led to sleep on a pile of sheepskins in the women's quarters. Only when she was well enough to rejoin the men by the blazing fire in the main room of the building did she discover that they were not prisoners at all but the honored guests of one of the mountain chieftains in his tribal hall. And with him they remained for all the long weeks of one of the worst winters the Welsh hills had ever known.

Snow drifted deep across the cwms and broad valleys; fast-flowing rivers froze from bank to bank and the mountains slept beneath an icy pall. Slowly, cared for by their Welsh hosts, the invalids grew stronger. Reassured that their pursuers could not reach them through the frozen hills, they regained something of their optimism, and with it made a new plan. As soon as the thaw came they would make their way west to the coast and from there they would cross to Ireland, where they could go to Margaret and Walter, and where they had many relatives and friends in a position to help them.

Matilda never asked their host why he had given them shelter; it seemed an abuse of his hospitality to query it. She supposed it was enough that they had been truly wanderers in the storm, thrown upon a sacred trust, or perhaps it was their common enmity with King John that had made them one at last with their Welsh neighbors.

As the thaw freed the high moorland trackways and the valleys of snow and ice, William and Matilda and their sons, accompanied by two Welsh guides, set off again into the teeth of the wind on their journey to the sea. They rode fast, muffled in sheepskins, nervous, in spite of the kindness and hospitality they had received, of penetrating so deep into the land of the Welsh, so often their enemies. But the journey, though bitter cold and wearisome, was without incident. They arrived at last at the broad Dovey estuary that separated north from south Wales, opposite the castle that guarded the river mouth, and looked down from the hillside onto the two ships tied up at the low wooden quay at the marsh edge. Will glanced at his mother and smiled. "Nearly there now. By tomorrow, God willing, we'll be safe."

She stared gravely at the ships. "I wonder how long it will be before John knows where we've gone. He could follow us to Ireland." She shivered, pulling the fur closer around her throat.

"He won't, Mother." Reginald took her hand. "The Irish lords are too powerful. He'd never challenge them. And between us, we're married into most of their families." He nudged his brother and chuckled.

The horses picked their way down into the village and their guide negotiated a passage for them with the dark, burly master of one of the vessels before carefully stowing their baggage in his ship. A strong onshore wind was crashing waves against the wooden quay and clouds of icy spray splattered onto the marshy track that led to the few fishermen's houses on the beach. They would not sail today.

Sadly Matilda bade farewell to her white mare. Their horses had been promised to their host as payment. Bowing, the guides made their formal farewell and then left, leading the string of animals behind them at an easy canter back up the track.

It was four days before the wind veered and dropped enough for the captain to risk putting his small vessel to sea. Matilda watched the hills behind them constantly during the short hours of daylight, expecting at any moment to see a line of horses and light-catching helms and lances that would show that the king had achieved the impossible and caught up with them. But they never came.

464

At last the boat nosed her way out into the bay. A brisk, cold wind sent her plunging sharply to her small sails. Matilda stood on deck gazing back at the receding land, half hidden under a pall of black cloud. Her hair was torn from the hood of her cloak and whipped mercilessly around her face and across her eyes but she ignored it. It was as though she still expected, even now, to see John galloping down onto the shore of the estuary and boarding the other vessel that remained tied to the quay. She shivered and Will put his arms around her. "The crossing doesn't take long, Mother. Do you feel sick?"

She glanced up and saw his grin, his eyes teasing. "You know I don't, you silly boy. I knew I would like the sea. I only wish we were crossing under happier circumstances." She sighed.

"Well, John can whistle for us now, so enjoy yourself." Will laughed. "You and I have the sea legs of the family, that's plain to see." He nodded over his shoulder. His father and Reginald had retired to a sheltered corner of the deck where they were seated on some stoutly roped barrels. Both looked very uneasy, and shortly first William and then his son slipped aft into the fetid deck cabin, where, wrapped in their cloaks, they lay down.

Before long the wind started to blow up again. It veered around to the east, whistling in the rigging, and the broad-beamed boat began to bucket up and down the troughs and waves with alarming violence.

Will's eyes were shining. "Be pleased the wind's getting up, Mother. We'll be there the sooner." Matilda laughed at his exhilaration.

Night fell early and with it the storm worsened. The passengers were sent into the stuffy cabin, where they lay awake, hurled from one side to the other amid a debris of falling cargo and luggage. The air stank of fish and vomit and outside the wind screamed in the rigging, until, with a rending crack, the tightly reefed mainsail ripped across the middle. Matilda, trying to brace herself, sitting with her back to the forward cabin wall, her arms round her knees, could hear the crewmen shouting and screaming as they fought with the thundering, shredding canvas.

At last the sail was subdued and only the crash of the wind and waves and the whistle of the rigging remained.

For three days and nights they tossed and rolled under bare spars until the gale blew itself out. Then on the fourth morning the master unbarred the cabin door and looked in, grinning. "Would you believe, the Blessed Virgin had guided us safely to the Irish coast?"

Matilda staggered out weakly and looked eagerly ahead at the long, misty, dark coastline. The waves were still huge, but the wind had dropped a little. The sailors were rigging a makeshift sail and, as she watched, it caught the wind and filled. At once the boat stopped rolling aimlessly and picked up speed, heading in toward the shore. Another blanket of rain swept past them, soaking the planking in a moment, but

Matilda and Will stayed on deck, watching as the boat nosed into the harbor. Above them, on a rocky cliff, a castle rose, guarding the harbor and the sea.

"Fitzgerald's Black Castle." The master was behind them for a moment, his eyes gleaming triumphantly. "This is a good fortune after the storm, indeed it is. Wicklow. That's where we are." And he was gone again, his eyes screwed up against the icy rain, guiding his vessel to her moorings, as the torn sails were lowered into heaps of sodden canvas on the deck.

The shore of Ireland seemed unsteady. Matilda staggered and nearly fell as she led the others up the wooden quay. Reginald grinned uncertainly for the first time in days. Even William looked pleased. He gazed about him, still pale and dazed, then at last he seemed to remember who he was. He straightened his shoulders. "Will, Reginald, we must find horses. Find out about this fellow Fitzgerald. Will he shelter us until we're ready to go on?" He turned to see the last of their coffers being swung ashore and stacked on the quay. Everywhere seaweed and debris had been piled high by the wind and tide. There was a strong smell of rotting fish.

The master approached them gesticulating toward the hill. "There you are, men from the castle. They'll be coming to greet you, no doubt," he called.

They turned and watched. Five horsemen were trotting down the steep trackway.

Will stiffened suddenly. "Do you see their livery, Father? Is it possible?"

William knuckled the rain from his eyes. "William Marshall's men, by God. He's always been a good friend to us."

"So were a lot of people, Father." Reginald put a warning hand on his arm. "Better be wary until we know how he stands."

The knight in charge of the horsemen saluted as he approached. He had not been told to expect passengers and seemed surprised to see the bedraggled party on the quay. However, it seemed the Earl Marshall was himself in residence at the Black Castle and, helping Matilda onto his own horse, the knight prepared to escort them back there.

The marshall received them in the high-ceilinged hall of the keep that echoed still to the crashing waves far below.

"My friends!" The old man held out both hands with a broad smile. "Welcome. Welcome indeed." His smile changed to a look of concern as Matilda sank onto a form by the hearth. "Poor lady, you look exhausted. You all must be. The storm was the worst I've ever known. It must have sent a good many unlucky ships to the bottom." He shook his head sadly. "Come, let me call servants to show you to our guest chambers. They'll bring you food and wine there. When you've slept we'll talk."

466

The phone was ringing. For a moment no one moved, then slowly Ben hauled himself to his feet and went to answer it. Behind him Jo stared around her in a daze. She took a deep breath.

Ann stood up. She picked up the bowl of water and emptied it decisively into the sink. "Lunchtime," she said loudly. "Nicholas, will you please pour us each a glass of sherry."

Ben hung up. "They want us to collect the kids about four," he said.

"Fine." Ann was stooping over the oven, looking at the pie that she had put there earlier. "Fifteen minutes, then we can eat. Jo, will you shell me some peas?"

Jo hadn't moved. She was staring down at her hands. The knuckles of her fingers were reddened and swollen.

Ann glanced at them sharply. "That's what a morning on a damp Welsh mountain can do for you, Jo," she said quickly. "Fearful place for aging bones! An afternoon in the sun will soon put you right."

Jo gave her a shaky smile. "That's what I thought," she said. For the first time she allowed herself to look at Nick. "Do you remember what happened?"

He nodded.

"What are we going to do?"

Nick stared at the bottle in his hands. "We can't change history, Jo." His voice was hoarse.

"You can't change the past, but it doesn't have to happen again, for chrissake!" Ann said through clenched teeth. She took the bottle from Nick and poured it into the glasses, slopping a little onto the scrubbed tabletop. "Shall we go eat outside? If so, someone will have to dry off the table and chairs."

The sun had finally broken through the mist, sucking it up in white spirals from the fields and mountainside behind the house. Below in the valley the whiteness still rippled and bellied like a tide, but around them now the heat was coming back. Thoughtfully Ben pulled off his sweater. Then he picked up his glass. "Well. It's been an eventful morning," he said dryly. "I vote we drink a toast. To the successful completion of Jo's article on *la famille Clements.*"

35

Jo was sitting on the wall looking at the mist in the distance as the sun began to sink behind it, sending shafts of crimson and flesh tones through the peach and saffron, when Nick found her. He pulled himself onto the wall beside her.

"I thought I might drive home tonight," he said.

Jo looked down at her hands. As Ann had predicted, they had returned to normal in the sun that afternoon. She nodded. "Perhaps it's for the best," she said slowly.

"Jo. You must stop the regressions," Nick said after a moment. "You do realize, it's getting near the end. Matilda is going to die."

She shook her head desperately. "Not yet. Not yet, Nick. There is still time to sort things out. Maybe the books are wrong. No one seems to know for sure what happened. Perhaps William Marshall kept them safe—"

"No!" Nick caught hold of her shoulders. "Look at me, Jo. Nothing can save her. Nothing. She is going to die!" He turned away. "Part of me wants you to go on, Jo. Part of me wants to see you defeated and on your knees." He stopped. In the silence that stretched out between them Jo did not dare to raise her eyes to his face. She felt the tiny hairs on the back of her neck stir.

"It's not you, Nick," she said at last. "And it's not John." She raised her eyes at last. "It's what Sam wants."

Nick nodded bleakly.

"And it was Sam who warned me not to go on with the regressions at the beginning. He didn't want to hurt me then—"

"He hadn't got this idea in his head then, that he was William," Nick said grimly. "Somehow he wants to assuage his guilt by playing you and me off against one another. I can't believe he really wants you to be hurt, and yet—"

"I won't be hurt, Nick. Not by the regressions." Jo gave a rueful smile. "Carl Bennet often takes people up to and through the death experience. After all, if we believe in reincarnation, then death isn't the end—"

"It is the end of your current life, Jo." Nick shook her gently. "Are you ready to die? Do you want to stop being Jo Clifford and go into limbo or wherever it is you think you go for another eight hundred years?"

Jo drew back, her eyes on his face. "Of course not. But it won't happen."

"It might." Nick's hands tightened. "Please, Jo. Promise me you won't risk it."

For a moment they looked at each other in silence. Almost without realizing he had done it, Nick reached up to touch her face. "I don't dare trust myself with you, Jo. If I were really John—" He paused, then he shook his head. "I don't—I can't believe I was—but if it were true, then God help me, as far as I can see, it was not a life to be proud of. Perhaps he was the kind of man who would persecute someone beyond the grave." He shuddered, then he gave a taut laugh. "What a strange new body he's chosen to inhabit! A fraught and at the moment not very prosperous advertising executive! No, I can't believe it. And even if I can, it's the person I am at the moment who interests me, Jo. I don't give a damn for King John. Or Sam. He's been having a ball, setting me up and manipulating me, and it's over." He paused. "But until I'm sure there is nothing lurking inside me bent on doing you harm I don't want to risk being alone with you. So I'm leaving."

Jo moved toward him, a lump in her throat. "Nick—"

Nick closed his eyes. Then slowly he put out his arms and drew her toward him gently. He rumpled her hair. "You can't trust me, Jo. Whatever I do, whatever I say. Don't trust me, and don't trust yourself."

"Ann can help us, Nick—"

"She can't, Jo, and it's not fair to ask her anymore."

"Carl Bennet, then."

"Possibly." He kissed her forehead. "But I think it must be Sam. I have a feeling he is the only one who can exorcise this nightmare, and I intend to see he does so." He released her abruptly and pushed his hands into his pockets. "There is also the matter of Tim." He tightened his jaw. "I want to find out just exactly where he fits in to this charade."

Jo bit her lip. "Sam never hypnotized Tim," she said, so quietly he could barely hear her.

"No." Nick turned away from her. "That doesn't fit, does it? Three men. Richard, John, and William. They each loved Matilda in their own way. And now here we are. Tim and Sam and me." He gave a cold laugh. "Are you the prize, Jo? Is that what this is all about? If you are, then two people are going to lose out in this little exercise in karmic handouts. There have to be losers." He was watching as a black thread of cloud drifted over the huge muffled crimson disc of the sun as it slid toward the mountain.

"I hope you win." Jo's voice was a tiny whisper.

469

Nick looked back at her, his eyes strangely impersonal. "I intend to," he said. "This time I intend to."

Somewhere on the hillside Jo could hear the plaintive bleating of a sheep. The sound echoed slightly in the emptiness of the night and she shivered.

Slowly she sat up. She pushed back the sheet and climbed out of bed, her eyes on the pale curtains that hid the moonlight. Drawing them back, she caught her breath at the beauty of the silvered mist lapping up the flanks of the mountain below the farm, and for a long time she stood staring out, her elbows on the stone sill. Her body ached for Nick. She wanted the comfort of his arms around her and the feel of his mouth on hers. Whatever the danger, she needed him. But he had gone.

She put her head in her arms and wept.

It was Richard who had come between them. If she had not met Richard, could she have loved the prince who had favored her with his passion? Richard. Always Richard. The name ran in her head. Had Matilda, in those last months, seen Richard again?

She raised her head and glanced at the door. Ann too had made her promise never to try to regress again alone, but surely, just once more, just to find out if there was news of Richard. After all, Matilda had not died in Ireland. There could be no danger yet. Just ten minutes, that was all she needed, to search her memory for a sight of him once more—to take her mind off John.

She tiptoed to the door and turned the key, then she sat down in front of the window. Putting her hands on the sill, she fixed her eyes on the huge silvered moon and deliberately she began to empty her mind.

It was late in the evening when they reached the castle of Trim. Somewhere a blackbird had begun to sing softly, warbling in the green twilight. At last the rain had stopped and a watery sun sent slanting shadows across the track. The great gates of the castle swung slowly open and their horses trotted over the drawbridge and into the shadowy bailey to safety.

Margaret greeted her mother with open arms, hugging her and trying to loosen her thick cloak at the same moment, laughing and brushing away the tears. Then Walter too came forward to greet her; tall and handsome as ever, a humorous glint in his eyes. "So my two reprobate parents-in-law come to see us at last." He bent to kiss her and took her hands. "Welcome to Trim, Lady Matilda. We'll keep you safe, never fear." He guided her to the fire, leaving his wife to greet her father and brothers, and he stood for a moment studying her face. Matilda avoided his eye, embarrassed, conscious suddenly of the silvered hair snatched untidily from her veil by the wind and of the lines that worry, hard weather, and fear had etched around her eyes, and of the swollen, ugly hands he held so gently in his own. He raised one of them to his lips and kissed it. "Have you the strength to see Margaret's pride and joy before you rest, Mother?" He spoke so quietly she almost missed his words against the background of noise in the hall beyond them. "I know she had no chance to tell you and you'll have had no way of hearing the news. Our prayers were answered at last. We have a little daughter."

"Oh, Walter!" Matilda's tired face lighted with happiness. She pulled away from him and turned back to Margaret. "Why didn't you tell me instantly, you wicked girl? Take me to see her quickly, my darling, before I really do collapse with exhaustion."

But with the best will in the world she found as she followed her daughter up the steep stairs toward the nursery quarters high in the keep that she was trembling violently. She pressed her hand against her heart, feeling its irregular fluttering, and took a deep breath at every turn in the stairs, forcing herself to follow steadily as Margaret, her skirts held high, ran ahead of her. "We've called her Egidia," the girl called over her shoulder. "Oh, Mother, she's the most beautiful child you've ever seen. She's a pearl."

Matilda followed her into the nursery and sank heavily onto the stool that the plump, motherly nurse left as they approached the crib. Her heart was pounding uncontrollably and she felt suddenly overwhelmed with nausea and faintness, but somehow she managed to force herself to lean forward and admire the small sleeping face, two tiny webs of dark lashes lying so peacefully on the pink cheeks.

"She's beautiful, darling." Matilda smiled shakily.

Margaret had been watching her closely. "You're not well, Mother. What's wrong? You shouldn't have let me rush you up those stairs." She dropped to her knees in the strewn herbs at her mother's side, suddenly contrite. "I was so excited at seeing you and knowing that you were safe at long last."

Matilda smiled and patted her hand. "I'm all right. It has just taken so long to get to you, that's all. The marshall was so kind to us, then the new justiciar appeared and threatened to betray us. The dear old marshall defied him, of course, but he had so few men. He thought we'd be safer here."

"And so you are, Mother." Margaret hugged her again. "You will all be perfectly safe here, you'll see."

Matilda smiled sadly and glanced back into the cradle, where the baby was screwing its tiny face into a thoughtful, wizened caricature of itself in its sleep. "Perhaps, my dear, perhaps" was all she said, but in her heart she knew their optimism was but a vain hope. Once again she found John's face before her, haunting her; the handsome, spare features, the straight nose, the cold blue eyes, the cruel mouth that once had sought and held her own. She felt something tighten in her chest again, but this time she knew it was fear.

471

When the letter came, Matilda had no premonition that it was from Richard. She had watched Walter unroll it and scrutinize the lines of close black writing, her eyes calm, her face serene as she listened to Margaret singing to herself as she worked on a piece of tapestry by the light of the high window.

Slowly Walter climbed to his feet. He passed the letter to Matilda with a grin. "News to please you, Mother-in-law, I think," he said softly. Then, beckoning Margaret after him, he strode out of the hall.

Matilda took the letter and scanned it slowly. The words were formal, dictated to a scribe, but nothing could conceal the happiness of the message they contained. Mattie had gone from Wigmore back to Suffolk and at Clare, on one of the mild December mornings untouched by wind and flecked with mackerel cloud, she had presented Will with a second son, a companion for little John.

And now that Will seemed settled for the time being at Trim, Richard proposed that he bring Mattie back to Ireland.

Matilda rolled up the letter and walked over to the fire, her heart beating wildly. Richard would be hard on the heels of the messenger; perhaps he was already in Ireland. She bit her lip to suppress a smile in a sudden moment of wry self-mockery. So much excitement, so great a longing, suddenly, in a woman of an age to know better!

Will, when he heard the news, was beside himself with joy, and ready to ride at once for the coast.

Margaret seized his arm, her eyes, so like those of her mother, blazing with fury when she heard his plan.

"Don't you dare go to meet them, Will! You must let her father bring her all the way here. You must!" She glanced over her shoulder toward Matilda. "For Mother's sake! Think how she would feel if Richard turned back at the port!" So Will curbed his anxiety and waited, watching the drying road and the burgeoning spring sunshine that should have brought his wife from the sea, and didn't.

And then at last they arrived. Richard de Clare was riding beside his daughter, the two babies following with their nurses and the escort.

Matilda stood back to watch Will greet his wife, and there was a lump in her throat as she saw her son examine the small bundle that the nurse held out to him. He saw her watching and laughed, unembarrassed, his arm still round his wife's waist, his face alight with happiness.

Then, at last, Richard was beside her. "I'm glad the children have found so much happiness in each other," he murmured by way of greeting, touching her fingers lightly with his own. His hair now had turned completely white and his face was marked by pain and exhaustion. He met her gaze squarely with a wry smile. "Don't look like that, my dear. I'm getting old. It shows, that's all."

"Richard, have you been ill?" She had forgotten her son and the crowds of people around them, conscious only, with a terrible sense of fear, of the deathly pallor of his skin.

He shrugged. "A fever, nothing more. I had my Mattie to take care of me. No harm has been done, save the delay in coming to you. Come now, you must take us to our hosts. Walter will be wondering what has happened to us."

There was no way that Richard could hide his failing strength from Matilda during the weeks he stayed at Trim, and, as if he were conscious how unhappy it made her to see him so stooped and weak as he watched the hunting parties ride out daily without him, he insisted at last on leaving before Easter. Nothing she could say could dissuade him, nor did he make any attempt to see her alone before he left.

"Good-bye, my dear" was all he said as she bade him farewell in the bailey at Trim. "God go with you, and protect you always." He raised her fingers to his lips for one lingering kiss and then he mounted his horse and rode slowly away with his followers over the drawbridge and out of sight. He never once turned back.

"Jo!" Ann was banging on the bedroom door. "Jo, for God's sake, can you hear me?" She rattled the handle again. "Jo, let me in."

"Here, let me." Ben pushed past her. He thundered on the door panel with his knuckles. "You are sure she's in there? She might have gone out for a walk."

"She's in there. Look, the key's in the lock on the inside."

Behind them the sun blazed down through the small skylight in the back roof, lighting up the stripped wooden boards of the floor and the charcoal and cream wools of the rug hung on the wall.

"Ben—what if she's done it? What if she regressed on her own and died—"

"Don't be stupid!" Ben's voice was sharp. "Jo is a sensible woman. She's not going to do a damn fool thing like that." He knelt and put his eye to the lock. "Fetch me a pencil and a newspaper or something. Let's see if we can push the key out and bring it through under the door."

"Why did she lock it?" Ann moaned as she watched Ben juggling the pencil gently in the lock.

There was a small metallic bump as the key fell, and with a satisfied grunt Ben pulled gently on the paper and brought it under the door. Ann grabbed the key and with a shaking hand inserted it in the lock.

Jo was lying on her bed, her arms across her eyes.

"Is she breathing?" Ann ran to her and dropped on her knees beside the bed. "Jo? Oh, God, Jo, are you all right?"

"I can see her breathing from here." Ben stayed firmly in the doorway, his eyes fixed on the low neckline of Jo's nightgown.

"Jo?" Gently Ann shook her shoulder. "Jo, wake up."

With a little sigh, Jo stirred. She opened her eyes and stared at Ann blankly.

"Jo, it's after ten. The children have been pestering us to wake you." Jo smiled faintly. "Egidia," she said. "And Mattie's boys. So sweet. So like Will when he was little. . . ." She closed her eyes again.

Ann glanced over her shoulder at Ben, who looked heavenward and disappeared back into the hall. A moment later she heard the sound of his feet running down the stairs. She turned back to Jo. "Not Mattie's boys, Jo. Polly and Bill," she said gently.

Jo frowned. "I slept so heavily," she said slowly. "And such a long sleep. Richard left. He had given up. . . . He was old, Ann. Old." Her eyes filled with tears. "I must have cried myself to sleep."

Nick leaned forward and turned on the car radio. Beside him was the map and the route Ben had given him to follow via Hereford and Ross. He had spent the night, in the end, at a pub somewhere in the mountains, leaving before breakfast to try to find his way back to the route after driving aimlessly for hours the evening before. He felt drowsy and very depressed.

He blinked, trying to concentrate on the blue car in front of him, pacing himself as the early-morning sun beat down into his face. He did not want to return to London. Every ounce of his being cried out to stay in Wales with Jo. Clenching his teeth, he put his foot on the accelerator and swooped past the blue car. In its place now was a green van. It slowed, blocking his way, and he braked, swearing.

It was somewhere just south of Hereford, as the A49 swept up toward the crest of a long hill, that he slammed on the brakes again. He was staring at the signpost on the opposite side of the road. The sound of the radio faded, as did the swish of cars overtaking him, the speed of their passing making the Porsche shudder as it sat at the curbside.

ACONBURY 1 MILE

He frowned. The name meant something to him. But what? Slowly, without quite knowing why, he pulled the car into the side road and drove slowly down it, staring ahead through the windshield at the woods and thick hedgerows on either side of what turned out to be a narrow, winding lane. He drove on, past some farm buildings, then the car drifted to a halt outside a small deserted church. His chest felt tight and his heart was beating with an uneasy, irregular rhythm as he climbed out.

Still without knowing why, he walked through the gate and past some old yews toward it. Two carved angels hung on the oak pillars of the porch, staring across the uneven flags. Walking in between them, he tried

474

the huge rusty iron ring handle of the church door. It did not move. Then he read the typed message pinned to the heavy oak:

NOTICE TO VISITORS

This church has been declared redundant and is now used as a diocesan store. . . . Visitors are always welcome to view the building and the key can be made available by prior appointment. . . .

Nick sat down abruptly on the narrow stone seat that formed part of the wall of the porch. He found himself breathing very deeply. There was a sting of tears behind his eyes and a lump in his throat. But why? Why should this small, lost church fill him with such overwhelming unhappiness?

Suddenly unable to bear the enormous misery that flooded through him, he stood up once more and, ducking outside, almost ran back to the car, climbing in and resting his head against the rim of the steering wheel. It was ten minutes before he reversed the car into the gateway and made his way back to the main road.

Jo reached London about seven that evening. They had tried to persuade her to stay, but when she insisted she had to go back, Ann's relief was almost palpable. They parted with kisses and promises that they would see one another again very soon—but there was no more mention of Matilda. Jo knew that if her past came to her again, it must be alone. She could ask no more of Ann and Ben.

After making her way slowly up to her apartment, she let herself in. There was only a second's hesitation as she looked around, wondering with a sudden feeling of nervousness if Nick were there, but the apartment was empty. She toured it once quickly, opening all the windows, then she let herself relax. It was good to be home.

She showered and changed and poured herself a glass of apple juice. Then she unpacked her notes and piled them on the coffee table. The Clements article was practically finished.

The sudden ringing of the phone made her jump. She climbed to her feet and went to answer it slowly, suddenly apprehensive.

"Jo? How are you?" It was Sam.

Her body went rigid. She felt her fingers lock around the receiver, her knuckles white as she turned to look out at the drooping flowers on the balcony. "I'm well, thank you." She kept her voice carefully neutral.

"When did you get back from Wales?" Sam's voice rang so clearly in the room it sounded as if he were there with her.

"Only an hour ago." She felt the rags of tension beginning to pull at her temples. Her head was beginning to throb. Put the phone down. She must

475

put the phone down. But she didn't. She stayed where she was, her eyes on the stone balustrade with its curtain of wilting green.

"May I speak to Nick?" Sam was speaking again.

Jo felt her stomach tighten. "He's not here, Sam. I don't know where he is."

"Did he go back to Lynwood House?" She could hear the amusement in his tone.

"I told you, I don't know where he is."

There was a pause. "I see. Do I gather you have quarreled again?" he said at last.

"No, Sam." Jo could hear her voice rising slightly. Desperately she tried to keep it level. "I'm sorry to disappoint you, but we haven't quarreled. We are the best of friends. We had a lovely time in Wales, and whatever it was you tried to do to Nick didn't work. And just in case you think you can come here again and repeat the charade, forget it. We know what you're up to. It won't work, Sam, do you hear? It won't work."

There was an amused chuckle down the phone. "I don't know what you're talking about, Jo, but I hope to see you again soon. Very soon."

"No, Sam, forget it."

"Whatever you say, love. But before you hang up on me forever, have you got my mother's phone number? I'm down in Hampshire with her at the moment."

"I shan't be phoning you, Sam."

"Perhaps not." He laughed again. "But Nick will. You make sure you've got it somewhere handy, there's a good girl. Someone may need to get in touch with me urgently. You never know." He laughed again. "Your life might depend on it."

The line went dead.

Jo stared at the receiver for a moment in disbelief, then she slammed it down. It was several minutes before she reached for a pen and scribbled Dorothy Franklyn's phone number down obediently on the notepad by the lamp.

Tim looked at Nick without surprise. "I thought you'd turn up one of these days," he said.

"Well, we have one or two things to sort out, do we not?" Nick followed him into the studio.

Tim swung around. "We have nothing to sort out," he snapped. "You don't own her, for God's sake."

"I intend to marry her."

Tim stood quite still. His mouth had fallen slightly open as the pain of loss hit him anew. With an effort he pulled himself together. "Then congratulations are in order. I hope you'll both be very happy." He turned away. "Does your brother know?" He was staring up at the high ceiling of

476

the studio, concentrating with elaborate care on the pattern of spotlights and tracks suspended beneath the shaded skylights.

"Not yet." Nick stood still just inside the doorway, his arms folded across his chest. "And neither does Jo yet. Keep away from her from now on, Tim. I'm only going to tell you once."

"There is no need." Tim did not look at him. "Jo has never felt anything for me. She and I were part of a dream, that's all, and my share of the dream is over, if it ever existed at all. Come over here." He moved slowly, as if every bone in his body were aching with fatigue.

Nick hadn't noticed the easel in the corner. He watched as Tim pulled the sheet off and turned the easel slightly toward the light. "My wedding present to you both, if you like," Tim said quietly. "I'll get it framed. I've no use for it now."

Nick stared at the photograph. He could feel a pulse beginning to flicker somewhere in his throat. It was Matilda de Braose. Not Jo. There was no trace of Jo left in those huge eyes with their suspicion of love and laughter, the straight, slightly long nose, the determined chin, its strength emphasized by the fine white linen of the headdress. His eye ran slowly down the photo, resting for a moment on her hands, then on down the heavy folds of the scarlet surcoat and pale-green gown to the point of one shoe that showed at her hem. He would have recognized her anywhere, the woman whose image had haunted him, tormented him, for eight hundred years, the woman with whom a prince had fallen hopelessly in love, the woman for whom his passion and longing had grown twisted and sour.

Abruptly he turned away, feeling the bile rising in his mouth. "So that was how she looked to de Clare," he breathed. "She never looked at me like that. She kept only sneers for me!"

Without another word he strode back across the studio.

"Where are you going?" Tim's voice was suddenly harsh.

Nick stopped. He half turned. "Where do you think I'm going?" he said. His eyes were hard.

He groped for the door, then flung himself down the stairs and out into the street, leaving Tim standing by the photo.

"Don't hurt her, Nick," Tim said softly as he heard the street door close. "For pity's sake, don't hurt her."

36

Jo pushed away the typewriter and stood up. She was too tired to work and too tired to eat. Sam had upset her, and she was angry and agitated, and her thoughts kept on going back to Nick. She wanted to see him so badly it was like a physical pain.

When the phone rang she stared at it for a moment before picking it up. "Jo, dear? It's Ceecliff. How are you?"

Jo's face relaxed into a smile. "Tired and grumpy. It's lovely to hear from you. How are you?"

"Agog to hear some more about your Matilda. Is she still with you?"

Jo managed a laugh. "You make her sound like a tenant. Yes, she is still with me."

"Good. Then you must tell me all about her. I'm going to ask a great favor, dear. I'm coming to town tomorrow. I have to see my dentist and I want to go to Harrods. Could I possibly stretch my poor old carcass on your sofa tomorrow night? I'm so ancient these days I can't face the journey both ways in one day."

"Of course you can." Jo's spirits had lifted at her words.

"Splendid. Now, don't chase poor Nicholas out if he's there. I'd like to see him and I'm not naive! I'll see you about five, my dear, if that's all right," and she hung up without giving Jo the chance to reply.

Jo smiled. "Naive. You!" she murmured to herself. "Never!"

She stood up and went out onto the balcony, staring down at the tub of geraniums at her feet. She had deluged the plants in water and already they were responding, the sharp, sweet-sour smell of sooty London earth filling her nostrils, as, suddenly, her eyes overflowed with tears. Don't think about Nick. Don't. Desperately she tried to concentrate on the scarlet petals of the flower, but they blurred and swayed before her eyes.

Before he left the Clementses' farm he had taken her hands in his. "I don't want to see you again, Jo. Not till this is over," he had said. "Don't call me. Don't let me come near you. Not for any reason whatsoever, do you understand?"

Abruptly she retreated indoors. She turned on the stereo and threw herself down on the sofa. If only Nick were here for Ceecliff to find tomorrow. If only he were here . . .

She closed her eyes, trying to force herself to listen to the music. Ten minutes of Vivaldi to try and unknot the tension behind her eyes, then she would go to bed.

As they dismounted in the castle ward at Carrickfergus, Matilda found herself looking upward at the solid keep glowing ruggedly in the evening light, and she shuddered in spite of the warmth of the evening.

Word had come on Midsummer's Day that King John, together with an army of men, had sailed from Pembroke and landed at Crook on the southeast corner of Ireland. From there he had ridden to Kilkenny and been received with all honor by the Earl Marshall.

"But what's happened? Where's William? Why haven't we heard anything? Why has the king come to Ireland?" Matilda had looked wildly from Walter to his brother Hugh and back, after they had heard the news from the marshall's messenger. In the spring King John had at last agreed William could return to Wales, where he would grant him one more audience.

"I don't understand." Walter rubbed his chin thoughtfully.

"I have a letter, my lord." The messenger fumbled in his pouch. "I was told to deliver it secretly to the Earl of Meath and no other."

"Well then, give it to me, man." Walter slid his finger under the seal, a worried frown on his face. Hugh and Matilda waited in silence, watching as he scanned the closely written lines. At last he let out a deep breath. He looked up at Matilda. "It's the worst news, I'm afraid. You'd better sit down while I tell you."

Matilda went pale, but she did as she was told, sitting upright on a narrow stool. Hugh put his hand protectively on her shoulder. He cleared his throat nervously. "Go on, Walter. Tell us."

Walter glanced down at the parchment. "It appears that William went to Hereford but at the last moment he refused to meet the king. Instead he began to rally men with a view to recapturing some of his lands by force." He glanced up as Matilda drew in a quick painful breath. "The king promptly set off for Haverford as he had been threatening, where his host was already gathering for an invasion of Ireland."

"An invasion?" Hugh repeated, appalled at the word.

"That's what it says here. Lord Ferrers apparently tried very hard to act as an intermediary and somehow persuaded William to ride to Pembroke after the king and there William actually saw John. According to him he offered him forty thousand marks to be paid at once if the king would restore him to favor."

Matilda gasped. "Forty thousand? He's out of his mind. Where would we get that kind of money!"

Walter licked his lips. "I gather that's what the king said. He also commented that it wasn't William anyway, but you who really headed the de Braose family now." He paused and glanced up quickly. "If anyone could raise any money it would be you and not your husband, and he intended to hold you and you alone responsible for the debt."

Matilda closed her eyes for a moment, conscious of Hugh's reassuring hand gently squeezing her shoulder. After another quick glance at her, Walter went on, his finger tracing the lines of writing that grew smaller and more cramped toward the bottom of the parchment. "The king offered William the chance of accompanying him here to Meath, where they could together confront you, but William refused. He has ridden to the March, intent on raising an army of his own. It seems the king let him go."

"Courage, Mother. We'll be safe here, you'll see." Will half turned, watching as his wife and children with the nurses trailed disconsolately after Walter and Margaret toward the stairway that led up into the keep at Carrickfergus.

Matilda tried to smile. "I keep thinking about your father, Will. Why did he do this to us? Why didn't he try to make peace with the king? It is almost as if he did it deliberately to set the king against me."

Will's mouth was set in a grim line. "It was unforgivable of him. He must have known that the king was going to try to find you, although Hugh reckons the king was coming anyway—and"—he hesitated—"well, Father has been behaving erratically, you must admit. I'm not sure all the time that he really knows what he's doing anymore."

They stood watching as the last of the party climbed the wooden stairs into the keep. Only a few attendants remained hovering behind them, waiting to escort them in. The last of the horses was being led off toward the stables. Overhead two gulls, their wings pink in the last light of the setting sun, wheeled and called over the high walls.

"The king has followed us across Ireland, Will." Matilda put her hand on his arm. "There is no safety for us here."

He smiled at her fondly. "I know. I've talked it over with Reginald and Walter and they agree. We must all get to France as soon as possible. It's the only way now. And this is a good place to embark from, so when we've rested a little, Hugh is going to find us boats."

She sighed. "Oh, how I long to see Giles again. Ask Hugh to hurry. I don't care about resting. Let us leave quickly. I don't think he'll take it as an insult to his hospitality." She made a brave attempt to smile.

But it proved much harder than they had anticipated to find a boat that would carry them south down the calm, blue sea toward France. The first two captains Hugh approached shrugged and gesticulated and bargained noisily and then sailed away without them on the first favorable wind.

Anxiously they scanned the waters of the lough for vessels that might be on their way to anchor in the sheltered little harbor behind the castle and could take them off; but in the calmness of a flat, unbroken sea no boats came near them. They could see flocks of gulls hovering and diving over hidden shoals of fish but no fishermen seemed interested. Tension mounted behind the high sandstone walls as the lookouts were doubled to the seaward side, and men spent hours straining their eyes toward the opposite shore of the lough as if expecting at any moment to see the massed armies of the king forming ranks upon the beach.

But no one came. High above the keep a lonely gull wheeled, its laughing cry echoing in the silent walls over the backs of the dozing men and the horses snuffling uninterestedly at wisps of hay in the heat of the courtyard.

Slowly the sun began to sink and the shadows lengthened across the translucent water.

The horseman could be seen a mile away, galloping down the track past St. Mary's Abbey and the houses in the little township from the direction of Bael na Farsad, the ford at the mouth of the River Lagan. Silently the guards at the main gate strung their bows and waited.

"Quickly! Quickly!" The man pulled his horse to a rearing halt, its hooves plunging into the dust of the road. "Tell the earl the king is less than a day's march away across there." He waved across the slowly darkening water. "He's reached Holy Wood. Others are coming from Rath. By sea."

"May the Blessed Virgin save us." Will crossed himself fervently when he heard the breathless rider's message. "What do we do now?" He looked at Hugh and then from Walter to his mother and back. They were standing on the eastern wall, feeling the light wind stir their hair in the warm night. High above, a shooting star cut a green arc through the velvet sky. Matilda strained her eyes into the distance to where Hugh had pointed, as the last fingers of the sunset reflected on the lough, but she could see no sign of lights or campfires. The distant shore was as dark as the lapping water.

Suddenly Reginald gripped her arm. "Look! A boat—and it's coming here."

They squinted into the dark as the small fishing boat, illuminated by the glowing brazier it carried amidships, ghosted in with the tide. Hugh waited long enough to see it round the point and head in toward the small harbor below them, then he turned and ran soundlessly for the steps.

They watched the boat nose in silently alongside the quay and the black figures of the men working on the deck swinging baskets of fish over the side to waiting hands. Matilda saw the dull gleam of silver as each load was lifted high, then suddenly she saw Hugh's men, their swords drawn, swarming over the quay. A basket of fish went flying and the silver trail spilled across the black stones, some of them slipping back into the dark

481

water. The fishermen put up only a token resistance as the armed men jumped aboard. From their position high on the wall, the watchers could pick out Hugh's tall figure pointing from the quay as guards were posted, and the sailors held at sword point on the deck of their boat. Then Hugh turned away and disappeared into the shadows. The whole exercise had been managed without a sound.

"He'll be at the postern gate," Walter murmured urgently. "Quickly. There'll be no time to lose. The wind is going around, it'll be in the right quarter to take us off if it doesn't drop."

The boat was an old one, open and shaky, its planks badly caulked, and there was barely room, with the fishermen to sail it, for the passengers. Mattie and Will and their two babies, Margaret with Egidia in her arms and the wet nurse following, Reginald and Matilda and Walter and, last of all, Hugh with a long regretful look behind him at the great fortress he had helped to create. Four guards stood amidships with drawn swords as the mooring ropes were cast off and the boat turned silently toward the sea.

There was a splash and a sizzle as Walter tipped the brazier over the side and then complete darkness, apart from the glow of the starlight on the square of bleached canvas above their heads.

It seemed to Matilda as she watched, breathless, that they were not moving at all. The black silhouette of the castle hung above them for what seemed an eternity before at last, imperceptibly, the sail began to curve and billow and the water started to cream gently beneath the vessel's bow.

Slowly the black coast of Ireland began to drop away into the night and they were left alone with the shooting stars and the fiery phosphorescence of the warm sea.

Jo opened her eyes, puzzled at the sudden change in light. Something dark was standing between her and the lamp. Pushing away the heavy clogging sleep, she struggled to sit up. The music had stopped and the apartment was very silent.

"So you thought you could escape by sea." The soft voice brought her upright with a jerk.

"Nick?" Panic shot through her. "How did you get in? What are you doing here?" She tried desperately to clear her brain.

"You were talking in your sleep. You should have bolted the door, Jo." He was sitting on the arm of the chair near her, in front of the lamp. She could see the faint, gilded halo of lamplight around his body in the shadows. The balcony outside the open door was in darkness.

"What have you come for?" She looked toward him, still frightened, not able to see his face.

"What do you think I've come for?" He turned sideways suddenly and she saw that he was smiling. Her blood turned to ice. It was not Nick. The man behind those steel-blue eyes was calculating and cold and full of hatred.

Without conscious thought she tried to get up, but he had anticipated her. Before she could move he had grabbed her, pushing her back against the cushions. "No, my lady," he said quietly. "No. Let us hear the end of this story, shall we? Let us hear it together."

"No!" She pushed at him desperately. "Nick, you're not supposed to be here. You must go away. I don't want to go on, Nick. I mustn't. It's too near the end. Please, Nick. You know I mustn't." She stared up at him, terrified. "Nick," she cried. "Stop it. Don't you see what's happening? It's Sam! Sam is making you do this. Please. Don't let it happen. Don't let Sam win!"

He frowned as he looked down at her. "Sam?" he said slowly. "There was something I had to tell Sam—"

Jo swallowed hard. "He is with your mother," she said. "He called earlier. He wanted you to call him back." His grip on her wrists had slackened slightly. "Go on, Nick, please call him. It's important." She tried to keep her voice steady, her eyes on his face.

She saw the slight flicker of uncertainty for a moment behind his eyes, then it had gone and he was smiling again. "You are very anxious I should phone him all of a sudden. I wonder why." His grip on her wrists tightened again and he bent over her until his face was only inches from hers. "Do you think he is going to distract me from what I came to do?"

Her mouth had gone dry. "What did you come to do?" she whispered.

From outside the open French doors the sound of a car hooting in the darkened square blasted into the room. Nick raised his head slightly, but his eyes did not leave her face. "I came to see you," he said evenly. "The woman I love."

Jo was breathing heavily, trying to control the panic that was threatening to overtake her.

"If you love me, Nick, you won't hurt me," she said pleadingly. She tried once again unsuccessfully to push him away. "Please, let me go. You're hurting my wrists—"

He smiled. "So little a pain, surely, compared with the pain you caused me."

"I didn't mean to cause you pain," she cried desperately. "You must believe me, I didn't. I love you—" Her voice cracked into a sob.

Nick did not move. His eyes narrowed cynically. "Love," he whispered. "What love?"

After transferring both her wrists to one hand, he touched her cheek gently. A teardrop stood for a moment on the pad of his forefinger. Slowly he leaned forward and brought his lips down on hers.

"Who did you really love?" he murmured. "Was it de Clare, all the time?"

483

Jo stared up into the eyes so close to hers.

"It was you," she whispered. "In the end it has always been you—" She relaxed at last beneath the iron grip on her wrists and felt at once a corresponding lessening of pressure from his hand as his mouth sought hers once more. Closing her eyes, she could feel the accustomed longing beginning to stir somewhere deep inside her. Almost without realizing it she was returning the kiss, feeling her body tremble as he reached inside her blouse. For a long moment she lay still, then frantically she tried to tear her wrists free of his imprisoning hand. Instantly his grip tightened. Leaning back slightly, he smiled. "Relax, Jo," he said softly. "Don't fight me." As he looked down at her she saw a new enigmatic blankness in his eyes, then he reached forward again and touched her face. "Now," he said, "the end of the story, I think."

"No!" She shrank away from his touch, but she could not move as his free hand, gently insistent now, moved slowly over her forehead and down her temples. Desperately she tried to turn away, but he caught her chin, forcing her to look at him as once more he stroked her forehead, soothing her, relaxing her in spite of her sick terror.

He smiled. "That's better. Stop fighting me, Jo. I'm not going to hurt you," he said softly. "This is what we both want, and you know it. To find out what happened." His fingers had not stopped caressing her temples and she lay still at last, looking up at him, conscious only of what intensely blue eyes he had. Nick smiled and, leaning forward, brought his lips down to hers once more. He was forcing her back, by sheer willpower, into the past. She was trapped and even through her fear she could feel the world around her slipping out of gear.

It was several minutes before Nick stopped the movement of his hand. He looked at her closely. Her eyes were closed and he could feel the tension leaving her body as she relaxed deeper into the cushions. Gently he released her wrists at last and, leaning over her, kissed her again.

"Now, my lady," he said. "I want you to tell me what happened next. You were on the ship, leaving Ireland . . . leaving me behind. You thought you had escaped me, didn't you?" He laughed, then stood up and walked over to the open door and looked out onto the balcony. "Come, tell me what happened next. Tell me how you fared on your voyage to freedom."

An hour or two before dawn Matilda, huddled in a fur blanket with her little grandson John in her arms, fell into an uneasy sleep, rocked by the gentle motion of the boat. When she awoke the sky was already graying, the clouds high in front of them touched with pearly pink above the misty distance that was the coast of Scotland. The little boy in her arms stirred and nestled closer into the warmth of her cloak and she held him close, ignoring the stiffness in her shoulders and the rime of damp that covered everything in a net of droplets. The steersman sat hunched at the steering oar, an old sack around his shoulders, his eyes fixed calmly on the horizon. She could see his brown face, weathered into a network of wrinkles, and the piercing blue sailor's eyes. He seemed oblivious of Hugh's guard holding a drawn sword at his back.

Close beside the boat a fish jumped, its body arching into a silver flash. Automatically the man's eyes flicked in that direction. She saw his fingers flex for a moment on the smooth oak under his hand.

"Where will we land?" She kept her voice quiet so as not to disturb little John.

The man looked at her for a moment, considering, then he jerked his head forward in the direction of the dipping bow. "Yon's the Rinns o' Galloway. I'll tak' you to the Blessed Patrick's port, if the wind holds and we make the tide." He squinted up at the masthead, where the blue pennant stood out strongly before the mast. "But I'm thinking the wind will drop come the sunrise." He had a gentle, lilting voice, unhurried and relaxed.

Matilda glanced behind at the white ripples of their wake. The sea humped and rolled gently behind them, darkening toward the horizon, where the night was slowly shrinking back.

"Yon king will have no better wind than us, lady." The old man read her thoughts with ease. "And I heard he's a day behind you. You'll be away over the hills long before he sets sail from the lough."

"And I trust my constable will keep him guessing at Carrickfergus for a while." Hugh's voice came suddenly out of the shadows. "It might be weeks before the king realizes we're not there. We could be in France by then. With luck."

"Scottish William has become the English king's man; you know that?" The fisherman spoke quietly. "You'll not look for support from him. The Lion is old and tired. He'll not defy England again."

"You know a lot, old man." Hugh chuckled. "I've no doubt we'll find lords enough in Scotland to support us, even so. They're no friends to John. Just long enough to find us a passage over to France. That's all the time we need."

As the old man predicted, the wind dropped as the light grew stronger. They watched the sun rise in a sea of flaming mist behind the Galloway hills as their sail flapped and hung empty. Somewhere a rope began to flap aimlessly against the mast, and one of the babies began to whine fretfully. The creaming of the sea stopped and instead the water was silent, every now and then eddying with a gurgle along the barnacled planking.

For a long time they lay becalmed, hardly seeming to move. The old skipper refused curtly when Walter suggested that they bring out the long oars. "Time enough when the tide changes, my lord," he insisted quietly. "She'll bring us in in God's good time."

Behind them the horizon hazed with pearl, remained empty of pursuing boats.

It was after noon when they at last drew in alongside the quay at Portpatrick and two waiting men, barefoot in their checked rags, caught the mooring ropes and made fast to the makeshift bollards, their eyes wide as they saw the naked swords and the women and children. The party stepped ashore, stiff and cramped, and stood together on the warm wooden quay looking around. A huddle of little huts stood back from the bay and a well-trodden road led away inland from the sea over the dry grass.

"We'll need horses." Hugh turned to the skipper who leaned thoughtfully on the side of his ship watching. He seemed in no hurry to slip his moorings and sail away even though the guard had left the ship and were standing on the quay. The fishermen were sitting idly on the deck, seemingly uninterested in what was going on.

The old man shrugged. "I doubt you'll be finding any here." He grinned across at the boy who was coiling down the rope on the quay and spoke to him volubly in the swift tongue of Ireland. The boy shook his head and shrugged. Then he pointed over his shoulder inland. "He says you'd best go to the castle," he translated, his eyes twinkling. "But only if you've gold enough to pay. The laird there is no friend to landless men."

Hugh and Walter exchanged a quick glance.

"Tell him to guide us," Hugh commanded. "We have the money."

"Oh, Hugh, we don't have to walk? Not with the babies, and in this sun?" Margaret put her hand on her brother-in-law's arm.

He hesitated. Then he turned to the boy. "Is it far, this castle?"

The sailor translated and the boy gave a slow grin. "It's as far as it is and no further" was the enigmatic answer. Hugh gave an exasperated exclamation.

"Perhaps the women had better wait here, in one of the cottages or somewhere. Will, you stay with them. Keep two of my men. The rest of us will go and find some horses from somewhere."

He wasted no time waiting for arguments. Matilda stood with Mattie and Margaret and watched as the men strode up the track after the barefooted boy. She stood till they were out of sight before turning to Will. "Spread our cloaks under the tree, Will. We'll wait there in the shade. See if you can buy bread and ale at one of the cottages." She felt almost lighthearted suddenly. Happier than she had felt since King John set foot in Ireland. At last it looked as though they had given themselves enough start over him to get away.

The sun blazed white now in the high arch of blue and the stones in the dusty road were hot to the touch. Behind them the shoulder of the hill was already afire with budding heather and from the winding, climbing dog roses and the creeping wild thyme came the hum of the scent-loving bees.

The children slept and with them the nurse, her head lolling back against the knobbly boll of one of the trees, snores coming from the slack mouth, the bodice of her gown falling carelessly loose, showing a heavy brown breast with its broad, reddened nipple. Aboard the fishing boat the sailors slept beneath the shade of a sail that they had slung across the deck to save the whitened planking from the relentless heat. They had shown no sign of wanting to leave on the turning tide.

It was much later and they were all hungry and thirsty before they heard the clatter of hooves and the jingle of harness in the distance and saw men approaching at last. Will scrambled to his feet, screwing up his eyes in the glare of the evening sun, as he gave his mother his hand. "There seems to be rather a lot of people and no spare horses that I can see," he commented at last, puzzled.

They stood beneath the clump of trees watching as the horsemen approached. There was no sign of Walter and his brother or Reginald. At the head of the troop rode a redheaded man with a scarlet chevron emblazoned on his surcoat. He reined in near them and looked down from his horse, one eyebrow raised in the thin, tanned face. "Are you good folk on a pilgrimage?" he inquired lazily. His eyes traveled from one to another, surveying them all in turn, missing nothing. Then his gaze came back to Matilda. Imperceptibly it sharpened.

"Surely it's the Lady de Braose?" He spoke so softly she wondered if he were talking to himself. Then he bowed in the saddle, a flash of merriment showing in his green eyes. "May I present myself, my lady. Sir Duncan of Carrick." He continued to eye her steadily and she felt herself beginning to tremble. His next words horribly confirmed her worst fears. "I only recently returned to Scotland myself. I couldn't help hearing then about your slight altercation with my beloved cousin, King John."

Out of the corner of her eye Matilda saw Will's hand go to his sword hilt. She bit her lip. "I think you're mistaken, Sir Duncan." She tried to smile, steadying her voice with an effort.

"Oh, no, my lady, I think not." He interrupted her before she could deny it. "And I think it would please His Grace mightily if I were to tell him where you are." He stopped smiling abruptly and gestured over his shoulder.

The troops of men broke rank and the party beneath the trees was surrounded. Will, with an ugly oath, unsheathed his sword and the two knights from Carrickfergus followed suit, putting themselves between the women and Carrick's men. But hardly had Will raised his arm when three armed knights rode him down, and he fell beneath their hooves, his blade flailing uselessly. Mattie screamed and ran toward him, but one of the mounted men, laughing, bent and scooped her slender body into the saddle before him as easily as if she had been a child, and held her there, her arms pinioned helplessly at her sides by his grip.

Sir Duncan sat watching as Will, his face bruised and bleeding, staggered to his feet. "Bind his hands," he ordered curtly. Dismounting, two of his men forced Will's arms behind him, tying them brutally tight with a leather thong. With an apologetic glance at Matilda her other two knights promptly threw down their swords, and she watched helplessly as they too were bound. "I think you will agree, my lady"—Sir Duncan bowed to her again—"that it would be foolish to resist arrest." He beckoned forward the young man who had been riding behind him. "My esquire will take you pillion with him. Bring the others!" he ordered his other men. "We'll return to Turnberry tonight." He wheeled his horse and spurred it toward the edge of the quay, where the sailors, disturbed from their rest, were leaning against the side of their boat watching the proceedings with impassive interest. Sir Duncan felt for his purse and flung a coin negligently across onto the bleached planking. The old man regarded it unmoving.

"Take the news to the king that I have captured the lady he is seeking," he commanded. "Tell him I'll wait for his instructions at my father's castle of Turnberry."

The old man chewed his lip indifferently. "I'll sail with the next tide, sir. I'll see that your message is given."

Matilda, from her seat behind young James Stewart, wondered if there was any pity in the old man's eye as he watched them wheel their horses and ride away.

They rode inland as the dusk fell, following the clearly marked road across the open flats and into the woods. At Craigcaffie the men lit burning torches to light their way as they followed the track around Loch Ryan and followed the coast road north. They rode fast. Matilda was forced to cling to the waist of the young man in front of her, half conscious of the glitter of starlit water to their left, half blinded by the streaming torch held by the rider who galloped at their right-hand side. She rested her head against the broad back before her and closed her eyes; beyond the circle of light and the thundering hooves there was nothing but darkness and despair. Somewhere close to her, among the riders, she could hear a child crying bitterly and she knew it was little John. She ached to hold him and comfort him and she tried to look around, searching for Mattie, but the figures near her on the thundering horses were blurred by the streaming smoke and the bitter fumes.

Apart from one brief rest to water the horses, Sir Duncan did not draw rein until they reached Turnberry. The sweating, trembling animals trotted over the echoing drawbridge and stopped at last, their breath coming in clouds of steam as they drew up before the high keep. After sliding from his horse, he came and held out his hand to help Matilda dismount. He seemed unruffled by the long, wild ride and maintained his scrupulously polite manner. "Welcome, Lady Matilda." He bowed low. "I trust you will think of yourself as my guest until we hear what His Grace would wish me to do with you."

Matilda was shaking, half with fatigue and fear, half with anger. "You're no friend of mine, Sir Duncan. If I enter your house it will be as your prisoner, never as your guest," she flashed at him, snatching her hand from his.

He smiled. "As you wish." He turned abruptly on his heel, barking a command to his men, and ran ahead of them into the castle.

They were hustled into the keep and up into one of the high chambers under the roof. There was no furniture and the wooden floor was swept bare. All three babies were crying now and Matilda, in the light of the candle that burned on its pricket near the door, could see that Mattie was near tears herself. The nurse was white, her eyes enormous with terror. Will had been taken away from them out in the bailey and Matilda felt sick with fear for him. It was a moment before she felt Margaret's hand on her arm, steadying her. "Help me with the babies, Mother. We must quiet them. Perhaps nurse can give them all a little milk, if she can, even John. At least we're sheltered here, and it's warm."

"He would have made us comfortable, if you'd let him," Mattie flashed. "We could have been his guests. There would have been a fire and blankets and food. Why are you so stubborn and proud? Must we all suffer for it all the time?" She turned away petulantly as Matilda bent to pick up little John and hug him tightly in her arms.

"Hush, Mattie," Margaret retorted warningly. "Mother did quite right to refuse. We don't need a fire. It's a hot night."

The child was heavy in Matilda's arms and she could feel them beginning to ache already, but she continued to hold him, feeling the warmth and comfort of his little body as his arms crept around her neck. Margaret had given Egidia to the wet nurse and was rocking Mattie's little Richard, trying to quiet his fretful wails, gently loosening his swaddling bands. "There's one thing we must thank heaven for, Mother. Walter and the others have got away. The villagers who were watching will tell them what happened and they will come after us. Somehow they'll get us out of here. They'll think of something."

Mattie looked up, a sudden ray of hope in her tear-reddened eyes. "Do you think so? Oh, yes, of course they will. They'll save us. Walter would never let you be taken a prisoner. They'll save us and find Will."

Matilda forced herself to smile, though her lips were dry and cracked from salt and sun and fear. "Of course we'll all be all right. Don't worry. I'm sure they'll think of something before the king sends for us."

Some time later as light was beginning to filter through the unshuttered windows they heard steps on the stone stairs outside. The door was unbarred and men appeared carrying mattresses and blankets. They brought in jugs of wine and plates of meat and oatcakes and a bowl of milksops for the babies, and set them down near the empty hearth. Then one of them turned to Matilda and saluted. "Sir Duncan sends his compliments, madam. If you and the ladies will accept his hospitality you will be most welcome to dine at his table tonight."

Matilda felt her cheeks flame. "I thought I told Sir Duncan what I thought of his hospitality. Please tell him I haven't changed my mind. I will never willingly stay a guest under his roof."

The man bowed without comment, his face carefully neutral, and withdrew with the others, barring the heavy door behind him. As soon as he had gone Mattie burst into loud sobs. "Why? Why did you refuse him? We could have tried to change his mind. We might have escaped if we had got out of this infernal room. We might have got away!" She flung herself at the door, beating her fists in anguish against the thick unyielding timbers.

Matilda looked at her, her face set. "And leave your babies as hostages?" was all she said.

37

Nick stretched slowly on the bed and looked up at the sunlight sliding through the curtains and playing on the plaster frieze around the bedroom ceiling. He smiled. It was a long time since he had awoken at Jo's on a Monday morning. He brought his wrist up in front of his face and stared at his watch. Christ Almighty! It was eight-fifteen. He was due at the office at eight-thirty. He leapt to his feet, then he stopped in his tracks.

The bed beside him was empty, the bedspread still in place, save where it showed the imprint of his sleeping body. And he was fully dressed.

Slowly, with a leaden heart, Nick walked up the passage to the living room. Jo lay where he had left her, on the sofa, very still beneath the blanket he had tucked around her.

"Nick? What time is it?" She opened her eyes slowly.

"After eight." He went and sat down beside her.

"What happened? Why did I sleep here? When did you arrive?" She pushed the hair out of her eyes.

Tenderly Nick leaned forward and kissed her forehead.

"Jo, I'm flying back to the States this morning."

She sat up. "Why?"

"I have to go, Jo. I have to get away from you, don't you see?"

Pushing herself up onto her elbow, she stared at him. "But why the States?"

"Because it's far away. I came here last night, Jo. I hypnotized you. I don't even know how, but somehow I frightened you into a trance against your will. I made you tell me some more of the story, Jo, knowing it was dangerous for you, knowing you were afraid. By rights I should be locked up!"

"Nick, that's not true." Jo stood up shakily. "I don't remember—"

"You don't remember because I told you you wouldn't remember. You were crying, Jo. You started to cry as you talked, and it brought me back to sanity. I told you to go to sleep and I told you to forget." He clenched his fists. "Until this is over I am not going to trust myself even in the same city

491

as you. Somehow I've got to find Sam and get him to straighten out this mess, if he's capable of doing it. I'll see if he's still down in Hampshire." He strode grimly to the phone and glanced without comment at the pad with his mother's number on it, then he began to dial.

Dorothy Franklyn answered at the second ring.

"He's just left, Nick," she answered in response to his curt inquiry. "He said he had to get back to town later today. Is anything wrong, Nick? He really was very on edge all weekend."

"Nothing's wrong, Ma." Nick drummed his fingers on the desk. "I'll call you again soon." He hung up. "He's on his way back to London. Jo, I don't want you staying here alone. You've got to keep away from both of us."

Jo bit her lip. "There's no way I'd ever let him in." She gave a tired smile. "Ceecliff is coming to stay with me tonight."

Nick's face lightened. "That's good news. I wish I could see her."

"So do I," Jo said sadly. "So do I."

The apartment was empty. Nick walked around it twice, alert for any sound, before he slid the deadlock on the front door and went toward the phone.

He booked a flight on the afternoon jumbo jet, then he called Jim Greerson.

Jim was desperate. "For crying out loud, old son! You were supposed to be here!"

"I'm sorry, Jim. I'm sure you are handling everything brilliantly."

"I doubt it. And if it's screwed up, it's no one's fault but yours! Mike Desmond was furious when you didn't turn up again. I've told him you will personally go over to his office tomorrow and grovel and lick his shoes."

Nick stared up at the ceiling. "Jim, I'm flying back to New York this afternoon—"

"Like hell you are!" It was the first time Nick had ever heard Jim sound really angry. "This is your firm, Nick. If you want to save it, you fucking will show up and pull your weight! There are other people's jobs on the line too, you know. You've got twenty people working for you, in case you've forgotten, and they all rely on you!"

Nick passed his hand over his forehead. "Jim—"

"No. No more excuses, Nick. Just get here, fast." Jim slammed down the phone.

"Damn!" Nick looked down at the memo pad on the desk where he had written down his flight number, then he ripped off the page and, screwing it up, flung it into the wastepaper basket.

As he did so something lying in the bottom of the almost-empty basket caught his eye. He stooped and picked it up. It was a cheap wooden crucifix with, nailed to it, a plastic figure of Christ.

Bet looked up from the flat-plan on her desk. "You want to work here? In the office?"

"Just today, Bet. Please. I have a reason for not wanting to be at home. I can finish the article off and leave it with you." Jo hitched herself up on the edge of Bet's desk. She leaned over and picked up the box of cigarettes lying by the telephone. Her hand was shaking slightly.

Bet marked up a couple more sections on the plan, then she threw down her pen and stood up. She went over to the coffee and poured out a cup. "You'd better drink this." Deftly she took the unlit cigarette away from Jo and tucked it back into the box. "I'm sure I can find you a desk here, love. In fact, there's one here permanently for you if you want it. You know that."

Jo shook her head. "Only for today, Bet, thanks all the same. Then I'm going home. And I'm going back to Matilda. I've finished all the research I'm going to do." She took a deep breath. "Now I want to write it all down quickly and get it out of my system once and for all."

Bet smiled. "I'm glad you've changed your mind. It would have been the end of a beautiful friendship if you'd let me down on that one. I've provisionally scheduled you three main feature slots starting in March. That gives you three months to write it. Will that be enough?"

"It'll be done in three weeks." Jo's voice was dry.

"Whenever." Bet raised her hands in an expansive gesture of compliance. "I've spoken to Tim. He's sending all the photographs to you direct before he leaves."

"Leaves?" Jo glanced up.

"He's going to Sri Lanka on Sunday, for six months or so, with the delectable Caroline." Bet carefully avoided Jo's eyes. "It's best, Jo. He'll destroy himself if he stays here."

Jo looked away, taken aback at the sudden, suspicious prickling behind her eyes.

"He'll get over it," Bet went on gently.

"Of course he will." Jo forced herself to smile.

"Will you put him in the articles?"

"No."

"But he is part of the story—"

"So is Nick, but I won't include him either." Jo stood up suddenly. "Don't worry, you'll get your money's worth. I shall pillory myself for my avid readers, but not my friends."

Bet shrugged. "As you wish, but you're omitting some of the most extraordinary parts of the story, Jo. And don't forget, the big bad world has already read about Nick and Sam."

493

"Then let them make their own connections." Jo picked up her file of notes. "I'm working on the Clements story now, so please, tell me where I'll find a desk, and I'll start."

Ceecliff paid off the taxi and walked slowly up the steps to ring Jo's bell. It was several seconds before the intercom buzzed into life.

"It's me, dear." She stooped toward the disembodied voice in the wall.

"Are you alone, Ceecliff?"

Celia Clifford stared around her carefully. "Totally. And I haven't been followed! I changed taxis twice to make sure," she said solemnly.

There was a gurgle of laughter from the wall. "Enter then and be recognized!"

"What on earth is all this about?" Panting after her climb up the stairs, Ceecliff watched as Jo bolted the front door behind her and fixed the chain.

"Nothing. I'm just being careful."

Ceecliff divested herself of her lightweight coat and dropped her handbag and shopping bags on a chair. "Have you locked Nicholas in or out?"

"Out. Oh, Granny—" Jo threw herself into the older woman's arms.

"You haven't called me that since you were quite tiny, Joey," Ceecliff murmured gently. "My goodness, look at you. If you cry like that, you'll dissolve, child." She led Jo to the sofa and pulled her down beside her. "Best let all the tears out first, then you can tell me everything."

It was eight-thirty when Ceecliff opened the front door to Nick. She smiled at him and gave him her cheek to kiss, then, taking his hand, she led him into the living room. "Joey is in the kitchen, Nicholas, fixing us some paella, so we can talk in here."

Nick put the bottle of wine he was carrying on the coffee table and sat down obediently. "I thought I might not be coming here again," he said slowly. "I had arranged to go back to the States this afternoon."

"Running away is not going to solve anything." Ceecliff sat down on the edge of the sofa beside him. She reached forward and took his hands in hers. "That's why I called you. Joey told me everything this evening. The whole story."

"Including what I did to her last night?"

"Including everything." She gave a small wistful smile. "Nicholas, amid all your problems, your anguish and your fear for Jo and for yourself, has it ever crossed your mind to acknowledge the fact that your spirit, the kernel of life inside you that is the essential you, has loved one woman for eight hundred years? That is some love story, Nicholas, and the way Jo tells it, it sounds as if there are three of you who have been given a second chance to redeem the mistakes you made all those years ago. A chance to fulfill your love, Nicholas, not repeat the terrible mistakes you made be-

494

fore. A chance for your brother, if he was this dreadful man, William, to prove he isn't a coward any longer, and for Richard—" She shrugged. "I don't know what Richard did, except perhaps grow old. But maybe there is to be another chance somewhere for him as well."

"You don't really believe all this?"

"Wait, I haven't finished." Ceecliff tapped him on the knee reprovingly. "I know nothing about psychology, or this frightening hypnosis business, but it does cross my mind that your brother has been practicing some kind of mental isometrics on you. He is using your resistance and your fear to fight yourself, within yourself." She paused, searching his face gravely for a reaction. "Have you thought of admitting to yourself that you were once another man? That that man made some terrible errors, for which his soul has lived in torment, and that a kind, not a vengeful, deity has given him the chance, through you, to make amends?"

Nick let out a deep breath. "No, I hadn't thought about it that way."

Ceecliff laughed. "You can say I'm gaga if you like, but I haven't lived nearly eighty years without learning something. And one of the things I've learned is that anything is possible, Nick. Why do you think you met Jo? It cannot have been coincidence."

"Sam introduced us."

"Perhaps that act was his first step on his own road to salvation."

"Perhaps." Nick looked skeptical. "Look, Ceecliff, I'm sorry, I'd love to believe this, I really would—but I can't." He stood up and began pacing up and down the carpet.

"But you do believe in your brother's power over you?" Ceecliff looked up at him, not moving from the sofa.

He stopped. "I've had proof of that."

"And you have had proof that your love for Joey is stronger than his evil intent. You nearly hurt her, Nicholas. You had it in your power to hurt her, even to kill her last night, but you didn't actually do it." She reached up toward him. "You were ungentle and ungentlemanly." She gave him a smile. "But you did not actually harm her, did you?"

Nick shook his head slowly.

"You could have forced her to tell you her story to the end last night, Nick. You could have forced her to experience once more the moment of death. But you didn't do it. You could have killed her, Nick. And if you were going to, if that was what you really wanted, you would have done it then. But you *didn't!*" She pulled herself up off the sofa and went to her shopping bags, which still lay on the chair near the door. "I bought us a nice bottle of Amontillado in Harrods before I came. Why don't you open it, Nick. And pour Jo one as well." She glanced at him with a gentle smile. "Think about what I've said, won't you? Don't just dismiss it out of hand."

Jo was in her bedroom, lying on the bed, her arm across her face. Nick sat down on the bed beside her. "I've brought you a sherry, Jo."

495

She turned and looked at him, her eyes still swollen from crying. "What do you think of Ceecliff's theory?"

He smiled. "I'll buy it. Anything is better than mine, and I hear John is next after Richard III for reappraisal and reinstatement by historians." He reached forward and pushed her hair gently back from her face. "I want to believe Ceecliff's love story, Jo." He leaned forward and kissed her on the lips. "I want to very badly. It would mean that at the end of the story you will marry your handsome prince and live happily ever after."

Jo gave a snort. She pushed him away and reached for the sherry glass he had put down on the bedside table.

"Don't overdo it, Nick." She swung her legs over the side of the bed and stood up. Her smile faded. "What about Sam? He's not going to want a happy ending, Nick." She couldn't hide the sudden tremor in her voice.

"I'll deal with Sam." Nick put his arm around her. "But you mustn't see him, Jo. You are too susceptible, and you do realize, don't you, that you must never, never go back to Matilda's world again? You know as much of her story as you need to know. There must be no more."

She nodded. "I had already decided that. I didn't want to know any more anyway. It was you who forced me to go on last night, Nick."

He grimaced. "God forgive me. Jo, just for a while, I still don't want you ever to be alone with me either. Not yet. Ceecliff has said she'll stay with you for a few days, if you want. I think you should let her."

Jo nodded. "I'd like that."

He grinned. "Good. It'll soon be over, Jo, I promise. It will soon be over now."

"Why so formal, Nicholas?" Sam eyed his brother across the table with grim amusement. "And so extravagant. Claridge's, no less!"

Nick was looking at the wine list. "I wanted to talk to you somewhere quiet."

"Then why not the apartment?"

"Because I don't trust you." Nick ordered a bottle of claret, then he leaned back in his chair and looked Sam straight in the eye. "It hasn't worked, Sam. You're a devious bastard, and I'll admit you had me shit-scared for a while, but it hasn't worked."

Sam smiled. "Pity." He put his elbow on the table and rested his chin in his hand, looking at Nick through narrowed eyes. "You are quite sure, are you?"

Nick felt a prickle of unease stir the small hairs at the nape of his neck. "I know it," he said firmly. "But tell me one thing. Why? Okay. You despise me. Fair enough, I suppose: a brother's prerogative. But why Jo? Why hurt her?"

"It amused me to see you both dancing like puppets at my command." Sam stretched his long legs under the table. "You and that wimp,

Heacham. His memories are genuine, you know. He's a real sensitive, poor bastard." He sat back in silence as Nick scrutinized the label on the wine bottle and then sipped thoughtfully from his glass.

With a curt nod at the wine waiter Nick watched the two glasses slowly poured, then he picked his up and extended it toward Sam. "I'll drink to your speedy and permanent return to Scotland."

Sam clinked glasses with him amiably. "It will be within the week," he said. "I have only one or two things left to do in London."

"Just so long as they don't involve Jo."

Sam smiled. "Jo barely exists for me any longer," he said cryptically. And he took another sip from his glass.

Nick reached into his pocket. Silently he laid the crucifix on the table. Sam looked at it. He set down his glass. "Where did you find that?"

"In the wastebasket. Is it a symbol of discarded belief or a prop you don't need anymore?"

After picking up the cross, Sam held it in his hand for a moment, staring at it expressionlessly, then he slipped it into the pocket of his suit. He glanced up at Nick, who was watching him closely. "Oh, I need it," he said softly. "I'll need it for another week at least. What's wrong? Did you think I would shrink back like a vampire and disappear in a puff of smoke when you confronted me with it?" He laughed out loud. "You are rattled, little brother." His eyes had grown suddenly very cold. "Rattled and rather stupid." He turned to the food that had been put down before him.

Nick fought back a wave of nausea. Doggedly he picked up his knife and fork. "Just keep away from Jo," he said again. "And just in case you feel like looking her up, I warn you, her grandmother is staying with her, so she won't be alone, ever."

Jim Greerson sat back in his chair and began to fill his pipe slowly. He glanced at the man opposite him. "Nick won't be too keen on us pursuing this King John business," he said with an apologetic smile. "It's one hell of an invasion of his privacy."

Mike Desmond smiled. "Privacy is there to be invaded, Jim. Look." He handed him a piece of paper. "One of your fellows slipped me this." It was an unmistakable caricature of Nick with, on his head, a lopsided crown.

Jim whistled. "You'd better not let Nick find out who drew that. He would be for the bullet."

"Or a raise. Look." Mike produced a second piece of paper. "See this? Get something along these lines on TV at peak time and it'll be worth a few bob on your account."

Jim shook his head slowly. "Nick will kill us if we suggest it."

"You want our account, Jim? Look, for Pete's sake! I've done all the work for you! There can't be a paper in the country that hasn't picked up that story about Nick. Everyone in the country knows what he does.

They'll all recognize him. It will sell, Jim, you know that. But for God's sake get your skates on. I want to be topical! Hammer out a storyboard fast. It will be worth it."

Jim grimaced. "You're the boss, I suppose."

"Right. I'm the boss. I pay your fat salaries and supply the fuel for that car of Nick's. Besides, you'll be boosting all your other clients by implication, so if it means Nick Franklyn has to lay his head on the block for a few nights, I'd say it was worth it, ten times over." He stood up. "Tell him that from me, Jim. I'll expect to hear from him this afternoon."

Jim walked over to the window and threw it up, letting in a blast of hot traffic fumes and noise. He ran his fingers rather desperately through his hair, then he walked over to his desk and pressed the buzzer.

"Jane? Where is Nick?"

"He's not back from lunch yet."

Jim glanced at his watch. "It's after three, for Christ's sake! Where was he going, do you know?"

"He was meeting his brother at Claridge's."

Jim sighed. "Okay, Janey, love. The second he appears wheel him in here. It's double desperate." He sat down and drummed his fingers on the desk top. Then he pulled the two sketches toward him and studied them critically. He grinned. They were really rather good.

The house lay bathed in moonlight. It was completely silent, the undrawn curtains turning the windows into dark pools, reflecting deeply into the interior of the building. Slowly the figure tiptoed up the grass on the edge of the drive and made its way around to the back. It crept up to the back door and tried it gently, before skirting the dustbins and pushing at the small rear window. That too was locked.

Systematically the dark-clad shadow tried every downstairs window before shining a powerful flashlight up at the second floor. The light beam slid over the wisteria around the front door, playing among the fronds, almost lovingly caressing the weeping greenery until it found what it was seeking, the blue, square box on the wall that marked the burglar alarm. There was a quiet chuckle in the silence as, slowly, he bent and picked up one of the large granite lumps that marked the flowerbed edge. After raising it above his head, he hurled it through the front window on the left side of the door with a deafening splintering of glass.

For a moment the wailing alarm seemed deceptively quiet in the black, back-lit moonlight of the garden as, without a backward glance, the figure slipped into the bushes and out of sight, but already, next door, the lights were beginning to come on.

Jo and Ceecliff were planning a visit to the watercolor viewing day at Sotheby's when the phone rang. Jo answered it, then, with a frown, passed it over to her grandmother. It was several minutes before Ceecliff hung up. Her face had gone pale.

"That was Julian Frederickson who lives next door," she said slowly. "My house has been burgled."

Jo stared at her, shocked. "Oh, no. Was much taken?"

Ceecliff shrugged. "They don't know. The alarm went off in the middle of the night and they've found a broken window. Julian is a key holder and he's been in and looked around. He says there's no damage as far as he can see, but—" She caught Jo's hand. "I'm going to have to go back."

"Of course." Jo gave her a hug. "I'll drive you down."

"No, dear. I know you have another meeting with your editor to choose your pictures this afternoon. You can't possibly come." Ceecliff smiled. "Julian would have known if anything had been touched. He knows the house well enough. It sounds as though that beastly alarm scared them off. I'll get dressed quickly and catch the first train I can get hold of."

Jo rummaged in her bag and produced her car keys. "Here. At least take my car. Please. By the time you've crossed London to Liverpool Street and found a train and made the connections to Sudbury it will be midnight. Take my car and I'll come up at the weekend and collect it."

"You're sure, dear?" Ceecliff stared at her doubtfully.

Jo nodded. "I'm sure."

"And can you get someone to come and stay with you? You mustn't be alone."

"I'll be okay." Jo kissed her on the forehead. "There are loads of people I can ask."

She stood on the pavement waving as Celia Clifford expertly slotted the blue MG into the traffic and disappeared, then she walked back slowly inside, feeling curiously bereft.

After shutting the door, she slipped the bolt automatically and fixed the chain. She glanced at her watch. It was just after ten. Plenty of time to call someone a bit later, but first there was something she wanted to do.

Ceecliff had been with her since Monday. Now it was Thursday. She'd finished the Clements article but started nothing new. She stood and ran her fingers over the pile of books and tapes and documents on her desk. Three weeks to write the three articles, she had said to Bet. But what about the book? The biography, the quest for her past existence. What of Matilda?

She sat down and pulled the first notebook toward her. Then she inserted a sheet of paper into her typewriter.

Once upon a time . . .

It was the way all the best stories started.

She worked steadily right through the day, commanding her brain to answer questions, marshaling memories, holding her emotions in an iron grasp as she wrote. It was hard to dissociate herself from the story. Her fingers would race more and more quickly over the keys, filling in detail she never knew she possessed, till, cramped and exhausted, she had to rest them. The time of her meeting with Bet had come and passed. Apologetically she called the office, promising to come in first thing on Monday, then she wandered into the kitchen for a glass of milk before going back and switching on the tape of one of her earlier regressions and listening intently as she sat down and put her feet up on the cushions.

At five Ceecliff called. "Just to let you know all is well, dear. They must have been scared off. Julian organized someone to mend the window for me, so I'm snug and safe. Let me know when you're arriving. You'll find my car in the station parking lot. . . . I only hope it will start after a week." She paused. "Is there someone there with you, Jo?"

Jo started guiltily. She had forgotten all about phoning someone to come and be with her. "Don't worry, everything is organized," she said. "Now take care. I'll call you tomorrow and let you know when I'm coming."

She broke the connection and then she dialed the office in Berkeley Street. "Please come this evening, Nick."

"Is Ceecliff still with you?"

"No, she had to go back."

"Then I shouldn't come, Jo."

"We have to believe her, Nick. We have to trust ourselves. Please come. I need you."

Nick sighed. "It's you who have to do all the trusting, Jo."

"I'm prepared to risk it. I don't want to be alone."

"Then I'll come." As Nick put down the phone he pressed the intercom button. "Jane, tell Jim I'm leaving in twenty minutes. If he wants me to countersign those documents he'll have to bring them now. And Jane, did you check the orders for tomorrow's champagne?"

"Have done." Jane's voice echoed lightly in the room. "Will there be anything else, Your Majesty?"

He cut off the peal of laughter with a good-humored curse. Was it really worth it? Allowing himself to be made a fool of for the sake of the firm. He deliberately put the thought out of his mind. This time tomorrow Mike Desmond would have signed the contract and the team going to the States would be three quarters of the way across the Atlantic.

Until then, there was Jo.

She met him at the door dressed in a soft silk dress of plum-red. He stared at her for a moment, unmoving, before he entered the apartment.

"What is it?" Nervously she fingered the skirt. "Don't you like it? Ceecliff helped me to choose it."

He smiled. "It's quite lovely." He took her in his arms and buried his face in her hair. It was loose, he noticed. No scarf, no ribbon. How could he tell her he had seen a life-size picture of her in Tim Heacham's studio, wearing a gown of just that shade of red?

He closed the door behind him and slipped on the chain. "Why did Ceecliff go so suddenly?"

"She had a phone call that someone had tried to burgle her house. They didn't get in, but obviously she had to go and check."

"And she's not afraid of being there alone?"

"Apparently not." Jo looked away suddenly. "That's my weakness at the moment."

"Not a weakness. It's common sense. You'd be a fool to be alone as long as Sam's around." Nick pushed her away reluctantly and walked through into the living room. "I had lunch with him the day before yesterday. The good news is, he's going back to Edinburgh at the weekend."

Jo sighed. "I hope he never comes back."

"Or not for a very long time. You've decided to go on and write it, then?" Nick was standing looking down at her desk. He picked up one of the books from the pile.

She nodded wearily. "It's the only way I'll be free," she said. "Otherwise Matilda is going to haunt me for the rest of my life." She hesitated, glancing at him. "Bet wants me to mention you in the story, Nick. Do you mind?"

He laughed. "*W I A* is about the only periodical that hasn't mentioned me yet. But isn't the story a bit over the top for them? I'd have thought such a tale of love and despair and unmitigated male chauvinism would have turned all those *Women in Action* readers off for good."

Jo smiled. "Perhaps. Bet thinks it will turn them on. But in fact, all it does is prove that some women at least were just as capable in those days, and had enormous managerial responsibilities, and that men were male chauvinist pigs every one, as ever. The readers will love it."

"And my role? The arch M.C.P., I suppose?"

Jo busied herself in the drinks cabinet, holding up empty bottles to the light.

"I shall be suitably diplomatic about your role. Would you rather be the villain or the romantic hero?"

"You decide. As long as you know which I am in real life." Nick looked down at her as she raised her eyes to his. For a long moment they stared at each other, then he reached down and took her hand. "That is empty," he said, firmly closing the cabinet. "If ever I saw an empty cabinet, that is it. I'll nip up to the liquor store and get something." He gave her a rueful smile. "While I'm there, glance at this. It's the storyboard for the TV ad Desco wants us to put on."

As the door closed behind him Jo stared at the sketches he had put into her hand. She felt numb. It was all reduced to a stupid, cheap joke. John. Handsome, powerful, malicious John, pilloried by a tatty TV advertisement; reduced to a trite little sketch, to be screened between *Coronation Street* and the evening quiz show. She shivered unhappily as she put them down.

Nick was back in ten minutes with a bottle of gin, four bottles of tonic, and a carafe of chianti.

Jo let him in silently.

"I take it you don't like the idea?" He glanced at her as he produced a lemon from the pocket of his jacket. "Is there any ice?"

She nodded. "It just seems rather . . . small."

"Jo, Mike has laid it on the line. He wants this idea or out. Our boys think it will work. It's an amusing script even for the people, if there are any, who don't know what the hell we're talking about. If I veto it, we lose the account."

"Then it must go on."

"Is it any worse than what you propose to do with your articles and your book?" He took her hands gently.

Jo shook her head.

He gave a small smile. "Jo, don't you think it's what we need? To send ourselves up a little bit? Humor is an awfully good anodyne."

"I know. It's just . . ."

"I know what it is, Jo." Releasing her, Nick turned toward the kitchen. "I've been there, remember?" He changed the subject abruptly. "Are you going to come to New York with me—" He broke off with a curse as, behind them, the phone rang. Swinging back into the room, he picked it up.

"Hello?" There was complete silence on the other end of the line. They both heard the connection go dead.

Nick slammed down the receiver.

"Wrong number," he said cheerfully. "Now, where was I?" He put his hands gently on Jo's shoulders. "Well, will you come?"

She nodded slowly. "Yes." She moved back slightly. "Will we ever be able to forget all this, Nick?"

He turned away and, picking up the bottles, led the way into the kitchen. "In time it will distance itself like a bad dream, I expect. I hope." He gave his boyish smile. "Till then we must just make sure nothing else happens—apart from the happy ending."

They ate their supper in silence, neither suggesting they turn on any music, watching the light fade in the room as darkness came.

The phone rang again. After a moment Nick stretched across and lifted the receiver. Once again, when he spoke the line went dead. "It's Sam," Jo whispered into the silence. He sat back, not looking at her, his eyes on the open French doors onto the balcony. The streetlights gave a pale, false moonlit wash to the stone of the balustrade. He did not dare move. He did not dare even think about her. Suddenly danger crackled in the atmosphere between them, held at bay only by the quiet.

Then it was gone. Nick turned and looked at Jo covertly. She was sitting uncomfortably, drawn to the edge of her chair by the urgency of the phone bell, her shoulders tense, the angle of her head defiant as she stared past him, as if she were listening to something far away inside herself.

Nick was suddenly galvanized into movement. "Jo! Jo, for Christ's sake, don't do it! *Jo!*" He caught her shoulders and shook her hard. "Jo, can you hear me?"

Her hands had come up automatically and she clutched convulsively at his shirt front. "Nick——"

"Hold on, Jo. Don't let it happen. Fight it, Jo. Fight it!"

She let go of him abruptly and clapped her hands to her head.

The blackness was whirling around her; there was a roaring in her ears, waves of sound annihilating her, like torrents of angry water toppling over onto a beach. There were chains on her wrists and rain, rain in the shadows, rain in the wind howling around her, tearing at the huge red-and-gold standard with the clawing leopards of England as it strained high in the darkness, tearing her clothes, and above all the sound of thunder. But Nick was still beside her. She could see his mouth moving. He was talking to her, his hands outstretched to hold her. It was Nick . . . Nick . . .

The telephone bell cut through the sound, echoing in the room for the third time that night. Neither of them took any notice of it. To Nick it echoed obscenely in the silence, for Jo it drove the whirling noise away. As suddenly as the dislocation had come, it passed, leaving her shaking like a leaf.

She collapsed into Nick's arms, tears pouring down her face. "It wanted to happen again, Nick. I was at the castle at Carrickfergus. You were there too. . . ."

"But you fought it, love." He gathered her tightly against his chest. "You fought it." Behind them the phone fell silent. "It won't happen again. You know now you can fight it. You can. It's all right, Jo. It's all right. You're safe."

She was still clinging to him desperately. "Don't go, don't leave me——"

"I won't leave you, Jo." He smiled down at her reassuringly. "Come on. It's all over now. You're safe."

"Make love to me, Nick."

He tensed slightly. "You know I want to, but——Jo, I have my own demons to fight too. I'm afraid of what I might do."

She was shaking her head, still clinging to his neck. "You won't hurt me, Nick. You won't. Just make love to me. Make me part of you. Please. You have to——" Her voice rose suddenly. "Please, Nick. Now. Here."

"No, Jo." Gently he held her away from him. "Not here."

He led her through into her bedroom and, closing the curtains, turned on the bedside light. She was standing quite still, looking at the floor. Her shaking had stopped. He put his hands on her shoulders. "You're sure this is what you want?"

She nodded. "Undress me, Nick."

He frowned. She was standing before him completely submissive, no longer hysterical, not moving as he raised his hand tentatively to the zipper at the back of her dress. The soft red silk slid to the floor. Beneath it she wore nothing but a black lace slip. He pulled the straps down over her shoulders and the slip followed the dress, leaving her quite naked. Keeping an iron control over himself, Nick led her gently to the bed and pulled back the covers, watching as obediently she turned to climb in. Across her shoulders was a fading welt, the mark of Sam's belt. At the sight of them Nick felt a wave of blind fury sweep over him. For a moment he did not move. He clenched his fists, feeling the icy drench of perspiration across his shoulders as he closed his eyes.

"Nick?" He heard Jo's whisper from the bed.

She had pulled the sheet over herself and was staring at him. He could see the sudden fear behind her eyes.

He forced himself to smile. "It's okay, Jo." He sat down beside her. "It's not you. I just had this tremendous urge to kill my brother." He touched her face gently, then slowly he began to unbutton his shirt. "I won't hurt you, Jo. I promise." He reached out to turn off the lamp. Then he pulled her into his arms.

She slept lightly, waking twice in the night to reassure herself that Nick was still there, snuggling against his warm, relaxed body before drifting back into a restless, dream-haunted sleep. Once she cried out and Nick turned to her without waking and held her close against him. They both woke early. Jo was pale and there were dark rings under her eyes as she made their coffee and toast while he was shaving. He glanced at her once or twice as they had their breakfast, concerned at her unnatural quietness.

"Jo, are you all right?" he asked at last.

She nodded. "Tired, that's all. I didn't sleep very well."

He smiled. "Not my fault, I hope."

"No, not your fault." She made herself smile back over her coffee cup. "Nick, Ceecliff took my car. If you don't need yours, would you lend it to me this morning?"

He glanced at her sharply. She was taut as a wire again, her knuckles white on the handle of her cup.

"Of course you can borrow it." He reached into his pocket for the keys. "Where do you want to go?"

"I've got one or two things to do." She made a visible effort to pull herself together. "I've been away so much. If I'm going to Suffolk tomorrow, I must get some things sorted out today."

504

"Okay." He finished his toast, drained his coffee, and stood up. "I'll call you later. If you're very good, there might even be a glass of champagne for you at the office this evening." He paused as he was about to put on his jacket. "Do you want me to come back here this evening?"

"You know I do." She stood up and reached up to kiss him. "I want you to come back here always, Nick."

As soon as he left she showered and dressed in a blue linen skirt and blouse. She straightened the apartment, put her camera and notebook in her bag, and picked up the keys to the Porsche. Then she hesitated. She looked at the pile of books on the table.

She knew what she had to do. She had to find out where Matilda had died. No more trances, no more hypnotism. Just plain fact, to finish the story off. When she got there she would know. She opened the notebook and stood staring down at the scribbled lines of writing; notes taken so many weeks ago, which had meant so little then. Now they were a short-hand mockery of a lifetime of love and hate and hope and fear.

She ran her finger down the page. "Matilda and her son were sent from Bristol to a dungeon at Windsor" . . . Windsor or Corfe. She gazed across the room unseeing. Windsor or Corfe. She would know at once. She would feel Matilda's fear. That would be enough. There would be no last trance; no more. Just the final stark sentence in her story.

She closed the notebook resolutely and, picking up her bag, let herself out of the apartment.

The Porsche ate up the miles to Windsor, streaking down the fast lane of the M4 without regard to the speed limit. From far away the huge towers of the castle showed from the road, shimmering in the haze that hung over the willow-lined water meadows which bordered the Thames. Jo swung the car into the old town and parked it in a side street below the massive castle walls. For a moment she did not move. She rested her forehead against the steering wheel and closed her eyes, trying to steady the uneasy pounding of the pulse beneath her ribs. Then, taking a deep breath, she swung the car door open and pulled herself out. The town was very crowded and she was jostled back and forth on the pavement as she made her way resolutely toward the gatehouse at the entrance to the cas-tle.

The lower ward was thronged with people. Gray stone; walls; towers; the flying buttresses of St. George's Chapel; emerald grass, clipped as if by nail scissors. Up toward the hill on which stood the huge round tower. Cameras; children; everywhere people staring; people laughing; people talking; people only superficially aware of the ghosts that walked around them. Hitching her bag up higher onto her shoulder, Jo stared up at the vast bulge of the gray walls. High above, rippling from the flagpole, was a flag. She felt her stomach tighten as she stared up, half expecting to see again the snarling leopards of John's standard against the stormy sky. Her mind made a tentative shadowy probe toward the dream, rejected it, and drew back. It was not John's standard. She could see the brash red, white, and blue now of the Union Jack with, behind it, wisps of high summer cloud and sunlight.

Slowly her hands unclenched in the pockets of her skirt as she walked around the castle perimeter, expecting nothing now, the moment past, the ancient stones absolved of her particular nightmare.

It was after five when she got home. She threw down the keys on the table and went straight to the phone.

"Jane? Is Nick there? It's Jo."

Over the line she could hear the sound of laughter from the office. Suddenly she felt cut off and very lonely.

Jane came back on the line in seconds. "Sorry, Jo. You've just missed him, but he was only going to the apartment. You'll catch him there."

Jo sat still for a moment feeling strangely let down. He had promised to return to her. She wanted to tell him what she had done. She wanted to tell him what had happened.

She leaned forward slowly and flipped her notebook open. "Matilda and her son were sent to a dungeon at Windsor . . ." Jo picked up her pen and crossed out Windsor and wrote Corfe.

Half an hour later she redialed Nick's number. It rang for several seconds before it was picked up.

"Hello?" It was not Nick's voice that answered.

Jo felt herself tense nervously. The receiver slipped slightly in her hand as perspiration started out all over her palm.

"Sam?" Her voice was husky.

"Hello, Jo. How are you?"

She couldn't reply for a moment. Neither could she put down the phone.

"I thought you'd gone back to Scotland," she managed to say at last.

"I'm on my way." She could hear the amusement in his voice. "Nick and I had a long talk about things on Tuesday and we agreed that perhaps I should go home."

Jo found she was pressing the receiver closer and closer against her ear. "I want to talk to Nick."

"He's not back yet, but I'm expecting him any second." His voice was very calm.

"I see. Look, Sam, I'll call back in a few minutes."

"There's no need, Jo," he said slowly. "He'll be back very soon. Talk to me instead."

"I don't want to, Sam," she replied in a panic.

"You do want to. You've been wanting to speak to me for days; you've been needing to speak to me, Jo." His voice sunk a semitone. "That was why you called, because you realized how much you needed to see me, because of your headaches, Jo. I want you to listen to me very carefully now. Can you hear me, Jo?" He paused for a second. "When you speak to Nicholas he is going to ask you to come to his office party. You are going to tell him you are too tired. You have a headache and you don't want to see him. You don't want to see him at all tonight, do you, Jo? You are going to sit down quietly at home and watch television, and later this evening I shall come to you and make your headache better. You do have a headache, don't you, Jo?"

"Yes." Her whispered answer was barely audible.

"Then you need me, Jo."

She stared at the phone for several minutes after she had hung up, a puzzled frown on her face. Why had she talked to him? Why had she listened to him for even a single second? She never wanted to see Sam again, and yet it was true, she did have a headache. It would do no harm, surely, if he came, just for a few minutes, to help her relax. . . .

When Nick called her she was firm and slightly distant. Her headache was worse, like a blinding ligature around her eyes, throbbing incessantly as she tried to focus her thoughts. "I'll be all right, Nick, really. I just need an early night." She hadn't congratulated him on the signing of the contracts with Mike Desmond. That was the reason for the party. She groped for the right words, painfully conscious that the room was beginning to spin.

"You are sure you'll be okay?" His voice came from far away. "Jo, I'll look in later. If you're asleep I won't disturb you. Take care, my darling. . . ." Darling. He had never called her that before. Smiling in spite of her pain, Jo felt her way almost blindly to the television and turned it on, then she sank onto the sofa in front of it and sat back, her eyes closed, letting the waves of crushing agony beat one by one against the back of her eyelids.

Sam came sometime after seven, inserting in the lock of the street door a shiny, newly cut key. It stuck slightly, then it turned and the heavy door swung open. The second key fitted perfectly. He held his breath slightly as he turned it, wondering if she had bolted the door, but it swung open silently and admitted him to the quiet apartment.

He listened. Yes, the TV was on softly, as he had known it would be. After closing the door carefully he slid the bolt home and slotted in the chain. Then he turned into the living room and stood looking down at Jo. She was lying back against the cushions on the sofa, her face white, her eyes closed, oblivious of the violent fistfight between two men going on on the screen before her. Her body was taut with pain.

"Hello, Jo." Quietly he walked into the room.

She opened her eyes wearily and gave him a faint smile. There was a quick shiver of apprehension, then it was gone. "Are you going to make my headache better?"

Sam nodded. He stood between her and the TV. "You know what I'm going to have to do, Jo."

"You're going to hypnotize me again."

Sam smiled. "Isn't that what you want?"

She nodded slowly. "But I don't want to go back into the past, Sam. I don't want to regress any more. . . ."

She wanted to stand up, but her limbs were too heavy. They would not obey her. She looked up at him helplessly.

"Were you really William?" she asked slowly. "Or did you just choose him?"

Was there a hint of a smile behind his eyes? Sam was feeling in his pocket. He produced a cassette and, moving across to the stereo, he inserted it into the player. The soft strains of the flute cut across the muted wail of a police siren on the screen in the corner.

"We do not choose our destinies, Joanna. They are given to us," he said. He folded his arms. "It's time to take you back. You shake your head. Poor Jo. You are already halfway there. You hear the music? You cannot resist the music, Jo. It takes you into the past. It takes you back to John. It takes you back to the king who has ordered you to be shackled like a common criminal and brought before him on your knees. . . ."

38

John was sitting by the fire in one of the side chambers above the hall when the prisoners, still ragged and damp from the sea and the rain, were brought before him.

He turned in his chair without comment as the three women and Will, reunited at last, stood before him and their guards fell back. Matilda raised her head and looked the king full in the eye for a moment, then proudly, without lowering her head, she knelt before him. The others followed suit, and she could hear, with a sudden snap of irritation, that Mattie had begun to sniff again. No one spoke.

The king held his hands out to the fire and began to rub them slowly together, not taking his eyes from Matilda's face. "So," he said at last. "We meet again."

She was the first, eventually, to look away, dropping her gaze to the border of his mantle, which brushed gently in the rushes around his chair. He stood up so abruptly she had to force herself to remain still and not flinch backward as he came to stand above her. He was so close she could smell the oil of lavender in his hair. The room was silent save for the rattle of rain against the window screens and the occasional hiss as drops fell into the glowing embers on the hearth.

She thought for a moment he was going to touch her, but he moved away again, walking over to the table that had been drawn up against the far wall of the room. It was laden with parchments and books and held the king's pens and ink. He picked up a letter and unfolded it slowly as he turned back to the prisoners who remained kneeling by the fire. His face was hard.

"Prince Llewelyn has, it appears, thought fit to join your husband, my lady, in making trouble for me in Wales." His voice was icy. "That is unfortunate." He strode back to the fire, the letter still in his hand. "Unfortunate for you, that is, if your husband persists in his rebellion when he knows that I hold hostages."

Matilda clenched her fists together nervously, very conscious of the iron fetters that encircled her wrists. She swallowed. "Will you give me the chance to raise the money to pay my husband's debts, sire?" Her voice came out huskily and too quiet. She wasn't sure if he had even heard her. Mattie and Will, side by side, were completely silent.

"Your Grace," she tried again, a little louder. "Before we fled from Hay I was able to put by a little money and some jewelry. I am sure with the help of our friends and my other sons we could raise some of the money we owe. If Your Grace would accept that as a start and—"

Her voice trailed away as he turned from the fire at last and looked down at her.

"It is no longer only a matter of money, Lady Matilda."

"I will persuade William to give himself up to you. And on his behalf I can surrender all the de Braose lands. . . ." She could not keep the note of pleading from her voice and, though she despised herself for it, the anguish in her tone was real.

"Your lands, my lady, are no longer yours to surrender," he said sharply. He looked from Margaret to Will and Mattie behind her suddenly. "It appears that Ireland has become a nest of traitors. The lands of the Lacys are all confiscated too, your husband's, Lady Margaret, and those of his brother. It is as well for them, perhaps, that they seem to have escaped, for if either of them show themselves again, their lives might well be forfeit." He spoke quietly. Margaret shrank behind her mother as the king's cold eyes fixed on her for a moment. Then he threw the letter down on his chair, talking half to himself, half to them. "I shall subdue Ireland. Every man here shall acknowledge me as king or I shall know the reason why. And when I return to Wales, make no mistake, I shall reduce that country—and its princes too—to ashes if I must. . . . Guards!" He raised his voice for the first time. Their escort sprang forward and the king eyed them critically. "Take the prisoners away," he ordered.

Matilda began to rise to her feet, awkward and stiff after kneeling for so long. To her surprise he stepped forward and held out his hand to help her. But his face was grim. "I shall consider your offer of money, Lady Matilda, but I feel that nothing short of the full amount of forty thousand will do now. And that may not be enough. Meanwhile you and your family will remain my prisoners. We leave Carrickfergus tomorrow, and you will travel with us back to Dublin."

The king sent for Matilda only after they had been encamped for several days at Dublin. She was brought to his tent, which had been set up in the midst of his army overlooking Dublin Bay, and appeared before him in midmorning, leaning on the arm of the tall knight who had been appointed her escort. The king had ordered her fetters removed when they had reached Kells, and she and Margaret and Mattie had been allowed serving women and provided with fresh linen and hot water, but Matilda was very tired.

There was no compassion in his face as the king looked at her. "The sheriff of Hereford has written to tell me that your husband has now attacked one of my castles. He requests my instructions and begs me to declare this man, once for all, outlawed. William has gone too far this time, Lady Matilda."

She went pale. Her escort had withdrawn from the tent and she felt suddenly weak, standing alone before the king. She half glanced around, hoping to see a stool. Finding nothing to sit on, she slowly sank to her knees.

"Give us one more chance," she whispered. "See, I beg you on my knees. Somehow I will find the money. I will make William submit. He will surrender. Only give us the chance to talk to him."

John pushed back his chair with an exasperated exclamation. "It seems to me we've had this conversation before. How many chances must I give this man?"

"Sire, I know where I can find the money," Matilda rushed on desperately, hardly taking note of what she said. "I have thought about it much and I am sure I can raise it. I know I can. Let me see him again. Please, Your Grace, give me that one chance."

John turned away. He went to stand at the door of the tent looking out toward the dazzling blue of the sea. Far out on the edge of the haze three small boats sailed slowly northward, trailing their nets. He watched them abstractedly for a moment, chewing his nails. Then suddenly he swung round. "Why do I find it so hard, even now, to refuse your pleas?"

For a moment she thought his face betrayed a hint of pity, but it was already gone when he spoke again. "Very well, one last chance. But this time I must have your promise in writing." He stepped to the desk and, reaching for his bell, summoned one of the chancery clerks. "An agreement; Matilda de Braose, the Lady of Hay, agrees to pay a fine of fifty—yes, fifty, you must pay for my patience—fifty thousand marks to the royal exchequer before"—he hesitated, counting on his fingers—"before Lammas next. That gives you a year, my lady. You will sign the document and on reaching Wales your husband will sign it too. You and your family will remain in my custody until your husband pays me the first installment. That is the last time I intend to discuss this matter. It seems to me that I have already been too lenient." He leaned forward, watching the clerk laboriously copying out the formal words of the document. "I mean to see the barons of this country learn to respect me, Matilda, whoever gets hurt in the process. I'll not be played with, remember that. You tell your sons and your precious friends the Lacys and the Earl Marshall and all William's cronies that if they defy me and compound treasons against the crown they will find out just how strong an arm their sovereign has. I'll not see the safety of the realm endangered." He bent and snatched the finished parchment from the clerk, who was blowing on the ink. "I've reduced Ireland

and now I'll reduce Wales." He took the pen from the clerk and held it out to Matilda, who rose to her feet with some difficulty. "And you had better pray that this time your husband respects this agreement, because I shall hold you and your son accountable, if necessary with your lives."

Matilda took the pen, glancing at his face as she did so. Two red spots of anger glowed on his cheekbones and his mouth was set in an uncompromising line as he stared down at the document before them. She felt the cold black shadow of fear hovering over her heart as she blinked back the sudden scalding tears. "Please, Holy Mother," she whispered as she dipped the pen in the ink, "let William come to the king." Her hand shook as she carefully wrote her name at the end of the lines of black, crabbed writing. Then she let the pen fall.

They landed at Fishguard on the northern coast of the Pembroke Peninsula two days later. It was raining. Matilda scarcely noticed the route they took, sunk as she was in misery and fear. Her eyes remained lowered, dully taking in the streaming chestnut mane of the mare she rode. For several miles she worried a burr out of the tangled wet hair, twisting it in her fingers, watching unfeeling as tiny spots of blood sprang up on her skin to be washed away almost at once by the rain.

As soon as they had landed the king had dispatched riders to take her message to William, if they could find him in the high fastnesses of Elfael, bidding him come to ratify his wife's agreement.

"You fool, Mother," Will had said. "You complete fool. You know he won't come. If they tell him how much money you've promised he'll run or die of shock, but he won't come."

"He will come, he will." She clenched her fists, gazing at her son's pale face with such an ache of protective tenderness that for a moment she was unable to go on. Then she gained control. "We have money, Will. Our tenants will raise it for us, and our friends. Reginald and the Lacys must have reached France and Giles. There are so many who can help us, my dear. And there is the money I hid. It will be there still."

"Did you tell Father where it was hidden?"

Matilda shrank at the bitterness in her son's voice, but she shook her head. "He could not find it, even if I had. It is in a secret place in the mountains. I think I would have to go there again myself to be sure. . . ."

"And, even then, you might not find it, Mother dear." His voice was gentle again suddenly. He kissed her forehead lightly. "It seems to me that we must pray for a miracle."

It was at Bristol Castle on the feast of St. Eustace that the prisoners were summoned at last to the great hall after the evening meal was over. John was listening to the carolers who had arrived from Gloucester. He sat on his great chair, his legs stuck out in front of him, a goblet of wine still in his hand.

"It appears your obedient husband has decided to accede to your wish, Lady Matilda," he called loudly as soon as he saw her. A hush fell over the crowded hall and Matilda drew herself up, feeling hundreds of eyes on her as she walked slowly toward the dais and waited, her eyes lowered. John gestured at one of the servants and he ran, bowing, to a door.

The two men had obviously been waiting just outside, for they came in at once, hastening to the dais, where both went down on one knee. Matilda saw with a sudden lurch of her heart that one of them was William. He did not look at her, and she saw his surcoat and tunic were torn and mud-splashed and his beard unkempt. The old, unhealthy pallor had returned to his cheeks.

John rose, belching slightly as he moved, and set his cup down. He clicked his fingers at a clerk, who brought forward a parchment, which Matilda recognized at once as the one she had signed only weeks before, in Dublin.

"You agree, I take it, Sir William, to your wife's terms." John spoke curtly. "Fifty thousand marks she has promised. You realize that?"

William nodded almost imperceptibly. Still he did not look at her. "Then you will sign the agreement?" John stood and watched as pen and ink were brought to William. Then the de Braose seal was produced from his companion's pouch. There wasn't a sound in the great hall as the red wax dropped slowly onto the parchment, the pungent smell for a moment stronger even than the aroma of food and fire and candles and the strong smell of sweat that came from the lower tables of the hall. There was a hiss as the seal met the wax and the clerk carefully removed the document and passed it to the king. John waved it away. "Enough. I want to hear the singers. The first installment, Sir William, by the feast of St. Agnes, and"— he shot his head forward suddenly, his eyes blazing—"not one day later."

They were all ushered from the hall as the minstrels struck up a merry tune for the king.

Outside in the icy ward Matilda flung herself at her husband as he turned away toward the stables. "William, will you not even greet me? Surely you're allowed to talk to me before you go? For pity's sake!"

He turned back and looked at her, his face blank. "What am I to say, Moll? I have to go to find this money. There is so little time."

Matilda threw herself at him, clinging. The guards made no attempt to stop her. "It's not so much, the first installment. Ten thousand marks, that's all, my dear. The marshall will help and Reginald and Giles, of course. You must write to them at once, and our friends in the Marches. Please, William. You will try?"

"Mother." Will was behind her suddenly, his hand on her arm. "Mother, come into the warm. My father knows what to do."

513

"You do know, William? You will do it? There's so little time. Oh, my dear, you will help me . . ." She was sobbing now, still clinging to him. William turned away, shaking her off. "I've told you, woman. I'll do what I can. What else can I say?" A gust of wind blew his cloak open as a groom brought two horses forward and the guard closed in on Will and Matilda, beginning to hustle them toward the corner tower where they were lodged.

"William, William . . ." Her voice rose to a scream as Will put his arm around her and pulled her away. "William, help us, please! *Please, Please help us.*"

But already his horse was trotting toward the portcullis as it slid upward into the darkness of the gateway. Seconds later the two figures had vanished into the night.

Matilda collapsed onto Will's shoulder as Margaret and Mattie ran, consoling, to her side, and slowly they led her back to the tower as the first drops of rain began to fall on the cobbles.

Sam was standing looking out of the window across the square. There were tears on his cheeks as his hand clenched in the curtains. Slowly he turned. "So William left you, my lady," he whispered, "to fetch the money." He laughed bitterly. "Did you believe him? Did you wish that you had been a faithful and loving wife? Tell me how it happened, my lady. Tell me how it felt when finally you realized that William was never coming back."

Jo's fingers moved restlessly over the cushions on the chair, scratching harshly at the tapestry work, shredding the wool beneath her nails. Her eyes moved unseeing over the flickering TV screen.

"William," she cried again. "William, for the love of the Holy Virgin, please, come back."

Tim knocked on the door, easing the heavy camera bag on his shoulder. He was panting heavily after climbing the long flight of stairs.

Judy opened it at the third knock. She was wearing her painting smock and old jeans. She looked slightly harassed as she saw him standing there.

He grinned. "I hope I'm not too late. You did say any time after eight would be okay."

"Oh, God, Tim, I'm sorry, I forgot. Come in, please." She dragged the door wider. "I never meant you to go to so much trouble. When I asked you to do the catalogue, I didn't realize you were going abroad."

"It's no trouble, Judy. You put quite a challenge to me. A catalogue of your inner thoughts, not just reproductions of your paintings. How could any photographer resist the temptation to photograph a lady's inner thoughts!"

514

She laughed. "I shall obviously have to censor them heavily." She closed the door behind him. "Can I get you a beer or something?"

Tim shook his head. "I think I'd rather get on. I want to look at the work that's going to the gallery in Paris and the studio, and I want to look at you." He smiled at her impishly. "You realize a lot of this will rely on the processing and I'm going to have to leave that to George, but he'll do it well. I think you'll be pleased with what he produces." He put down the bag and pulled it open. "First I want a picture of you in front of that sunset before it fades."

The back window of the studio was ablaze with crimson and orange. Judy glanced at it. "I'll change—"

"No! Like that. Jeans, paint stains, everything." He caught her shoulders and propelled her toward the window, turning her in profile to the light. "That's it. You'll be almost totally in silhouette. Just the slightest aura of color around your face and those streaks of red on your shirt. They look like overspill from the clouds."

He photographed her dozens of times against the window as the light faded to gold and then to green, then at last he turned his attention to the pictures. One by one she brought them forward into the strong studio lights.

"Are you really leaving tomorrow?" She studied his thin, tired face as he raised the light meter in front of a huge, unframed canvas.

He nodded. "Tomorrow evening."

"And you'll be gone months?"

"At least three." He squinted through the viewfinder and then retreated several paces before clicking the shutter.

"Are you going to see Jo before you go?"

He was suddenly very still. "I don't know. Probably not." He stepped away from the camera and helped her replace the canvas against the wall. "I had thought I might call in on my way back from here, but I'm not sure. Perhaps it would be better if I didn't see her again."

Judy raised an eyebrow. "You made that sound very final."

Tim gave a harsh laugh. "Did I?" He helped her lift the next picture onto the easel. "Jo has plenty to occupy her without me intruding. I want you in this one, standing facing the painting, that's it, back to the camera with your shadow cutting across that line of color."

"It's only a catalogue, Tim. You're turning it into a work of art—"

"If you'd wanted anything less you'd have asked your boyfriend to bring his Brownie," he retorted.

Judy colored. "My boyfriend?"

"Is Pete Leveson not the latest contender for the title?"

Judy stuck her hands in the seat pockets of her jeans. "I don't know." She sounded suddenly lost. "I like him a lot."

"Enough anyway to dish the dirt on your ex-lovers into his lap."

"Why not?" she flared suddenly. "Nick hasn't been exactly nice to me. I hope he rots in hell!"

Tim laughed wryly. "I think he's been doing that, Judy," he said.

The king rode out of Bristol three days later, leaving his prisoners behind in the custody of the royal constable. They were allowed the use of several rooms in the tower and their babies and the nurses were lodged on the floor above them, but nothing hid the fact that there were guards at the doors of the lower rooms and two men on duty always at the door out into the ward.

Matilda spent long hours at the window of their sleeping chamber gazing out across the marshes toward the Severn and the mountains of Wales beyond. Slowly the last leaves dropped from the woods, whipped off the leaden branches by cutting, easterly winds that blew gusts of bitter smoke back down the chimney into the rooms, filling them with choking wood ash. In spite of the fires they were cold, and though clothes and blankets were brought for them, Matilda seldom stopped shivering. She could not bear to allow the northern window shuttered, watching through the short hours of daylight for the sight of her husband's horse.

But he did not come.

The feast of St. Agnes passed and no word came, from William or the king. Then as the first snowdrops were pushing their way up through the iron-hard ground a detachment of men arrived escorting two of the king's household. They were lawyers.

Matilda stood before them alone, wrapped in a mantle of beaver fur, watching their gray, bookish faces for any sign of human feeling or concern.

One, Edward, held out her signed agreement. "Your husband, Lady de Braose, has failed to produce the said sum of money by the agreed date. Are you able to produce the money in his stead?" He looked up at her, mildly curious, uninterested.

Matilda swallowed. "I have money hidden. It may be enough, I don't know. I'm sure my husband is on his way. Can you not give him a little longer? I'm sure the king—"

"The king, my lady, has had word that your husband is fled to France." It was the other man speaking. He was seated at the side of the table, idly paring his nails with a knife. "There is no mistake, I'm afraid." He too was watching her now.

Matilda bit her lip. Now that it had happened she felt calm, almost relieved that the waiting was over.

"Then I must raise the money myself. I hid it with the help of my steward at Hay. There was some gold, jewelry, and coin. We put it in coffers and carried it up to the mountains."

"This money." Edward was tracing the writing of the document. "Would it amount to fifty thousand marks?"

"As your husband has defaulted we would require the full amount at once, you see." The younger didn't bother to look up this time. He was still working on his thumbnail.

"I was thinking in terms of the first installment," Matilda groped for her words cautiously. "There would be ten at least, I should think. I could raise more if I were allowed to go to Wales to—"

"Out of the question, I'm sorry." Edward drew a parchment toward him on the desk. "Did you make no note of the value of the money you hid, Lady de Braose? Perhaps your steward could be found to bring it. If I may have his name we can send riders."

"There were about four thousand marks in coin, if you must know." She shrugged. "Most of my jewelry was there. That must be worth a lot, and my husband's rings and chains, and gold." She glanced from one to the other, but both men were shaking their heads.

"I'm sorry. It's not enough." Edward rose, licking his lips nervously. "I must tell you, my lady, that His Grace has ordered that the judgment of the realm be carried out against your husband. He is now an outlaw in this land. The king has also decreed that unless you were able to meet to the last penny the amount required within three days of St. Agnes' feast, the day stipulated in the agreement you yourself signed of your own free will, you should suffer the full penalties for your husband's default."

He paused as the other lawyer too rose to his feet and began to push the pile of parchments together into a heap. The gesture was somehow very final.

"What penalties?" Matilda heard her voice as a whisper in the silence of the room.

He shrugged. "I have letters for the constable. You and your son, William, are to be removed to the royal castle of Corfe. The other ladies and your grandchildren will remain here for the time being, I gather."

Matilda looked from one to the other. She could feel her panic rising. "When must we go?"

"Today. As soon as an escort has been mounted." The two men bowed together and made their way past her to the door. Then they had gone and for a moment she was alone, before the knight who had brought her from the tower was again at her side. "You'd best go and make your farewells, lady," he murmured kindly. "The constable had an inkling of what the letters were going to say. The men are already summoned to escort you."

"Corfe," she whispered bleakly. "He uses that as a prison."

"No more than any other place. It's a favorite residence of his sometimes. Don't worry. You'll be out of the way there. He'll forget about you soon enough, and then your friends will be able to buy you out." He put his hand for a moment on her arm, a small gesture of comfort, but she could not help a shiver of terror at his words. She looked at him bleakly for a moment, then, slowly, she followed him back to the chamber she had shared for so many long nights with Margaret and Mattie and bade them a tearful farewell. Then she hugged the two babies and, last of all, her beloved little John, who clung to her, crying.

"We'll see you again very soon, Mother, never fear." Margaret took her hand for a moment and held it close. "Don't worry. You have many friends and they will all be working on the king to release you. He won't hold you to blame for long for Father's faults. You'll see."

Matilda forced herself to smile. "Yes, my darling, we'll see," she whispered slowly. "I'm sure it will all come out right in the end." And she reached to kiss her daughter one last time.

"Enough!" Sam moved across the room and stood before Jo, looking down at her, his face haggard. "It is too soon. John may intend to kill you, my lady, but I can still save you." Taking a deep breath, he steadied himself with an effort. "This time I can. This time I shall follow you to Corfe. I shall atone." He knelt before her and took her hand in his. "Dear God, I didn't mean to make you suffer so. Only a little longer, Moll. Only a little longer. You have to go there. You have to go, but I shall follow you." He was crying openly now, his face twisted with anguish. "My brother has much to answer for! But he will not be the one to save you. I will get there before him, Moll, I will save you." He raised her hand to his lips and pressed a lingering kiss upon her fingers. Then slowly he stood up. "And now, to keep you safe till morning. You will stay here, my lady, not moving, until dawn breaks. Then and only then will you set out on your last journey to Corfe. I have one last debt to pay tonight." He smiled suddenly, straightening his shoulders. "Then I shall follow you and tomorrow you will be mine."

Letting her hand fall, he went to the TV and turned up the sound. Then, slipping the cassette from the stereo into his pocket, he glanced around the room. Jo had not moved. Her eyes were once more on the TV but they did not register any movement. Her face was pale, and on the shredded cushion below her hand her fingers were still. He tiptoed out of the apartment, banged the door behind him, and ran down the stairs. In Gloucester Road he hailed a taxi.

Judy put the two mugs down on the table and pushed the packet of sugar toward Tim. "You know, I never expected you to spend so long over this. I really am grateful."

He took two spoonfuls, scattering crystals over the table, and stirred them slowly into the black coffee as, far away below, the street door banged. Footsteps began climbing the flights of stairs toward the studio.

"I'm sorry I can't see the whole project through." Tim smiled at her.

"Perhaps, if I'm honest, I spent longer than necessary. I wasn't looking forward to spending this evening on my own. Caroline is packing and washing her hair and convincing her mama she is not going to join a guru and never be seen again. I'm meeting her at the airport tomorrow afternoon."

Judy glanced at him. There was a touch of humorous sympathy in her eyes. "We could split a take-out dinner if you like—" She looked up in surprise at the sudden knocking on the studio door.

Tim climbed to his feet. "You're on," he said. "Chinese or what?" He pulled open the door and stepped back abruptly as Sam thrust his way past him into the room.

Judy jumped to her feet at the sight of him.

"Sam?" Her voice was frightened. "What are you doing here?"

Sam had stopped dead as the door swung back against the wall. He looked swiftly from Judy to Tim and back, then he smiled. "So." He took a deep breath. "You two?"

"Get out, Sam." Judy put her hands on her hips. "I don't know what the hell you're doing here, but get out. Do you hear me? If you don't, I'll call the police again!" Her voice was unnaturally shrill. "You are not welcome in my studio."

"Come on, Sam." Tim took a step toward him. "You heard what Judy said. Just leave quietly, there's a good fellow."

Sam laughed. "There's a good fellow," he mimicked mockingly. "Oh, no, my friend, not this time. This time I think we have some scores to settle, some scores that go back a very long way." As he stepped menacingly toward Tim, Judy turned and dived into the bedroom. She grabbed the phone, but Sam was immediately behind her and with a quick jerk he had torn the wire from the wall.

"No more police, Judith, my dear," he breathed. "I think we can manage very well without them this time."

Judy went white. "You're crazy, Sam," she shouted. "Crazy!"

Behind Sam, Tim had appeared in the doorway, and for a moment none of them moved. Then Sam threw down the end of the wire. "It was you I came to see, Judith. I seem to remember we had an unfinished piece of business to settle. Each time I leave Joanna I have this urge to come here, it seems. To visit another whore. All women are whores. Even my mother, or she would never have had another child. A whore to my father!" He took a deep breath, controlling himself with an effort. "You should be flattered that I share my brother's taste in beautiful women. As you do, of course." He turned to Tim. "I'm almost glad you are here, so I can deal with you once and for all. My wife's eldest daughter, remember . . . ?" His eyes were suddenly blazing with emotion.

Judy backed away from them as Tim eyed him warily. "Forget it, Sam," Tim said coldly. "Forget it. It's all in your imagination."

"Is it?" Sam took another step toward him. "Joanna doesn't think so."
He laughed.

"If you've been near Jo again—" Tim suddenly squared his shoulders.
Though of much lighter build than Sam, he topped him by several inches.
"If you've touched her, I'll kill you, so help me God!"

"Of course I've touched her." Sam sneered. "Did you think I would
leave her alone? She admitted everything, you know. How she had
cheated me. How she slept with you. I beat her for it, did she tell you?
And if I beat her, what more should I do to the lousy bastard who seduced
her!" He was only feet from Tim now.

Tim backed away hastily. "Sam, for God's sake, calm down. Let's talk
about this."

"Not this time. I sat back and let it happen long ago. I pretended I
didn't know. I watched people snigger and laugh behind their hands and
call me cuckold. I could do nothing about her fornication with the king,
but you—you are a different matter. I was never entirely sure. She was too
clever for me in the past, but now things are different. Now I am in
control. And now I know the truth." He picked up the brass candlestick
from the low chest near him and held it up menacingly. "You are going to
pay for what you did, de Clare!"

"No!" Judy screamed as he lifted his arm.

Tim, his face white, dodged back toward the bedroom doorway. As he
did so his foot caught on the Persian rug that covered the polished boards.
He staggered for a moment, then he slid sideways, crashing against the
edge of the door.

Sam laughed. "Now I have you, de Clare! On your knees like your
paramour!" He raised the candlestick high above his head as Judy
launched herself at him, catching his arm. As they wrestled for a moment
Tim slipped slowly onto his hands and knees, then on down to the floor.
There was an ugly bleeding gash from the door latch on his temple.

Abruptly Sam let his arm fall. He stood staring down at Tim.

"Tim?" Judy threw herself down on her knees beside him. "Tim, are
you all right?" She raised a white face toward Sam. "He's unconscious."

For a moment Sam did not move, then almost reluctantly he squatted
down beside Tim and felt below his ear for his pulse. Judy held her breath.
She felt very sick.

"He's okay," Sam said at last. His voice was calm again. "But you'd
better call an ambulance in case." He stood up. "I'm sorry. I lost my
temper."

Judy backed away from him. "You lousy shit!" Her eyes were blazing.
"Get out of here, Sam! Get out, or I swear I'll see you go to prison for the
rest of your life. You should be in a straitjacket!"

She ran to the bed and grabbed the phone, then with a sob she flung it down. "I'll have to go and call from the apartment downstairs. Shall I put a pillow under his head?"

"No, don't touch him." Sam was still standing looking down at Tim's inert body. After a moment he pulled a blanket off the bed and tucked it around him, then he looked at Judy. "You'd better phone quickly," he said.

Music echoed out of the open windows in Berkeley Street as the party warmed up. Jane was sitting on Jim Greerson's lap when the phone rang and for a while neither bothered about it. Then finally Jane leaned forward and picked up the receiver.

"Nick?" she called. "Anyone here seen the boss man? There's a guy here on the end of the line says it's an emergency."

Nick materialized at last, a glass of champagne in his hand. He was grinning. "A phone call at this hour? It's probably a complaint." He pulled himself onto the desk. "Hello?"

On the other end of the line the voice of Judy's downstairs neighbor launched into an excited and apologetic monologue. For a moment Nick listened, puzzled, then abruptly he stood up. "An accident, you said? Who's hurt?"

"I don't know," the unknown voice at the other end was out of breath. "A very nice gentleman, very tall. He hit his head. Miss Curzon went with him. They took him to St. Stephen's. . . ."

Judy was sitting alone in the dimly lit hospital waiting area. Her eyes were red with crying.

"What happened?" Nick put his arms around her and held her close.

She shook her head and sniffed. "They think he's cracked his skull. They've taken him up to the operating room."

"Who?" He pushed her away from him so he could see her face. "Who is hurt, Judy?"

"Tim. It's Tim Heacham!"

"Tim?" Nick stood quite still for a moment. "But for God's sake, what happened?"

"He came over to take some photos of my paintings and your brother arrived. He threatened Tim, and . . ." She began to sob again.

"Sam hit him?" Nick sat down abruptly next to her.

"No." She sniffed hard and groped in the pocket of her jeans for a soggy tissue. "No, he tried to and Tim dodged. He slipped on my stupid rug. Oh, Nick! Supposing he dies!"

"What were they fighting about?"

"Sam called him de Clare. I think they were fighting about Jo. He talked about his daughter."

Nick's lips tightened imperceptibly. "My brother really is insane," he

521

said at last. He rested his elbows on his knees and put his head in his hands. "God, what a mess! Where is he? Did he come to the hospital?"

She shook her head. "I don't know where he went."

They both looked up as a young fair-haired woman in a white coat appeared. She carried a clipboard.

She sat down beside them with a tired smile. "I understand you came in with Mr. Heacham?"

Judy nodded. "How is he?"

The young woman shrugged. "He's still in the operating room. We'll know more later. I wondered if you could give me details of his next of kin?"

Judy clutched at Nick's hand. "He's dying?"

"No, no. It's normal procedure. We have to try to contact his family."

They looked at each other. "I know nothing about his family," Nick said slowly. "I'm sorry. We're just friends of his."

"I see." She slipped her pen back into the pocket of her coat. "You don't know his wife?"

"He has no wife," Judy said softly.

The young woman frowned. "He was conscious for a few minutes upstairs before he went into surgery. He was talking about his daughter. Matilda, was it? Perhaps if we could find her?"

Nick stood up. His face was very tense. "He has no daughter either," he said.

As the woman disappeared through the swinging doors Nick turned on Judy. "Aren't you going to rush to the phone and call Leveson? I should imagine this will make a juicy headline!"

Judy colored. "Of course I'm not." She sat slumped in her chair. "How long do you think the operation will take?"

Nick shrugged. "I suppose I should call Bet Gunning. She knows Tim best. She must know where his family is." He glanced at his watch.

"Jo might know," Judy said softly. "I wonder if Sam's gone back there? He said he had come from her apartment. Nick?"

Nick had stood up. His face was white. "Are you sure?" Already he was striding toward the door. "You stay here, Judy." It was all he said, then he was gone.

Judy subsided onto the chair and began to sob again. It was midnight.

"Jo? Jo, can you hear me?" Nick crouched beside her and took her hand in his. It was ice-cold. She was staring unblinkingly at the blank TV screen. Automatically Nick reached to switch it off, then he passed his hand up and down in front of Jo's eyes. Her eyelids did not move. He felt cautiously for her pulse. It was there, very slow and unsteady.

"Jo? Jo, love, listen to me! You must listen. Please." He chafed her hands vigorously in turn. "Jo, I need you. For God's sake, my love." He took a deep breath. "Jo, I am going to count backward from ten. When I reach one, you will awaken, do you hear me?" His voice was shaking badly. Gently he pushed her back against the cushions. He touched her forehead. Her skin was strangely cold. "Ten, nine, eight, seven, six, five, four, three, two, one." He caught her wrists. "Wake up, now. Wake up!"

She did not move. She still had not blinked. Nick looked around wildly, then he leapt to his feet. Jo's address book was lying by the telephone. He ran his finger down the second page and found the number he was seeking: Bennet, C. Office—home/town—home/country. Praying, Nick dialed the second number.

The phone was answered by the sleepy voice of Mrs. Bennet. It was only four seconds before her husband was on the line.

He listened to Nick intently. "It sounds like a catatonic trance," he said almost to himself. "I'll come straight over. Don't try to wake her, Nicholas. I'll be with you in twenty minutes. If she seems cold wrap her up warm, then get yourself a drink. I'm on my way."

Nick glanced at his watch. It was one-fifteen. Grimly he found two blankets in the closet and tenderly he folded them around her, then he went into the kitchen and put on the kettle. It was nearly two before the doorbell rang.

Bennet crossed the room in two strides. Gently he pulled the blankets away from Jo's face. "How long has she been like this?"

Nick shrugged. "Maybe since my brother left her, I guess about nine or ten."

"He put her in this trance?" Bennet scrutinized Nick's face.

"I suspect so," Nick said grimly. "But we both know she's capable of doing it herself. I thought she was beginning to learn to fight it, but maybe she couldn't manage it when she was alone. Is she going to be all right?" He knelt beside her and took her hand.

Bennet smiled. "I think so. She is showing signs of eye movement—see? I think she's coming out of it naturally." He sat down next to Jo and, putting his hands on her shoulders, pulled her gently to face him. "That's it, now, Lady Matilda, can you hear me? That's right, you recognize my voice. You can speak to me without fear, my dear, you know that. You are tired now, are you not? And very cold. I think it would be nice if you woke up, my dear. You are going to wake up slowly—"

He broke off as Jo jerked backward in his hands. Her eyes had lost their vague unseeing stillness and were focusing past him on Nick's face.

Nick stood up, smiling with relief. "Jo, thank God—"

But she had torn herself out of Bennet's hands and pulled herself shakily to her feet.

"Please," she said wildly. "Please, give me more time. I have the money. I told you, it is hidden in the hills above Hay. Please, give me more time. Please." Tears were pouring down her cheeks. "William will come back. He promised. He will come back, if not for me, then for our son. Please, Your Grace, please—" She threw herself on her knees in front of Nick. "Please, punish me if you must, but not my son. Not Will!" She was sobbing violently. "Take me. Do what you wish with me, but spare my son! He has done nothing. It is my fault. It is all my fault!" She looked up, her hair, trailing across her eyes, wet with tears. "You loved me once, Your Grace. Can your love have turned so completely to hatred?"

Bennet caught her shoulders gently. "Come, my dear. This will do no good—"

"No!" Her voice rose to a scream. "I will not go! You must listen. My liege! My lord king. Please, spare me—"

She was sobbing hysterically, clinging to Nick's sweater.

Quietly Carl Bennet turned to the case he had brought with him. He swung it onto the coffee table and, opening the lid, produced a hypodermic syringe. "Hold her still," he commanded in an undertone. "I'm going to give her a shot to make her sleep."

Nick caught Jo's wrists gently. "Come on, love," he said. His voice was shaking violently. "I will spare you. I will . . ."

She did not seem to notice as Bennet pushed up her sleeve, swabbing quickly and efficiently before he inserted the needle in her arm. Within seconds her fingers loosened on Nick's sweater and she slumped at his feet.

For a moment he could not move. His throat ached with anguish. Carl patted his shoulder gently. "I'll help you carry her to bed. I've given her thirty-five cc's of Valium. That will knock her out for several hours. When she wakes she will be all right."

Nick pulled himself together with difficulty. "You're sure?"

"Quite sure." Carl's smile was brisk and reassuring. "I'll come back about"—he glanced at his watch—"about ten o'clock tomorrow morning. I would like your permission then to rehypnotize her and very strongly implant the suggestion that she never take part in any regressions again, induced by others or by herself. I think it will work this time. She is sufficiently afraid of the consequences to cooperate." He stooped and lifted Jo's shoulders from the floor. "Come, help me put her to bed."

Carefully they laid Jo on the bed. Nick removed her sandals and covered her with a blanket, then, smoothing her hair back from her face, he kissed her gently on the forehead. Five minutes later he had shown Carl Bennet out. After pouring himself a gin, he went to the French windows and pushed them open. The sky was still completely black above the glare of the streetlights around the square. The air was cold and fresh, cutting through his thin sweater, making him shiver. It was clean though. Clean and good and it bore the hint of rain.

He turned his back on the window and threw himself down on the sofa. Tomorrow—no, today—it would all be over. Jo would be made to forget any of this had ever happened. But he would remember. He and Sam, and Tim.

Poor Tim. With a groan he stood up, glancing at his watch, then he dialed the hospital.

"May I ask who is inquiring?" the impersonal voice on the other end of the wire said in response to his question after a series of clicks and silences.

Nick spelled out his name patiently. "I was at the hospital earlier," he said. "Tim is a very old friend."

"I'm sorry, then, Mr. Franklyn." The voice suddenly became compassionate. "But I have bad news, I'm afraid. Mr. Heacham never regained consciousness after the operation. He died at a quarter to three."

39

Sam braced himself against the aircraft seat and closed his eyes. He hated the moment of take-off—the pressure against his body as the plane accelerated, the speeding tarmac beneath the wheels, turning into a blur outside the window that defied eyesight, the knowledge that he was trapped, strapped into the fuselage as it hurtled forward out of his control, bearing him helplessly to whatever destination it chose. He focused his eyes desperately on the No Smoking sign, waiting for the slight bump that would indicate they had left the ground.

His head was whirling. A monumental hangover, no doubt, though he couldn't remember drinking anything at all. He remembered walking up Park Lane as dawn was breaking. It had started to rain and he had thrown back his head to feel the cool droplets on his face. Exhausted, he had reached the apartment at last. Nick was still out, presumably at his office party.

Sam meticulously packed all his things, checking for anything left behind. Then he turned out the lights and drew back the curtains on the gray early morning. Outside it was raining hard.

Before he left the apartment he reached into the pocket of his jacket and pulled out the crucifix. He stared at it for a long time, then he kissed it gently and stood it on Nick's writing desk, propped against the lamp. He stood looking at it for several seconds, then, crossing himself, he turned for the door. After slamming it, he slipped the keys through the letter box, then he made his way toward the stairs. He still needed to walk, exhausted though he was. He would walk now, through the rain, to Green Park Station and take the Piccadilly line to Heathrow. Only at the last minute had he turned his back on the Edinburgh flight and asked instead for a standby ticket to Paris. He had no reason to think that Judy would tell the police about the fracas in her studio, but if she did, perhaps it would be better if he made himself scarce for the time being. He smiled grimly as he reached for his American Express card and then slowly made his way toward the departure lounge.

He leaned toward the window and stared out at the landscape of minia-

526

ture houses and roads, so meticulous, so square, laid out beneath the steadily climbing plane. Then there were meadows and the silver curve of the river. For a second he caught sight of the majestic towers of Windsor Castle, then the plane sliced up into the soft, enveloping down of cloud. Sam sat back and unfastened his seat belt and for the first time thought of Jo.

He closed his eyes again, feeling icy sweat drench his shoulders. He had abandoned her. He had sent her to Corfe and abandoned her. He had failed. Once more he had fled. Fled to France. And so history was to repeat itself after all.

He could feel the ironical laughter welling up inside him. For a moment he tried to stop it, fighting the explosion building up inside his chest, then he pressed his head back against the seat and opened his mouth to let the sound escape. It came out as a huge heart-rending sob. Within seconds his face was coursing with tears.

It was eight o'clock when Nick looked in on Jo. He stood watching her tenderly, tucking the blanket more tightly around her deeply sleeping form, then he stooped and kissed her gently and lingeringly on the lips. "Jo, my love," he whispered. "I'm going to the office to pick up the contracts, then I'm coming straight back. Can you hear me, Jo?"

She did not move. He could see the blue veins on her eyelids, the almost transparent quality of her skin against the vivid dark hair with its hints of chestnut on the white pillowcase.

"I'll be back in forty minutes, Jo, I promise," he whispered again. "Then I won't leave you again."

Outside the front door he hesitated for a moment. Should he run upstairs and ask the Chandler woman to come and sit with Jo until he got back? He glanced up at the dim stairwell, barely lit by the rain-splashed skylight three floors above, then he began to run downstairs. Jo was still deeply asleep. Dr. Bennet had said she would be out for at least eight hours. He would fly to the office in a cab, grab the contracts and outline presentations, and be back before nine.

As the door closed behind him, Jo opened her eyes. Her head was spinning and she felt violently sick. Fighting to make her heavy limbs move, she climbed out of bed and made her way to the bathroom.

Forty minutes, Nick had said. Just forty minutes to get away.

She stood under the cold shower until she was shaking but wide awake. After toweling herself dry, she dragged on her jeans and a thick sweater, then she drank a mug of scalding black coffee. The caffeine hit her like a hammer and she felt it jolt her system, making her heart palpitate uncomfortably as she groped on the shelf for a road map.

She took a denim jacket, a scarf, and her bag with the map, then looked

527

for the keys of the Porsche. They were still there where she had dropped them on the desk. With a faint smile she slipped the key ring over her finger and let herself out of the apartment. It was eight twenty-seven.

Nick returned at eight forty-five, paying off the cab and running up the stairs to the apartment two at a time. He knew she must be awake as soon as he opened the door. He could smell coffee, and the lamp on her desk was switched on.

"Jo?" With a little stab of unease he slammed the front door and put his pile of folders down on a chair. "Where are you?"

He knew instinctively that the apartment was empty, but even so he searched it, throwing open the bedroom door and staring at the bed, where the blankets on the floor showed the speed with which she had gotten up. Her dress was lying on the bathroom floor, the shower in the bath still dripping where she had failed to turn it off properly.

He leaned over and tightened the tap, then he turned back to the living room. The notebooks on her desk were haywire as if she had been searching for something. He pulled one toward him, running his eyes down the page of close writing. One line caught his eye.

Matilda and her son were sent to a dungeon at Windsor. Jo had crossed out Windsor so hard that her pen had torn through the paper. Over it she had written *Corfe.*

He went cold. He ran to the French doors, tore at the handle, and flung the door open so he could step out onto the balcony. The rain was pouring down now, splashing up from the flowerpots, drenching the passion flower till it hung in heavy garlands away from the wall. Leaning over the balustrade, Nick squinted down into the street to look for his car. He had noticed it earlier as he ran for a taxi and debated swiftly whether to go back for his keys. Then a taxi had cruised past and slowed as he flagged it down, and he had forgotten the car. God, how he wished now he had taken it! The parking space was empty.

His hands shook as he dialed Bennet's home number. "I know I was a fool to leave her, but she was asleep and I had to fetch these damn contracts. She's taken my car."

There was a brief silence. "She will be in no condition to drive. Do you know where she might have gone?"

"Corfe." Nick's fingers drummed on the phone. "That's down in Dorset on the coast somewhere, I think. I've never been there. But it must be three or four hours' drive at least."

"I'll bring my car and come and collect you," Bennet said briefly. "How much start has she got?"

"It can't be more than half an hour."

"Another half hour before I pick you up. That makes her an hour ahead of us. Be ready!" Bennet slammed down the phone.

528

* * *

In her hotel room just outside Frome Ann Clements stared out at the rain and groaned. She hated driving in bad weather. It took all the joy out of it. She looked at the boxes of pamphlets on the bed. She had been a fool to unload them from the van the night before. She had been so afraid they might be stolen from the parking lot, but now she was going to have to carry them back through the rain. She had collected them the day before from the printer, now she had to get them to London. She made a face. London in wet weather was worse, if possible, than London in the sun, and she didn't even know anyone to go to the theater with.

She stopped in her tracks. Jo.

The phone was answered after just one ring. She grinned, sitting down on the bed as she inserted her diary, with Jo's number, back into its place in the huge straw tote bag. "Well, hi, Nick. How are you both?"

His reaction was less than reassuring. "Ann. It's not good. Jo's in a bad way."

"I'm sorry." Ann could hear the depression in his voice as she slumped back onto the bed. "I was calling to say I'd be in London this afternoon. I wondered if I could come over and see you both. I'll still come if I can help. I came down to Frome last night and now I'm—"

"Did you say Frome?" Nick's voice cut through hers. "Frome in Somerset?"

"Well, I'm just outside the town actually—"

"Ann. Please, you've got to help. Jo is on her way to Corfe. You know what that means. She mustn't be there on her own, Ann. I'm leaving now to follow her but she's got my car and it's fast. Can you get there? Please?"

"Why, sure." Ann stood up anxiously. "But where is Corfe?"

"It's in Dorset. Nearly on the coast. It can't be more than an hour from where you are. Have you got a good map?"

"Yes, but the old van doesn't go very fast."

"Ann, I don't care how fast it goes. You can be there before us. Please."

Ann took a deep breath. "Okay, Nick, I'm on my way."

She slammed down the phone and turned to look at the boxes. Damn the things! They would take at least ten minutes to load.

Jo peered through the windshield, fighting the heaviness in her eyelids as the long wipers drew great arcs on the rainswept glass. Back and forth. Back and forth. The road stretched out endlessly, the verges beyond the windows blurred gold and mauve with wet ragwort and rosebay, the visibility ahead cut to nothing by the heavy spray thrown up by trucks as they thundered westward.

Once she pulled in at a service station and filled the car with gas. In the bright garish café next door she ordered a cup of black coffee and sat at the plastic-covered table, staring at a jam jar full of ox-eye daisies. She ached with fatigue. The long drive through the heavy Saturday morning traffic, the strange muzzy feeling in her head, above all the knowledge, unquestioning and certain, that she had to make the journey, overwhelmed her. She did not think of the future, or of the past. Her mind was drained and empty. She drank the coffee quickly, barely tasting it, and stood up. There was still a long way to go. Wearily she climbed back into the car and headed once more toward the south west.

The traffic slowed, crawling past some roadworks, then on again, plunging into the New Forest, speeding up as it swept on, then abruptly the highway ended and she found herself impatiently driving down narrowed roads, her speed held in check by the double white line. The rain was still heavy, the windshield wipers endlessly working. On and on. Back and forth. With a sudden shot of adrenaline in her stomach she realized the Porsche had drifted toward the opposite side of the road. She dragged it back as an oncoming car, its lights blazing, blasted her with its horn.

Keep awake. She must keep awake.

She peered at a signpost as it flashed toward her out of the silver streaks of rain and vanished before her eyes had time to focus.

Through Wareham, where she was forced to stop three times at traffic lights, chewing her nails, as the car stood waiting its turn to move, then at last on up the last miles of narrow road.

Corfe Castle loomed on a hill in a gap among the Purbeck Hills, the high fingers of its broken towers reaching up toward the sky, stark sentinels, visible a mile away above the trees, on the narrow, winding road. Jo slowed the car with a jolt of fear. The rain had stopped at last and streaks of vivid blue were showing in the sky to the south. In the rays of sunlight the colors were vivid. Dazzling white convolvulus trailing through the hedges, heather on the sandy verges a brilliant purple, and everywhere the trees washed to deep emerald by the glitter of the sun. Within minutes steam was rising from the tarmac and strings of mist were spiraling up from the trees.

She drove, slowly now, around the foot of the castle hill, staring up with a dry throat at the towering white ruins above her, then she drew up in the center of the old stone village south of the castle and, pushing open the car door, climbed out in a daze.

Slowly she walked toward the ruins, her eyes fixed on the walls ahead of her, and over the bridge and beneath the shadow of the entrance gatehouse. There she was brought up short by the ticket kiosk and a turnstile. A man was staring at her and dimly she realized he wanted some money. She had to pay to get in! A wave of hysterical laughter swept through her and was gone as soon as it had come, as, still in a daze, she groped in the pocket of her jeans and found a pound coin. Then at last she was inside the walls, walking up the steep, narrow tarmac path toward the grotesquely broken towers of the Martyr's Gate.

The castle was still comparatively deserted after the rain, but she noticed little. She did not see the ancient stones, reduced by Cromwell's sappers to their present state of ruin, nor see the wildflowers, the thistles, the yarrow, the ragwort, the wild marjoram, or the festoons of clinging ivy. She did not see the blue sky, or the white Purbeck stone with its gray shadow of lichen. Her eyes were growing dark.

Carl Bennet swore roundly as he stamped his foot down on the accelerator and threw the blue Mercedes at a gap in the traffic. It roared past two trucks, cutting in with only inches to spare in front of the line of oncoming traffic. Unconsciously Nick was clutching the sides of his seat. He closed his eyes briefly, but said nothing. When he opened them again it was to see the streak of blue in the leaden sky. He glanced down at the road map on his knee.

"Ten miles to go," he said tautly.

Bennet nodded. His tongue showed briefly at the corner of his mouth as he negotiated a tight bend in the narrow road, then he allowed himself a quick smile. "The rain has stopped, at least," he said.

The constable was waiting for them, his face set grimly in the flickering light. The king's orders were still in his hand. As the horses drew to an exhausted standstill before him, he read them silently once again, still not wanting to believe. Then slowly he reached for one of the flaring torches and held the parchment in the flame until it blackened and curled.

The oubliette lay beneath the floor of the western tower. Will fell heavily as they pushed him through the trapdoor, his legs buckling under him, and he lay still in the dark. With Matilda they were more gentle, lowering her down beside him and flinging down a sheepskin and some sheaves of straw. She looked up, dazed; faces peered down, torches flashed and smoked above her and there was air. Then the great stone slab fell.

Light came fitfully, creeping icily through the drain gulley in the base of the wall. Kneeling to peer through it, she could see the hill opposite the castle. It was white with snow. The silence was profound, save when Will groaned. She had tried, groping in the dark with gentle fingers, to ease his leg; feeling the splintered bones and the blood, she had wept.

The light of the setting sun slowly faded from the gulley and no one came. They had no food, no water. She gnawed at the heads of wheat still clinging to the straw. Will burned beneath her hand. "Blessed Virgin, save us. Sweet Lady, intercede." Daylight came again and brought no comfort. She clawed at the walls, tearing at the stone, and wept again.

As it grew dark once more Matilda took Will in her arms, his limbs already wasted by the fever, his face beneath her hand contorted with agony. Twice he screamed out loud as she held him close and she remem-

531

bered the day of his birth—the agony of the black wizened face in her arms; and she knew there could be no hope.

When the light appeared again at the drain and a white sea mist drifted up across the hills, her eyes were too dim to see. Will lay already stiffening in her arms and she unbraided her hair, spreading it across his face, cradling him close, rocking gently to ease the pain.

Sam found a room in the rue Saint Victor.

His eyes were still swollen with grief as he pulled open the double mansard window six stories up and pushed back the shutters looking out over the rooftops of St. Germain. Then, turning, he managed to smile at the concierge, who, puffing from the steep climb up the stairs, had followed him into the room. Giving her a wad of francs, he persuaded her to fetch him a bottle of cognac with the promise that she could keep the change. His thoughts were all of Jo. Not once had he remembered Tim.

When the bottle came he locked the door. From outside the window, above the distant roar of traffic, he could hear a church bell ringing. He stood, glass in hand, looking at the street far below. He could smell new bread from somewhere and coffee and garlic and wine. The smell that was the smell of Paris. From the room next door he could hear the sound of muffled laughter.

He refilled his glass. He hadn't eaten for over twenty-four hours, and already the drink was going to his head. Another glass followed, tipped down his throat, and then, impatiently, he threw the glass into the corner and drank straight from the bottle. His vision was beginning to blur.

He stared up at the sky, frowning, trying to see. The clouds were lifting. A faint ray of sunlight illuminated the line of raindrops on the wrought-iron railing outside the window in front of the parapet, turning each one into brilliant diamonds. He stared at them hard. The tears were coming back. He made no attempt to stop them, feeling them coursing down his face, soaking into his shirt. He took another drink, then, carefully putting the bottle down on the table, he stepped up onto the low sill. It was no problem to climb over the railing. He rested his hand for a moment on the warm slates of the roof and then, swaying slightly, stepped up onto the parapet.

His last thought, as he leaned forward into space, was of Matilda.

Ann stared ahead of her at the gap in the Purbeck Hills. There was no mistaking the angry silhouette of the castle, rising high above the sea of forest. Above it lay the huge cold arc of a rainbow as the last of the soft black clouds slipped away.

She saw the Porsche at once, parked carelessly, next to the market cross, and drew up near it, stiff and aching from the concentration of her journey. She wasn't used to driving any distances these days, never mind the tortuous cross-country trip she had just made from Frome.

After slamming the van door, she set off at a run toward the broken masonry arch over the bridge across the dry moat, her sneakers silent on the road. Like Jo, she was brought up short by the need to find her entrance money. Then, already panting, she ran up the lower ward, following the path across the huge area of grass toward the causeway that crossed the inner moat and ran between the massive towers of the Martyr's Gate.

There she hesitated, looking around her, her hair blowing in the wind. There was no sign of Jo. To the right rose the King's Tower and all that remained of the main castle. To the left a second area of grass formed the west bailey, surrounded by gray stone walls, at the far western end of which stood the bare remains of the Butavant Tower. She walked on slowly, and hesitated. Then, turning left, she peered around the end of a wall. Jo was sitting there on the short, damp grass.

Ann let out a little sob of relief. She ran toward her, stopping six feet away from her.

"Jo?"

Jo did not turn. She was staring in front of her, her hands hanging loosely between her knees, her hair blowing in the southwesterly wind. Her hands were bruised and bleeding, her nails torn.

Ann stared at them in silent horror. "Jo, are you all right?" Crouching beside her, Ann gently touched her shoulder. There was no response. Jo's skin was cold.

Behind them two men and a woman, cameras slung around their shoulders, had appeared through the Martyr's Gate. Slowly, enjoying themselves, they turned away up toward the remains of the keep. The sound of laughter echoed through the bright, windy air.

When Bennet and Nick arrived they were both still sitting there on the swiftly drying grass. The tourists had come past them, stared surreptitiously, and gone. Ann held Jo's hand gently. She could make no contact, get no reaction at all from the empty shell that was Jo. Once or twice she took her pulse. Each time it was weaker.

Bennet sat down next to them. "How is she?" he murmured.

Ann shook her head. "I can't get through to her. She blinks. When I lift her hand it falls naturally. Her eyes are quite normal, look. But she is completely cold."

Nick was staring round at the ruins of the castle. He was full of pent-up anger as he glanced back at Jo.

Bennet had opened the small case he had brought from the back of the Mercedes and was rummaging in a drawer, but suddenly Nick was beside him. He put a restraining hand on Bennet's wrist. "No more drugs," he said.

"Nicholas, I must."

'No. Leave her to me. Please."

Ann scrambled stiffly to her feet and backed away. Reluctantly Bennet followed suit. Both were watching Jo's face.

Nick stooped and caught her shoulders, pulling her to her feet. "Stand up. Do you hear me? Stand up. Don't give in. Fight." He shook her hard so that her head snapped back and forth as she sagged toward him.

Bennet took a protesting step forward, but Ann put her hand on his arm. "Wait," she whispered.

"Fight it. Live. I want you to live. Do you know who I am?" He held her hard in front of him.

Slowly and painfully Jo focused on his face.

"I want you to live. Come back to me. Do you hear me, Jo? It is all over!"

Darkness and pain were swirling in her head, dragging her down into the earth. Blackness, sleep, escape. Peace. She did not want to return. She felt no anger. Only regret; regret for the sun and the sky and laughter that was behind her. Soft eternal blackness waited. Blackness where her son was already at peace. . . .

She did not want to come back. A second chance. A reprieve; the sun blazing down from behind the high towers of white stone. She put her hands up to her eyes, but he caught her wrists and pulled them away, the man who had been her king. His eyes were full of compassion now. He was ordering her back. Her life was not being demanded. The body in her arms was dissolving, fading into the mist. There was a new life inside her waiting to be born. She had to come back. She had to obey, to give him the chance to atone. . . .

"Jo?" Nick was willing her back to life. "Jo, can you hear me?"

There was a very slight change in her now. He couldn't name it, but it was as if her resistance were weakening. She had changed her mind. She was going to return. "Jo, my darling, you're going to make it." He shook her again. "It's all over, love. All over."

She touched his jacket experimentally, as if testing the command she had over her fingers, and winced at the pain. "Over?" she repeated, dazed.

Behind them Ann and Carl Bennet exchanged glances. Ann was smiling, but there were tears in her eyes.

"It's over," Jo repeated slowly. "She died. Here, beneath this tower."

"I know, love."

"They took the bodies out of the oubliette after eleven days. They laid them in a single grave. Will was in her arms. They couldn't separate them at the end. There was no cross, no stone. The king wanted to forget. . . ."

"He never forgot, Jo. He never forgot."

She extricated herself from his arms slowly and for half a second he moved to try to restrain her, then he stood back as she walked, shakily, across the grass to the crumbling wall behind them. "Here," she whispered. "They are here, in the foundations of the wall. They threw them in the rubble and piled the stones on top of them." Slowly she stooped, then, gently snapping off a stem of wild marjoram, she walked to the shadow of the wall and laid the flower on a shelf in the stone. For a moment she stood staring down at it, then she turned and began to walk back toward the shadowed entrance to the Martyr's Gate.

Nick hesitated, then he followed her as she made her way slowly back down the lower ward and out across the bridge. The Mercedes was parked outside the pub. Bennet opened the rear door and obediently she climbed in, sitting back, her eyes closed. In silence Ann climbed in beside her and put her arm around her shoulders.

"She needs a brandy," she said.

Bennet shook his head. "That's the last thing this girl needs," he said curtly, "on top of all that Valium. I've got some coffee in the back."

Nick was standing uncertainly beside the car, watching as Jo clasped the mug of hot sweet coffee in her hands, sipping it. He glanced at Ann, then at Bennet. They were both preoccupied with Jo. Quietly he turned and began to retrace his steps into the castle.

Bennet looked around. For a moment he did not move. He frowned, then he handed the Thermos to Ann. "Take care of her," he whispered. "I'll be back in a moment."

Nick was standing looking down at the spray of tiny mauve flowers lying in the shadow of the stone.

Her hair had been redder than Jo's, her eyes a little greener perhaps. She had been so full of life, so graceful, so vivacious. And she had been broken by him.

"Forgive me." He did not realize he had spoken aloud. Slowly he knelt in the wet grass in silence.

It was five full minutes before he rose slowly to his feet. Without looking back he turned and headed toward the cars. Bennet was waiting for him in the shadow of the huge stone gateway.

Suddenly noticing him, Nick stopped, looking embarrassed.

"I thought I was alone."

Bennet smiled gravely as he fell in step beside him. "You were not alone," he said. "Someone was listening. I think, for some reason, you have been given a second chance."

Nick nodded. "I believe I have."

In the back of the car Jo reached across and touched Nick's hand. She was staring at the wet, muddied knees of his trousers. "Thank you," she whispered.

He put his arm around her. "It's finally over." He pulled her against him.

"For them." She gave him a shaky smile. "But what about for us?"

"For us it is the beginning. A new beginning."

"And Sam?" she whispered.

"I don't think Sam will come back." His arms tightened around her. "And nor will Tim, Jo. They had a fight last night. Tim slipped and cracked his skull." He hesitated, feeling her body tighten. "He's dead, love."

She tried to swallow her tears. "But why? Why Tim? He never hurt anyone."

"It was an accident—"

"It wasn't an accident," she cried miserably. "Nothing has been an accident. It has all happened by design. Every single thing, from that first time I met Sam in Edinburgh. I should have known then. I should have recognized the danger." Her voice rose. "It has all been Sam, hasn't it? Every bit was staged by him. It wasn't real. You weren't King John. I wasn't Matilda. He set the whole thing up. He's been laughing at us all the time."

Nick said nothing. He was gazing past her out of the car window, up at the silhouette of white stone against the brilliant blue of the sky.

He did not see the huge cracks in the masonry. He did not see the fallen slabs of stone or the weeds and the ivy. He was looking at the solid, newly built keep of a powerful great castle, with the three huge snarling leopards of England streaming in a blaze of red and gold from the topmost battlements.

He had been there before.

536

EPILOGUE ONE

10 OCTOBER 1216

Margaret de Lacy pushed back her hood and carefully straightened her gown, shaking off the rain. The roars of merriment from inside the dining hall showed the people of Lynn were enjoying the feast they had prepared for the king as he progressed through the eastern counties of his realm. She took a deep breath and nodded to the page at the door, who, having bitten her coin, had pocketed it cheerfully. He pushed it open with a flourish and winked at her. The hall was packed with people and noisy, but determinedly Margaret pushed her way toward the high table where the king was eating.

He did not notice her at first, raising his goblet to toast the fat sheriff. There had been supplicants on and off all evening and he was disposed to be benevolent. Then he turned and saw the woman who waited at his elbow, her green eyes fixed quietly on his face. Slowly his smile faded and he lowered his goblet. Sweat stood out on his brow and he wiped it with the back of his hand. Rising to his feet, he pushed back his chair with sudden violence. Silence fell over the table as curious faces watched on every side.

John crossed himself, and she saw his lips move, questing, toying with a name.

She curtsied to the ground. "I am Margaret, sire. Her daughter."

She heard the whispers running down the hall and saw the excitement and puzzlement on the faces near the king. He had grown pale as he watched her and his expression was guarded.

"I have come to beg a grant of land, Your Grace. To build a convent to my mother's memory. I hoped you would do that much for her—now." She looked down, not wanting, suddenly, to see the pain in his eyes.

"Of course." She hardly heard the words, but she saw his lips move. "Where?"

"In the Marches that she loved, sire."

He saw her eyes through a swimming haze, green and beautiful, flecked with gold; the eyes of another woman.

Suddenly the king doubled over, racked with a spasm of pain. He

537

clutched his stomach, retching, and the silence around him turned to cries of concern, but he waved help away. "Bring me pen and ink." He gasped. "Quickly. You shall have your convent, Margaret de Lacy. For her sake."

The clerk took down the record of the king's grant of land in the royal forest of Aconbury, south of Hereford, and the royal seal was appended to it, there in the hall at King's Lynn, before he allowed himself to be helped, groaning, to his bed. In the chaos that surrounded his illness Margaret slipped away, clutching her parchment.

Eight days later John Plantagenet was dead.

EPILOGUE TWO

PARIS—JANUARY 1986

Judy was wearing a 1920s dress sewn with thousands of reflecting beads, her red hair brushed into a glossy cap over her forehead as she mingled with the guests. The paintings looked good. She was pleased with the exhibition, even more pleased with the catalogue, which under George Chippen's tender nursing had already gone into two reprints before preview day. There had been a huge demand for Tim Heacham's final piece of work.

Behind her Pete Leveson was supervising the champagne. She smiled at him over her shoulder. They had been married three days before.

Catching her eye, he put down the bottle he was holding and reached out for her hand. "Happy?"

She nodded.

"There's a huge crowd. I can't believe we asked this many."

"I don't care how many come. Just as long as everyone enjoys themselves."

Behind them, in the doorway, Bet Gunning flourished her invitation and took a glass of champagne from the nearest tray. Threading her way toward them, she smiled at Pete. "So are you going to write this exhibition up for me as well?"

"Try to stop me." Pete stepped forward and gave her a kiss. "Aren't Nick and Jo with you?"

Bet took a sip of champagne. "They changed their plans," she said. "When they got back from the States on Wednesday they decided to go straight on to Hay-on-Wye." She glanced at Pete with a sudden glimmer of malicious humor. "Perhaps I owe you this one, Peter. I think they've gone to get married."

"I see." Pete chuckled. "And the story comes full circle."

"As good stories always must." Bet smiled. "I for one will drink to them."

"And to the baby." Judy lifted her glass innocently.

"What baby?" Bet swung around on her. "Jo is supposed to be writing a book!"

"I'm sure the two are not mutually exclusive," Judy purred. "It's due at the beginning of May. Nick called us from New York to tell us."

"And being the sweet, charitable girl she is," Pete said softly, "Judy couldn't help but start wondering."

"Wondering?" Bet echoed. She looked at Judy suspiciously.

Judy smiled. "The way I see it, there are two candidates for paternity. Nick or King John."

Bet took a sip from her glass. "For that matter, dear old Tim and the handsome Earl of Clare could also put in a claim, I suspect," she said softly.

Judy raised an eyebrow. "So—" She whistled through her teeth.

"And you've both forgotten William de Braose himself," Pete put in.

They all looked at each other in silence for a moment. Then Pete raised his glass. "Well, here's to Jo, God bless her," he said. "To her safe confinement and to the total discretion of the press!"

HISTORICAL NOTE

King John and Matilda de Braose were real, but their personal relationship, if any, is a matter purely of surmise. That she goaded him about the murder of his nephew and, on more than one occasion, provoked him to outbursts of fury, is recorded. Matilda's affair with Richard de Clare is purely imaginary, as is my speculation as to the possible illegitimacy of any of her children.

The circumstances surrounding the death of young William and Matilda are mysterious, but the chronicles are more or less unanimous in saying that John deliberately had them starved to death, either at Corfe or at Windsor Castle.

The king's actions have never been satisfactorily explained, even though his patience must have been considerably strained by William's behavior. The viciousness of his treatment of Matilda and Will caused such an outcry at the time, when cruelty and revenge were commonplace, that the king himself felt it necessary later to issue a statement explaining the course of events leading up to the outlawry of William senior. The death of the two hostages he could not or would not explain, but his statement was signed by various friends of Matilda and relatives, including Adam de Porter, Earl Ferrers, and the Earl of Clare himself.

There were two generally accepted reasons put forward to explain John's behavior: one, that Matilda had unforgivably taunted the king about the murder of Arthur of Brittany, and the other that John had decided anyway to make an example of a rich and powerful baron and selected the brash upstart William for the role. It is possible that when he had eventually to carry out the sentence of death against the hostages he could not bring himself openly to order execution.

For whatever reason, the downfall of the de Braose family, if it was intended to intimidate other powerful nobles, succeeded in achieving the opposite effect. It scandalized the country and the signatories of John's statement were among those who, four years later, signed Magna Carta, with its famous clause 39, which stated:

No man shall be taken, imprisoned, outlawed,
banished or in any way destroyed, nor will we
proceed against or prosecute him, except by
the lawful judgment of his peers or by the law of the land

William de Braose died in exile in France on 9 August 1211. His funeral service was conducted by Stephen Langton and he was buried in the Abbey of St. Victor in Paris.

Giles, Bishop of Hereford, returned from exile in France in 1213, ostensibly ready to make his peace with the king, but when John showed no signs of returning to him the confiscated de Braose lands, Giles sent his brother Reginald to the Marches, and eventually the castles of Abergavenny, White Castle, Skenfrith, Brecknock, Hay, Radnor, Builth, and Blaen Llynfi were recaptured by the de Braose family with the help of the Welsh. Reginald's wife, Gracia de Burgh, had two children, William and Matilda, and died young. He then married Gwladys, a daughter of Llewelyn, allying himself to the Welsh, who supported the de Braoses in their efforts to regain their lands. Paincastle returned to the Welsh and was held by Gwallter, the son of Einion Clud.

Giles died in 1215 and the following year the new king, Henry III, at last recognized Reginald as inheritor of the de Braose estates.

Margaret and Mattie were released unharmed. Mattie returned to her father, Richard de Clare, who until his death held the wardship of her eldest son, John, although her sons were technically kept hostages until January 1218. John later married Margaret, another daughter of Llewelyn, and challenged his uncle Reginald's right to the family estates.

Richard de Clare died in the autumn of 1217.

Matilda's eldest daughter, the young Matilda, died on 29 December 1211 at Llanbadarn Fawr and was buried, as she wished, next to her husband at Strata Florida.

Of Isobel Mortimer little is known. Her husband, Roger, died in June 1214 and was succeeded by his son, Hugh.

Margaret de Lacy was still living in 1255. She had three children, Egidia, Katherine, and Gilbert.

Three carucates of land in the Royal Forest of Aconbury were cleared at Margaret de Lacy's order, and there was founded, sometime before 1218, a rich Augustinian convent and chantry chapel to commemorate, in perpetuity, the souls of Margaret's parents and her brother Will.

All that remains today of the priory on John's gift of land is a small, redundant, haunted church, locked and used as a store.

PRINCIPAL DATES

(Dates in italics are approximate)

1154	Accession of King Henry II
1160	*Birth of Matilda de St. Valerie*
1174	*Marriage of Matilda*
1175	Massacre of Abergavenny
1176	*Birth of William de Braose the Younger (Will)*
1176	Betrothal of Prince John to Isabella of Gloucester
1177	*Birth of Giles*
1178	*Birth of Matilda the Younger (Tilda)*
1179	*Birth of Reginald*
1182	Fall of Abergavenny
1182	*Birth of Margaret*
1184	*Birth of Isobel*
1188	Summons to the Third Crusade
1188	Betrothal of Mattie to Gruffydd ap Rhys
1189	Marriage of Mattie to Gruffydd
1189	Death of Henry II. Accession of Richard I
1189	Wedding of Prince John
1189	Prince John visits the West
1191	William seizes Elfael and builds Castel Mallt (Paincastle)
1192–99	William Sheriff of Herefordshire
1195	Siege of Paincastle
1196	William itinerant justice for Staffordshire; gains co-rights in Barnstaple and Totnes
1197	Year of Pest and Plague. Death of Trehearne Vaughan
1198	Second Siege of Paincastle
1199	Death of Richard I
1199	William one of John's supporters at his coronation
1200	William succeeds to the Honor of Limerick
1200	John grants William the right to take land from the Welsh
1203	William becomes Lord of Gower
1203	William in attendance on John in Normandy at time of Prince Arthur's death

1205	William becomes Lord of the Three Castles
1207	First signs of William's impending fall from grace
1208	23 March. John's conflict with Rome over appointment of Stephen Langton as Archbishop of Canterbury leads to interdict of Pope Innocent III
1208	The de Braoses flee to Ireland
1209–10	William back in Wales
1210	Spring. King John arrives in Ireland
1210	Matilda flees to Scotland
1211	Death of Matilda and Will
1211	9 August. William dies in Corbeil. Buried in Paris by exiled Archbishop Langton
1215	Magna Carta
1216	10 October. The authorization of a grant of land at Aconbury to Margaret de Lacy is one of the last pieces of business John transacts
1216	18 October. King John dies

NOTE ON NAMES

The name of de Braose is variously spelled in the chronicles and subsequent history books as de Briouse, de Breos, and de Briouze as well as de Braose.

Matilda was as frequently referred to as Maude or Maud (the names having the same derivation as Matilda), quite apart from her nicknames in local history and folklore as Moll Walbee, Malld Walbri, and Mallt or Mawd.

Margaret, her daughter, is in some records referred to as Marjorie.